"Those are the best big waves on the planet. It must be seventy, eighty feet down there, and it's perfect!" said Heath Larson with a voice of authority no surfer in the world could match.

"Hey! Look over there!" exclaimed Roberto Mercante, "There's something floating in the middle of the lagoon! Some kinda Polynesian trimaran!"

"Fergit about that one inside the lagoon," said Clem Charleton as he circled the PBY into a final approach, "What are y'all gonna do 'bout the one down there in front of the entrance? It's floating right where we gotta go!"

"I bet they've seen us by now," said Luan, standing on the prow of the center hull and shading her eyes from the sun.

"I'm sure they have. And no, Taveka, they didn't forget their surfboards. Those are jetskis hanging under the wings."

"Well, David, that's better than the bombs those seaplanes sometimes carried during the war."

"You think so? I don't. Ka'unua is our sacred reef, but that will mean nothing to them."

Waves of Warning

Glenn Hening

Surfing Your Ocean Publications

Glenn R. Hening, Inc.

Oxnard Shores, California

First Edition

10 9 8 7 6 5 4 3

To order additional copies, go to www.wavesofwarning.com

Or contact:

Glenn R. Hening

Surfing Your Ocean Publications

5212 Moonstone Way Oxnard Shores California 93035

805-382-0657 glenn@wavesofwarning.com

Contents

Acknowledgments

Bill Gould, the Woods brothers, George Segala, Gary Hansch, Casey Morgan, Hal Jepsen, Steve Merrill, Juan Loma, Brown Dog and Mati Waiya;

Jeff Hunter, Barret Stoller, Susan Stoia, Drew Kampion, Chris Martin, Flip Cuddy and Dr. Dume for their perspectives on the surf industry; Tom & Paul for their timely help; Manasa Baravilala for the trip to Lekemba and Tarakua Point in the Lau Group, Fiji; Lt. Com. Ken Hobeman and Lt. Com. Jerry Feltz for their interviews and materials on Antarctica; Charlie Clements for his PBY5A expertise; Robin Tuttle-Maguire and the Oxnard Public Library for rare books about Polynesia; Janet Troxel for Felix Reisenberg's classic book "Cape Horn" (1939); Dr. David Lewis for his pioneering 'wayfinder' research and book "We the Navigators" (1972).

Special thanks in remembrance of Rick Vogel. Rest in peace, old friend.

Special thanks to Dr. Bill Patzert, Randy Laine, and Chip Bell for their classic characters based on true integrity.

Special thanks to Len Kelemoana Barrow, PhD, for his special insights about the Hawaiian surfing family.

Thanks to Jim Traynor for his encouragement and guidance; to Erin Eamer for her invaluable suggestions and sensitivity to nature and human nature; to Tom Southern, Garth Murphy and especially Mike Pearson for editing from a well-read surfer's point of view; to Jayne Jartved and Peter Østrin for their pinpoint observations. Thanks to Pat Darrin for his timely input.

And many thanks to Mr. Phil Kellogg.

Thank you Jericho Poppler, Mike Salter, Jeff Beals, and R.J. Smerling for making things work at crunch time.

Cover photo by, and many thanks to, Brandon Aroyan.

Thanks to David Truong at Flyer Web Printing, Oxnard, California.

Dedication

To my daughter Helen Grace
    and
    my son Pierce John-Michael

&

To surfers everywhere
    who give away waves
    when they don't have to.

Foreword

It's rare for a surfer to take up the ancient literary themes of courage, betrayal, greed, love, and exploration and bring them to life in the world of modern surfing, but that's what Glenn Hening does in this book.

I've known Glenn since he started surfing's most successful environmental organization, the Surfrider Foundation, some 20 years ago. Over the intervening years, through all his writings and efforts as a surfing activist, I have come to appreciate him not only for his cultural edgework but for his insatiable appetite for knowledge and making just the right connection to trigger new understanding. His personal background is unlike any surfer I've met, plus he's a really good surfer!

So, Glenn Hening is uniquely qualified to set in motion all the great themes of this major fictional work, to underpin them with experiential truth, and to take them in surprising directions. I doubt that anyone else in the surfing world could accomplish what he has in these pages.

Over the course of my rather extensive career as a surf writer (I've published several books and over a thousand feature stories), I've learned how challenging it is to write from "the core" while also speaking coherently to non-surfers about the ephemeral reality of riding waves.

Glenn Hening's grand tale rings true precisely because he is the genuine article - a core surfer with a unique gift for communicating (and revealing) some fundamental truths about human nature and the never-ending questions we ask ourselves about what are we doing with our lives and what the future will offer our children.

Enjoy and learn from *Waves of Warning.*

Drew Kampion

Bio note:
Former editor of Surfer magazine and currently American editor of The Surfer's Path, Drew Kampion is the author of *The Book of Waves, Stoked! A History of Surf Culture,* and *The Way of the Surfer.* A collection of his surf stories, *The Lost Coast,* was published in the spring of 2004.

Introduction

For the first twenty years of my surfing career, I dreamed of the day when the most important thing in my life (other than my family and children) would be recognized by Jacques Cousteau or National Geographic as being worthy of their attention. I dreamed of the day when surfing would be honored and presented on a par with the great human endeavors and cultures.

That dream was part of why I came up with the ideas that grew into the Surfrider Foundation in 1984 and the Groundswell Society in 1995. One of the main reasons those organizations exist is to hopefully nudge surfing towards, dare we say it, respectability, while retaining the challenge and spirit that has driven so many, including myself, to make surfing our lifelong passion.

In 1998, that recognition finally happened. For the first time ever, there was a picture of a surfer on the cover of National Geographic. It was Laird Hamilton, one of surfing's all-time legends, dropping down a really big wave that filled up the space inside the famous yellow border.

For a moment, I was stoked! It was a validation of sorts and honored surfing and people like Laird who pushed limits and found new frontiers to challenge themselves and others following in their footsteps.

Then I took another look at the cover, and my next thought drove me to write my first novel, *Waves of Warning*.

I wondered, "Do we really deserve this? Does surfing really measure up when it comes to all the great human endeavors covered by National Geographic? What is surfing compared to exploring Antarctica, sailing the tall ships a hundred years ago or today's transoceanic racing yachts? How does the integrity of modern surfing measure up when examined from the perspective of the Polynesian wayfinder societies?"

I dug even deeper and more things occurred to me.

"What about the environment? Do surfers really care that surf spots, and by extension the world's oceans, are endangered?

"What are the consequences of the global consumer economy of which surfing is such a hedonistic example?

"What about the selfishness and localism that has stained the soul of surfing?

"And if waves are for free and you can't buy a storm or a reef, how do we reconcile surfing's natural spirit with the huge amounts of money being made in the surf industry?"

To answer these questions in contemporary terms may have resulted in a collection of essays, and indeed I have written for publication on localism and others that bear an activist scrutiny.

But to really get at some answers, I concluded that I would have to extrapolate, or grow logically, current trends in the surfing world to their extremes. I would have to throw together a lot of stuff about the accomplishments and cultures of surfers, explorers, blue-water mariners, and Polynesian societies and then heat up a story over time. Thus the idea for a novel was born.

Waves Of Warning is the result of six years of research, interviews, and acquiring dozens of books and hundreds of articles about surfers and the fields and individuals to which I would like surfing to be favorably compared. The process included interviewing Antarctic veterans, talking with Thor Heyerdahl, discovering rare books of Polynesian culture, researching the facts and lore of World War Two seaplanes, finding eyewitness accounts from the Age of Sail in maritime museums, and visiting ancient archaeological sites in Peru. And since I am also an active surfer, riding completely new surfboard designs and being a part of current events in modern surfing further added to the body of knowledge behind my first novel.

Yet throughout all the research, writing and editing, I became increasingly aware that conclusions will remain elusive when asking such questions as:

Do we, as surfers, really measure up as people of the sea?

Do our heroes merit genuine respect by surfers and non-surfers alike?

Do the accomplishments of our 'surf culture' outweigh the greed, violence, and selfishness so easily found in surfing today?

And most importantly, what are the dangers when modern surfers find themselves losing contact with the timeless nature of the ocean?

Of course, by the very nature of surfing, there can be no one answer to any of these questions. Indeed, each surfer will have his or her opinions based on their own ultimately unique and entirely personal experience in the surf zone, an oceanic wilderness where the waves we ride have been breaking for thousands and millions of years.

Yet, I wrote *Waves of Warning* because it is important to try and think clearly about the issues that prompted me to write this book. Here's why.

One of my heroes is Fred Rodgers, the man who was on public television for thirty years reaching young and old with a gentle and powerful message about being true to one's self and others. Towards the end of his career, he was asked if he could sum up any thoughts about the world as it has changed over his lifetime. He said, "I don't know if, as human beings, we are made for the world we are making for ourselves."

Waves of Warning is about the world of modern surfing that, in some ways, we are in danger of making for ourselves. Of course, there are thousands of surfers who are active stewards of the 'aloha' spirit, and we will never be able to 'make' the storms, winds, and waves that define the surfing experience. And if we get a bit arrogant and full of ourselves, getting caught inside on a big day will always put us in our place pretty damn quick.

However, if we don't tend the soul of the surfing community, then we are not contributing to a positive legacy for future generations. If we allow commerce, competition and technology to erode our sensitivity to the simple experience of being with Nature, we lose our sense of curiosity and wonder about the fascinating world around us.

And if we, as surfers, ignore social and environmental trends that distance us from the feeling we had on our first wave, then what do we have to show for all that surfing has given us? Maybe we're buying new surfboards and equipment all the time, collecting contest trophies or memorabilia without end, always dreaming of our next surf trip, and constantly trying to live the surfing lifestyle to the hilt. Yet something will be missing, and someday we might not even remember what it was, even though it will always be just beyond our finger tips, right in front of us every time we paddle out.

Glenn Hening, Oxnard Shores, 2005

[signature] 293/500

Note: This single volume edition of "Waves of Warning" is the edited and condensed version of the entire story as first published last year. Readers of that original manuscript two-volume edition will note many similarities and yet some differences which I believe have enhanced the story and deepened the characters.

Part One

The First Winds of Winter

A Wayfinder

A star-filled dome of deep blue ran down to the horizon all around the voyaging craft, its three hulls slicing relentlessly forward through the waves of the South Pacific. A crisp north wind filled the sails as the last edge of the night's storm swept away to the east. A sharp, thin crescent moon was setting in the west.

A lone figure emerged from the streamlined shelter on the deck of the center hull. For six nights and days he had voyaged across the Nebula Archipelago, a vast array of reefs and islands, with no charts or GPS to guide him. He was a modern man navigating with the knowledge and skills of ancient Polynesian mariners. He was a wayfinder.

He made a final course adjustment while the last of his guide stars was still visible in the sky ahead. He dragged his hand through the water and noticed a slight change in its temperature. Then he sat down in front of his mainmast and closed his eyes to feel the swell patterns now that the storm was gone. He waited to absorb and interpret all the motions of his voyaging craft before he finally smiled. He knew exactly where he was – and he would soon arrive at his destination.

The trance of his concentration softened. He envisioned his wife, her face glowing in the candlelight, looking down at their two children fast asleep. Then he saw the three of them standing at the edge of the lagoon next to his mentor, decades of knowledge in his wrinkled face framing a broad smile and bright eyes. They all raised their arms and voices in greeting as he drifted home across the still water.

The voices faded to silence as a low roar grew in his ears, bringing him back to the present moment and the tasks before him. He opened his blue eyes to the tinge of light in the east and the sight of spray rising from the open ocean dead ahead. Seconds later he heard the distinct explosion of a big wave breaking, like a herald announcing a message of power from the mighty spirits of the timeless seas.

The sun touched the horizon. The tri-hulled craft rose to the top of a rolling wall of water. From its summit he caught a last glimpse of his guide star and a clear view of his goal. The first bright rays of dawn lit up the sea. A wave of emotion flooded through David Helmares, a feeling of revelation and promise he had known only once before in his life, when he first saw the Pacific Ocean.

David was eight years old and his family had just flown across the country from New York following his father's career to Southern California. They had arrived at night, and he was barely awake during the taxi ride from LAX to the Surfrider Inn overlooking Santa Monica Bay. His mother put him in his pajamas, and he was sound asleep the minute his head touched the pillow.

The next morning came cold and clear. It was January and a low winter sun brightened the room and opened the boy's eyes. His family was asleep, but David was too excited to stay in bed. He got up, opened the sliding glass door, and went outside to the balcony.

Below him was a broad beach of white sand. Beyond it, the blue Pacific stretched away to a crisp horizon. Santa Ana winds whistled a breeze out across the sea. Small rippling waves lapped against the shore. David stood transfixed for almost a minute as the colors and the vista created a memory that would last a lifetime. Then his mouth opened wide. "Wake up, everybody! We're here!"

The sun rises quickly in the South Pacific and was soon three hands above the horizon. David could see rainbows starting to form in the spray of the waves breaking less than half a mile off his bow. He looked into the transparent sea below him. The deep blue of the open ocean was giving way to the emerald and turquoise of Ka'unua, the most revered place in the wayfinding traditions of the Marulean sea people.

Located at the focal point of an underwater mountain range, Ka'unua transformed raw oceanic power coming up from the Southern Ocean into perfect patterns of wave energy. The reef was a timeless source and center for the navigators of Marulea. It was their Valhalla, and it was where David Helmares would perform rituals to become the next chief navigator of his adopted people.

He lowered his sails near the southern end of the reef and drifted in slowly. He needed an exact understanding of the challenge ahead. He saw the next set of swells approaching. He raised a sail for a few moments to let the wind push him a little closer to get a clear view of what he had to see.

The first swell was about twenty feet high when it peaked and split into two breaking waves that went in opposite directions and continued breaking down both sides of the elliptical reef. Each swell in the set was successively bigger, yet they all broke with the same symmetry. The waves followed the curves around the reef until, like soldiers closing ranks, they met at the entrance to the lagoon where they stopped breaking and re-formed back into rolling swells to continue their journey northwards across the Pacific.

David Helmares was in the presence of the ultimate surfing dream come true. Yet he was not watching with a surfer's eye for riding the waves, but with a wayfinder's gaze of study and respect.

He checked his position and set a sea anchor to keep his voyaging craft almost stationary in the current and the wind. He continued to watch the swells until the last and biggest waves of the set had rolled all the way to the north end of the reef. Having learned all he needed to know, he turned his attention to the first task that would take him into the heart of the energy at Ka'unua.

He paused and considered his timing and the conditions. The winds from the north blew clouds of spray off the peaks of the swells coming from the south. The rays of the morning sun were shining out of the east at a perfect angle. He smiled with well-earned confidence, dove off the bow, and began swimming west to see the crystal circle of all colors.

The impact zone was quiet except for the foam swirling in eddies of white and turquoise. He heard the call of a bird and was no longer alone. He looked up to see the kindred spirit of the Marulean wayfinders, a wandering albatross, circling on motionless wings.

He swam into the shallow waters until he could stand on the reef. Breathing rhythmically, he riveted his attention on the horizon to the south. He thought of the countless times he had scanned horizons as a surfer, impatient for another thrill, and realized he was now waiting for something of much greater meaning.

He did not wait long. The horizon itself seemed to rise up. The next set of waves was approaching Ka'unua. He began swimming with all the strength he'd built up in anticipation of this moment.

He made it over the first swell before it broke, and reached the crest of the next with seconds to spare. Then he saw what he came for.

The third swell was much, much bigger but he knew where it was going to break and he knew he was in exactly the right place. He became one with the last moments of silence all around him, watching as Ka'unua transformed raw oceanic power into exquisite natural perfection.

The wave began to break. A thousand tons of water arched up and out into mid air, forming a translucent arch high above him. For an instant he was inside a wondrous liquid cathedral. Then gravity and momentum began to change ineffable beauty into deadly force.

One last look and he dove deep.

A massive liquid guillotine slammed down behind him and detonated an explosion. Shockwaves bounced off the coral, but David was ready. With his long arms stretched above his head and his body streamlined for maximum speed, he was propelled out of the impact zone and towards the surface.

He surfaced kicking hard with his arms raised high. He was surrounded by the cloud of spray left hanging as the wave roared on down the reef. The sun was to his left. He looked to his right.

A fantastic prismatic vision was revealed in the cloud of spray. The crystal circle of all colors was about twenty feet from him, a completely round rainbow floating just above the surface of the sea.

His hands reached out as if he could touch the circle's apex. He opened his arms wide and lowered them slowly tracing the rainbow from top to bottom. When his hands finally touched, he stopped kicking and settled back down into the sea.

He quieted his mind and soul to secure the image in his memory forever. Seconds later the spray began to dissipate in the wind. The vision slowly disappeared until suddenly there was nothing left for him to see.

Now it was time to survive.

The next wave of the set was even bigger and already breaking. David exhaled all the air out of his lungs and dove quickly to the bottom to firmly grasp handholds on the reef an instant before exploding turbulence enveloped him. He released his consciousness and banished panic from his mind while he waited for the maelstrom to subside. Then he rocketed to the surface.

He inhaled three deep breaths, emptied his lungs to reduce his buoyancy, and dove to the bottom. Once more he held on to the reef with all his strength to withstand the energy scouring across the coral. Then he surfaced, inhaled, and dove again, and again and again and again, matching his cycle of survival with the rhythm of the set. Though each wave was successively bigger, he held his ground through all of them by holding on to Ka'unua.

Finally he surfaced and saw nothing to the south but the flat line of the horizon. He smiled, and then began to laugh loudly. But his laughter was not of arrogance. He was full of life's purest joy, and it was close to a minute before he returned to the world around him.

David swam back to his voyaging craft. He lifted himself up on to the low deck in the stern, water falling off his tan body in warm clear rivulets. He looked to the south and saw another set of swells approaching the impact zone of Ka'unua. He did not watch them break. They were no longer a part of his quest. He went to the bow and pulled up the sea anchor. He stepped to the foremast and raised a small sail. He walked back down the center hull and sat with his hand on the tiller. He brought her around and headed north, staying well clear of the breaking waves, using the unbroken faces of the swells to push him to other end of the reef and the passage through the coral.

He reached the entrance, lowered the sail, and drifted towards the center of the lagoon. The roar of the huge waves breaking around the reef was incessant, but there was an exquisite quiet of protection surrounding him. The wind blew a low song through the rigging of the voyaging craft, and again David heard the cry of the albatross, now circling directly above the center of the lagoon where he would perform his next task.

David ducked into the shelter and moved the sleeping mat and pillow where he had taken his short rests during the voyage. He lifted a small board from the deck and reached down into the hull to retrieve a polished box of wood, its blond and purple grain smoothed from centuries of care. His mentor, Taveka, had given it to him when he began to teach David the history of the fifteen chief navigators of the sea people. While learning about each of the men who had voyaged throughout the Nebula Archipelago back through the centuries, he carved fifteen small objects out of black coral. They were all distinctly different, and after the three years of his apprenticeship the box was now full in anticipation of this day when he would present them to the fifteen souls swimming in the waters below.

He returned to the open deck, sat on the bow of the center hull, and opened the box. He extracted the first of the carvings, closed the box and dove off the bow. The water was crystal-clear and David could see concentric rings of colored coral below, and then around him as he went deeper and deeper. It took him almost twenty seconds to reach the final center of the formation and touch the white sand. There he buried his offering to Taveka's father.

He began to sense the presence of Taveka's ancestors all around him. He exhaled a long breath, and suddenly he felt as if he was surrounded by happy children watching bubbles dance to the sky.

With a broad smile on his face, David floated to the surface. He retrieved another carving, angular yet balanced, for Taveka's grandfather. Again he dove to the white sand. This time he thought he heard laughing comments about the carving from the souls surrounding him. And for the next two hours the banter never ceased as an unmistakable presence of a brotherhood filled his soul while he honored each of Taveka's ancestors.

Finally, the ancient box was empty save for one last object. It was for the navigator who first ventured out into the Pacific from the coast of South America. The stone carving flowed and curved from bow to stern, replicating a sea-going craft made of bundled reeds, shaped to voyage the oceans as the crescent moon sails the skies. David made his last dive and placed it gently on the white sand. He paused for a second, almost as if he expected to see the black coral craft float away and set sail for a distant shore.

Then he rose from the depths slowly, his heart filled with the gratitude and approval of the navigators as their souls spoke to his.

He surfaced to see the albatross gliding in a wider circle. He swam a short distance to the south until he was above the coral rings that encircled the heart of the lagoon. The coral formation had expanded with a new ring growing outwards during the lifetime of each navigator. He dove, touched the inner ring, and surfaced. He swam around its circumference, diving now and again to touch the coral, until he was back where he started. Over the next hour David repeated the ritual above each of the rings until there were only two left, the ring that had grown during the lifetime of Taveka's father, and the outer ring of Taveka. This time he dove to find the most sacred object in the tradition of the chief navigators of Marulea, placed there by Taveka's father at the end of his life.

When he came to the surface, he was wearing a heavy necklace carved from a single piece of aquamarine coral, its links symbolizing the unbroken spirit of the navigators and sea people of Marulea.

David found himself struggling as he swam the last lap above the ring of Taveka. Diving and touching the ring became more and more difficult until he found himself almost completely exhausted. But as he traced the lifetime of his mentor, he saw the beginnings of another ring that would grow during his own lifetime as Taveka's successor.

5

Finally he completed the last circle and looked down into the depths at the apex of the ring. There Taveka would soon place the necklace where it would remain until David's successor would find it a generation from now.

The sun was now low in the west, and as he swam back to his voyaging craft his thoughts ranged back and forth in time. He had seen the crystal circle, brought gifts to the souls of the navigators, traced their rings of coral and retrieved their necklace. He had arrived as a wayfinder. He was departing as the next chief navigator of Marulea.

He lifted himself out of the water and began his preparations for the voyage home. For a moment he had another thought of the future, of a day many years from now, when he would take his final voyage to this very place with the navigator who would succeed him. He looked up at the albatross circling ever higher above him, its effortless flight a graceful reminder of life's eternal transitions through time in this world and beyond.

Then his body stiffened and his world stopped. Far above the albatross, metal wings began to shine in the golden light of the setting sun.

His heart froze. His mind reverted to logic, his first thought one of assessment. He was near the edge of the Nebula Archipelago and many hundreds of miles from all commercial, military, and cargo transport routes. There was no reason for a plane to be flying anywhere near Ka'unua.

Yes there was. There was a reason, and a jolt of recognition told him exactly what it was. Someone was looking for perfect waves - and had found just found them.

His heart convulsed like the sea in an earthquake. A raw bottom of deep and painful emotions was revealed. Then a tsunami filled with the dredged slime of his past slammed into his soul with an unstoppable force.

The selfish and thoughtless aggression of so many surfers, including himself at his worst moments, filled his mind. The nobility of the Marulean navigators was swept away in a tidal wave of black rage. Like the violent cursing locals of so many great surf spots, he began screaming at the intruder.

"Out! OUT! GET THE FUCK OUT OF HERE!"

As the words left his mouth, the metal flashed even more brightly. More obscenities filled the air. Then the wings banked towards the northeast.

The raging screams continued until the plane vanished into the sky. Only then did David Helmares begin to gain control of himself. When his voice finally went silent, he realized the albatross had vanished. No waves were breaking around the reef. All was quiet except for the echoes of his own words.

Then it hit him. The toxic suspicion and fear that had contaminated so many surfing communities around the world had now been brought to this holy place by his outburst.

His heart was overwhelmed by a surge of shame and remorse. The surfer in the plane had done nothing wrong. He was not the man whose actions had now brought hate to the waters of Ka'unua.

6

The last rays of the sun had long disappeared below the horizon before David Helmares began to compose himself by thinking of Taveka. His mentor had always talked about the importance of recognizing one's failings, of being honest with every part of one's self. David now realized the utter truth of those words, knowing he would live to the end of his days with the fact that his own selfishness had stained the most sacred day of his life.

Addicted to Perfection

L.J. Merrill strained to keep his camera steady against the porthole window of the rear door. The reef ten thousand feet below him was shrinking in his viewfinder as the turboprop began to turn back towards Easter Island. He pressed a tiny button on the camera to use the digital zoom and get a last few seconds of data. Then the pilot made a final adjustment to his course, and Merrill lost sight of his target completely. He pressed the stop button, lowered the camera, and pushed his face sideways against the glass to get a last glimpse of the nameless reef with perfect waves all around it.

Turbulence rocked the plane and Merrill instantly wrapped his arms around the camera and crouched to the floor. Then the turbo-prop fell into an air pocket, leaving him weightless for a second before bouncing him hard on his ass. For a moment the plane steadied, and with a surfer's grace and balance he stood up, ready to make his way back to his seat. Though he was wearing a button down shirt tucked into pressed khakis and a leather belt with matching walking shoes, he looked every bit the consummate waverider as he gracefully stepped across the floor moving unpredictably beneath his feet.

The turbulence worsened and the plane's tail began to flex. Merrill stayed low, as if going through the tube of a wave, while protecting the camera like a baby. Passengers were starting to panic, but not him, not with his goal only a few steps away. Oblivious to the erratic roars of the engines and the frightened cries of the passengers, he waited for the precise moment when opportunity would come out of chaos. Years of surfing gave him perfect timing. His chance came in a split second, and with two quick steps and a lithe movement, L.J. Merrill was back in his seat.

He quickly placed the camera between his knees and buckled the seat belt. Then he held it tightly to his chest and closed his blue eyes. The plane did a sudden turn to the left, and then back to the right. It went into a dive and came back up, all the while shuddering and shaking like an off-road racing jeep on Mexican dirt road.

"Shit, maybe this is really it!" he said loudly.

He heard the man next to him begin to pray in a soft voice. Merrill's thoughts raced through his life the way he heard it happened at death's door.

Suddenly the turboprop was flying perfectly steady, almost as if nothing had ever happened. He continued to grip the camera tightly until he realized they were flying in "clean" air again. He heard passengers talking excitedly to each other and the voice of the captain apologizing for the rough ride and promising smooth going for the rest of the flight.

8

He loosened his arms, and looked at the camera. He was not going to die. In fact he had a whole new life right there in his hands. He smiled, until a jolt of desire shot through him with the urge to power up the camera and see the images he had recorded. But he resisted the impulse, though not without a conscious effort. He put the camera in his aluminum briefcase and snapped closed the latches. He did not need to look at the forty five seconds of digital images right now. What he had witnessed through the viewfinder was clear in his mind's eye, having seen it in his dreams for years.

* * *

For the cognoscenti of world-wide surfing adventure, L.J. Merrill was a legend. He always traveled alone, showing up solo on the epic days at surf spots around the globe, from France to South Africa, from Central America to Western Australia, in jungle zones, lonely atolls, offshore islands and the inaccessible edges of every continent. He had survived in the most primitive conditions imaginable without giving it all a second thought: third world trains, malaria and dysentery, buses bulging with peasants, fetid ports full of thieves: nothing fazed him. His survival instinct had seen him through tight spots time and again as he discovered new destinations while always searching for the same thing.

L.J. Merrill was strung out on the rush that could only be found inside the liquid tunnels of perfect waves.

However, L.J. Merrill was no ordinary surfer addicted to the adrenaline and endorphins of surfing's ultimate moments. He was meticulous and focused as he chased the dragon around the world. Meteorology, topography, oceanography, wave physics and historical research were the keys to getting what he needed. He had been able to turn his jones into a career scouting for surfing's largest commercial travel company, Geosurf, and escort clients to the company's resorts.

But as with every junkie, the threshold high became harder to find. Although the waves were great at the Geosurf resorts, to L.J. Merrill they were now little more than methadone. He was able to maintain, but the craving of those pure first hits never left him. The time came when he became convinced he needed one more big score, one final discovery of a high that would last.

For years he had used archival satellite imaging and detailed hydrographic maps to discover new surf spots. But now what he needed seemed to be in the gaps not covered by the photos or the charts. He turned to the Internet, but the results were disappointing. The on-line satellite images of the distant regions of the seven seas were crude at best and he was unable to locate what he was looking for.

However, out of all his research he slowly distilled data pointing toward a zone of seamounts and atolls in the far reaches of the South Pacific. He re-focused, knowing he needed to dig even deeper by seeking out eyewitness accounts from those who had actually sailed those waters.

Whenever his flight paths gave him a day or two of layover anywhere near a maritime museum, he would spend every possible minute looking for clues in the charts, logs and voyage reports from the age of sail. Once, when Geosurf needed him to get from the Caribbean to Southwest Africa, he arranged to fly from Miami to London instead of directly to Cape Town so he could spend a day at the British Navy's Admiralty archives.

Though he was researching primary sources as if he was a doctoral candidate, the information was sketchy at best. Sea captains of tall ships were rarely more than cryptic in their daily logs, and their end-of-voyage reports were usually just as terse. Occasionally he found an entry such as, "Water discolored brown. Breakers." or "Reef sighted. Course altered." If the latitude and longitude had been recorded, he'd check to see if the ship had been within range of known seamounts, atolls and islands.

He then scoured maritime museums and on-line catalogs to find the original charts used by captains sailing through nearby island archipelagos. One in particular attracted his attention. It was from a voyage of a French ship in 1827 to the Gambier Islands, southeast of Tahiti. The chart had a number of handwritten annotations, which translated into "Hazardous Reef" and "Large Breakers". The zigzag of the captain's course through the reefs and low-lying atolls showed how lucky he had been to escape after risking his ship by sailing through those waters. To Merrill, the chart looked like a beautiful, celestial constellation. To that lucky captain, however, his chart was a navigator's nightmare.

Merrill then cross-referenced the chart against de-classified undersea topo surveys done for the U.S. Navy by NASA. When he found some rough evidence corroborating the account of the French captain, he knew he was on to something.

His next step was to research ships reported lost anywhere near those remote waters before charts were printed delineating sea lanes giving wide berth to the archipelago. He found a smattering of data from survivors' accounts, and one or two logs that had survived along with the captains who wrote them. But this turned out to be a dead end as there was no indication that the ships were wrecked by running aground on the type of reef he was looking for. In the end he could only conclude that if such a catastrophe had happened, and indeed several ships were reported missing with all hands lost and no wreckage found, then the logs would never be found since they – and the captains who wrote them – had gone down with their ships.

For a while he was stymied until his thoughts turned to a story familiar to anyone interested in the history of the sea, the famous tale of the mutiny on the H.M.S. Bounty. The course of the mutineers might have taken them through the archipelago in question. Perhaps they had witnessed what no man had seen before or since and, other than the French captain and his crew, survived to tell the tale.

After almost two years of digging, L.J. Merrill finally found exactly what he was looking for in the research library of the University of the South Pacific in Fiji. The librarian gave him a reproving look as he let out a surfer's hoot of excitement while turning pages over two hundred years old of log entries written by Fletcher Christian.

After deliberately setting a course into uncharted waters to avoid capture, the mutineers sailed for days without sighting any atoll or island, only to be suddenly surprised at night by the sound of booming explosions. They dropped sail and waited for dawn. As the sun rose they could see, dead ahead, a reef that surely would have sunk them. Only through sheer providence were they able to sail around its perimeter and avoid catastrophe. Christian's account concluded with a key phrase: "The large rollers became breakers when obstructed by the reef. Our ship could have been swallowed by their gaping mouths had fortune not been with us. We avoided the shoal and stayed with the swells to continue our voyage."

Merrill closed the log, knowing the reef narrowly avoided by the mutineers of the H.M.S. Bounty could very well be where he'd find the waves of his dreams.

He began to build up his theory piece by piece. The mutineers had sailed from Tahiti to their last redoubt, Pitcairn Island. Since they took no latitude and longitude sights, he had to recreate their probable course by comparing the speeds of normal winds and currents with the hull speed of the Bounty. Double-checking the mutineers' diaries, he narrowed his search to a triangular zone of a hundred square miles due south of the Actaeon Islands.

Now he needed to directly address several critical issues.

First, he needed reefs fully exposed to the south and thus well outside the effect of any swell "shadowing", or reduction, caused by blocking atolls and islands, a common situation throughout Polynesia. He went back to his database, re-checked all his charts, and found an area free of any shadowing. There were several seamounts in the zone, though no reefs were indicated. But he pressed on as if there were.

Next he needed water temperatures warm enough for the propagation of certain species of coral which grow gradually into long, gently sloping reefs. He checked existing temperature data for that part of the Pacific, and though the data was rough, there were indications of warm currents flowing through the area.

This was a major advance for L.J. Merrill because it solved what had been a recurring problem in his explorations to find perfect waves in Polynesia. The biggest waves were often too hollow and too powerful to ride because they came out of extremely deep water and broke all too abruptly on shallow coral shoals. However, there was an excellent chance that, thanks to prevailing water temperatures, the reef that almost sank H.M.S. Bounty would have a gentler slope that would build waves more gradually and cause them to break less precipitously.

He began to feel he was definitely on the right track. All the preliminary indicators were in place: the ship sinkings, the mutineers' diaries, the lack of swell shadowing and the water temperature. When another piece of the puzzle fell into place, L.J. Merrill knew he was closing in on the reality of his surfer's dream in a very remote region of the South Pacific.

He knew that *El Niño, a warm water phenomena that caused sea levels to rise, was being exacerbated by the Pacific Decadal Oscillation, a large scale transfer of heat around the Pacific Ocean. And now, global warming was accelerating both natural phenomena, resulting in sea levels rising as much as a meter in a few specific areas of the South Pacific. One of those areas included the zone identified by Merrill through his research. There might be a chance that the reef, if previously too shallow to ride, might now be surfed safely thanks to an extra cushion of water.*

Finally, one last body of information had to be acquired. He needed to know about the prevailing winds in the triangular zone, and he got what he wanted from the oceanography department at the Jet Propulsion Laboratory in Pasadena, California. His contact there, an old surfer and world famous scientist named Bill Patzert, had helped him find the water temperature data he'd used to solve the coral species problem.

Merrill gave him another call and was lucky that Patzert had the time to find and analyze the detailed wind information Merrill needed. He was even luckier when Patzert called back and told him it was possible for passing fronts to generate northerly winds instead of the normal southeast trades that dominated the area. Those rare winds would be critical, because the raw power Merrill wanted would have to be refined for the waves to be ridden safely. When Patzert told him the northerlies could occur any time from August to October, Merrill knew there was only one piece left in the puzzle. And he already had it.

He knew there could be some big swells coming up from the Southern Ocean during those months, and in fact, the biggest Southern Hemisphere swell to ever hit Malibu had occurred in August.

L.J. Merrill knew what he wanted, he knew where it was, and he knew when to go. The totality of his theories indicated a high level of probability concerning the reef, the weather, and the waves. He was ready to score his high. Now he had to figure a way around his next big problem: he had a job.

Merrill's scouting skills had once been the key to Geosurf's success, and in the beginning he had been treated like a partner by the company's owner, Ian Clark. However, the relationship had become strained over the years as his love of the far frontiers began to clash with the facts of life in the surf travel industry. Clark had more than enough business at existing sites and didn't need him making more discoveries. But Merrill had never saved up much money, and when Clark offered him contracts to guide tours to places he'd discovered years ago, Merrill signed them.

Yet despite the fact he was on a short leash, L.J. Merrill felt blindly optimistic when he sent Clark an outline of his plan to find the last, best big wave arena on earth. Without divulging too much of what he knew, he tried to convince Ian Clark that chartering a seaplane simply had to be done.

The response was not what he expected. Even though he had found all the company's prime surf sites, Clark told him in no uncertain terms the days of chartering seaplanes to follow his hunches, with Geosurf paying the bills, were over.

Merrill was stunned by Clark's rebuff. But like a child who just cannot face the realities of a divorce, he convinced himself if he just tried hard enough, he could make everything all right again.

Then L.J. Merrill got lucky. After giving surfing lessons to some French millionaires at the Geosurf resort in Tahiti, he received instructions from Clark to catch a flight to Chile where he would shepherd a group of California surfers to the rugged southern coast.

Merrill knew the flight would take him close to the remote archipelago of his research. Since Geosurf flew clients on Trans Pacific Airlines quite frequently, he tried to go through channels to see if the pilot could make a change in course to allow Merrill to possibly shoot some video from the plane. The flight operations manager at the airline office in Papeete listened politely to Merrill, and then just as politely refused the request.

That only made him more determined. He had been in situations like this before, dealing with officials in countries around the world, and he knew what to do next.

On the day of the flight L.J. Merrill arrived early at the airport. Having learned the name of the flight's pilot, he waited until he saw the man coming through the lobby an hour before the flight was scheduled to depart. He struck up a conversation with him, and a minute later an envelope changed hands containing a slip of paper with several sets of latitude and longitude figures. The envelope also contained a thousand dollars in cash.

Two hours after take off, the plane made a change in course. The captain radioed he was avoiding some threatening clouds, and thus nothing was perceived to be amiss back at Trans-Pacific's flight operations office in Tahiti.

A few minutes later, L.J. Merrill checked his GPS unit. It confirmed they were flying over waters once sailed by the Bounty's mutineers and now affected by both the cycles of natural change and the follies of man's excesses. He turned on his digital video camera as he took it out of his briefcase before heading to the rear of the plane where he would get the most unobstructed view possible. He was looking for the ultimate wave, and though it was October and late in the season for the Southern Hemisphere, he knew a big swell was running – and he might never get a chance like this again.

* * *

L.J. Merrill had a familiar warmth inside him, that of an addict who had just scored. He had found the ultimate perfect wave breaking in the most remote archipelago in the South Pacific. No one but him knew of its existence. Certainly it had never been surfed, since the ruler edged waves breaking perfectly along both sides of the wide, elliptical reef would have been impossible to ride before the latest and most powerful El Niño had raised sea levels to all-time heights. He was sure of his data and sure of his instincts. This was it, the last great find in modern surfing: the most distant, the most powerful, and the most beautiful waves on earth.

13

He pulled the seat belt a little tighter as he stared out the window and watched the Southern Hemisphere's panoply of constellations begin to brighten the deep blue of the heavens. He finally let go of all the tension in his body and thought of the wonders of the universe and life itself.

But just as he began to float on his high, anxiety sliced through his mind. He came down fast, but it was a familiar feeling and he reacted with the aplomb of a veteran addict. He opened his briefcase, put a data stick in the side of the camera, and downloaded the image stream to make sure the data was secure. Then he put the seat back and ran the images over and over again behind his closed eyes, knowing that this time the high was going to last for a while.

Four hours later he came to when the captain announced they were approaching Santiago. He buckled up and considered Clark's instructions to meet the tour group and guide them to surf spots he had discovered years ago. But, like a junkie who knows exactly who he is, he knew he'd have no second thoughts about blowing off an appointment that clashed with his need.

And how long do you plan to stay in our country?" asked the customs official.

"Unfortunately my plans have changed and I'll be leaving for California as soon as possible," said Merrill.

The official stamped his passport, and he went to the nearest payphone. He knew Geosurf's owner would not want to hear about any change in plans. And even if Clark was willing to listen, he'd tell Merrill now was not a good time and any ideas about scouting would have to wait.

But patience is not a word from an addict's vocabulary.

"Ian, this can't wait! This reef has got the best waves I've ever seen! I've got to get out there right away!" Merrill said to himself, rehearsing his pitch as the call went through.

Two Seconds

"No, you can't come back right now and I won't send you a ticket! All you've got is a few seconds shot from a plane, and there's five clients at fifteen grand each waiting for you to take them surfing!"

Ian Clark listened for a second before holding the headset away from his ear. Dressed in Armani behind a tech-and-teak desk, he was the image of a successful executive except for the gaunt look on his face and the deep lines around his brown eyes.

"Listen, L.J.," he interrupted, "I don't have time right now. Go over to FDX, use their secure web site and send me the file. Then give 'em the data stick. You did make a backup, didn't you? Tell 'em I want it on my desk tomorrow at 9 a.m. Then do what you are paid to do, okay? Take the clients out to dinner, drink some Pisco, and get some sleep. And tomorrow go to that spot, uh - - " he swiveled around and glanced at the map behind his desk, "that place near Valparaiso and go surfing with those guys."

Merrill started to argue, but Clark wasn't listening. His attention was on his computer and the market ticker flowing below a packed spreadsheet. He scribbled down a stock price before it disappeared while Merrill described the turbulence that almost broke up the plane and how he thought he was going to die.

"L.J., I understand you went through a lot. We all go through a lot. Call me back in twenty-four hours. Just give our clients what they paid for and we'll do just fine."

"Yeah, but Ian, why can't you get someone else down here? I've just found the best surf spot in the world with the most amazing big waves I've ever seen! We've got to get on it right away!"

As far as Ian Clark was concerned, the only thing he had to do right away was get off the phone, execute a trade and make some quick money.

"Ian? Didn't you hear what I said? This place is perfect!"

"Yeah, yeah, I'm listening, L.J. I can't wait to see it. Send it right away and call me to confirm, no, don't call me. Have the FDX guy e-mail me the tracking number. I'll talk to you in exactly twenty-four hours. Use the direct line on the cell phone I gave to the group. Don't worry, this will work out unreal. Just do what I tell you to do, but do it right now, okay? Talk to you tomorrow. Later, bro."

* * *

L.J. Merrill and Ian Clark were once the ultimate team when it came to guiding well-heeled surfers to perfect waves all over the globe. Ian was the industry insider, L.J. the pure-hearted adventurer. Together they founded Geosurf Expeditions, although Clark structured the "partnership" to make him sole owner of the company while maintaining a contractor arrangement with Merrill. That was fine by L.J., who didn't care about business details so long as he was scouting, or riding, perfect waves. Over the past ten years their surf camps and remote resorts had made Clark a millionaire on paper. But now he needed liquidity, because without it he was liable to be indicted.

Ian Clark was a sometime surfer with a degree in journalism from Cal State Long Beach when he got his start in the surf industry writing up glib video reviews and contest results at one of the magazines. He was a quick study and soon understood what the publication was really about, and it wasn't surfing.

From a strictly business point-of-view, the mag was little more than a catalog for corporations using surfing to sell everything from clothing to cars to deodorant. Therefore, his job depended on ad revenues and making nice with people who didn't surf. That meant the only way he could get ahead was to keep one foot in editorial and one foot in advertising by building relationships with surf stars while helping companies with branding and market penetration.

It was brutal work, and he spent five years climbing the masthead before finally making associate editor. The salary was good and he had stock options in the conglomerate that owned the magazine. Yet as an employee, no matter how much he made it was never enough for living large in Orange County. He was stuck – until he did a prospectus on himself and came up with an idea that could be leveraged bigtime.

He could sell the soul of surfing. He could deliver on the endless dreams of surfers craving perfection by establishing a global network of resorts near the world's best waves. And being a veteran of the surf media, he knew how to create myths and heroics out of practically nothing. So it would be easy to create an aura of exclusivity that would have the O.C. surfing elite begging for reservations and paying five figures for high-end excursions to the places he controlled.

First, he needed the waves themselves. He needed a scout, and in all the surfing world there was only one person who knew how to find the quality product high-rolling customers would demand. Clark knew him by reputation only, but from the stories and legends he learned all he needed to know. It took some time and some sleuthing, but the day came when Ian Clark finally found L.J. Merrill on the other side of the world, in Western Australia, camped out on a deserted headland overlooking perfect, empty waves.

He laid out a proposal to start Geosurf Expeditions, correctly guessing Merrill would see it as a way to turn his addiction into a profession. Clark knew Merrill was a Type-A surf junkie, but what he didn't know at the time was that L.J. Merrill was also a good person at heart. Merrill had always respected the locals he'd met around the world as he searched for bigger, better and faster waves. Clark's proposal gave him a momentary flash of inspiration: with hard currency coming in from Geosurf clients, they could help impoverished coastal communities throughout the Third World. Without going into a lot of details or learning more about each other, Ian Clark and L.J. Merrill shook hands outside the tent and then went for a surf at what later became one of Geosurf's first resorts.

Ten years later, the company owned twenty surf camps and eight high-end resorts on five continents, throughout Polynesia, and all around the Indian Ocean. Reservations were booked years in advance and locals had jobs building the camps and working at the resorts. The "Glimmer Twins", as Clark and Merrill were nicknamed by the surf media, were getting all they wanted in terms of Orange County "juice" and endless tubes, respectively.

It was all good, as they say, until the singer decided he wanted to be a pop star right when the lead guitarist wanted to take the band deeper into the pure fix of the blues.

In the beginning, and for some time afterwards, Geosurf was welcomed by indigenous communities who were grateful for the positive economic impacts on their village economies. But after ten years of double digit growth, the locals began to want a bigger cut of the action. Merrill could not help but agree with them and, remembering Clark's promises from the early days, began to talk about turning the resorts into surfing preserves locally owned and operated by cooperatives that would share the profits to the benefit of families and communities.

This was not what Ian Clark was about by any means, since Merrill's "share the wealth" attitude would have done nothing for Clark's upward climb in cash-conscious Orange County. Clark had indeed made a lot of promises to Merrill at first and had kept some of them, but he found it increasingly difficult to endure Merrill's shrill tirades about the rich getting richer, the social inequities of the Third World, and Geosurf's profits.

After one particularly boring dose of Merrill's naïveté, Clark had snickered, "You only know the half of it."

"What did you say Ian?"

"Oh, nothing, L.J. You only know the heart of it, of surfing, that is. I've got a lot of other things I gotta think about to keep Geosurf going."

Geosurf did business in a variety of currencies and Ian Clark had become adept at moving money from one country to another. The upside was not big in the beginning, but there came a time when he was able to skim off enough cash to start playing the international commodities markets. He would keep the money moving until he had enough to invest in offshore corporations on the advice of brash young stockbrokers driving Ferraris around Newport Beach.

Soon he was looking and acting like a player, and that was good enough for them, and him. It was a fast crowd to run with, and Ian Clark found himself golfing and partying instead of doing much surfing. After all, he was the owner of a major company in the surf industry, but truth was, he never liked to *ride waves all that much. He was always afraid of being pushed underwater and hitting the bottom. The day came, however, when he learned that wipeouts in the world of money could be just as bad, or worse.*

Thanks to Clark's fast-and-loose use of the company as his personal piggy bank, Geosurf's business plan began to fray at the edges. The waves never changed, so he could only make more money by first increasing his volume, then his prices. Geosurf was turning big dollars, but it was never enough. His problems began to gather steam as his worldwide exposure to market fluctuations increased. Because of the amounts of money he was moving to cover his growing losses, he found himself skirting laws first devised to snare drug dealers. That's when he began to realize there was only one solution to his downward spiral. He needed a pile of cash, and he needed it fast.

* * *

The forty-five seconds went by all too quickly, so he ran the data stream again in slow motion after enlarging the video window in the center of the screen until it covered more than half the spreadsheet displaying his daily investment positions.

He stopped the motion on one particularly clear frame. Then he stared at the three registered letters sitting on his desk: one from his accountant, one from his lawyer, and one from the I.R.S. He looked again at the waves arrayed around a perfect reef, but a phone icon began to blink at the top of the screen. He saw the number, knew who it was, and knew he had to think fast.

"You weren't supposed to call back until tomorrow, L.J., but yeah, I got it and just looked at it. It's hand-held, slightly out-of-focus, not long enough and you were up at what, ten thousand feet? So I'm going to have it re-processed to see what's really down there."

Ian Clark paused and took a deep breath before taking a fateful step.

"I'm going to need some time to figure out how we're going to market this place, L.J., because you did find the best surf spot in the world and the most amazing big waves ever!"

Clark heard the excitement in Merrill's voice and for a moment his heart felt heavy - until ticker numbers running across the bottom of the screen reminded him he had no time for nostalgia.

"No, you're staying there. I need you to take those guys surfing. You can fly back when they do. They paid a surcharge because they wanted to surf with the legendary L.J. Merrill, so you're going to make an extra three hundred a day!"

Merrill started to protest, but Clark cut him off.

"L.J., we can sell some big ticket packages when we open up your reef. We can get some local fishermen involved and really help out their villages. It's way out in the ocean, isn't it?"

Clark caught himself before saying another word. Keeping the exact location of a new discovery secret until they were face-to-face was an important tradition for L.J. Merrill.

"That's why I want to come back now! I can show you where it is and we can get started right away!"

"L.J., you'll be back in two weeks," said Clark in a firm-but-friendly voice, "Right now you need to do what you're paid to do. Go surfing, keep the customers happy, and make some good money. And trust me, when you get back, I'll have a game plan ready to go."

"Ok, Ian, maybe you're right. Besides, the place probably won't be good again till March or April. We're gonna need a seaplane and all kinds of stuff, but it will all be worth it."

"I'm sure it will, L.J., I'm sure it will. See ya at LAX."

He pressed delete on the keyboard and the phone icon disappeared from the display, leaving the biggest perfect waves in surfing's history superimposed over the spreadsheet that mapped his world of money. He looked at the computer screen for a long time and saw his future begin to take shape - until he realized Merrill would never agree to selling out to a big corporation for the kind of cash he so desperately needed. Maybe he could flip a deal before Merrill got back? But as soon as the thought occurred to him, he knew it wouldn't work. The legendary scout had found surfing's Shangri-la and would demand to know why his once-in-a-lifetime discovery had been sold to the highest bidder.

"And then what would I tell him? That I needed a lot of cash to pay off debts because I've been skimming profits instead of keeping promises?" he said in a voice that only his conscience could hear.

The relentless data streaming across the bottom of the screen never stopped, and he knew he was cornered by two alternatives with but one way out: he'd either have to admit his mistakes and trust L.J. Merrill, or betray him and stay out of jail.

It took Ian Clark all of two seconds to make his decision.

Surf for Sale

It was an unusually gloomy day in the heart of the surf industry. The Catalina eddy was blowing a thick, dirty mist against the glass curtain walls of Wavelife International's corporate headquarters in Newport Beach. The view from the top floor was anything but grand, and the mood in the executive conference room was just as gray.

Ian Clark was waiting outside the room, ticking off his pitch points, when the door opened and he was motioned to come in. There were seven people sitting around the table and they were all staring at him. No introductions were made, and no one said a word. The silence put him off balance. Then he realized that if he lost control of the meeting, he'd never get it back, and if that happened, he'd be walking out the door empty-handed. The very thought practically drained the blood from his gameface. But then his survival instinct kicked in, his mind switched to autopilot, and he began his well-rehearsed presentation to the people at the top of a corporation in trouble.

"Ladies and gentlemen, five thousand miles southeast of this room there is a range of undersea mountains crowned with coral reefs that have been avoided by sailors for centuries. They are not on any maps, and are hundreds of miles from the nearest inhabited islands. Now, most open ocean reefs are too shallow and irregular to surf safely, but - - -"

Clark was immediately interrupted by a voice from the back of the room.

"But what, Clark? My surfers aren't about to surf some death reef in the middle of nowhere no matter what you try to sell us," said Roberto Mercante, founder of the company, "So why are we here?"

The interruption was just what Clark needed. He snapped out of his fear and the adrenalin kicked in.

"Times have changed, Roberto, so why don't you just relax and pay attention? You might learn something," said Clark, his tone of voice purposefully sharp.

"Global warming is here to stay, and for a lot of people that's bad news. Of course, some are trying to reduce their contributions to this ecological disaster, although by all the chrome SUV's I see down there in the parking lot, I'd say we still have a ways to go."

Clark didn't see the dirty looks he got from June Wilson, Wavelife's Wall Street liaison, and Bill Massara, the company's chief financial officer, who had both made a lot of money in recent years at Wavelife as evidenced by their ostentatious urban assault vehicles parked conspicuously near the front door.

20

"And who knows? Maybe Mother Nature will be able to absorb the excesses of our society and begin reversing the trend. In the meantime, the world ocean is becoming a stern judge of man's folly, the sentence will not be commuted; and a parole hearing is a long way off. We have fallen from grace with the sea, or so the environmentalists would have you believe.

"The reality is, of course, that as long as you can sell t-shirts and trunks in Kansas, the consequences of rising sea levels won't mean squat to your bottom line. Yet, somewhere in your cash-strapped conscience there must be a twinge of regret over the current situation – I'm referring to global warming, not the downturn in your stock price."

The vibe in the room was now becoming really edgy, exactly as planned.

"Ok, so much for the tree-hugging. After all, in our wonderful world of modern surfing, is there anything more important than contests, big wave reputations and price points?" said Clark, daggers of sarcasm stabbing with every word.

Now he had their complete attention, and especially that of Cheryl Corlund, the CEO of Wavelife. With her blond hair cut short, piercing green eyes and a steel-trap mind, she intimidated everyone in the surf industry. And now here was a guy trying to yank her chain.

"Get to the point, Clark. I don't have all day, much less another five minutes for this bullshit."

"Ok, sorry for all the doom-and-gloom. I forgot, rising sea levels and global warning really have nothing to do with the sinking stock of a company drowning in debt. Or do they?"

Clark paused and made careful eye contact with each and every person sitting around the table. He had them right where he wanted them. He looked straight at Cheryl Corlund.

"So let's get down to business. I'm here to offer you the chance to get in on the discovery of waves that could not have been ridden until global warming caused a rise in sea levels, waves that are now bigger and more perfect than anything ever seen in the history of surfing. It is my guess that such an opportunity may have some value to Wavelife International given your current situation."

He took a disk out of his shirt pocket and sailed it down the table without breaking eye contact with the CEO.

"Here you go, Roberto, let's take a look at this."

Mercante's dark Brazilian eyes glared at Clark. He inserted the disk into the DVD player and lobbed the remote control back to Clark. A color balance image appeared on the huge plasma screen mounted on the wall. Clark moved out of the way to reveal shaky images of a briefcase, a seat, a window, and then a zoom down from a plane flying at ten thousand feet over a vast blue ocean.

The group watched in silence. Forty-five seconds later, Clark hit stop as the camera turned away from the plane's window. Nobody said a word. Clark sensed he had exactly what Wavelife needed. A second later, he knew he was right.

"Where is this place? And when can I go there?" demanded Mercante.

Clark's smile was just this side of a smirk. The bait had been swallowed. Now he'd set the hook.

"All in good time, my friend. Let's talk about the surf for a moment, why don't we? The waves are twenty-five feet high, maybe bigger, coming in every twenty seconds, and the ride will be almost a mile long. Oh, it also looks like the wind is straight offshore."

"Show it again," said Heath Larson in a commanding tone backed up by his reputation as the best big wave surfer in the world.

Ian Clark sensed the challenge and confronted it directly.

"What for?" he asked with disdain, "You can't see anything anyway."

"So what the hell are we doing here, Clark?"

Mercante's temper was at the boiling point. He had been one of the pro circuit's hottest surfers until his favela roots took hold and he began to compete in the surf industry. But he quickly found out that in the garment business, surf savvy was nowhere near as important as bean counting. That was why his wife continued to use her maiden name, and that was why a quick darting look from her green eyes was all he needed to know he was to shut his mouth immediately.

Clark saw the silent exchange and played off it perfectly to take total command of the room.

"I'll tell you what you're doing here, Roberto. You're trying to save your company, and you're listening to me because I know how you're going to do it. Now stop wasting everybody's time and just pay attention."

He tapped two clicks on the remote and up came Geosurf's logo and a column of icons, each containing moving images of perfect waves from Geosurf's exclusive surf zones. At the bottom of the menu was a final selection labeled "Under Development" with just a generic icon and an "X" on it. Clark scrolled down to it and clicked the remote.

The last frame from the original clip began to grow as if through an unlimited zoom lens, simultaneously coming into perfect focus until the frame was full of swells arrayed around the reef like spokes on a wheel. Then they began to move.

Swell after swell came from the top of the screen, splitting into matching perfect waves marching in formation around both sides of the reef, their smooth faces rolling over into huge tubes with perfect precision.

"Hey", said Sonny-boy Noaloa, winner of pro surfing's world tour two years in a row, "that mo like it, brah. You show dat one again, yeah?"

"Hold on there, champ," said Clark. "Wait till you see what's next."

* * *

After his last conversation with L.J. Merrill, Ian Clark knew exactly what he had to do. Merrill never divulged the locations of new surf zones until they met face to face. This time, however, that meeting would never take place.

22

Clark quickly called Trans-Pacific and told his contact that a *Geosurf* employee had seen what looked like good surf on a flight from Tahiti to South America. *Was it possible that the flight recorder could provide the GPS position, and the altitude, just before the plane had experienced some turbulence about two hours into its flight?* The airline executive was only too happy to oblige *Geosurf's* owner, and with the GPS data on its way, Ian Clark started working on his pitch to Wavelife International.

He had sold surf tours for years using real video, but all he had was Merrill's distant footage compressed into a data file, and that would not be good enough for his purposes. So he sent the file to a CGI company that had done a lot of work for *Geosurf* enhancing surf video images. He remembered discussions he'd had with them about the state-of-the-art work the company had done for NASA using software developed to simulate landings on Venus and Mars. He got on the phone to the VP of the company, and an hour later, Clark was in business.

The last frame of the image stream showed a shadow angle on the tail stabilizer. Combined with the GPS and altitude data, that single frame would help the programmers to reverse engineer a series of calculations, similar to sea captains using sextants and trig tables, to determine the sun's precise position when Merrill had shot the images. This would give them a exact reference angle for the almost imperceptible shadows of the wave's hollow tunnels. With the ability to then extrapolate the geometry and dimensions of the forms on the sea's surface, the programmers and computer graphics artists could then create a three-dimensional digital tour of the waves. The VP assured Clark that it was quite doable, and in seventy-two hours Clark saw a rough of exactly what he needed. In the end the two-minute tour cost almost thirty thousand dollars, but that was cheap considering the bet Clark was placing on his future.

* * *

All eyes in the conference room were glued to the screen displaying a perfect vision of some of the most, if not THE most, extraordinary waves they'd ever seen. The "video" was not real, but Clark was almost certain that neither the executives nor the surfers would ask questions about the stunning images.

They didn't.

Although Mercante and Corlund were used to cutting-edge pitch meetings, neither they, nor anyone else sitting around the table had ever seen anything like this. The "camera" seemed to drop until it stopped just above the surface of the water facing a wave that filled the screen. The wave started breaking. The "camera" did not move, and the waterfall/avalanche got closer and closer until it finally closed right over the "camera".

There was a stifled gasp from the lone female surfer in the room.

Aleja Gracellen caught her body involuntarily responding to something outside the boundaries of her skills. She was the woman who danced with the sea, but deep inside, she knew riding such a wave would be no dance.

The "camera" went underwater as the liquid mountain rolled overhead. Then it came up to the surface into the sun only to have another wave fill the frame. The "camera" panned slowly to the right. Now they were looking directly into a hollow tunnel big enough to swallow a school bus. The arc of the wave curved out into space like a nautilus shell. It was a ruler-edged waterfall peeling perfectly like the honing blade of a lathe.

The "camera" pulled back as the power roared forward, all the time maintaining the view into the tube. Ten meters back in the tunnel a maelstrom of certain death was clearly visible.

"Nice wave," said Larson.

"I thought you'd like it Heath. That's why I want you to be the first to ride it." Clark felt confident enough to lay it on a little thick even though both he and Cheryl Corlund knew what was really going on had nothing to do with anything other than a lot of money.

The "camera" floated up to a safer position. The low angle of the sun gave the thirty foot waves an ominous look, their concave, translucent faces glowing a deep blue before feeling the reef and breaking perfectly.

It was nothing but a sophisticated illusion, but the visceral reactions of the people around the table were anything but digital. They were like awestruck climbers looking at Mt. Everest as the jet stream blew a plume of snow off the summit, their hearts and minds transfixed by a hypnotic vision of glory and danger.

Roberto Mercante mind-surfed the waves, lost in delusions of surfing at a world-class level. Sonny-boy Noaloa imagined himself shredding turns and getting big air all over the huge walls as if he was skateboarding giant half-pipes. Heath Larson saw himself so far back inside the tunnels that he couldn't be seen at all. Aleja Gracellen was wondering if she'd ever be good enough to ride what she was seeing, and both Wilson and Massara were wishing they knew how to surf just to be able to appreciate what was on the screen.

But to Cheryl Corlund, however, it was like watching a person screaming behind soundproof glass. There was just too much raw energy for her to absorb, and she didn't bother trying. By the reactions of the surfers, she didn't need to know anything more about Clark's find. Unnoticed by the others, she opened up a laptop screen built into the conference table, clicked an icon, and began to study a spreadsheet full of data. Her mind went into high gear, knowing she would have to strike a deal with Clark to integrate his find into her plans for Wavelife's future.

The "camera" began to fly free and clear above the swells revealing a mirror image set-up on the other side of the lagoon. Just as perfect and powerful as the "rights", the "lefts" peeled like Pipeline, with two important exceptions: instead of stopping abruptly after one quick tube section, they kept going for almost a mile. And they were much bigger than anything ever ridden at Pipe, second reef included.

The POV pulled back up to ten thousand feet. A seamless edit brought them back to the real images shot just before the camera angle became impossible. The screen went blank for a second. Then the Geosurf logo appeared.

Ian Clark and Cheryl Corlund locked gazes. She knew he needed cash, like a prospector needed a grubstake, in exchange for the promise of a bonanza based on a mere forty-five seconds of reality and two minutes of simulation. He knew he'd successfully made his pitch as if each frame was a grain of gold found in the sand of a creek bed leading to surfing's "Treasure of Sierra Madre". There was no misunderstanding between them. Each knew exactly what was on the table: Wavelife needed a shot in the arm.

* * *

Waves have always been at the heart of a multi-billion dollar industry because their wild energy makes them an endless source of wonder and respect. Dozens of companies used man's fascination with waves to sell apparel to everyone from awestruck tourists to veteran surfers. For years, Wavelife International had done it better than anyone else.

When Roberto Mercante founded the company, he understood firsthand the unique affect of waves on human emotions. He knew the world of surfing to be a truly awesome place of raw energy, where waves are like wild beasts roaming at will across the vast curved liquid space covering much of the planet. He'd found a lot of romance in man's relationship with the seven seas, but he'd learned more than once that no one can ever take their hospitality for granted as long as waves move across their surface. Their beauty can be inspiring, but at the same time, he knew that waves are, in a purely primal sense, an enemy.

Wavelife's success was based on this paradox, and another paradox as well. Surfing is the antithesis of business, and sharp as Mercante was about how to use waves as a marketing tool, he quickly learned he wasn't going to be able to make real money without the smarts of an MBA. Though it wasn't a marriage of convenience by any means, Mercante had found the perfect match in Cheryl Corlund, Harvard grad, looking to make millions and finding fertile ground in the world of her husband. It was a dream team that took the surfing world by storm.

The early advertising campaigns emphasized the power and subliminal terror of big waves. As the company grew and began to target non-surfers, marketing experts were brought in who designed campaigns around the carefree joy of children letting the gentle surf chase them up and down the sand. Then, when sales numbers began to slack off, Wavelife went back to its "core surf" identity. One campaign traded on the survival instincts triggered when tourists are caught unawares by rogue waves. Mercante re-branded waves as if they were sharks shattering the complacency of a day at the beach. "Never Turn Your Back on the Ocean" took on a "Jaws"-like resonance in the media - and sales soared.

25

When the fear angle began to wear thin, Wavelife went back to fun in the sun and sales jumped again. Within a few years they'd perfected a marketing strategy of constant motion across a broad spectrum from panic to joy, trading on the fathomless natural power of waves that can elicit primal instincts from dread to ecstasy.

Wavelife mined these veins of fear and fun, refined them into sophisticated branding campaigns, and marketed quality clothing at premium prices. It worked like a charm, and revenue went through the roof. The company became the most powerful in the surf industry and, almost like a diamond cartel, eventually controlled supply and demand of surfing's media identity as if they were the anointed gatekeeper of "genuine surf" to the New York apparel industry. Corlund's excellent management kept the profits rolling in, and when the company went public, Wavelife International was an instant hit on Wall Street.

But as with every trend in the rag trade, what once was coveted eventually became commonplace. Garmentos who didn't know Heath Larson from Frankie Avalon realized that they could move product simply by slapping surf lingo on their stuff. They flooded distribution channels with cut-rate knock-offs at hard-to-beat price points. They knew there was plenty of business to be done selling to people who didn't surf but wanted to be cool because nothing could be sold as "cool" as easily as surfing. And as long as they were paying less for the same image that kept the kids happy, parents were happy to save a buck at the expense of Wavelife's "core authenticity" branding campaigns.

At the same time, management ran into problems keeping shareholders happy by selling strictly to surf shops and better clothing stores. Executives of publicly traded corporations always need ever-increasing volumes to keep the share price up, and Wavelife was no different. Mercante and Corlund had to start doing business with big box chains and off-price outlets. That drove the surf shops crazy and incensed the buyers from the up-scale retailers.

Within a year Wavelife's "core surf" credibility began to erode. Wavelife had strip-mined its way to all-time highs on Wall Street – by sinking to retail's rock bottom world in the cut-rate bargain bins. But that meant there was nothing special about the brand anymore, and investor analysts and institutional shareholders began to lose interest in Wavelife as a "hot" buy. A day of reckoning was now on the horizon like a set of swells that would soon turn into waves of problems that threatened to overwhelm Mercante, Corlund, and the company they'd built from scratch.

Ian Clark learned of Wavelife's dilemma over a year ago while on the golf course. Word was the stock, once a status symbol in the surf industry, had been downgraded from "buy" to "hold", and if analysts began to issue "sell" recommendations, rumor had it the consequences would be quite serious. Clark knew the rumors were based in fact because like all the clothing companies in the surf industry, Wavelife borrowed heavily each season in order to pay cloth and sewing contractors upon delivery so that garments can be shipped to the retailers. The problem was Wavelife didn't get paid until the garments "checked through". Until a sale was rung up, Wavelife didn't get paid. From his days with the magazines and late-paying advertisers, he'd learned that banks lending to apparel industry corporations keep a close eye on sales figures, and loans covenants are very strict. The banks always got their money first, and depending on the amount of orders placed at trade shows versus sales projections, even Wavelife had sometimes been unable to get working capital during times of economic uncertainty – or marketing ineffectiveness. That time had finally come for Wavelife, and Corlund had been forced to take a drastic step to secure working capital.

It became common knowledge that she had to start borrowing from "factors", who work exclusively in the clothing business and who charge extremely high interest rates and often are nothing if not heavy-handed. She had no choice, even though she knew the dangers of working with factors. If they called in her loans for any reason whatsoever, Wavelife would have to pay in full on the spot, and she'd seen what happened to other companies when they didn't: offices were padlocked, liquidators showed up the next day with moving vans, and a company was out of business in a heartbeat.

Corlund walked the tightrope like a pro for several product cycles, but in a strange-but-true version of how things sometimes worked for publicly traded corporations, even though revenue was up, the value of the company was down. All her efforts to appease Wall Street had only created a whirlpool of diminishing returns. By trying to compete in mass-market channels, she'd only diluted the brand, which forced her to try to sell even more, which only cheapened the brand. And when the stock began to sag, she knew something had to be done, and fast.

Although Wavelife owed hundreds of millions of dollars to a consortium of banks and factors, payments had always been made on time. But now the stock price was making everybody nervous, including the Orange County brokers who had made fortunes recommending Wavelife stock. Meetings with investment analysts and creditors were growing testy, and the word on the street was not good. The bankers were seriously considering reductions in the amount of money they were willing to loan Wavelife, and the factors were upping their interest rates. Unless something drastic was done at Wavelife to keep the creditors happy, the wolf would soon be at the door.

When Clark asked his broker buddies what they thought Corlund was going to do, they told him how corporations in trouble often find new waves of cash to ride down Wall Street. Everything depended on perception, they said. Shareholder enthusiasm had to be ignited one way or another, and the easiest way to do that was to re-define the company with a fresh and powerful branding campaign. Clark had that skill set wired from his days at the magazine, and in his growing desperation for cash, he thought of how he could work up a pitch to Corlund that would hold up under her scrutiny and net him a fat consulting fee. He knew he'd have to come up with an ingenious and innovative publicity campaign and unparalleled market penetration, but to do that he would need something extraordinary and unlike anything ever seen before in the history of surfing.

And then one day he saw exactly what he needed.

27

* * *

"What's to stop us from simply finding this place ourselves?"

"C'mon Roberto, if it was that easy, I wouldn't be here. The South Pacific is a big place, and even if you found a reef that looked like it might have potential, who knows how long you'd have to wait for the right combination of swell, weather and wind. No, Roberto, you'd be better off working with me, because I know where it is and I know when the waves will be good."

"What do you want out of this?" asked Cheryl Corlund.

"The honor of your presence when I open the place up."

Corlund smiled. She knew this was just a smokescreen and she didn't say what she was thinking because she knew what was coming next.

"Plus expenses," added Clark, "and future considerations."

As in buying Geosurf when the time comes, thought Corlund. She, too, had done her homework and knew all about Clark's money problems and what kind of deal he needed to make, and soon, to extract himself from the financial vise that gripped him.

Heath Larson felt tension fill the room like a set of huge waves coming in from the horizon. So he did the same thing he always had when, despite his true courage and determination, he sensed he was out of his element. He relaxed an let discretion be the better part of valor.

"Hey Sonny-boy, we go check surf, yeah?"

Larson was born on a ranch in Wyoming but had grown up in Hawai'i and spoke pidgin easily, though only to Hawaiians. He knew that Noaloa liked confrontation and would want to watch the deal go down, but he knew the hot-headed Hawaiian could only make things more difficult for Mercante and Corlund.

"C'mon, brah. You need recover if you want party tonight like last night," teased Larson.

"Uh, yeah, okay, Heath," said Noaloa reluctantly.

"How about you, Aleja?" asked Larson. Although he'd had problems with women all his life and a bad divorce to show for it, he knew when to be a perfect gentleman, and he was nothing less to Gracellen.

"Want to go for a run?"

Aleja Gracellen glanced at Cheryl, who nodded.

"Yeah, but I don't know if I can keep up with you guys."

The three surfers got up from the table and walked past Clark without shaking hands. He did no more than nod to them. There was no point in being social with the surfers when he was about to face off with Mercante, Corlund and her two lieutenants.

The doors closed behind the three surfers and silence filled the room. Clark knew he was in good position and felt even better when Cheryl Corlund spoke first.

"June, I think you and I can talk later this afternoon. Bill, I'll come over to your office as soon as we're finished here."

28

The stock market expert and the chief financial officer stood up from the table. Clark thought to make some points, so he stood up, too.

"Nice to meet you both," he said.

They nodded to Clark, and walked right past him. Suddenly Ian Clark didn't feel so confident. The door closed, and Clark sat back down. He didn't know what to say, and it showed. Corlund sensed his nervousness and played off it.

"Roberto, please give the disk back to our friend here."

Mercante ejected the disk and nonchalantly skimmed it down the table like a Frisbee.

The disk stopped well out of Clark's reach. Mercante's carelessness was not accidental. The future of surfing's biggest corporation was on the line. It was time to play hardball.

Deal

"Well, that was a waste of time. I wonder why Cheryl had me show up in the first place. I can't surf those waves."

"Sure you can, haole girl. Tow-in easy, no problem."

"No problem until you fall, Sonny-boy," said Heath Larson.

The elevator door opened and they walked across the lobby past several Wavelife employees who were surprised to see the two Wavelife heroes in person on a normal business day. As for Aleja Gracellen, nobody quite knew who she was, but she must have been somebody if she was with Larson and Noaloa.

"Have you ever done any tow-in surfing?" said Larson as he held the door open for her.

"No, and I don't plan to, although I must admit the footage I've seen of you makes it look like fun."

"I surf da place no problem, dey gimme mo money."

"You already make more money than you know what to do with, Sonny-boy," said Gracellen, never one to mince words with surf stars. She noticed the cold, damp wind had picked up a bit.

"Heath, there's no way the surf's any good."

"Yeah, but getting some exercise beats sitting in a conference room. And fifty bucks says the world champ is too hung over to run to the pier and back."

"You're on, brah!"

The Hawaiian took off across the parking lot, last night's party hound turned into a competitor who hated to lose.

Larson looked at Gracellen. She shrugged.

"Sure, why not?"

They caught up to Noaloa half way across the lot. When they got to the street, the men turned left but Gracellen cut to the right.

"Sonny-boy, wait a sec! Hey Aleja, where are you going?"

Gracellen turned and ran backward as she yelled, "The Newport Pier is right down the street. Anybody can do that. Let's see you guys run to the Huntington Pier!"

Noaloa and Larson looked at each other, but Gracellen did not wait for them to decide.

"And if I beat you both, you guys each owe me a hundred bucks!"

* * *

"We'll give you a hundred grand worth of shares and you can use Wavelife surfers in your ads free of charge. And we'll throw a five-star contest at any Geosurf resort you want. Plus a t-shirt," said Roberto Mercante.

"Your stock's headed south, I don't need surf star endorsements, and contests are more trouble than they're worth. But we can start negotiating on the shirt. Just what are they worth these days?" said Clark, knowing that Sonny-boy Noaloa liked wearing t-shirts with his fat paychecks silk-screened on them to intimidate his competitors.

"About 37 cents net, but for you we'll make up a special one with a check for a million dollars on it," Mercante said.

"A million dollars? You know it's a sign of the times when seven figures sounds like chump change," said Ian Clark, feigning a yawn. Then he leaned forward, clasped his hands on the table in front of him and zeroed in on Mercante.

"How much do you think it will cost you to exploit that place?"

He glanced at Cheryl Corlund, who appeared to be paying attention. But just to make sure, he began firing off costs one after another.

"You've got to bring it all to the customer, no? Design new lines around the conquest of the reef! Production costs! Point-of-sale displays! Sales team training! Travel costs! New trade show booths! Trade show parties!" Clark winked at Mercante, knowing his wife was obviously not amused.

"Need I go any further? Oh, wait a sec, what about the upside? The stock goes up, the points you pay the banks go down, the factors are your pals again, and you're flush! So, a million bucks? Try again, but first take a look at this."

Clark pulled another disk from his shirt pocket and sailed it across the room. Mercante caught it with one hand.

"What's this?"

"It's a copy, yours to keep, deal or no deal. Why don't you take another look to remind yourselves of exactly what's on the table."

Once again, the Geosurf logo dissolved into a menu of the best waves in the world. Only this time, the last item said "The Wavelife Ring of Power", with a glowing blue circle surrounded by perfect waves.

Ian Clark noticed Mercante's eager body language and was reminded of an old movie about a mysterious map and a remarkable discovery.

"You could call it surfing's 'Eighth Wonder of the World'! It could be your King Kong, Roberto," he said while making no attempt to hide the snide tone to his remark, "And Aleja could be the beauty who tamed the beast! With Heath to save her in the nick of time!"

Cheryl Corlund knew the comment was right on target, but she said nothing and let Clark dig himself in a little deeper.

They watched the simulation again. Clearly, it was the heaviest surfing environment imaginable: the biggest, most remote, and most perfect set-up in the world.

When the clip ended, Mercante turned back to Clark and laughed.

"Ok, Clark. You can have the keys to the front door. You can have anything you want. I want to surf that place!"

31

Clark laughed, too.

"That's big of you, Roberto. Your whole company for the best wave in history - now that IS being authentic. Thanks, but no thanks - the rag trade would be bad for my health," he said with a knowing laugh.

He turned to Cheryl Corlund because it was time to get serious.

"Ok, Madam CEO, what's your offer?"

Cheryl Corlund had barely glanced at the screen and had paid scant attention to the antics of Clark and her husband. They were like two monkeys scurrying around for peanuts compared to what was on her mind.

When Wavelife's troubles began to mount, she had called in some old Harvard MBA chums to tackle the problem, and a number of scenarios were fleshed out after weeks of work with division heads and marketing experts. However, when Wilson and Massara reviewed the various alternatives, they sliced the proposals to pieces. At the end of the day, nothing penciled out for the company in its existing incarnation.

Then Wilson and Massara had come up with an idea. The way out was to pull off something rarely done on Wall Street anymore: a leveraged buyout. If she could execute an LBO, and then sell the company, her seasickness in the surf industry would be over. It would be like stepping onto dry land after a season in hell trying to sail a drunken boat across a stormy ocean. However, to get investment bankers interested in underwriting the buyout, she would have to show them something to pique their curiosity, if not their greedy instincts, and after seeing Larson's reaction to Clark's reef, she had exactly what she needed. And, as it turned out, she could treat the reef as if it was a lease on some wilderness acreage where there "might be" oil and gas reserves.

There are no guarantees the reef could ever become a fixed asset. Its value is unknown, and that would be the key to skirting around the insider trading laws. And it may never be worth a dime to anyone until Heath and Sonny-boy ride the place. After the LBO is executed.

And the beauty and the beast angle with Aleja? I hate to admit it, she thought, *but the idea had merit.*

She looked back at Clark and responded in a soft, friendly voice.

"We'll joint venture a surf camp on the nearest island under Wavelife's name, pay for all the infrastructure, pay you to run expeditions to the reef, give you 10% of the net profits from sales of site-related garments, and cross-promo with Geosurf for three product cycles."

Cheryl Corlund low-balled with the best of them, but that was exactly what she wanted Clark to be thinking, and his response was pretty much what she knew it would be.

"You pay for everything, provide an unsecured loan of fifteen million to Geosurf, give me twenty-five percent of the gross on everything coming out of, what did I call it, the Wavelife Ring of Power? And I run the show, period, on-site."

"What about contests?" interrupted Mercante without having to look at his wife to know his part in her strategy.

"No."

"Special events?"

"Not yours. All mine, and your employees have to surf in 'em. With you as sole sponsor, of course. One-point-five mill would buy you signage above the title."

"Then what's in it for us?"

"The honor of doing something for the sacred soul of surfing," said Clark, with just a hint of a tent-show preacher in his tone.

Cheryl Corlund's voice cut between the two men.

"I'm here to do business, Mr. Clark. Apparently, you are not. Why don't you just go peddle your ego someplace else?"

Her husband caught his cue and quickly added, "But when can I go surf that place, bro?"

Ian Clark laughed loudly.

"Good cop - bad cop! You two are really something. Biggest company in the surf industry, and I hear your parties are pretty wild, too. Oh, by the way, how are the kids these days? Did they graduate yet?"

Clark was really pushing it. He knew that he was up against a powerful tag team in Cheryl Corlund and Roberto Mercante, so it was no holds barred. The two Mercante teenagers were infamous in Orange County for their parties and had been already been kicked out of two private high schools. It was below the belt, but to Ian Clark it was fair. This was not about making nice.

"Okay, let's cut the crap. What's your best offer?"

"Why don't we just buy Geosurf and you can work for us?" Roberto liked the idea of owning access to the best waves in the world, and Geosurf had every license worth having.

The CEO glanced at her husband. It was time for him to butt out.

Her eyes locked with Clark's.

"I don't want anything more to do with you than I have to. Here are my terms," she said, having already considered her SEC filing dates, next year's trade shows, production lead times, sales teams orientations, LBO due diligence issues, her current cash-on-hand, and the fact that next year's selling season coincided with the Southern Hemisphere's winter surf.

"Heath Larson, and/or possibly other surfers to be named later, in the water riding the place exactly as you showed it to us between June 21 and August 17, or you sign Geosurf over to us lock, stock and barrel," she began.

"June 21 is the first day of summer, but what's August 17 about?"

"Don't interrupt me again, Mr. Clark," said Corlund, knowing this all had to happen according to schedule and that the reef could not come with any strings attached.

"All rights to the reef will belong to Wavelife and all permits will be in our name. If we decide we want to do anything out there we own all on-site events and you will not be involved in any way, shape or form other than consulting at our discretion."

Clark wasn't about to say a word. He knew there was more to come.

"I will hand you a check for two million dollars as soon as the first wave is ridden by Heath Larson within the given performance period. We will subsequently pay you twenty-five percent of net profit from site-related apparel up to another two million. If you cannot get Heath on these waves," she pointed to the screen, "between the specified dates, you give us the keys to Geosurf Expeditions."

"Well, uh, I don't know, uh, but what - - -"

"But what?"

Clark knew the term "net profit" didn't mean a thing, and he knew Corlund understood that as well. He detected an urgency in her voice, despite the clipped tones she used to intimidate him, and so he countered without ever forgetting for a second that he needed cash, and fast, or remembering what would happen if he didn't deliver.

"Two now, two when Larson takes off. No back end."

"One point five now, one point five on his first wave, paid end of August, no back end."

"If he surfs the place on June 21, I don't want to wait."

"Understood."

"Deal."

"There will be a check waiting for you at the reception desk on your way out." She pushed her chair back, went around the conference table and picked up the disk before walking over to Clark and extending her hand. "It's a handshake for now. Tell your lawyer to clear his calendar for next Tuesday at 10 am. We'll all meet right back here to sign papers. Now if you don't mind, I've got a corporation to run."

Just before she walked out the door, Cheryl Corlund paused and turned around. "I want a game plan from you guys before you leave the premises," she noticed her husband was staring at the screen, "So listen carefully," Mercante heard her words and immediately turned around. "I don't care what it costs as long as it comes out of your surf team budget, Roberto. I'll need forty-eight hours notice before Heath hits the water, and none of this 'Well, we thought a swell was coming' bullshit. Is that understood?"

Corlund's husband took a deep breath. He owed Wavelife's success to his wife, and he knew she expected results.

"Loud and clear," replied Mercante.

"What about you, Mr. Clark? Can you do it?"

"Well, - - -"

"Well what? We've got a deal, or don't handshakes mean much to you?"

"I can do it," he said, though he knew he would have said anything just so he could walk out the door with cash-in-hand.

"I'm sure the two of you will be a great team together," she said without looking back as the door closed behind her.

The two men sat for almost a minute looking at the image on the screen. Neither wanted to say the first word, but Clark was prepared with an icebreaker.

"You know, it must be hard to stay in touch with reality in a place like this," said Clark, leaning back in his chair and sweeping his arm around the conference room, "so I thought I'd bring along a little air freshener."

He pulled out a small joint of Durban Poison, the near-psychedelic weed grown in South Africa. He lit it up and offered it across the table.

"Fucking Clark, what the hell are you doing?" said Mercante, holding up his hand in refusal.

As the fabled smoke from the African Horn expanded in his lungs, Clark started to get up to exhale out a window. Then he realized that they don't open in skyscrapers, so he simply exhaled over the table.

"Sorry to smell up your inner sanctum, but I forgot there's no way to get fresh air into these corporate monuments," said Clark, "and I just thought we could get on the same wavelength, Roberto."

But within seconds he was rambling on about how Wavelife's surfers should not use special boards or technology, the publicity angles they could push, t-shirt designs, floating houseboats filled with spectators, and worse.

As Clark spewed, Roberto thought about what his wife wanted from him. The company's future depended on his creating a new surfing sensation, something he'd done many times at trade shows, contests, and parties. But this time there would be no fall-back position if he failed. This had to be the genuine article, and there was no room for Clark's stoned nonsense.

"Shut up, Clark. Maybe you didn't hear some of the terms, but as I recall you are now a paid consultant. Heath Larson would never go for what you are talking about."

"But he has to have some sense of real adventure - real risk - survival on pure instinct –"

"Clark, we're going to minimize every risk. Jet skis, personal GPS locators, oxygen bottles, – that stuff is standard these days, although maybe not for guys at San Onofre. Next thing I know you'll be telling me no lifeguards!"

Clark didn't miss the dig in the reference to the surf spot known for its gentle waves, so he came right back at Mercante.

"How'd you guess?"

"Fuck you, Clark. You must have spent too much time with Merrill or something. Oh, and by the way, what's he going to think about your deal with my wife?"

"He's got nothing to do with this," said Clark, and he felt himself lose some ground.

"Oh yeah? What, some seagull just plopped that disk down on your desk? Well, that's neither here nor there. What concerns me is that you're sitting here stoned trying to think straight about survival surfing."

Clark may have been floating on a cloud, but he was ready with a lightning bolt.

"And your polluted version of life has you thinking any straighter? Just what kind of place you got here, Roberto? A monument to man's best instincts for making a buck? What's it all worth when it is nothing but marketing?

Here's a chance to stand for something - or can't you get to your feet anymore when its time to go for it on the wave of the day?"

That one stung as Clark could see from the reddening of Mercante's face. But though the mogul was ten pounds heavier after years of trade shows and hospitality tents, he was still a Brazilian surfer with a lot of pride.

"Well, at least I'm not afraid of drowning every time I get caught inside."

That one stopped Clark in his tracks, until he remembered Mercante had spent a week with Merrill on a trip to a stretch of Moroccan coast leased by Geosurf to control access to a series of excellent point breaks. They must have talked some story about Geosurf's owner.

"Fuck you, too, Mercante. You and your surf stars! How about just a compass? Turn 'em into real sea-faring ocean adventurers! You could have square-riggers as a backdrop at the trade shows! And just think! Wavelife would finally be totally core authentic! You know, kinda like climbing Everest without oxygen!"

"Clark, I'm not getting through to you! Without lifeguards and a personal locator system we'd never get the insurance. And you can't catch those waves without jetskis."

Clark lit the joint and took a hit.

"Oh, come on, Roberto, you're Wavelife International! Think big!"

He handed the joint to Mercante, who took it and then surprised Clark by snuffing it out and flipping it back at him.

"Locators, jetskis and lifeguards or I won't be able to get insurance. And Response/Rescue will be a Stateside operation and not the local boys you have working for you at your island resorts. This thing has to work for my wife, Clark. Real money doesn't believe in Polynesian traditions, or haven't you learned that yet?"

Clark was too stoned to parry the thrust. His conscience was sliced open and a cascade of memories drowned his thinking.

He remembered all the promises to the locals he'd made while thinking he could do it with someone else's money. He remembered the investment bankers on their yachts in Newport Beach glazing over when he tried to talk about indigenous franchises needing seed capital to create self-sustaining communities at surf sites around the world. Then the money market numbers started flashing through his brain and the meeting with his lawyers and his accountant about the registered letter from the IRS. The thought of handcuffs brought him back to reality in a millisecond. A big check was waiting downstairs. All he had to do was shut his mouth and go get it.

"All right, Roberto. Anything you say. What's next?"

"I've got to see this place for real, Ian, and as soon as possible."

"I'll book us first class roundtrips to Tahiti. I've got to do some business down there, so I'll meet you at Papeete harbor next Friday and we'll go have a looksee, just me and you. Oh, one thing, now that I think of it. I'll need a non-disclosure from you."

"And I'll need an invoice for the tickets. We'll square it up when we sign the contracts on Tuesday, okay?"

He stood up and extended his hand to Clark, who also got out of his chair. The two men shook hands, first as businessmen, then with locked thumbs in the classic "brother" grip.

"Ok, Ian. We've got some mutual interests, don't we, bro? Speaking of which, where's that DP?"

They sat back in their chairs and Clark lit the last of the joint and passed it across the table.

Now that the deal was done, Mercante saw no harm in getting high. He sucked a hit deeply into his lungs, and then tried to hand the glowing joint back to Clark.

"No thanks, I've had enough. See you in Tahiti."

Clark stood up and walked towards the door as Mercante coughed a cloud of purple smoke into the room.

Clark looked back at him. Mercante was trying to say something, but nothing came out.

"Don't forget, Roberto, its better to be straight wishing you were high than high wishing you weren't," said Clark as he opened the door and walked out without closing it.

Behind him, a disoriented millionaire surfer was fumbling with the remote control. He couldn't figure out which button would make the perfect waves start rolling again.

.

Geevum, Brah!

Cheryl Corlund walked into her office through a side entrance. The gray weather outside her window had not changed, but the disk in her hand was like a shining medallion worth much, much more than its weight in gold. Now the challenge for her was to realize the potential it represented by combining its promise with the surfers who represented the future of her company. She reached for the phone to have her assistant get them up to her office right away, only to remember she had no idea where they were.

* * *

"George, did you see who just ran by? I think she surfs for Wavelife!" said the excited fresh-faced co-ed, the boredom of her dead-end job suddenly broken up by a star-sighting.

Her harried boss, a veteran surf shop owner on his last legs, barely bothered to look up from a pile of invoices on the counter. The surf was flat, the weather lousy, and business was bad at Pier Surf 'n Sport. Vintage surfboards hung from the ceiling, but now the only surfboards for sale were crammed into a small corner in the back. Shoes and shirts dominated the sales floor of what once was a classic California surf shop now fighting a losing battle with big box outlets.

"What do you care who surfs for Wavelife? And what are you doing standing around by the door? Go straighten out the shoe section."

She rolled her eyes and walked across the showroom floor as two more surfers flew down the sidewalk.

"Wow! That was Heath Larson and Sonny-boy Noaloa! I wonder what's going on?"

"I don't care if it was Laurel and Hardy chasing Madonna! Get to work!"

"Have you ever met them? I wonder what they're like?"

"Who knows? Probably no different than all the other surf stars working for the big boys."

* * *

On the five mile run from Wavelife's headquarters in Newport Beach up Pacific Coast Highway to the Huntington Beach pier, twenty-five year old Aleja Gracellen had no trouble setting a pace for Larson and Noaloa. A little jog was nothing compared to the ballet workouts she did three times a week.

She had taken her first dance class when she was five, the same year her dad gave her a tandem ride across a small wave at Malibu's Surfrider Beach. Growing up, she never stopped dancing or surfing with styles all her own in both disciplines. As a result, nobody flowed with the beauty of Malibu's perfect wave the way she did. Once when she got out of the water a tourist complimented her, "I didn't know surfing was so beautiful! You reminded me of when I was learning ballet in Russia!"

That is how she met Cheryl Corlund. Two summers ago, Roberto Mercante had the idea to take Wavelife's regional managers and buyers from their biggest accounts to watch some new Wavelife team members in action at Malibu. Corlund went along because schmooze was part of doing business.

It was a Saturday morning and the waves were good at Surfrider Beach, famous around the world as the home of Gidget and Mickey Dora. But she hadn't surfed for almost fifty years and he had died of cancer, so now the only thing special about Malibu was the insanity of the crowds.

From their first wave, things did not go well for the Wavelife surfers. The locals did not give them any slack and although Roberto was calling the play-by-play for his guests, the suits had a hard time appreciating the talent of the Wavelife professionals who could never get a wave to themselves.

However, Cheryl Corlund did see a young woman stand out from the mob, the only surfer who consistently rode wave after wave in smooth contrast to the radical shortboarders or lethargic longboarders jostling each other, five to a wave.

She began to think of how Wavelife's image didn't reflect the grace of surfing so much as it did the aggression, though as long as sales continued to climb in the 14-24 male segment she wasn't going to question her husband's judgment. Still, she wondered how much of a market could be found if Wavelife started selling a new women's line. She kept her eye on the wahine with the idea of talking to her when she got out of the water.

After an hour the surfing exhibition was going downhill fast. Corlund saw the managers and buyers were getting restless, so she took her eyes off the wave dancer and tried to distract them with some eye contact and personable chitchat about next season's new styles.

Then a big set came through and Roberto directed everyone's attention to the four Wavelife surfers all riding one wave together. Corlund watched them for a second, only to realize she'd lost sight of the young surf dancer. She scanned the crowd to find her again, but never did because Aleja Gracellen was long gone.

She was starting her shift at one of Malibu's better restaurants down the coast. With her hair wet and her heart content from her surf session that morning, Gracellen got right into the flow of running the front desk, taking reservations, greeting people and seating them with a fresh and friendly smile.

By the time the Wavelife surfers got one more wave and came up on the beach, it was almost noon. They were beat from battling the crowds. The managers and reps were hot from the midday sun. Everyone was getting cranky, so Roberto Mercante suggested they all go get something to eat.

Half-an-hour later, he ushered everyone into the crowded waiting area at the Point Café. He walked over to the front desk, ready to impress everyone.

"Hi, I own Wavelife, and I need a table for ten."

Aleja Gracellen checked the reservations list.

"No, nothing for Wavelife. You'll just have to wait, and I'm afraid it is going to be about two hours right now."

Mercante hit the ceiling.

"Maybe you don't understand. We are THE biggest company in the surf industry. We have the BEST surfers in the world, and some of them are standing RIGHT over there. We're hungry and we want a table right NOW. Here, make it happen."

"Oh yeah, you were at the beach today, you and your surf stars," said Gracellen. She took the proffered hundred dollar bill, tore it in half, and stuffed it in the front pocket of Mercante's aloha shirt. Then she went back to the reservations chart in front of her.

"Well, Mr. Wavelife," she said, without a trace of a smile, "You've got a couple of hours, so why don't you soak your head in the ocean and learn some manners? Maybe then I'll have a table for you. Party of ten, correct?"

She entered the reservation, and then looked up with a bit of a grin.

Mercante was raging when he came back to the group. Cheryl Corlund looked across the floor at the target of his anger and recognized the young surfer from Malibu, now handling the front desk with style, just as she had surfed so beautifully through the crowds in the water. Roberto insisted they go somewhere else. On the way back to their cars, Cheryl Corlund had an idea. She always let her husband have complete control over the surfing side of the company's operations. Now she was going to make an exception.

A week later, Roberto Mercante was sitting in his corner office watching a video of young Brazilian surfers battling each other in a contest with first prize being a Wavelife sponsorship. His wife walked in unannounced, and he almost fell out of his chair. Standing next to her was Aleja Gracellen.

"Roberto, meet our surf team's new member," said Cheryl Corlund in a tone of voice that brooked no dissention.

It was all he could do to smile and apologize for his behavior at the restaurant. With his wife standing right there, Mercante politely explained how the surf team worked and what Gracellen's responsibilities would be. Things seemed to go well, and Cheryl Corlund went back to her office to run the financial side of the corporation.

Roberto called in Wavelife's surf team manager to take Gracellen downstairs for her fittings and then to legal to sign a contract. He wished her good luck as she went out the door. Then he sent an e-mail to tell the manager the new-hire was to be given no preferential treatment whatsoever, and in fact if he washed her out, so much the better.

That didn't happen, at least not right away. Gracellen appreciated the opportunity and did her best to live up to what was expected of her as a professional surfer. Not until after several months of surfing in contests around the world did she begin to have doubts about working for Wavelife.

Give her a smooth blue wave at Malibu and Aleja Gracellen was a vision of elegance and style on a liquid stage, her arms and hands held just so, while turning and flowing through the curves of the curl with matchless beauty.

But give her fifteen minutes of choppy, knee-high surf – and three aggressive, hard-core competitors who knew how to surf for points in marginal conditions – and she never had a chance. And to compound her frustration, Aleja never got any help from her teammates. To them she was Cheryl Corlund's pet: how else to explain her staying on the team after a string of first round losses? The team manager did nothing about the sniping and behind-the-back gossip, and though Gracellen tried to be nice, her sweet disposition only made her rivals more vicious.

Had Corlund known what was going on, she might have stepped in. However, running an international corporation took all of her time, and it wasn't until a mid-year budget meeting did she have a chance to ask her husband about the woman who danced with the waves.

"Well, as far as I know she's going through the normal adjustments of a surfer new to the world of professional surfing. And in any event, her contract runs through the end of the year. If we have to make any changes, we'll talk about it at renewal time," he said.

As her first season drew to end, Aleja Gracellen was sick of the whole thing, not to mention living out of a backpack, the obligatory trade show appearances, in-store autograph signings and industry parties. Then came December on the North Shore: the surf industry's annual crescendo of everything she hated about being a pro surfer competing on the tour.

The first contest was at Haleiwa and the waves were big with a cross-wind chopping up the faces. The other Wavelife surfers had Hawaiian experience, but with contracts coming up, they needed all the points they could get and weren't about to help the rookie. So she paddled out in the wrong place and immediately found herself caught in a rip that pushed her right into the impact zone. She got nailed by a set, her leash broke, and as the horn sounded to signal the beginning of her heat, she swam back to the beach to find her board – broken in half. She had a backup, but it was too small for the powerful waves, and so she tried to borrow a board from her Wavelife teammates. But they claimed, with some justification, that they couldn't take the risk of having their boards broken, too.

Though there was time left in the heat, Aleja Gracellen knew it was all over. She took off her jersey and tossed it at the judges. She changed into her sweats, gave her extra board to a young girl waiting for an autograph, and hitched a ride straight to the airport. The next day she got her job back at the Point Café and began to forget all about her year of hell as a professional surfer.

Two weeks later, Cheryl Corlund noticed Aleja was not at Wavelife's Christmas party. She asked Roberto what had happened to Gracellen on the North Shore.

"Well, I guess she just couldn't handle it. The other girls did quite well. We wash out surfers all the time after their first year," he said matter-of-factly.

Cheryl Corlund had no patience with underperformers at Wavelife, but she was not going to let business-as-usual ruin what might someday be a valuable asset to the corporation. Just after New Year's, Wavelife's CEO drove up to Malibu alone to eat lunch at the Point Café.

Gracellen was on shift. She looked up and said, "Table for one?"

Then she did a double take.

"No, Aleja, table for two. Can you break away for a minute?"

The two women sat in a window table overlooking the tiny, empty waves of Topanga. It was raining, business was slow and they talked for hours about Aleja's experiences on the tour. Cheryl Corlund gained fresh insights on Wavelife's total dependency on competitive surfing as the most powerful component of the company's marketing efforts around the world. She realized she'd made a mistake by not fully appreciating Aleja's version of riding waves versus the cutthroat world of professional surfing. And she realized she wanted Wavelife's image to start being more about the former and less about the later.

It was almost four and the sky was getting dark when Cheryl Corlund offered Aleja a new contract with no strings attached: no contests, no trade shows, no obligations of any kind. All she had to do was go surfing and simply let the beauty of her surfing speak for itself and, of course, the company.

Gracellen said she'd think about it and call Corlund in a few days. When she did, she told Wavelife's CEO she did not feel right about collecting a paycheck for doing nothing but riding waves. She did not want to turn surfing into a job. However, Aleja Gracellen had an idea. She suggested that Wavelife underwrite a summer surf school for young girls with impoverished backgrounds that might also involve chartering buses to bring inner city kids to the beach. If Corlund was interested in spending that kind of money, Gracellen was willing to manage the program.

The CEO agreed, and during its first summer of operation, Gracellen's program helped hundreds of young people find themselves in the fresh world of surfing for fun. It did nothing for Wavelife's bottom line, but when Wavelife received a community service award for Gracellen's work, Corlund had a brief vision of adding a new component to Wavelife International's business plan. The only problem was, as a publicly traded corporation, she didn't know how she'd sell altruism to shareholders who wanted to make money, not give it away.

* * *

Corlund remembered her original ideas about changing the business plan thanks to Gracellen's inspiration. She thought back to watching the three surfers leave the meeting with Ian Clark and how she'd once again caught a glimpse of a new Wavelife arising from its current quagmire by tapping into

Gracellen's special spirit and the potential of Clark's reef. But those waves would be impossible to deal with unless Heath Larson's character and courage were part of the plan, and she knew that might end up being easier said than done.

* * *

The performance of the world's professional surfers in two-to-ten foot waves was remarkable. But double the size of the surf, and the level of performance was cut in half. And once the waves got up to twenty and thirty feet or more, the top surf stars would more often than not be sitting on the beach - watching Heath Larson just starting to warm up. His performances were almost unimaginable, and yet no one really knew how he did it.

When he had first signed on the dotted line years ago as a pro surfer, he gave himself away to the sponsors, writers, and filmmakers who eventually defined his life as the best big-wave surfer in the world. He soon found himself less a brave explorer than an emissary of a flawed and greedy society whose stabs at nobility and courage were but line items in marketing budgets.

We want you to be one with nature, to go where no man has gone before, but wait until we've reloaded the cameras, ok?

That changed when he signed with Wavelife. It started with his first press conference. Heath Larson had never quite found the answers, or patience for that matter, when interviewers asked him endless variations of the same question, "Why? Why do you risk your life?" So when they started up by asking that time-worn question, he answered sarcastically, "It pays the bills."

Everybody laughed at his insouciance. And right away Mercante had Wavelife's marketing team design a sales campaign around Larson's nonchalant attitude.

The real answer, however, was nothing to laugh at. It was nowhere near as simple as "Because it's there", first uttered by the British climber George Mallory when asked why he was climbing Mt. Everest, where he died on his summit attempt. By contrast, Heath Larson had never come close to buying the farm. He knew when to pull the plug on sessions if the winds or tides made the waves too tricky. No, Heath Larson did not ride big surf "because it's there." He surfed huge waves because there was nothing there.

When he was in a tube the size of a house, there was nothing inside the wave with him, and when the ride was over the wave was gone. So for Heath Larson, surfing was about nothingness, and he clearly understood that fame was a function of riding waves that usually didn't exist. They disappeared for months, sometimes years at a time. And even after he rode one, it was gone seconds later.

But his relationship with surfing was not casual at all. He was not blasé about huge surf by any means. Even though his mountains came and went, Heath Larson was completely aware of the dangers of big wave surfing and had a healthy respect for their power. Yet, he was able to detach himself from their world, and exist on his own terms when surrounded by danger, thanks to the writings of an obscure French philosopher.

Jean-Paul Sartre had written a massive book called "Being and Nothingness" during the Nazi occupation of World War Two. While most professional surfers could barely get through the surfing magazines, Larson read and re-read Sartre to train his mind for the challenges of surfing massive waves in life-and-death conditions.

From Sartre, he took the philosophy of his surfing even further. Only humans know truth because only humans lie, and there was nothing human, or even earthly, when a liquid avalanche roared across a reef. There was no 'truth' to be found - only a place devoid of human existence far back in the innermost hollows of a massive wave. There his soul could breathe because a wave has no soul. That was when he felt alive, alone, and complete.

So he returned to that transient, ephemeral place year after year, wave after wave, where his track was the only trail through the spinning caverns of collapsing force. And every time he reached the end of the ride, he would look back, and where he had just been no longer existed. And days, weeks, and months later, Heath Larson could go down to the sea and see nothing. The surf would be flat. There would not be a wave in sight, and only he knew exactly where he had been.

* * *

Cheryl Corlund pondered Heath's version of surfing and knew she still did not quite understand it. But she knew she'd needed him at the meeting with Clark to ascertain the true value of Clark's discovery to the company that employed him, though entirely on his own terms. After hearing Clark's initial pitch concerning "the last, best big wave discovery on earth", she had fired a shot across his bow by telling him that Larson would be there to see if he was full of crap or not. When Clark welcomed the idea, she called Larson right away, though she knew he'd see the situation as a crucible where surfing, greed and ambition would be fused together in the name of corporate priorities. But she knew he would live with the result if it allowed him to be released into the wilds of the sea and the power of its waves, where he could be free on his, and Sartre's, terms.

Now, given Larson's reaction to what had appeared on the screen in Wavelife's tenth floor conference room, she was confident he was going to find new inner and outer limits in his existentialist approach to experiencing massive energies and absolute nothingness in the most perfect big waves he had ever seen.

When it came to Sonny-boy Noaloa, however, it was a different story. He was Wavelife's top competitive surfer and defending world champion. On a hunch she had her husband make sure that Noaloa, never a big wave rider by any means, was also at the meeting. Trying to combine the spirit of Gracellen with the strength and power of Larson was a pretty radical idea in itself. Bringing Noaloa into the mix was just about over the top. That's why she did

44

it, though she knew there'd be a lot of work to do if Sonny-boy Noaloa was to play a significant role in her plans. And just exactly how that could be done remained as unfocused as the gray day outside her office window.

* * *

Wilson Smith Noaloa was, like most Hawaiian surfers, actually a nice person when he wanted to be. His parents had split up when he was young, and though he was born in Hawai'i, his mom had taken him back to her parents home in Florida when his Hawaiian dad had started drinking after the construction jobs dried up in Waikiki. His dark skin and Polynesian black hair put him in between the blacks and whites at Cocoa Beach High School, and he experienced a prejudice that could only be left behind when he went surfing.

And surf he did, every waking moment. The small waves of the East Coast were almost impossible to ride. As it turned out, they were actually a blessing in disguise. He learned to make the most of each ride, and his Hawaiian roots gave him a feel for the ocean even though he was seven thousand miles from his island birthplace.

By the time he was seventeen he was the best surfer Florida had ever seen. After winning the State Junior Championships, he was contacted by a sports agent. Noaloa was told he had a future as a pro surfer, with a lucrative sponsorship, especially since a Hawaiian had not won the world championship for almost ten years. He would have to go to Hawai'i to build his career, and of course the teenager was flush with excitement over the agent's pitch about making lots of money, surfing all the time and maybe leaving Florida to live in the Islands.

His mother turned down the agent's proposal without a second thought. Her memories of the party years in Hawai'i never went away, and no way was she going to let her son go down that road. She had kept him on a very short leash, driving him to the beach and back, watching him surf endless hours, and entering him in contest after contest just to keep him focused on something healthy. She thanked the agent for his time, but her son was going to stay home and graduate from high school, and that was that. Or so she thought.

The sports agent did not make a living by letting hot young prospects get away, and he never let a week go by without a phone call or a 'chance' meeting at a contest. He knew the kind of money he was talking about could not be ignored since Noaloa's mom was barely making ends meet working a night shift at a truck stop.

At the end of Wilson's junior year, the agent proposed he spend the summer training in Mexico at Puerto Escondido. The waves were almost as fast and powerful as those on Oahu's North Shore, and the plane flight was only five hours from Miami. The agent would cover all expenses, hire a surf trainer to work with Wilson, and fly his mom to Mexico whenever she wanted to see her son.

It was a pitch she could not turn down, and within weeks the daily workouts and pounding tubes of Puerto turned Wilson Noaloa into a

45

supernatural surfer. The agent began to show footage from sessions to some of the big surf companies, and soon there was a buzz in the industry about the unknown from Florida, or Hawai'i, depending on who was being pitched.

The week before Wilson was to start his senior year of high school, the agent took him and his mom out to dinner and laid out a scenario to take the surfing world by storm. He wanted Wilson to spend the winter on the North Shore and he would pay for all expenses. He talked about sponsorship dollars for the boy that were twice his mother's yearly take-home pay. Wilson would have a tutor to keep up with his classes, and he would come back to Florida to complete the spring semester and wear a cap-and-gown in June.

There was not much his mother could say. Two days later she watched him get on a plane, barely eighteen years old, her heart telling her she didn't know when she would see her son again.

The first thing Wilson did when he arrived in Hawai'i was find his father. Johnny Noaloa was sleeping off a hangover in a small apartment on the down side of Honolulu when he heard a knock on the door. The knock turned to a pounding, and he yelled for whomever it was to go away.

"I'm not going away."

"Who the hell are you?"

"I'm your son."

That got Johnny's attention. His stupor began to lift as he opened the door to see a strapping young man in new clothes standing in front of him, with a nice car parked at the curb and a guy in sunglasses leaning against it.

"Well if it isn't Sonny-boy!" said his dad, "And who's your backup?" gesturing towards the car.

"My agent. C'mon, dad, we've got some catching up to do."

The winter surf on the North Shore begins in mid-October, and after the first two swells, Sonny-boy Noaloa was turning heads at all the major spots. His ascendancy was remarkable. Making a big entry into the Hawaiian surf scene was no easy deal. Broken boards from the waves, broken noses from the locals, and the fear of both day in and day out, had sent more than one budding young surf star back to Brazil, Australia, or California. But Noaloa gained entré at Sunset and Pipe, where the pecking order was as vicious as the surf, thanks to his Hawaiian looks, his amazing surfing ability, and his dad on the beach watching his back after the agent put him on the payroll.

Noaloa was training hard in waves of all sizes and his performance was impossible to ignore. His agent was on the phone working potential sponsors against each other by pushing the story line of "local boy come home". Wilson, the dutiful son, talked to his mom almost every day, and the tutoring was going well - until the world Pro Tour and all the surf media came to Oahu – and a star was born.

Sonny-boy Noaloa was everywhere, surfing shoulder-to-shoulder with the biggest names in the world, going to parties, and taking meetings with his agent and prospective sponsors. By Christmas the young phenom was on the verge of becoming a very rich young man. There was no way he was going back to Florida. High school would have to wait, and he would get a diploma when he got the chance.

That chance never came. Roberto Mercante signed him to a one year contract, with incentives. He proceeded to win almost all the pro tour qualifiers around the world. When the tour hit the North Shore, Wavelife had enough pull to get Noaloa into the big contests, which he also won. Mercante then signed him to a long-term, record-breaking deal, resulting in two world championships in two years. But now it was year three, he was out of contention, and the brash young surfer was coming face-to-face with a reality for which he was ill-prepared.

* * *

Cheryl Corlund knew he was going to be flying to Hawai'i tomorrow, and although he was technically the world champion, there was no way he would hold on to his crown. He hadn't been able to handle the pressure, pure and simple. Roberto had convinced her that his value to the company remained high, and there was nothing in the numbers that pointed to Noaloa as being responsible for the company's problems, even though he had not made it into a single final all year. She knew he had lost to competitors who surfed beyond themselves when given a chance to knock off the champ. What she didn't know was that now he had just been beaten by a girl.

* * *

"I no used ta lose, Aleja," said Sonny-boy Noaloa, "and I no lose yet. We got run back, you know."

He could barely get the words out trying to catch his breath. Gracellen was serene, looking out to sea from the end of the Huntington Pier. She had barely broken a sweat.

"That's right, Sonny-boy, the bet was to the pier and back. I'll give you a few seconds. Then we'll race back."

She looked at the waves, then turned to Heath Larson.

"See, Heath! I told you it wasn't any good!" she said, glancing at her watch, "Hey, I gotta get up to LA. Ok, guys, let's get going!"

But the surfers were not ready to to run another step. They were in excellent shape, but they were completely out of gas.

"Oh, come on! I can't believe it! Larson the Living Legend and Sonny-boy Surf Star! Losing to a girl? Well, then, why don't you just both give me your hundred bucks right now?"

"Uh, er, um, I left my wallet in my car?" said Noaloa.

"Here's twenty, can I owe you?" said Larson sheepishly.

"Keep your money, Heath, you'll need it for a cab. But I better see two envelopes on my desk by this time next week, guys, or you'll each owe two hundred to the shelter. Oh, did I tell you I've been taking boxing lessons lately? Great for the cardio! See ya, guys!"

47

The two men watched her run back down the pier and into the overcast partially obscuring the hotels and shopping malls of Surf City.

"That chick is just unreal," said Larson.

"We geev er all kine shit on the tour, and Haleiwa worked her ovah good. I thought nevah see her again. Why she stay at da meeting?"

"Well, she just worked us over pretty good, Sonny-boy, so maybe Cheryl Corlund knows something about her we don't."

"Yeah, Mercante no give one shit afta she quit Haleiwa. Maybe you right. They stay up to something."

"They better be. Has Roberto given you a contract for next year?"

"Nah, but I no worry. He no pay me good I go surf for Gnarlaroo or Island Beach. Make da kine money for reals. You watch cuz."

"I wouldn't count on it, brah. You may be the world champ, but the tour ain't what it used to be. The whole industry is in trouble, and Pricemart doesn't have a surf team."

"So what you do, Heath? Who goin pay for your jet skis? You get contract fo next year?"

"Nope, and maybe I won't want one."

"Bullshit, brah. You no turn down six figgahs."

"We'll see, Sonny-boy. Maybe I need to just surf for myself again. Maybe its time to forget all this," he swept his arm across the skyline of Surf City, "after I surf the place we saw today."

"Yeah, we go surf dat place, no problem, but first we get back Newport. Let's get one taxi, ok brah? No way we gonna run back."

Larson laughed. "Yeah, my knees are already feeling it."

"And we gotta get a beer fo da road."

"I only got twenty."

"Dats ok. I got da credit card, brah. Part of my contract!"

The sun was burning off the haze over the beach while Sonny-boy's brain was only getting hazier by the minute. His dad's alcoholic genes were catching up with him, and it was a bad time to be thinking about his future.

"So what makes you think you can get another sponsor, Sonny-boy? I hear you're not gonna win this year."

"Brah, fuck dat. I da bes on da tour. You watch. I goin win Pipe fo sure."

"Yeah, but that's only Pipeline, and we both know you're not in shape for Sunset, or even Haleiwa. You're going down and I bet your agent is already scouting for someone new."

Noaloa knew every word was true. The fact that Roberto Mercante had avoided him before the meeting with Clark only confirmed his fears.

"Den why dis meeting wit da guy Clark if I stay washed up and you tired being a surf legend? And what da deal with da chick? She onna payroll but no even surf!"

Noaloa was practically shouting across the table.

"They needed us to intimidate him to see if his pitch was for real. As for Gracellen, I got no idea, though Corlund knows, that's for sure. Maybe she wants to turn Wavelife into some fashionista boutique and us getting killed at that reef will make a good excuse."

"Larson, you stay on drugs or wat? You watch. Dey goin sign me an I goin jam on da tour. Den we go surf dat place mo biggah then evah!"

Noaloa raised his glass and his voice was heard throughout the bar.

"Geevum, brah!"

Heath Larson smiled at Noaloa but grimaced inside. He had heard that pidgin bravado before, a surfer's challenge to give his all against impossible odds. It was pure Hawaiian pride, and as such there was a little sadness to it. But he had never backed out of a wave in his life, no matter how big, and he wasn't going to start now.

"Yeah, Sonny-boy, we geevum!"

The *Skyhook*

"Where the hell have you been?" said an impatient Roberto Mercante, sweating in the mid-morning sun across the street from the harbor in Papeete, "First you tell me to meet you here at nine, and now it's ten! And why here? I thought we were going to go see the reef!"

"Roberto, did you re-set your watch to Polynesian time? And as for our recon of the reef, that's exactly what we are going to do," said Ian Clark, emerging from the taxi in aviator sunglasses and a khaki outfit. He paid the driver and took a look up and down the street. Traffic was heavy, but he saw a gap and that was all he needed.

"Let's go!"

He grabbed Mercante's arm and they hustled across two lanes, paused on the center divider, and then ran across two more. Mercante slowed down when they hit the sidewalk, but Clark didn't stop.

"Clark! What the fuck is this?"

"I'll explain in a minute, Roberto. Let's keep going."

They jogged down a long wharf, dodging trucks and forklifts going in and out of large warehouses. At the end of the wharf they went down a gangplank to where, in complete contrast to everything behind them, a true Polynesian outrigger canoe was tied up.

"Clark, you've got to be kidding! We aren't going to paddle this thing to the reef, are we? I don't need to be put through a bunch of bullshit!"

"Just get in and sit down. Up front, please."

Clark released the line from the cleat on the dock and hopped in. There were two paddles in the bottom of the hull. He grabbed one and pushed them away from the dock. He offered the other to Mercante.

"Here's your paddle, Roberto. It will be easier if you help."

"What kind of crap is this, Clark? I don't want to go on some harbor tour!"

"Just paddle!"

The noise from the city and the docks receded as a fresh wind blew into their faces across the clear, blue water. Mercante's shirt began to dry out. Had he been a tourist, it would have been fun paddling a canoe in the heart of Polynesia. But Roberto Mercante was not having fun.

"Listen, Clark, we don't have time for this nonsense. My wife expects a phone call from me today, and I'd better have good news for her."

"Will you stop whining and just paddle? Here, together. Stroke, stroke, stroke."

"All right, Clark, this isn't a roman galley."

The canoe started to pick up speed, and within minutes they were both putting their backs into it.

"Where the hell are we going?"

"To meet our ride. See that buoy?"

"No."

"You will once we get outside the harbor. Keep paddling. Ramming speed!"

Clark picked up the pace and used his paddle to change their course. The wind was stronger in the channel, and Mercante was getting wet all over again.

"Now do you see the buoy?"

"No I don't. Clark, this is getting me edgy."

"Just keep going. We're almost there."

They didn't stop paddling for almost ten minutes, and when Mercante finally saw the buoy he thought they would stop and simply glide up to it. But Clark kept going, and Mercante kept up with him.

Finally Clark slowed down and then stopped. Although it had looked only a few feet high from a distance, the red and white stripped pole now towered almost eight feet over their heads, bobbing up and down in the low swells rolling through the light chop.

"Roberto, tie up the bow to that steel ring on the buoy. Use a bowline knot. You remember, the rabbit came out of the hole, around the tree –"

"Yeah, yeah, Clark, I remember. So now what?"

"We wait for our ride. They'll be here any minute now. Nice day, isn't it?"

"Who'll be here? Why aren't they waiting for us? Clark, if this is all bullshit, my wife, will, I mean I will make sure you never do business in the surf industry again."

"Yeah, I know Roberto, and you'll be running Geosurf as per the contract. But patience, my man. In fact, I think I see them coming right now."

"I don't see anything, Clark."

"Try looking straight out to sea and up around ten o'clock."

Mercante turned to where Clark was pointing. Then he heard the engines, a strange sound to him in a world of jets and helicopters. He could make out a long wide wing, and then a fuselage hanging down from it, and then two circles of props as she leveled out at an altitude of no more than a hundred feet.

"Clark, you can't be serious!" he shouted over the roar as the pilot went into a tight 180-degree turn and came back over the buoy. Mercante saw a face framed by a baseball cap and a headset looking down at him from a side window of the cockpit. The seaplane headed out to sea, banked another hard turn, and lined up with the buoy. It slowly lost altitude and the tips of the wings swung down on struts and turned into pontoons. Then the bow touched the water and a perfect V of spray shot up from the keel of the fuselage going seventy miles an hour. The pilot kept the power on and was closing fast.

"Ian! They're gonna hit us!"

With fifty yards to go the pilot throttled all the way back and the seaplane settled down dead in the water. A touch on the throttles and she began to drift slowly towards the buoy. She was all white trimmed with international orange. Her name was in flowing blue script beneath the cockpit window: *The Skyhook.*

The cargo bay door opened up behind the wing. A barrel-chested crewman wearing a flight suit appeared.

"Y'all got the cash, Ian?"

"As instructed. Permission aboard?"

"Lemme see."

The plane was now floating close to the buoy with the outrigger in the shadow of the huge wing. Clark took a clear plastic bag out of his pack and held it high.

"All right, Clark. Permission granted."

"Ok, Roberto, this is it. You go first."

Mercante stood up unsteadily in the canoe and hesitated.

"C'mon, pal. In we go!"

A strong arm grabbed his hand and practically lifted him bodily into the cargo bay. Then Ian Clark gripped a handhold on the seaplane and stepped up quickly into the cargo bay opening. He wasn't going to get any help from the *Skyhook*'s flight engineer, and he knew why.

"How cum L.J. ain't with you?"

"What do you care? Isn't this what you need to see?"

Clark handed him a plastic bag with a wad of hundred dollar bills clearly visible inside.

"It all better be here, Clark. Took us twenny hours to get here, an' the Captain wasn't happy 'bout it t'all."

"Well I figured you guys wouldn't pass up a quick charter. Mac, this is my client Roberto Mercante."

The flight engineer extended his hand.

"Mac Owens. Welcome aboard the *Skyhook*."

"Uh, yeah, nice to meet you too," said Mercante, but his eyes were on the bag in Owens' hand.

"Uh, Ian, I think we have to have a little talk."

Clark cut him off.

"Not now, Roberto. Mac, where do you want us?"

"Back in the sunroom."

Ian Clark led the way towards the rear of the seaplane into a compartment with two large Plexiglas blisters built into each side of the fuselage.

"Sit over on the port side, Roberto."

"Ian, we've got to - -"

"No, on the port side, the left side. Don't forget port and left have the same number of letters. And you'll get a better view when we take off," said Clark as he sat down opposite Mercante and strapped in.

Mercante did as he was told until – and then went back to losing his cool over the bag of money.

"Clark, how much is this costing me?"

"Don't worry, Roberto. You'll get an invoice."

Owens came through the hatch and glanced at the seat belts of the two passengers before touching a button on a small box riveted to the bulkhead.

"Passengers aboard, Captain."

"Do you have their boarding passes?" said a gruff voice on the intercom.

"Don't worry, Captain Sanchez, its all there," said Clark, raising his voice so he could be heard over the intercom, "Ten grand for eight hours, as agreed."

"Clark you SOB, where the hell are we going?"

"To check out the best surfing reef on the planet, Captain Sanchez. And madam co-pilot! Set your course to one-eleven east. How's it going, Tina?"

"Just fine, Ian. But one-eleven? There's nothing out there that I know of. You're sure about that course?"

"I know exactly where we're going, so don't worry, Tina."

"We won't as long as you're paying cash. Mac, passengers ready for liftoff?" interjected her husband.

"We're go, Captain."

"Copy that, Mac. Tina, systems?"

"All go."

"Ok, talk to you guys later."

Mac Owens strapped himself into a folddown seat bolted to the bulkhead at the rear of the 'sunroom'. Sanchez revved the starboard engine to turn the *Skyhook* into the wind. As she came around, Roberto Mercante became even more disoriented: the outrigger, the *Skyhook*, the cash, Clark's vague directions, and now he was in the tail of a seaplane about to take off.

"Hey Roberto," yelled Clark.

Mercante stopped looking out the canopy and turned to Clark.

"Let's go check the reef!"

"Uh, yeah, Clark, but - - -"

His voice was drowned out by the engines throttled wide open and the noise of the hull slicing through the sea like a racing powerboat. The sound changed as the *Skyhook* came "up on step" and began clipping through the tops of the swells. Suddenly there was only the roar of the engines as the Catalina PBY-6A, first flown on its maiden flight in 1943, broke free and climbed into the sky.

The *Skyhook* was flying about eighty feet above the sea surface. Clark and Mercante were all eyes looking out the domes as submerged reefs went by in every gorgeous shade imaginable of blue, aqua marine, and turquoise. Mac Owens just sat there watching the two passengers, remembering what it was like to simply enjoy the ride from a first-timer's point of view.

But within minutes the spell was broken. Roberto Mercante couldn't help himself when he remembered what Clark had said about time and money.

"Eight hours? Ten thousand bucks for eight hours?" he said, turning to look across the compartment.

"Yup. Thousand bucks an hour plus charter costs."

"But eight hours? I've got to be back before then!"

"Not a chance, Roberto," said Clark, not bothering to look back, "The plan is to get to the reef, set down and taxi around to check it out. Then we take off and fly back. Now, if we run into storms, or the winds are bad, or something mechanical happens - -"

"What do you mean something mechanical? Is this plane going to get us there and back or not?"

"Roberto, if there's one thing about a PBY, it's that they always brought their crews home safely."

"Yeah, pal," interjected Mac Owens, "an' tain't polite ta run down a plane while yer flyin' in 'er. Kinda bad luck, in fact."

"Well, I've got a call to make this afternoon. Will my cell work where we're going?"

"Prob'ly not."

"Well then is there a radio I can use?"

"Tell ya what, Mr. Mercante, lemme give ya a tour, an' then we'll go up to the flight deck an' see what we kin do ta keep y'all in touch with yer busy life. C'mon, bud, this way."

The flight engineer unbuckled his seatbelt and stood up near the rear of the 'sunroom'.

"Besides, if we go down ya' need ta know how ta exit the aircraft."

"If we go down?" he said, darting a dirty look at Ian Clark who was completely absorbed in the view of the South Seas streaming by.

Owens led the way through the hatch in the rear bulkhead separating the "sunroom" from the last compartment of the PBY.

"This used ta be a machine gunner's station. Now we kinda use it fer cargo an' such."

Mercante stepped in to the aft compartment. Fins, masks, snorkels, and several spear guns were mounted on the curved walls of the final tail section.

"Dependin' on conditions, we usually exit back 'ere. Keeps tha rest the aircraft dry when we're goin' divin', an' if we hafta ditch, this section stays afloat longest. 'course, that ain't never happened in tha seventy-one years of this aircraft's operation, but ya never know. Now Roberto, ya need ta unnerstand how ta work tha hatch. She opens up an' secures with this latch, so if yer the first guy out, be sure she stays open fer the rest of us. Jes' like on a regular jet."

Mercante looked down and saw the ocean blurring by seemingly only a few feet away through a clear Plexiglas window centered in the emergency hatch on the floor.

"Uh, why are we flying so low?"

"Takin' 'vantage of a trick they used durin' the war. We pick up a little extra lift from tha push o'f tha wing 'gainst tha air squeezed between us an' tha water. End up usin' a little less fuel."

He started to open the hatch but a nervous Mercante held up his hand to stop him.

"That's ok, I get the picture."

"Oh c'mon, yer having fun, ain't cha? Now let's go forward an' I'll show y'all everythin' alla way forward."

Back in the 'sunroom' Ian Clark was studying the display of a small GPS unit. "Mac, can you get a position check for me? I've got 148 degrees 34 minutes west, 18 degrees 10 minutes south."

"Nice gadget ya got there, Clark. Since when didja care 'bout such minor details as latitude and longitude? Thought that was L.J.'s department."

"Since I started paying cash, Mac."

The flight engineer didn't miss the intent of the tone in Clark's voice.

"Mr. Mercante, would you kindly wait fer me in tha cargo bay? 'nd here," he said, taking a thin plastic binder out of a built-in rack on the bulkhead, "This will answer a lotta yer questions 'bout the *Skyhook*. I'll be right with ya."

The flight engineer held the hatch open and Mercante stepped into the cargo bay. The hatch closed abruptly, and once again he wasn't quite sure what was going on. He looked around, and other than several metal boxes bolted to the forward bulkhead, it was completely empty. There was nowhere to sit, so he crouched with his back against the bulkhead and opened the binder.

Welcome aboard the Skyhook, owned and operated by the Skyrider Foundation, a non-profit organization dedicated to increasing educational opportunities for the youth of Polynesia.

You are flying in a Catalina PBY6A amphibious airplane, one of 2,943 such planes built during the Second World War. Their acronym, PBY, signified their purpose as patrol bombers, with the Y designating their manufacturer, Consolidated of San Diego, founded by the colorful Reuben H. Fleet.

The PBY flew in every naval theater of war around the world. It was a PBY that first saw the Japanese fleet steaming towards Midway, and a PBY that dropped the first bombs on Japanese soil. It was a PBY that spotted the German battleship Bismarck in the North Atlantic and PBY's that were the first line of defense against the U-boat wolfpacks. But for many veterans, the real legend of the Catalina stems from the countless missions flown to rescue them after their planes crashed or ships sank.

After the war, hundreds were converted to serve a wide variety of purposes. For several decades Catalinas were flown for adventure tour companies, oil exploration outfits, fire-fighting crews, and even private owners who had them re-fitted as global air-yachts. To this day they can be seen flying in air shows around the globe.

The lineage of the Skyhook can be traced back to her squadron known as the Snafu Snatchers. She followed B-29s on bombing runs and P-40s into battle and picked up any pilots who were shot down or had to bail out. In fact, some fighter pilots knew they would run out of gas on the way home but they also knew the Snafu Snatchers would be right there to fish them out of the drink.

In 1944 the Skyhook was painted black for midnight missions to retrieve downed flyers hidden by native Polynesians from the Japanese. A roar coming in from the horizon, a white wake appearing on the sea – and many a young pilot waiting nervously in an outrigger knew he would soon be out of harm's way.

After the war a special squadron of Catalinas, led by the Skyhook, spent two years searching for the remains of pilots in the wreckage of downed aircraft on reefs, atolls, and islands across the Pacific. Flight crews pushed themselves and the planes to their limits to recover dogtags - or anything - that would serve to identify the fallen and bring closure to their kin.

The Skyhook was then flown by the Navy in support of nuclear testing operations conducted during the fifties and sixties. In the seventies she was sold to the newly independent government of Fiji and used to transport medical services, patients and government officials to the far-flung islands of the new nation.

Into the eighties and nineties she saw service in the States and Europe flying a succession of wealthy owners to their yachts in the Caribbean, secluded islands around the Bahamas or private lakes in Switzerland. She was owned and operated by a tourist adventure company in Africa for several years before being bought by the government of India during the conflicts with Ceylon.

Finally, she was acquired by Australian businessmen to fly surfers to remote islands throughout Indonesia. But after a few months in service, she was replaced by high-speed power yachts in response to the demands of the fast-paced surf travel industry. She was mothballed to a hangar in Brisbane and gathered dust for several years until she was tracked down by Victor Sanchez.

Captain Sanchez' father had flown her in World War Two and his stories of recovery missions during and after the war left a strong impression on Victor, who vowed one day to find the Skyhook and get her in the air again. After flying jets for the Navy in the Gulf War, Captain Sanchez decided to muster out of the military and start a new life in the South Seas. He had a vision of providing passenger service, ferrying medical services and patients, and even taking divers and surfers to remote sites inaccessible by boat. Captain Sanchez met his wife Tina on a flight to a remote island in French Polynesia, and thanks to her concern for her people, they formed the Skyrider Foundation. Supported by charter income, grants, and retainer fees from Polynesian governments, the Foundation operates a school for promising youth from throughout Polynesia to prepare them for university studies in medicine and other careers in service to their home islands.

We hope you enjoy your flight aboard the Skyhook. Please read on for more information about her exact specifications, a list of missions flown during the war, a timeline of ownership, and other fascinating facts about our beloved Catalina flying boat.

Mercante reflected for a moment on what he had just read until his mind darted quickly to wondering what was taking so long with Owens and Clark.

When Owens saw the hatch close, he pushed a small dead bolt on his side to secure it completely. Then he turned to Ian Clark, looking out across the ocean as if he did not have a care in the world.

"What tha hell is this about Clark, an' don' gimme any crap. Tha plane commander don't like yer style one bit, an' I'm inclined to 'gree with him. Where we goin' an' what's tha deal with L.J.?"

Clark turned slowly, letting Owens see his annoyance at being distracted.

"Listen, Mac, I don't have to tell you a thing about Merrill. You have ten grand in your hands, and exactly where we are going is classified information for now. Which reminds me, I need you, Victor and Tina to sign these."

He pulled three forms out of his backpack and handed them to Owens. Without breaking eye contact, the flight engineer tore the papers in half and handed them back.

"Clark, I'm not goin' fer yer bullshit. Besides, if we signed yer pissant non-disclosures and then violated the terms, whatcha gonna do, sue us? So try bein' straight with me or y'all never gonna fly on this aircraft agin."

Clark knew Owens was a man not given to idle threats, and with his entire plan depending on the capabilities of a Catalina, he knew he had better come clean, and fast.

"Ok, Mac, here's the deal. I found a reef with the best big waves on the planet. I sold the rights to Wavelife International. Their surfers are going to ride the place and I'll need you and the *Skyhook* to make it happen."

Mac Owens looked at Clark with a sharp eye for more than a few seconds. "Nuff said."

The flight engineer turned and slid open the dead bolt, but before he opened the hatch, he looked back at Ian Clark.

"Oh, jes one thing, Ian. I don' know where we're goin', but I do know y'all didn't find the place. So I'd 'preciate it if ya don' ever lie to me again, pal."

The hatch closed and Ian Clark was very much alone. Owens' comment made him wonder what L.J. Merrill was doing at that very moment. He didn't have a clue, but one thing he did know: not only did he owe the reef to his former scout, but also the *Skyhook*.

Before they had met that fateful day in Australia, Merrill had twice hitched rides on the seaplane to remote islands throughout Polynesia on his search for surf. Once Geosurf got going, they chartered the *Skyhook* on numerous occasions, and though Clark didn't like the bills, the investment had paid off with several major finds. And for years afterwards, the *Skyhook* flew Geosurf customers to remote resorts. Clark smiled at the thought of the prices he used to charge, but the smile faded when he remembered how things changed overnight.

Two years ago he bounced a check to Tina Sanchez drawn on a bank in Samoa when one of his Third World commodities schemes did not work out. He quickly made good on it, but Victor Sanchez took it personally given that the whole idea of flying the *Skyhook* was to support the Skyrider Foundation and its work with young Polynesians across the Pacific. He let Clark know that although the *Skyhook* would continue to be available for charter, the terms would strictly cash in U.S. dollars from then on.

That condition precluded any further business since Ian Clark was always skimming the cash and thus never had any for operations. And at the time, it didn't matter anyway. He found he could save money using light planes and chartered yachts instead of the *Skyhook* while charging his clients the same top-dollar rates. Although the PBY continued to be pictured on Geosurf's brochures and website, she had never flown again for Clark since the bounced check.

But now here he was, paying top dollar and yet having to put up with Owens' attitude, because he knew had no choice: his entire plan depended on the *Skyhook*. She had the range, the cargo capacity, and the ability to set down in the middle of the ocean. Merrill's video gave no indication of what it would be like to anchor a large yacht anywhere near the reef. The PBY Catalina, unlike a Grumman Albatross or other smaller seaplanes, could carry a dozen people plus a lot of equipment, including jet skis. Of course, that meant burning aviation fuel no matter what the cost, and at eighty gallons an hour, the Catalina was not cheap. But then again, he smirked, it wasn't his money.

He looked down through the bottom pane of the Plexiglas dome. The ocean speeding by seemed so close he could almost touch it. It reminded him of the blur of data across the bottom of his computer screen. The stark contrast of the two images had a powerful effect on him. He turned away and saw the empty compartment, but he found no relief from his discomfort.

His smirk was replaced by a downcast stare when his first thought was of the machine guns that once protruded from the Plexiglas blisters, of the Japanese fighter planes zooming past, some on fire, others firing back, bullets ripping through the thin aluminum cutting into young flyers, blood spurting everywhere. He could almost hear their screams over the roar of the engines. He saw his reflection in the opposite dome, his shades and his khakis and his GPS, and he felt very out of place and then embarrassed. This was a place of honor - and not for posers from Newport Beach who made fast money, thanks to golf and gossip, along with promises that were never kept.

His mind went blank for a second. He looked at the hatch and gave a thought to joining Owens and Mercante and how wonderful it would be to trust some real friends for once in his life.

But he didn't make a move – until he turned his downcast eyes back to watching the South Pacific blur past him.

Mercante looked up as Owens came into the cargo compartment.

"I see yer doin' yer homework, Mr. Mercante. Any questions?"

"Yeah, just one. How safe are we flying in a plane built in 1943?"

"Well, sir, we jes' came back from the States to renew our FAA certificate allowin' us to carry passengers. She's actually a better plane now than when she was first built."

"You know, I've only seen them in movies. I think there was one in a surf movie, as I recall."

"Yeah, 'In God's Hands', when those guys escaped from jail an' were rescued by Shaun Tomson."

"You know him?"

"Sure, flew 'im out to one of Merrill's special reefs cupla years ago. Nice guy. Anyways, that was a PBY, but she was a 5A. The *Skyhook* is a 6A. The Navy came up with a re-design called the Nomad PBN-1 back in '43, but she weighed too much an' had less range, so they sold 'em to the Ruskies an' came up with tha 6A. Her top speed was one eighty five, but that was only in a steep dive. She had a ceiling 'round - - -"

Owens could see that Mercante was glazing over.

"Say, how'd ya like something to eat? I'm gettin' hungry. Follow me."

Owens led him forward to the mechanic's compartment between the landing gear wheel wells. The noise of the engines was deafening in the cramped space crowded with tools and smelling of lubricants. Mercante looked up into a hollow superstructure ringed with cables, tubing and wires connecting the controls and systems between the fuselage and the wing. Halfway up the "tower" were windows on each side and a seat mounted between them.

"Yeah, that used ta be the flight engineer's station. Ya needed three people to fly a PBY durin' the war, but FAA regs changed in the early sixties and required everythin' to be controlled by no more than two people from the flight deck. So I don' go up there much anymore."

"You mean this plane has been flying since the sixties?"

"She bin flyin' since World War Two, remember?" said Owens impatiently, "You know, Pearl Harbor, the Nazis, John Wayne fighting the Japs!" A thought of *What-the-hell, the guy is a rich surfer, what does he know?"* helped him change his tone back to the friendly voice of a tour guide. "Mr. Mercante, the *Skyhook* wuddn't be in the air if I didn't make shure she complied with every safety reg known to man. Cum on in, please. Y'all be more comfortable."

Owens stepped through the hatch into the galley. In contrast to the 'sunroom', the cargo bay and the mechanic's station, the galley of the *Skyhook* had wall-to-wall carpeting. Thick insulation cut the engine noise to a minimum. Four cushioned captains' chairs swiveled around a clean formica table. He closed the door behind them and Mercante was surprised at how quiet it was.

"I guess yer used to flying first class, so have a seat, Mr. Mercante."

"Well, actually I - -"

The intercom buzzed on.

"Everybody hold on for a sec, we're going to hop an island coming up."

"Better sit down an' strap in," said Mac Owens, pointing to the chair nearest his passenger.

Not ten seconds after the seat belt clicked Mercante was pushed down in his seat as the *Skyhook* suddenly went from eighty feet off the deck to two hundred and fifty feet. She leveled off, and then dove back down, only to repeat the process a second time almost immediately.

"Ok, that should do it for now. Hey Clark, you sure about that course?" said Victor Sanchez, laughing. The intercom clicked off.

"Yeah, Mr. Mercante, do you know where we're going?"

Mac Owens didn't get an answer, but he did get a plastic bag out of a drawer as fast as he could.

"Here ya go, pal, use this. Next time lemme know 'fore we take off. We got some fast-actin' scopolamine, 'though it won't do y'all much good right now."

He pushed the button on the intercom.

"Flight, we've got a passenger who don't like roller coasters all that much."

"Roger that, Mac, but orders were one-eleven at cruising speed, and one-eleven it's going to be until I'm told differently."

"Of course, we can fly a bit higher, but that's more fuel, with an appropriate surcharge, of course," said Tina Sanchez.

Mercante's stomach emptied itself a second time into the bag. He looked at Mac Owens with a green face and nodded.

"That's a go, Flight, but I think a gradual climb would be in order," laughed Owens.

"Climbing to one thousand. Say, when we level off why don't you come up to the cockpit? We'd like to say hello, Mr. Mercante."

"I'm not feeling too, uh," he dry heaved into the bag, "social right now, thanks," the words barely getting out of his mouth amidst a stream of breakfast and bile.

"Well, let's hope y'all gonna enjoy the rest of yer flight," said Owens, almost feeling sorry for the vomiting millionaire sitting in front of him.

"Mac, could you go up in the tower and give me a visual on number two? I've got a low oil pressure indicator up here."

He handed Mercante a plastic sports bottle from the refrigerator and reached into a metal cabinet with a red cross on it to remove a small bottle of pills.

"Roger that, Flight. Here, drink this an' take three of these. It'll settle yer stomach. An' stow that bag in the trash when yer done. An' don' fergit to close it first. That smell really gits ta me."

Mercante nodded, one hand holding the medicine and the bottles, the other holding the bag. Owens headed aft to the mechanic's compartment and opened the hatch. The noise and smell of engines flooded the galley.

Mercante opened the container and washed down two pills with a long swig from the sports bottle. He started to feel better almost instantly. The hatch to the mechanic's compartment was open, and he could see the flight engineer up inside the superstructure, looking out through a small window, and then coming back into the galley, closing the door and buzzing the intercom box.

"Flight, no apparent oil leaks on number two. Must be the gauge. I'll run a test on 'er when we get back to Tahiti."

"Roger that, Mac. How's our passenger doing?"

Owens turned to Mercante.

"Feelin' better?"

"Uh, kinda, I think."

"He's ok, Flight. Ready fer some introductions?"

"Sure, come on up. And grab some juice bottles, will you please?"

"Will do."

"Say Mac, what is this stuff? Seems to work pretty fast."

"Soda water and kava, plus summa those scopolamine pills. Settles yer stomach an' gets yer mind off yer nausea. Y'all might be getting' a bit drowsy pretty soon, so let's go visit the cockpit."

Mac Owens stood up and walked forward and opened the bulkhead hatch. The doorway was filled with light.

"Go on in," he gestured to Mercante.

Roberto stood up and suddenly didn't feel all that well. But he knew he couldn't wuss out now, so he ducked through the hatch and found himself standing between two seats mounted on platforms three feet high on either side of him. The man on his left didn't look at him, seemingly quite busy with flying the plane. But the person on his right was another story entirely. The first thing he saw was her long black hair in a ponytail coming out the back of her baseball cap. Then she turned and extended her hand to him, her nails done perfectly. "Welcome aboard, Mr. Mercante. I am Tina Sanchez. Sorry about getting you sick. Are you feeling better?" she smiled.

"Yes, thank you," nodded Roberto, somewhat mesmerized by the smooth feeling of her hand and her classic Polynesian beauty. He was barely able to remember his manners and cover his mouth as he yawned. Then he fully snapped out of it when she introduced the pilot now looking at him from not more than two feet away.

"This is my husband Victor," she said. The pilot had his hands on the controls and nodded at Mercante, his firm jaw not allowing anything more than a thin smile.

"Gangway there, mate!"

Mercante was startled by Mac Owens behind him. He walked forward a few steps and found himself almost ducking under the instrument panel into a forward compartment.

Owens handed two plastic bottles to Tina Sanchez. She held one up so that her husband could see it and he nodded. She gave him a bottle and he took a long swig from it before giving it back to his wife. He took his headset off and ran a large hand through his dark wavy hair. He looked down at Mercante from his pilot's perch.

"So you're paying the bills at Ian Clark's direction. You sure you know what you are doing?" Sanchez wanted direct eye contact and took off his sunglasses to get it. His bluntness caught Mercante off guard.

"Uh, yeah, hi, I'm Roberto Mercante. I own Wavelife International. Nice to meet you."

"Oh, I thought Wavelife was owned by the shareholders. We tried to raise some money once from you guys and got the run-around."

"Now, Victor, be nice. He's not feeling that well."

"Right dear," Sanchez turned back and looked at Mercante.

"So, are we on company time, or is this just a junket for the hell of it?"

"Victor!"

"Oh all right, but any friend of Ian Clark, is, uh, ah forget it. Where's L.J.?"

"I don't know. But I trust Ian Clark, as does my wife and she's the CEO. He pitched us an idea and we're going to take him up on it."

Mercante yawned and his eyelids drooped.

"He knows where there's an unknown reef with the best waves I've ever seen, and we want Wavelife surfers to be the first to ride the place."

"Yeah, there was a lot of surf two weeks ago, but it is pretty flat right now."

"Well, I just want to see the place with my own eyes," said Mercante, fighting to stay awake.

"Knowing Clark, that's probably a good idea," remarked Sanchez, prompting a withering stare from his wife. He quickly put on his sunglasses and headset and went back to giving the PBY his undivided attention.

"Yeah, that reminds me, Clark wanted ta double check our position against his GPS gadget." Mac Owens touched the button on an intercom box. "Hey bigshot, ya wanna check yer GPS? Cum'on up here."

There was no answer.

"Clark, y'all back there sleepin' in the sun or sumthin'?"

Still no answer.

"Hey Ian, we're almost there!"

"No, we're not. We're only at one four seven five two west, two one one zero south," said a very alert Ian Clark with a sharp tone to his voice.

Tina Sanchez looked at a display in front of her.

"That's right Ian," she said into her headset patched into the intercom.

"I'll be up there in a minute. Thanks for remembering me, Mac."

The box clicked off, and Owens shrugged.

Tina Sanchez knew that Owens' attitude was entirely due to how her husband felt about the owner of Geosurf Resorts. And she knew she had to do something about it.

"Say, Roberto, why don't you go forward there and lie down for a while. We'll wake you up when we get there."

"Thanks, I think I'll do that. Nice meeting you both," said Mercante. He yawned again, and ducked under the instrument panel into the forward compartment where he curled up on some loose cushions and coiled ropes.

He was out like a light, but Tina Sanchez was taking no chances. She motioned for Owens to put on an intercom headset hanging from the bulkhead. Then she spoke in a low voice that could be not be heard over the engines.

"Ok, Mac, why the attitude?"

"He said he knows exactly where we're going. Says he found it, but of course that's crap an' I called him on it."

"Well, I bet L.J. is out of the picture because Clark screwed him, one way or another," said the Captain.

"Now listen, and that means both of you. L.J. was a nice guy, but times change, and we've got paying customers aboard, and don't forget it."

"Yeah, had sum fun with him, didn't we? You'd think Clark would remember all tha places - - - "Owens stopped in mid sentence when he saw the look of a woman who didn't want to hear another word about L.J. Merrill, "Oh, right, the money. Here you go, Tina."

Owens handed her the zip-lock plastic bag. She opened it and started to count the bills.

"And there's more where that came from, believe me."

Ian Clark poked his head through the hatchway into the cockpit. Mac Owens shouldered past him back into the galley so that Clark could step forwards into the cramped cockpit.

He extended his hand to Victor Sanchez.

"Hi Victor, good to see you."

Sanchez turned and barely nodded to him. Clark felt the vibe and tried again with the Captain's wife.

"Hello Tina, how are you? Sorry again about that problem we had."

That was all her husband needed to hear, and he made no effort to rein in his dislike for a man trying to sweet talk his wife after bouncing a check for over twenty thousand dollars.

"We didn't have a problem, Clark. You did, and that's why you're paying cash now and forevermore. Is it all there, Tina? Better count it."

"Yes, Victor, its ten thousand, as agreed, although you may have to cover some extra charges, Ian. Our fuel consumption has gone up."

"No problem. As long as we're on course, I'm stoked."

"One eleven dead on and steady as she goes. Where are we headed, Ian?"

Clark looked back into the galley at Owens.

"I wasn't going to tell you until I had signed non-disclosures, but Mac tells me they won't be needed."

"Actually I just tore them up when you tried to hand them to me," said Owens in a loud voice, standing back in the galley.

"Yeah, Clark, what makes you think I'd sign anything for you anyway? First you bounce a check, then you show up with some story about a magic reef, and by the way, where's L.J.?"

Victor Sanchez' tone was ominous. His wife could sense the tension, but with ten thousand dollars in her hand, she was not going to lose an account just because male egos were turning the men into growling dogs.

"Ian, why don't you and I go sit down in the galley and discuss this? And Victor, I think you should come with us. Mac, could you come up here and keep an eye on things?"

"Uh, yeah, sure Tina," he said with some hesitation. But Ian Clark was ready to clear the air. He turned and ducked back through the hatch, bumping into Mac Owens. Tina Sanchez got out of her seat and followed Clark through the hatch.

"Let's go, Victor!"

"All right, I'm coming. Mac, one eleven due east. And bring her up to top speed. Let's get this over with."

"Aye-aye skipper, one eleven east. Full throttles."

Victor Sanchez sat next to his wife and glared across the table at Ian Clark.

"You didn't answer my question about L.J. And I want to know where we're going, Clark."

"Ok, Sanchez. But first forget about L.J. Merrill. And as for where we are going, I'll show you in a minute."

"You said we're going to the best surfing reef on the planet, but there's no place to surf on this course for thousands of miles!"

"Keep your shirt on, skipper. We're not going thousands of miles."

Clark pulled a portable DVD player out of his pack, opened it up, touched the "play" button, and pushed it across the table.

"Here's the place we're looking for."

The husband-and-wife team watched the forty-five seconds of shaky video shot from ten thousand feet.

63

"I know those waters like my own hand, but I've never seen this place. Where is it on the chart?"

"Don't bother, Victor. It's not on any chart."

Sanchez narrowed his eyes.

"Clark, I've just about had it with your - - - "

His wife pinched him painfully on the knee and he stopped short of saying another word.

"Maybe you've never seen this place before, but seeing is believing, and you'll see it in person soon enough."

"Ian, are you sure about this?"

"I'd bet my life on it, Tina."

"Seems like you already have," she replied.

"I've bet Geosurf on it, that's for sure. I've got a good deal with Wavelife and all things being equal, you will, too. I - - -"

"What kind of deal, Clark? And what kind of deal did you give L.J.?"

Clark's focus snapped into survival mode.

"Victor, just shut up about him and listen. I'm offering you a retainer of fifty thousand dollars in cash for sixty days starting June nineteenth. Plus a matching cash contribution to the Foundation. Plus all expenses, fuel, and two fifty per diem each. Mac, too."

"And where does L.J. fit into all this?"

"He doesn't. You know as well as I do that he would never work with a corporation like Wavelife. So I had to make some changes and - - -"

"That's ok, Clark, I can imagine what happened with Wavelife in the picture. He never trusted you all that much anyway."

"Victor, enough is enough. He brought cash, and Ian, if you put fifty grand in our hands and another fifty to the Foundation, we'll be able to work with you. And you did say all expenses, plus fuel and per diem?"

"Correct. There will be at least two flights in and out of the place, possibly more. The *Skyhook* will be doing air-ferry with a lot of equipment and passengers."

"I think we can do the job, Ian. What do you think, Victor?"

"As long as its cash, we'll be ready."

"There will be two hundred and fifty thousand US dollars deposited in your Fijian account as soon as I finalize the details with Wavelife. Fifty thousand will be yours to keep no matter what. Satisfied, Captain Sanchez?"

"That will be just fine, Ian," said Tina Sanchez before her husband had a chance to respond to the obvious challenge in Clark's tone of voice.

"Good. That's what I was hoping you'd say. Only one more thing: I will give you the coordinates, but they stay aboard the *Skyhook*. I've got to keep this place under wraps or - - -"

"Or somebody might steal it from you the way you stole it from L.J? Well, Clark, collecting on your karma is not my job. So exactly where do we set down?"

"Come and get me when you're within a ten mile radius of one three seven west and twenty-one south. And I have your word?"

Victor Sanchez hesitated, but his wife did not.

"You do."

She extended her hand to Clark and shook it firmly. Then she looked at her husband, who was looking at the DVD display and watching the images play again. She closed the lid of the player firmly and handed it to Clark.

"Victor!"

"Uh, yeah, okay Clark."

He extended his hand, but kept his eyes averted.

Clark left the galley and made his way back to the 'sunroom'. Tina Sanchez leaned back, looked at her husband, and sighed.

"Ok, dear, let me give it to you straight. Our job is to keep the *Skyhook* in the air and the Skyrider Foundation solvent. We're making good money on this flight, so I want both Clark and Mercante to enjoy themselves and feel welcome."

"Yeah, but - - - "

"No yeah-but, Victor. That's the way it's going to be, for one simple reason: Wavelife grossed over a billion dollars last year. I will NOT have you guys jeopardizing a relationship that could really help us. Are we understood?"

Victor Sanchez looked liked a cowed boy glad he wasn't going to be spanked. Tina Sanchez took that as an answer.

"Now I'm going up to relieve Mac. When he comes back here, I want you to tell him exactly what I just told you. No tone. No sarcasm. Be nice. We've got commitments that are way too important for you to screw things up because of L.J. I feel for him too, Victor. Now is not the time to deal with it. Period."

She got up out of her chair and opened the hatch to the cockpit.

Mac Owens was concentrating on the temperature gauges to make sure she wasn't overheating.

"Mac! Victor has some things to discuss with you."

Roberto Mercante slowly opened his eyes, and he didn't know where he was. He sat up, looked around the small compartment and saw two anchors atop piles of thick, neatly coiled rope. Slowly he remembered exactly where he was: on a World War Two seaplane flying out over the South Pacific on its way to the most perfect big wave reef he had ever seen. In his excitement, he stood up and hit his head on the skylight. He turned and bent over to go through the hatch leading aft. Ducking through it, he came up into the cockpit and was startled to find Tina Sanchez alone in the co-pilot's seat.

"Well, glad to see you're up and around, Roberto," she said with a smile as she looked at her nails.

Mercante just stood there soaking in the image of a beautiful woman sitting at the controls of a seaplane. Then he saw the control yokes moving slightly and it took him a few seconds to figure it out. Autopilot.

"Uh, can I sit up there in the other seat, Tina? May I call you Tina?"

"Sure. Just don't touch anything."

65

He climbed up into the seat on the port side of the plane. He looked out the window and saw an ocean of rich blue to the horizon with coral reefs surrounding lagoons of turquoise.

"I've got to get me one of these!" he said in a voice audible over the full sound of the twin engines.

He barely touched the steering controls and his imagination ran wild. There he was, flying his own plane to undiscovered waves that only he would surf, with a Polynesian beauty at his side.

"Roberto, I told you not to touch anything," said Tina Sanchez, pretending to scold him.

He quickly took his hands away from the controls, abashed at the reprimand.

"Well, go ahead, get a feel for her," she said, relenting coyly, "Just don't grip her too tightly, ok? You need to feel how she moves on her own before you try to control her."

She got out of her seat and stood right next to Mercante.

"Here, let me explain what all these dials and displays are for. Oh, excuse me for a second before we get started."

She smiled at the speechless Mercante and hit the button on the intercom.

"Victor, why don't you make us some lunch? And Mac, could you do a run through of all the maintenance we've been deferring this year? We will be giving the *Skyhook* a re-furb when we get back, thanks to Roberto."

She looked at him, her smile bright against her dash of lipstick and rich Polynesian skin.

"Now, where were we? Oh, you want to learn how to fly her, do you? Well, there are some important things you've got to learn."

"Boy, I like this!"

"You like it now. You'll learn to love it later."

For almost half an hour the millionaire surfer was living a dream come true, flying to the best waves in the world in a Catalina with a knockout dame standing next to him in the cockpit. Though they were both married, the Brazilian millionaire and the Polynesian beauty were not above some serious flirting while winging above an idyllic ocean paradise.

But Tina Sanchez knew what she was doing, and when to do it at exactly the right moment.

"You know, I think we're getting a bit too hot, don't you Roberto?"

"Uh, er - - -"

"The temperature gauges, remember? Gotta keep an eye on 'em all time!" she purred as she withdrew to the co-pilot's seat.

She eased off the throttles slightly.

"There, that's better. Mac! Come on up and fly for us, ok?" she said into the intercom, "Roberto, let's go get something to eat. I hope my husband has lunch ready for us by now. After you!"

Tina Sanchez never took her eyes off him as she gestured to Mercante. He followed her hand and almost fell out of the captain's seat. His face reddened as Sanchez laughed.

"Oh, don't worry. It's always a little awkward the first time."

Mercante stumbled a step and caught his balance by holding on to the bulkhead. The hatch opened and he stepped through it like a drunken sailor, bumping into Mac Owens in the process.

"Oh, sorry, Mr. Mercante! Did you have a nice sleep? Everything ok?"

"Sure, Mac. Just great!"

Owens lifted up into the captain's chair.

"Everything's steady, Mac. Did you and Victor have your little chat?" The tone in her voice was strictly no-nonsense.

"Yes, ma'am. Captain's orders understood loud and clear."

She swung gracefully out of her seat and went through the hatch all in one motion, ready to share an excellent lunch and conversation at the captain's table with her husband and their new-found patron.

An hour later, Roberto Mercante was in excellent spirits. Tina Sanchez saw her chance and excused herself.

"Victor, can I have a word with you? We'll be right back, Roberto," she said, motioning her husband to follow her to the engineer's compartment.

She closed the hatch behind her.

She gave her husband a long, luscious kiss, and then did it again.

"Are you okay, Victor? I know this is hard for you."

"Yeah, I just can't get L.J. out of my thoughts. I KNOW Clark ripped him off for this place and then sold it to this guy. And now I've got to keep them both happy? C'mon, Tina!"

Tina gave him another kiss and put her arms around his waist and pulled him tightly to her.

"Victor, if we can land Wavelife as a donor, we'll put that many more kids on full scholarships. Do it for them, Victor. Wavelife can really help us."

"Ok, now that you put it that way, I'll be the nicest guy you've ever seen," said Victor, putting his arms around his wife and looking into her deep eyes.

She kissed him once more. "You already are the nicest guy I've ever seen. Now, you go hang out with the boys up front and I'll go get Ian."

Tina Sanchez went aft until she reached the 'sunroom'. She opened the hatch, and found Ian Clark fast asleep. She looked at him and thought about just what drove human beings to end up so far from heart and home. She knew Clark's story from endless hours of flying with L.J. Merrill, and all she could do was hope that some good would come of Ian Clark's plans. She stepped back into the cargo bay, and slowly closed the hatch. Then she made some noise with the winch before pretending to struggle with the hatch. Then she said in a loud voice, "Hey, Ian, I think we're almost there!"

She waited a few seconds before stepping into the 'sunroom'. And just as she'd anticipated, Ian Clark was waking up.

"We're getting close, Ian. C'mon, let's go up front and see what's cookin'," she said with a smile almost angelic in its charm.

67

"Oh, I'm sorry, I fell asleep," he said, looking up at the first friendly face he'd seen in a long time. Then he looked at his GPS and his heart skipped a beat.

The air in the cockpit was charged with excitement. Mercante was in the captain's seat and loving it as Mac Owens was showing him all the dials and going on and on about the mechanical aspects of flying a Catalina PBY. Victor Sanchez was giving pointers to Mercante about how the *Skyhook* handled. Ian Clark crouched in the forward compartment watching the numbers displayed on his GPS and glancing from time to time through the observation porthole.

Finally he saw what he was waiting for on the GPS display.

"We're here," he said, almost to himself.

Nobody heard him, and that was just as well, because as he looked out the window, he saw a dozen reefs scattered across the sea. Every one of them was fringed with white on their east-facing shores from wind chop coming from the trades. None of them showed any signs of swell from the south, but then he realized that the swell was the least of his problems.

"Oh shit."

He looked at the coordinates from the airline and at his GPS. They were almost identical, but the airlines had only given him degrees and minutes, but not seconds. And with a second equal to about six nautical miles, the numbers from the airline could be off by as much as three hundred and sixty miles. They didn't pinpoint the reef, and now there was no way to tell which of the reefs far below, if any of them, was the one Merrill had discovered. He took a deep breath to suppress a panic not unlike that of a drug dealer about to display product to a cash customer when he discovers he's been burned up the line and his stuff is no good. But he caught himself as the instincts of a salesman kicked in. The first thing he had to do was stall for time.

"Ok, steady as she goes," he looked down at the GPS, "Victor, maybe you better take the controls. We'll be setting down soon. Roberto, why don't we go back into the sunroom? I'm sure the view will be great from there."

"Yeah, good idea you guys," said Mac Owens.

Mercante got out of the seat and Sanchez swung up and took the controls after carefully turning off the autopilot. He followed Clark aft, passing Tina Sanchez in the galley.

"We're almost there, Roberto! You must be really excited!" she said.

Mercante smiled at her, tongue-tied at seeing such a gorgeous woman tidying up the place. Clark didn't even notice her. He was sweating bullets as he led Mercante back to the 'sunroom', but he knew he was lucky they were flying at a thousand feet. If the *Skyhook* had been close to the sea surface, he wouldn't have seen all the reefs arrayed across the ocean, nor would he have seen that none had the perfect elliptical shape in the images captured by Merrill.

Mercante looked out the port dome like a kid staring through a window at a toy store. Clark pretended to look out to starboard, but his mind was far away.

The intercom box came on.

"Ok, Ian, I'm going to take her down. Where do you want me to go?"

Clark looked up at the sky in resignation and closed his eyes. He wanted to pray, but he knew God was not going to help a liar and a thief.

"Yeah, Ian, where is it? Can you see it?" said an excited Roberto Mercante. Clark opened his eyes, and looked into the deep ocean. Then he saw the handle at the bottom of the Plexiglas dome. Anxiety attacked from all sides. Merrill, Geosurf, Wavelife, Victor and Tina Sanchez, Mac Owens, the lawyers, the cops, the IRS, the surf stars, the Newport crowd: they were all flashing across his mind and looking straight at him. He looked down at the handle. Then his gaze went right through the window.

Off in the distance he saw a faint ring of white set against the blue of God's ocean. And then he thought he saw yet another ring of white just on the horizon. He felt something powerful turn his heart around. He steadied himself. Now he had to think fast. He waited for a few seconds, and yet a third ring appeared. They were about eight to ten miles apart. The surf was flat, and there was no way of telling which one was the reef in Merrill's video. But any one of them would do for now, and that was all that mattered.

"Right there, Roberto! There it is! That's the reef!"

He pushed the intercom button.

"Hey Victor, set her down next to the first reef just ahead of us. We're right where we want to be!"

The Sea People

David Helmares guided his voyaging craft slowly through the reef passage into the quiet lagoon. With the trade winds at his back, the return voyage from Ka'unua had taken but two days. He could see Taveka standing at the water's edge, his white hair and broad smile in sharp contrast to his dark brown skin, holding his weathered hands high above his head in greeting.

David's eyes filled with tears, and for a moment, he could no longer see his mentor. The tears turned to laughter, as David remembered the first time he had sailed through the passage into this lagoon when the welcome had been quite different.

* * *

"You do not have permission to land here. You do not have permission to anchor in these waters."

The spry and surprisingly strong Polynesian was standing knee-deep in the still waters of the lagoon and holding firm to the bow of the fiberglass sailboat to keep it from touching the shore. From the lines on his face he could have been sixty or seventy years old. Yet his physique, half-hidden by a traditional lavalava wrapped around his waist and up over one shoulder, was of a man in the prime of life. He spoke in the voice of one who had commanded others for decades.

"What do you want?"

"My name is David Helmares, and I want to learn from the sea people of Marulea," he replied from the cockpit near the stern of the boat, "And your name, sir?"

"My name is Taveka. Who are you, Captain Helmares?"

The deeply tanned Helmares was wearing sunglasses and a visor to protect his eyes from the glare of the ocean. He was bare-chested, and his surfing trunks were as sun-bleached as his hair.

"I've just sailed over three thousand miles and - - -"

"Captain, that is not what I asked you."

"Sir, uh, I mean Taveka, I have everything you need right here. This bag contains my passport, ships' papers, and all my documents."

He began to walk forward from the cockpit, only to see Taveka raise a hand in a clear signal to proceed no further.

"Please just stay where you are. I am not interested in your documents. Now, Captain Helmares, what did I ask you?"

The question was posed in a quiet, patient voice that nonetheless demanded a response.

"May I at least come forward and speak to you more directly?"

"Tie your helm down so your boat does not drift. Then come and sit on the bow. And take off your sunglasses."

The young sailor did as he was told. He sensed the man standing before him had all the authority of a customs agent, a harbormaster, and more.

"I was born in the United States, in the state of Texas, in - -"

"Texas? Well, you are a long way from the Lone Star State, partner!"

Taveka looked straight into David's eyes.

"Just one minute please, Captain. I think others will want to hear this."

He turned and waded through the shallow water to the beach and continued to walk across the sand.

"Remember," said Taveka, calling to the unexpected visitor from the trees fringing the beach, "Do not drop anchor under any circumstances!"

Within minutes a crowd of people gathered on the beach. They were wearing sarongs, canvas shorts, traditional loin wraps, and muumuus in bright yellows, reds and blues that contrasted with their rich brown skin. There were strong young men and women, many with children of all ages and sizes. There were older couples hand-in-hand, and the people up front made way for them as they sat down near the water. Only when they were seated did everyone else sit down, though some of the young children could not contain their curiosity and went swimming around the modern sailboat. There was a lively murmur of conversation, and David could pick out words in English, French, and a dialect that he had not heard while sailing throughout Polynesia. A small group of elders appeared behind the crowd and did not sit down. Taveka emerged from that group and walked through the crowd to the water's edge.

"Captain David Helmares, we are impressed you were able to find us, and for that you have our respect. Now, who are you?"

David was about to begin when a voice came from the middle of the crowd. "And be brief – we have to go fishing in a few days!"

Everybody laughed, except for the elders and Taveka.

"I'll do my best. I was born in Texas, but my father died when I was only three."

"What city in Texas?"

"What day were you born?"

"Was your birth painful to your mother?"

"Do you remember him?"

There was so much curiosity in the air that Taveka did not try to tame it for almost a minute. Then he slowly raised his hand and the questions stopped momentarily.

"First he must present himself to us."

David Helmares realized he was in a truly foreign place far, far from California in more ways than one.

"Of course, I'll be happy to answer any and all questions. I'm not going anywhere."

"That remains to be seen. Although I am the chief navigator for our people, the decision about you is not entirely mine."

One precocious boy about ten years old just couldn't wait.

"I want to know how did he get here from Texas?"

"Yes, and why did he find us?" said another youth, possibly six or seven.

"Did you build your boat?"

"Can you catch fish with it?"

"Are you married?" That question came from a blushing young girl, barely a teenager, sitting near the water.

"Yes, are you available?" asked a large woman seated in the middle of the crowd. A wave of laughter rolled through the crowd as David blushed. Taveka suppressed a smile and raised his hand. This time the quiet would not be broken.

"He does not have permission to land. We do not know who he is or if he is welcome. First he must present himself to us."

The chief navigator turned to the young man sitting on his fiberglass craft.

"First you must present yourself to us. Then we will council and decide if we want to ask you any questions. If so, we will all take part in questioning," said Taveka, eyeing the children starting to splash and laugh in the water again, "even the young ones if they so choose."

He turned and looked across the crowd. All were seated and silent. Only the elders stood their ground.

"Now, Captain Helmares, look me in the eye. Who are you?"

"Yes, thank you. May I say one thing to you all before I begin? I have been through many countries and across many borders, and I have never been through anything like this."

"Of course not. That's why you came here. Please continue and do not interrupt yourself."

"I was born in Texas - -"

"Yes we know that!" said a teenager.

"Let him speak! Let him speak!" said voices from around the crowd.

"I don't remember much about living in Texas. We had a nice house. My father died when I was only three and my sister not quite one. I don't think of myself as being a Texan and I don't remember my father or his death."

The crowd was silent. Some of the children and their parents moved closer to each other as David talked about the early years of his life.

"After my father's death my mother moved us to New York and we lived with my grandparents on Long Island. The ocean was right down the street. I do remember clearly going to the beach with my grandmother when I was maybe four or so. Then my mother got a job in New York City. We had to move and for a long time I never saw the ocean again."

"That's really sad," said one of the children, "How did you ever grow up without the ocean?"

"I don't know, maybe I'm still trying to grow up!" Helmares laughed, but he noticed Taveka was not laughing. He resumed his story with a serious tone to his voice.

"We lived for four years in an apartment building made of bricks." David soon found himself recalling things he had not thought about in many, many years: going to school for the first time, sledding down hillsides in the winter and falling out of a tree when he was seven years old. He remembered his best friend with whom he traded baseball cards and going to Yankee Stadium with his grandfather and learning how to swim at the YMCA.

"My mother met a nice man who would take us places on weekends. They were married, and next thing I knew we left New York and moved to California. That's when the most important thing in my life happened."

"And what was that?" asked Taveka.

David related the story of waking up on his first sunny morning in California and seeing the Pacific Ocean for the first time.

"Are you sure that's the most important thing that ever happened to you?" asked an elder. David had been so proud of his story that he was at a loss to answer the elder's question for almost a minute.

"Yes, I think so. We lived in a city called Santa Monica and my new father took us to the beach all the time. That's when I first learned to bodysurf, next to the Santa Monica pier. My dad - - -"

"Your dad? But he wasn't your real father, was he?"

"No he wasn't my real father, but to this day I can hear his voice when I'm not doing my best. I learned a lot from him, especially when he would take us fishing. One Saturday he took us to a pier up the coast in Malibu. The fishing wasn't that good and he said, 'Why don't you go over to the beach? Maybe you'll find something to do.' I did, and that's the first time I saw people surfing.

"Right away I wanted to be a surfer. But my parents were not going to make it easy for me. In fact, I had to buy my first surfboard with my own money."

"They were good parents to you," said an elderly woman sitting in the middle of the crowd.

"Yes, they were. I was the only one of my surfing friends to get a university education because of them. Had I not listened to my parents, I don't know what would have become of me because, except for my education, nothing could distract me from surfing, not even girlfriends."

"You were crazy!" came a voice from one of the men, and laughter rippled through the Maruleans.

"Well, not so much crazy as enthusiastic. Even when it came to my career, I chose to study history at university because the schedule of the required classes gave me more time to surf."

David laughed to himself and made eye contact with Taveka.

"Don't interrupt yourself, please," he said, and once again David looked into eyes that spoke of timeless youth and ancient wisdom.

"When I graduated, my parents asked me, 'And now what?' My hair was bleached blond and I was working at a surfboard shop. But I had a good answer for them.

"'I'm going to be a history teacher!' They were always supportive as long as I kept my word. They even let me take time off from university to go to Hawai'i and Australia, although my dad made a deal with me. I could go with his blessings, but I had to pay for the trip myself and I still had to get my teaching license on time."

"Did you keep your word?" asked Taveka.

"Yes, I did. And the strange thing was, when I came back from that trip, I was more stoked on education - -"

"Stoked? What is stoked?" asked a young man with a fishing net over one shoulder.

"Don't interrupt him!"

"That's ok. Stoked? I guess it is being crazy, enthusiastic, and very rational about staying that way."

"Sounds like you were just short of being a fanatic," observed Taveka.

"Let him talk!" said a teenager. Taveka covered his mouth to hide his smile.

"My parents became resigned to my passion for surfing, although my mother often expressed her worst fear that I would become 'an educated drifter, an itinerant vagabond never to have real roots in his life', to use her exact words."

Helmares sighed at the memory.

"I can still see her at the kitchen table, asking my dad to please do something about what surfing was doing to me. He just said if that was what I wanted to do, he wasn't going to stop me. He knew surfing gave me energy and inspiration. He was very wise and trusted me - and that's how I learned to trust myself."

People from various parts of the crowd stood up and began to leave, apparently having to get back to something important. They waved at David as they left. He waved back, and then looked at Taveka with questioning eyes.

"Oh don't worry, they'll be back."

"Ok, where was I? Oh yeah, teaching."

"And surfing," added Taveka sternly.

"Uh, yes," said David, a bit chastened, "I got my credential, and found a job right away. I really loved my profession. Yet, within a few years I started to think about leaving Southern California."

"Why?"

"The waves were more and more crowded, and tension in the water started to ruin surfing for me. Getting good waves required more aggression, more cunning, and a selfishness that changed me in ways I did not like."

"And teaching?"

"I was good at it. Surfing taught me a lot about determination, planning and facing challenges. But after several years at an inner city junior high, I realized I was no match for the endless stress of L.A.'s city schools. And so I changed course."

"You became a sailor!" said a young teenage boy sitting up close, listening to David's every word.

"Yes, I became a sailor. I spent three years designing and building this boat. She has a retractable keel for sliding through shallow passages just like this one," he gestured back at the lagoon behind him, "and I named her the *Morning Light*."

David was lost in thought for a moment. The sailors in the crowd knew why: it is a special thing when a builder names his ship, almost as important as when a parent names a child.

"The day came when I said goodbye to my students and handed my letter of resignation to the school principal. He said good luck, shook my hand, and went right back to the papers on his desk. He was always writing me up for violating policies and regulations, and I was just a headache to him."

Taveka narrowed his eyes just a little. But then he winked at David, who was not a little relieved as he continued his story.

"My parents and friends came down to see me off the day I set sail, and now that I think of it I believe even my mom was actually happy to see me pursuing my dream."

A few mothers in the crowd wiped a tear from their eyes.

"First I sailed down the coast of the Baja Peninsula, staying for weeks at a time to surf - -"

"South of California, in Mexico?"

"Yes, Taveka. There were good waves, but there was no place to make a living as a teacher. So I kept sailing south and ended up in El Salvador. I landed a job teaching kindergarten at a bi-lingual school only thirty minutes from one of the best surfing waves I'd ever seen. But El Salvador became a dangerous place. A civil war began between the rich and the poor. When Americans began to be targeted by both sides, I bade farewell to my students and friends and sailed away."

"Yes, we bid farewell to you now, David, maybe we'll see you again tomorrow," said a man with a brotherly voice as his wife pulled him away from the group along with two small children. Others also took the opportunity to take their leave. They all waved a friendly goodbye to him. David looked away from Taveka and waved.

"Captain Helmares, you're off course."

"Oh, yes, uh, Taveka, I'm sorry. My next stop was Costa Rica, south of El Salvador. It is one of the few countries in the world without a standing army. Their motto is, 'Our children are the soldiers'. I spent six months anchored in beautiful emerald coves, with monkeys chattering in the trees at night and good waves breaking in the bays. But there was no way to make a living, and for a while I even thought about returning to California.

"Then I got lucky. I got a chance to charter my boat to some scientists in the Galapagos Islands. What a wonderful place! It was a priceless experience that sharpened my intellect. The only problem was - - -"

"You weren't surfing!" said the teenage boy who had been listening carefully.

"That's right, I wasn't surfing. So when I heard of excellent waves in Northern Peru, and a theory about the origins of surfing and ancient Peruvian cultures, I set sail immediately after my last charter. In Peru my training in history helped me research surfing's remote past. I studied ancient festivals celebrating the sea and from carvings on the walls of archeological sites, I learned a lot about a culture strongly influenced by waves in their social structure, art and architecture."

"Cite an example, please." Taveka's command cut with precision.

"They had a rite of passage for young men requiring the initiate to ride a wave. They used what is called a 'caballito'. That is Spanish for 'little horse'. It is made of dried reeds bundled together. And again, when I helped excavate a temple near one of the longest surfing waves in the world, we found a ceramic pot with art depicting a god riding a caballito across the sky like a crescent moon. When I talked to Thor Heyerdahl - -"

"You know Dr. Heyerdahl?" Taveka's voice was surprisingly sharp.

"No, I can't say I know him. I had a chance to interview him once at an archaeological conference. He was studying a particular society that had built fleets of reed craft he believed sailed from Peru to Polynesia."

Taveka looked at the elders. One nodded in return.

"Maybe you will tell us more some day. For now, continue."

David noticed a distinct change had come over both Taveka and the elders, and that Taveka had used the words 'some day'.

"I was inspired by Dr. Heyerdahl's ideas and again set sail in the *Morning Light* to research his theories connecting ancient Peru and Polynesia."

Taveka and the five elders stared at David intently. The crowd sensed the tension. Even the children who had been playing in the waters stopped and went to sit down with their families. David proceeded cautiously.

"I made landfall at over a dozen inhabited islands, looking for artistic, botanical, and cultural parallels between Peru and Polynesia. On Rapa Nui," he paused, shifted his glance for just a second, and noticed that every set of eyes was looking directly at him, "I found ocean-going reed craft and ancient stone carvings of seacraft that were almost identical to artifacts I had seen in Peru. I also learned of a rite-of-passage ceremony involving a legend that - -"

Taveka held up his hand.

"Enough! Remember you are only to present yourself at this time. Please finish, Captain."

His tone was direct and serious, the crowd was dead silent, and the elders all had their arms crossed.

"Yes, well, I'm almost done, actually. In the course of my research throughout eastern Polynesia, I began to hear stories about a very old and very remote island society. It was said they could make passages of hundreds of miles with no charts or navigational equipment, though exactly where they could be found no one quite knew. But I pieced together a rough idea and set a course through this archipelago, sailing for days over shallow reefs and atolls with my keel fully retracted. But finally, I found the sea people of Marulea. I found you."

Taveka and all the people sitting on the beach turned to look at the elders. One gestured with his hand at the people sitting near the shore. They stood up

76

and walked down the beach without turning and waving to David as others had. Taveka walked across the empty sands to the elders. They sat down to make a decision about the man who had found them.

For the next twenty minutes the only sound David heard was the gentle lapping of tiny waves on the sand. He thought of everything he had said and of things he had left out that might have been far more important than those he had included. Then Taveka left the elders and walked across the sand to the water's edge. David resigned himself to having to leave immediately.

"Thank you for presenting yourself, Captain. Normally a visitor must have a herald announce his coming and act as intermediary until certain issues are settled. You had no herald, so we had no choice but to let you present yourself. Now I have questions for you, as do others. Will you answer them?"

"Yes," he said in surprise, "I will!"

Taveka turned and nodded. The elders stood there unmoving for a second. Then they turned around and walked back into the palm trees.

"We are going to start at the beginning. Who was your father, what did he do for a living, and why did he die?"

Several children who had left with the crowd saw Taveka talking to the visitor and ran back to sit at the navigator's feet. They were shy at first, but then they too began to ask him questions.

"Did you have toys?"

"Did you have to go to school?"

"What games did you play with your friends?"

Others came and joined the group. The crowd soon grew to over two dozen, once again representing a cross section of the Maruleans, from children to young adults to parents and grandparents. Everyone had questions for him, and the thread of information wove through times and places David had not considered for many years. Taveka was always in control, and when David digressed, the chief navigator always remembered the original question and steered David towards the next logical waypoint on the chronological voyage through his past.

Three hours later, David was still sailing with a long way to go. The curiosity of the Maruleans knew no bounds. Even more daunting was just how much his interrogators knew about the world he had left behind even though they were thousands of miles from 'civilization'.

Another hour and the lowering sun was starting to shine directly into David's eyes. Yet the questions never stopped. If he seemed to leave something out, he was politely asked to, "Remember more, please."

And he did so, knowing his patience and honesty were being tested. Finally the sun touched the fronds of the tallest palms as David finished explaining why he had never owned a Beatles album.

"I think we are done for today. If you want, we can continue tomorrow," said Taveka.

"Yes, I will continue."

"Fine. You may drop anchor. You do not have permission to land. You must stay aboard the *Morning Light*."

David noticed that Taveka had used the name of his boat and took that as a positive sign.

"Understood. Until tomorrow, then."

"Yes, until tomorrow."

Taveka turned and walked across the sand to the tree line. Most of the crowd dispersed up and down the beach. Some went swimming, some walked back to the palm grove, and David could see lights starting to flicker here and there between the trees. But some of the children stayed close to the boat, and they continued to ask questions until darkness began to close in. One brought him a coconut and cracked it open so David could drink its refreshing liquid. The stars came out and lights could be seen all throughout the forest of the island. David could no longer see the faces of the Maruleans on the beach.

Finally a voice said, "You must be tired."

It was the young woman who had been particularly interested in David's experiences with dance and ballet.

"Oh no, I'm fine thanks! How are you?" he said, suddenly refreshed. But his question was not answered. The Maruleans all said goodbye to him at once and next thing he knew, he was alone.

David got up stiffly from his perch on the bow. He smiled at the thought of going to sleep as quickly as possible, knowing that the sooner he slept, the sooner tomorrow would come.

* * *

The questioning took another two days. The Maruleans would come and go as if the uninvited visitor was little more than an aberration in their daily routines warranting but a small fraction of their attention. Sometimes only Taveka and a few children would be questioning him. An hour later they would be joined by the very oldest members of the community. Towards late afternoon, several families appeared with lots of food and turned his "inquisition" into their picnic.

Sometimes he saw nubile young women with their families and it was not easy for the sailor, after months at sea, to stay focused on his answers. But when a dozen men showed up after a day of fishing, an aura of challenge filled the air that could not be taken lightly. They asked him many specific questions about building the *Morning Light* and his sailing experiences.

By late afternoon of the second day, the crowd had grown to its original size and Helmares was peppered with many questions from all sides. But finally the questions tailed off, and Taveka let almost another hour pass without anyone asking David Helmares any further questions. Nobody seemed to mind the silence, and there was nothing expectant or impatient about the crowd. Then Taveka joined the five elders for a few minutes before walking back to the water's edge.

"If no one wishes to know anything more," he said in a loud voice and pausing, "then I will ask the last questions."

He turned and looked deep into David's eyes.

"Why did you come here?"

"I want to learn everything that you can teach me."

"About what?"

"About your history, your culture, how you survive, and how you navigate throughout the Nebula Archipelago."

"What about yourself?"

"I'll be doing that the rest of my life, Taveka."

"Good answer, David. I believe you."

Taveka turned to the crowd.

Many nodded. Most importantly, so did the elders.

Taveka took a step forward and extended his hand.

"You have permission to stay and learn from me and our people."

* * *

The sea people of Marulea were descendants of ancient mariners whose exact origins were known only to the elders. There was some interface between the Maruleans and French Polynesian officials when necessary, but the great distances made governing the sea people almost impossible. Their home islands were close to the center of the Nebula Archipelago, a maritime region which, though having no specific boundaries, was recognized as a cultural preserve by the French government. They left the Maruleans alone, and for good reason.

The Maruleans were descendants of an island society that had once numbered over six thousand. In the early 1800s, a Frenchman named Gambier had tried to establish his own fiefdom over the isolated people. It was a disaster, and before French authorities finally came and removed the madman to exile, less than four hundred Maruleans were still alive.

Due to the distances involved, the French authorities in Tahiti were unable to help the survivors and left them to their own devices. The Maruleans left their home islands and its horrific memories and retreated to another group protected by an almost impenetrable zone of reefs and shoals. There they were able to stabilize their community and their contact with the sea by maintaining the integrity of their seafaring traditions.

At the onset of World War Two they re-established contact with French officials to help fight the Japanese and rescue downed airmen by transporting them secretly out of harm's way. When the war ended, their self-imposed isolation resumed. They wanted no part of a modern world capable of destroying itself.

The story of their service in World War Two brought their history to the attention of a group of influential Frenchmen. A trust fund was established to repay the Maruleans for Gambier's genocidal policies. This gave them access to as much of the real world and its wealth as they wanted.

As it turned out, they did not want much. They were well aware of global politics, economics, and technology, and from their perspective, there was not a lot to be gained by boarding those runaway trains. They knowingly strengthened their cultural identity with their dependence on the resources of the Archipelago for their survival. They used some modern tools or materials on a limited basis when it suited a specific need, but they would let nothing erode the values of family and community developed over the past thousand years. The Maruleans had almost been wiped out once, and they were never going to risk it happening again.

* * *

The fact that David was endlessly inquisitive about the Marulean culture earned the respect of the sea people. Taveka possessed a keen intellect and saw in David a child-like curiosity combined with mature responsibility. Taveka enjoyed being David's mentor, and that joy brought a new hope to his heart.

Taveka was the last in the line of Marulean navigators. The deepest secrets of wayfinding knowledge were passed from father to son, but that vital tradition was endangered when Taveka had lost his wife at the birth of his daughter, Luan. The line of navigators was threatened, but Taveka's love for his lost wife did not permit him to consider ever re-marrying.

Taveka raised his daughter with the help of their community, and she had grown into a warm and lighthearted young woman. Luan began to attract eligible young men from throughout the nearby islands. As she came ever closer to taking a lover who might then become her husband, her father kept his counsel to himself and offered no advice unless asked. Even though she was his only child, he honored her integrity and would play no part in her relationships with suitors. Although this was not easy for either father or daughter, it was even harder for her suitors. Luan was wise beyond her years, and none were able to adjust to her combination of innocence, intelligence, and beauty.

As Taveka grew older, the Marulean elders considered how to name the next chief navigator for the sea people. Many solutions were proposed and then discarded. He could not take on a Marulean as his apprentice without issues surrounding Luan being raised. It was an almost tragic quandary until David Helmares found the sea people. When the elders gave permission for him to remain with them, they were invoking a wisdom allowing them to gracefully respect an important Marulean tradition while possibly finding a way around it. Since David was not of Marulean blood, the blood-tie tradition did not technically apply to him.

When he accepted Taveka's offer, David committed himself to never being anything less than an attentive and responsive student of Taveka. His apprenticeship involved every aspect of sailcraft from making ropes and sails from natural fibers to finding trees on distant islands for hulls. When Taveka began to teach him wayfinding skills around the Nebula Archipelago, it took Helmares several months to grasp the fundamentals of concepts that would eventually take years to master.

Another aspect to challenge him was his status in the general community. Self-sufficiency is hard work. Hunting fish in the wild, growing fish in 'farms', and actually farming the land on various islands throughout the archipelago were never-ending tasks. The Maruleans were not shy about telling him when they could use an extra hand no matter what the task. He was always a cheerful volunteer, and soon there was a running joke between him and the community: when anyone would need some help, they would come and say, "David, I am going to volunteer you to help me today."

Helmares' assimilation into the Marulean daily life was not quite a year old when he was asked by the elders to help with the schooling of the young Maruleans. He started with geography, history and biology as the core curriculae, branching out into the arts and math, using music to teach fractions and other mathematical concepts.

Throughout all this, David Helmares never gave Taveka's daughter even the most innocent of thoughts. He had made enough mistakes with women in California, and he depended on a strong sense of self-discipline to preclude any chance of a fatal faux pas with the beloved daughter of Taveka.

In the same way, Luan saw David as her father's student and nothing more. This was a point of honor given her respect for the traditions of her people and the Marulean navigators. Yet there was one thing about her father's apprentice that intrigued her.

David rarely had time for surfing thanks to Taveka's mentoring and the school. However, there were fun waves practically all the time on the reefs surrounding the central island of the Maruleans. From March to October, there were days when the waves never stopped. On each side of the passage into the main lagoon, perfect waves peeled across smooth reefs. He could ride the waves only rarely, and then for only an hour at most, sometimes at midday, sometimes at dawn, and even once or twice under a full moon at night. He always laughed when he thought of the irony: having chosen teaching as a profession so that he could surf, he was now also a student and not surfing much at all.

But no matter when he paddled out on one of the boards he always stowed on the Morning Light, Luan tried to be on the beach to watch him. The beauty of surfing was something she could appreciate with special immediacy given her mastery of traditional Polynesian dance. There was a wonderful grace to David's style while racing through blue tunnels or dancing along the white spray of the peeling crests. But there was a limit to his art: the length of the ride. Luan got to thinking that she would like to see him surf a wave for minutes instead of just seconds. One day she talked to her father about it.

"Yes, his surfing is quite special, isn't it?"

"It is, father. It is a dance with the sea, and I want to study it. Maybe he can teach it to us, but first I want to see what he does when he has to be creative on a much bigger stage."

"I know of a reef much longer than ours. It points in the same direction, and the waves are bigger. It would be a good test of his skills to voyage there

and back," he thought for a second, "No, it is not that hard to get there. He'll make it, and if he gets lost, you'll make it back."

Luan looked at her father carefully.

"You want me to go alone with him?" she asked.

"Why not? He would never jeopardize his research and apprenticeship by dishonoring my daughter, or our traditions, in any way. And if he does, throw him to the sharks!" They both laughed.

"And now that I think of it, there are several ancient ceremonial sites that might interest him on an island near there," said Taveka, "just to keep his mind off other things."

"Father!"

"Of course, who knows, maybe he doesn't want to be alone with you!" Taveka was laughing loudly.

"Now you stop that! This is about dance, not romance."

Taveka stopped laughing and looked into his daughter's eyes. "Yes, I can see that. Forgive an old man, will you?"

She hugged her father and said, "One thing at a time, father."

A week later the daughter of the chief navigator of the sea people, and the surfer-teacher-sailor went on a short voyage lasting just a day, leaving before dawn with Luan sitting in the bow and David astern. It was every surfer's dream to be heading out to ride perfect waves because a beautiful young woman wants to watch him. But as the student of Taveka, Helmares was entirely focused. He was a navigator first and foremost, and in the time honored tradition of the wayfinders, Luan did not speak to him while they were under way lest his concentration be affected.

When they arrived in late morning at the atoll Taveka had suggested, David's self-discipline was rewarded by long waves six to eight feet high breaking continuously along the barrier reef. He spent the afternoon riding flawless symmetrical waves along the reef like it was a racetrack. He was executing maneuvers only possible at very high speeds with a graceful, erect, arms-open style seldom seen anywhere in the surfing world. He was an inspired danseur lighting up a stage. Luan studied his pas de deux with the sea, noting his instinct for grace and flow with the eye of one who saw dance as almost a sacred act.

When Luan and David came back under a late rising moon, they could both look Taveka in the eye without hesitation. The old man was more pleased than he would ever admit. His student had passed more than one important test on the trip.

With dance as common ground, David and Luan established a genuine friendship based on mutual respect. It was the kind of friendship that, without either person doing anything about it, sometimes becomes the rich soil for the first flowers of true love. That is what happened to them, though the flower bloomed very slowly. At first Luan was not going change the natural course of her life as a young lady with many male friends and David could not let himself be distracted from his apprenticeship by falling for his teacher's daughter. His becoming a navigator was far more difficult than anything he had ever done. Almost a year passed, after their first voyage, before David and Luan began to spend more and more time together with the blessings of Taveka. A year after that, they declared their intent to be married after consummating their relationship, and soon they were able to tell Taveka that he was to become a grandfather.

During this time, David gained a new level of oceanic awareness. With all his sailing experience as a foundation, his wayfinding skills eventually surpassed that of other Marulean men his age. They were gracious in accepting him as Taveka's student, and one became a very good friend to him.

Under other circumstances Manasa might have succeeded Taveka as chief navigator for the Maruleans. However he had recognized, as did other Marulean men, that David was worthy of great respect for choosing to leave his world and serve an apprenticeship of hard work and self-discipline to become one of them. There was no resentment or jealousy, and when Luan gave birth to twins, the surfer, teacher and sailor from California became a full member of the Marulean society.

Another year passed, and the day came when David was ready to take his final test as Taveka's apprentice by voyaging to Ka'unua, performing three ceremonial rites of passage, and then returning safely with the necklace symbolizing the line of succession of the chief navigators of the Marulean sea people.

* * *

It was late afternoon when David brought his voyaging craft right up to the sand. He jumped out and pushed hard to bring it as far up the beach as possible. Taveka helped him, as did Manasa and several other Marulean men who had seen David coming through the reef passage. They saw the jade necklace around David's neck, and dared not speak a word. Neither did Taveka.

David was too overcome with emotion to know quite what to say, but the Marulean men clearly understood what was going on. They just gave him a short wave and a smile and went back to their work. David was about to say something in greeting, but Taveka put a hand to his mouth. The mentor motioned to the apprentice, and they began to walk north along the water's edge around the curving shore of the lagoon. When they were out of sight of the village, David and Taveka were joined by the five elders dressed in deep blue garments David had never seen before, with feathers, shells, necklaces, and bracelets of coral adorning them.

The group of seven now headed for the far end of the island, walking abreast across the wide, sandy beach, the elders separating Taveka and David. For the better part of an hour they walked in silence, towards a low, black cliff he had seen from the sea while sailing to other islands. When he had first asked Taveka about it during the first year of his apprenticeship, he was told it was off limits to all Maruleans.

"Except for certain people under certain circumstances. Don't ask any more questions. Maybe someday you'll learn more, and maybe not. Just don't ever go there."

It was an ancient place. The black rock outcropping, eroded by eons of time, was the tip of the volcano that had formed the island millions of years ago. The half-dome face of the rock was twenty feet high, sheer and smooth. At its base was a waist-high circular platform of flat, black stones. The group stopped and faced the rock formation. Though the sun was low in the west, David could feel heat from the rocks. He could also feel the cooling trade wind at his back blowing stronger here than at any other place on the island. From the center of the group an elder sprang up on to the platform in one motion. She turned around and spoke though her eyes were on the horizon.

"We will now hear of a voyage," said Kalala.

The other four elders stepped up and turned in unison to face Taveka and David below them.

"And leave nothing out," whispered Taveka. He winked at his apprentice, sharing a moment from long ago. The elders smiled in recognition of the bond between the navigator and the young man who they hoped could succeed him.

David gave a detailed account of his six days of voyaging to Ka'unua. He told them of the storm he had survived and his first sighting of the reef. They questioned him carefully as to his exact actions and the sequence of events leading up to the moment when he saw the circular rainbow.

"Come up, David, and show us how big it was," said Mara, the senior female of the elders.

David stepped up on the platform and walked to the black wall. He wiped the moisture from his forehead with both hands and drew a large circle on the face of the stone, starting at the upper apex of his reach. The hot, black rock burned his fingers, but he did not stop until he was finished. As he stepped back, he heard Kalala speak.

"Don't turn around, David. Just watch."

The circle began to disappear from the point above his head and then down and around the entire circumference of the circle. As with the rainbow he had seen at Ka'unua, the circle was soon gone.

"Now, turn around," said Otava, the senior male of the group.

David did so. When he looked down at Taveka, a flood of emotion went through his heart.

"David, tell us of your visits to Taveka's ancestors," said Matua, another female elder.

He described the dives into the lagoon and the gifts he had made for each in the lineage that stretched for generations into the past. He told the tale in reverse order, starting with the stone boat for the ancient voyager from the coast of South America. When he got to Taveka's father, Kaho, his voice began to falter as he realized who would be next to join the ancestral spirits in the lagoon at Ka'unua.

84

The fifth elder, Sukuna, motioned to Taveka, who stepped up on the platform to join them. David looked at his mentor and was surprised to see him smiling with a look of reassurance.

"David, you are wearing the necklace of the navigators. Tell us of your finding it," said Otava.

When he finished describing the third task, all were silent. They did not ask any more questions, and David did not break the silence, aware only of the low sound of the trade wind blowing through the rocks as the sun disappeared below the horizon.

The elders formed a circle around the chief navigator of the Marlueans and the young man who was about to take his place.

"David, Taveka will now wear the necklace," said Kalala.

David carefully placed it on Taveka's shoulders, their eyes never wavering. Taveka took the feather of the albatross from behind his waist and held it up between them.

"David, you are now who I once was. When the albatross flies above this very place, I will prepare for my voyage to Ka'unua."

They touched foreheads and David took the feather in his hands. He touched his heart with it, and then placed it behind him in his waistband.

Taveka moved to one end of the line of elders, David to the other. They all turned to the west, joined hands, and raised their arms to the first sliver of the crescent moon low in the western sky.

* * *

The line of navigators was not to be broken, and true love was, as tradition prescribed, the key link in the chain. For the first time ever, the wayfinder's lineage would pass through the heart of a daughter to a man who would become the chief navigator for the Maruleans.

Two weeks passed and the 'official' marriage of Luan and David took place. Maruleans came from all the islands of the Nebula Archipelago for the ceremonies marking the succession and the marriage. Three years ago, David had been accepted in the community without hesitation, because no one questioned the judgment of Taveka. Now the old man was able to enjoy the final step that linked the sea people to their past and their future.

All was quiet, though the island was full of visitors. Honeymoons were not a part of the Marulean tradition, and when the sun went down, the celebration slowed and then stopped. This was how the Maruleans demonstrated their sincere respect for the union of husband and wife.

The full moon was almost overhead, shining so brightly that even the tiny waves touching the reef could be seen clearly across the lagoon. The wind moved through the palms, fronds rising and falling in the breeze.

Alone with his thoughts, Taveka walked down to the beach and launched his voyaging craft. He slowly paddled through the waters crowded with visiting outriggers and voyaging craft from across the Archipelago. Finally, he was out near the barrier reef where small breakers punctuated the silence in a regular rhythm. He turned to gaze at the island where almost two thousand Maruleans now slept. He thought about the heritage of his people, their trials and extraordinary history, and the lineage of navigators now to remain unbroken. He looked at his tri-hulled craft and thought of the voyage it would soon make, the last voyage for both of them. He set a sea anchor to steady the craft against the current and the swell. He laid down on the bamboo thatched deck. His eyes closed slowly as he drifted to sleep soothed by the sound of the surf.

He dreamed of his youth, of a time when the moon was bright and he was in a canoe near a reef far away. He was not alone. Three injured American pilots were with him. They were waiting for a PBY to take the flyers to safety.

The roar of engines grew loud. A large shadow dropped out of the sky. A white wake sliced across the black sea. The sailors waved goodbye to him, gratitude clearly visible on their faces fading into the stars.

The faint sound of engines echoed in the mind of the dreamer. The dream ended, but the sound did not. Taveka's eyes opened to the moon directly overhead. Across the white light flew a silhouette, just as it had so long ago.

Surfing the Street

The sound of rushing water drowned out the ring of the phone. The answering machine clicked on.

Hello, you have reached 714-797-1357. If you have this number, it must be important, so please do leave us a message and we'll call back soon.

"This is the international operator. I have a collect call from – sir will you say your name, please?"

"Roberto."

"I have a collect call from Roberto. Will you please accept the charges? Hello, hello? I am sorry sir, but no one is answering. Pleased try your call again later."

"I can't try again later! Cheryl! Pick up the phone!"

"Sir I cannot allow any communication – and could you please turn down the noise in the background? I can barely hear you."

"I can't turn down the noise – those are engines and I'm in a seaplane! Operator, this is an extremely important phone call. I own Wavelife International and I simply must get through! Cheryl! Pick up the phone!"

"Sir I'm sorry but you'll just have to call again later."

"Listen, I'm in a plane in the South Pacific and we've only got a limited radio connection right now and I'm calling my wife. I know she'll pick up the phone in a minute."

Eight thousand miles away, Cheryl Corlund turned off the water and stepped out of the steaming shower. She heard the voice on the answering machine and ran across the bedroom floor holding the towel to her wet body.

"Sir, I'm sorry but - - -"

"Let me speak to your supervisor, please," he said in a last ditch effort to buy time. His wife lunged for the phone.

"- - - you'll have to call again later. Thank you for using - -"

"Hello, operator, I'm here."

"Operator, that's my wife! Cheryl it's me!"

"This is the international operator. I have a collect call from, uh, sir please say your name again."

"Roberto Mercante!" he yelled. If there was one thing that ticked him off, it was when people forgot his name.

"Will you accept the charges?"

"Yes. Roberto, where are you?"

"You may proceed with your call, sir. Thank you for using TransCom International."

"We found it! It is so beautiful you just won't believe it!"

"Why didn't you call on time? I tried your cell and then I tried the hotel. You were supposed to call me hours ago."

"I couldn't call! We were out at the reef, and it took us four hours to fly there and - - -"

"Four hours! Roberto, you can almost fly back to Hawai'i in four hours!"

"Not if you are in a PBY! Oh and wait till you see this plane! We've got to get one!"

"We're not getting a plane, Roberto. We'll be lucky if we get a bonus this year. And what is a PBY?"

"It's a seaplane, and we flew from Tahiti out into the Pacific and we were only eighty feet above the ocean the whole way, well, except for when we had to fly higher so that we wouldn't hit any islands. But that was ok because - -"

"Hitting islands? Roberto, what the hell are you doing?"

"You told me to work with Clark and that's what I'm doing! Now listen for a second, ok? He chartered a seaplane for us - - -"

"How much did that cost?"

"They gave us a deal, and it wasn't that much money because we needed this plane to get to the reef. It can land on water so we had to have it and - - -"

"How much, Roberto, and don't lie."

"Ten thousand, plus some extra costs, but honey, we had to - - -"

"You and Clark spent ten thousand dollars," she let a moment of silence pass, "Roberto, I don't like this."

"This place is magic, Cheryl, and it was worth it, even though I got really airsick. And anyway, you said it had to come out of my budget, so I'll worry about the money, ok?"

She knew he was right. Ten grand for a plane flight was peanuts compared to the real stakes involved, and so for the moment she decided she didn't want to think about money.

"Well, I'm sorry you got sick. Are you okay now?"

"Yeah I'm much better. How are the children?"

"I suppose they're fine. Donny stayed over at a friend's house last night and Anna is downstairs, I think. They're okay, Roberto." Light began to glow through the curtains, reminding her she had to get back to business. She had an early conference call to New York and had to get out the door.

"Roberto, I've got to go in two minutes. Is it what you expected? Is it what we need?"

"Yes and yes," he said, hearing the urgent tone in her voice, "It looked exactly like the video, except the waves were about three feet, but they were absolutely perfect."

"Then it wasn't exactly what we saw, was it?"

"Well, uh, no, but," Roberto knew he was running out of time, "but we taxied around the reef and went snorkeling and the bottom is perfectly smooth and goes down into the water forever. When a swell comes it will be unbelievably good."

"Roberto, we're betting our future on it. Anything else I need to know? I've got exactly one minute."

"I talked to the pilots and told them what we will need and they said they can do it. A Catalina PBY is the only way we can get everything to this place without a lot of hassle. They are really great people. Right now we're headed north to catch some tail winds back to Tahiti and - -"

"Roberto, call me when you get to Tahiti. Love you. Bye."

"- - - and we're flying in the moonlight and it is so beautiful and, Cheryl, are you there? Hello, hello?"

Roberto turned to Tina Sanchez. "Did something happen to the radio?"

"No, the connection's ok. She must have hung up. Was that your wife?" she asked inquisitively. She knew full well it was, but she wasn't going to let all the flirting that afternoon go for nothing. Roberto took off his headset and looked at her bathed in the moonlight coming through the Plexiglas domes.

"Yeah, that was my wife," he said with just a hint of resignation, "also known as the CEO of Wavelife International. She's really busy right now getting things organized for this project."

"Well, I hope to meet her someday," she said with a bit of a huff.

"You will for sure, Tina," said Ian Clark, amused at the vibe between her and Mercante, "or maybe give her a call when we get back. How much longer before we arrive?"

Sanchez caught Clark's comment and looked right through him.

"Shouldn't be too much longer. Now that I think of it, why don't we just cancel the extra charges, Roberto? Our original arrangement with Ian will be ok."

"Thanks. The boss will appreciate that," said Mercante with a smile that was returned with a little extra thrown in.

"Isn't it beautiful flying like this? Oh, look! That's the Nebula Archipelago down there."

She turned and looked over her shoulder and brushed against Mercante's arm.

"I wonder what kind of surf you could find on those islands, Roberto?"

Mercante looked down and saw islands surrounded by reefs as far as the eye could see. He looked up a little and the moonlight had caught a reflection in the Plexiglas of the Polynesian beauty sitting next to him. The vision clicked, and Mercante took note of it for his next meeting with marketing.

"Yeah, maybe we could fly around and check 'em out sometime, Tina! Yeah, What do you think Ian? Maybe there's even more spots down there!"

"Well, let's just get our original deal done first, and then we'll think about new places, ok?"

* * *

"Hello Bill, everybody there?"

"Yes, Cheryl, but let me warn you: the market is skittish this morning and they're a bit distracted."

"I know about the market. That will work in our favor. They'll be itching to make some money."

"They're ready when you are."

"Three minutes."

Cheryl Corlund clicked off the intercom and walked into her private ladies' room to check her hair and makeup. She did not want to appear flushed on camera, and the video conferencing images were sometimes a bit color-saturated. She straightened her Italian business suit and was satisfied she had the look for dealing with Wall Street. She came out and walked briskly to the door of her office, grabbing a slim portfolio off her desk on the way. She went past the desk of Dolly Artensa, her executive assistant, without stopping. Artensa was Corlund's senior by almost ten years and had been with her since the beginning. Both knew this was no time for chitchat. Except for one thing.

Halfway across the carpet Cheryl Corlund stopped and turned around. Artensa was impeccably dressed in shades of yellow that contrasted perfectly with her deep brown skin. She took off her glasses and looked Corlund up and down. She smiled, reached into her desk, and tossed a heavy, carpenter's nail across the room.

Cheryl caught the nail with one hand. Without another word or glance, she left the office ready to pitch a deal worth a billion dollars.

Bill Massara and June Wilson were in the room. Their video images were in small windows on the plasma display. There were five larger windows on the screen. Four of them displayed heavy hitters sitting in their offices on Wall Street. Then Cheryl Corlund took her seat and the display was complete.

Her camera angle and lighting had been set up for a perfect shot of a powerful businesswoman. She set the portfolio down so that the camera could not see it. She opened it to glance at Wavelife's share price at the opening bell, the numbers already traded, and the current worth of her company.

"Good morning June, Bill, gentlemen. Thank you all for your time. I'll be brief and to the point."

She put a hand in one pocket of her business suit and touched the point of the nail. Not a trace of emotion could be seen in her face.

"Given Wavelife's current valuation on the market and my responsibilities to our shareholders, I will be submitting a proposal to the company's board whereby my management team will execute a leveraged buyout of the company's stock. I need to know if any of you would like to be a part of such a transaction. Gentlemen?"

"Hello Cheryl!" boomed Ben Jeffries, one of Wall Street's most famous dealmakers, "Good to see you, though it has not been so good to see Wavelife's stock performance lately. The tide's gone out on the surfing angle, and you're looking for investors in an LBO?"

Corlund smiled back at Jeffries. His slicked-back hair, bow tie and suspenders were almost a cliché, except for the fact that his power was very real. But she didn't say a word because she knew she didn't have to.

"And your point is, Ben?" said Bill Massara, his wire-rim glasses set against a broad face and a buzz cut. He knew when to step in front of his boss and take a bullet.

"His point is, Mr. Massara, that your price has been heading south and I don't think it will be getting much of a tan this winter," said Peter Lasserman, a street-smart New Yorker who headed a firm that often competed with Jeffries, sometimes ruthlessly. But they were actually good friends, belonged to the same country club, and their wives supported the same charities.

"Yes, Cheryl, I must say, an LBO does seem a bit optimistic, wouldn't you think?" John Vutara, also a friendly competitor of Jeffries, was known for his careful attention to even the most insignificant of details when it came to underwriting investment banking deals. He was born in India, schooled at Oxford, and wore the pinstripes of Saville Row. His proper British accent added to his authority. "I know you surfers like to, how do you say, 'go for it', but aren't you risking a, and no pun intended, wipeout here?"

"I don't surf, John," shot back Corlund, letting the statement hang in the air until June Wilson caught her cue.

"Yes, John, don't be short-sighted," she said, wearing a gray suit to contrast with Corlund's fashion statement, though at three grand hers was slightly more expensive, "We have our sights set on next summer. That's why we are talking to you now. Apparel is a cyclical industry, the wheel is going to turn this summer, and Cheryl's going to turn it. You gentlemen have a ground floor opportunity here. By underwriting a buyout of Wavelife's shareholders, you'll be in a position to do quite well a year from today."

"Which will be the height of your selling season going into the fall shows. But still, the timing is a little tight, and with profit margins so razor thin in your segment, there's no room for even the slightest error." Bruce Kaufman wore a polo shirt to set him apart from the other investment bankers because he wasn't pals with them by any means. He knew the only reason he was there was because he had outperformed them three quarters in a row.

Cheryl Corlund knew her response had to be airtight since Kaufman obviously didn't care about the stock or the shareholders.

"Point taken Bruce, and that is why I'm doing this. We have assets under development we believe may be of significant value to the company. However, to take advantage of them and increase profitability we need a new management structure to execute efficiently."

Massara and Wilson looked straight into the camera's eye. This was no time to break ranks with even a hint of anything other than full commitment to Corlund's words.

"What, you're gonna bring Gidget out of retirement?" said Jeffries, and everybody laughed.

"No Ben, she's happy being the legendary Gidget, no more no less. Actually, I was thinking of opening a surf shop in New York and teaching you guys to surf the Street!" said Corlund, sugar-coating her sarcasm with just the right amount of charm.

Everyone laughed again, though with a brevity that made it obvious there would be no more jokes.

"How much are you going to pay?"

"Twenty-two a share, Ben," said Wilson.

"But, but that's almost eighty percent over your current price!" exclaimed Lasserman. John Vutara was also obviously taken aback. Bruce Kaufman, however, didn't blink. The fact the stock was undervalued was moot to him.

"Well, Peter, that is what the shareholders deserve and it will keep them quiet next year when Wavelife will be worth a lot more than it is now."

"If you're right about everything, Cheryl. What is your board going to say about all this?" asked Kaufman, "And when can I see your numbers?"

"They'll agree that it is in the best interests of the shareholders. I'll be in New York mid January. I'll have complete data sets with me at that time."

"My dear lady," said Vutara, looking her straight in the eye, "Why are you doing this?"

Corlund was well prepared for this moment of truth.

"I need to be able to respond to a changing marketplace without the constraints of a stock that is performing poorly because of outside factors over which I have no control. With a new business plan and a fresh marketing approach, we anticipate a return on your investment up to twenty basis points above any valuation as represented by Wavelife's share price within the past five years. We have an all-star cast and a dynamite script and the curtain will be going up next summer. You can either be backstage or in the audience."

"Well," said Jeffries, "My wife is always dragging me to premieres on Broadway, and I don't need any more front row tickets. Count me in."

"Thanks Ben," said Corlund, consciously not letting her excitement show, "John? Bruce? Peter? What else can I tell you?"

"Nothing for the time being," said Lasserman, taking his cue from Jeffries, "I'm in."

"I'll look forward to your visit, Cheryl," said Vutara, "and my team will be prepared to look at your numbers when you present them to us."

"I'll see you when you get here," said a non-committal Bruce Kaufman.

"Say Cheryl, can you bring my grandkids some swag? They've got that surfer stuff all over their rooms!"

"Will do, Ben. Bruce, John, it has been a pleasure. Peter, say hi to your wife for me."

"No can do, Cheryl. If I even mention your name, she starts in on why New York sucks and we should move to Newport Beach!" Lasserman said with a laugh instantly shared by Corlund.

"Yeah, Peter, she always told me she hated snow with a passion, even on ski trips. Gentlemen, the best of holidays to you, and I'm confident it will be a happy new year."

Everyone said their goodbyes. Then the video displays went to blue before the Wavelife logo appeared dead center.

Corlund sat down and took a deep breath to suppress the rush of victory pumping through her veins. Massara and Wilson waited for her to speak. She looked at them but was thinking of her husband and Ian Clark, flying in the moonlight high above islands of paradise thousands of miles away. Then she flipped the moment around completely just to prove she had mastered it.

"You know, if this doesn't work, we'll have to go into exile someplace. How does Tahiti sound?"

"Well, it would be better than Siberia!" laughed Wilson.

"I hear you can buy your own island down there," smiled Massara.

"Well, first, let's see if we can't make enough money to buy our own jets to fly there," said Corlund, not laughing or smiling, "Let's get on it."

The Clean-Up Set

"Y'all never guess who I slept with last night." Daisy, a tall and deeply tanned girl from Texas, was standing in front of the bathroom mirror, making sure she didn't spill the coke she was snorting off her fingernail.

"Who cares? The question is, who are you going to sleep with tonight?" Sheila, a hardbody bottle blond from L.A., glanced over at the other face in the mirror and then went back to making sure her look was just right.

"No really, y'all never gonna guess. Here, you want some of this?"

"Is it any good?"

"Not bad. Got it from the Brazilians."

"As long as it's not the speedy shit from Town. So, you laid some big surfer, did you?"

"Yup, the biggest."

"Well, then it was one of the Westside boys working security outside."

"Oh don't be stupid. I'm talking about the best surfer in the world."

"The best surfer in the world wouldn't be caught dead around here in December. Whoever he is, he's surfing someplace we've never heard of."

"Well, what about the world champ?"

"You mean Sonny-boy?"

"That's right. Had him all to myself all night."

"Well, I guess congratulations are in order, dearie, except for one little thing," she said sarcastically.

"Oh yeah, what's that?"

"He's not going to win this year, so fucking him all by yourself doesn't mean much, unless, of course, he told you he loved you!"

"I ain't that dumb, but he did tell me to meet him here tonight."

"Now why would you want to spend another night with a has-been? Listen, I'm setting up a thing for a couple of the Australians. Maybe you'd be interested."

"Just me and you?"

"You've got to be kidding me. Haven't you learned anything since you've been here? I met some hookers from Town, and so far its gonna be three on two. But you'd make it four on two, and that would be wild."

"Well, I don't know, I - - -"

"Of course, you can always go on your date with your world champ. Who knows, maybe he'll even hold your hand and ask to meet your parents or something."

"Oh shut up! Ok, who are these guys?"

94

"Well, one of them could win it this year."

"You mean you know Mick Lennox?"

"That's right, and his friend is just as hot. They'll go all night long and want more for breakfast."

"All right, but what do I say to Sonny-boy?"

"What's there to say? He'll figure it out. Happens all the time on the North Shore."

In most respects it was just another December on a stretch of beach five miles long that temporarily becomes the center of the world for every surf company, touring pro, would-be surf star, sponsor, filmmaker, and surf magazine writer from around the planet.

This year, however, there was a little extra buzz in the air. Sonny-boy Noaloa, two-time defending world champ, was not going to repeat. Even if he won all three contests on the North Shore he still wouldn't have enough points to beat Australian Mick Lennox, the current points leader.

Lennox had kicked off the year by winning the events on the Australian leg of the tour while Noaloa was working on his pub crawling skills and showing up a little too hung over to make it out of the preliminary heats. The rest of the year was more of the same. Lennox and the other touring pros were hungry, and with no one to keep him focused, success had finally caught up with the young Hawaiian champion from Florida. The agent, now expanding into basketball where his talent for recruiting high school phenoms was paying off big, had left day-to-day minding of Sonny-boy to his father. Johnny Noaloa formed an entourage of Hawaiians, on the payroll thanks to the agent, to babysit the champ and intimidate his opposition around the world. But there was not much the Aloha Patrol could do when their boy sometimes only caught one or two waves during a heat. And Roberto Mercante didn't give the situation much thought until it was too late. He'd spent most of the year recruiting local talent around the world to boost Wavelife sales and cred, and when it became obvious Noaloa wouldn't repeat after his dismal showings in Europe, he simply had marketing work up a new campaign, "When It Counts!", anticipating victories on the North Shore that would cover Sonny-boy's bad season.

"Hey, baby, last night no good enough fo you?"

Sonny-boy Noaloa had a bottle of whiskey in one hand and a fat spliff in the other. His words could barely be heard over the din of a shredding band and a packed crowd at the beach house rented by GroundZero, the surf industry's edgiest company.

Daisy was walking out with the Australians, L.A. Sheila and the hookers from Waikiki. She ignored Noaloa completely. Mick Lennox didn't.

"No mate, its whose gonna be good enough tomorrah, and it won't be you."

"Fuck off, Lennox, you fuckin' Aussie haole fuck!"

"Well Sonny-boy, sounds like you can talk a lot about it, but looks like talk is all you'll get tonight."

Noaloa dropped the whiskey bottle and threw the joint away as he lunged at Lennox. The party was so wild that nobody quite noticed what was happening. Noaloa didn't see much of the fight either as Lennox took one step back, cocked a right, and delivered to Noaloa's jaw. Fortunately for Sonny-boy, he was so drunk that he didn't feel the punch. With the girls laughing at him and the Aussies stepping over him, the world champ was laid out on the deck overlooking the moonlit waves of Pipeline. Noaloa's dad and a crew of brick-house Hawaiians had just gotten their drinks when they turned around to see their boy flat on his back. Sheila saw them and pulled the Aussies toward the steps to the beach with Daisy right behind them.

Noaloa's father saw the Aussies going down the steps to the beach. It didn't take him more than a few seconds to figure out what happened. He slugged back the drink in his hand and told the posse to give chase.

"You get dose guys. I wanna have talk wid 'em."

Daisy saw the Hawaiians coming and screamed. The Aussies went into high gear down the beach, the blondes right behind them. The Town chicks stayed put. They had nothing to fear, and besides, they weren't going to take off their high heels to walk in the sand. They briefly melted back into the party before sidling up to Noaloa's dad and his fallen paycheck.

As for Mick Lennox and his friend, they didn't stop to talk story with the big Hawaiians chasing them. They kept running – all the way to the airport and back to Australia.

The next morning, Sonny-boy Noaloa, with two stitches in his lip, struggled to second place in what was to be a four man heat at the Sunset Beach Pro. Mick Lennox was a no-show, and Noaloa only had to beat a Brazilian to advance. No problem there. The posse made sure the Brazilian knew what was good for him. Sonny-boy made it to round two, and that was good enough for now.

When the agent called to check the results and Johnny Noaloa said Sonny-boy was unable to come to the phone, the agent smelled trouble. First he called Mercante, who told him to catch the next non-stop out of New York. Mercante then got himself a ticket out of LAX that afternoon, but it was not until he was boarding his flight that he was finally able to get through to the one guy he thought could help salvage the situation.

"Heath, I need you to get over to the North Shore. We've got a problem and I need your help."

"Roberto, the last place on earth I want to be right now is on the North Shore," said Larson, sitting on a cliff overlooking his favorite big-wave reef on Maui, "I hate that circus and you know it."

"Listen Heath, I need you to get through to Sonny-boy because - - -"

"How am I gonna do that? Kids these days, you can't tell 'em anything!" Larson laughed, but Mercante only got more serious.

"No, Heath, listen. Mick Lennox left Hawai'i thanks to Sonny-boy's dad. He didn't show up for his heat, so Sonny made it through, but just barely thanks to his dad scaring the shit out of some Brazilian. Heath, this looks really bad for the company."

"Well, so what, Roberto? What's so bad about a cold shower every once in a while?"

"Hawaiians don't like cold showers, Heath, and neither does my wife. We can't have this whole thing blow up over a bunch of bullshit."

"Roberto, the whole North Shore contest scene has been bullshit since day one. Now its even worse, and you want me over there? No way."

"Heath, I NEED you to help us. I'll be there about six your time."

Larson sighed. The last thing he wanted to do was fly to Oahu, especially since he had a training session scheduled that afternoon.

"It's gonna cost you, Roberto."

"I've got my checkbook with me. See you at the airport."

Larson hung up the phone and called out the back window.

"Bruddah! What say we go North Shore?"

A large, smiling Hawaiian looked up from his work in the lush garden in the backyard. Ilano Kolana drove the jetski that pulled Heath Larson into the huge waves. Kolana was bigger and stronger than Larson, but he could throw a net, weave palm fronds into hats, and was a native son of the islands almost without peer. He was Heath Larson's only friend.

"No tell me you like do dat again! Dat ten year ago!" said Bruddah, referring to Larson's legendary outside reef sessions while the contests had been conducted close to shore within camera range of the media.

"Nah, no surfing, Bruddah. We go save some big bacon for Mercante."

"Sure, brah!" he laughed loudly, "We nevah roast pig long time!"

The agent was there. Mercante was there. Larson was there. Noaloa's dad was there. Cheryl Corlund was on the video conference screen. The only person missing from the VIP room at the Honolulu airport was Sonny-boy. He was sleeping off another hangover in a rental house overlooking the North Shore with Bruddah watching over him.

"First off, my client fully understands his responsibilities to his contract and definitely intends to fulfill them," said the agent.

"Oh shut up, why don't you? Your client doesn't understand a thing right now and neither do you." Even over a conference line, Cheryl Corlund's voice had all the authority she needed. "We lived with his behavior on the tour, but I can't have him winning contests thanks to thugs scaring off the competition."

"Who you calling a thug, bitch?"

Noaloa senior was nursing his own hangover. Mercante cringed, but he didn't step up to his wife's defense. He was in Hawai'i, and he knew his place. His wife had no time for such niceties.

"You and your thug friends, Noaloa. You screwed up and that's going to stop right now."

Mercante turned white, but Larson stepped in.

"What I think needs to stop is the pressure on Sonny-boy."

"What do you mean, pressure?" said Mercante. "He's got a fat contract and all the surfboards and women he could ask for. Maybe he won't be the world champion again this year, but we still love him - - -"

"You don't love him, Roberto, and neither does anybody else at this table," said Larson, "or on the phone."

"What I no love him? I his dad!"

"Yeah, a dead-beat dad who really doesn't give a flying fuck about his son. And you're not the only one." Mercante and Corlund felt a little uneasy and said nothing. Not so the agent.

"Listen, Larson, I've been representing Sonny-boy for a long time and I've done everything to - - -"he said.

"You've done everything to make a buck as fast as possible. And didn't you hear the lady tell you to shut up? Now mind your manners and listen. Here's what's going to happen if you all want this to go away." The best big wave surfer in the world was setting up a tube ride through a tunnel of human chaos. As long as he was in control he could trust the situation completely. He was going to ride this wave his way, and everyone around him knew better than to disagree.

The bucket of water wasn't ice cold, but the effect was the same.

"What the fuck you do dat fo', asshole?"

It took a few moments for two bleary eyes to focus, and even when they did, his brain couldn't quite get in gear with what was happening.

"Heath! What you doin' heah? And why did - - -"

"It's called an intervention, young man, and you're coming with me."

Larson lifted him up in one motion and put him over his shoulder in a fireman's carry.

"Hey, what da hell you doin'? You can't - - -"

"Oh yes I can, champ, and I even have Bruddah's permission."

"Where my dad? Where my agent? Where my cell phone?"

"Calm down, brah," said Bruddah, stepping out of the doorway to let Larson walk through with his burden, "Heath stay your friend."

Larson looked like a linebacker carrying a wiggling sack of potatoes. Waiting outside was a crew cab pickup with Roberto Mercante at the wheel. Larson dumped Sonny-boy in the back seat and slammed the door closed. The locks clicked.

"What the fuck you guys doin'?" screamed Noaloa.

Heath settled into the shotgun seat and looked over his shoulder. He saw that Bruddah had jumped in the back of the pickup and was ready to go.

"Put your seatbelt on, Sonny-boy. Its time you learned the meaning of the word 'restraint'! The whip's coming down and you're going to like it. Punch it, Roberto!"

Mercante spun the wheel, stepped on the gas, and Noaloa flew backwards into a seat as Larson cranked up the volume and the Stones came blasting out of the speakers.

At that very moment Wavelife's press release was being read over the P.A. system at the contest site announcing Sonny-boy Noaloa's withdrawal from the event due to a severe shoulder injury.

Two days later the winner of the contest was being crowned on the podium, the agent was waiting outside Cheryl Corlund's office, and Johnny Noaloa was back in his Waikiki apartment wondering how he was going to pay the rent without going back to day labor. Up in the hills of Maui three men were sitting on the porch of a rustic cabin listening to slack key guitar. In the bathroom the defending world pro surfing champion was throwing a tantrum.

"I no clean da toilets no is matta what you guys do to me!"

The men tried to minimize the interruption of the soothing music that wafted across the green valley.

"Roberto, brah, maybe we outta da Ajax," said Bruddah.

"I'll put it on the list when I go to town. Anything else you can think of?"

"Quiet, guys," said Larson, "Listen to this. It's from the sixties when Ry Cooder came over here."

Sonny-boy Noaloa didn't give a shit about slack key guitar.

"When dis gonna stop? I gotta get outta heah an' get ready fo da Haleiwa! People gonna wonder where I stay! I need talk to my agent right now!"

Larson bit his lower lip and pushed pause on the CD player. Sonny-boy had been a handful, and so far it had been a stand-off tempered only by Larson's patience, Bruddah's Hawaiian roots, and Mercante reminding Noaloa that he was still under contract. But Larson liked Hawaiian music, and he REALLY liked Ry Cooder.

"Well, maybe when you can learn to appreciate good music, we'll let you talk to someone, but it sure won't be your agent."

"Ah fuck you, Larson!"

There had been some dicey moments, but Mercante and Bruddah knew this one could get ugly by the look on Larson's face as he slowly stood up and walked in the house.

Sonny-boy Noaloa was standing in the bathroom, his clothes stained and dirty from two days of scrubbing floors, washing walls, and giving the cabin a complete going over while the men had camped outside on the lawn.

"Ok, Heath, I've learned my lesson, but I am not going to clean the toilets, and there's nothing you can do about it," said a suddenly very frightened Sonny-boy Noaloa, speaking good English the way his mother had taught him. Larson saw the fear in his face and adroitly reversed field.

"Wilson, you've done such a good job I wouldn't want you to blow it so close to finishing. C'mon, let me help you." Larson found an old scrub brush and a canister of cleaning powder under the sink. "First thing you do is turn off the water to the unit, and then flush it. That way you can scrub the inside and get it really clean. You know, like a cleanup set coming through at Sunset."

The winner of the Sunset Beach Pro two years in a row looked on in amazement as the man who used to surf Sunset just for the fun of it got down on his knees and began to scrub the toilet.

"See, Sonny-boy? Sometimes it's just easier to do what you need to do."

A week later the second contest of the series was run in excellent waves at Haleiwa, and for another week Noaloa rumors continued to float from the parties to the press to the surfers out in the water – and back again. But nobody knew a thing, and when the surf report predicted a powerful swell for the final and most dramatic contest on the pro tour at Pipeline, everyone pretty much forgot about Noaloa in the building excitement.

Over on Maui, four men were covered in mud and laughing their heads off. A pure-bred Hawaiian pushed his best friend into the pool at the base of a waterfall, but not before he could quickly grab the chairman of surfing's largest corporation and pull him in too. Then pro surfing's champion jumped up on the Hawaiian's huge shoulders and they fell in sideways.

Heath Larson climbed out of the pool, up the short cliff, and slid over the falls back down into the pool below. He was quickly followed by the others, and for the next half hour it could have been a backyard in Ohio with kids going down a waterslide, yelling and screaming and having the time of their lives. Finally, the four emerged from the clear water and sat in the warm Hawaiian sun. Larson looked up at the sky, and noticed some clouds beginning to form to the west.

"You know, guys, it might be blowing offshore at Pipe tomorrow. Maybe we go over there and see if it is any good."

"Nah, fuck dat place," said Sonny-boy Noaloa, "Let's stay heah. Maybe Honolua stay good tomorrow."

Larson exchanged glances with Bruddah and then nodded to Roberto Mercante.

"Well, Sonny, if I'm not mistaken, you work for me. Heath, what do you have in mind?"

* * *

A wall of whitewater pushed up the sloping sand and under the restraining ropes that lifeguards had strung along the beach. Out to sea, the last two waves of the set were shutting down on the second reef. Thanks to a strong offshore wind, the waves coming across the inside reef were pushing fifteen feet and holding their perfect shape.

A horn sounded, and with lifeguards on jet skis and a medevac helicopter on the beach, the Pipeline Pro Championship was underway. The first surfer took off, fighting the wind down the face. He was going to try and backdoor the tube, but he didn't have enough speed and the tunnel swallowed him whole. The crowd gasped as pieces of a broken board exploded out of the white water and the waverunner sped in to pick up the dazed surfer. The next surfer paddled into takeoff position. He caught the wave, looked down at what awaited him, and pulled back at the last instant. His nerve had failed him completely, but now things were even worse as he turned around to see a rogue set fifty yards outside of him and the other two surfers abandoning their boards to dive under the wall of whitewater.

Twenty minutes later, the horn sounded, and heat number one was in the books without a wave being ridden. Although a new world champ would be crowned at the end of the event, all the touring pros knew it was going to be a long day.

By mid morning, several thousand spectators were watching as the last of the preliminary heats was getting ready to enter the water. The contest officials gave three colored jerseys to three nervous surfers. The fourth jersey, for the automatically seeded world champion, remained unclaimed. The competitors got their last instructions and headed towards the surf. They paddled out and sat waiting for the previous heat to end. When the horn sounded, they moved into position.

The contest officials were busy tabulating scores. They didn't notice the fourth jersey disappear. A lull in the sets prompted them to delay the start of the heat. The announcer was giving short bios on the three competitors in the water, noting that Sonny-boy Noaloa was an apparent no-show and what a sad ending it might be to the career of surfing's most meteoric star.

"Yes, Noaloa seems to have given up, and so this heat will proceed with only three surfers. Attention water patrol, will you please clear the water of non-competitors," he said, noticing that a surfer had paddled out to the left of the contest area.

A set of waves loomed on the horizon. The horn signaled the beginning of the heat. The three competitors scrambled to the takeoff zone as a lifeguard on a jet ski roared toward the intruder.

The first wave of the set stood up on the second reef, where it was met by the lone surfer. He ignored the lifeguard and took off down the long, steepening slope of the wave. It reeled across the inside reef and jacked up an extra five feet into a perfect tube ten feet in diameter. The unknown surfer disappeared deep into the tunnel. Everyone on the beach knew he wasn't coming out. Everyone, that is, except three men standing under a palm tree near the judges.

Five long seconds elapsed before the crowd gasped. Coming out of the tunnel, the surfer did a cut back, stalled, and put on the jersey! He ducked through another inside tube and exited the wave with a graceful turn and a salute to the beach. The crowd went wild. Sonny-boy Noaloa was given a perfect score of ten on his first wave.

Late that afternoon, Noaloa had the Pipeline contest first place trophy at his feet after winning every heat and scoring a record point total in the final. During the awards he was laughing and friendly while tour officials crowned a new world champion, a Californian who had not survived his first heat at Pipeline but who had finished with the most points on the world tour, barely beating the missing Mick Lennox.

Heath Larson and Bruddah were watching Noaloa graciously applaud as the slightly bewildered Californian soaked in the cheers of the crowd. Bruddah caught Sonny-boy's eye. He cocked his head slightly, and Noaloa slipped down off the platform leaving the new world champion in the spotlight.

Noaloa was like a little boy who had finally won the approval of a big brother. He even looked the part as he struggled with his first place award, a traditional heavy koa-wood carving that was almost as big as he was.

"Gimme that thing," said Heath Larson and he carried it casually with one hand as Bruddah opened a path through the crowd ahead of them. When they got to the pickup Roberto Mercante was in the driver's seat on his cell phone to California giving the green light to the "When It Counts" campaign. Larson tossed the trophy in the back like a piece of firewood.

"Don't forget Sonny-boy, it's only Pipeline. Soon we'll be riding some real waves, and no matter how good you are, there won't be any trophies."

Gifts

After the tyrant missionary Gambier had decimated the Marulean people in the early 1800s, the survivors faced many hard challenges. One of the most difficult was to reconcile their hearts with Christianity. Gambier had forced the Catholic religion on them in a manner no different than the Jesuits had used in California. The effect on the Maruleans was, at first, almost the same as that experienced by the Chumash. Unfortunately for California's seafaring coastal tribe, the Spanish stayed forever. Fortunately for the Maruleans, the French eventually left them alone.

This gave the sea people, with their heritage of island independence and common sense, a basis to reject formal Christian religion. They could not accept that the Son of God, a living embodiment of love and life, would have to die to save them. They had no use for the image of a vengeful Father who would burn sinners in an everlasting hell if they didn't believe in Him. They could not believe that Jesus had died for their sins – there was no logic to that idea at all. The cross was a symbol of human failure – nothing more. The image of a tortured man dying a horrible death and the Catholic teachings about suffering, guilt and sin, were discarded.

But the Maruleans remained Christians, using love as taught by Jesus as the cornerstone of their faith. And the more David Helmares understood the Marulean version of Christianity, the more he embraced it. When it came to celebrating Christmas, however, David maintained one tradition from his youth, and again this year he made sure the batteries were fully charged on the Morning Light *as he strung lights from his rigging and put a set of speakers on deck.*

The evening star appeared above the horizon where the sun had set on a hot and windless day, the longest day of the year. On this night the sea people of Marulea began a week of fasting and feasting, of games and solemn ceremonies, to celebrate the solstice – and the birth of Christ.

Taveka was standing in the doorway of his home thinking about the love Jesus had taught and the hope and faith in the goodness of man being celebrated by the Maruleans. He also thought of the next solstice, in June, when the season would change to winter, when he would begin the steps of his final journey to the arms of angels, his ancestors and his wife. Then tears came to his eyes when Handel's Messiah came wafting across the water.

Early in David's apprenticeship Taveka had wanted to learn something from the young Californian that held some special significance from his past.

David had responded by suggesting Taveka listen to the set of CDs he'd made so that he'd always have his entire music collection with him wherever he went. So, over a period of months, Taveka listened with respect to everything from the Allman Brothers to "The Sound of Music", but when David played a special homemade compilation of Christmas songs, starting with a series of classics from the Percy Faith Orchestra, Taveka felt his soul truly touched. That Christmas, Taveka suggested David share the music with the Maruleans. They loved it as much as Taveka did and considered it a wonderful gift and a welcome addition to their celebrations.

The next song was "Away in the Manger", and Taveka thought of the passing of his beloved wife so many years ago. Their new-born daughter had been in his arms when he kissed her mother goodbye. Now that Luan had married his successor, Taveka could look forward to the day he would be with his wife again. He stood smiling as the tears ran down his face, his heart filled with the simple song about a child's birth and what it meant to an old man whose time was coming.

Three children were walking by and one of them noticed the old navigator had not greeted them in his usual friendly manner.

"Uncle Taveka, are you sad?"

"Yes, Uncle," said a little girl, "why are you crying? It's Jesus' birthday and we're going to my auntie's house for stories and then we're going to make gifts for our parents. Isn't anyone going to give you presents?"

"Yes, little one, I already have many presents. Sometimes people cry when they have much happiness inside them."

"So you are not sad, Uncle Taveka?"

"How can anyone be sad if a new year is coming with all sorts of surprises and fun?" he said with a smile on his face.

The music faded to silence for a moment.

"Uncle Taveka, are you going to die soon?"

"Shush, you weren't supposed to say anything to him!"

"No, it is a question I will answer. Yes, I am going away, and it will be before next Christmas. So why don't you all make me extra gifts this year?"

His smile turned to laughter, and the eyes of the children lit up as they felt the joy of giving fill their hearts.

"Yes, we will! We will bring them Christmas morning, Uncle!"

The children skipped off down the path. Taveka smiled in acknowledgement of the endless passing of generations, with the innocence and joy of children being the only eternal constant of life in its every breath. Then he heard the opening notes of "We Three Kings."

* * *

Two thousand miles to the west, the Skyhook was sitting just outside her hangar near the headquarters of the Skyrider Foundation. Victor and Tina Sanchez were dressed up as Mr. and Mrs. Claus. Mac Owens had an elf's costume on. Two dozen high school students carrying brightly colored packages formed a line at the cargo bay door. Though time and distance made it impossible for the students to go home, the Skyhook was going to stand in as Santa's sleigh on its annual Christmas flight to some of the most remote islands of Polynesia bearing gifts to the students' families and friends.

"Did you weigh this?" asked Mac Owens.

"Uh, yeah, kinda."

"An' how much did it weigh?"

"The scale said forty six."

"Was that pounds or kilos?"

"Uh, I don't remember."

"How much is it 'sposed to weigh?"

"Under fifty, I think."

"Yes, that's right. That's fifty pounds – not fifty kilograms!"

The boy's lip quivered as if he was going to burst into tears.

"You mean it can't go on the plane?"

"I didn't say that, Mister Nathan Bailala. However, you'll hafta pay the excess baggage charge."

"But I don't have any money!"

"Ok," said Owens, "Please print your name, an' the weight, an' then sign right here." He handed a clipboard to the grateful teenager. The young man did as he was told until he stopped and looked at Mac Owens. He had quickly scanned the list and realized that several students, whose gifts for their family and friends were already stored in the *Skyhook,* had submitted packages that weighed as much, or more, than his.

"Hey, these others are overweight too!"

"Look a little closer, young man. Their weights are in pounds!"

"Oh, ok. All right. Well uh - - -"

"Merry Christmas, Nathan!" said Mac Owens. The finality in his tone told the teenager further argument would be useless.

"Uh, Merry Christmas, Uncle Mac. What should I do now?"

"Why don't you go an' see if Mr. an' Mrs. Santa need some help."

Thanks, Uncle Mac! Merry Christmas!"

"Kids these days! They jes' don' pay 'tention when they should!" he said to himself, only to remember NASA had lost an eight hundred million dollar Mars mission because some engineers had confused pounds and kilograms.

"Oh, well," he thought, "What's a little excess baggage?"

The thought reminded him of the load he'd have to deal with on the Wavelife mission, and he began to ponder, as he had for several weeks now, just how he would deal with all their equipment, especially the jetskis, as he positioned the Christmas gifts securely in the cargo bay. He was arranging the packages in reverse order according to the flight plan whereby they would be distributed to the families of the students at rendezvous points outside a dozen barrier reefs, several of which were where the *Skyhook* had rescued sailors and pilots during the war. He remembered how the Catalina had been re-fitted especially for the purpose of those touch-and-go missions by having all the external bomb and torpedo hardware removed since she would no longer be tasked with delivering death.

Mac Owens stopped everything. He climbed up on the *Skyhook*'s wing. He removed a panel, and sure enough, the cable and pulley mechanisms for bombs weighing up to two thousand pounds had never been removed when the *Skyhook* had been converted for rescue missions. He checked the other wing, and suddenly he was in business.

"Well, that solves that problem!"

* * *

The Mother Ocean Shelter occupied a building that had once been the home of Synanon, right on the beach in Santa Monica. Over the years it had been sold and converted into condos, but when the most recent owners went bankrupt, the building came up for sale at a foreclosure price. Aleja Gracellen had seen the sign announcing the sale on her way to Newport Beach for a meeting with Cheryl Corlund. She had an idea, and now the downtrodden once again had a home on the beach.

Gracellen had mastered the surfing mobs at Surfrider Beach and the ritzy crowds of Malibu's restaurants. People were needy, off balance and helpless whether competing for waves or flaunting their wealth. Both experiences were surprisingly relevant when it came to running the shelter.

The tree was tall and green and the presents wrapped in recycled paper. A dozen children were listening to their mothers sing "Silent Night" in the large utility room that was converted to a dormitory every night. When the song ended with hugs and tears all around, Aleja Gracellen thought of Cheryl Corlund and how she had quickly come and gone before the children could give her the Christmas gifts they had made for her.

"Wait a minute, everyone, if you please! Everyone! Just quiet down for a second. I don't know how many of you saw the lady who was here a little while ago - - -"

"You mean the one who parked her Escalade over near the pier so we wouldn't know who she was?" said a voice from the back.

"She's the one who is taking care of us, isn't she?" said one of the children.

"Well, there's no getting anything past you guys, is there?"

"You live on the streets and go through hell for years, and you'll be pretty sharp too, Aleja!" said one woman with a laugh that was more rueful than happy.

"Yeah, that's her. Well, even though her company gives us a lot, she stopped by this year with a special gift, though she didn't want anyone to know about it."

"Is that what anomin – anony – what is that word?" said one of the children.

"Anonymous, dear, and yes, that's what she is. Our anonymous benefactor. Well, I want us all to bow our heads for a second and give her a gift straight from our hearts."

Aleja Gracellen touched the envelope in her pocket, containing a Christmas card from Cheryl Corlund and a check for fifty thousand dollars made out to the shelter.

"Can we pray for her? I can do that!" said a little one up front.

"Yes, child, that is what we can do for her. And of all the gifts we could ever give her, I think prayers are the ones she needs the most."

* * *

The tree was plastered with fake presents, clumps of tinsel, plastic ornaments, and blinking lights. It looked just like last year's to Cheryl Corlund, standing outside the entrance to Wavelife's headquarters, as did the "Surfing Santa" party in full swing swirling through the lobby. Her husband had gone over the top, as usual. A dozen models were scantily dressed as Santa's helpers and helping her husband, dressed as Santa himself, hand out the bonus checks to dozens of happy employees. For the moment she cared not to think about how the glow would soon fade from the bright eager faces once they discovered the checks were less than half of last year's.

She caught her husband's eye for a second and then walked across the lobby and hit the button on the elevator. He caught up with her and pulled her to one side.

"There you are – what took you so long?"

"And Merry Christmas to you too, dear! I'm surprised you even missed me," she said, glancing back at the bevy of beauties handing out the checks, "Can't you think of something other than eye candy for your party mix?"

"Oh Cheryl, c'mon, it's Christmas, have a drink! You look like you need one! And there are some people from home I want you to meet."

"I've already met half of Brazil, Roberto. Who are they this time?"

"Buyers from a new chain in Sao Paulo. They've got steel mill money behind them."

"Ok," she said, knowing Wavelife sales had slipped a little in Brazil, "Give me a minute. Have you heard from Maui?"

"So far, so good. They're back up in the hills even as we speak. No parties, no women, no nothing. Bruddah and Heath are keeping the pressure on and Sonny-boy is doing quite well from what I understand."

"Did you talk to Bruddah?"

"Yeah, and if it wasn't for his friendship with Heath, we'd be sunk. He's turning out to be the key in all this, Cheryl."

"Well, if he's going to be that essential, do we have him under contract?"

"I gave him one with the salary left open. He signed it on the condition that we pay him a dollar a year."

Corlund was taken aback for a second. The spirit of aloha was one thing, but turning down a blank contract to be a dollar-a-year man said a lot. She wasn't sure if it was a reflection of Bruddah being a proud Hawaiian – or a well-considered decision based on an accurate opinion of what Wavelife did and didn't stand for. Then she knew it was both. The elevator opened and a crowd of employees pushed their way out.

"Merry Christmas everybody!" said Roberto heartily, "C'mon over and get your bonus checks!"

He let himself be swept away while she entered the empty elevator and hit 'ten' to find some peace and quiet above it all.

When the elevator doors opened, Dolly Artensa was standing there, tired and ready to go home. But when their eyes met, Artensa knew her boss could use some company.

"I'm surprised you didn't just stay there," she said, "After the year we just had, a shelter doesn't sound half bad."

Corlund nodded silently and Artensa gave her a hug before they walked slowly to the CEO's corner office. For a long time they simply stood near a floor-to-ceiling window and looked out at the lights of the 405 streaming through fields of office buildings that had replaced the groves of orange trees.

The silence was eventually broken by a whisper.

"I parked two blocks away, Dolly, so nobody would see my car, and walking in felt like, well it felt like - - -"

"Like you were coming in off the street and needed some shelter yourself. Honey, loneliness cuts just as deep whether you're driving a Cadillac or a shopping cart."

Corlund laughed softly.

"And now I've got to get back downstairs and schmooze some Brazilian money. And for what? Flying surfers around the world and fake Christmas trees?"

"Well, don't look at it that way. Aleja and the shelter and those women with their children can use all the help they can get. So turn on the charm and get some business done."

An hour later the models were in a conga line around the tree and Roberto Mercante was as happy as he could be. He and his wife were getting along famously with the wealthy industrialist and his entourage, regaling them with stories about how Sonny-boy had won at Pipeline and why the "When It Counts" campaign was going to work. Then Mercante saw a sharp-dressed man come through the front door and excused himself for a moment.

"Ian, bro! Merry Christmas!"

"Roberto, nice party! I bet there's no shareholders at this gig, are there?" Clark said with a knowing laugh.

"Ah, fuck 'em! We gotta party sometime! What can I get you to drink?"

"Well, I'm driving, so I'd - - -"

"Ian, c'mere," said Mercante, putting his arm around the tall Californian, "Listen, I know all about DUI's an' corporate liability and all that shit. See those girls dancing around the tree? Guess who they are?"

"Don't tell me – the designated drivers!"

"See how smart you are? So have a drink, no have two! And let me introduce you to your chauffeurs!"

Soon Ian Clark was dancing around the Christmas tree with his driver and her backup. The Wavelife employees were now long gone, replaced by the Orange County party patrol in their silicone and stilettos, silk shirts and gold chains. Clark was enjoying every second of his new life as a Wavelife insider surrounded by beautiful women, hot-shot surfers, and flashy new money all living it up in the lobby of the surf industry's number one.

A guy sailed by Clark, did a double-take, and extended one hand in a bro handshake while spilling the rest of his drink with the other.

"The man himself!"

Clark knew the look, generic OC in tinted hair and loose silk shirt, but he didn't who he was.

"Uh, yeah, hi! My name's Ian Clark - - -"

"Shit, man, I KNOW who you are! Mr. Ian Clark! I've spent a lot of money with Geosurf! Got great waves in the Mentawais! Spent a week at your place in New Zealand! The Azores! Loved the place, man! I'm one of your regulars!"

The party was really loud and the guy had had a few, so Clark didn't pay too much attention until the guy said something that was not what he wanted to hear.

"Say bro, I hear Santa gave you a pretty bitchen Christmas gift this year!"

"Uh, what? What did you say? Couldn't hear you!"

"I said, I hear you've found a new reef – and you're gonna sell trips on a seaplane to surf the place!"

"What reef? I don't know what you are talking about!" stammered a surprised Ian Clark.

"Sure, Ian, no problem," he winked, "Here's my card. Just call me when you've got the package all wrapped up and ready to go, ok? Merry Christmas, bro!"

A New Man

Dirty oil came spurting out of the drain hole and began to puddle on the garage floor. Sonny-boy Noaloa cursed loudly and re-positioned the drain pan. He wiggled out from underneath the truck with oil on his shirt and a pissed-off look on his face. Heath Larson was standing at the work bench repairing the footstraps on a high-speed surfboard. He glanced over his shoulder and quickly guessed what happened.

"You'll find some clean-up stuff over there in the corner. And don't forget to put the plug back in before you start putting in the new oil. And when you're done with the truck, we'll get started on the jet skis."

"Yes, sir. Anything you say, sir. Right away, sir."

Larson was caught offguard by the tone in his voice. For the past three weeks they had been making real progress turning the bad boy surf star into a sober-minded waterman. Now that the January rains were pouring down, the training had shifted to Larson's garage where the focus was on the machines that were a part of riding big waves. It was a completely different kind of surfing that had to be understood from the ground up, but the look on Noaloa's face told Larson it was going to be a longer climb for the former pro champ than he'd first imagined.

* * *

An hour after the victory at Pipeline, they had both been in the same airport conference room where the decision had been made to change Noaloa's m.o. ten days previously. Roberto Mercante was sitting at the table, and Bruddah was standing near a window looking out at a view of Diamond Head. Mercante's flight was leaving in twenty minutes, and his wife was smiling on the video conference screen. Thanks to the intervention, marketing didn't have to trash the "When It Counts" campaign and scramble a new sales angle before the upcoming trade shows. Heath, Bruddah and her husband had pulled it off, and things were looking up. She thanked them all before getting to the point.

"Sonny-boy, I won't see you until Surf Expo in Florida, but I want you to know how proud I am of you. And I've got great news. You won't be on the pro tour next year. As of right now, I want you to start preparing to become a true surfing legend as a big wave rider."

Noaloa didn't know what to say. For him, surfing had been all about competition, starting with his mom driving him to contests up and down the east coast of Florida every weekend.

"Yeah, but, uh, I like surf da contes', and if I drop offa da tour, what I do? And what kine talk people make?"

"Let 'em talk all they want," said Roberto Mercante, following his wife's lead, "That will only work in our favor. I can see our press release right now: No Tour for Noaloa - He's Got More Important Things to Do!"

"That's pretty good, Roberto. Have the P.R. and marketing people get started on it right away. Heath, can I count on you to continue your excellent work with Sonny-boy?"

"Uh, well, that's not in my contract, Cheryl," said a surprised Larson.

Corlund sensed she had to put out a fire. "Well, that's easily solved. Why don't we up your numbers by half, retroactive to the beginning of December, plus a performance bonus on a per wave basis at our new reef?"

"Well, that sounds good, Cheryl, I guess," he said with genuine hesitation, stalling for time, feeling like an outside set was coming and he was in the wrong place. Before either of them could say anything, Noaloa jumped in.

"Eh, I goin surf dat place too! What I get? I mo bettah talk my agent."

"He's not working for you anymore, Sonny-boy. I bought your contract from him. But don't worry. You can have the same deal as Heath, and now you'll keep the 10% you used to pay that guy."

"Yeah, but - - -"

"But what, Sonny-boy?" said the CEO, now no longer smiling, "Call it a well-deserved Christmas present. Haven't we always taken good care of you?"

Corlund took Noaloa's silence as acquiescence.

"Good. Roberto, go over to the fax machine and make sure it's on," said Corlund, "Now Sonny-boy, you're going to stay with Heath on Maui, and Heath, you're going to get him ready to be your partner when you surf the reef."

Now Larson had to speak up. It was one thing to bulldoze a business deal. Telling him who to trust his life with was something else.

"Cheryl, I already have a partner. It takes a long time to set up a tow-in team."

"Roberto tells me we've got until May before the reef starts breaking, and I don't need you guys at full strength out there until August. Heath," she softened her tone, "I'm sure you can do it with Sonny-boy training full time. And of course we'll cover all your expenses."

Mercante walked back to the table with the two contracts.

"Here's the deal, guys," he said, "Take it or leave it."

Corlund winced at her husband's words. Sometimes people snapped when they heard that cliché at the bargaining table. When it came to Heath Larson, she was right. He made no effort to read the contract. He knew exactly what Corlund was doing. For the first time in his association with Wavelife, he was ready to walk away from the table. The thought gave him a distinct sense of freedom and his heart sang for a second. He got up and indeed left the table.

111

Corlund and Mercante were speechless. Sonny-boy, too, was surprised, but he couldn't ignore the idea of making more money.

"Heath, bra! We can do dis! We gonna do sometin' nobody evah dream of! Brah, we goin blow minds!"

But Larson didn't hear a word as he walked over to talk with Bruddah who had been listening to every word and understood the situation perfectly.

"Heath, I know you hates dis shit," he said quietly, "Dey tryin' to buy you wid a lotta bucks, brah. But mebbe we change dis kid forevah and make him one da kine role model for other kids on da islands."

"You sure about that, Bruddah?"

"Yeah, brah, we gotta chance and we gotta go for it. What we gonna do, let da Tui and GroundZero turn alla da kids into thugs?"

"Ok, Bruddah, you're driving, as usual."

"Dat's ok brah, we pull dis off and he gonna be da model citizen!"

Bruddah grinned, and Larson saw a look in his eye that couldn't be denied. He turned and walked back to the table. It was one thing to be cornered by a CEO. That he could walk away from simply on principle. But Bruddah's words hit home all the way to his surfer's soul.

"Yeah, Sonny-boy, we can do it," he said, "But Cheryl, Bruddah is in on this or else I'm out."

"Yes, well, uh, of course! Roberto, work out the details, ok? And so can I get your signature, Heath? Sonny-boy?"

The two surfers signed the contracts, and a relieved Cheryl Corlund smiled again.

"Great! Mala kalamaka, and happy new year! Gotta go, guys! Bye!"

The video screen turned blue. Cheryl Corlund leaned back in her chair and smiled at June Wilson and Bill Massara. With signed contracts in hand from Larson and Noaloa, she could now get back to the work in front of her.

"Ok, let's see the financials we'll be taking to New York," she said.

In Hawai'i, her husband also had work to do, but before he could get started, Bruddah had the first word.

"Hey Roberto, betta tell you wife its Mele Kalikamaka, ok, brah?"

The day after Christmas, Larson and Noaloa went back to the training regimen that had cleaned up the former world champ. They started every day at dawn with a jog through the mountains at dawn and a light breakfast before a morning workout of stretching, yoga and low-impact free weights. After lunch was a different story. With Bruddah as their drill sergeant, they would redline all afternoon with surf-centric exercises Larson had developed over the years using sand for resistance work. They finished every afternoon doing swim sprints with Bruddah pushing them to exhaustion.

"Here come da shark, boys! I one hungry mako today!" he'd yell, and if he caught either of them, he'd grab a foot and drag the laggard under water. For all his strength, Larson got caught every once in a while, and though he got some slack in the beginning, Noaloa was soon swimming almost as fast as he could paddle a surfboard.

But they never surfed. Noaloa didn't need to become a better surfer - he needed to prepare for an entirely different way to ride waves from another realm. On New Year's Eve they watched the ball come down in Times Square on the small black & white TV in the kitchen and raised a toast of spring water to the new year. The former world champ was looking forward to tomorrow so much he was glad to go to bed. The sooner he fell asleep, the sooner it would be day one of a new year as a new man.

When Noaloa jumped out of bed an hour before dawn he found a note on the kitchen table. Within minutes he was running down to the coast, and as the sun touched the horizon he found Bruddah sitting on a cliff overlooking an ocean full of waves. Below them, in the water all alone, was Heath Larson riding perfect waves at one of the best surf spots in the world, Honolua Bay.

The Bay was often the most crowded surf spot in the entire Hawaiian island chain, but the surf had been good for days and the surf reports had called for the swell to drop. So most of the surfers on Maui had indulged in the usual over-the-top New Year's revelry, not knowing that the surf report had got it all wrong, leaving Larson to reap the fruits of self-discipline by shredding the ten footers as if he was surfing chest-high Malibu. Noaloa had rarely seen Hawaiian waves surfed with such casual power and style. And he had never seen what Heath Larson did after one particularly stand out wave: he simply sat and watched a set go by without trying to catch even one wave.

The sight of empty perfect waves was too much for the young surfer.

"Say Bruddah, we out deah! Git da kine tubes 'fo da crowd come, yeah?"

Bruddah's response put him back in his place.

"Nah, let da guy surf alone. Let some da waves go by wit nobodys on dem. We just sit and watch, brah. Good fo' da soul."

Noaloa knew better than to say another word, but it took a while for him to swallow and digest his frustration. He and Bruddah exchanged some small talk about Larson's technique on a few waves, but it wasn't until the wind changed directions and clouds began to form on the horizon that Bruddah changed the subject as other surfers began to show up and Larson caught his last ride.

"Look like da Kona winds come. Gonna rain real good. I tink mebbe we change da training, Sonny-boy. You in great shape. Now it time we gonna train you fo' da jetskis."

* * *

Riding big waves once required only two things: a big, fast board and a lot of guts. Then board design reached a limit at the intersection of paddling speed vs. performance on the wave itself. The bigger the wave, the faster it moved through the ocean, but bigger boards that paddled fast enough could not be made with the necessary maneuverability to surf the waves successfully.

The solution was smaller, highly maneuverable boards that didn't paddle at all but were towed behind jetskis that went faster than the waves. Now catching the wave was no problem, but that was just the beginning.

After several years of development by a small group of veteran big wave riders in Hawai'i, the 'tow-in' technique changed big wave surfing forever in three important aspects. First and foremost was the fact tow-in surfers could not go surfing alone. They needed a jetski, and the jetski needed a driver whose role was crucial not only for catching the waves, but also rescuing the riders when they fell. Second was the jetski itself. They had to be maintained, and surfers had to become gearheads. Finally, to accommodate the excessive speeds and torque found in waves forty to sixty feet high, the boards became like waterskis, with footstraps and extra weight, and could not be paddled at all.

And thus was broken a basic thread tying all surfers together going back to the days of the Duke when surfing was simply a man, a board, and a wave.

For many, the loss was a small price to pay for the adrenalin and exhilaration now orders of magnitude greater than anything previously experienced by surfers. Tow-in surfing became the subject of dozens of articles in the mainstream media, and the fact that surfing was once called the sport of kings became ancient history in a new world powered by jetskis.

The Duke was dead, and a new king was crowned: Heath Larson. Yet in some ways, Kahanamoku's spirit lived on in Larson's soul. Although he was on the cover of Outside and National Geographic, he refused to be a part of the surf magazine popularity polls or participate in their annual "biggest wave" photo contests. Once he was offered a script for a TV commercial that had him comparing big waves to Mount Everest. He turned it down. He knew there was no comparison. No one ever claimed victory over the highest mountain on earth after first using a helicopter to get close to the summit the way a jet ski was used to get a surfer on a big wave.

Heath Larson had no illusions about his dependency on a machine or, to a much larger extent, his tow-in partner. Mechanical aptitude could be learned, but trust was something else again. He had worked with several jetski drivers who knew the machines and the tow-in techniques backwards and forwards. But it wasn't until he met Bruddah, a Hawaiian whose integrity went back generations, that he finally was able to find the kind of bonded friendship that allowed him to reach the pinnacle of a sport-within-a-sport with its life-and-death challenges.

Now he and Bruddah were facing a new challenge that had nothing to do with nature and everything to do with human nature.

* * *

"Why I gotta do all dis? I no like work on cars – why we no jus take da car dealah and have dem fix?"

114

Larson let the words hang in the air while another downpour hit the metal roof over their heads. And it took almost a minute for him to make sure he was calm and centered before he spoke.

"Because you're contract with Wavelife averages out to fifty bucks an hour, and the poor guys who change oil for a living make about ten. Who do you think is going to do a better job?"

"Wavelife pay me fo' surf. I nevah was paid fo dis kine surfing."

"That was last year's surfing. This year you're going to have to be more than just a guy who can win surfing contests."

"What you talkin', brah? I beat da bes' surfahs in da world, and mo' dan one time! It was fuckin' hard! Brah, I deserve to win!"

Noaloa was digging in. Larson was ready for the confrontation.

"Listen Sonny-boy, maybe you have forgotten, or maybe you don't even know, I grew up on the North Shore. If I had wanted to turn surfing into a dog-eat-dog job, I would have probably won the tour just like you.

"But I didn't want to surf shitty waves or psyche out opponents or get into the judges' heads. Waves are a God-given gift, and to use them to make myself number one out of a pack of competitors just didn't make sense to me."

"What you stay doin' now? You use jetskis to be da bes' evah in big waves! What da difference? We both da best surfers in da world!"

"Are we? Is it about the fame, or the feeling? What about the seven year old kid who gets his first wave all the way to the beach? Or the mom who somehow gets a wave all to herself at Malibu? Do we feel any better than them, or are we just more famous?

"Think about it, Sonny-boy. Just who is the best surfer in the world? Is it some paid pro getting air for the hundredth time because the magazines need a cover shot, or it is some poor guy with four kids and a mortgage who gets the wave of his life at some empty beach nobody's ever heard of? Believe me, Sonny-boy, being on top in surfing is not about judges and sponsors. It's not about getting your picture taken in the tube a split second before the wave eats you alive and breaks your board. Just ask any of those old guys in their eighties at Waikiki or San Onofre."

Noaloa had never heard anyone say anything like that before, and he didn't know what to say. But he tried.

"Shoots, Larson, you know who you are and what you do is mo' pono dan anybody evah do in surfin'. No try bullshit me."

"Ok, maybe I'm not getting through to you. Let's look at it this way."

He walked over to the jet skis and the rack of hybrid surfboards on the wall. For a moment, Heath Larson was framed by equipment like an astronaut standing in front of the space shuttle.

"I guess it boils down to this, Sonny-boy. You've never had to depend on anyone out in the water. Everything I've done has always depended on Bruddah. When we surf that reef, I am going to have to depend on you and you'll be depending on me. If either of us thinks of ourselves first, the other guy just might die."

115

"Yeah, but how stay surfin' if need alla dis stuffs, one guy fo' drive noisy machine fo' pull inna da wave? An' why I have depen' on you fo' anytin'? I no like be responsible fo' you, anyway."

The two surfers just stared at each other. It was a showdown and neither was going to give an inch.

"You guys get da truck ready? I gotta go Town go shoppin'. Moms and Pops comin' ovah for dinnah. Gonna bring da family, too."

It was Bruddah, coming in out of the rain with some well-timed and much-needed Hawaiian aloha.

"Yeah, we were almost done. Go ahead and put five quarts in her, Sonny-boy, or was it six? Better check the manual," said Larson without breaking eye contact with Noaloa.

Sonny-boy averted his glance and saw Bruddah looking at him.

"Shoots, I gonna get um done," he said, tossing the oily rag towards the trash can. He missed, on purpose.

Heath Larson saw the gesture but let it slide. He went back to his work, but not before catching Noaloa's eye and then looking at Bruddah.

"Yeah, when you go town, I think we're close to running outta toilet paper. Better get some. We gotta lot of shit to clean up around here."

* * *

A week later, the rain had stopped, the skies were blue, and the surf was big enough to begin actual training with the jetski and the tow-boards. On the other side of the island, at a deserted reef far from the cameras, Sonny-boy Noaloa got his first real rush as a tow-in surfer. Heath Larson had positioned him perfectly, and all Sonny-boy had to do was stand there and cruise through the biggest tube of his life. At the end of the ride his euphoria was that of a child who had just experienced something for the first time, something so wonderful that it made him oblivious to the world around him.

Then he heard the jetski and saw Larson coming towards him at full throttle – being chased by a rogue wave twice as big as the one he just rode. And just like a child, the former pro surf-star froze in panic. Larson was frantically signaling for him to be ready for an evacuation pick-up. But like a deer in the headlights, Noaloa couldn't move. And to make matters worse, his feet were still in the footstraps.

Larson didn't slow down until the very last second. He saw that Sonny-boy was attached to the board as he pulled up right next to him.

"Leave the board and get on the sled!"

His words were drowned out by the roar of the oncoming wave and Sonny-boy continued to struggle to get his feet out of the straps.

"Grab the sled, NOW!"

Noaloa reached for the handropes of the rescue sled attached to the waverunner and pulled himself up onto the sled.

"Get the board up in the air!"

The white water was now mere few yards away. Noaloa rolled up on to the sled and had the board out of the water.

"Hold on!"

Larson redlined the jetski just before the white water hit them.

The acceleration was so abrupt that Noaloa was thrown sideways. The nose of the board caught in the water, but Noaloa held on, his legs twisting and straining until the straps broke.

Raw ocean power chased them towards the shore lined with large boulders. Larson began to edge to his right, aiming for the break in the reef where the wave would back off for a few seconds before smashing into the cliff.

"Get ready to bail out!"

But Noaloa didn't hear him over the roar of the wave about engulf them both. He was holding on tight in sheer panic when Larson jammed the ski into a hard turn at the last second to zoom out to the safety of the deep water channel as the wave slammed into the rocks and exploded up against the cliff.

They were safe, but the experience seemed somehow surreal because suddenly the ocean had become completely quiet. The rogue had been the last wave of the set. The entire surf zone, where huge waves had been breaking with tremendous force and where Sonny-boy had been rescued just seconds ago, was now covered with nothing but a layer of soft white foam.

As they drifted to a stop, Larson turned around with fury in his face.

"You trying to get us killed? Didn't you see my signal? Remember what we did in training? Why didn't you - - -"

Noaloa wasn't listening. He was grimacing in pain.

"Hey brah, I tink my knee is fucked."

Kicking

The rain came down hard and L.J. Merrill's thoughts spiraled into darkness. It was another cold, wet day of an endless El Niño winter. A constant string of storms had turned the blue Pacific into a sickly brown, though that made little difference to him. He was kicking, and he didn't care about the ocean anymore.

The lights were off and the curtains closed. He listened to the water pouring through the gutters outside his bedroom at the bottom of his parents' home overlooking Laguna Beach. He thought of his once fantastic life now down the drain. A squall rattled the windows and he laughed softly to himself.

Ah yes, so this must be what they call rock bottom.

He raised his hand in empty, sweeping gestures.

The legendary L.J. Merrill! Free citizen of the surfing world! Explorer, adventurer, surf guide without peer! The man who had ridden a thousand perfect waves!

He let his arm fall to the side of the chair.

Stuck in a dark, damp room trying to change his life.

* * *

When he came back to Southern California with the tour group from Chile, L.J. Merrill knew something was wrong right away. Ian Clark was not at LAX to meet him. He caught a shuttle to John Wayne Airport and then another down to San Clemente. Even though it was long after dark, he asked to be dropped off at the Geosurf office. There his fears were confirmed when his key didn't turn in the lock. He panicked for a second. He had been in dozens of tight spots around the world, but this time he knew he'd finally reached the end of the line.

He took the key out of the lock and for the first time in years he thought of his parents. He looked down the street and saw some phones near a gas station. He remembered calling them once a long time ago when he was in a jam in Central America, only to be told he had made his choices and he was on his own. But he knew his parents had never given up hope that one day he would leave his wanderlust behind him because they knew what he'd been like before surfing took over his life. They were under no illusions as to what the rush of surfing could do to a young man, but he'd always scoffed at their fears and refused to think of riding waves as an addiction. It was only surfing, he'd told them, and he could walk away from it any time he wanted. Now, he realized, it was time to see if he could keep his word.

It was a surreal moment at the kitchen table late that night. A prodigal son had come home, and there was an unspoken understanding the word "surfing" would not be mentioned. There was small talk about the plumbing and his dad's new car, and his mom's hair looked good. She offered to go and make up the bed in his old room. Before he could reply, she bustled off to get clean linen for him. While she was out of the room, his dad asked him to stay home through the holidays. He said he would think about it.

Merrill woke up late the next morning and went upstairs to the kitchen. He kissed his mom and noticed she looked like she had been crying. His dad was reading the morning paper. He put it down right away. L.J. had never seen him do that before.

"Say, John, the Angels are in the playoffs. Want to see the game tonight?"

"Maybe. Yeah, that sounds good, dad. Can I use the phone for a minute?"

"Why don't you have some breakfast first? I can make you some waffles if you want."

The tone in his mother's voice was pleading, and waffles had always been his favorite breakfast.

"Uh, yeah Mom, that would be great," he said, feeling her tug at his heartstrings while reaching for the yellow phone on the wall, "But I've got to make a call first."

"I'm sorry Mr. Merrill, but he is out of the country," said a voice he did not recognize, "Mr. Clark did instruct me to say that if you called would you please come over to the office at your earliest convenience?"

Merrill thought for a second. "Ok, I'll be over there right away."

"Uh, could you make it in an hour or so?" she replied in a suddenly nervous voice.

"Sure, why not. How about two this afternoon?"

"That would be fine Mr. Merrill."

L.J. hung up the phone. He was instantly back on the plane looking through the viewfinder, on the phone to Clark, getting drunk with the tour group, at LAX with no one to meet him. Yes, this was really happening. This time he didn't panic.

"Hey, mom, can I have some eggs, too?"

His mother almost feinted, and his dad suppressed a smile.

"And Dad, you need any help around the house today? How about I mow the lawn? And, uh, I'm sorry, I should have asked first, but can we stop in San Clemente for a minute this afternoon on the way to the game?"

When they pulled up at the Geosurf office, a large security guard was standing outside the door. L.J. got out of the car and walked right up to him.

"Sir, could I see some identification?" said the rent-a-cop.

"I don't need any identification. I'm L.J. Merrill and I helped build this place. Who the hell are you?"

"Ah yes, Mr. Merrill. I'm sorry sir, but I have my orders. You are not to enter the building." The guard grabbed the radio mic on his shoulder and spoke quickly. "Hey Joe, he's here."

"Listen, asshole, get the fuck out of my way!" Merrill started to see red, literally, as his blood pressure shot up and his brain flushed with anger.

The guard took two steps back and planted his feet. One hand went to the mic on his shoulder, the other went to the gun at his side. The door opened and another guard walked out with a board under each arm. Merrill's jaw dropped. They were yellowed with age and had dings and scratches all over them. They had been around the world four times.

"Joe, we've got a problem."

The guard dropped the boards on the concrete and put his hand on his gun.

"Hey, what the fuck are you doing? Those are mine!"

"Yessir, I know. I'll have to ask you to step back and keep your hands visible, please. Al, keep an eye on him. I'll be right back."

"What the fuck is this? You guys can't do this to me!"

The guard said nothing. His hand on his gun and his feet spread wide said everything.

"If your buddy damaged those boards I'll - -"

The door opened and the other guard emerged carrying two boxes and a clipboard.

"Any trouble, Al?"

"Not so far."

The guard put the boxes on the pavement next to the boards. "Mr. Merrill, here are all your personal items and an inventory. Sir, Could you please sign this? I'll thank you to cooperate. We're just doing our job."

The legendary surf scout looked at his boards lying on the concrete. All the memories of riding them in paradise surf around the world came rushing back to him. The boxes contained maps, photos, and souvenirs from a career of finding perfect waves and a partnership now destroyed.

L.J. Merrill snapped the clipboard out of the guard's hand and scribbled his name across the form without even looking at it. He put the pen on the clipboard and tossed it back to the guard, who then handed him an envelope with his name typed in capital letters and marked "Confidential". He was about to open it right then and there when the whole thing hit him like a rogue wave on an outside reef. He was fucked, and he knew it. But he also knew his dad was watching, and that gave him just enough courage to somehow salvage a shred of dignity.

"Do me a favor, guys. Put all that stuff in the dumpster around back, and tell Ian Clark I'll see him again someday," he said before tearing the envelope in half and tossing the pieces at the dumbfounded guards. Then he turned around and walked to the curb where his father was waiting in the car.

"You all right son? Shouldn't we get your boards and take them home?"

120

He looked at his dad and saw the pain of a father who had lost their only son to years of selfishness. And he thought of his mom and what it would mean to her if surfing no longer had a grip on his soul.

"I won't need them anymore, dad. I promise. Let's get out of here."

* * *

L.J. Merrill had made good money working for Geosurf, but had never saved a dime. Though technically an independent contractor who paid most of his own expenses, he was much more the classic vagabond surfer living as if the money would never end. He landed in California knowing a check for eight grand to cover the trip to Chile was waiting for him. He also knew that check had been in the envelope when he tore it in half and tossed the pieces at the security guards.

So the legendary L.J. Merrill moved back in with his parents. He took all the old surfing pictures off the walls of his room. He put up curtains over windows. He didn't want to see the ocean when he woke up. There were some old boards in the rafters of the garage. He gave them away to some kids down the street. After a while word got around he was in town and some of his old surfing buddies started calling. He told his mom to simply take messages which he never read. For the first time in fifteen years he was home for the holidays. He kept busy helping around the house, running errands for his mom and spending time with his dad in his shop. He went to church with them on Christmas Eve. Never once did he go down to the beach. After two months away from surfing, L.J. Merrill was starting to feel like a changed man. He got a job framing houses and found he had his dad's talent for carpentry.

But a chance meeting doomed his recovery.

It was at a New Year's party. Merrill thought he could risk seeing some friends and toasting in a New Year for which he had high hopes. He was greeted warmly by people he hadn't seen in a long time. Some of them asked about Geosurf, and he was proud of himself when he politely and firmly refused to talk about it. But then he ran into an old client, and Jack Richards just laughed when Merrill told him about the promise to his parents, throwing away his passport and his New Year's resolution to never go near the ocean.

"Don't you know that once a junkie, always a junkie? Kicking is a lot harder than you think, L.J. Like they say about heroin, 'You can get it out of your body, but you can't get it out of your mind.' So when you start chipping again, here's my card. You can work for me as my personal trainer and surf scout, on year-round retainer. No freeways, no pounding nails, no living at home with Mom and Dad. And all the waves you want."

Merrill told him to fuck off, and they both laughed.

"Ok, L.J. good luck. Oh, yeah, I hear Ian Clark's selling some secret reef to Wavelife. Know anything about that?"

L.J. Merrill knew he dare not even begin to think about Richards' question. He simply smiled and said he had to get going.

* * *

Another squall hit the windows, and Merrill gave up. There were tears in his eyes as he dialed the number on the card. He heard Richards' voice telling him to leave a message.

"Sure, Jack, I'll leave you a message. You're right. I can't handle it. When can I see you? The number at this phone is - -"

Just then the other line picked up.

"See you at Aliso Creek Beach Park in half an hour."

Merrill hung up knowing he was going to be used, again. But he was a user himself, and as long as he could feed his need, he didn't care. He collapsed in a chair like falling into a pit of personal failure. He thought of his parents. What was he going to tell them? For the hundredth time he kicked himself for trusting Clark with the digital video of the most perfect big waves on earth. Then he remembered what Richards had said about Clark and Wavelife.

The tears stopped. His eyes opened wide. A surge coursed through his veins with a kick more powerful than a thousand perfect waves. The rush hit his brain with simultaneous thoughts of betrayal, a corporation, the most amazing surf he had ever seen, and a way to get even.

I will tell Richards the whole story! This is the chance of a lifetime!

It was as if a patch of blue sky had opened in the black clouds for God to shine a light on him, though he knew it was not the grace of the Good Lord warming him, but the fires of revenge.

But what about mom and dad? What am I going to tell them?

He knew he'd tried his best, but kicking his surfing addiction was not going to happen without first getting even with Ian Clark.

Mom, dad, I've got to do this. And it will be my last surf trip, ever.

Even as he mouthed the words he was going to say to them, he knew they sounded no more sincere than those of a crack addict vowing to take a last hit and not one more. He felt bad for a second, and then the moment passed. It was time to score, and he had an appointment with his connect. He got out of the chair and crawled across the floor, his eyes searching beneath his bed. He wedged under it and reached into the farthest corner against the wall. He grabbed an aluminum briefcase he had not touched in a long time.

* * *

"Well that's just too bad, L.J., but what do you expect, trusting Clark? Business is business, bro, and that's what you get for thinking you could just surf forever."

L.J. Merrill was just staring ahead as the rain came down harder. He couldn't see the ocean through the rain or his tears. The momentary rush of elation in his bedroom had been replaced by the deep depression of an addict on a roller coaster ride.

"Yeah, but if people knew what happened, if I could just tell 'em - - -"

"Don't be a dumb shit, Merrill." Jack Richards saw no reason to go easy on an addict who needed him for a fix. "Clark PR'd your exit so smoothly most people think you're retired in Hawai'i even as we speak. And listen, pal, nobody would pay attention to you anyway because you're not a player anymore. You're useless. You are now nothing but flotsam drifting away on the tide. Besides, even if the facts were known, as long as Clark supplies the goods to people throwing money at him, why should they care if some surf junkie gets trampled in the process?"

"Yeah, but this is surfing! It's supposed to be something special! We're supposed to be a brotherhood!"

"What are you, high or something? Loyalty, friendship, right and wrong – none of that means a fucking thing when there's a buck to be made. Believe me, I know what I'm talking about."

"Yeah, but Jack," he sobbed pitifully, "If someone ripped you off for the most important thing in your life, wouldn't you want to get back at them?"

Jack Richards paused. He had never thought about just what was the most important thing in his life. His wife and kids? No, better not go there. Surfing? Maybe. Money? Probably.

"L.J., if someone took surfing away from me, I'd probably think about doing something. But money? Now you're talking. Tell me the deal you had with Clark. Maybe my lawyers can shake him down for five, six figures."

"Fuck money! I want something else."

"What do you mean, fuck money? You're broke! What else is there?"

"I found the best big waves on the planet! Clark stole it from me and - - -"

"Yeah, I know all that. You already told me. What does that have to do with me?"

"What if we get there before Clark and Wavelife - and you're the first one to ride the most perfect big waves in the world?"

"Merrill, that's the same pitch you used to sell me a trip to Peru, remember? And it turned out to be nothing but huge storm surf pounding against sheer cliffs."

"Well, this time it's real! It is the heaviest thing I have ever seen! Here, see for yourself." Merrill pulled his digital camera out of his aluminum briefcase and turned the power on. The "battery low" light came on as he swung out the small LCD screen. He pushed play and handed the unit to Richards. Forty-five seconds later, Richards pushed the back search button and ran it again. He stared intently at the images, then hit the slow-motion button. He held the camera even closer, but the image suddenly went dark. "Battery out" flashed across the screen, and the unit switched off.

"Has anyone else seen this?"

"No, not except for Clark."

"And Roberto Mercante and Cheryl Corlund and Heath Larson and Noaloa and who know who else. Mercante and Clark flew to the South Pacific last fall and Corlund's in New York pitching an LBO. And Sonny-boy quit the tour and is training with Larson on Maui."

"How do you know all that?"

123

"Gossip on the websites, friends in the islands and connections on Wall Street. Something's up at Wavelife, that's for sure. Jeez, Merrill, you really want to take them on? Cheryl Corlund plays for keeps. Somebody who would trust a guy like Ian Clark doesn't have a chance in her league."

"That's why I need you, Jack. You are the only guy who can help me. I know how we can get there first and score the place as big as it gets. You offered me a job, and that's the job I want. We'll fuck Clark and Wavelife, and you'll get to ride the best waves of your life, I promise you."

"What's this going to run me?"

"C'mon, Richards," said Merrill, sensing his pride coming back to him, "If you have to ask how much it costs, you can't afford it. Isn't that what the rich always say?"

Richards burst out laughing. The rain had stopped and the skies were clearing a bit. He checked his watch and pulled out his wallet.

"Ok, L.J. You're on. I gotta get back to my office. Here's five hundred against fifteen hundred a week. What's next?"

* * *

Jack Richards took a look at the huge world map covering a wall of his office. The blue pins showed all the places he had surfed since he'd started in junior high school. The green pins showed all the places he had made money, starting with his first million, when he was fresh out of college with degrees in computer science and business administration, short selling stock in a start-up software company. More pins clustered around the Bay Area until the dotcom bubble burst and he got a law degree, turning to IPO's, junk bonds and takeovers nationwide before striking it rich in the arcane world of shareholder lawsuits. Now he was forty-three, and although he had surfed all over the world, there were more green pins on the map than blue ones.

He thought about Merrill's plan. The waves looked phenomenal, and there was something about Wavelife's involvement that got some old juices flowing again. It would be no problem to break the news at home that he was going to be training for a big surf trip that might last two to three months. His wife and two children were used to him being around only when it worked into his schedule. They had their gold credit cards and all the toys and gadgets they wanted, not to mention a huge house with a full time cook and go-fer to take care of them. His announcement would make little difference to them one way or the other.

That made him remember why giving them everything money could buy didn't give him any satisfaction: his wealth was nothing more than his obsession to always outdo himself. And here he was, once again, out to prove something, and as always, nobody but him would even care since the only thing he every truly cared about was himself. He knew his relationship with

124

his family had turned into nothing more than another transaction. He didn't have their love or their respect, and he knew why.

His therapist had told him the last time he saw the guy a few years ago. The only time his self-esteem was real was when he was making lots of money or surfing really well. But now, he realized, he didn't need more money, and if Merrill's plan worked, his surfing career would reach an ultimate plateau. Then what would he do with his life? Tell his wife and kids he was sorry and he was going to make it all up to them from that moment on? Maybe he should give his therapist a call.

He turned on his computer to find the number in his database. The desktop screen came up and his automatic programs kicked in, first to show his positions in the market, and then the swell models for surf around the world.

A half hour later, he remembered why he had turned on the computer in the first place. He opened a drawer and wrote "Call therapist" at the bottom of a long to-do list of things he never quite got around to. Then he went back to his stock analysts' on-line newsletters and prepared to make some trades while checking the wave action models for the Southern Hemisphere.

Blizzards

The line of cars stretched unbroken and unmoving down 7th Avenue. Cheryl Corlund sensed something wrong and looked up from her briefing book. Across from her in the limo was June Wilson, leafing through Wavelife's latest internal financials, completely immersed in data and unaware of time or space. Corlund glanced at her watch and at the traffic ahead of them. At this rate they would be late, and she did not want to start her pitch by apologizing for anything, even if it was a blizzard.

She looked out the window and saw the snowfall abating somewhat. That did it. She looked at her shoes, and then at Wilson's.

"June, June! Give me your shoes."

The analyst looked up and it took her a second to process what she'd heard.

"You aren't going to - - -"

"Just give me your shoes."

She took off her Guccis and put on Wilson's fur-lined snow boots. She pulled a snow hood up out of her parka and cinched it down around her head. The limo inched forward, but Corlund's mind was made up in more ways than one. She was ready to deal with New York on its own terms, a state of mind that gave rise to the thought of pulling the plug on the Wavelife surf team.

"And use the extra time to run through a valuation if we decreased marketing's surf team budget by ninety percent," she paused and opened the door, "And make it across the board: salaries, travel, contests, everything."

The driver looked in his mirror and couldn't believe what he was seeing. He jumped out and came around the back of the limo but there was nothing he could do except get out of her way.

Wavelife's CEO walked down the middle of the street between the line of cars until she got her bearings. She was in the heart of the garment district, and she knew all the shortcuts. She cut between two taxies and ducked into a doorway to enter the huge open assembly floor of a big women's wear label. She walked briskly through the aisles of Puerto Rican women concentrating at their industrial sewing machines. She avoided the glassed-in offices inhabited by old garmentos yelling at each other in their usual conversational tone. She dodged open bins filled with assembled garments and made a mental note to call Wavelife's design team. It looked like preppy was coming back. At the far end of the floor she pushed through two scarred and battered double doors into the cold of the loading dock. She walked down the concrete steps just as a truck backed in.

"Hold it Mack! Hey, lady, what the hell youse doin'?"

Corlund was not about to stop for any chitchat with the warehouse crew. The shortcut had saved her two blocks and she didn't have a minute to lose. She glanced at her watch and smiled. She lowered her shoulder and headed into the storm, becoming more invigorated with every step. She didn't mind dealing with a blizzard in New York. She could have cared less that she wasn't safe in first class at thirty thousand feet or poolside dozing in the warm winter sun in Newport Beach. She was exactly where she wanted to be, and a brisk walk through the garment district in a blinding snow storm was a good time to remind herself of the facts of life on her way to Wall Street.

There was no more room to grow in the surf industry because the action sports apparel business is notoriously volatile in the young male segment.

Our early investors made money thanks to creativity, innovation, and offering customers new choices. We hit a peak in the department stores, and did it again with the big box retailers.

But now creativity and innovation don't mean a thing. Bargain hunters have put us in the off-price outlets. Our shareholders made a lot of money for a long time. They bought in low and sold out high, and while we were climbing all the time, it was easy to find new investors.

But now our return on capital is turning negative, and that's the only thing of consequence to the analysts. Our sales numbers are up, and we're the undisputed leader of the surf industry. But margins are down, revenue growth has stalled, and that's the only thing that matters on the Street.

Being on top means nothing in a world where greed is everything. No matter how well we've done, they always wanted more, and when they didn't get it, our stock went south.

So I have to change everything. I have to start over. And I'm going to do it on my terms, not theirs.

Corlund turned a corner and saw her destination through the heavy snowfall where she would tell a panoramic story of her plans to use Wavelife's current plateau as a launchpad for herself and a few backers.

* * *

"Cheryl! Come in, come in! I'm happy to see you! Isn't this weather the worst! When I didn't hear from you I thought something must have happened!"

Ben Jeffries was a people person because it was good for business. The people who made money with him didn't know, and probably wouldn't have cared, his heart was alone and aloof and his being the gregarious sort was just a cunning and shrewd strategy.

"Why would I call? We said ten o'clock, and here I am."

She extended her hand to Jeffries. Her manners were impeccable, as she knew they had to be.

Sit down, sit down! I'm afraid the gang will be a little late, what with this storm and all."

"Well Ben, if a California girl can make it through a blizzard, I guess you New Yorkers are getting soft!"

His smile let her know he appreciated her moxie.

"Can I get you anything, Cheryl? Coffee, tea, a shot of brandy?"

"Yes, thank you, Ben. Coffee, black with a shot of Courvoisier. Oh, and while you're up, will you also get me nine-hundred and seventy-two million dollars?"

Jeffries looked her straight in the eye, his eyebrows lifting slightly.

"Well, nothing like a woman who knows exactly she wants!"

They both laughed. It was a good beginning.

* * *

It was past noon when Cheryl Corlund pushed her chair back from the conference table. The men around the table moved their chairs to stand as she rose. The meeting had gone well so far, and Corlund was confident she could leave the room for a few minutes.

"No, please, gentlemen, be seated. I'll be right back."

As soon as the door closed the best-dressed man at the table got straight to the point.

"Ben, I think we can do a bit of business here, don't you?" said John Vutara, leaning back in his chair and taking the reading glasses from his nose.

"Should be a piece of cake!" said Jeffries, looking at Peter Lasserman who'd seen enough executive summaries to know this deal was within spec, so far. It wasn't big money, but things were a bit slow on the Street and with Jeffries leading the charge, the downside for his company would be minimal.

"Concur," said Lasserman, who then looked at the man sitting next to him. But Bruce Kaufman was engrossed in a legal pad that Lasserman could see was full of abbreviations and figures.

"Don't you have a staff for that stuff, Bruce?"

Kaufman looked up and stared at Lasserman. "Well, I don't like to waste their time if things don't add up for me. And since it is my name on the door, I don't have the luxury of double-talking my investors."

Ben Jeffries quickly moved in to de-fuse the friction. "Well, I think we'll all do just fine here, don't you, Bruce? Say, its lunchtime! Oh, and I hope you guys like swordfish. Can't get it in the restaurants anymore but I flew some in from the West Coast. Let me call my chef and see if it's ready."

Cheryl Corlund walked with authority down the richly carpeted hallway. She opened a side door into a room looking like someone had left a window open and the blizzard had blown in. But there were no windows. It was a blizzard of paper and data that covered the table and all four walls.

The room was filled with a dozen men and women along with sheaves of documents, spreadsheet print-outs and laptops. June Wilson was carefully guiding three men through Wavelife's cost centers displayed behind her on a huge white board covered with product icons and sales figures. A small group was seated at one end of the table watching a powerpoint. Others were deep into spreadsheets printed on fanfold printouts hanging from the walls. One guy was standing in the corner waiting to feed a document into the fax machine after it was done spewing out a stack of faxes.

Wilson saw Corlund come in and excused herself from the presentation to the lead analysts representing Jeffries, Lasserman and Vutara. All the other people in the room worked for them.

"Jeffries' people seem pretty excited, though Lasserman's wish there was more money in it just to make things interesting."

"Well, we're not here to entertain them with a 'Barbarians at the Gate' circus. How about Vutara's crew?"

"Steady as she goes, though they do count their pennies."

Corlund saw the guy at the fax machine.

"I told you nothing was to leave your sight!"

June Wilson was a pro. She reacted as if Corlund's comment had been a snake crossing her path. She didn't hesitate to pin its head to the ground with a spiked heel.

"Here are the non-disclosures. That guy is faxing an order for some Chinese takeout. I've got everything under control, and why aren't Kaufman's people here?"

"The money isn't big enough, so he'll be running the numbers himself," admitted Corlund sheepishly while remembering that Kaufman had not signed a non-disclosure, "I'd better get back to Ben's office."

"Yeah, good idea, Cheryl, and don't forget their non-disclosures. And wiping out surf marketing increases our return on capital by point-eight-zero-three per share," said Wilson with a look that almost had Corlund cowering.

"Uh, that's great."

"That's better than great, Madam CEO, as I'm sure you are well aware. Anything else you want to know Miss Big Shot?"

"Touche!" she laughed, "How much longer do you need?"

"After lunch, about another two hours should do it. Oh, and I want my boots back. These stupid Guccis are killing me!"

Cheryl Corlund smiled as she closed the door on the boiler room and headed back to the eagle's aerie.

* * *

The light through the floor-to-ceiling windows was fading early thanks to the storm blowing hard outside. It was pushing four o'clock, but Cheryl Corlund's clothes were still pin perfect. As for her pitch, it had been equally expensive and decisive thanks to a mind that had only become sharper as the meeting wore on.

"And you are certain your board will pose no difficulties?" asked John Vutara, thinking about the optics of the deal.

"Since today's exploratory talks have gone well, I strongly anticipate getting the directors to act, and quickly."

"Well, as you know, board cohesiveness and unanimous approval are essential in these situations. We can't afford any delays, or else - - - "

Vutara left the implications hanging in the air. Peter Lasserman flew them home. "With the company in play, who knows who else will try to match our bid. And we don't want that, now do we?"

"Gentlemen, the directors recognize their fiduciary responsibilities to the shareholders. This buyout is very much to that end. We will execute it quickly and quietly."

"That's good enough for me. How about you, John?" Lasserman looked at Vutara. He was taking the wire-frame glasses off his nose and putting them carefully away in his breast pocket.

"Yes, there is nothing amiss here."

They both looked at Cheryl Corlund, and with a slight nod of their heads they confirmed their readiness to back her plan. All three then looked at Ben Jeffries, but he was looking at Bruce Kaufman and didn't like what he saw. Kaufman was examining a painting on the wall, obviously ignoring the exchange between Corlund and the investment bankers. Too obviously.

"Say Ben, I didn't know you collected Pollock. A bit abstract for a guy like you, no?"

Jeffries instantly got the message from Kaufman. He was out, and this had all been a waste of his time.

"Well, it's tripled since I bought it, and I'm never one to pass up a good investment," he said. The implication was clear, but Kaufman didn't bite, and that was that.

"Cheryl," said Jeffries, turning away from Kaufman and beaming a fresh smile across the table, "Barring any surprises from down the hall, and I'm sure there won't be any, you can count on us."

"Thank you. And thank you for your time gentlemen. I know you all have bigger fish to fry - - -"

"Or bigger waves to ride!" chuckled John Vutara.

"Or bigger waves to ride," said Corlund. She knew any sign of wavering or contingency plans would hurt her cause. She touched the nail in her pocket and concluded with one last pitch.

"Gentlemen, thanks to your support, the Wavelife LBO plan will stand the test of time and deliver substantial returns on your investment."

"Cheryl, I think we all agree with you," said Ben Jeffries.

Speak for yourself, Jeffries, Kaufman smirked to himself, *Once these old guys get a hint of their sexuality revitalized, they're goners.*

"Well, I'll give you a call if I need to see all the data for myself someday," he said, "and but for your excellent hospitality, Ben, I might have been more comfortable with the bean-counters down the hall. It has been a pleasure, Cheryl, and we'll be in touch."

He stood up quickly, surprising Corlund and the men at the table. Kaufman reached over to shake hands with Vutara, Lasserman and Jeffries, all sitting within arm's reach. But Corlund was at the far end of the table. For a moment he hesitated, waiting for her to stand up and walk around the table to extend her hand as is customary for a lady to do to a gentleman. She stood up, but that's as far as she would go. The slight was not lost on Bruce Kaufman, though of course he didn't let it show.

"Thanks for your time, Bruce," she said, "I look forward to providing you with more information as necessary."

They both knew that was bullshit, but they both smiled anyway. Kaufman turned and walked towards the double oak doors. Jeffries quickly stood up and hastened to open one of them.

"Thanks for a great lunch, Ben."

"Thanks for coming, Bruce."

Jeffries gave him an old boy slap on the back. Kaufman returned the gesture with a thin smile and a nod. Jeffries watched him walk down the hall and the smile disappeared from his face. He let the door close slowly before turning around and back into his usual beaming self.

"Say, guys, ready for a martini? How about you, Cheryl? You did very well this afternoon."

"Thanks Ben, but I've got to get going," said Corlund with a wink, now that she could let her guard down, "I just hope it was as good for you as it was for me. I'll give you a call tomorrow!"

"That's what they all say!"

Everyone laughed loudly, and the cordial goodbyes from the three gentlemen to Cheryl Corlund left a glow in the room that was the essence of a good deal in the offing.

Downtime

The morning breeze was dying in the palms. It wasn't quite seven a.m. and the day promised to be a scorcher. The South Seas may be the romantic idyll of dreamers around the world, but with a long day of problems ahead of him, it was just another place to earn a living for Mac Owens.

He walked across the hangar floor, entered a small office and was happy to see a trail of paper falling out of the fax machine. He took the fax to the machine shop and straight to a long metal table where the parts of a disassembled motor were arranged in an orderly fashion. Checking the cutaway diagram and parts list on the fax, he then studied several parts in the center of the table. They were bent, twisted and torn. Next to them was an open box with the replacements. He picked up each broken part, then the new one. His eyes went back to the fax, then back to the parts.

"Son-of-a-" He caught himself just in time, or it would have cost him a buck. He fined himself every time he broke his New Year's resolution, and the jar on his desk was already half full of bills and a lot of change. He went back to his office and hit the send bar on the radio transmitter.

"Victor Tango, this is Grease Monkey, cum in please."

"Grease Monkey, this is Victor Tango. Good morning Mac. Wrong parts, right?"

"Morning Tina. Yup. Ya know I wouldn't be havin' these problems if it wern't fer Ian Clark an' his damn jetskis."

"Don't get started, Mac. What do you want to do?"

"Fly back ta Florida an'd walk in the factory an' throw this piece o' crap at whoever can't read simple English."

"Well, you did say trying to use electric hoists instead of hand-winches was something that might work, as opposed to something that would work."

Owens had to laugh.

"That's correct, Madam Captain. Six differnt makes, five pieces of s-h-i-t. An' the one that did survive still failed 'fore she got ta two thousand pounds. An' then I do 'em a favor an' pinpoint the damn problem, an' they send me the wrong damn parts!"

"Hmm, so far that's four bad words, even if you spelled one. But to a lady, well, better put a twenty in the jar, Mac."

Owens almost cost himself another five, but bit his tongue.

"Will do, ma'am. My sincere apologies."

"Apology accepted. Any good news?"

"Engine work on schedule. Electrical panel re-wired. Landin' gear greased, and - - -" Mac Owens stopped in mid-sentence. He grabbed a pencil and scribbled a quick sketch to cut his jetski lift problems in half.

"What, Mac, another idea?" Tina Sanchez knew her flight engineer well.

"Mebbe. Anyway, the starboard engine is almost ready to re-mount, an'I'll get on the port one next week. Valves within spec, but I can tell ya with alla this weight an' drag, if we have any seaway problems gettin' outta there, we'll hafta run tha heads at max temp to git on step. An' then the problem won't be the valves, it'll be the head itself. An' if we ever hafta replace it, she's gonna cost an arm and a leg."

"Well, if memory serves correctly, all our costs will be covered."

Mac Owens had another idea.

"Say, Tina, why don' I go ta Florida? Only way I'll ever be able ta trus' this 'lectric hoist is ta go ta their factory, stress test the units, an' have 'em make me sumtin' that won't break."

Tina Sanchez could hear a lot more in Owens' voice than just his need to go to the source of his problems to solve them.

"Mac, I think that's a wonderful idea."

"What's a wonderful idea?" It was Victor Sanchez, walking onto the porch of their open air home with a Hawaiian sling spear and goggles in one hand and a string of fish slung over his shoulder.

Tina turned to her husband with a smile. "Mac thinks he needs a vacation."

"No I don't, Tina!" said Owens, but his tone had a laugh behind it, "I jes need to git 'xactly what I need an' there's only one way ta do that."

"Well, let's just call our friend Ian Clark and tell him we'll be spending some of his money," said Victor, "How about first class to Paris, and then a hop to Miami at your leisure?"

"As much as I'd like ta stick it ta Clark under entirely honest circumstances, January ain't much fun in France. I think straight home would suit me jes fine, thankee!" Owens let his Florida drawl syrup all over his words at the mere thought of seeing St. Pete again.

"What do you think, two weeks?"

"Nah, Tina, I don' like the place all THAT much. I'm only goin' fer parts, not a snowbird vacation."

"Only going for parts! You DO need a vacation," said Victor Sanchez, "Three weeks then. Let's get you out of here tomorrow morning. I'll call Clark right now. I hear he's a pretty good travel agent."

"No, I'll call him, dear. You go make us some breakfast!"

"You want to fly Mac Owens Tahiti-Miami round trip first class for some parts? You can't be serious!"

"Ian, I don't think you understand, so let me spell it out for you, ok?"

"Sure, Tina, go right ahead."

"The problem is you sold Wavelife on using the *Skyhook* to get everyone and all their equipment to the reef. The wings can take the load of the jetskis, but the problem is the original bomb hoists for a PBY were cable-and-crank

133

systems to be used on a runway, not the ocean. So hand-cranking won't work. It's too slow."

"Well, so what? We're in no hurry."

"We would be if for some reason we'd have to get airborne quickly. It's our biggest problem right now, and Mac's been testing electric hoists that'll fit in the wings."

"So that's what those invoices were for. Couldn't you have found cheaper ones?"

"How cheap do you want to go when your whole project is on the line?"

"Ok, ok, I get the picture," he said reluctantly, knowing she was right.

"Ian, we simply have to trust Mac when it comes to anything mechanical. You may not like him, and he certainly has his feelings about you. Shackleton didn't like McNeish either, but he saved the entire expedition."

"Yeah, I know. L.J. told me that story too and - - - "Clark caught himself at the mention of his old partner. Back in better times they had some ideas about adventure surfing in the Southern Ocean after Merrill became fascinated with the lore surrounding Ernest Shackleton's expedition in 1914. They even went to South Georgia Island to scout surf sites close to where Shackleton had landed after a miraculous voyage in a small boat fixed up by ship's carpenter Paddy McNeish to survive the Southern Ocean.

"You know, Ian, maybe you should - - -"said Tina Sanchez, thinking wistfully of L.J. Merrill and how this whole thing was somehow off kilter. But Clark closed down his heart fast. One glance at the data stream on his computer and it was back to business.

"I should get off this phone and get Mac his tickets. Anything else?"

"Mac needs the jet skis themselves when he gets back in three weeks. We want to start test runs by early April."

"Ok, will do. Bye, Tina."

"Take care Ian," said Tina Sanchez sincerely, her woman's instinct sensing a man who was his own worst enemy and doing nothing about it.

* * *

A tall Florida boy in his mid-50s, dressed in bulky overalls and a woolen cap, was working on the port engine of his PBY Supercat. A cold snap was wrecking the orange crop across the state, but Clem Charleton wasn't about to slip his maintenance schedule for anything short of a hurricane – or the surprise appearance of an old friend.

"Son of a gun! Mac Owens!"

"Clem, if I'da known it was gonna be this cold I'da stayed in Tahiti!"

"Well all ya gotta do is get on the ol' Internet these days. Got alla info ya need fer practically everythin', ol' boy!"

"Yeah, I know, but who wants ta know more'n they needs to? One thing did catch my eye, though. Saw ya got yer own website an' all tryin' to sell yer Cat. Any bites?"

"Nah, not yet."

"Mebbe half a mill is a bit steep, doncha think?"

"Nope. I'm pre-qualifyin' her next owner, so ta speak. Say, Mac, ya ever run into a problem with the clutch discs inside the starter motor? The dang things keep crappin' out on me."

"Yeah, they started usin' auto tranny discs. Git 'em in Mexico 'cause they ran outta the 'riginals. Ain't aircraft spec anymore."

"Yeah, I thought twas sumtin' like that," said Charleton as he finished tightening the motor mounts before climbing down to greet his old friend.

"How long ya stayin'?"

"'bout three weeks. Didja git my e-mail?"

"Probly. What it say?"

"'bout the 'lectric hoists fer the wings."

"Well, Mac, as I recall I did git an e-mail fulla cussin' when y'all broke a bunch by tryin' to put twice the spec load on 'em!" Charleton laughed.

"Yeah, the one ya recommended lasted longer 'n all the others, so - - -"

"So lemme guess – they sent ya the wrong part, an' you're here to raise hell with 'em!"

"Yup, an' mebbe raise sum hell with you, too!" laughed Owens as a cold winter wind blew through the hangar, "Say, how long ya gonna work out here in the frozen north? Let's go get a drink, whaddayasay?"

Clem Charleton needed no encouragement.

"Someone flies seven thousand miles fer parts, I'll buy 'em a drink!"

* * *

"Remember when we worked tha orange groves 'round Orlando? You wouldn't believe what they got goin' on up there now. Damn convention center so big they run four shows at the same time. This week ya got yer hotel operators, yer mainframe computers, motorbike 'cessories, an' surfin' stuff. Next week gonna be diesel engines, water beds, an' who knows what all. I tell 'ya, Mac, only way to make a livin' anymore is sellin' stuff!"

"Well, here's to the great marketplace, Clem, may it never darken the doors of our hangars!"

The two men clinked their tumblers of whiskey and rye as Tom Petty came over the jukebox and the men sang along, *"One foot in the grave, one foot on the pedal, I was born a rebel!"*

"Clem, ya say they got a surfin' show runnin' up there?"

"Yeah, m' daughter told me 'bout it. She 'n my son-in-law got themselves a surf shop. She's mindin' the store with my grandson cuz Tommy's over there buyin' stuff. An' he's got hisself a booth, too. He's tryin' to drum up a bizzness sellin', hell, I think he's sellin' surf trunks made outta plastic or sumtin'. "

135

"Hey Clem," drawled Mac Owens as the whiskey was starting to soak in, "Let's take a ride. I haven't seen yer daughter since she was this high, an' I better take a look at yer grandson. Make sure he ain't takin' after you!"

"Sure, Mac, why not? The little guy's gonna be a pilot sumday, I tell ya," said Charleton, "Here's to the future o' aviation!"

Glasses were drained and re-filled.

"But mebbe first we should stop by an' say hello to Tommy while we're at it," said Owens, "I gotta hunch 'bout sumtin'."

"Nah, parkin' round there's a nightmare. We'll jes wait 'till Tommy comes home. 'sides, why the hell would we wanna go to sum goddam trade show?"

"'Cause there might be a guy there who wants to buy a PBY. An' he can meet yer price!"

"Well, in that case, what are we waitin' fer? Let's git on it!"

They knocked back the rest of their drinks, tossed twenties on the counter, and told the bartender to keep the change on their way out. The veteran seaplane pilots had their engines revved, their flight plan agreed upon, and they weren't about to wait for clearance to take off.

The run up A1A brought back a lot of old times for two ol' boys in a vintage black Charger. But memory lane ended at the Orlando off ramp, with Disney World, Magic Mountain, Sea World and dozens of restaurants and hotels in every direction. It would have been a bit of a shock except for the 110 proof fueling their impromptu adventure. They were oblivious on their own terms and loving every minute of it. Finally they saw the huge convention center buildings in the distance and Clem Charleton pulled out his cell phone.

"Tommy, Clem here! Y'all never guess where I'm callin' from. I'll give ya one hint. Jes which of those hangars you in?" he asked, looking out across the thousands of cars at two huge buildings the size of a dozen football fields.

"What the hell ya doin' here, Clem? Come alla way up ta visit yer grandson? Dana an' the baby are at the shop."

"I know, an' that's where we're goin'. But I got an' ol' buddy a' mine sittin' here, an' he wanted to stop by first cuz he says he knows sum honcho who might be here. Guy's lookin' to buy a PBY!"

"Well, first we gotta gitcha in here, Clem. Look fer the signs that say west pavilion, concourse one, an' park close as ya can. Then head fer the main gate."

"We gonna need passes ta get in or sumptin?"

"Damn right. I'll have 'em ready fer ya at will call."

"Ok, boy, where we gonna find ya in there?"

"Ask 'em fer a map. I'm way out in the low rent district!" he laughed.

"All right, Tommy, here we come. Over an' out."

Charleton clicked off the phone as he wheeled into the main parking lot keeping the Dodge power plant at a rumbling idle.

"Ok, Mr. co-pilot, we're looking for a tie down somewhere close to that big hangar to port. Say, Mac, this runway don' have any landin' gear skid marks on it – we must be the first blackcat to ever set down here!"

"Yup, well, why doncha jes fix that right now!"

Clem Charleton slammed the Hurst into first and floored it. He peeled rubber for fifty yards, and you could hear the rebel yells over the roar of the four twenty seven.

Roberto Mercante had stationed a Wavelife employee outside the pavilion's main entrance to call him the instant Sonny-boy Noaloa, Heath Larson and Bruddah arrived. When he got the call, Mercante signaled his trade show manager to get ready to start up one of Wavelife's famous show-stoppers announcing Noaloa's arrival. Then he made his way quickly to the front entrance to get his surf star ready. But when he saw the three men waiting just outside the entrance, he suddenly had big problems. Sonny-boy Noaloa was on crutches and people were starting to recognize him and Larson. Mercante saw some space behind the palm trees and plywood facade that had been set up as a portal to the show.

"C'mere, guys."

A second later, the four men were effectively hidden from public view as Mercante tried to hatch a plan.

"Jeez, Sonny, I didn't know your knee was that bad. That kinda messes things up."

"Roberto, this whole place is messed up," said Heath Larson.

"Yeah, Heath, I know what you think," said Mercante with no patience in his voice, "But it pays the bills, including yours. Next time we're surfing fifty footers, I'll listen to you. Right now, you and Bruddah kill some time and then come over to our place. Sonny, here's the deal."

He flipped out his cell phone and hit a pre-set. "Johnny, hold off the parade until I call you back." He listened for a second.

"Oh, shit."

He glanced through the plate glass doors and saw a phalanx of gorgeous women in high heels and bikinis marching down the main concourse towards the entrance. Two were holding a banner that read, "When It Counts!" Six more carried surfboards, and the rest had their arms full of goodie bags. Mercante had to think fast.

"Ok, Sonny-boy, lose the crutches and just take a few steps towards the door, ok?"

"Roberto, I do a lotta walkin' it gonna hurt like hell!"

"Then it will hurt like hell, Sonny-boy. There's a lot of money riding on this," said Mercante, turning to Larson and Bruddah, "See you guys inside. Wait for me in my tent around the back."

The arena PA came alive.

"Now arriving at the main gate, this year's Pipeline Champion, Sonny-boy Noaloa. The two time world champion will be signing autographs over at Wavelife."

Mercante knew Sonny-boy's entrance needed to have as much impact as his first wave at Pipe, and it did. When the women got to the door, Mercante spoke quickly in Portuguese. The two strongest, volleyball players from Brazil, immediately lifted Wavelife's top surf star to their shoulders. A second later, a booming rap bass came out of the arena sound system. A samba beat dropped in on top of it. Buyers from Midwest chain stores stopped fingering t-shirts made in Malaysia. Strippers grinding for the sunglass companies were ignored. The beat got louder as business stopped in its tracks throughout the arena. Even the noise from the skate ramps was drowned out.

A crowd began to gather and exhibitors along the trade show city's Main Street gritted their teeth. The surfboards were held high and surrounded Sonny like spears. They were molded plastic made in Romania and looked exactly like the one Sonny had ridden at Pipe. Each had a large number attached. Then the trombones picked up a groove over the rhythm tracks on the P.A. and Wavelife's chairman became the Music Man leading the big parade.

"Win a board just like Sonny's! Find the ticket and win the board!" shouted Mercante, throwing raffle tickets high in the air.

Quickly a ringer picked one up off the floor and handed it to Mercante.

"We have a winner!"

Mercante gave the daughter of a Wavelife manager one of the boards, and she marched off with a big smile on her face and out the front entrance, as instructed. People started to scramble around on the floor grabbing the raffle tickets. Teenagers began running towards the main concourse. The schwag bags were tossed to the crowd like loaves of bread to a starving mob. Things would have been out of control in just a few more seconds except that Mercante was a seasoned pro at this stuff. Security was right on time and six thick men and women in Wavelife tanktops stretched yellow "Do Not Cross" tape around a moving perimeter to protect what was, for the moment, the core of Wavelife's marketing machine as it paraded through the heart of the trade show.

At the red carpet entrance to the Wavelife sales center, Noaloa's bearers turned so he could face the cheering throng as the last of the surfboards was given away. Mercante liked the "Caesar entering Rome" imagery, though for Sonny-boy Noaloa it felt more like a shot of whiskey to a dried-out desert prospector. He was on top of the world smiling in the sunlight of stardom - until the v-ball betties lowered him to the floor. A shot of pain went from his knee to his brain, but Roberto Mercante was right there to hold him up until an assistant slid a chair under the former world champ. Mercante hit a preset on his cell phone, barked an order, and a second later, the horns-rap-samba music cut off and the P.A. announcer read his script.

"Sonny-boy Noaloa is signing autographs right now at the Wavelife center – don't miss your chance to see this year's Pipeline Champion! He's at Wavelife right now! Get your poster of Sonny in the barrel at Pipe – right where he'll always be when it counts!"

As the slogan echoed throughout the arena, the banner was stretched behind Noaloa by two smiling models falling out of their bikinis. The music cranked up again, though now through the mega-amp sound system built into the Wavelife installation. Two Wavelife models positioned a table in front of Sonny-boy. Two more brought boxes of Pipeline posters and souvenir pens. The security detail used more yellow tape to herd the crowd into line.

Within minutes Noaloa's scribbled name was practically illegible, but penmanship was hardly an issue at this point because there were fans lined up around the block. Mercante waited a while until the end of the line was finally in sight, and Noaloa's hand was a massive cramp, before he made his next move. With a showman's instinct to always leave 'em asking for more, he picked up the stack of posters and began to give them out to the people in line.

"Come back tomorrow and Sonny will sign 'em for you! Thanks for coming! And don't miss our fashion show at five!"

"Well, finally! Yer out in the boonies, aintcha, Tommy!" said Clem Charleton as they walked up to a bare-bones booth next to a nose-ring wholesaler and across the aisle from the latest skater shoe company.

"Hi Clem, hi Mr. Owens, how y'all doin'?"

"Jes fine, son. How's business? Anybody stoppin by?"

"Nah, Wavelife jes' did sum big shebang when Sonny-boy Noaloa showed up. I'll be lucky to see anyone down here fer the rest o' the day."

"So Tommy, where'd ya git the idea fer these trunks?" asked Mac Owens, fingering a sample on the display table.

"Long time back an outfit called Patagonia did a line of clothes made from the same stuff. But no one ever followed their lead, so I figgered I saw me a niche."

"Helluva good idea! Keep all dat plastic outta the landfills! I bet yer gonna do real well, young man!" said Clem Charleton.

"Well so far I'm gittin' nowhere. All the big industry players got contracts signed to kingdom come with offshore cotton mills an' garment 'semblers jes this side o' sweat shops. An' I can't sell 'em to the surf shops o' the chain buyers neither. They never take a chance on anythin' new."

"Well, mebbe I kin talk to someone over at Wavelife," said Owens, "Say, Tommy, tell me, ya ever heard of a guy named Roberto Mercante?"

"Hell yes. Guy's an asshole fer as I'm concerned. Why ya askin'?"

"I met 'im cupla months ago an' we're gonna be flyin' him 'round Tahiti later this year. Said he's interested in a PBY."

"Hell, with the kinda money he makes, he kin afford it!"

"Well, let's go see what he's up to. We'll be back in a little while," said Clem Charleton.

His son-in-law watched the two men walk away down the empty aisle. There wasn't a buyer in sight, so he settled back in a folding metal chair and wondered what it would be like to own a seaplane. He closed his eyes for a second and rubbed the weariness out of them. He thought of his wife and baby boy and realized he still had hours to go before closing. He looked at his samples, and then looked up to see a buyer walking down the aisle. He jumped to his feet like a surfer who wasn't going to let a wave go by.

"Hi, I'm Tommy Pratte, an' kin I show you something new an' important for the future of surfin' an' our environment?"

Roberto Mercante did a quick walkthrough of the sales center on the way to his "office". He made sure the "When It Counts!" graphics were everywhere. He checked the point-of-purchase displays of all the shoes, shirts, jackets, hats, watches, wetsuits, backpacks, cellphones, bikinis, surf shorts, and three dozen other products branded by Wavelife International. Marketing had signed off on the entire installation before it was shipped from the setup warehouse, but business was brisk, and he had to keep checking on everything since as soon as Surf Expo ended, he'd be doing it all over again in Vegas for CIGAM and then on to New York for the spring runway shows. He felt like a rock tour manager, complete with backstage problems.

Heath Larson and Bruddah were sitting with Sonny-boy Noaloa after two models had carried him on their shoulders around the outside of the Wavelife sales center to the enclosed pop-up. The tent flap opened and Mercante stepped in like a man who'd just been through a hurricane and now had to deal with a mudslide.

"Ok, Sonny-boy, What's the deal with your knee?"

"Da guy on Maui say I have to stay off it much as possible. Heath got me take alla dis homeo stuff fo' help to heal, but - - -"

"What about the jet ski training? What happened to that?"

"We got him one da kine brace, get lotta driving practice," said Bruddah.

"But marching in parades was not something we'd anticipated," said Larson with a distinct edge to his voice. But Sonny-boy didn't mind the parade so much as what he had to do when it was over.

"Hey, mahalo fo' da parade an' stuffs, but next time, no make sign so many postah, ok Roberto?"

"What else can you do with a bum knee? And now I've got to figure out what we are going to do with you for the rest of the show."

It was obvious to the receptionist at the Wavelife sales center that the two flyers, in their leather jackets and smelling faintly of good whiskey, were not buyers with appointments. But they weren't going to take no for an answer.

"Lissen, honey, I jes know Mr. Mercante wants ta see us eeemeedeeatly," drawled Mac Owens.

"But sir, your names are not on the list. And I'm sure he's very busy."

"Well, kin ya do us a favor, dear, if ya please? Kin ya page 'im? An' jes tell 'im the flight engineer from the *Skyhook* is out front. An' thankee very much fer yer trouble, ma'am."

While the receptionist dialed a number, Clem Charleton got a bit antsy.

"Mac, ya sure 'bout this? Tommy didn't think too highly of this guy."

"Well, Clem, les jes see what happens next," grinned Mac Owens, "I think y'all jes might be pleasantly surprised."

140

"What he gonna do da rest of da show? He gonna do nutin, brah, cuz he need stay offa da knee," said a glowering Bruddah.

"Yeah, Roberto, we're here because Cheryl needs us to meet your new backers. Then you tell us to stop by here on the way," said an equally unhappy Heath Larson, "but you never said we'd have to deal with a bunch of trade show bullshit!"

"Yeah, I know, but hell, that parade was something, wasn't it? C'mon, guys, gimme a break!"

His cell phone beeped.

"Mr. Mercante, two men are here and said you'd want to talk to them, but their names aren't on the list."

"Well, then don't let them in."

"I know, but one said to tell you he was the flight engineer on the *Skyhook*. Should I - - - "

"I'll be right there! Sonny, stay off the knee. Heath, Bruddah, I'll be right back. There's someone you guys should meet."

Mercante exited the tent and walked through the sales area where a buyer was starting to make a stink and getting loud about it.

"You never made me put 50% down before! This is bullshit! I don't need to be treated this way! I've got a fat open-to-buy budget, and - - -"

Mercante recognized the guy as the owner of a chain of surf shops in Texas. He knew there wasn't any money in servicing those small accounts, but he didn't need any more headaches.

"Bob, good to see you again! Is there a problem? Julie, be sure to give Bob his usual terms. Good to see you, bro!" Mercante nodded to the Wavelife rep, who immediately re-engaged her customer.

"Two ten e.o.m. - does that work for you, Bob? And no interest for ninety days, ok? Now, can I show you our new thongs?" She called over to where a group of models waited salaciously. "Maria! Tawny! Why don't you change into the Rio line! I'm sure you'll like what you see, Bob."

"Now that's more like it," said the Texan.

"Mac Owens! What are you doing here? I thought you were working on the *Skyhook*!"

"Well, Roberto, that's what I'm doin' in a roundabout way. In fact, Clem here helped me with the hoists we're gonna need to get yer jet skis under the wings. Lemme introduce ya, an' by the way, he's got a PBY fer sale."

"Well, that's, that's, that's great, Mac!"

It took Mercante a few seconds for everything to register. But since glad-handing was a core competency at trade shows, Mercante's auto pilot was functioning as he extended his hand to Clem Charleton.

"Hi, I'm Roberto Mercante, pleased to meet you, and thanks for helpin' out on our project. And you've got a PBY you want to sell?"

141

"Yeah, well mebbe," said Charleton, sizing up the Brazilian millionaire as if was the last guy in the world to whom he would sell his beloved Catalina, "I don't know if I want to sell her right now."

"Well, let's go in and talk about it. Is she a 5A or a 6A or is she a SuperCat? Does she have the 1830-92 engines? How many hours you got on 'em? What's her fuel consumption fully loaded? Oh, and that reminds me, Mac! I want you to meet the boys who'll be surfing the reef!"

Big Time, Being and Nothingness

A thirty foot power boat nosed out into Tampa Bay with four surfers, two seaplane flyers and a slum-kid-turned-millionaire aboard.

"I thought we gonna meet the boss onna yacht! She no onna dis boat!"

"Of course not, Sonny-boy. This isn't the yacht. That is!"

Heath Larson pointed across the bay to a palace of lights floating on an illuminated sea.

"Look like one kine aircraft carrier in Pearl Harbor!" said Bruddah.

"I hope he's not another big time wheeler dealer looking to make some money in the surf industry," moaned a jet-lagged Aleja Gracellen, "But Cheryl said he was a nice guy, so here we are, I guess."

"Well, Aleja, for one thing, there isn't this guy's kinda money in the surf industry, and for another, you don't get this rich being a nice guy."

"Uh, Heath, no talking about money, ok? It just isn't done in certain circles," stammered Mercante, unable to take his eyes off the megayacht.

Bruddah and Larson couldn't help but laugh at that one. And Mac Owens was right behind them.

"Mr. Mercante," said Mac Owens, who had switched to bourbon in the limo, "I shore du 'preciate you in-vitin' me an' Clem to cum 'long, yup. An' you kin count on us to make sure y'all make a helluva good impression!"

"Shoots, I wonder how much that sell for?" said Sonny-boy, completely awestruck.

"Well, young man, as J.P. Morgan once said, 'If yuh hafta ask how much, yuh cain't afford it." said Charleton, who had been around big time wealth before and wasn't all that keen on being stuck with the experience yet again. But the bourbon was the best, spending time with Mac Owens was priceless, and so far, Roberto Mercante had asked a lot of good questions about his PBY without asking how much it cost.

The tender came up behind the megayacht. "*Aeolusean* – New York" was painted in swirls of blue and gold across the transom almost forty feet wide. Lights built into the hull below the waterline lit up the water all the way down to the sandy bottom.

"She'd make a helluva squid boat, if ya didn't hafta pay yer fuel bill," said Mac Owens, "Prob'ly cost ya close to hunnerd grand to fill 'er up."

"Hundred tousand dolla? For gas?" exclaimed Noaloa.

"Hell yeah, an mebbe more," said Charleton, "Boat this size probly got thirty, forty thousand gallon tanks. Enough ta fill up a damn swimmin' pool. 'Course she's probly got one of those, too."

143

"Fo' reals!?"

"Yessirree, young man," said Mac Owens, "Yer 'bout to have yer eyes opened. Didja ever read Fitzgerald?"

"The rich are different than you and I," quoted Heath Larson.

"C'mon, Heath, Cheryl needs us to make a good impression, so let's try to be good guests, ok?" said Mercante.

"Yeah, Heath," said Gracellen, "We owe Cheryl at least that much."

"Yeah, maybe," said Larson sarcastically, "But you don't end up owning a megayacht by being Mr. Mellow."

Cheryl Corlund knew Ben Jeffries was an astute judge of character, and after the meeting in his office, she had suggested he meet the surfers who would be the core of Wavelife's new image. He thought that was a grand idea and suggested a weekend on his yacht. Corlund checked her calendar, and Jeffries made arrangements to move the *Aeolusean* from the Bahamas to Tampa Bay for the weekend of the surf expo in Orlando. Corlund then had her husband call Heath to have him, Sonny-boy and Bruddah fly in from Hawai'i, and she'd personally called Aleja Gracellen because she knew Jeffries would appreciate her bearing and personality, key image points in Corlund's vision for expanding outside the surf industry. She also suggested that June Wilson and Bill Massara be a part of the weekend aboard the yacht, and Ben Jeffries wholeheartedly agreed. And when Roberto called from the trade show to tell her the flight engineer from the *Skyhook* was in Florida visiting a friend and that they'd happened to stop by, she had her husband invite him to come along for the weekend to round out a complete picture of her plan. Now it was all coming together, and Corlund couldn't have been more pleased as the tender approached the megayacht. She was standing with Wilson and Massara on an upper deck, watching Ben Jeffries and two of his grandchildren welcome the surfers and the flyers aboard the *Aeolusean*.

After a complete tour of the megayacht, or as much as they could see in an hour's time, they all sat down to a four-star Michelin dinner on gold leaf china embossed with the image of the Greek god of the wind, Aeolus.

The after-dinner movie in the private theater was a classic western, "Red River". It was an unlikely choice, but Jeffries had picked the classic Howard Hawks western for good reason: it was about as far from a fifty million dollar megayacht as one could imagine. That suited Charleton and Owens just fine. They knew the movie by heart and, between sips of bourbon, were saying lines from the movie word for word. After the movie Sonny-boy went off to play video games with the kids. In the main salon, Aleja was poised and delightful discussing the art on the walls with Jeffries, Wilson and Massara. And Owens and Charleton talked seaplane story with Roberto and Bruddah. It was all Cheryl Corlund could have hoped for, except for one thing. Though she did her best to make him feel comfortable by getting him to engage in the conversations around the room, she was unable to prevent Heath Larson from becoming increasingly ill-at-ease as the night wore on.

144

The clock was climbing towards midnight when Ben Jeffries gave everyone a copy of the *Aeolusean* guidebook and suggested they pick out their suites for the night. Sonny-boy was obviously going to stay with the kids in their room stocked with food and video games, so everyone else began to make their choices. Aleja Gracellen liked the Grecian Isles, and since it was a double, she was joined by June Wilson. Owens and Charleton took one look, thanked Ben for his hospitality, and asked for a couple of berths in the crew quarters. Jeffries couldn't stop laughing and was glad to oblige them. Massara and Bruddah took the British Admiralty, Corlund and Mercante took the Oriental Black-and-Red lacquer room. But once again, Heath Larson seemed the odd man out. Corlund suggested he take the Polynesian suite, thinking it might do him some good to sleep in somewhat familiar surroundings to brighten his spirits. He agreed with little more than a shrug of his shoulders.

It was pushing two a.m. and Heath Larson was wide awake. He just couldn't shake a sense of being detached from reality aboard the *Aeolusean*. He was comfortable with that sensation while surfing, but to have it be triggered by something man-made irritated him to the point that sleep was hopeless. Then he realized there was only one way to deal with it. He left the suite and, with guidebook in hand, set out to embrace all that surrounded him exactly as if it was just another huge wave to be ridden.

He went down the passageway of the VIP suites deck assimilating the first of many images he would coalesce into a collage to be considered later. He walked past antique table and chair arrangements in small alcoves set between the doors to the suites. When he came to a wide swirl of a stairway leading to the upper decks, on a whim he went right past it to the rearmost of the *Aeolusean*'s three elevators.

For the next hour he used elevator doors like the shutter of a camera to take mental snapshots of wealth undreamt of by any person he'd ever known, much less himself. Sometimes he'd take a step out of the elevator and just stand there for a minute or so, emptying his mind of all its pre-conceptions about money and absorbing images of a world as far from the inside of a wave as any place he could imagine. In some ways he felt like a kid riding up and down elevators. He liked the sensation of innocence – it provided welcome contrast to the deep thinking going on in his powerful mind. He finished his odyssey at the top deck of the forward elevator that opened on to the captain's bridge. From the bowels of the engine room to the control center of the megayacht, Heath Larson had collected enough images to create a broad mosaic for his intellect to ponder. And he knew just the place to do it.

He pushed a button to go back down a deck. Exiting the elevator he walked straight towards an oak door under a brass sign that said, "Library". He opened the door and the lights came on automatically to reveal shelves of custom bound volumes in a variety of leather bindings with an oversized porthole in the wall opposite him. He began to scan the titles and authors' names embossed in gold. When a volume caught his eye, he perused the first few pages. Not only were they all first editions, but extremely rare ones at that.

He handled them carefully, knowing some must have been worth five or six figures, easy. *Ah, but we mustn't think about money at a time like this. It just isn't done in certain circles!* His inner voice chuckled at the incongruity.

He walked over to an alcove with indirect lighting where a lone book was positioned as if it was an illuminated Bible in the Pope's private collection. The title was in French, but the name of the author caught his eye. He picked the book up from its altar and walked over to an overstuffed leather chair. He switched on the green shaded reading lamp positioned above and slightly behind his head. Not knowing a word of French, he was nonetheless attracted to the idea of paging through *L'etre et le Néant*, by Jean-Paul Sartre, in the original. He opened the volume, and was surprised to find the title printed in English. He was even more surprised when he began to page through the custom-bound book in his hands. Whole sentences, even paragraphs, were highlighted in florescent yellow. A fine point red pen had been used to underline certain key words and phrases. Notes were carefully printed in the margins. Here and there a star was placed next to a cryptic notation.

Larson's curiosity was truly piqued. He thought of the falling-apart paper back version of the same book sitting next to his bed back up in the hills of Maui with many of the same underlinings and highlights. He remembered his purpose for coming to the library: to contemplate all that he had seen on the *Aeolusean*. But now his mind was even more alert, eager to use the book for reference during his meditation.

Then he laughed when he thought of the catalyst he preferred for moments like this, but he'd left the pakalolo back at the hotel, so he got up and went over to a small liquor cabinet next to the porthole. He opened the cabinet to find it contained only one bottle. *Aeolusean – blended for Ben Jeffries* was embossed in gold leaf against a royal blue velvet label. He took a glass out of the small rack and opened the bottle He poured two fingers and took a sip.

"Now that's good Scotch!" he said aloud to the authors on the shelves. He took another sip, looking out the porthole at the lights of Tampa Bay. He took the tumbler and went to curl up with "*Being and Nothingness*", the principal text of modern existentialism, and consider the parallel realities of waves and wealth. He had barely gotten comfortable when a voice surprised him from the door of the library.

"I see you have an interest in the existential, Heath."

Ben Jeffries had immediately noticed the absence of Sartre's tome from its customary place in the alcove. His long strides took him right past Larson and directly to the liquor cabinet.

"Where does that come from?" he said as he poured himself a stiff one.

"The bowels of waves big enough to swallow the *Aeolusean*, Mr. Jeffries."

"Heath, please, call me Ben!"

"Well, as you might imagine, that's hard to do in the bowels of a megayacht, Mister Ben!"

Jeffries smiled at Larson's similes and raised his glass. Their eyes locked for an instant.

146

"A toast! To the bowels!"

Larson considered the moment, and then slowly raised his glass. They each took a sip of the golden-amber liquid.

"Funny, sometimes I think I come aboard her so she can swallow me," said one of the most powerful men on Wall Street, "and I see your point, Mr. Heath. This setting challenges one's sense of authenticity, does it not? But Sartre has been good company, as you can see, so that version of personal anguish has been obviated by his, how shall we say, sage advice. Are you familiar with such situations?"

"Yes, quite familiar. However, I've found him relevant in places that present a somewhat less tangible reality than yours, I'd say."

"Reality? Now how would Sartre respond to that, my friend?"

"Touché, Ben. which takes us to the heart of an issue, since your yacht is here, and my waves are not."

"Insofar as the fact that after you ride one, it is no longer existent? Whereas the *Aeolusean* exists in space moment after moment after moment?"

"Precisely. Ben, it seems we've arrived at an appropriate point of departure for a conversation. What say another round and let's have at it," said Larson, with a mischievous grin matched by the look on Jeffries' face.

"My sentiments exactly!" Jeffries went back to the cabinet and retrieved the bottle, relishing the idea of matching wits with a highly unusual guest.

"May I say, Heath, that I am grateful for your company. So many times I've had guests aboard and more often than not the talk devolves into chatter about the market or the costs of everything in this day and age. Not this time, however, and so let me propose a toast to Cheryl Corlund!"

"To the CEO," said Larson, rising to his feet, "may she continue to manage us with a deft hand!" The room echoed with full-throated laughter.

"Yes, we must thank her for the opportunity to while away the wee hours considering the finer existential distinctions between waves and wealth!"

"May I propose the points of our discussion, Heath?"

"Something along the lines of 'where does all the money go?' and/or 'whither the energy of the wave?'"

"I couldn't have said it better myself," laughed Jeffries as Larson stood and proffered his tumbler. He poured his guest, then himself. He set the bottle down on a small round table inlaid with mother-of-pearl and an iridescent mosaic depicting Aeolus, the Greek god of the wind.

"To Sartre! Without him we'd be lost!"

"To Sartre! With him we'll never be found!"

The two men first examined their respective experiences dealing with massive amounts of ocean energy and financial power and the necessary courage and flair essential to scaling the heights of success in their chosen arenas. Then they probed their respective senses of detachment from "réalitié", as Sartre had posited the concept, with regards to the securities market where nothing was secure and the reefs where, more often than not, there were no waves to be found.

From time to time they referred to the volume on the table, like a touchstone for a conversation of the sacred, never letting themselves stray beyond the boundaries of logic they had defined for themselves. So fully engaged was the discourse that time itself seemed to stand still. Not until a shadow was cast by the bottle across the table did Jeffries make note of the night's passing.

"Light! In the east! I must say, young man, you've absorbed our French mentor well."

"Have I? As I recall, when students flocked to his lectures in 1968, he upbraided them!"

"Point taken, Heath. I think his words were to the effect that if they had read his philosophy, they would have known better than to listen to him!"

"Run aground on the reef of their own solipsism! Stranded like castaways seeking guidance though forever blinded by ignorance of their folly as would-be followers! How pathetic they must have seemed to the master!" Larson was letting go a bit, almost like ending a wave with a comic pratfall.

"Speaking of which, the master of the *Aeolusean* will be coming on watch at eight bells and waiting for instructions. Why don't we continue our conversation up on the bridge?"

"Actually, Ben, let's leave the conversation here, where it existed, intact, whole, untouched, complete."

"Well put, Heath. To stoop to some pedestrian level of possession would be unseemly."

"Yes, Ben, the essence must be left elusive. Anything less, well, it just isn't done in certain circles!"

Both men laughed so hard tears came to their eyes.

"Say, why don't we get everyone out of their bunks with a little joke of sorts? I have an idea for the captain that might just meet with your approval."

Jeffries grabbed the bottle and took a straight swig.

"Down the hatch!" He handed the bottle to Larson, who drained it dry.

"Hey, ho, and up she rises," Jeffries began to sing in a sailor's baritone, "Hey ho, and up she rises!"

Larson eyes lit up like the sunrise and he came in right on time.

Hey, ho and UP SHE RISES! Err-lie in the morning!"

"What shall we do with a drunken sailor?"

"What shall we do with a drunken sailor?"

"WHAT SHALL WE DO WITH A DRUNKEN SAILOR? ERR-LIE IN THE MORNING!!"

Harmony and light filled the library to overflowing, and soon the salty verses of the old sea chantey echoed down the passageways as two titans from worlds apart made their way to the bridge. The captain of the *Aeolusean* smiled at the two new shipmates delivering his orders for the day. Within a few minutes, powerful winches were engaged and heavy anchor chains came up through the hawsepipes. Twin diesels longer than limousines roared to life and huge propellers began to spin. The megayacht turned slowly to leave the land astern on the tide that was on the turn.

Out on the bow of the *Aeolusean,* a big wave surfer and a Wall Street tycoon were joyfully dancing a drunken sailor's jig as the morning wind carried their voices to the horizon.

Dog Days in the South Seas

David Helmares pulled the large chunk of coral up hand over hand. The night fishing had been miserable and the early morning sun getting hotter by the minute. The oppressive humidity of February in the Nebula Archipelago reminded him of teaching summer school in East L.A. with no air conditioning. He remembered how, as soon as the final bell rang, he and his students would run out the door and within minutes he'd be on his escape route down the freeway to the beach. He smiled thinly to himself because now there was no escape on a dog day.

Across the channel he saw a set of four beautiful waves peeling along a distant reef. It occurred to him he was actually not much of a surfer anymore and that he could not surf the waves that were so beautiful and yet so out of reach. He had to be back in a few hours because he had to teach school all day, and he realized he might never get to surf them with his responsibilities as a father and navigator increasing all the time.

With a final heave the coral anchor came up on board and the outrigger began to drift through the channel. But instead of raising sail, David sat down and watched the perfect waves in the distance. He thought of the self-discipline he'd mastered as Taveka's apprentice, and for the moment he purposefully ignored it. He emptied his mind of all he'd learned, and within seconds a wave of self-doubt washed through his mind when he thought of his life as being little more than a wandering drift rather than a well-chosen path. He did not think of the sincerity of the Maruleans' respect for him. He did not think of the trust he'd earned. He did not remind himself that that there was no reason to second guess Taveka's faith in him. He did not let these thoughts enter his mind, because there was a reason to question himself deeply, and he knew exactly what it was.

He looked at a vision of surfing's ultimate dream waves and knew no one had ever seen them through a surfer's eyes. That fact prompted a single thought so insistent and invasive that he could no longer avoid where his mind was going. Maybe he couldn't ride them right now, but those were his waves, and his alone. The thought flowed easily through him, and he felt comfortable for an instant until, just as it had at when he saw the flash in the sky at Ka'unua, a storm of black and selfish emotion flooded through him. The same rage filled him as he imagined surfers invading HIS world and polluting HIS waves with conflict. Familiar screams of anger began to well up in him, only to be swallowed in shame when he remembered he hadn't told the elders about what happened when he saw the plane fly over Ka'unua.

150

He closed his eyes, and it was only when he could no longer see the waves did his mind begin to slowly clear and find new thoughts to heal itself. Acknowledgment. Confession. Forgiveness. Trust. Love. He stood up and opened his eyes. He would tell his wife about what happened at Ka'unua. Then he would tell Taveka. And then he would tell the elders. He pulled on the sheet, and the mainsail began to rise up the mast. The fishing craft caught the trade wind immediately. David tied off the lines and quickly stepped back to the tiller to bring her around. He steered away from the reef and set his course.

"You've made a serious mistake, David," said Luan, breastfeeding their daughter while David played quietly with their son, "When Kalala said to tell them everything, you didn't. Instead you deceived her, and the elders, and my father. This just may change everything for us David, you know."

"Except we love each other and we love these two."

"Yes, except for that. But who knows, maybe I'll be looking for daycare for them in Santa Monica if the elders decide you are not worthy of being our chief navigator. The elders don't take things like this lightly, I can tell you. So get going, David, or you'll be late for your students. And then after school you have to go see the principal."

"I know, I'm in trouble again, just like I always was back in Los Angeles," he said with a bit of a laugh.

"That's right David, except this time it's not a matter of paper work or policies. This is very serious, David," she said, "And nothing to laugh about."

"Why did you tell me today?"

"Because when I saw such perfect waves and realized no one else had ever seen them, I had the same selfish emotion run through me that I felt seeing that plane at Ka'unua."

Taveka broke eye contact with David and looked out across the lagoon to the horizon where a bank of clouds was turning purple in the setting sun. The two men sat in the sand for another five minutes without a word passing between them. Then Taveka stood up.

"Your mistake was not in hiding what happened at Ka'unua. Your mistake was waiting for life to unfold and push you to reflect on it. As a navigator, you are always going to make mistakes. Only if you recognize them honestly can you adjust your course and get to your destination. The error lies in ignoring them in the hope they go away. Of course, David, they never do."

"Can they ever be undone?"

"No. You can only change course."

"What about forgiveness?"

"As opposed to what, guilt? Guilt has no currency with a navigator. It is not a truly human emotion. It is a violent act to induce it in others, expect it from others, or inflict it upon yourself. Guilt is not the same as conscience. We Maruleans understand the difference.

"David, every man has something inside him that he'd rather forget, but if he's lucky he never will because it will often be what keeps him honest. I was wondering what that would be for you, and now you've told me. You have it in you to be selfish, arrogant, and maybe even violent. That's not unusual, but in your case, the question is all in the name of what? Some momentary pleasure?"

"I never thought of 'localism' in surfing using those terms, but - - -"

"But what? You know better than to use that word with me. What are you really saying, David?"

"I never thought of surfers and their selfishness as being anything more than common immaturity. After what happened at Ka'unua, I began to wonder if there is something more insidious about it, something deeper. Then after seeing perfect waves this morning, it was triggered all over again. Even after all I've learned from you, it is still there."

"David, you're a history teacher. What do you think was the most violent confrontation ever between human beings?"

"I don't know, Taveka, that's a pretty big question. Maybe the rape of Nanking by Japanese soldiers?"

David had struck a never, but Taveka's face revealed nothing.

"No. Think about surfing, David, think about selfishness, about invaders, about what do you call them, locals? Think, David.

"I know. The Battle of Stalingrad."

"Why?"

"The German invaders trying destroy the Russians fighting for their homeland."

"And what made it unique?"

"Hand-to-hand savagery that lasted for months. They fought over a concrete wall, a room, a courtyard, and the frozen dead were stacked like cordwood. Hitler challenged the pride of the German army by shaming them into a battle they could not win. Stalin gave orders that there would be no retreat, and the Russian soldiers were followed into battle by blocking squads. If any of the front line troops turned and tried to retreat, they were shot by their own countrymen."

"And why did this battle take place?"

"Okay, I see your point. So am I Adolph Hitler or Josef Stalin?"

"Neither, because you've never murdered another human being."

"How do you know that?"

"Because I would know if you had."

"How?"

"Because, as the cliché goes, it takes one to know one."

David was now very uncomfortable. During his years of training to become a navigator, he had been put through wringers by his mentor, and he had always emerged with the nonsense squeezed out of him and feeling better for the experience. He was not sure that would happen this time.

"So many people around the world like to think of Polynesia as a paradise, a place for exotic, romantic adventure. They easily forget the fratricide, infanticide, internecine warfare, and human sacrifice which not long ago were as much a part of Polynesia as palm trees and lagoons full of colorful fish. David, there is a thread that ties every human being to every other human being. It is the ability to commit murder or destroy in another any part of their essential human spirit.

"David, when you saw those waves, and when you saw that plane, and when you didn't tell us everything about your experience at Ka'unua, you were being tied up by that thread running through you. You failed a test of character in your own eyes. David, there are much more telling tests of the soul. You did not have that thread become a steel cable. That's the real test, David, the test most difficult to pass, because that's what happens when murder makes sense. It may never happen to you, but it happened to me, and I failed that test."

Taveka was silent for several very long minutes. David lost track of the time, his mind empty except for Taveka's words. Then the chief navigator of the Marulean sea people spoke again.

"I killed a man once, and then I killed again, and then again. It was during the war, they were the enemy, but it was not combat. It was murder. You have not crossed that threshold, and you probably never will. Yet your character is flawed in a way that has shocked you. David, there is no way to alleviate that. You must carry it with you, as I have done. And that is conscience. For you it is but a common thread of humanity. But for me it is a woven steel mesh net from which I'll never escape because nobody knows what I did but me.

"So here we are, two brothers in deceit, each with something inside him that would blow our worlds apart in the light of day. I've kept my secret to myself, David, and I suggest you do the same. The elders don't need to know what happened at Ka'unua because you will remember it every time you see a perfect wave. Every time you see what you've always dreamed of, you will remember the curse of your one failure. I know what I am talking about, David, because it happens to me every time I see a little boy."

The sky was almost completely dark. Venus and Mars were visible, as were the brighter stars of the Southern sky. A bare rustle of a breeze came across the lagoon. Taveka's words hung in the thick, damp air. There was no wind to blow them away.

But David was blown away. He opened his mouth and a question formed on his lips, but he was quickly silenced by Taveka.

"I know what you are thinking, David. You want to know what happened during the war. You want to know more about who I am, as if that will somehow help you when I'm gone."

"Yes, Taveka. I want to know what happened because it seems to be very important."

"For you it will never be important. You have your own memories to haunt you, the ghosts of your past you wish would go away. You don't need to meet mine."

The two men were now almost invisible to each other except for the faint glow from the warm lights of the village coming through the palm trees.

"Tell me, David, have you ever witnessed a death?"

"No, I haven't. I saw corpses in El Salvador, and I've been to funerals and read eulogies."

"Well, there is nothing I can tell you about it. Nobody can tell anyone about death, I think. You will see mine before long, and it will be partly due to you. You are part of what will kill me, David, because I could not ready myself for Ka'unua until my successor had been identified."

He paused and saw the tears behind David's downcast eyes.

"Strange, is it not? That an enlightened people, as we Maruleans like to think of ourselves, would have an important tradition dependent on the thread that binds all humans together? For you it takes the form of rage about waves. For us, it is death at the hands of another."

Taveka patted the necklace beneath his shirt.

"The chain of navigators is that thread. I will die because of your actions, because you successfully proved yourself worthy. All your self-discipline, all your courage, all your dedication, and in the end I will die because of it. So what does that tell you about guilt?"

Taveka waited for David's true spirit to come through, and his heart was gladdened when it did.

"Fuggedaboutit!" David laughed ruefully at the old New York saying.

"Right!" exclaimed Taveka with a huge smile, "You will not be a stronger man if guilt is your response to your failing. Conscience does not thrive on guilt. It can only become stronger with love. David, if you are to be the navigator our people need, you will need strength beyond your imagination. You will find it, as I have, if you do not shy away from your failings. Conscience quickens your resolve and steels your determination if it is driven by love, not guilt."

"Surprising words from a murderer," said David without thinking.

"Ah, your soul speaks again! Good! You really are the man to succeed me, David," said Taveka, rising to his feet.

"And as for me being a murderer, understand that what you are aware of from this conversation about what I did in the war has nothing to do with Luan's mother dying at her birth. Yet I was also the cause of her death, David. Had we not conceived a child, she would not have died, and when I lost her I breathed the poison of guilt until it almost suffocated me. But God gave me a child to love, and that was my way out of the trap of guilt that could have killed me. But as for the blood on my hands from the war, I keep it close to my heart to this very day because it keeps me honest."

David was ready to stand up, but the sight of Taveka's profile kept him on his haunches. A half moon was above the navigator in the deepening blue of a clear night sky. For a moment Helmares saw his mentor as a man possessing a wisdom that has been sought be people from time immemorial.

"Taveka, I wish there was a way to share all your knowledge with the rest of the world."

The mentor turned, looked at his apprentice and could barely keep from laughing at the words.

154

"Well, David, that is very nice of you, and thanks for the compliment. But I had my fill of the outside world during the war, and it is hard enough just to hold on to my own path, and be who I am to my people, without trying to be a guide for total strangers. I've done that once with you, and that's been more than enough for one old man to handle, thank you!"

Helmares laughed. "Yes, I guess you are right, Taveka."

The Marulean navigator put his arm around the Californian surfer.

"Of course, the idea of going on tour like some kind of traveling mystic does have some appeal," he said with a hearty laugh, "if it's all expenses paid! Problem is, I've got a more important destination in my immediate future now that you are chief navigator. So the world will have to somehow survive without me. Speaking of surviving, did you catch any fish last night? And what are my grandchildren going to eat for dinner?"

The Mariners

"Last one! Go!"

The gut wheels rolled back and forth on the parking lot pavement. L.J. Merrill and Jack Richards were in perfect synch with James Brown's "Gravity", the last cut of the warm-up playlist. For the past hour, and for the past six weeks, they had used songs on their iPods as relentless drill sergeants to drive them through increasingly difficult two-a-day workouts. Today, however, they were just getting in a quick session to work out the stiffness after the drive up from Laguna Beach. They were overlooking a beach in Oxnard, a few miles from their destination in Ventura Harbor where they had an appointment in less than an hour at the world headquarters of the Order of Southern Ocean Mariners.

"Sixty-one, sixty-two sixty-three, sixty-four! Ok, I'm ready."

"Are you?" replied Merrill, "I've got you in pretty good shape, Jack, but have you been doing your homework on the Southern Ocean?"

"Fire when ready, L.J.!"

"Ok, Richards, twenty questions, and a hundred buck fine for every wrong answer. Cape of Storms?"

"The original name for the Cape of Good Hope. Southern tip of Africa. 15th century. Vasco De Gama, Portugal."

"First circumnavigation?"

"1522. Ferdinand Magellan, sailing under the Spanish flag."

"Wrong. That's a c-note. Magellan never made it. He left Spain with five ships. Only one made it all the way, under Del Caño. Ok, here's an easy one. What did Magellan accomplish that's remembered to this day?"

"He discovered the Straits of Magellan."

"When, where and why?"

"1520. The protected passage at fifty two degrees south latitude. Because he had to get around the tip of South America to get into the Pacific. He could have gone a little further south and rounded Cape Horn. Discovered by Schouten, Holland, 1516."

"Didn't ask you that, Jack, but glad you know it. Now what is almost six hundred miles wide between Cape Horn and Antarctica?"

"Drake's Passage, first sailed by Sir Francis Drake of England in 1578. He was a pirate with Queen Elizabeth's blessing to make life miserable for the Spanish."

"What English captain sailed for purely scientific purposes through the Southern Ocean?"

"James Cook. Three voyages in the *Endeavour*. 1770s."

"How did he meet his end?"

"Same as Magellan. Killed by islanders due to poor cross-cultural awareness of the sensitivities of people who'd never seen white men before."

"Pretty good, there, Richards. Oh, by the way, what is the Southern Ocean?"

"The combined waters of the South Atlantic, the South Pacific, and the Indian Ocean south of the equator. C'mon, L.J., give me a hard one."

"What about the mariners of the Southern Ocean in the 1800's?"

"It's been called the Golden Age of Sail thanks to the romantic illusions evoked by the tall ships of the era such as the clippers carrying miners from New York to San Francisco, the *Sovereign of the Seas, Flying Cloud, Lightning, Cutty Sark.* Later you had the *Parma, Penzing,* and the Cape Horners carrying cargos for the China tea trade, Australia wheat and lumber. But it wasn't it so golden for the sailors. The captains were tyrants. Speed was everything and the tall ships were really dangerous places to work, especially when sailing through the Southern Ocean and around Cape Horn in winter."

"Not bad, Jack. What did they call their roughest sea route?"

"The Roaring Forties. The term was first used by sailors given the constant wind blowing from east to west that roared in the rigging above them in the band of ocean between forty degrees south latitude and fifty degrees south latitude."

"Ok, now tell me about the men who sailed the Roaring Forties alone."

"Well, Joshua Slocum did the first solo circumnavigation in 1896. But he sailed east to west and avoided the Roaring Forties. So I'm gonna go with Vito Dumas from Argentina. He did the first solo round the world in the Roaring Forties using the winds and waves to push him west to east. He did it during World War Two, and at the time it was the longest single non-stop passage ever."

"How about Sir Francis Chichester?"

"The classic English adventurer. Wanted to sail around the world in less than a hundred days. Wanted to break Dumas' record. Gypsy Moth IV. 1967. Had to stop once."

"Bernard Moitissier?"

"France. The ultimate romantic. He became a national hero in France. He was far in the lead of the first non-stop solo circumnavigation race in 1969 when he decided going back to the accolades of a fawning public was not for him. After passing Cape Horn, instead of setting his course north up the Atlantic, he simply kept going east and sailed for another three months. He ended up in Polynesia where he lived for a few years before eventually sailing back to France."

"Who actually won that first solo race?"

"Robin Knox-Johnston. England. Was the first to go around the world non-stop by himself."

"Well, Jack, you have done your homework. Now, what about modern sailing in the Southern Ocean. There have been all these races."

"Yeah, the Golden Globe, the Vendee, the Whitbread, the Volvo Ocean Race, The Race - - -"

"What was the Race?"

"Unlimited maxi catamarans around the world. Non-stop. Six hundred and fifty miles a day. First run in 2001."

"Now, there was one thing all these Southern Ocean voyages had in common. What was it?"

"All the voyages were made during the relatively calm months of 'summer' in the Southern Hemisphere, from October through March."

"Why?"

"For most sailors it is suicide to attempt winter passages in the Southern Ocean. Except for the Order of Southern Ocean Mariners."

"And if we are going to surf a reef in the South Pacific on waves coming out of the Southern Ocean, where and when are the waves coming from?"

"The Roaring Forties. In winter. June through September in the Southern Hemisphere. That's twenty, Merrill. Now let me ask you a question."

"Well, that's actually only nineteen. You jumped the gun about the races. I actually didn't ask you anything about them."

"Don't get smart, Merrill!" laughed Richards, "Remember, I'm the guy paying the bills, and you do work for me."

"Yassuh, boss. But if I wasn't smart enough to get smart with you, we wouldn't be here. But what's your question?"

"I wrote OSOM a check for two hundred grand to cover our passages if we're accepted. If we're not, I get the money back, correct?"

"Jack, you already know that. What's your real question?"

"And you haven't told either Atkins or Bucher what we're really trying to do?"

"No, haven't talked to them at all. No point in it, Jack, and you know that, too. First we have to make it through today, and if we do, the shakedown cruise is no bargain from what I've learned."

"You know, L.J., this feels like we're interviewing for a job, and yet I'm paying them!"

"Yeah, Jack, something like that. And the thing is, all your millions ain't gonna mean spit in a few minutes."

"I know, L.J., I know. That's why I'm doing this."

Charles Atkins pulled into the OSOM parking lot at the far end of the harbor near Ventura, California. His corroded '83 Ford van fit right in with the slouching four-door sedans patched with duct tape and the pick-up trucks with beds battered and gouged. The place almost looked like a junk yard. One would never guess these street legal rust buckets were owned by men and women who, when not ashore, coursed around the globe in the most advanced oceanic voyaging craft ever built.

He went into the lobby of the OSOM HQ, signed in the day log and checked the bulletin board. Atkins smiled at the flyer announcing a tug-of-war between the Aussies and the Russians. They were two of the four crews, selected on a revolving basis from the Order's world-wide membership of over a thousand mariners who supported and sailed aboard the fleet of Alba_Swords representing fourteen countries, that would be sailing around the world through the Southern Ocean this year in OSOM's annual Roaring Forties Regatta. Along with the Germans and the Peruvians, they were already working on their Alba_Swords in the hangar-sized prep facility adjacent to the headquarters building, and though the event wouldn't start for another four months, Atkins was not surprised that the energy level was obviously already pretty high.

But he was surprised when he saw a 3x5 card announcing a '64 Dodge Dart sedan for sale. He'd had his eye on Tak Kurosawa's ride for several years, and now that the mission prep manager had traded "up" to a '61 Ford Ranchero, Atkins had his chance. He looked around the lobby and quickly grabbed the card off the board. Fair's fair and all that, but Charles Atkins was taking no chances when it came to a vintage straight six in good condition.

He went back out the front doors and around the corner to a double flight of stairs running diagonally up the side of the building. Just under six foot with the graceful build of a ballet dancer, Atkins had extremely fast reflexes and his aerobic capacity was second to none in the Order. As usual, he took the stairs three at a time up to a landing where, with one graceful motion, he opened a wooden door with a porthole in it to enter OSOM's nerve center.

The main deck of the Bridge, as the command center was known, was built with an open view down into the vessel prep facility simply called the "Shed". The Bridge was ringed by an upper balcony and tinted windows that allowed a clear view from the docks and mountains to the east all the way around to the Channel Islands and the ocean to the west. As he walked around the balcony Atkins gave a quick glance out to sea. He couldn't see the waves breaking, but he could hear them, and with the wind offshore, he knew it had to be good. He checked his watch and knew he had to get on it if he wanted to get some waves before the orientation began in a few hours.

Sliding down the railings on his hands he landed lightly on the main deck of the Bridge next to a multi-screen plasma display covering a large part of one wall. Sixteen individual screens made up a grid of images filling the display, but he was interested in just one: a map of the entire Pacific Ocean covered with a series of jagged lines like a small child's attempt to connect numbered dots. He touched the display, and its image instantly expanded to fill the entire grid. A row of icons appeared across the center screen and Atkins touched one. Then he stepped back as the display was updated with new downlinked data from a tracking satellite. Numerous jagged lines began to appear all over the grid. When the updates were finally in place, Atkins smiled.

Thousands of miles from land, the wandering albatrosses of the Southern Ocean were foraging to feed their young. Among them were sixty-four birds with GPS signal units delicately attached to their backs. Come July and August, he and his fellow mariners would use data from some of those same birds to help locate the most efficient courses and continuous wave trains through the Roaring Forties. The birds would be the scouts, and the mariners of OSOM would be able to use data from the albatrosses to help them voyage through the Southern Ocean in winter at the helms of the Alba_Swords, the most unique open ocean sailing craft ever built.

Atkins stepped back from the display and went up the stairs to check the surf. Another set was breaking, and he was starting to get antsy. He turned and looked down at the docks to focus on the original Alba_Sword prototypes that looked more like swordfish than oceanic yachts. They were the breeding pair for the entire fleet, and he quickly considered the different characteristics of the *Serena* and the *Tom Swift*. Though they were practically identical twins, he remembered words written long ago about mariners and tall ships.

> *She is more than a ship to the sailor; she is a personality. He knows her; he has watched her make her voyage. He knows what she can do and what she can't; he knows when she is being asked to do too much and when too little. He always speaks of his ship as if she lived.*

Atkins decided to go with the *Tom Swift*. He knew she was practically interchangeable with the *Serena*, but Atkins liked the *Swift's* steady helm when conducting shakedown cruises for candidates who wanted to join the Order. He went back down the ladder to a desk console display and called up a real-time satellite image of the Eastern North Pacific. A front was passing above Point Conception, about forty miles north of Ventura. A fresh gale was following the storm that would pass over the Santa Barbara Channel just around dusk Sunday night. With a big late-winter groundswell already running in from the deep North Pacific and a full moon rising behind them, it looked like a good set up for a very rough, and visually threatening, passage around the outermost islands on the other side of the Santa Barbara Channel.

Atkins cackled in delight. Plenty of wind and swell, and probably even some rogue waves to surprise the candidates IF they made it through the orientation. He e-mailed his "flight" plan to Ray Seranen, the chief meteorologist for OSOM, and then realized he was running out of time if he wanted to go surfing. His mind paused a second as his eyes studied the monitor before him. Then his fingers spun the track ball and the arrow pointed to the *Tom Swift*'s icon. With a double click, the smile melted into steely-eyed concentration. Up came the internal website displaying work zone icons for every thing connected with and to the *Tom Swift*: electronics, structural stress, provisions, sail plans, the propulsion system, and much more. He selected 'Voyage Preparation', and then selected 'Able Bodied Passenger Orientation' about halfway down the menu. He checked the downlink to the peripherals bus, and when its integrity was confirmed, he headed down the open stairs from the Bridge to the aft end of the Shed. And as chance would have it, his timing was perfect.

"Hey! Tak! Just the man I wanted to see!" smiled Atkins, holding up the card from the bulletin board, "when can I take delivery?"

160

"Two grand in cash and you can drive her off the lot today!" laughed Tak Kurosawa, carrying a laptop and some rolled up blueprints on his way towards the four Alba_Swords at the other end of the Shed.

"Can I give you a twenty as down payment?"

"Why don't you just go to the bank right now?"

"Well, I was hoping to get in a few waves across the street, and, uh - - - "

"Surfers! You guys never give up, do you? Ok, but Tuesday for sure!"

"Tuesday for sure, Tak. Say, got a minute to help set up the simulator?"

"Sure, Charlie. Scuttlebutt has it that you're shaking down some candidates this weekend. Gonna be some fun in the Channel after this blow goes by tomorrow," said Kurosawa with the glint in his eye of a veteran OSOM mariner, "IF they survive you today!"

The two men walked over to the side of the building and swung two doors wide open, revealing an exact replica of the cockpit of an Alba_Sword supported by a series of hydraulic cylinders. The simulator was mounted on a large flat bed platform resting on steel rollers. They grabbed two handles protruding from the unit, twisted the hand grips slightly, and began to roll the Alba_Sword simulator slowly across the smooth concrete floor. They guided it through a ninety degree turn to the left and lined it up with docking clamps embedded flush into the floor. Kurosawa went around checking the alignment with the socket hold-downs. Then he flipped levers around the base and clamped each hold-down to insure the simulator was anchored rock-solid. Atkins went to a control panel built into the wall. He touched a button and a large concave screen, flanked by recessed speakers, lowered slowly from the ceiling to partially surround the simulator.

"Ready to rock and roll, Charlie," said Kurosawa.

"Thanks Tak, but I prefer jazz with my seasickness. How goes it with the Regatta crews?"

"On schedule – no anomalies. The Russians and the Aussies are going at each other pretty good. Funniest one-liners I've heard in years. The Germans have a new watch system that they're working on with the Peruvians. Ship-shape and Bristol fashion all around."

"Well, sounds like us gringos better get in gear," replied Atkins. He went back upstairs to the Bridge while Kurosawa stayed below to visually check the mechanics of the simulator. From the main data console Atkins initiated the 'Motion Sickness Stress Test', and the simulator below him came alive. He ran it through a full routine. Everything was working perfectly. Kurosawa gave him a thumbs up before turning away toward the work zone of the shed. Atkins powered down the simulator and went back to the computerized pre-voyage system. He selected 'San Miguel Island' from a menu and left the program, now directly connected to the on-board telemetric sensors and data files of the *Tom Swift*, to run through over a hundred system checks controlled directly by the computer. Then he climbed the ladder to the balcony with a pair of binoculars. He focused on the *Tom Swift* and could see that the wheel in the cockpit was rotating slowly as the computer ran the checklist on her. It was all one system now, and he did not need to be there. He put down the binoculars, walked over to the exit door and pushed it open. He saw a cloud of seaspray hanging in the air over the surf zone, and seventeen seconds later another appeared, telling him all he needed to know.

He closed the door quickly and began to tap-dance in cross-over steps down the stairs. Halfway to the bottom he reversed his step and went backwards up to the landing. There he did a Prince spin on one heel before descending all the way down to the bottom of the stairs, keeping perfect time with heel clicks on each step. Charles Atkins was happy as a lark, dancing the stairs to warm up his surfing feet, and vice versa.

A brisk wind blew offshore towards Santa Cruz Island, green and vivid fifteen miles out in the ocean across the Santa Barbara Channel. Endless swells were rolling in from the western horizon. Across the street from OSOM headquarters and two hundred yards out to sea, deep blue waves were being transformed into turquoise tunnels as they moved across a perfectly groomed sandbar. And no one was out.

It was a classic northwest groundswell, and there were hundreds of surfers in the water at other spots up and down the coast. But the surf reports had overlooked a rare sandbar that had built up next to the jetty at the Ventura harbor mouth. It was still early, and for the moment the place was empty, but not for long.

Standing on the wet sand with a high performance surfboard under his arm, a lone surfer contemplated what was in store for him. He was about to jump off the continent and enter a surfer's dream-world.

Ken Bucher looked up at the sky and mouthed a *Thank-you!* Not only was the surf perfect, but his session would also be a celebration of his coming-of-age. The night before, his mother had given him her blessing, and later today he would begin his candidacy to crew for his dad on an Alba_Sword in the Roaring Forties Regatta.

"Yeah!" he exclaimed as he literally leapt for joy into the ocean as the last gasp of a wave's energy exploded at his feet.

Bucher's timing was that of a matador leaping over a bull. He came down prone on his board with his arms extended and fingertips just touching the cold Pacific. At eye level he now faced endless waves, shaped by the sand bottom and groomed by the offshore wind. It was a superb surfing arena.

He paddled out through the fields of foam as the broken waves swept laterally along the shore. Each one tried to push him back to the beach, but soon he was a football field's distance from the sand. There he paused just before entering the impact zone where the groundswells became a surfer's playground. He waited until the last wave of a set broke and its white water rolled past him. He timed his passage across the sandbar and quickly made it out to the smooth waters seaward of where the waves had been breaking. There he stopped and sat up on his board. Though resting, he was absolutely alert and observant. It was not long before he saw what he had come for.

A set of swells began to unload its power upcoast from him. Less than a minute passed before the first of six waves formed up where Ken Bucher waited. He was sitting in water too deep to be able to catch the first wave and he made no move to position himself to ride it. He was, for the moment, not studying its form as a surfer, but as a photographer.

Bucher had an old Nikonos waterproof camera slung around his neck. He brought it to eye level and examined the wave even more closely through the viewfinder. He saw it begin to break gradually from right to left. Abruptly it hit the sandbar and the tube opened wide into a deep tunnel. Ken could see directly into the innermost limits of the wave as it sped towards him with perfect shape.

He sat poised on his board not thirty feet from the maelstrom of energy clearly visible through his viewfinder. He floated up the steep face of the swell, ten feet high and threatening to break, without moving a muscle. His patience was rewarded. Through the viewfinder, Bucher saw a vivid rainbow arc to the left in the spray blown back as the peak of the wave pitched forward. In the center of the frame there appeared the elliptical eye of a perfect wave, and to the right he could clearly see, though many miles away, the peaks of the Santa Ynez Mountains covered with snow. The composition was perfect. He clicked the shutter and captured an extraordinary vision, and although the combination of such beautiful elements was very rare, Ken Bucher was about to see it again and again.

For the next five waves of the set, and then for another three sets, Bucher constantly maneuvered his surfboard to position himself in and around the impact zone, snapping image after image of natural perfection from all angles. Sometimes he filled the frame with the wave's blue face set against the white snow. Another angle displayed nothing but floating crystal droplets with the arc of a rainbow slashing through the spray.

Once he got so close to the energy that he slipped off his surfboard, after snapping a shot, and dove through the wall of water to avoid the crushing force coming down towards him. He emerged unscathed as the wave rolled over him, his board firmly connected to his leg by a long leash. He reeled in his board, got on it and started paddling to get out of harm's way, though he had the presence of mind to snap another picture of the on-coming wave while he was paddling, with the nose of his board in the foreground to create a point-of-view perspective.

He finally lost count of how many photos he had taken when a large set stood up outside, the biggest of the morning. The water around him was now a golden gun metal blue as the tide was beginning to go out and the waves were dredging up sand inside their cylinders.

He made a quick assessment, paused, then paddled his board straight towards the highest peak of the first wave. It stood up ten feet tall in a solid wall that offered no escape. The crest threw out into space over his head. The pointed nose of his board pierced through the face of the wave as he pushed his board underwater to let the energy roll over him. He held on tightly, feeling the wave try to suck him back towards shore. But his duck dive was deep, and his timing was lucky. He emerged out the back of the wave. The cloud of spray enveloped him and he couldn't see a thing for a second. But then the air cleared for an instant, revealing a perfect rainbow ring five feet in diameter to his right lit up by the morning sun behind him. It seemed almost close enough to touch, and he was transfixed for a second. Then he quickly brought his camera up to his eye and tried to take the picture before the vision disappeared. He clicked the shutter, but nothing happened. He looked at the camera for a second, and then realized he was out of film!

He shook his head and remembered what his dad had once said, "Don't always use the camera to record what you're seeing. Just use your brain." Then he realized he had no time for such thoughts when he looked up to see another, much bigger wave about to break directly in front of him. He dove off his board holding the camera tightly to his chest. The camera was protected, but not the surfer. The wave crashed down on Bucher and his board, pushing him underwater and tumbling him like clothes in a dryer. The buoyancy of his board caused it to be pulled away from him and his leash stretched almost to the breaking point.

But the leash held, and a moment later he surfaced. He put an arm through the loop of the camera strap, and with the camera now safe and secure behind him, his arms were free to swim as hard as he could. He grabbed a lungful of air, and dove again under the white water of the next wave. Up for air, another wave, another dive, and then once more before he could finally reel in his board and lay at rest on its deck.

He looked across the smooth sea surface towards the horizon, only to see a new group of waves coming on strong. The photographer now became a surfer. He paddled out into deeper water and waited in perfect position for the third wave. He pivoted his board towards the shore, paddled two strong strokes, and stood up to glide down the slope of water golden in the morning sun. He turned hard off the bottom, not a muscle flinching, standing fully erect and ready to enter a sunlit tunnel of liquid light. He bowed his head at the last instant as the crystal ceiling came over and around him. He disappeared from the world for almost five seconds before coming out of the tube, his body arched slightly forward with his hands held lightly over his head. It was a moment to savor, and although the wave kept going, Ken Bucher turned his board back towards the horizon in a graceful exit.

A sharp whistle broke into his trance. He turned to see Charles Atkins sprinting across the beach with a board under his arm. Kenny gave him a double whistle in return as he paddled back out to the take off zone to wait for his godfather – and the next set.

Atkins timed his launch perfectly between the pulses of waves and paddled directly to the take-off zone, his powerful arms and shoulders pulling him out to sea with surprising speed.

"Nice barrel Kenny!" Atkins exclaimed as he slowed down and drifted towards his best friend's son, "Does your G.P.A. look that good?"

"Straight A's Uncle Charles! Hey, here come some waves!"

Bucher spotted a set lifting up out to sea, and the two surfers instantly pulled their boards around and began paddling rapidly toward the oncoming waves. These were the biggest of the day, rolling in like a convoy of eighteen-wheelers.

164

"Which one do you want?"

"Number two! Thanks!" said Atkins.

As he paddled into position, Atkins noticed a couple of SUVs had pulled into the parking with boards stacked high on the roofs.

Well, he thought, *let's give these guys a show.*

The wave steepened and began to pitch out as he caught it and took off down the face. In that instant, Charles Atkins, husband, physiologist and sailor, turned into Charlie Atkins, arguably one of the most stylish and perfectly choreographed surfers in the world. He transformed a wetsuit, surfboard and wave into a tuxedo, dancing shoes, and a polished wood floor. He was the surfer as dancer extraordinaire, moving with the grace of the original Temptations, emulating their smooth moves on a smooth wave.

Charlie Atkins got in rhythm by surfing just ahead of the wave's backbeat as it broke down the line of the sandbar. After an initial run to come up to the speed of the wave, Atkins carved a cutback like an octave change before weaving through the next section of the wave as if it was eight bars of solo space. He was the epitome of nonchalance as he set up a final statement going into the shorebreak. Atkins drifted down into the heart of the energy just as the wave, born thousands of miles away in the North Pacific, began the last moments of its life.

The climax solo passage came right on time as he turned his board in synch with the multi-plexed curves of the liquid crescendo building around him. And then, just as a musician will leave a clear note hanging in the silence at the end of a song, he exited the wave with a virtuoso's touch as it finally collapsed on the sand. And for a few seconds, he paused with his hands flaired out for style before lowering himself gracefully back to a prone position on his board to quietly culminate a ride intended to be nothing less than a perfect statement about one man's version of soul surfing.

He looked out to the takeoff zone and saw that his godson had caught a great wave. He watched Bucher's every move with keen attention. Initial drive off the top of the crest. Perfect set up to gouge a turn off the bottom. G-force catapult – absolutely vertical. Launch into mid air, a full meter between his fins and the pitching lip of the wave. Land it. Charge down the face. Extend out a turn with a cross-over step, then backstep to carve a drop knee cutback thirty feet in diameter.

Atkins was not surprised with Bucher's performance, but the next thing he saw made his jaw drop. Ken brought his high performance short board around in a complete 360 degree turn. It was not the tail-slide trick often seen in surfing contests, but a true carving circle few surfers in the world have ever executed properly.

Bucher went speedsurfing towards the last vertical section of the wave ahead of him. He glided down the face and used all the g-force of a hard turn to launch once more into midair off the exploding lip. A full three seconds later, he landed on the back of the swell just as it died on the beach. He stood poised on the board, as the water drained back to sea, and then stepped lightly to the sand.

Bucher and Atkins looked at each other. They snapped their fingers in unison and cracked up with laughter.

"Oh yeah, that reminds me Kenny, do you have my Sam Cooke tape?"

"Right up there in the parking lot. But you can't have it back until you return my Pearl Jam!" They both laughed even louder.

"So you ready for today?" Atkins shifted gears a little.

"Yeah, I'm ready. My paper work's in the van. You want it now or what?"

Atkins smiled at Bucher's attitude. Only yesterday Kenny had been playing with blocks and riding around on his first bicycle that his uncle had given him for his sixth birthday. Now he was, without doubt, the son of Frank Bucher, though with shades of James Dean, thought Atkins.

"No, just give it to Chip. The only thing I want right now is some more waves before it gets crowded!"

Charles Atkins turned to the ocean and paddled back out for more soul encounters with the blue power. The surfers in the SUVs had scrambled into their wetsuits and were running towards the water with their boards. Bucher turned and walked towards the parking lot. He recognized one or two of them and was going to say something, but they were so intent on getting in the water that they barely nodded to him. He just smiled at the instant crowd about to burst the bubble of what had just been a surfer's dream. They would be getting some great waves, but he'd had his share for the day. And he had more important things to do.

"Morning Kenny, how was it?"

"Uh, pretty good, I guess. And I got some photos."

"That's so amazing you surf and - - Good morning OSOM, how can I direct your call? Certainly, I'll put you right through."

Chip Bell punched four numbers on the key pad and spoke briefly into his headset. He had worked the front desk at OSOM practically since day one. He spoke fluent Spanish, French and German and could handle calls from around the world like an automatic transmission. He did not fit the stereotype of a receptionist, with his long hair and tattooed forearms, but there was no one better at the job, and his perfect attendance allowed him to build up enough vacation time to crew on two Regattas, and he'd be going again this year.

He put the call through and turned his attention back to Ken Bucher.

"Yeah, so you got good photos. Bring 'em in when they get - - Good morning, OSOM, ah, Guten Tag Frau Kistenberg, wie gehts?"

Bucher knew from experience that talking to Bell when he was on-shift was at best hit-and-miss. He sat down on a couch across the room and opened his briefcase. He extracted the manila envelopes containing his paperwork, and then carefully addressed them to *P. McRane, Membership Director and Crew Coordinator*. He made sure his handwriting was large and legible, and labeled the envelope, *"Candidacy documents for Kenneth Bucher."* ell was still speaking German into his headset, so Bucher placed the envelope on the desk. Bell glanced at it and gave Bucher a thumbs up without missing a beat of the conversation.

166

Walking out of the lobby, Ken Bucher looked across the street. The offshore wind was dying, but the surf was probably still really good. He gave half-a-thought to another go-out, but with three more cars in the lot he knew his surfing was done for the day. He had some time to kill before the orientation, so he walked to his VW van to stretch out in the back and shift his focus from being a great surfer riding some of California's best waves to the challenge of being a humble greenhorn hoping to ship out on a voyage where the surfing was of an entirely different realm by orders of magnitude.

The Orientation

Jack Richards hit the brakes just inside the OSOM parking lot.

"Maybe I should park out on the street," he said, apparently not wanting to flaunt his wealth for the first time L.J. Merrill could ever remember.

"That won't make any difference, Jack," replied Merrill with a sigh, "There's a space."

A somewhat chastened millionaire squeezed his chrome-trimmed SUV in between a '61 Ford Falcon and an '82 AMC Eagle. They were barely able to open the doors and slide out sideways. Out of habit Richards beeped the doors locked and set the alarm.

"Ain't wealth wonderful!" Merrill muttered under his breath.

The two men walked through the front doors of the lobby to the front desk. Chip Bell gave them a friendly greeting and had them sign a clipboard.

"You guys are a little early, so if you'll just have a seat, Captain Atkins will be with you at ten sharp. Good morning, OSOM, how may I - -, oh - -, Top of the morning to you, Frank! Ah, no, not yet, but as soon as he gets here I'll - -, wait a sec, here he is. Do you want to talk to him?" Bell paused, and then laughed, "Ok, bye."

Richards and Merrill turned to see Kenneth Bucher walking in the front door and straight towards them as Chip Bell answered another incoming.

"Hello Mr. Merrill! Ken Bucher. You may remember me from the trip to Baja four years ago."

"Of course I remember you, Kenny. You were caught inside the whole time, but looks like you can paddle through just about anything these days!" said L.J., noticing the young man's full shoulders and long arms, "Good to see you again. Let me introduce you gentlemen. Kenny, this is my long time friend and client, Jack Richards."

"Maybe we should go sit down over here," said Bucher and he steered them away from the reception desk.

"What brings you here, Kenny?" asked Richards as they walked past a scale model of an Alba_Sword.

"Same as you guys, I guess. Ship out on an Alba_Sword in this year's Roaring Forties Regatta. But first we gotta make it through today's tests."

"Yeah, and then there's the shakedown cruise tomorrow," said Richards.

"Well, that's only if you make it through today," smiled Bucher.

Jack Richards instinctively decided to roll him, just as he'd done dozens of times to get inside information from company employees before making investments, planning a takeover or filing a shareholders' lawsuit.

"Wow, Ken, here we are on Saturday morning and it feels like we are taking the SAT or something," he said, forcing a nervous laugh, "And you know the guys who wrote the exams. What do you think it'll take to pass?"

Ken Bucher stared at the floor for just a second. Then he looked Richards in the eye. "Well, I'm pretty young, and this is a rite of passage for me, in a way. Not that you guys are old or anything, but maybe it will be something different for you. Like they used to say on the old ships, I'm coming up through the hawsepipe. I'm green and laying my keel, so to speak. But you guys, well, my dad once said that the older people get, the harder it is for them to change."

"Sure, Ken, but I was just wondering - -"

Bucher ignored the interruption.

"That's the only thing he's ever said to me about people trying to get a berth on an Alba_Sword. Other than that, he's never talked to me about what it takes to join the Order. I guess he wants me to learn certain things on my own. Does that answer your question?"

Richards frowned. He did not know if Bucher was being sarcastic or not. He had trouble reading young people given the way he had raised his own children. L.J. Merrill saw Richards' reaction but could only smile at Bucher's words. He was relishing the personal challenge of making his scheme work by going through what promised to be an ordeal. It would make the revenge that much sweeter, and he didn't need any insider tips or shortcuts. And for an instant, Merrill thought maybe he didn't need Jack Richards after all.

"Nice weather we've been having lately," he said with a reproving look at Richards. He turned to the son of OSOM's founder. "Been surfing much, Ken?"

Before Bucher could reply, double doors opened at the far end of the lobby and two people walked towards the three men.

"Candidates Bucher, Merrill, and Richards," said Charles Atkins as he shook hands firmly with them. "May I introduce Mariner Patricia McRane."

Standing next to him was a clear-eyed, muscular woman wearing a pony tail and a smile that was strictly business. They were both wearing black jumpsuits with the OSOM coat of arms over their hearts and a pattern of endless waves running around their waists.

McRane extended her hand to each of the men.

"I've been reviewing the information you've submitted and so far, there are only a few problems. Mr. Bucher, you'd better clear up those parking tickets at school. They'll start going to warrant next week."

"Yes ma'am. Will do."

"And Mr. Richards, do we have the coke under control these days?"

"Absolutely," he said without skipping a beat, "Not an issue. Can I give you a blood sample?"

"That won't be necessary for the moment. And Mr. Merrill, why does Customs always red flag your passport?"

Merrill's face didn't register even a hint of surprise. He knew the drill. When it comes to people with access to government data, there is only one thing to do and that's to tell the truth.

"Too many trips to too many countries. Their computers track every time I use my passport. I guess they assume that I'm in the commodities trade, so to speak. Of course I was, but instead of bringing drugs to customers, I brought the customers to the drug."

That brought a scowl to Richards' face but Charles Atkins let out a laugh.

"Quite refreshing there, Merrill. I'd never quite thought of surf guides in those terms. Ok, gentlemen, let's hope no more anomalies turn up, or we might have to ask you to withdraw your candidacies."

"Of course, you may also choose to withdraw voluntarily at any time during today's activities," said McRane, "If you'll excuse me, I've got some calls to make to the references listed on your apps."

She exchanged nods with Atkins before turning away to walk back through the open doors. He watched the eyes of the candidates to see where they went. During past orientations, those candidates whose eyes had followed the striking figure out the door were the eyes of men who washed out sooner as opposed to later. This was not a time to be distracted. Atkins was glad to see not one of the three failed this telling test.

"Gentlemen, I commend you for having the character that would bring you here seeking a berth on an Alba_Sword. Today, however, we will begin to see if your reach exceeds your grasp, and for many people that has been the case. If the past is any guide, by three this afternoon at least one of you won't be here. This isn't written in stone and I'm not here to purposefully wash out any particular candidate. But I can tell you being cocky will not serve you well today. If anything, let me suggest humility as a far more appropriate emotion. To that end, will you walk this way, please?"

He directed the men through the open doors. Richards walked ahead of the others down the hall towards another set of double doors that were closed. He put his hand on a crash bar to open one of them when Atkins stopped him.

"Not yet, Mr. Richards. And who knows, maybe not at all. Let's start in here, please."

He opened a side door marked with a simple brass plate. The Chapel was a small room with a center aisle between a few rows of short, wooden pews. Richards quickly sat down in the first pew on the left. Merrill sat across the aisle from him. Ken Bucher went down the aisle and sat in the front row.

The side walls were covered by plaques of various sizes and shapes. Merrill looked at them carefully and saw that each one was engraved with the image of a ship, her crew list, and a date. Richards looked off into space, while Bucher stared at the stained glass wall in front of him, with daylight glowing through the transparent panes of ocean blue, gold, amber and turquoise, swirling around a centered circle of white translucent marble.

Atkins closed the door and walked to the wall of light. Standing ramrod straight, he established eye contact with each man before beginning his sermon.

"Ye men who would be mariners in the great ocean of the south! Hear now the invocation of the souls resting beneath the seas where ye would voyage." He closed his eyes and turned his back on them to fully transform himself into a man of the cloth.

"Dear Lord we ask You to send us a host of shipmates to look upon these men who would sail upon Your great waters. Let the souls of the departed come and measure these men here today with their weather eye. Let them come and stand a watch as guardians for them. Fill their hearts and minds with wisdom, and help them search their souls, so that they will not share the fate of those shipmates forever lost in the eternal dark of the endless deep."

Atkins turned back to the candidates to gauge their first reactions. Ken Bucher was looking him right in the eye, as Atkins had expected from the son of OSOM's founder. L.J. Merrill was looking at the plaques on the walls before he, too, met Atkins' gaze with respect. Jack Richards had "What kind of bullshit is this?" written all over his face.

"Hear now, candidates! Welcome the souls who've sailed the great waters before you. Let them enter your innermost thoughts as you are tried and tested today. Hear their words of encouragement – but ignore at your peril their words of warning.

"You are here today because you have imagined yourselves voyaging across the blue deep, with roaring winds at your backs and huge waves beneath your hull, and excitement charging the very air you breathe. You are here because you have set a course, but a sailor never speaks of setting a course as if he could just draw a line across a map of the seven seas. No, the wise mariner only *shapes* a course *toward* his goal, knowing there is no certainty in life, and to assume such is to tempt the fates.

"Candidates, this chapel is your first port of call if you would voyage across the Southern Ocean. Here we honor the mariners whose tall ships once put to sea from this very port to make that same voyage a hundred or more years ago – and who never stepped foot on land again. In recent years, many have sought to voyage with the Order, captivated by the so-called romance of the sea. They hoped to find it by becoming an able-bodied passenger on an Alba_Sword or indeed joining the Order. Yet more than a few came to their senses in this very place. And no harm done. They went home to their loved ones and a life made more real by admitting their folly."

Atkins glanced at Richards and knew he had his full attention.

"You've seen the pictures of the majestic ships with clouds of sails running before the wind. They embody the romantic notion of the seven seas, do they not? Yes, the sea is a beautiful thing to a landlubber. To a wise sailor, however, she is a siren who lures the unwary to their deaths."

L.J. Merrill shifted uncomfortably in his pew.

"Picture in your mind's eye a tall ship tied to a wharf. Up the gangplank comes a raw-boned country boy. He has always dreamed of becoming a sailor and seeing the world. Now his chance has come. He steps on board and is immediately reprimanded by a gruff voice of authority. It is the first mate.

"'Stop right there, boy. First I want to know who you are. Then state your business, and then ask for permission to come aboard. If given, THEN ye come aboard."

"The boy steps back to the gangplank.

"Tom Blake. Looking to sign on as a sailor. Permission aboard, sir?"

"'Permission granted, Looking to ship out, are ye?'

"Our young man nods his head. The mate knows they are short-handed, and though a landlubber, the country boy looks strong enough. Soon he signs the ship's articles and then turns away full of pride. He cranes his neck at the masts rising hundreds of feet to the skies above. He scans the decks of his new home, walks aft to the wheel and then forward to the bow.

"There sits an old salt carving a model ship from a hunk of hardwood. The greenhorn introduces himself. Says he's signed up for their voyage around the Horn. The ancient mariner takes his measure and nods in token recognition before returning to his work.

"Then the intrepid young man asks, 'Sir, do you think we'll see the graybeards?'

"The old mariner hears excitement in the question and pauses in his work because, candidates, our young man knows not whereof he speaks. The greenhorn is excited about the prospect of seeing waves as tall as the masts above him, rolling from the horizon, one after another for days upon end, with crashing white water spilling down their faces like beards on old men.

"But the wise mariner knows the greybeards are older than men, aye, much older. He knows they have roamed the seas from time immemorial and make no mistake, they do so to this very day. Age has not weakened them. They are not bent and stooped by the centuries. Their strength is reborn with every storm that sweeps across the Southern Ocean, and God have mercy on those who meet them in their full fury!"

Atkins' voice filled the Chapel as if he was calling down hellfire on the heads of unrepentant sinners. He paused and looked at each of the men in the Chapel, before continuing in the voice of the ancient mariner.

"'Do I think we'll see the graybeards? Aye, there's a chance they'll be wandering across our path. Is that what you want? To see the big waves?'

"The mariner looks up to catch the greenhorn squarely in the eye. The young man hesitates, and then nods, as if courage is expected of him.

"The mariner's eyes return to his work, and as his knife once again carves into the hardwood, he but speaks these words of admonishment.

"'Son, once you see those waves, you'll never want to see them again.' "

Charles Atkins let a minute of silence elapse before speaking his final words in the Chapel.

"I will now leave you here with your own thoughts and the names on these walls. Let the souls of the departed shine a light on your true reasons for being here. Make your peace with them, and then decide if you would still dream of voyaging to the Southern Ocean. Take as long as you like, for your time is your own, even as your life belongs to no one but you. I will await your decision."

Atkins turned once more to the wall of light and said a prayer that could not be heard by the candidates. Then he walked out in silence, leaving the candidates alone with their thoughts.

The Chapel door had barely closed when Jack Richards emerged and locked eyes with Charles Atkins.

"Ok, I'm ready. What's next?"

"Your shipmates, Mr. Richards. We wait for them."

Richards narrowed his eyes briefly before looking away and walking slowly down the hall towards the doors to the lobby. But he stopped just short of them and leaned against the wall to wait.

Five minutes passed before Kenneth Bucher came out of the chapel.

"Ok, Uncle, I mean Mister Atkins. I want to keep going."

Atkins had been pretty sure the young man would understand the visit to the chapel in no uncertain terms. Just to be certain, he spoke a few words to test the young man's concentration.

"It got really good out there after you left," he said in a low voice.

Bucher was caught off guard and his response was pure instinct.

"I had more important things to do than surf more waves. So I didn't really miss anything, did I?"

The young man winked at his godfather and stepped aside when L.J. Merrill came out of the Chapel.

"Captain Atkins, I want to thank you for what we just did. It gave me a lot to think about, and reading the names of the crews lost at sea - - -"

"No, Mr. Merrill. They were not lost at sea. Those plaques commemorate crews whose ultimate fates were never known. Those sailors are simply missing. Theirs was a fate feared most by sailors, because nothing was ever found of them or their ships. Therefore, their loved ones never found closure, if you will, and suffered endlessly with grief. We honor them as best we can, although we really don't know what happened to them except neither they nor their ships ever made it home."

L.J. Merrill thought of his parents as he heard the words deep in his heart.

"Mr. Richards, are you with us?" called Atkins down the hall.

"Of course, CAPTAIN Atkins. Let's get going!"

This time Jack Richards hit the crash bar without breaking stride.

They entered the Shed and were confronted by the fully exposed hydraulic cylinders, hoses and heavy duty fittings of the Alba_Sword simulator. At the other end of the shed they saw four fully-rigged Alba_Swords. Working on the pair closest to the huge open doors were two groups of men and women in OSOM uniforms. The easy banter and laughter of a relaxed working atmosphere was in stark contrast to the menacing machine directly in front of them. Charles Atkins walked around the simulator to a tall room divider attached to the wall. It unfolded easily like an accordion as he stretched it across the smooth concrete floor, blocking half the candidates' view of the vessel preparation work zone. When it was fully extended, he went to the other side of the building and repeated the process. Before securing the two sections together, he poked his head into the work zone.

"Hello, Charles Atkins here. Ok, we'll be starting up in a minute. As you all remember, it gets pretty loud. You saw the notice on the bulletin board, I hope!" he said to the dozen or so people working on the Alba_Swords.

"What notice, mate? That dinky card with yer name on it?" came the crackling Aussie voice of Brad Farmer, engineer on the Alba_Sword *Eden*.

"Zhats ok, Atkins, ve Russians saw ze notice! Ze Auzzies can't read, you know!" said watch leader, Rudolph Velelov.

"Read good enough to know yer behind schedule, Rudy!"

"Zhat's ok, Mr. Farmah, ve are ready right now," said Misha Yevgenev, navigator, "You Auzzies, you are zee ones need more time!"

"We could sail tomorrow and sink you in our wake!" Helen Cooper, the captain of the *Eden*, was not going to give an inch.

Several of the Russians and Aussies started jawing at each other good naturedly, giving Atkins a chance to close the doors quickly before they turned on him for the sport of it.

He walked back to where the candidates were waiting, but the divider was not soundproof.

"Zay, Atkins!" boomed Velelov, "Ve agree with Farmah. Ve zid not zee da notice. Zere was no notice! But ve git za message. Ve all agree you owe us for our, how do you say, yes, for our inconvenience! Ve all eat lunch on your tab in ze mess hall, okay, Atkins? Yes, done deal."

"And we eat steak, mate! Training for the tug of war tomorrah!"

"You vill need more than steak, you Vickies! You need whole cow!"

Atkins smiled and shook his head as he walked around the simulator. He stopped smiling upon hearing the last of a remark by Jack Richards.

"- - - the chapel, now he puts up a veil between the novitiates and the devotees," Richards muttered, "What is this, some kinda religion?"

Atkins didn't hear all of Richards' words because Richards didn't want him to hear them. In and of itself, that was more than sufficient grounds for a sharp response and a challenge to the candidate.

"You got a question, Mr. Richards? Or something you'd like to share with all of us?"

"No, not at this time."

"Richards, you sure you want to do this? Maybe you're worried you don't have what it takes. Is that it, Mr. Richards?"

"No, that's not it, Mr. Atkins. I've got what it takes, you'll see. I was just wondering what kinda cult you got going here, SIR."

Merrill and Bucher blanched at Richards' words. Atkins didn't even blink.

"Well, we haven't asked you to drink the kool-aid yet, have we? And you can leave any time you want. So Mr. Richards, if you've got something to say about what we're doing, I want to hear about it. Is that clear?"

"Yessir, Mr. Captain, sir."

Atkins' glare was met with Richards' obvious defiance. Atkins had seen this before, after leaving the Chapel, in the attitudes of candidates who hadn't touched matters of the soul for a long time.

"Gentlemen, let's begin." He turned and climbed cat-like up the rope ladder to the deck of the Alba_Sword simulator. He cut an imposing figure looking back down at the greenhorns. Ken Bucher was first in line.

"Well, candidate, what do you say when you are about to step onto the deck of a ship?"

"Permission aboard?"

"Not quite. First identify yourself. Then state your business, then request permission aboard."

"Ken Bucher, candidate for able-bodied passenger. Permission aboard?"

"Permission granted."

Bucher went up the ladder and his example was not lost on L.J. Merrill.

"L.J. Merrill, sir, candidate for able-bodied passenger. Permission aboard?"

"Permission granted."

Richards looked up at Atkins with a wry grin.

"Jack Richards. Looking to sign on as a sailor, sir. I want to see some graybeards, SIR. Permission aboard?"

"Permission granted, MISTER Richards. You strap in over there, in the co-pilot's seat. Mister Merrill, remain standing and take the helm. Mister Bucher, right here in the engineer's seat."

Richards breezed past Atkins, his attitude unbowed. This whole thing was now a takeover bid, and Jack Richards had that skill set wired. He'd never lost when "take no prisoners" was a best management practice. He wasn't going to lose now. He started with a snide comment to L.J. Merrill when Atkins turned his back for a moment to pull up the rope ladder.

"Hey, L.J., you seem pretty comfortable around here. Maybe OSOM can be your new drug," he whispered, "You know the kid's gonna make it, so if I end up the odd man out, you can try and sweet talk these guys into taking you to your reef. Is that it, bro?"

Bucher knew something was going between Richards and Merrill and ignored them. Atkins didn't.

"Ok, Richards, what's your beef now?"

"Not a thing, MISTER Atkins! Just telling L.J. what a great time I'm having!" he said evenly. Atkins saw right through him, as intended, but L.J. Merrill said nothing because he knew there was some truth to what Richards had said. In the Chapel he had repeated the vow to his parents that this would be his last surf trip. When he said the words it occurred to him that joining the Order of Southern Ocean Mariners was an idea that would meet with their approval, and no matter what happened to Richards, he'd still have a chance to settle his score with Ian Clark.

Atkins stepped over to a console with a clear view of the three candidates.

"All right gentlemen, let us begin. Candidate Merrill, helm hard to port."

It took Merrill a moment to remember which way to spin the wheel, but when he did the cockpit began to rotate.

"Helm hard to starboard!" said Atkins when they had done one full revolution.

Merrill spun the wheel in the opposite direction, and the simulator reversed its motion.

"Set your course for true north!"

Merrill looked at Atkins with a big question mark in his eyes.

"The compass in front of you, candidate! Steer by the compass!"

The simulator was revolving, as was the compass rose in its brass case. Merrill quickly adapted to the situation. He slowly reversed the wheel. The simulator came to a stop and so did the spinning compass rose. Then he brought her back around and was back on course in no time.

"Well done, Mr. Merrill. Bucher and Richards, your turn at the wheel will come later. Call out the course, helmsman!"

"Zero degrees north, captain!" said Merrill in a confident voice. It was all Richards could do to keep a smirk off his face. Bucher was all eyes and ears, noticing the response lag between the wheel and the motion of the simulator.

"Gentlemen, let us proceed."

Atkins pressed a button, and the sound of wind filled the space around them, creating a sense of floating isolation in the cockpit. On the screen, spray began to appear before turning into waves spiraling around OSOM's insignia on a pennant snapping briskly in a gale force wind. Then the wind died slowly into silence, the flag disappeared, and the waves were replaced by two lines of plain text.

The Order of Southern Ocean Mariners
Able-Bodied Passenger Orientation

"Candidates, let us first mark the last known positions of those gone forever missing after venturing out into the Southern Ocean."

The display changed to a map of the Southern Hemisphere to graphically impress upon the men just how little land there is below the equator and the immensity of the Southern Ocean. A timeline appeared at the base of the display stretching across the centuries from 1400 to 2000. A pointer began to move through the years. Slowly, one at a time, black crosses appeared near coastlines, and then farther and farther out into the empty blue spaces of the map. Each cross marked the last known location of a sailing ship, starting with the sinking of a Portuguese caravelle off Good Hope in 1484. When the display advanced to the 1800s, the crosses multiplied rapidly. A zone southeast of Cape Horn became blacked out: thirty-five crosses were added there in 1905 alone. The appearance of crosses slowed in years when sail was increasingly replaced by steam, and then diesel. Yet the crosses continued to pop up until a final two marked the last locations where human life had been lost during a recent yacht race through the Southern Ocean.

Charles Atkins had conducted the orientation many times, but never once did he find himself inured to what was on the screen. The timbre of his voice was not that of someone just going through the motions.

"Now gentlemen, let us take a closer look at what may have happened to a ship of good men a long time ago."

All the crosses disappeared except one about two hundred nautical miles east southeast of Cape Horn. The map dissolved to a black and white image of a square-rigged, four-masted cargo ship on a calm sea. The timeline disappeared. Text began to crawl across the bottom of the screen.

Glenburn, Falmouth, England, launched April 10, 1886.
Five thousand tons. Crew of twenty four.
Built for the grain trade with Australia.
Loaded timber March 1, 1893 port of Glasgow.
Destination Adelaide, Australia.
Reported overdue July 21, 1893.
Declared missing. Lloyds December 16, 1893.

"Candidates, the cross on the screen marks the last known position of the *Glenburn*, but in reality we know not where she sank. And as for her crew, there are no tombstones to mark the final resting place of their corpses. Their souls were released at the bottom of the sea. Candidate Merrill, will you please read their names."

"Aye aye, sir."

L.J. Merrill began to read the names as they crawled across the bottom of the screen from right to left.

"Peter Lewis, 52, Captain, William Adams, 28, First Mate, John Bertram, 23, Second Mate, Michael Charing, 41, carpenter, - - -"

The sails of the *Glenburn* filled with wind and the sea began to rise. Within minutes she was heeled over, the very picture of adventure and gallantry so often associated with "the golden age of sail." Then a very large rogue wave appeared and swept across the decks of the ill-fated four-master. The point-of-view closed in, and sailors could be seen high in the rigging attempting to shorten sail. The wind began to scream and then one, and then another sailor fell from the ratlines. A spar broke, and the screams of eight men were heard over the wild wind as they fell a hundred feet into the exploding sea. A mainsail blew out, knocking more men into space. Another huge sail was torn from the mast, and then a wave almost a hundred feet high smashed into the wounded ship. The *Glenburn* began to disintegrate. Above the roaring wind could be heard the terror-stricken voices of drowning men gasping for their last breaths, and screaming the names of their loved ones, until they were silenced by another mountain of cold water that buried the ill-fated ship.

"EDWARD WARREN, 21, ABS, CHARLES WILLIAMS, 18, ABS, ARTHUR CHARLES, 14, cabin boy, PATRICK LEEDS, 14, cabin boy."

Merrill read the last of the names as the *Glenburn* sank without a trace. Then Atkins' baritone rose above the roar.

"Candidates! THERE is your romance, your nostalgia, your armchair adventure! A beautiful ocean? No, a KILLER of men! A proud tall ship? No, a SMASHED coffin! Brave sailors now CORPSES trapped in her sinking wreckage! Their wives now widows, their children never to see their fathers again. Let their black fate touch your souls - that you may now know, and will never forget, the truth of the Southern Ocean."

The candidates stared at the screen. Their minds told them it was all computer-generated imaging. Their hearts felt something else altogether. Merrill held on to the wheel with a death grip. Bucher was visibly shaken, and Richards' once steely gaze was now reduced to darting glances from the display to Atkins and back again. The simulator began to vibrate from the sound of the screaming Force Twelve wind. It seemed the screen itself would be shredded to rags.

Then, slowly, the sound subsided and the raging ocean that destroyed men and ship became, once again, a placid sea. All was quiet, the candidates even more so. But not quite. The simulator was now matching the motion of the gently rolling surface of the open ocean on the screen.

"Excuse me gentlemen, but I have business to attend to. Candidate Merrill, you have the helm. Set your course for thirty one degrees north. I'll return presently. Mr. Bucher, please store the ladder."

Before he turned away, he pressed several icons on the touch screen panel facing Merrill. A small digital timer mounted on the console began to count down from sixty. Atkins tossed the rope ladder over the side of the simulator deck and descended to the concrete floor. Bucher pulled up the rope ladder and strapped himself back into his seat.

When the time reached zero, the calm on the screen quickly changed. The wind came up from the northwest. A large groundswell appeared from the southeast. The course announced by the Captain required Merrill to steer between the opposing forces. It was like a giant video game, perfectly simulating the motion of the waves and the minor shock as they "hit" the craft he was steering.

Richards and Bucher watched the screen and felt the effects of Merrill's helmsmanship as if he was driving a four-wheel off road vehicle through an obstacle course. Of course, the "sea" was not that rough, but the sensation was quite real as the wind built up to a Force Three.

The simulation continued for almost ten minutes and Merrill found himself increasingly tasked by the challenge of wave after wave slamming into them. Then the simulator stopped its motion completely. The wheel in Merrill's hands froze in place. It was another few seconds, though, before the three men realized they no longer had to be holding on tight.

Atkins climbed up the rope ladder so that his head and shoulders appeared over the railing.

"Gentlemen, Mariner McRane tells me that for now your candidacies can proceed if you so choose."

The simple sentence shocked the men back to a moment of mixed emotions. They were relieved their documentation was accepted, and yet they felt a sense of dread at what lay before them, as if half-hoping they could go home without having to ever face what they now knew might await them.

"You can unbuckle yourselves now. If you are going to continue, follow me. Once we've had some grub for lunch, we'll do the motion sickness and other tests this afternoon."

Just after four p.m., and fifty miles up the coast, the founder of the Order of Southern Ocean Mariners was sitting next to his wife on a bluff near their home overlooking the Santa Barbara Channel. Frank Bucher knew the orientation had just ended. He pulled a phone out of his pocket, pressed a button, and was connected with Charles Atkins.

"What news, Charlie?"

"Good news, Frank. We will be shaking out to San Miguel noon tomorrow, and with a full crew, as it turns out. Richards was a bit of a pain in the ass, but in the end he kept his mouth shut and passed all the tests. Merrill did fine. As for the third candidate," Atkins paused, "He seems to have the right genes."

Bucher looked at his wife and nodded with a smile. But the smile was not returned, and she got up and walked away from him.

"May I assume we'll be taking the sunset cruise towards the Western Gate," continued Atkins, "Followed by a channel transit with a surprise or two to see what Jackie Wallet and the Soul Survivor are really made of? I think we already know about the other candidate."

Bucher couldn't help but grin at Atkins' nicknames for Richards and Merrill until he thought of his son – and his wife.

"He did really well, honey," he said to her, but she had her back to him and was watching the sun begin to set behind the growing clouds of the approaching storm front. A pang went through his heart when she didn't answer. A moment later Frank Bucher realized he was still in communication with Atkins.

"Uh, yeah, uh, Charlie, I'll meet you at Razorblades on the way up. It might be good to, uh, check their bonafides as surfers, and, uh, then head out into the Channel after dark."

Atkins sensed what was going on between a father and mother now that their son was ready to become a man.

"Do you or Sophia want to talk to your boy?"

"No, just tell him to call home when he gets a chance."

Bucher clicked off the headset and walked over to his wife. He knew she needed to be alone with her thoughts, and yet he knew she needed him by her side. He sat down on the dry grass beside her but did not touch her.

The wind was blowing hard out to sea. Pelicans were gliding in formation above the surfline. Small waves rolled through the kelp beds, their crests blown to spray as they crashed and died on the beach. For some the solitude and beauty were picture-perfect. But for a mother whose son was about to go to sea, the world was as bleak and lifeless as the moon. It was some time before she finally took her husband's hand and put it to her cheek.

* * *

Charles Atkins walked out into the lobby where the three men waited.

"Gentlemen, your candidacies may proceed. Please be back here at noon tomorrow if you wish to continue. You can bring your surfboards if you like. We might have a chance to surf Razorblades on the way up the coast."

"Do we need to bring anything else, Captain Atkins?"

"No, Mr. Merrill, we have everything you need," Atkins glanced at the gathering storm outside, "including foul weather gear."

"How'd I do on the reaction time tests, Captain?" edged in Jack Richards.

"Within specs, Mr. Richards. In fact you all were within specs on today's tests, else I'd be washing you out right now. Do not forget to maintain your motion sickness meds. It will be the real thing tomorrow. Mr. Merrill, Mr. Richards? Can I ask you to step outside for a minute. I'll join you presently."

"Ok, Kenny, see you tomorrow!" said L.J. Merrill. Richards just nodded at the young man, who politely smiled back.

The two men walked out of the lobby to where they had a view of the *Tom Swift* and the *Serena*. The afternoon had clouded over and a wind from the south was now picking up. The surf across the street was rough and ragged, ruined and unrideable by the approaching storm.

"Need any help, Uncle?" said Bucher.

"Ok, Kenny, you're off duty as a candidate, I guess. Yes, in fact you can help me put away the simulator, and then you can swab the decks! And then there's probably clean-up stuff you can do in the work zone, and then you can fix my board because I think we could get some good waves tomorrow. And when you're done with that I might need some more help."

"Well, I, uh - -"

"Too late, young man. You piped up, and your offer has been accepted. Besides, you want to come up through the hawsepipe, don't you? This is how it's done. The Captain keeps the new cabin boy busy until the poor chap drops from exhaustion. Then we splash a bucket of cold water on him and work him some more. Believe me, Kenny, you've got it easy compared to the real thing a hundred years ago. Now, where was I? My car needs washing - - -"

"But its gonna rain!"

"Pipe down, shipmate, and follow orders. You are lucky I don't have you cooking me dinner. Well, now that I think about it, that's not a bad idea at all!"

Kenny Bucher slugged him in the arm.

"So get busy while I have a few last words with the other candidates."

"Gentlemen, we'll be shipping out on the *Tom Swift*. She is the Alba_Sword closest to us. You are welcome to take a closer look at her, but you are not to go aboard without permission."

Merrill's eagerness was stopped short as Atkins finished his sentence. Then a shot of anxiety jabbed his heart. He wanted to be in OSOM right now, but he couldn't, and the junkie came down hard and fast. Then he chuckled at his little emotional loop-de-loop, and smiled deeply when he thought of how ridiculous it was to be so tightly wired to the toggle switch between euphoria and depression.

"Thanks, Mr. Atkins, I'm sure we'll see more than enough of her tomorrow. Jack, we better get going if we want to beat traffic across L.A."

"Yeah, thanks," said Jack Richards, "Do we owe you anything for today, or is it part of the deal?"

"The orientation costs are included in the price of your passage - IF you do make passage. If you don't we'll subtract what you owe us from your money in escrow and send you a refund after the shakedown cruise. Of course, if you're out right now, just say so. We have your mailing address."

"No, that's okay. Just checking," said Richards, reacting quickly to the challenge he perceived in Atkins' tone.

"Fine, then, gentlemen. There is one thing more I'd like to know if you'll permit me. I have a question for you, Mr. Merrill, and your client. When was the last time you cried?"

L.J. Merrill thought for a second, and then smiled at a pleasant memory from long ago. "The last time I saw a local girl get her first wave on a board I gave her at a Geosurf resort in Samoa."

"And you, Mr. Richards?"

"Uh, when, uh, it was, uh, I think it was when I and my wife, or no it was when my daughter told me she loved me and I was on a plane last year, or, uh, yeah I think that was it."

"Thanks, Mr. Richards. See you tomorrow, gentlemen."

Richards was about to say something, but Merrill raised a finger. Atkins turned and went back into the lobby. Merrill and Richards watched him walk away. They avoided each other's looks, knowing they'd both lied.

Richards turned away first and started to walk across the parking lot.

"Fuck, L.J., why don't we just get a room and stay up here? I don't want to surf tomorrow."

"You will if Razors is firing! Our boards are down in Laguna, and besides I want to sleep in my own bed tonight. Don't you?" said L.J. Merrill, now a few steps behind. He stopped in his tracks, realizing he was following Richards and wanted to get out ahead of him again somehow. But nothing came to mind except a biting remark.

"And you can spend some time with the wife and kids!"

"Fuck you, Merrill. Let's go."

Not another word was said until they were sitting in the big SUV, its engine warming up while the first drops of rain touched the windshield. It had been a long day and there was a long drive ahead of him. The stress of the tests had taken its toll, and Richards' patience was shot.

"Listen, L.J., don't give me any shit. And I don't like the way you treated me today, asshole."

"Treated you? What are you talking about?"

Richards' anger took over he drove out of the OSOM parking lot.

"Listen, L.J. you'd be holed up with mom and dad if it wasn't for me and you know it. And - - -"

Merrill cut him off.

"No, YOU listen, Richards. YOU just went through a stop sign and you didn't even see it. If a big rig had been coming, You'd be dead right now," Merrill paused, "Well, maybe not. This thing does have side airbags, doesn't it? Sure it does, the best that money can buy. But money can't buy what we need, Jack, and you know it. So why don't YOU shut up and just drive, ok? This isn't the simulator."

"Don't tell me to shut up, Merrill. Just because you've found your new best friends - - -"

"Oh, THAT'S it. Now I get it. Now what would it tell you about a man to hear him say something like, 'Your new best friends'?" he said, but he knew the answer right away: a man whose feelings had been hurt. L.J. Merrill knew what that felt like and softened his tone immediately.

"Jack, we're in this together, ok? Maybe I got carried away a bit today, but Clark fucked me over and it went pretty deep. So I'm sorry, but the only way to get even is with Bucher and Atkins, and you know why."

"Yeah, I know, L.J. The permits and the predictions."

"Right. Ian Clark and Wavelife have a lock on that reef. I know how Clark works because I worked for him. He got an exclusive to a hundred square miles of open ocean by telling the Tahitians he wanted to scout some reefs and islands and keep it secret from his competitors. That's how we used to do it, Jack, but this time he cemented the deal with a ton of Mercante's money so nobody could buy their permit out from under them. And if they get there first, the Tahitians will give 'em a ninety-nine year lease and its all over."

"Yeah, but you only found out about that deal last week!" said Richards.

"Listen Jack, I knew what the deal was going to be when I met you last January. I knew the only way to beat Clark and Wavelife is with OSOM. Bucher sails under the UN flag and he can go anywhere he wants."

"Yeah, I know all that, L.J.," said Richards as he carefully stopped for a yellow light about to turn red near the freeway.

"Well let me tell you something else, Jack, just so you don't forget what we're really doing here. Not only are we going to boat in with the most respected sailors on earth, but we'll be riding the biggest waves of the year when we get there. That's what these guys wait for, and they always get it when they run the Regatta. Geosurf uses WaveAlert, and those guys get it wrong all the time in the Southern Ocean. So Clark and Mercante might over-amp and go out there only to find it shitty. But knowing Larson, he'll want to wait until he KNOWS its going to be really big. So with OSOM, we'll win either way. We'll surf it bigger and better for sure if they've blown it, or else we'll show up uninvited at their PR event and surprise the shit out of 'em."

Richards accelerated up the off ramp on to the southbound 101.

"Jack, we need each other to do what we want to do, and we need OSOM no matter what. We're doing fine so far, and we'll make it okay if we stick together. So let's just both back off and cruise for a while, okay?"

A steady rain began to fall. Jack Richards switched on the windshield wipers as he headed up the grade and into the Valley. They swiped at the rain and cleared the glass for a second, only to have the droplets come back again and again. Richards kept trying to clear his mind with Merrill's logic, but his heart kept raining thoughts without end.

Merrill's shot about his family had hit hard, and Richards could not stop thinking about it. He reached for the cell phone, then put it back in its cradle on the dash of the SUV, knowing he would just get an answering machine even if his wife and kids were home.

He thought back to a day during training when Merrill had been on his case about his paddling. He didn't like Merrill's tone, said something about it. He couldn't remember exactly what, but he remembered Merrill's reply.

"Sure, Jack. My apologies. Just remember, you only know who your friends are because they are the ones who call you on your shit."

Merrill was asleep with his watchcap pulled down over his eyes. They were almost to the airport when traffic slowed to a crawl and stopped. Richards was so lost in thought that only at the last second did he slam on the brakes. The big SUV slewed sideways and he lost all control. He spun the steering wheel, luckily in the right direction just as the tires found some grip.

L.J. Merrill's head bounced against the door window as the SUV came to a sudden and lurching stop with its front bumper only an inch from a big rig.

"Jack! What's going on? Where are we?"

"Nothing L.J. We're stuck in traffic, so go back to sleep."

Traffic began to move again and the after-action adrenaline rushed through Richards' veins. It brought him back to his senses, and a few seconds later he shook his head with a cynical laugh. He barged the big SUV into the carpool lane, stepped on the gas, and switched the windshield wipers to high speed as the rain began to come down hard.

The Shakedown Cruise

Charles Atkins kept a weather eye on the horizon and the incoming surf as he steered towards the point of land offering a safe anchorage. L.J. Merrill and Jack Richards sat on either side of him in the cockpit of the *Tom Swift*, but their eyes were on the headland known as Razorblades, its name derived from the sharp, angled rock formations jutting into the sea. They were coming into the lee of the headland and were now close enough to the waves for the surfers to see clearly into the open mouths of the rolling tunnels.

Atkins turned the Alba_Sword's bow out to sea and made sure they were safely in deep water where no waves could break.

"Drop anchor!"

"Aye, aye, Captain!" responded Ken Bucher standing out on the bow. He released the clamps and chain rattled through the hawsepipe. The hook sank quickly to the sandy bottom below. Atkins gave the propulsion system a short burst in reverse to set the anchor, and then came ahead a touch as Bucher pulled her up snug. The *Tom Swift* was now at rest.

"What orders, sir?" asked Jack Richards without a trace of sarcasm in his voice now that he'd gotten his attitude out of his system the day before.

"You guys go surfing if you want. It looks pretty good out there," answered Atkins, smiling at Richards and glad the man had come around.

"Aye, aye, sir!" responded the men in the cockpit who quickly went below to get into their wetsuits. Ken Bucher was close behind them.

"You on it too, Kenny?"

"Nope, I've got more important things to do than go surfing."

No one was in the water late this Sunday afternoon when the *Tom Swift* arrived. Access to Razors was highly restricted to owners of land surrounding the place, most of whom didn't surf very well given the demands of making the kind of money required to buy property in the area. They were no match for the heavy swell mixed with storm surf, and the dirt parking lot was deserted. To the trained eye of surfers with real talent, however, the waves were excellent.

"All yours, Jack!"

Jack Richards heard L.J. Merrill yell to him as a set of ten footers pulled into the bay like spokes on a wheel. He had been the first to get into his wetsuit and launch his board off the transom of the *Tom Swift*. For a moment he had endless perfect waves all to himself. True to form, Jack Richards took the first one he could get.

One stroke take-off into a kick stall. Down the face to set up a first power turn off the bottom right on the sweet spot. Accelerate to full speed flight down the line. A touch on the inside rail up into a drift along the pitching crest. Last second release into mid air free-fall. Land it, then another carving arc.

He glanced at the cockpit of the *Tom Swift* to see if Atkins was watching his performance. He was, but now the wave demanded Richards' full attention.

He gouged another culvert into the base of the wave, driving his board up from the flats into a concave wall peeling like a lathe shaving down the Razor's reef.

"Nice move," said Charles Atkins, using a spyglass to check Richards' facial expression up close with one eye while using the other to see the entire wave unfold, "A man possessed – though not by joy, Mr. Bucher. No childlike glee for the wallet, no fun on his face."

Below decks, Ken Bucher was examining Alba_Sword schematics displayed on a console when he heard the comment through the hatch and thought his uncle was talking to him. He looked up for a second, only to hear a voice he'd known all his life.

"He's a millionaire on a perfect wave with his friend cheering him on. What more could a man want? Seems like the guy doesn't quite know how to be happy, I'd say."

Broad-shouldered with a deep tan and a naval crew cut, Frank Bucher had paddled out to the *Tom Swift* after coming down to the beach from his home in the hills overlooking that deserted stretch of coast. He'd joined Charles Atkins to watch Merrill and Richards ride waves, though not to see their surfing skills so much as to look for clues to their characters like dancers trying out for a master choreographer.

Richards finished his ride with a final turn through the tail-end section of the wave. He looked at the *Tom Swift*, but Atkins had his spyglass raised towards the horizon. He quickly spun his board around and began paddling with short quick strokes without thinking about the fact that there were now two men in the cockpit when he saw what Atkins was watching out in the take-off zone. L.J. Merrill was facing wave number four of the same set.

The wave would have closed out the place had the tide been a foot lower. It looked powerful and threatening, but Merrill knew he had a chance to ride it. The liquid wall was now almost vertical. His position was absolute edge-of-disaster, a situation he'd faced a thousand times surfing around the world. He knew he would go, no matter what.

Three strokes and quick to his feet. Elevator drop ten feet straight down to the trough. Soul arch off the bottom, relaxed and arms spread like a hood ornament on a Rolls Royce, riding through a perfect double-overhead liquid tube. He drifted slightly sideways before his fins caught, giving him critical forward momentum at the last instant. He disappeared completely inside the tunnel of the perfect wave.

Bucher and Atkins watched with not a little bit of awe.

"Now that's the genuine article!"

"Let's see if he makes it."

185

Jack Richards had his head down and paddled hard to make it over the wave, unaware that Merrill's trail through the tube had put them on a collision course. Though almost blinded by spray inside the wave, Merrill shifted his weight back a hair, slowing his board just enough to miss his friend by inches. But the loss of speed had consequences. He was swallowed completely by the clam-shell collapse of the wave's last section. Yet his determination was that of a bulldog in a wide stance so solid nothing could budge him. The energy of the wave rolled forward. He popped out the back of the wave, completely unscathed and standing on his board.

Cheers were heard from the *Tom Swift*, though not from Jack Richards. There were two more waves in the set, and he wanted one real bad. And indeed he got the last one, a smaller wave marred by residual white water from the previous waves, and the ride was bumpy and frustrating. He milked it all the way to the beach, but his two waves could not match what Merrill had done with one. With no satisfaction in his heart, Jack Richards began to slowly paddle back out to sea where L.J. Merrill sat in the sunlight.

"Hmm, these guys are pretty good. But there's something about Richards that I don't like."

"Well, Frank, why don't you paddle out there and get a closer look?"

"Not a bad idea. Can your other crewman come along?"

"As of last report, he had more important things to do than go surfing," said Charles Atkins with a grin, "So I suggest he not be disturbed."

Frank Bucher paused, and then sighed, before giving Atkins a smile and diving off the taffrail.

Below decks, Kenneth Bucher was completely immersed in studying the muscle and brains of the *Tom Swift*. Years ago he had asked his dad why they were called Alba_Swords.

"Well, my boy, I want them to ride waves as effortlessly as an albatross, and I think they will with a hull copied from the curves of a swordfish."

Now the young man was finally aboard an Alba_Sword, and he wanted to learn everything he could about his father's incredible invention.

From watching his dad build scale models in his workshop at home, Ken Bucher knew that the hull's strength came from the use of materials developed for the SR-71 spy plane along with bamboo veneer and an epoxy process to give the featherweight material the strength of stainless steel. His dad had also spent a lot of time researching every Polynesian sailing craft known to modern man and a variety of high tech materials for the sails and masts to allow an Alba_Sword, like the wandering albatross, to always use the wind, no matter how weak or how strong, from gentle zephyrs to full gales.

After going through the digital schematics stored on the *Swift*'s computer, he traced the cables and hydraulics of the control, thrust and trim systems, noting how they interfaced with the ballast transfer tanks through a central processing unit connected to sensors throughout the entire hull. He marveled at the powerful gimbals and cylinders of the forward fins and hydroplanes,

186

positioned like the pectorals of the swordfish for maximum maneuverability. Making his way back to the propulsion units, he developed a mental picture of the remarkably integrated systems, lightweight components, and ichthyodynamic design required to voyage through the ocean with the agility of a fast attack apex predator. And then, in a flash moment of comprehension, he finally understood how his dad had solved the problem of voyaging thousands of miles from land, in huge waves too violent to be survived, by being able to find quiet safety with the touch of a few buttons.

"Candidate Bucher! You will be the duty cook. All hands will dine at 1800 hours. Commence galley duty in thirty minutes," said Charles Atkins, not wanting to cut short the young man's exercise in discovery too abruptly.

"Aye-aye, sir!" came the cheerful response from below decks. For a moment Ken Bucher looked out a porthole and saw a set coming in. Two surfers were in the takeoff zone, and a third was paddling towards them. But his curiosity got the better of him and he went back to examining the ballast sensor system. He didn't think twice about it, since he'd seen his dad surf a hundred times, but he smiled when he realized that for L.J. Merrill and Jack Richards, it would be their first.

Frank Bucher timed his arrival at the take-off zone to coincide with that of an outside set. Not missing a stroke, he kept going right past Richards and Merrill, giving them only a nod as the first wave approached. They were completely surprised by the presence of another surfer in the water. They didn't know who he was, but when the guy just kept paddling out to sea they figured he must have been one of the landowners since they didn't know what he was doing paddling out so far - and concluded he didn't either.

Suddenly they saw a wide carving curve of white water arc up and around wave number three. The surfer they'd dismissed as a kook suddenly appeared coming out of the trough, arms spread gracefully, gliding like a great sea bird across the unbroken face. The rider bore down on them at full speed before leaning back and carving a cutback that drenched them with a powerful blast of cold spray.

It was quite a shock for the world-traveled legend and the wealthy connoisseur of surfing at its best. L.J. Merrill realized he had just seen something beyond anything in his experience. Jack Richards was even more shaken. Atkins had told them that their surfing abilities might be judged as part of their candidacies. Now, not only had Merrill upstaged him, but some guy they didn't even know had almost literally sent him to the showers.

The two dazed surfers looked at each other, but before they could say anything, they suddenly realized they were seriously caught inside by the rest of the set. There was no escape. They tried to duck dive under the first collapsing wall. No sale. They were thrown backwards over the falls holding on to their boards. They came up to the surface only to be bulldozed by the white water of three more waves.

While Merrill and Richards were taking it on the bean in the impact zone, Frank Bucher was finishing his ride inside. He looked over at the *Tom Swift*.

Charles Atkins, snapping his fingers and dancing around the cockpit, gave a big thumbs up to Bucher, who waved and then slowly paddled back out in the deep channel, smiling at the thought of two old pros putting a couple of rookies through some serious hazing that had only just begun.

Bucher arrived at the take-off zone just as Merrill and Richards were recovering from their ordeal. Their clocks had been thoroughly cleaned by mother nature, and there was no trace of ego or resentment as the stranger paddled up to them.

"How'd you do that? That was an unreal takeoff!"

"Did you make it all the way? How'd you do that?"

Their enthusiasm violated the code of cool amongst the best surfers, but Richards and Merrill knew they had just been put in their place by a master surfer, whoever he was.

"Hi guys! Mind if I join you? My name's Frank Bucher."

He saw the awe-struck look in their eyes and turned it to his purpose.

"Some pretty good waves out here. Say, you boys surf pretty good! Who made that board, Richards? What kind of fins you got there, Merrill? Hey, here comes another set!"

Bucher began paddling out to sea, and Merrill noticed something unusual about the deck of Bucher's board. But he never got a chance to ask him about it as the waves became very consistent, each groomed to perfection by the wind blowing from the land. The three surfers took turns riding the long waves down the headland for set after set. The sun was bright over the islands on the horizon. Their boat rested at anchor in the bay. It was a surfer's paradise that couldn't get any better, until a yellow flag with a black ball went up the mast of the *Tom Swift*.

"What do you make of that?" exclaimed L.J. Merrill.

"Simple, L.J., the Captain's telling us to come in! No more surfing today!" said Frank Bucher without a moment's hesitation.

"You can't be serious! This is perfect out here!" protested Jack Richards.

"Yeah, uh, Frank do you think we can - - -"but L.J. Merrill never finished his sentence. Frank Bucher was already paddling toward the Alba_Sword. Merrill had thought to wait out the lull and ride a last one in, but with Bucher paddling and not looking back, he shrugged at Richards and both men reluctantly began to follow in his wake.

They were climbing aboard the *Tom Swift* in the gathering dusk when the next set of waves came marching in toward the deserted coast, their smooth liquid faces no longer to be marred by the slicing tracks of man. And behind them, in an endless parade across the timeless ocean, more waves were coming, as they had for ten million years, to break perfectly where an ancient accident of geology had created a small bay to shape the ocean's energy into spirals not unlike those of nautilus shells - or interstellar galaxies.

* * *

The dinner conversation was lively, with Charles Atkins and Frank Bucher speaking of nothing but how well Merrill and Richards had surfed, how good their waves were, and on and on. They knew that surfers like nothing more than to yap interminably about their rides, and the candidates were no exception as they fell for the ego-building hook, line and sinker.

"So Mr. Merrill, my son spent a week at one of your camps in Baja. He was impressed with your knowledge of the ocean. I take it you are still working as a surf guide?"

Merrill didn't quite know what to say. Jack Richards did.

"Yes, he's working for me, and that's why we're here."

Frank Bucher then turned to Richards and sized him up as a very rich man in very good shape. About the same height as Merrill, same weight, but when Bucher's gaze drilled into Richards' eyes, set deep in a head freshly shaven, and he knew the man was not about innocence. There was something like fresh air in Merrill's quiet, though well-traveled face. Jack Richards was another man entirely.

"Well, Jack, why would you have your surf guide bring you to OSOM?"

"I'm fortunate enough to be in a position where price is no object. You have my check for two hundred grand in escrow. Mr. Merrill has put us through a rigorous training regimen for the past six weeks in preparation for not only sailing with you, but for something even more challenging, we think. So I've brought along what I think will cover the price of a proposal we'd like to make."

He pulled a piece of paper out of his pocket, unfolded it, and put it on the table. It was a check, the kind used for major transactions on Wall Street, and it was made out to OSOM. It was signed and dated. The amount had been left blank. Merrill held his breath. He was well aware of Richards' audacity when it came to money, but this was over-the-top. He fully expected Frank Bucher to tell them to shove off right then and there.

"We're not tour guides for hire, Jack. You sail under our command, and that's that. So what's this about a proposal?"

He ignored the check and shot Richards with a look that demanded an immediate answer.

"Captain Bucher, you'll find I am quite prepared to make a significant contribution to your non-profit organization."

"Yeah, I'll bet. In fact, you probably need every tax write off you can get. Thanks just the same, but OSOM doesn't need your largess. Now let's cut the crap. You want to surfsail the Roaring Forties, that much is known," said Bucher with a cutting edge to his voice, "Now, what else do you want? What's the deal here, Merrill?"

"We want to be the first to ride the last undiscovered perfect wave on the planet. We want to time it perfectly to be there on the biggest day imaginable. I think the only way it can be done is by sailing with you. I know you have the best data on weather in the Roaring Forties, and I'm sure you'll be out there looking to ride in front of the most powerful storm of the winter. In fact I've surfed throughout the Southern Hemisphere riding waves that you were

189

probably also surfing before they got to me. If we can charter you and an Alba_Sword and set a course for the reef I found, we've got a chance to be there on the biggest day of the year in July or August."

"You want to crew on an Alba_Sword just to get a surf session, L.J.? Why don't you get Jackie Wallet here to rent a cruise ship and belly up to the bar?"

"Because someone else wants to surf this place, too, and we want to surprise them when they get there. Kinda like what happened when Amundsen beat Scott to the South Pole."

"So who you are trying to beat, Richards?"

"Wavelife International."

"Oh, and I bet your former employer must be in one this, is he not, L.J.? Well, that explains your newfound independence. And Richards, you must be interested in trying to take down a big corporation. So, tell me, why hasn't anyone surfed this place?"

"Because it's not on any map I could find," said L.J. Merrill, "and I've seen a lot of maps, Frank, believe me. But I did a lot of research, found some evidence, and now that water temperatures have risen dramatically in this one remote zone of the South Pacific, I figured there might be some reefs with some perfect waves that nobody could have surfed even a few years ago. And I found what I was looking for."

"Well, we have our preferred routes from New Zealand to Cape Horn and I'm sure your reef is well to the north of where we do our surfing. In fact we never go near all those archipelagos near the Gambier Group. Way too dangerous. And then there's the issue of getting a permit from the Tahitians. What about that?"

"Wavelife already has it," said Merrill, barely able to respond after Bucher's perfect assessment of the entire situation.

"And so you need someone who can get you there without violating maritime law, and that means OSOM," said Bucher with a knowing smile on his face for the legendary surf scout, "Pretty smart, Merrill. And I must say your theory about warm water incursions and new reefs to ride has piqued my curiosity, not to mention all the trouble you guys are going to – a big fat blank check just to outsmart a big corporation, not to mention a little revenge on the side, right L.J.?"

L.J. Merrill could look Frank Bucher in the eye. He had him dead to rights and he knew it. That's why Bucher blithely made a decision he knew would surprise the legendary surf scout.

"So your candidacies as able-bodied passengers will proceed for the time being. As for your surf trip, that would be a wait-see at best. So tell your client to put his check away, because you're not anywhere near your reef, L.J.," he said with a slight scold to his voice, "That is, of course, if you even want to keep going at all."

"By all means, Captain Bucher," replied Merrill.

The Captain turned to Jack Richards.

"And you Richards? What say ye?" said Frank Bucher, his wicked grin and Gregory Peck-as-Ahab imitation catching Richards off guard, as intended.

"Affirmative, sir. Count me in," said Richards, but not before his voice betrayed an instant of doubt.

"Well, that's settled," said Charles Atkins changing the subject after catching a quick glance from Frank Bucher, "Candidate Kenny, if nothing else you certainly qualify as a galley slave. Nice dinner."

"Thanks, sir. Now with your permission I'll secure the galley area."

"That won't be necessary, candidate," he said, turning to Merrill and Richards, "Gentlemen, the cook never does the dishes. OSOM tradition. Need I say more? We weigh anchor in thirty minutes. Be on deck in a timely fashion for our departure. Frank let's run a check of all systems. Mr. Bucher, please accompany us. You might learn something."

Despite the intensity of the conversation with Frank Bucher, L.J. Merrill and Jack Richards were in high spirits and thought the assignment to clean up was just a good-natured part of the shakedown cruise. They divided the work of busing the dirty dishes, washing and stowing them. Everything in the galley was labeled, and they finished up so fast they were left wondering what else they could do. Now alone with time on their hands, they had a chance to reflect on the events of the day.

"You know, L.J., I think this is really going to work! Bucher's an unreal surfer, and though he grilled us pretty good, I know he saw that check, and I bet he's already thinking about how he can help us beat Clark and Wavelife."

But L.J. Merrill wasn't so sure. His addiction to surfing perfection had put him in dozens of tight spots over the years, predicaments Jack Richards liked to think he understood but had never really experienced. Of course, sitting on a ultra-high tech transoceanic surfsailing craft was not the Third World by any means, but Merrill's instincts were never wrong.

"I don't know Jack. Listen, there's no way this is supposed to be this easy. Good food, great waves, all that chit-chat at the table, and so far all we've had to do is enjoy a coastal cruise, surf our brains out and do the dishes."

"Nah, bro. These guys aren't all that interested in working us over, not when our passages will net them major six figures and a lot more if we surf the reef. I bet you a grand Bucher takes that blank check and fills it out for a million bucks."

"We're a long way from that happening right now. First let's see if we make it through the rest of this trip."

"Listen, L.J., what could possibly happen? When it's our watch, well, you did a good job learning how to drive on the way up the coast, and I was watching everything you did with the propulsion jets and all that. Our surfing was good, our seamanship will be good enough, and I'm sure Bucher won't pass up that blank check when the time comes."

"All the same, Jack, we'd better keep our guard up."

It was easier said than done. After a great surf session and excellent food, the motion of the *Tom Swift* left both Jack Richards and L.J. Merrill more relaxed than alert. Even when they heard the anchor winch crank up and the systems of the Alba_Sword come alive, neither man's confidence was replaced by humility when the Buchers raised sail just as the last of the sunset faded to dark blue. The wind was blowing stronger down from the hills and whistling out to sea, but since offshore winds create a surfer's perfection, neither Merrill nor Richards felt any cause for alarm. As the *Tom Swift* left the protection of the bay with the moon rising over the Santa Ynez range, the two surfers were unaware that the winds of their paradise near the beach were the same winds of a sailor's hell out in the Channel.

* * *

"Take the helm, Mr. Richards!"

Charles Atkins turned away from the wheel and spewed a stomach-full of dinner all over the deck. L.J. Merrill and Jack Richards were strapped in on either side of him beneath the thick Plexiglas dome protecting the cockpit. Their knuckles were white on their handgrips as the *Tom Swift* crashed through yet another swell the size of a box car. For the second time during the shakedown cruise, they were shocked into paralysis, but this time from raw fear, not admiration. It was one thing to be caught inside by a few big waves near the beach on a sunny afternoon. It was quite another to be facing waves that never stopped coming out of the night, far from the coast, on an ocean getting rougher by the minute.

Merrill looked at Richards, his face white with fear. Atkins was spewing and the Alba_Sword was losing headway. Someone had to take the helm, and Jack Richards was practically catatonic. This was a moment of truth, and Merrill stepped up.

"Aye-aye, sir!"

L.J. unhitched his harness, waited for Atkins to slide away from the wheel, and then grabbed it just as the captain let go with another gush of partially digested food spewing from his mouth.

"Forgot my seasick medicine. Steady as she goes, candidate. Maintain course but do not take in sail. Thruster use at your discretion. You'll be relieved at midnight."

Atkins opened the floor hatch and went below. The Buchers were in their hammocks wearing alpha-wave headsets that prevented seasickness and soothed their minds to sleep. Atkins swung up into his bunk. He pulled a headset over his ears and breathed from an inhaler developed by OSOM to combat seasickness. He smiled at his planned incapacitation, knowing that leaving Merrill and Richards to deal with what seemed to be an emergency would stress them bigtime. He checked his wrist chronometer. There were forty-five minutes to go before the watch changed, and that would be enough time for the two unwitting surfers to reveal much about themselves.

L.J. Merrill was now in control of the *Tom Swift*. He'd done exceptionally well at the helm on the passage up from Ventura, but that was nothing more than guiding the family sedan around the parking lot for his first driving lesson. Now he was behind the wheel of a four-wheel drive with no brakes on a mountain road twisting in three dimensions simultaneously. But he was a great surfer and soon he was climbing and dropping around sections using the *Tom Swift* like a huge surfboard.

Richards should have been impressed with what Merrill was accomplishing and grateful to him for responding to Atkins' order the way he did. But the millionaire was in no mood to compliment or thank his partner for anything. He knew Atkins had put him on the spot, and that Merrill was right and they had been set up. He was angry all over again, just as he'd been in the Chapel, but this time he was ready to quit completely.

L.J. Merrill was loving every second of being in command at the helm, keeping the Alba_Sword on course, and feeling up to the challenge of facing wave after wave with skill and even a little daring. Finally there was a brief lull, and with no waves to deal with, he looked over his shoulder.

"Want to give it a try, Jack?" he said sincerely, though he knew full well Richards would not take the helm. So did Richards, who took Merrill's offer the wrong way.

"That's ok, L.J. You got us into this, now you get us out."

Merrill shrugged and turned around to see a black wall of water dead ahead, its crest clearly higher than the foremast. He swung the wheel hard over to bank off the white water of the breaking wave. The *Tom Swift* sideslipped and her lee rail went under. She was about to roll right over when Merrill turned the wheel at the last second, hit the thrusters, and brought her around to let the wave pass harmlessly under the keel. His eyes were now riveted on the prow of the Alba_Sword and the waves clearly visible ahead in the moonlight coming out of the black North Pacific. He helmed her over, around and through the swells getting bigger with each succeeding set. He was fully up to the task, and his confidence grew by the minute.

Jack Richards felt nothing of the kind, knowing he was just supercargo now, irrelevant and useless. It was a feeling he hated, a feeling he knew all too well as a husband and a father. He suppressed his frustration with a smirk at thought of Merrill being nothing more than his flunky being paid to come through with the pressure on. He regretted the thought almost immediately, but he was almost at the end of his rope.

They were now twenty nautical miles out in the channel, at sea in a window wide open to the full fury of the North Pacific. The cold winds coming down the coast pushed a steep and relentless chop across the remains of the storm surf to mix with the massive swells coming from a thousand miles away. The *Tom Swift* was in her element as was L.J. Merrill. Adrenaline and endorphins rushed through his veins. He had mastered the moment, and all the insecurities, fears, and self-doubts chasing him through life were left far behind. In the midst of pure power he was in complete command, fearlessly facing wave after wave on a course straight into darkness. He was so comfortable with the situation and confident in his skills that he wouldn't have minded all that much if he'd had to stand his watch at the helm for the rest of the night.

Jack Richards was hoping their watch would soon be over. The rough seas were getting to him big time, and after a long weekend, he was burning out fast. And the more exhilarated Merrill became, the more Richards hated the whole thing. Finally he could control himself no longer.

"Hey L.J.! Fuck this! You're such a hot shot, you don't need me! I'm going below!"

The tone took Merrill by surprise. Richards' words trip-switched a delicate synapse that crashed his euphoria into the anxiety of an addict about to be abandoned by his connect, someone he thought was his friend, a feeling he knew all too well. He closed his eyes to fight it off, but he couldn't quite do it because he did need Jack Richards. He thought of what he wanted to say in reply and opened his eyes. It was then he faced the reality of a true nightmare.

The biggest wave of the night, well over thirty feet high, was about to come down hard on the *Tom Swift*. Merrill thought to turn down the face to run with it. The thought came too late. A thousand tons of cold water buried the Alba_Sword. The masts laid down automatically into failsafe deck fittings as the *Tom Swift* was completely submerged. The cockpit went black for a few seconds that seemed like minutes until the moonlight became stronger as the Alba_Sword's buoyancy brought her up to the surface. L.J. Merrill and Jack Richards looked at each other with wide eyes for an instant. Then they saw what was directly ahead - the angry face of King Neptune himself.

A rogue wave of immense proportions loomed high above them. Merrill was frozen at the controls. The peak of the wave pitched forward and blotted out the sky. The Alba_Sword was swallowed whole. Strapped into their cockpit positions, the two surfers were helpless, and this time the moonlight did not reappear.

Charles Atkins was awakened by a sensor attached to his wrist. He glanced at the display over his bunk. They were thirty feet down, riding at zero bubble, with all systems in run-silent mode. He heard Frank Bucher roll out of his bunk, feet landing lightly on the deck, followed by his son. Atkins smiled when he thought of the two men in the cockpit who were by now probably ready for some relief.

An Open Window

Three lights were blinking on the phone console. Two more were steady and bright. A new e-mail was appearing every minute on one of her computer displays. And Dolly Artensa was humming "Get Down Tonight", her favorite battle hymn when things started to get hectic. She was in her element, busy as busy could be, loving every minute of it, in rhythm and in control. Her boss was on her game, and it felt like old times.

"No, but I'll be happy to take a message," she said into the tiny mic on the transparent stem of her headset. She listened another few seconds and then rolled her eyes before interrupting the growing tirade in her ear.

"Excuse me, but she can't take your call, and that's that. I will give her the message. Thank you." Artensa wondered if Roberto Mercante would ever remember that her instructions were to never let him through on days like this. She pushed the blinking light of a call that was much more pleasant.

"Sorry to keep you waiting, Aleja. Miss Corlund is looking forward to seeing you and," Artensa glanced out the window at the 405, "I'm sure she can see it's backed up, so don't worry about being late. Just take your time. Oh, and I rode my bike today, so you can park in my spot. See you when you get here. Bye!"

Artensa pushed another blinker.

"Sorry to keep you waiting," she lied with a straight face, "She'll have to call you back later today, Mr. Clark."

Aleja Gracellen found Artensa's spot between a white Escalade and a black Mercedes convertible. Her Jeep Wagoneer was a bit rusted and the back was cluttered with towels, surf wax and bags of donated clothes for the shelter. She felt a bit self-conscious and thought about parking somewhere out in the lot. But she straightened her shoulders with self-assurance and confidence, set the brake, turned off the engine, and opened her door.

It banged into the Mercedes, leaving a small rusty scratch on the shiny black paint. She frowned for a second and felt a little guilty until she saw the name on the sign 'Reserved for Mr. Mercante'. She felt a lot better.

Long strides took her across the lot and into the lobby past the walls with blow-ups of print ads showing happy, smiling people in Wavelife's latest lines. She knew they were all models who had been paid bottom dollar but were grateful for the exposure, and she thought of the real joy she saw at the shelter when a load of Wavelife seconds and close-outs had arrived a few weeks ago.

"Wonder what the surf industry would say if they saw THOSE smiling faces in the magazine ads!" she laughed to herself.

"Go right on in, she's waiting for you."

"Now don't go losing too much weight there, girl. We don't want the stick chick waif look, now do we?"

"No chance of that! But it sure feels good to not be fighting the pounds anymore. You've changed a lot of things for Miss Corlund and me, Aleja."

Gracellen grinned and her eyes were bright.

"Just doing my job!"

"And I better get back to mine." Artensa swiveled back to her computers and phones as Aleja Gracellen walked into the CEO's office.

"Well, I'm glad I made a good impression, but are you sure about that, Cheryl?"

"Ben Jeffries doesn't do anything unless he's sure. I'm going to make the presentation to the board next Tuesday, Aleja, and although you won't be there personally, you will be there in spirit."

"Well, I'll be glad to show up if you need me."

"Thanks for the offer, but you'll be in Hawai'i."

"What! Why?! I hate that North Shore scene!"

"We don't like it either, so you won't be on the North Shore. You'll be training with Heath on Maui. We've got a whole new world for us just around the corner, and we want you to be ready for it."

Training with Larson could only mean one thing to Aleja Gracellen: she was going to be surfing the waves she'd seen in the conference room last October. Ever since that day she'd thought about what it would be like to ride them, and every time she drove through the tunnel from PCH to the Santa Monica Freeway she thought about surfing through it. She took a deep breath and didn't flinch.

"Ok, I'm game, but what about Sonny-boy?"

"Ben's grandson Pierce really liked him, and Ben trusts the young man's heart. We got a green light to fully develop our new business plan, and he's a part of it, too. As is, I might add, expanding your shelter."

Now Aleja Gracellen looked very surprised.

"Expanding the shelter? You guys are really throwing a lot at me here."

"It will be one of the first things we do after we roll out a new Wavelife," said June Wilson, "Now don't forget, all this is confidential, and that's really important, Aleja. The last thing we want is for someone to get wind of our plan, especially the press."

"Ben and two other investors are helping us buy the company from the shareholders. If we can do it without having to fend off any unsolicited offers," said Bill Massara, "there will be more money left over afterwards, which translates directly into things like expanding the shelter."

196

"I got the part about buying the company, and I'll take your word for the rest of it. But what does this all have to do with me, other than surfing the reef and expanding the shelter?" she asked with skepticism in her voice.

Cheryl Corlund laid some cards on the table.

"We've been thinking about changing Wavelife's image for a long time, Aleja, almost since the first day I saw you surf Malibu. Opening the shelter was part of that, but now we want to go much further. When we met with Clark, it was part of our strategy, and I wanted you there, though at the time we didn't know exactly how it would all work. But now we do."

"We think there's a new and bigger market out there waiting to be developed that is not dependent on the fourteen to twenty-four male segment," said June Wilson, "Remember what we talked about on his yacht that night? And the questions I asked you about women and surfing?"

"Yeah, but I didn't think you were doing market research. Stupid me."

"Well, Aleja, I'm sorry if you feel misled in any way, but my business is to understand trends long before the trendsetters even know they are setting them, and then translate that information into multi-million dollar investments," said Wilson.

"Ben and his associates needed to know if transforming Wavelife is going to make money for them, plain and simple," said Massara, "All the market research told us good things, but we needed to put a face on it - - -"

"And that face is mine, right?" said Gracellen, thinking about the photos in the lobby and turning to look straight at Cheryl Corlund without saying a word. They locked eyes for several seconds, long enough for "You are using me" to be rebuffed by "Get with the program."

"Aleja, you are exactly the right person to be a role model for our female customers. You are going to be at the center of the plan, as is Heath for his segment and Sonny-boy for his. This is how it works. I can't shelter you from our business anymore. Your time has come."

"Until my time's over, and you go on to the next big thing."

"Aleja, business is nothing more than riding waves of what sells," said June Wilson, "We ride them all the time on Wall Street. In fact, I think I'm just as much a surfer as you are, only I wear silk suits instead of wetsuits. The important thing here may not be a career, but it is a window of opportunity to gain some independence for yourself and the shelter."

"If we ride this wave with courage and style, we'll have a lot to show for it when we kick out," said Massara, "You saw what successful financial surfers have to show for their rides, Aleja. Imagine a mega-yacht transformed into a program for the homeless, with you as captain."

Gracellen paused for a second. She didn't know if the problems of the homeless could be solved by piles of money. What worked more than anything was simple human kindness, and nothing about a mega-yacht said that to her. But Ben Jeffries had made an impression on her, too.

"And Ben Jeffries is making all this happen?"

"Yes, he is," said Cheryl Corlund.

Gracellen should have been ecstatic but wasn't. Even after she'd flown to Florida to meet Ben Jeffries, she never imagined herself becoming Wavelife's next big surf star. Now Cheryl Corlund was depending on her to do just that. She knew it was no time to lose her nerve, and she didn't when, an instant later, she remembered the lefts in Clark's video. They were picture perfect and they were going her way.

"Then shouldn't I have started training in January? March is pretty much the end of the big wave season in Hawai'i."

"We didn't know then what we know now," said Corlund.

"You still haven't told me how long I'll be gone."

"As long as it takes for Heath to get in some serious training with you. At least two weeks, maybe three."

"Well, in that case next time you come to the shelter, you have to park your car right out in front and meet and greet every single person, ok?"

Corlund was taken aback at Gracellen's alacrity. Wilson and Massara exchanged astonished looks.

"Including the ones that really smell?" said Corlund, trying to be cute with a shy look.

"Especially the ones that really smell!"

Well, I, I, sure, okay, that's no problem."

"Good, 'cause there's more. I'll be gone the full three weeks. I want all the training I can get before Easter. While I'm gone you'll have to take my place for two days a week at the shelter. Same for June and Bill. That covers my usual six days, right? And you three will be the organizing committee for the Easter Sunday event. And May Day, too. After all, if the shelter is part of the business plan, you all need training and first hand familiarity with how it runs. Or as Ben might say, what part of 'due diligence' don't you understand?"

The C.E.O. knew when she was outfoxed. She tried not to let it show, but when she looked at June Wilson and Bill Massara, her resolve melted.

"Yeah,! Due diligence! Why didn't the two of you think of that?"

The smile on Aleja Gracellen's face was so sweet they all had to laugh.

"So when am I leaving?"

"Day after tomorrow, but you won't be flying to Maui right away. First you're going out to the reef."

Ian Clark's eyes kept darting back and forth between two monitors displaying market data and tracking his investments. He was ready to pull the trigger on some trades, and if his timing was right, he'd be up five grand.

Then Dolly Artensa came on the line.

"Call from Cheryl Corlund. Go ahead please."

"Ian, stop what you are doing and pay attention," she said. She knew exactly what Clark was doing: watching the markets and not listening.

"Uh, yeah, just a minute, I've just got to do this one thing, and can I put you on hold for a second?"

"No, Ian, you can't put me on hold. Your quick trigger deals can wait, goddamn it!"

Clark knew he couldn't stop what he was doing without missing a chance to make some money. He stalled for time.

"Hello Cheryl! How are you? Everything ok?"

"No, everything is not ok. I wrote you a check for one and a half million dollars. I own you and you've got work to do."

There was no mistaking the tone in Corlund's voice. Clark reluctantly turned away from his monitors to concentrate on the voice in his headset.

"Yes Cheryl, good to talk to you. Things are going just fine. I've been in contact with the seaplane people, and - - -"

"Don't tell me what you've been doing. I'll tell YOU what you're going to do, understood?"

"Well, I've been pretty busy lately," said Clark, glancing at the monitor, "and right at the moment I don't have much time for - - -"

Corlund cut him off.

"You signed a contract. If you haven't read it by now, I'll read it to you. Do I make myself clear?"

Clark remembered a sheaf of documents approved by his lawyer that he'd signed without a second glance last October. The lawyer hadn't given them much of a look either. They both knew he needed the money, and neither was going to upset the apple cart by probing for details. It wasn't until a few weeks later that he'd actually read the contract, only to find out he was now just another apple on Corlund's cart.

"Uh, yes, clear as an azure blue sky, Cheryl," he said, trapped and knowing it all too well.

"I want you, Roberto and Aleja Gracellen, plus Heath and Sonny-boy, in Tahiti by Friday. I want you all at the reef on Saturday, and everybody back in Hawai'i by Sunday night. I need on-site documentation of the place. Roberto will tape it all then catch a red eye and be in my office Monday morning."

"You're kidding me," said Clark, "There is no way - - -"

"There better be for your sake, Ian. You're a travel agent: figure it out and make it happen."

"I don't know about the *Skyhook* - - -"

"And I don't want to hear about your problems. Is that understood, Ian?"

Clark saw a quote he needed running along the bottom of his screen.

"Clark, I told you to pay attention. Don't you understand English?"

For a second, he didn't. The only thing he understood was what the numbers on his screen were telling him: he'd just missed his chance to make a short term killing.

"All right," his sigh was easily heard over the phone, "Anything you say."

"That's right Ian, anything I say. Get busy and call Dolly with the flight information within the hour."

* * *

There wasn't much small talk on the flight to Tahiti. It had been a hectic forty-eight hours getting things squared away at the shelter on a moment's notice along with everything else Aleja Gracellen needed to think about before going on a trip for three weeks.

Clark had gone through hell making all the arrangements for the trip, including tracking down the *Skyhook* and negotiating with Tina Sanchez. On the plane he simply stayed stressed, glued to his laptop, with his investments and Geosurf running full bore around the world.

Roberto Mercante was somewhere in between. He was happy to be in charge, heading to the reef, and looking forward to another flight in the *Skyhook*. At the same time he was dreading seeing Heath and Sonny-boy and delivering some news that would shock the two surfers. They were waiting at the airport, and Mercante figured he'd better get it over with right away.

"There's no way that can happen. No way. It takes years to get it wired! And you're giving us three weeks?"

"Listen Heath, this goes all the way to Ben Jeffries and the entire business plan. And we've got until this summer to pull this off, and you can't tell me she isn't in great shape."

"You no understand da deal wit da drivah and da surfah, yeah?" said Noaloa, suddenly an expert on something he was barely qualified for, "I been work out fo' months, know da skis from a inside and out, and - - -"

"That's good, Sonny-boy. We're still going to need you, I'm sure," said Ian Clark, knowing his next paycheck depended entirely on Heath Larson getting his first wave.

"Ok, Roberto, we'll talk about all that later," said Larson, "Let's talk about what we're going to do when we get there. It will probably be flat, so I think it will be a good time to dive the reef and check the bottom."

"Ok, yeah Heath, that's a good idea, but don't forget my wife needs shots of the three of you and the *Skyhook*."

Larson groaned, but Noaloa perked right up.

"Ok, brah, no problem! Do one photo shoot, no big deal. So Aleja, how come you no bail outta dis like you jump da tour? I tot you hate da pro surfer stuffs," he said with a smirk.

Aleja Gracellen chose her words carefully.

"Listen, Sonny-boy, the future of my shelter is riding on this, so don't give me any shit. And that goes for all of you. I'm ready for the training, Heath, and Roberto, you make sure your employees here are with the program. You guys got that?"

The men didn't say a word.

"Uh, yeah, ok. When do we get into Tahiti, Ian?" said Heath Larson, changing the subject as fast as he could.

* * *

200

The *Skyhook* circled into the wind, and once again made an indelible impression on those who had never seen her before.

"Wow, this is going to be fun!" exclaimed Aleja, trying to be a good egg now that the men were showing her some respect, "You guys ever seen anything like it?"

Larson didn't know what to say. For a moment he was drawn out of his existential shell and was a bit awestruck by the sight of the *Skyhook* circling into the wind. Sonny-boy Noaloa was staring at the seaplane coming in, but he had nothing to say to Aleja Gracellen. When she had turned up in Florida for the weekend on the mega-yacht, Noaloa was not thinking about anything other than more glory and fame for himself. Now, however, they were actually going to the place where it was all going to happen, and here she was. It was a situation for which Sonny-boy Noaloa was not in the least bit prepared.

"An' how's mah good buddy, Roberto?" asked Owens as he helped Mercante up through the cargo hatch.

"Just great, Mac, just great. Say, Clem hasn't sold his Cat yet, has he?"

"Don' think so. I thought ya'all might have kep' in touch on that."

"Well, yeah, but when I'm around the missus - - -"said Mercante.

Owens just laughed. He had hearty greetings for Larson, Noaloa, and Gracellen. But when he pulled Clark in last, his face turned into a scowl.

"Ya know y'all cain't just order us around, Clark, an' I don't care how much money ya throw at Tina an' the Foundation. I had ta work a double shift ta git us air-ready. What in hell made ya think ya could git us on that kinda short notice?"

"Tina and the Foundation," retorted Ian Clark, holding up his hands, "See! No cash boarding pass this time, buster!"

Owens laughed, and for a moment a smile came to Clark's face.

"Yeah, I know. Jes kiddin', okay Ian? We're gonna have a good time! Roberto, why doncha take Sonny-boy an' the lady back ta the 'sunroom' an' get 'em ready fer takeoff. Ian, Heath, let's git up front. Roberto, once we're airborne cum on forward. We gotta talk sum 'bout yer big plans."

Victor Sanchez put the *Skyhook* on autopilot but remained in his seat while listening to the conversation through the hatch. His wife, Clark, Owens, Mercante, and Larson were hashing out details and making real progress. Basically, Larson told everyone what he needed, Mercante nodded his head, Owens took notes, Tina Sanchez wrote down ballpark costs, and Clark scowled because he was no longer in control.

"That's good news you've already been testing the hoists," said Larson, "I was wondering about that. Those SUVs are pretty heavy."

"She's built ta carry two tons a' torpedoes, but ma' problem was gettin' 'em out of the water quick-like. But with the 'lectric hoists, she'll work out jes fine," he said, glancing at Clark and knowing when to throw him a bone,

"Goin' ta Florida ta git some 'special parts made turned the trick. Thanks fer gettin' me there, Ian."

Clark nodded.

"Yeah, thanks Ian," said Tina Sanchez, "Mac's been his old self since he's been back. He really needed a vacation."

So do I, thought Clark, glancing out a porthole only to see a solitary, submerged reef with not another thing in sight as far as the eye could see. "No problem," he said, remembering the next check for one-point-five mill depended on the people sitting around him, "Now, where were we?"

"Wait a sec, are you going to hang two jetskis under each wing?" asked Roberto, "That's a lot of drag compared to torpedoes."

"Well, Roberto, y'all jes gonna hafta wait an' see how I solved that problem, too!"

"So we got Heath and Bruddah on one ski, Sonny and Aleja on another, one more for safety, and one for backup, right?" said Clark.

"Uh, I don't know about that yet," said Heath Larson, knowing the two surfers back in the 'sunroom' were probably not saying a word to each other. He'd already sensed a brewing problem between them because adding Gracellen to the team had marketing written all over it. Sonny was probably worried he'd be lucky to be the board caddie, And Larson knew Gracellen was not about to try and make nice to a pouting surf star.

"Ok, Heath. We'll figure that out later. Mac, you've got a draft cargo list. Tina, you're set for fuel, food and medical?"

"Yes, and we'll be ready for a shakedown run last week in April, first week in May."

"Gotta question fer ya, Heath," said Mac Owens, "Y'all shure yer jetskis kin run aviation fuel?"

"Guys are doing it all the time going after speed records. I won't crate 'em up for shipment until I KNOW they are ready. We don't want any problems when we get there."

Clark glanced at the GPS numbers on his watch and then looked out the porthole. He saw the first reef come up over the horizon, this time surrounded by a thin ring of white water.

"Speaking of getting there," he smiled around the table, "And let me tell you, its not flat this time!" Larson and Mercante looked at each other. "Go back in the sunroom and strap in. You'll get a perfect view of the place."

"Shit! Where's my camera?" exclaimed Mercante.

The two surfers scrambled out of their seats and went aft like kids running down stairs for Christmas. Tina Sanchez went up to the cockpit to co-pilot the descent and Mac Owens went up in the engineer's tower to give the engines a visual check.

Ian Clark fished a scrap of paper out of his backpack with new latitude and longitude numbers determined by the programmers. He'd spent another five grand to pinpoint the exact location of the reef in L.J. Merrill's footage. He pushed the GPS display button on his watch as they did a lazy circle over the elliptical reef. The waves were good, but he closed his eyes as his heart turned cold. The numbers didn't match.

The minute the *Skyhook* came to a rest at the northern end of the reef, Mac Owens deployed an inflatable with an outboard attached. He took Ian Clark with him to check him out on the rig while delivering Aleja Gracellen to the most perfect lefts she'd ever seen. Clark drove Owens back to the PBY, dropped him off and picked up Mercante and Noaloa. They went over to the rights with Mercante taping everything. It was a long distance swell, and during the extended lulls Clark motored to the other side of the reef where Mercante shot Gracellen's beautiful surfing. The two men now knew for sure that the place was in a class by itself, and with the *Skyhook* as a backdrop, they knew they were going to deliver exactly what Cheryl Corlund needed.

An hour later, Larson came up from his deepest dive and confirmed the quality of the reef where Noaloa had just ridden the best wave of the day. Gracellen, a goofyfoot, was surfing the lefts all alone, taking full advantage of waves going her way. Everyone couldn't have been more stoked. Mercante had been shooting every ride he could from every possible angle with Clark driving him around. He would have kept going but Clark had an idea.

Say Roberto, why don't you go ride a few yourself? And Heath, get out there, too! I'll shoot you guys from the wing of the plane."

The two men jumped at the chance. Heath went to share the lefts with Aleja, and Roberto went to the rights with a sense of release he hadn't felt in a long time. Things were coming around, and Mercante couldn't have been happier. Up on the wing, Clark shared Mercante's emotions. The quality of the waves was superb, as was the surfing of Gracellen, Larson and Noaloa. Everything was in synch. During a lull in the action, Clark stood up, stretched, and took a relaxed look around. He noticed something on the horizon that hadn't been there an hour ago. He looked through the zoom of the camera and saw a bank of clouds to the east.

"Hey, Mac, what's that on the horizon?"

In less than a minute he heard Owens call to Victor Sanchez to come up into the cockpit. In less than ten seconds, he heard the Captain's booming voice.

"Tina! Prepare for takeoff! Ian! Get down here, now!"

Sitting out on either side of the peak off the southern tip of the reef, the four surfers were startled to hear the sounds of the big Pratt and Whitney engines cough into life. They were even more surprised to see the *Skyhook* moving towards them, and fast. In less than a minute they saw Clark and Owens in the cargo door yelling at them. The engines drowned out their words, but the frantic motioning of their arms got the message across. The surfers and their boards were pulled into the plane through the cargo bay instead of the rear tail-gunner's hatch just as the wind kicked up to twenty knots in less than five seconds.

"Get in the back, strap in an' hold on!" said Mac Owens to the surfers. The *Skyhook* swung around so fast they bumped into each other trying to get to their seats in the 'sunroom'. "Two to a side, and one on the fold-down seat on the rear bulkhead. Here we go!"

The *Skyhook* went to full throttle and fishtailed around into the wind. She gained speed, shuddered, and accelerated off the surface of the sea with a sudden motion that churned the stomachs of the passengers. Victor Sanchez put the Catalina into a steep climb, and the PBY was bumping and bucking through the turbulence of the gusting winds and sheets of rain.

But in less than a minute, the *Skyhook* had lifted them up into a clear blue sky and leveled out. Mac Owens poked his head into the compartment. It smelled of puke thanks to the five wide-eyed, people looking at him.

"That's ok, y'all kin clean up later," he said with just the hint of a grin on his face, "So, how were them waves? Sorry we had ta get out of there so fast, but yer lil' paradise jes turned into a churnin' toilet a' chop an' confusion."

"Does that happen all the time?" asked Aleja Gracellen.

"Well, ma'am, yes an' no. Ya never know what's gonna happen in tha open ocean 'less ya monitor yer weather radar alla time, which I was sorta doin' while takin' care of sum maintenance in the cockpit. Captain an' the missus was eatin' sum lunch, so, well, it all turned out ok 'cause Ian saw 'er comin' for I did, so thanks ta him, it was no big deal," said Owens with a nod to Clark that erased some more of the past between the two men, "'sides, Capt'n figured it was a good time ta do a drill. Y'all had an open window there. Then she closed, plain an' simple. But y'all got whatcha needed, right Roberto? So no big deal!"

Roberto smiled, but Heath Larson's mind was way ahead of Mercante's and he wasn't smiling.

"Yeah, but if the surf's big and the wind comes up that fast, we'll have all kinds of problems in the water. This is a big place, and riding huge waves is hard enough without random variables that can happen without warning."

"Well, now y'all know why I been working on the winches, Heath. Say, Ian, why don' you an' Roberto jes open up the canopies a bit, get some fresh air in here? I'll be back in a minute. We got some stuff up front that'll help y'all feel better."

Owens closed the hatch and Larson looked at across the compartment.

"Ian, what's the deal on the weather out here?"

A composed Ian Clark was getting used to doing some fast thinking in the 'sunroom' of the *Skyhook*.

"Those squalls usually taper off in July, August. And even if one blows through, I bet the wind turns around offshore in its wake. We'll just ride it out, and get even better waves after it goes by."

Larson thought for a second. Clark's explanation couldn't be challenged, at least not yet.

The flight back to Tahiti was smooth. After they each got a stomach full of the airsickness concoction there was time to think about what they'd just experienced.

"Heath, you say the bottom seemed perfectly formed?"

"Yeah, but only what I saw of it."

"One thing for sure," said Roberto Mercante, "The surf was perfect. It's exactly what we want. The waves, the water, and - - -"

"And no one has ever surfed the place before! And wait till it gets big!" said an excited Ian Clark now that he could feel some genuine satisfaction for the first time in months, "This is going to work out great!"

"Yeah, lemme see da one kine tube ride I got," said Sonny-boy Noaloa as Mercante turned on the video camera and Clark moved over to watch it with them.

But neither Heath Larson nor Aleja Gracellen was interested in watching handheld surfing on a tiny camcorder screen, so they got up and went forward. She spend the rest of the flight up in the cockpit with Tina Sanchez learning about the Skyrider Foundation while Larson discussed mounting the jetskis, fuel consumption rates, and weather issues with Victor Sanchez and Mac Owens.

The sun was on the horizon when the *Skyhook* dropped off her passengers at the buoy where the outrigger canoes were tied up. Happy goodbyes were exchanged and everyone was in good spirits. Clark had pulled off the trip, Mercante had the footage his wife needed, the surfers were stoked, and Victor and Tina Sanchez had just made twenty-five thousand dollars they would split with Mac and the Skyrider Foundation. They'd had an open window and come through successfully. The reason it closed was soon all but forgotten.

Waxing the Board

Cheryl Corlund looked over the room where the board of directors of Wavelife International would be meeting in less than an hour. Not that she ever had to worry about the board's actions, but nevertheless she gave these meetings her utmost attention. The seating, the pencils, the water carafes, everything was by design. She turned on her heel and went back to her office. She had one last detail to attend to.

"Everyone here is ready to go. Anything else you can think of, Cheryl?" asked a smiling Ben Jeffries.

"No, Ben, we're set. The numbers speak for themselves. Oh, yeah, one thing. Bruce Kaufman."

Jeffries smile flattened a little.

"He's out. We don't need to waste time on his account. Oh, and be sure to give my regards to Roberto. The video was impressive. Tell Heath I appreciate his plumbing the depths and Aleja! My goodness, now that's modern dance! And can Sonny-boy surf! Great! Just great!"

"Give you a call in a few hours with the good news?"

"Nah, it can wait till tomorrow."

"Till then, Ben."

The video screens went blue and Ben Jeffries got back to business in his private dining room.

"Cheryl sends her regards. How's the fish?"

"Excellent, as usual," said Peter Lasserman.

"Say, Ben, can I steal your chef for a party I'm having next week?" asked John Vutara.

"They liked the video," said Cheryl Corlund.

"Yeah, I'm glad we had the time to edit it down," said Bill Massara, "Next time we better send a team of pros, that's for sure."

"I think that's the idea, Bill," laughed June Wilson, "But first things first. Did you get a final disposition on the reef issue?"

"The issue is the value of small waves versus the value of big waves. Our position is that big waves are an 'if', not a 'when', just like a big oil find is not a sure thing based on nothing but geological data. Therefore storms, swells and big waves cannot be treated as fixed assets. We're assuming the SEC will be all over the deal, and we'll be happy to comply with their requests."

"And on that note, what was it that Sonny-boy says?" asked Corlund facetiously, fingering the lucky nail in the pocket of her business suit.

"Geevum!" said three voices simultaneously.

Just as she'd done while walking through the blizzard in New York headed for a big meeting, Cheryl Corlund ran through a list of all the issues.

This is not a hostile takeover per se. There is nothing overtly hostile about the laws of the marketplace.

We cash out the shareholders at a price well above current share price. And they have to sell thanks to the board's decision. And the board has no choice because this is classic "gun-to-the-head".

Bill ran final assets and liabilities numbers against sales projection. June met with Ben to refine the loan structure. Our position is airtight, our bid is more than fair, and the board can't say no.

We even let them look like they are in charge. They will come back and demand an extra dollar or so to keep up appearances. Exactly as planned.

"Gentlemen, item 1A is a report from the chief executive officer," said Roberto Mercante.

"Thank you Mr. Chairman. Gentlemen, the company's market share has continued to grow. We are the acknowledged leaders of the surf industry. Unfortunately, that has nothing to do with the price of our shares," she said, her voice clear, confident and strictly business even while delivering bad news.

"As we all know, the apparel industry has been under pressure for some time to perform against standards based solely on growth year-over-year. We have met those standards and often exceeded them for almost a decade. However, investors are no longer interested in surfing. Only a tidal wave could get their attention," said Corlund, changing her pitch just slightly, "and with the quality of our surf team promotions thanks to Roberto, our surfers would be riding it!"

She injected levity into the room like an anesthesiologist, and everyone laughed almost on cue.

"But seriously, we have studied any number of ways to increase shareholder value and have made substantial changes in our operations to reduce costs and overhead. We've developed new lines, new markets, new publicity events, and new distribution channels. And indeed sales are up, but the share price remains flat. Therefore the only way we can realize the true value of the company for the shareholders is for management to execute a leveraged buyout."

Everyone in the room knew about leveraged buyouts, though none had ever actually been through the process of having senior management, using borrowed money, buy a company from its shareholders. Some called it stealing the company, and the all-time classic LBO, the story of RJR Nabisco, was fresh in the mind of at least one director.

"How far has this gone, Cheryl?" asked Richard Black, once Wavelife's senior V.P. of marketing during the early years but now making twice as much money consulting across the apparel industry.

"In order to preserve confidentiality, we haven't gone very far, Richard. We don't have a dime, but if the board allows us to go forward with this proposal, we will move quickly. Everyone benefits when management takes over, and our proposal is without a doubt in the best interests of the shareholders."

She continued her presentation without violating four important rules of these kinds of deals. She didn't tell them about potential assets not currently on the balance sheets. She didn't tell them of her future plans for the company. She didn't tell them anything about the financing behind her proposal. And she knew in advance what the reaction would be.

Within minutes Black was mollified when she outlined the process by which management would tender an offer for the company that included a generous incentive for shareholders to sell their stock. She knew that would be good enough for the rest of them. Still, each felt the need to weigh in.

"How generous? It would have to be north of the highest value ever traded," said Steve Palua, former Hawaiian surf legend and a board member because of his name and his contacts. He knew a leveraged buyout would benefit the investment group he represented. He had not been able to deliver good news to them lately, and he was anxious to know how much Corlund was offering.

"Try twenty-two a share, Steve," said Bill Massara, not blinking at the fact they'd be paying close to a billion dollars.

"Well, you're the CFO, Bill, so I'm sure you know your numbers, and that's a lot more than we're trading at right now," said Bart Thomas, on Wavelife's board because he would have been called a 'macher' in the old days though his current title was "contractor relations'. Thomas knew everything about the garment industry and had contacts from the design salons to the warehouses thanks to growing up in the heart of the New York garment district pushing carts for his father's shirt company.

"Yet it is, Bart, but that's what the company is worth, and that's what we are prepared to pay."

"Don't vee have zu do zis carefully? Und Cheryl, you und Bill und Roberto vill have zu quit from zee board," said Gunter Jacobsen, the German president of Wavelife's European operations.

"That's true, Gunter," said Cheryl Corlund. "In your board packets you'll see the appropriate letters of resignation."

"I'm sure everyone here would like to express their gratitude to all of you for your service to the board and the company," said Richard Black, as chairs were pushed back all around the table and the four remaining directors could shake hands with soon-to-be new owners of Wavelife International.

When the door closed behind Corlund, Massara and Mercante, Richard Black looked around the table. Everyone had a reputation to protect, so no one was going to be the first to say anything. But he knew that would get them nowhere, and he had clients to meet later that day.

"Ok, we need a chair, don't we? And we'll need to set up a special committee to examine her bid. Who wants to serve on it?"

"Well, I'd say the horse is out of the barn," said Bart Thomas, "and said committee won't be much more than a rubber stamp. But there's still gonna be some work to do."

"Yeah," said Palua, "and if someone decides to bid higher, the committee is going to be on the hot seat. But that's not going to happen, not at twenty-two. And so we'll just raise the price a buck for appearances, and we're done. So why don't you and I volunteer, Bart? Keep everybody happy and get it over with. Gunter, you're on, too, ok?"

"Well, if we had a chairman, he'd call for a vote," said Black.

"We got one, Black," said Thomas, "And you're it. All in favor?"

Everyone raised their hands.

"Done deal," said the New Yorker, "Now, the committee. We have three names? All in favor?"

"Hold on there, Bart! I'm the chairman. Ok, all in favor?"

After half-an-hour of wrangling over the exact wording of the minutes, Richard Black called Cheryl Corlund back into the room.

"Ok, Cheryl, the board is prepared to direct you to proceed. We have elected a committee that needs to see your proposal as soon as possible, and we'll have to issue a press release stating management has tendered an offer for the company."

"Fine. Here's the draft filing for the SEC. They will appreciate getting notice of your intent before reading about it in the press. We want everything to go smoothly."

Nobody cared that she was railroading them, least of all Gunter Jacobsen who was already thinking of his exit from the board with a good severance package to help him get out of apparel and in to telcom. He did make a token effort to look professional.

"Zee committee vill need all zee financials. Three copies, please."

"Bill has them waiting for you outside, Gunter. I'll warn you, though, it's a stack about a foot high."

"How long do you think this is going to take, Cheryl?" asked Steve Palua, anxious to get working on new investments with the money his friends would be making on the deal.

"Well, after the LBO disasters of the eighties, you can't do this kind of thing in a few weeks anymore. But if all goes as expected, we should be done by the middle of June."

Sunrise Services

"No way, Heath! I'm not letting go too soon! I'm releasing on his signal!"

Aleja Gracellen was floating on her back with her feet in the straps of the tow-in board. They were practicing whips, a technique they would be using to launch her into the big waves at the reef. For the past two weeks she had fixed the jet skis, run the mountains, and paddled for hours along the coast, and no matter what Larson had thrown at her, she had never said a word. Now Heath Larson was looking down at her from the driver's seat of the waverunner and as soon as she came right back at him, he knew something was wrong. They both looked at Sonny-boy Noaloa, sitting behind Larson as spotter and safety.

"What? I tott she goin' too fas'!"

"Don't worry about me, Sonny-boy," said Gracellen evenly, "I can take it just as much as you guys."

"Den what da hell you need me fo'? I thought a spottah want fo' da safety first! That's how you say, Heath!" Noaloa turned and was just about chin to chin with Larson.

He knew there was no love lost between Gracellen and Noaloa. But his existential detachment from people left him unable to construct bridges across the gaps and inconsistencies of human nature, much less two surfers at polar opposites, the pro surf star and the woman who danced with the sea.

"Ok, let's try it again. Sonny-boy, I'll let you know when we're up to speed before you give her the signal, ok?" said Larson, wrongly assuming forward momentum would ease the strain.

"Den what you need me fo?" retorted Noaloa.

Gracellen had heard enough. "Let's get going and we'll get it right the next time."

"I'm sure you will," said Noaloa, not a trace of pidgin to his words. He took off his safety vest and dove off the ski. He stayed underwater for almost thirty yards, and when he surfaced he kept swimming towards the beach.

"Now what's his problem?" said Gracellen.

"No big deal. He'll drive next time, I'll spot, and we'll get it right."

"Why don't we try to get it right without him? I can handle the speed, and I need to know how to do this before I leave, don't I?"

There were only two days left in their three week training schedule. They'd almost made it, but Larson knew he had finally lost control of the situation between Gracellen and Noaloa.

"All right, let's go," he said, gunning the ski engine. Aleja smiled and braced herself.

It was noon when they pulled up to the launch ramp. Bruddah had been watching the session through binoculars from the beach.

"Barbie from da 'Bu! You geevum good out deah, sista!" he said.

Gracellen smiled at Bruddah. She didn't mind his nickname for her since she'd more than proved she was no plastic doll trading on her looks.

"Thanks," she said in a quiet voice. Larson's voice was anything but quiet.

"Where's the kid? Did you tell him mutiny is a capital crime on the high seas?" He was only half-joking.

"Run back up da house. He no wanna talk. I figgah bes' leave 'im alone."

"Maybe you're right, I guess. Let's get something to eat and get back out there. Bruddah, you drive. We gotta practice more whips."

A late afternoon rain was beginning to fall when they slowly pulled up to the house. An exhausted Gracellen was asleep in the back of the crew cab as Bruddah and Heath added their voices to a soft, old song by Cecilio and Kapono. The joy and peace of the words filled their hearts, until Larson remembered Sonny-boy and switched off the ignition key without waiting for the song to end. They went inside and straight to Noaloa's room. No surfboards, no clothes, no Noaloa.

"Oh shit, where da guy?" said Bruddah.

"This isn't good," said Larson.

Bruddah went back out to the truck to get his cell phone while Larson looked around for a note of explanation. First it was a mutiny, now it was AWOL. He came back out on the porch just as Bruddah snapped the phone closed.

"Champ bail back Oahu-side. Call my cuz at Aloha Airline. The kid on da inter-island two hour ago."

"When's the next flight?"

"Nutha hour, but don't know we find him so easy. Maybe stay heah and tink first."

"What do you mean? Think about what?" said Larson.

"My cuz say he check his boards tru Sydney. And dat flight leave Honolulu in twenty minutes."

Roberto Mercante could not believe his ears.

"You mean he just left? How could he do that? He works for me!"

"Oh c'mon, Roberto, you know this thing with Gracellen really got to him. He knows Cheryl is thinking of firing the entire surf team, and he probably thinks that includes him!" said Larson, sitting on the porch steps.

"Well, she did fire 'em all, but not him. He's part of the deal! He KNOWS that, doesn't he? Where do you think he went?"

"I just told you Roberto. He bought a one way to Australia. Pretty expensive ticket, too. Last minute first class. Bruddah's cousin said he paid with a Wavelife credit card authorized for his use."

"Oh shit, that's right! He still has it!"

"There's more, Roberto. Here, let Bruddah tell you."

"He do all you ask him. He work hard but you no tink he got feelings. I like da Barbie. She got good mana. But he just a kid. You wife shudda known mo betta. Dis mo' than just business, brah."

Mercante bit his lip and thought of how his son and daughter were turning out after being raised around a schedule where business always came first.

"Ok, now what do I do?" asked the self-made millionaire.

"Bettah call your wife, and then call da guy Clark. We got go get him 'fo some thing bad happen."

Mercante's mind went blank.

"What do you mean, Bruddah? Why do we - - -"

Then it hit him like a thick lip of a suck-out tube over a shallow reef.

"Oh, shit! Mick Lennox!"

"Well, things could be worse. How are things going for Aleja?" said Cheryl Corlund, sitting in an L.A. garment district design studio looking at sketches for new lines of women's wear.

"I guess just fine, but listen, Cheryl, - - -"

"No, YOU listen Roberto. I don't want anything to interfere with Aleja's training. She has to surf the reef."

"But - - -"

"But nothing. When are you going to understand what we're doing, Roberto? Oh, and you did follow up on the surf team issue, right?"

"Uh, yeah, well, I started making calls two days ago. But some of them have been hard to find. It's not easy tracking down three hundred surfers around the world."

"Just put the pink slips in with their final paychecks. You don't need to be running up a phone bill making explanations. As for Sonny-boy, if Bruddah wants to go get him, that's fine with me. But Heath stays and finishes the training with Aleja on schedule," she said, smiling at a sketch for beautiful summer dress that would compliment Aleja's spirit perfectly.

Ian Clark was at his desk early the next morning and for once not watching the market data on his computer. Mercante had guessed Noaloa would try to get into Australia's biggest contest held during Easter Week, so tickets in Bruddah's real name were waiting at Quantas for a first class seat to Melbourne, the closest city to Bell's Beach. And Clark made sure a Geosurf employee would be waiting at the airport to pick him up. But the big Hawaiian had never traveled anywhere except the mainland and needed a passport. Forms were downloaded, signatures faxed, and now Ian Clark had to somehow get around a bottleneck in the Honolulu passport office.

"No, Mr. Clark, applications received under expedited circumstances today will not be ready until tomorrow. Security checks, you understand."

"Thanks so much for trying to help us, I appreciate it," said Clark switching gears and thinking fast, "If it wasn't a matter of someone's safety, I wouldn't be calling. Who am I speaking with?"

"My name is Rellsunn Laniakai, sir."

"What a beautiful name! And she was a great surfer. So much aloha in her heart. Quite an honor to be named after such a wonderful person."

"My parents were friends of hers. She was like my auntie."

"Well I won't keep you any longer, Rellsunn. Oh, one quick question," he paused and played the Hawaiian one-big-family card, "Does, uh, let me get his name, yes, does Ilano Kolana have to be there to sign for his passport?"

"Yes, he, excuse me, but did you say Ilano Kolana?"

"Why yes, he's a good friend of mine," said Clark. Bingo!

"Uncle Bruddah! Why he go Australia?" the passport office clerk couldn't help but lapse out of Fedspeak.

"He's got a friend in trouble. In fact, you may know him. Sonny - - -"

"Sonny-boy Noaloa! Oh big problem that one! But Uncle Bruddah got big heart. Okay, you tell him come see his niece right now. Window B, third floor. I got passport waiting he get here."

"I'll call him right away," said Clark, "Thanks so much for your help, Rellsunn. Aloha!"

"Goodbye sir, and thank you for calling the Honolulu Passport Office," said the young Hawaiian, jumping back across the gulf that separated blood from water.

* * *

"What the hell ya doin' heyah, mate?" said the pro tour director, sitting in his office overlooking the clean waves of the Gold Coast, five hundred miles north of Sydney, "Ya didn't show up at the Superbank contest and we figgered you'd quit the tour fer good!"

"Yeah, lotsa peoples tink dat. So how I get into da Bells?" said Sonny-boy Noaloa, calling from a hotel in Melbourne, a thousand miles to the south, but only an hour's drive from Bells Beach.

"Whatcher mean, Sonny-boy, how do you get in? Wavelife didn't send in a form on ya. In fact, they just pulled their whole fuckin' team mate. Mercante fired eight guys with no notice and never sent in their fees."

"Well, gimme one dose guys spots. I pay da entry fee."

"Can't, mate. They got picked up two days ago by Gnarlaroo and they're all back in."

"Even da Brazilians?"

"No, they went with Coral Brazil. I got a call from Rio, and we're waiting on a bank transfer, so - - -"

"So what's it gonna take fo' me get in? Fuck, I win dis ting two year ago. Dat worth sumtin'. Play up da press, get you paybacks no problem."

The organizer of the longest continuously running surf contest in the world, the Bells Beach Easter Championships, knew Noaloa had a point. The

Aussie tabloids were always looking for a cheap angle and he still had time to make tomorrow's Sunday sports supplements.

"Well mate, ya hafta start in the first round. And after what happened in Hawai'i, we gotta let the locals have a chance at every contest this year. So you'll be surfing against Aussies for two days, and you gotta win every heat ta advance all the way. Gotta be there Monday, six am. Its gonna be raining, and the surf is shitass, but that's your chance. The entry fee is two-fifty US."

Sonny-boy Noaloa opened his backpack and found the Wavelife credit card. It had a twenty grand limit with four to go.

"I'm in."

"Don't fuck with me, mate! No way Noaloa is heyah!" Mick Lennox was letting the morning sun rise on his hangover. He didn't need anyone playing games with him at the moment.

"Read it yerself, Mick!" said his old friend, Col Ritchie, his running mate around the world on the tour and the guy who'd been with Lennox when they had been chased out of Hawai'i. The headline said "Hawaiian Surf Star Wants Bells Trophy!" and the story went on for an entire column. Lennox didn't bother to try and read the fine print through his bleary eyes.

"Fuck that arshole! Let's get down there and kick his fuckin' arse back to the Islands!"

"Yer sure you want to do that?"

"I'm not gonna let that wanker run me outta the North Shore and then waltz around free Down Under! I gotta couple of friends from Narabeen who don't like him much either."

"Those guys play rough, Mick. You sure you know what yer doing?"

"Fuck, we'll just scare the shit outta him, bloody his nose a bit, and drop him off at the airport. No worries. Where's the fuckin' mobile?"

"Sir, can you tell us the purpose of your visit to Australia and why you are traveling alone? "

"It long story, but you no worry 'bout me. I come see good friend mine, help him out."

"And how long you will be in our country?"

"Uh, I don't know. First I gots to find my friend."

The official caught a signal from his superior.

"Sir, I'm going to ask you to keep your hands visible and please come with me."

"What you mean? I no got nuthin'."

"We will determine that in a few minutes. Routine procedures, you understand, and I'll thank you for your cooperation," said the immigration official, holding Ilano Kolana's brand new passport in his hand.

It was close to noon when Bruddah emerged from the immigration offices at the Melbourne airport, freshly fingerprinted and not a little bit shaken. He answered every question truthfully, but to the officials, things didn't add up. They made several phone calls to Hawai'i before asking more questions. But after almost two hours, Bruddah had earned their respect by keeping his cool and politely cooperating throughout his ordeal. He may have been a two-hundred and fifty pound pure bred Hawaiian the likes of which they had never seen, but he was also a very smart human being. When he was finally free to go, the immigration officials wished him luck during his visit to the lucky country. It was Palm Sunday morning, and he wondered what the week ahead was going to be like for an Island boy a long way from home.

* * *

A half moon was rising late Saturday night over the hills of Maui. Two attractive athletes were sitting on a veranda after dinner, trade winds wafting through the palms and the open windows of the house. Under any other circumstances, there might have been love in the air instead of a conversation that was quickly becoming a duel. She'd been dealing with come-ons for years and could see one coming a mile away, knowing her beauty was only enhanced by the low glow coming from the lights inside the house. But he was a confirmed bachelor trying to make sure she didn't misunderstand him, his existentialist intellect a constant reminder that she was not part of his personal life because the only personal life he had was the life within his person. He'd been alarmed by the suspicion in her voice and was backtracking as best he could because he didn't need anything to complicate the process of being ready to ride waves bigger than any she'd ever seen in person.

"But I just don't know if you're ready, Aleja. We need another week so we can work on the whips into some real waves. I know Cheryl has planned this whole thing for June through August, but the storms are starting up around Antarctica, and I just think - - -"

"Didn't we already go through this? I have to be back at the shelter by Wednesday, and tomorrow is our last session, period. And I am ready, Heath. You said yourself that once I'm up and riding, all I have to do is relax and not fall off. And I can do that, ok?"

"That's not the point. You haven't actually ridden a big wave on a tow-board, or wiped out and been picked up with the sled, or - - -"

"No, and I won't unless the surf comes up and we get in a session on the way to the airport. But one way or another, I'm on a plane tomorrow afternoon. I want to sleep in my own bed and not a cot in your garage, and that's that."

"Well, I'm sorry about that, and, uh, we could change that, I guess. You could sleep in Sonny-boy's room if you want."

"No, Heath, I'm going home."

"Aleja, you have to trust me," he said, but suddenly he didn't know if it was his mind talking, or his heart. "Why are you even doing this? If you aren't going to trust me, aren't you being less than honest with Cheryl Corlund telling her you want to surf the waves we saw at that meeting?"

215

"I trust you, and I'm honest with Cheryl. I couldn't do either if I didn't first trust myself, and know when I'm being honest. And the honest truth is I want to go home," parried Gracellen, "Any other questions?"

Even as it is truly impossible to adequately write about love, or convey erotica with words, it was not possible for these two human beings to bridge a gap that one could not leap across because the other didn't even see it. Yet Larson would not give up.

"What if I was to tell you that love was part of what we are doing?"

"Love of me? Love of self?" said Gracellen fiercely, more than ready to match wits with the existentialist when the 'L' word came up, "The love you think I must have for you if I am to be trusted with your life, or the love you think you must have for me if you are to be trusted with mine?"

Larson let the words lap against the strongholds of his mind like ripples against a jagged shore from a stone dropped into a lake. Gracellen waited patiently for him to speak, giving him the time and respect that he, like most men, needed.

"What we will be doing out on that reef depends on an absolute partnership in what can be, and will be, a life-and-death situation. Life is all about love, is it not? Isn't that part of why you are doing this, for the love you have for the people you shelter?"

"Point taken," she said.

Off in the distance a low roar could be heard. The waves of a new swell were starting to echo in the night. Heath saw a chance to include the ocean in the conversation.

"Maybe there'll be some waves tomorrow, and we can at least make sure we can work together in some real situations."

"Yeah, maybe. You know, Heath, I don't know much about you, and given all that's ahead of us, I don't think love should have any bearing on anything we do together."

"I know that, Aleja. What I'm speaking of here is a love that really has nothing to do with us, per se."

"Then what's all this about, Heath? You've got me up here, alone, with no Bruddah and no Sonny-boy to distract you. And now you are talking about love?"

"Not love as you may understand it. What I'm talking about is - - -"

Gracellen turned and looked straight into his eyes. She wasn't going to be less than direct with Larson. She expected the same from him and wanted him to know it. He did, and he didn't skip a beat.

"Shelter. You need it, the people you help in Santa Monica need it, and that is what love is. I find shelter inside waves. I don't find it with my heart in the hands of others. So this is not a matter of our hearts, yours or mine. It's a matter of the shelter to be found inside waves when you ride them as I have. And that will depend on our partnership when we're out at the reef."

"Did you say all this to Sonny-boy? Did you talk to him about love? Or did you stay safe in your macho world and talk around it?"

"Sonny-boy doesn't know enough about the mana of surfing to understand what riding a wave means. I think you do, and that's why I'm broaching the subject. A wave in its transient energy is the most unusual form of shelter there is. It comes and goes, and most people would never equate it with a warm fire, a family, sleeping in one's own bed, or the arms of a lover. But that's what it means to me. If we are to be partners in riding the biggest perfect waves in the world, you have to know that."

"How can a wave be shelter? How does it protect you?" asked Gracellen skeptically, "I saw the Malloys' movie and I liked their point of view. But as far as you and I are concerned, well, thanks for sharing, Heath, but I think you're full of shit."

She smiled, and Larson couldn't help but laugh in the knowledge they'd reached a denouement.

"You're right! Please excuse me while I go use the men's room," he said as he stood up and stretched, "You know, a guy won a Nobel prize for physics thanks to ideas he had while - - -"

"Please, Heath, you don't have to go into details, thank you," laughed Gracellen, "And if you'll excuse me, I've got to pack."

The first big set of the new swell hit the offshore reefs where they had been practicing. The explosions, amplified by the valleys, reverberated clearly and distinctly up to the house almost five miles from the beach.

"I think I'll go and prep the waverunner," said Larson, "just in case we have time for a session tomorrow."

"We'll have time," replied Gracellen, "Let's be ready at dawn. I'd love to ride some really good waves before I leave."

Larson looked at her for an extra second and Gracellen laughed.

"I'd LIKE to ride some really good waves before I leave."

They atmosphere was now completely relaxed between them and Gracellen was no longer on guard. She had a thought for Sonny-boy, and her heart softened at the thought of the former world champion.

"It's too bad what happened with Sonny-boy. Going to Australia was a pretty radical thing to do. I hope he knew what he's doing."

"He didn't, so let's hope Bruddah finds him fast."

* * *

"Hey, all I want is go surf!" said Sonny-boy Noaloa, trying to concentrate on the waves now slowly becoming visible in the cold, rainy dawn on day one of Australia's biggest pro surf contest.

"Fuckin' A, mate, that's all any of us want to do. We just don't want you to do it heyah!"

The cocky young Australian local had two of his mates standing on either side of him. All three were burly bricklayers by trade, though now on the dole, while trying to become professional surfers.

"Yeah, ya fuck! Ahfta what ya did to Mick on the North Shore, maybe we'll just break ya fuckin' surfboards and solve the whole fuckin' problem!"

The Sunday papers had announced Noaloa's last minute entry. The news was like electricity coursing through the traveling pro surf circus. TV crews and surf journos were looking all over for him, but Noaloa had deliberately stayed out of sight until the last minute. But even through the rain in the pre-dawn darkness, the Australian locals knew who he was. He didn't know what was going to happen next and realized he'd never been this scared before, not even when getting hassled in high school back in Florida. Of course, back then he didn't have a rep for having other people fight his battles for him, and right now his dad's posse was long gone.

Just then the traditional signal to start the day at the contest exploded out of the speakers. It was Australian surfing's national anthem: AC/DC's "Hell's Bells". He remembered how he'd been saved by the bell starting classes in Florida and he quickly took advantage of the temporary distraction. He grabbed his double board bag and practically ran to the judges tower.

"See ya in the watah, surf stah!"

"Yeah, he's gonna kick your ass!"

"And then we'll help ya get the fuck outta heah!"

"Five minutes. Five minutes. Competitors in the water, you have five minutes left in your heat."

The four surfers already knew how much time was left because they could see the big digital clock on the judges' tower even though it was raining steadily. But like all big surfing contests, the show went on at full blast and the announcement was easily heard out in the water like a sound check at an empty arena before a rock concert. In fact, there were no spectators anywhere because the fabled surf at Bells Beach was not even a shadow of itself.

This played to the strengths of Sonny-boy Noaloa. He had won a dozen such contests and knew exactly what he had to do when forced to hassle and grovel for crumbling mush breaking only a few yards from the beach. He ignored the dirty looks from the other three surfers in the water. He ignored the loudspeakers blasting speed metal music in between the announcer's lame attempts at commentary. He concentrated on getting "three to the beach", and he already had ridden two of them.

His first "wave" had been only about a foot high. Before going out he'd taken the leash off his board, knowing it could get tangled around his feet in the tiny waves. He had also replaced the normal fins on his board with much smaller ones so he could slide the tail around and slash skateboarder maneuvers while riding right up on the sand. His second wave was barely a ripple, but he was able to get to his feet and score points on a wave that was impossible for his competitors to ride. They were lifelong Bells Beach surfers and normally wouldn't have been caught dead trying to surf in such impossible conditions. They had entered the contest with dreams of making it to the big show by ripping the long even waves for which Bells was famous. Now, thanks to the realities of competitive surfing combined with the vagaries of the ocean in transition from one season to the next, they were sitting in the rain twenty yards from the beach and unable to even get to their feet.

The heat was coming to an end and Noaloa only needed one more wave. A rain squall hit and the judges could barely see the surfers through the downpour. Two of the Aussies simply gave up and came in, getting off their boards in the waist deep water and walking the short distance to the sand. But one wouldn't give up. It was one of the locals that had cornered Noaloa before the event started. The two sat almost within arms' reach of each other, stone-silent as if the other guy didn't exist, one ready to ride another ripple to make his victory complete, the other ready to explode in frustration.

A tiny wave began to form up and both surfers paddled for it. Noaloa was able to get his board moving on the swell, but the Aussie, who outweighed Sonny-boy by fifty pounds, just couldn't catch the wave. Noaloa got to his feet, and by simply crouching low on the short ride to the sand, was going to win the heat and advance to the next round. The bricklayer was enraged, and out of frustration he leaned back and let his board shoot out like a projectile. The board went over Sonny-boy's head, but he was so intent on riding the wave to the beach he didn't even realize what happened. The board missed him and, still attached by its leash, came back at the local like a slingshot.

"You fuckin bahstard! I'm gonna kill ya!" he screamed, as if Noaloa had intentionally tried to spear HIM. He ran through the waist-deep water, came up behind Noaloa, spun him around and cold-cocked him with a fist to the face. Noaloa was knocked flat on his back, but for an instant knew what was happening and tried to use his board as a shield. The local leaped on him and slammed a fist right into the Wavelife logo before ripping the board out of the way and going to work on Noaloa's face. The horn sounded, ending the heat and signaling the beginning of another fifteen minutes of competition between four more surfers trying to make it into the pros. Contest officials came running from the scaffolding and pulled the assailant off his victim. Noaloa tried to get to his feet, stumbled, keeled over and passed out.

The former two-time world professional surfing champion opened his eyes slowly. He was in a brightly lit room, with faces all around him. They moved back from the hospital bed until there was only one man smiling down at him.

"Bruddah, what, what - - -"

"You rest now, you safe. We talk latah."

"Did I, did I win? When's my next heat?"

Noaloa tried to struggle upright in the bed. A doctor and a nurse came to the bedside and helped ease their patient back down.

"You'd better go now, sir. We'll call you as soon as possible."

Bruddah turned and left the room, tears in his eyes and rage in his heart. He'd made it to the contest site just as the ambulance was leaving. When he got out of the rental, a contest official saw him and put two and two together.

"Uh, hello, uh, we had something happen, and if you are a friend of Noaloa's, well, I - - -"

Now the same official was sitting in the waiting room as Bruddah approached him, grabbed him by the shoulders and lifted the frightened man up out of his chair.

"No be scared, bra'. I guest in you country. I no punch you out. Go back run you contest. We no need you heah."

Bruddah set the man down gently and watched him head for the door. Then the big Hawaiian sat down and waited for doctors to tell him what was going to happen next.

But for the next two days, nothing changed. Noaloa remained sedated in the hospital and, back at the beach, the surf stayed flat. Contest organizers were able to force through the qualifying rounds and seed the winner into the main event. When Wednesday dawned and the surf was still terrible, officials put the contest on hold in hopes that some waves would appear the next day. They didn't, and now they were getting heat from the corporate sponsors. A TV show was planned, bleachers had to be filled and a champion had to be crowned. It all had nothing to do with the true spirit of surfing, so on a cold, overcast coast with not a wave in sight officials had no choice but to run the first round of pro surfing preliminaries.

The next day's dawn was even more dismal. It was Good Friday, and at Bell's Beach there was nothing good about it. The surf was dead flat, not even a ripple. There was literally not a wave in the ocean, and the contest had to be postponed again. Organizers were now in a panic. They began to make plans to run the entire event on Sunday, with shortened heats and a twelve hour schedule. The weather was supposed to change, and a new swell was tentatively predicted. Noaloa was still in the hospital with a severe concussion and a broken nose from the blows of the bricklayer. Doctors kept him under constant watch in case any swelling occurred in his skull that might damage the brain. He was conscious, and Bruddah never left his side.

Noaloa's assailant was jail. When contest officials had pulled him off Sonny-boy, the guy started throwing punches wildly. The whole thing turned into a pub brawl, except alcohol hadn't fueled the fight, though exactly what caused it would never be an easy thing to explain. Surf rage is sometimes beyond words.

Easter Sunday dawned at Bells Beach. The sound system came alive with "Hell's Bells", followed by a voice booming out of the huge speakers.

"G'day, everyone, and Happy Easter Sun - - - "

A screech of feedback drowned out the words until the announcer turned down the volume knob and started over.

"G'day, and happy Easter to us all. We've got the best surfers in the world 'ere t'day at the Bell's Beach Pro Surfing Championships. And the action will be startin' in a few minutes. First call heat number one, first call heat number one. Wearin' yellah will be Mick Lennox. Mick almost won it all last year and you can bet he's hungry for a shot at the title. Mick Lennox please report to the competitors' waitin' area! Wearin' red will be - - -"

Mick Lennox and Col Ritchie were sitting on the bluff overlooking Bell's Beach. The sky was clear but the surf was almost non-existent. It was the last possible day for the event, and fortunately the winds that had cleared the sky were also kicking up some chop that could be surfed. The comp was finally going to happen and everyone felt a little relieved as the first rays of the sun illuminated the three-story high scaffolding and sponsor banners at sunrise on Easter Sunday.

Yet to Col Ritchie, it was as if a curse had flattened the ocean because Neptune himself was enraged that the wonder of riding a wave had been twisted into a business and a battlefield of violence for which there was no excuse.

"Well, mate, Noaloa's still in the hospital, so you just may win this one."

"Yeah, well, he got what he had comin' to 'im, fair dinkum."

"Fuck off, Mick," said Ritchie, his Aussie sense of fair play now fully aroused, "There wasn't anything fair about it and you fuckin' well know it. I mean, what the fuck is it all about when a guy gets put inna 'ospital ovah some shitass waves and a fuckin' trophy?"

"Well, sometimes you just have to defend what's yores."

"Oh shut yer mouth, mate, the ocean ain't yores. Waves don't belong to you or anyone else," said Ritchie, "Anyway, ya can 'ave 'em today, all ya want, and maybe you'll be the champ, or was that chump?"

"Well, we've come alla way down heah. I bettah get goin'."

Lennox couldn't look him in the eye as he got up to get ready for his heat. Col Ritchie watched him walk down the bluff to face the realities of a professional surfing contest invading what used to be a pastoral and beautiful place. It was sunny, and thousands of people were filling the parking lots to overflowing. He knew the sponsors were going to be ecstatic to have their banners seen by the huge crowds, and when he saw the TV camera scaffolding, he almost began to laugh out loud. The surf was so bad they wouldn't dare broadcast it live, but he knew what the plan would be. After extensive editing and insertions of the sponsors' commercials, the show would end up filling an hour, complete with crowd shots, nervous competitors waiting for their heats, good looking sheilas lounging in string bikinis, and, hopefully, an Aussie raising the famous trophy above his head on a beer-soaked winner's platform.

Ten hours later, the sponsors did indeed get their money's worth. Mick Lennox was a relentless competitor when it came to outfoxing his international rivals. He breezed through the prelims, quarters, and semi-finals, taking down surfers from around the world who were out-of-synch after all the delays. In the finals he faced the current world champion from California who had won on points alone last year. The crowd chanted "Aussie – Aussie –Aussie" while the surfers battled it out in the sloppy waves. And when it was all over, Mick Lennox had won the Bell's Beach Pro Championships. Oversize cans of beer were shaken and sprayed all over the trophy stand. TV cameras and surf mag photographers covered it from every possible angle. When Lennox hoisted the fabled bell trophy over his head, he caught sight of Col Ritchie, and the smile faded from his face for a second before another wave of flash cameras reminded him to keep smiling.

After all the beer had been sprayed and all the cameras turned off, Lennox walked over to his friend.

"Well, ya did it, mate, for what its worth."

"Worth twenty grand and a lot of points, I'd say. You still got somethin' up yer arse, Col?"

Ritchie looked the champ in the eye, then looked over his shoulder and nodded. Standing next to a rental car was a big, dark skinned man.

"He's been waitin' for ya, Mick, 'cause there's someone in the car ya need to see, mate."

The passenger door opened, and at first he didn't recognize the person getting out of the car with a bandage on his face. Then realization hit Mick Lennox. He put the trophy down and walked towards Bruddah and Sonny-boy Noaloa. He stopped about five yards from the car. He turned and looked back at Ritchie holding the trophy. Then he looked at the envelope in his hand containing the check for his first place victory.

"I heard you lookin' fo' me, Lennox. I just want make sure you find me before I get outta heah."

"You got that right, mate. 'ere you go. 'ospitals ain't cheap," he said, and he handed the envelope to Noaloa.

The two surfers looked at each other, and neither knew what to say next.

"Eh, Sonny-boy, say mahalo," said Bruddah.

"Nah, no thanks necessary. The surf was so bad, ya would'a won, ya know. I heard ya knocked the stuff out of those guys in yer first heat."

"Fo' reals, but den da heat end, and dey come bleed my face!" laughed Noaloa.

Col Ritchie came over and put the trophy on the front of the car.

"Ya wanna ornament for the bonnet?"

"Nah, he got plenny dose at home," said Bruddah, and they all started laughing.

A local surfer in a wetsuit with a board under his arm came running past the four men standing around the car. He recognized Lennox and slowed to a walk.

"Good on ya, Mick! Bring us a title this year!"

"Thanks. Where you goin'? There's no surf!"

"Oh yeah there is. Look!"

All eyes turned toward the ocean. A set of head high waves was rolling in.

"'appens every time, mate. Soon as the tour leaves, the surf comes up. She'll be big by sundown, and tomorrow'll be perfect, mate. And the circus will be long gone. See ya next year, champ!"

The surfer ran down the pasture toward the fresh new waves as the banners were being rolled up and the scaffolding began to come down.

* * *

"But I found it and I want it!"

"Now Katy, let the other little girl have it," said Aleja Gracellen.

"No, I want it! I want it! I want it!"

222

The four year old dropped her Easter basket and clenched her fists. The mother was nowhere to be seen. She had been in the shelter for two weeks before a Saturday night turned into a slippery slope, leaving the little girl to wake up alone on Easter Sunday morning. Aleja had seen it happen before, and she knew a hug was not going to work. She did know what would.

"I think I know where there's the best egg in the whole world, and if I tell you where it is, will you come with me to get it?"

"Where is it?"

"Cheryl, take over for a second. Katy and I are going to find the best egg in the whole world!"

"But, what will I do? There's a lot going on and I've - - -"

Aleja Gracellen looked the CEO in the eye.

"This is part of the deal, remember? Don't worry, we'll be right back. Oh, and if you get the chance, check the porta-potties and make sure there's enough toilet paper in 'em."

Gracellen took the little child's hand and walked away from the shelter's Easter Sunday breakfast and egg hunt. "Now, we're going to find you a special Easter egg, and we're going to find it where no one else can see it."

"Will it be pretty?"

"I think so. The Easter bunny sometimes hides eggs right next to the ocean because she likes the sound of the waves. Do you like the ocean, Katy?"

"Yes. Do you know where my mommy is?"

"Your mommy is looking for Easter eggs, but they are really hard to find. I think God is trying to help her."

"I hope so. She needs a lot of help."

"Look, Katy, there are the dolphins!"

The little girl ran to the water waving her arms.

"Hello dolphins! Hello! Wait for me!"

Gracellen stopped and watched the child. She took an Easter egg out of her pocket and half-buried it in the sand near the high tide line. She watched the homeless child running along the edge of the water following three dolphins swimming along the surf line. A small set of waves came in. The dolphins took off and rode one underwater down the beach. The child was waving to them and running to keep up with them. Maybe miracles happen, maybe they don't, but Gracellen could have sworn the dolphins saw Katy and jumped high out of the water - and then kept riding the wave as she ran along the beach.

Gracellen wiped her eyes, and the dolphins were gone. Katy came running back as full of joy as a child could be.

Then she saw the egg, and picked it up.

"I found it! I'm going to save it and give it to my mommy! Ok, we can go now. I found the egg!"

They walked back across the beach. Aleja Gracellen looked over her shoulder and saw another set of waves coming in. They were very small but stretched for a hundred yards parallel to the beach. They were from the same storm that produced the waves she had ridden with Heath only a few days ago, three thousand miles out in the Pacific, where she'd ridden the biggest surf of her life. Now the last remnants of the winter's last swell, so very far from their birthplace in the North Pacific, had allowed some dolphins to bring true joy to a little girl running along the shore.

When they got back to the Easter egg hunt, Katy's mother was standing near a tree off to one side, looking chagrined and more than a little worse for wear.

"Mommy! Mommy! Look what I have for you!"

Mother and child embraced, and Aleja Gracellen had to say something before her heart would have choked her up completely.

"See you later, I hope?" she said, looking the mother in the eye.

"Yes, if you'll have me."

"Well, you'll have to start all over, but that's what we're for."

The two women nodded to each other and Gracellen turned away, only to see her chief volunteer on a cell phone at the food distribution table.

"- - - but call me tomorrow at the office and we'll discuss it," said Cheryl Corlund, "Uh, excuse me, could you please leave your shopping cart, oh, uh, sorry, that's ok, you can keep it with you. Uh, yes, yes, Heath, I heard you the first time. I'm here helping Aleja with the Easter event she puts on at the shelter. I'm really busy, Heath, and no, no, please just take one plate of food, ok? There is plenty more and you can come back for seconds."

Heath Larson was sitting very alone on the porch in the low glow of light from the sun just below the eastern horizon. With Gracellen gone and the Hawaiian winter surf over, he was beginning to amp in anticipation of surfing the raw power of the Southern Hemisphere's winter storms.

"Cheryl, I'm going to call Ian Clark and get this thing in gear. Aleja is ready to tow in and I just talked to Bruddah, and we have to - - -"

"You did? What happened? Is Sonny-boy ok? Uh, Roberto! Check the porta-potties! There's more toilet paper in that box over there. Heath, is he ok?"

"Well, he'll be fine, and actually the whole thing worked out ok down there. But we have to get on track right away and - - -"

"Heath, Call Clark and tell him what you want. Then call me, no, call Roberto. Gotta go."

Cheryl Corlund quickly put the phone away as Aleja Gracellen gave her a reproachful look.

"Ok, I'm working! Don't worry! It was Heath, but everything is okay!"

* * *

Halfway between California and Hawai'i and three thousand miles to the south, the sun was two hands above the horizon. For almost all the sea people of Marulea, Sunday was always a day of rest, though without any formal services, even on Easter. However, they did follow one tradition faithfully.

Just after sunrise, many would gather in small groups because for the Maruleans, "Sunday services" were about helping each other, neighbor-to-neighbor. And so three youths had come to the home of Luan and David Helmares to care for their infant children so that the parents could go off to spend the day being a couple in love.

The circle of pleasure flowed effortlessly, steady and true, strong, then a pause, then stronger once more, he on his back, she above. The sails were full of wind and the tiller tied against the tide and current. The three hulls of the voyaging craft were on course, leaving husband and wife free to find each other, skin to skin, in love and lust while voyaging to an isle on the horizon.

"Oh, oh, that's wonderful, oh, yes, yes, yes!" The words flew through David's dream under the shelter dome of the voyaging craft. There was a pause, and David stirred in his sleep. In the dream he could hear the words as they echoed. Then a laugh, almost a scream of delight, and David was awake.

"Go! Go! Oh, yes!"

Luan was standing on the bow, her rich skin supple and shapely, her shoulders broad, her waist trim, her legs long and lean. She glowed warm in the mid-morning sunlight with a voice full of excitement and wonder.

"Luan! What are you - - -"

He saw that they had arrived at their destination, at the reef across the channel from the fishing grounds, the place of perfect waves he thought only he had seen. Luan turned and laughed, revealing a surfer off in the distance behind her. He was up and riding, and his wife couldn't get enough of it.

"Luan! What's going on?" he said, the anger rising in his voice.

"Oh don't get your panties in a bunch, David, or whatever your old State Beach buddies used to say. It's my father!"

"Oh, uh, yeah, ok, yeah, sure it is, who else could it be?" he said, suppressing an inner intensity less about jealousy than it was surprise. He joined his wife to see Taveka gliding motionless across a wave, leaning back and raising an arm in a classic pose. David remembered his mentor studying a photo above David's bunk on the *Morning Light*, a photo of surf legend Joey Cabell, in full 'danseur' pose, at a reef in the Indian Ocean.

The wave finally tapered down to nothing, but the wooden board had a momentum of its own, and Taveka continued to glide for seconds after the wave backed off. He remained balanced and elegant, until he relaxed and lowered himself to kneel on the deck of his board. David felt a twinge of selfishness. Despite having his wife at his side, he found it hard to accept the fact that the wave he once thought of as his was being ridden by someone else, even if it was the man who had taught him so much.

Taveka slowly maneuvered his board around and pointed it back out to the take-off zone. He looked up and saw the voyaging craft. He stopped, thought for an instant, and then began to gesture and yell as loud as he could, his tone harsh and abrupt.

"Out! Out!! This is my wave now!"

A twinge exploded in David's soul. He heard the thread of steel woven into Taveka's voice and realizing his mentor wasn't kidding. He quickly walked back to the stern.

"Ready about, Luan!"

She was dumbfounded. She'd never heard her father scream like that, and the reaction from her husband was just as shocking.

"David, its dad! He's just kidding! C'mon, David!"

"Ready about, Luan! And I mean it!"

His wife came back to where the lines controlled the sails.

She released the lines as he pushed the tiller hard over. The craft turned hard away from the reef. Sails filled with wind, and David set a new course towards an empty horizon. Luan came back and sat next to him. She held his hand, and touched his cheek with her fingers. For a moment he was stoic and stared straight ahead. Then he began to cry.

"Why would he do that? Why? What, what did I do? He surfs because I taught him, he knew about the reef because I told him, and - - -"

"David, stop talking. You don't have to stop crying. But stop talking."

Luan could not have loved him deeply if his heart was not sensitive and true. And now his heart was pained. So she let him cry, her husband showing the real courage it takes for a man to feel deeply, and let it show. For a moment he buried his head against her breasts, until a thought opened his eyes.

"I know what he was doing. He was testing me. He was giving me a taste of my own poison, and he made sure it was as real as possible. He wanted to give me a strong dose, almost like an anti-venom, to inoculate me from ever letting myself lose control again. He knew what went through my mind the last time I was here, and he wanted to make sure I got the point, even if he had to use something deep inside him from a long time ago."

Luan's mind was reeling from the energy created between the two navigators. She could not absorb it, and so she let her body do the thinking. That gave her something to say.

"Well, David, we can always wait for him to leave," she said, the vivacious smile in her eyes but a glimmer of the love she felt for the man in her arms, "Or how about that reef we went to the first time we sailed together? And that way we could be alone, David."

"Oh, Luan, what would I do without you?"

She smiled at her lover, but then her smiled faded just a bit when he stood up quickly in a burst of excitement.

"Yeah! And on this swell it's going to be firing!"

He went to the tiller and changed their course. She adjusted the sails, and the voyaging craft gained speed and began to make passage towards a reef off in the distance. He checked the current, she tightened the rigging and there was nothing else to do but glide across the clear turquoise water to their destination.

"Now, Luan, what else did you have in mind?"

"Hey, this localism stuff ain't half bad!" Taveka thought to himself as he saw David's voyaging craft heading out to sea. He almost laughed at how he'd played his little joke on David. But he knew, and he was sure David certainly knew, that it was no joke. He had tested his successor with but a drop of the bitter memory from his past, and he'd used the pain of his own failing to reinforce the message. Now he was confident David would be a better man for having to come face to face with what it was like to be on the receiving end of man at his worst.

Taveka looked up the reef, and a wave was breaking perfectly towards him. He noticed the mouth of the rolling tunnel was almost oval in shape, almost like an egg, reminding him that people had celebrated Easter as the morning sun shone down on churches and children around the world. Then he remembered it was Monday across the date line just a few thousand miles to the west and his moment of reflection flew away like a bird leaving a nest.

He turned his surfboard and aimed it down the path the wave would take along the reef. Two strong strokes and he slid down its face, the weight of his board causing it to accelerate with its own momentum. Quickly he was on his feet, leaning slightly and turning to set up a long effortless glide through an almost magical space.

David's surfing had made such a strong impression on him that he'd begun to consider becoming a surfer himself, and then did exactly that. They'd built a special board for him, and with a few lessons from his former apprentice, the navigator found a new way to match his instincts with the ocean's energy. He'd quickly mastered the basics, and now he was able to stay right in the pocket the entire wave, adjusting his speed now and then to trim through the best path down the curving wall of water. Spry and in great shape, Taveka had become a good surfer.

At the end of the ride, he looked out and could barely see the mast of the voyaging craft on course to another reef off in the distance. Now he was floating alone, surrounded by the aquas and emeralds of a lonely paradise, with more perfect waves coming down the reef as far as his eye could see. He didn't waste an instant and began paddling to the takeoff zone, knowing that after the sun had set on this Easter Sunday, he would never surf these waves again. His thoughts were on new places to ride waves all throughout the Nebula Archipelago and on the place where he would ride his very last wave.

May Day

The eyes of the passengers were glued to the portholes and observation domes. They had all seen the original video and the computer graphic version of what the waves might look like. Now the real thing was only two hundred feet below them. Victor Sanchez was all business at the sluggish controls, keeping the *Skyhook* in an easy circle while his wife gave him a final set of observations and clearance to set down.

"Apparent wind southeast five knots. Light chop. Wave train interval five minutes. All conditions go."

"Roger that," said Victor. He clicked on the intercom. "All passengers prepare for landing in one minute. Seat belts mandatory. Mac, cargo secure?"

"Affirmative, Victor. We're go," said Owens.

Victor Sanchez had executed hundreds of open ocean 'landings' with the *Skyhook* in the prevailing southeast trades that blow across most of Polynesia. The only variable was timing his final approach and splashdown between the sets, so he waited until the last wave of a set began to break at the southern end of the reef before setting up the *Skyhook*'s final approach and aiming for the shelter of calm water in the lee of the reef. Two minutes later, the seaplane's V-hull sliced into the sea about a hundred yards from the entrance to the lagoon at the northern end of the reef. Sanchez quickly throttled back to maneuver the Catalina towards her anchorage. It was a textbook execution of an open sea landing in a large groundswell, and he brought the *Skyhook* to a rest exactly as planned.

"Ok, Heath," he said over the intercom, "Here we are, and I hope this is what you wanted."

* * *

Surf season in the Southern Hemisphere began with arrival of the first swell at Bell's in the hours just after the contest ended. Those waves came from the lead storm of a series of low pressures coming up to full winter strength while whirling around Antarctica like spinning tops. For days the surf grew steadily, as did the storms, until one broke out and up into the Roaring Forties and metastasized into a major surf producer.

At its birth in the Indian Ocean twelve hundred kilometers south-south west of Australia, the system produced waves that lit up the reefs of Indonesia. The storm rolled eastwards in a path comparatively close to the Antarctic continent, broadcasting swells all across the southern coasts of Australia and

New Zealand. The core winds weakened a little when the low slowed its eastward motion for almost twenty hours south of New Zealand. There it sat until a jolt of energy from cold Antarctic winds powered it up again. The result was unusual. One day the surf was only two to four feet along the eastern shores of Australia. The next day it was twelve to fifteen feet. The surf report companies completely blew the prediction. Intermittent technical delays often caused a full twenty-four hours to elapse between satellite snapshots. Hence, surprise was still a factor when it came to surf in the Southern Hemisphere, and this swell was a prime example.

After shocking surfers up and down Australia's east coast, the storm resumed its march eastward loaded with wind. The "coconut grapevine" began to hum all across the Pacific, thanks to cell phones and satellites, with a simple message: drop everything and go to the best surf spots because great waves were on the way. Hundreds joined the frenzy, including Heath Larson.

With a phone call from a friend in Australia, Larson was alerted immediately when the surprise swell hit Australia on the last Sunday in April. He had done some data mining to get the information about what had produced the surf in Clark's video. He knew what he was looking for. He quickly checked the US Navy Wave Action Model site – and saw almost the exact same swell pattern.

Despite his considerable intellect, Larson succumbed to the siren call, "Surf's up!" A surge of anticipation washed through his brain, a feeling known only to surfers when the anticipation of great waves overpowers all reason. His eyes lit up with energy and euphoria.

He knew the Wavelife-Skyrider agreement didn't kick in until June 21. But all the jetskis were waiting in Tahiti and Mac Owens had completed all preparations, including the electric hoist system, necessary to turning the Skyhook into a floating expedition base camp. There were no technical issues that would preclude the run to the reef.

So he knew exactly what to do. But when he picked up the phone, his euphoria met its first challenge. Cheryl Corlund was too busy running the Easter event at the shelter and had no time to talk to him. And he had no way to contact Clark on Sunday, so he did the next best thing. He skipped Clark and went straight to the people he'd need to get to the reef. But again, he struck out when he called the offices of the Skyrider Foundation, only to be told that the Skyhook wasn't home. And then he slapped himself in the forehead. He remembered Owens telling him that they'd be ferrying a self-contained medical clinic around the outlying atolls of the Tuamotus on a UN grant to check for genetic anomalies in new-born Polynesians that could be traced to atomic testing by the United States and France. But then his luck changed and he was able to call the Skyhook direct and got Victor Sanchez over the radiophone patch through Tahiti.

* * *

229

"Hold on a second, Heath, let me get her up and level," he said, pausing to make sure he wasn't distracted until he had the *Skyhook* at cruising altitude, "Ok, so what's up?"

"The surf, Victor, and I think we need to make a run out to the reef in the next three days. I know about your contract, but this swell will be perfect and we need to practice."

"Well, there's no way I can help you, Heath. We can't just drop everything and go surfing. We won't be done out here for a while and then its twenty hours back to base and we've got a maintenance scheduled 'cause we have two charters next week. So no can do."

"I understand, Captain, its just that - - - "

"Listen Heath, I like what you are about and how you conduct yourself. But this whole thing is Clark's deal, and going out of my way for him just isn't in the cards."

"Well, yeah, but - - -"

"No yeah-but, Heath. Now let's shoot straight here, shall we? As far as I'm concerned, this whole thing is about nothing more than money. So I'd rather not spoil things between us, you know what I mean? Skyrider has a contract with Clark and Wavelife, and we're yours starting June 21. Unless that changes, there's nothing I can or will do."

Heath Larson appreciated Sanchez being direct, but he could think of nothing in reply. Then he thought about Sanchez' last sentence for a second.

"Aye-aye, Captain, understood loud and clear. Let me make some calls. Maybe something can be worked out tomorrow morning."

"Yeah, maybe," replied Sanchez, "but don't count on it."

* * *

"Wow, Heath, sounds great, but no can do," said Roberto Mercante, answering his first call of the day, "Bad timing. The LBO and all that. We just have to wait until the contract with Skyrider kicks in. Too bad. I hear its going to be a really good swell."

"What about Clem Charleton's plane in Florida? Can't you call him and tell him you're interested in buying it and would pay for a quick charter?"

"C'mon Heath, you know how that would go over with Cheryl."

"But Roberto, there's got to be a way to make this work."

"Well, call Ian Clark. He's the travel agent. I bet he's in his office right now even if it is Monday morning. Good luck Heath!"

* * *

"I'm sorry, but Mr. Clark is in a meeting. Would you like to leave a message on his voice mail?"

"Uh, yeah, sure. Thank you."

"Ian, this is Heath. The surf is gonna be unreal at the reef, and we need to be out there three days from now. You need to call the *Skyhook* - - - "

Clark was listening to the message without letting it distract him. He was always 'in a meeting' when calls came in. But at the mention of the *Skyhook*, he picked up the phone.

"Heath! Just got out of the meeting and heard your voice. What's up?"

"We've got to get down to the reef, and we've got to do it right away. There's a swell coming from a storm in almost the exact same place as the storm last October that you, or uh, - - -"

Clark quickly interrupted the conversation.

"I know about the swell. We've been swamped with last minute bookings to Fiji, Tonga, and the Society Islands. I'm really busy right now, so what can I do for you?"

"I got in touch with the *Skyhook*, and they aren't available without a contract modification. So you've got to call them, and right away."

"Oh, really?" said Clark barely containing his irritation that Larson had jumped him in contacting the *Skyhook*, "Well, that's something I can't do, Heath. We've got a contract with them and after June 21, we'll be able to practically live down there waiting for a swell. But now's impossible."

"Ian, we both know you can't count on the ocean! It may be flat June, July, and August! It's happened before, and if it happens again, we'll be SOL."

"That's true," and Clark realized what that would mean, "but, uh, I don't know, Heath, even if we can get the *Skyhook* by some miracle, who's gonna pay for it? Wavelife won't."

"Yeah, I know, I just called Roberto. But can't you pay for it? I'm sure you are doing ok out of all this."

Clark's clear thinking turned to anger. His end was none of Larson's business.

"No, Heath, it doesn't work that way. Look, I'm really busy right now. I'll call you if I have any ideas, ok?"

"Ok, I get the picture," said Larson, bristling at Clark's "don't call me – I'll call you" attitude, "I've got more calls to make, Ian, and I am going to make this work. And when I call YOU back, don't have your secretary tell me you are in some fucking meeting. I don't like being lied to."

* * *

"Heath! Good to hear from you! How's the surf, my friend? Stupid question! I bet it's always perfect in Hawai'i!"

"Not quite, Ben, but it is going to be perfect out on the reef, and we need to be there."

"Well, I don't surf, so why do WE need to be there?"

"Well, not you exactly, Ben, but the company you are buying has a big interest in me surfing the place, and Aleja, and Sonny-boy. So we need to get out there and get started."

"Heath, I'd love to help, but everything is on hold right now while the SEC scrutinizes the deal. In fact, as a current stockholder and member of a potential investor group, I can't be talking to a Wavelife employee outside the due diligence process. It's called 'passing on insider information'. It's a big red light for the Feds. How's the weather been over there?"

Larson didn't know what to say except simply answer the question.

"Just fine, Ben, just fine. Looks like it's gonna be a beautiful summer. You should come over sometime. We'll hunt pigs and have a luau for you," he said, making some friendly small talk to get back in synch with Jeffries.

"Yes, Heath, that would be great. Let me check my calendar, and I'll give you a call. Gotta go, Heath. Best wishes!"

"Same to you Ben. Bye!" he said cheerfully, having thought of who he could call next.

* * *

"Heath, let me tell you for the last time," said Cheryl Corlund, "the contract between Wavelife and the Skyrider Foundation cannot be modified. We are in the quiet period mandated by the SEC. I can't do anything other than work within the business plan established before the date I tendered our offer. If I spent company money to enhance the value of the corporation, I'd have to tell the whole world about the place or the Feds would pull the plug on our deal in a heartbeat."

"So, uh, ok, I get the picture. If I wanted to go surf the reef, I'd have to pay for it myself, is that it?"

"You would be free to do that, yes Heath," said Bill Massara, speaking clearly so the conference phone in Corlund's office could pick up his voice, "Just don't involve the company in any official or financial manner."

"It would have to be a freelance expedition on your part, Heath," chimed in June Wilson, "though as a Wavelife employee, anything you learned about the place as it relates to increased value to Wavelife would have to be disclosed publicly."

"Okay, I gotta do it on my own dime, and if the place turns out to be what we expected, I'd have to go public with the news."

"Well, not quite, because if it turns out to be anything less than a sure thing," said Corlund, remembering her strategy concerning the reef, "then the value of the reef would be of a speculative nature, and we wouldn't have to disclose it since there would be no value-add. So that's about it for now, and unless you have something else?"

Larson knew Cheryl had just told him something important between the lines but off the top of his head he didn't know what it was.

"No, that was it. Sorry to take up your time, Cheryl," he said.

"No problem Heath. Give our love to Bruddah and Sonny-boy. Oh, and if you figure something out, be sure and call Aleja at the shelter."

"Will do," said Larson. He clicked off his cell, and broke down the problem. He needed the *Skyhook*, but he'd have to pay for it himself while convincing Victor Sanchez to take his money. Then he remembered why Sanchez was flying charters in the first place.

* * *

"Maui Real Estate, Maureen Nirema speaking."

"Maureen? Heath Larson. Good to hear your voice. Say, how much is my place worth? Including all the acreage?"

The top real estate agent on the island didn't waste words.

"Two point five as is. Thinking of selling, Heath? I'd love to have the listing."

"Well, if I was thinking of selling, of course I'd call you first. But right now I want to pull some money out of the place."

232

"That would decrease the value of your holdings, but with the market as strong as it is for properties like yours, you would probably be back at par within a few months."

"Good. Who do you like for a loan broker?"

* * *

"Hello, Heath. What's up?"

"A contract is a contract, Victor. You were right about that. Can I have a few words with your better half?"

Sanchez pressed a button on the headset.

"Tina! Heath Larson calling."

There was a sudden increase in the volume of the engines as now two microphones were picking up the roar of the Pratt and Whitney turbo props.

"Got it! Hello Heath, how are you?" said Tina Sanchez. Then the volume of the engines was halved as Victor clicked off.

"Tina, I have a proposition to make to the benefit of your Foundation."

"Well Heath, Victor already told me of your idea, and I don't think there's any way we can - - -"

"What if someone put a million dollars in a new endowment fund for Skyrider? Would you have any special customer services available for such a benefactor?"

She instantly knew what he was doing, because they both knew that when it comes to running non-profits, money doesn't just talk, it screams.

"We certainly would, Heath. How can I help you?"

* * *

"That's brilliant, Heath, and for such a good cause! My wife has always wanted to own a time share in Hawai'i, so I guess our partnership in Sartre will now extend to the hills of Maui. Who do I make the check out to?" said Ben Jeffries.

* * *

"Let me get this straight. You're putting up five, and raising the rest by selling time shares in your place at two-fifty each. How did you come up with this, Heath?"

"By thinking about how a non-profit works and by having a great real estate agent down the road. And don't forget, Cheryl, I'm only doing an endowment, just like you've done for Aleja, though without the tax advantages. But that's ok, because the waves will be worth the price of admission."

"Well, you certainly don't take no for an answer when you want to go surfing! Ok, if Ben's in, so am I."

* * *

"Yes, Heath, what is it?" said Aleja Gracellen in a strictly business voice sitting behind her desk at the shelter.

"We're going to the reef day after tomorrow."

Her composure had no chance against visions of perfect waves.

"But I thought we weren't going until June at the earliest! And oh shoot, we have a special event for the kids coming up. I don't know if I can - - -"

"Well, I hope you can miss it, because the reef will be firing. Isn't there someone who can fill in for you?"

"Uh, no, there - - -, wait a sec, let me put you on hold ok? I'll be right back," she said, hitting a preset on the phone

"Cheryl! Remember our deal about the May Day event? I hope so, 'cause I need you to take over for me, ok? Thanks!" Click.

"Ok, Heath, when's my flight?"

* * *

"Randy Laine? Heath Larson. You busy right now?"

Surfing's premier jet ski and safety expert had exactly the answer Larson wanted to hear.

"Nope, and you're lucky, Larson. I heard about the swell, and you're the first phone call. So what's my flight number?"

* * *

"No can do, Heath. After that last run to Cortez, I'm not gonna get lowballed for surf photos ever again."

Bob Rowe was once a premier surf photographer who had been crowded out of the field by a new generation of auto-focus wanna-bes who worked dirt cheap. He was now a L.A. County lifeguard but did the occasional freelance for the mainstream outdoor magazines because they paid him what he was worth. Larson knew what he was worth.

"Name your price, Bob. You'll be working for me. At full rate. You retain all the rights. And all expenses paid."

"I assume you want me to bring all-digital and the steady-cam chest harness and the helmet with a heads-up display on the visor?"

"Absolutely. Bring everything you can, but don't check anything with the airlines that might hang us up."

"Heath, for the kind of money you're gonna pay me, do you think I'd make a rookie mistake like that? Where are we going, and when's my flight?"

"Call you back in an hour. We're gonna be in Papeete to meet a seaplane at dawn day after tomorrow."

* * *

"Ok, Clark, it's me and I know you are listening, so get on the phone. No, wait, I don't need to talk to you right now. Bill me for five first class roundtrips LAX Tahiti arriving Papeete thirty six hours from now. Names are Aleja Gracellen, Randy Laine, Bob Rowe, Roberto Mercante, and of course, you. And three more from Honolulu for Sonny-boy, Bruddah and me. Get back to me with flight numbers in an hour. We're meeting the *Skyhook* at sunrise on Thursday."

* * *

"Heath, if you weren't such a nice guy, I'd hafta give y'all a piece a' my mind 'bout this, this - - -"

"Chinese fire drill, Mac? Yeah, I know, but we've just got to get out there and get a feel for the place when it's big. Come this summer, we may only get one chance, and we won't be able to afford any screw-ups."

"Well, why aren't the Wavelife honchos payin'? I unnerstand ya took out a loan 'gainst yer house or sumtin'? Fer a surf trip?"

"I'll get it back, with interest, if this all goes well. If it doesn't we'll all be screwed anyway, except you guys, of course."

"Tina Sanchez keeps us flyin', that's all I know," said Owens, circumspect about his boss and her financial acumen.

"Speaking of flying, let's talk about the waverunners. Have you flown with them in place yet?"

"Yup. Wing mounts worked jes fine, but I had ta reinforce tha landin' gear ta handle tha side mounted units. Now 'bout tha rest a' yer stuff, let me git the list."

"Don't bother, Mac, I've got it here."

"No Heath, I'll git mine an' we'll go through 'em together. I don' want no screw ups."

"Well, actually, Mac, the more screw ups the better on this trip. That way we'll be able to fix them before the real deal this summer."

* * *

"Tell me one mo time, brah. We go surf da place now?"

"Pack it all up, Bruddah. The locator stuff, the suits, everything. Sonny-boy, you're on the boards, the ropes, the - - - "

"Heath, if we be flyin' Tahiti tomorrow, we gotta be outta heah inna bout two hours ta catch the last inter-island tonight. We no got time fo' stand-around and yak. You got da reservations?"

"Uh, well," for the first time in hours, Heath Larson came up short, "I'll be making that call in a minute. You guys got your passports?"

Bruddah and Sonny-boy looked each other, knowing Larson was trying to get back in total control.

"Passport? What passport? No need a stinking passport! Tahiti is Polynesia, and anyways I thought use 'm once, den trow 'em away!"

"Yeah, Heath, mine go lost inna laundry, or mebbe leave wid my pops? Or wait a sec, no, I no see him fo' one long time. Maybe my agent got it."

The two Hawaiians looked at Larson, with deadpan faces, and then all three started laughing.

* * *

The *Skyhook* arrived just before dawn outside the harbor where a fishing boat was waiting with eight people, ten surfboards, and a good number of equipment cases. It took a good half hour to methodically load and position everything for the flight to the reef with Mac Owens giving directions. Finally the cargo and passengers were ready, the engines roared to full power, and Victor Sanchez got her slowly in the air and soon she was heading straight towards a weak sun rising higher in the east. By the time the sun was overhead, the *Skyhook* was once again floating on the Pacific Ocean.

"Looks pretty good! Looks REALLY good! We gonna geevum! Dey peelin' all down da reef! Hey, Aleja, check out da lefts! Dey perfect!"

"Oh, yes! This is gonna be fun! Wait till Ben and Cheryl see me dance on these waves, Roberto!"

"Yeah, it looks like what you showed us back in October, doesn't it, Ian?"

"Yup! I told you, Roberto, this place is the best big wave ever!"

Noaloa, Gracellen, Mercante and Clark were too stoked to notice that Bruddah, Heath, Laine and Rowe were not saying a word. They knew what they were looking at. Larson finally put it into words.

"No, Roberto, it doesn't look like what we saw, because the wind isn't offshore. So no, Ian, it isn't the best big wave ever. In fact, it's no good."

"Huh?" said four incredulous voices.

"You guys take one mo look. See da chop from da trades?"

"The trades?"

"Winds, Barbie, da trade winds. Dey called dat by da old sailors 'cause dey blew right way fo trade routes. But dey blow wrong way fo' us."

"Take a closer look," said Randy Laine, "We've got a southwest swell with southeast trades – that's like skateboarding down a hill with speed bumps coming at you from the wrong angle."

"So now what, Heath?" asked Bob Rowe.

"Well, basically I don't think this place is going to work for us."

"What do you mean, Heath?" said Clark nervously, "It looks pretty good out there!"

Rowe and Laine knew they were not a part of this conversation and retreated to the 'sunroom' in the aft section of the plane. Bruddah kept an eye out the porthole, but he gave Larson a look and shook his head.

"Yeah," said Roberto Mercante, "I mean, for sure it's too big for me, but you should be able to handle it."

The next set began to break at the far end of the reef. It was hard to tell exactly how big it was. Soon the set was breaking from one end of the reef to the other, and the *Skyhook* was starting to rise and fall from the swells in lee of the reef.

"Listen, Roberto, I paid for this trip. I really want to understand this place, and right now, the only thing I know for sure is that the prevailing wind is from the wrong direction and the waves are shitty."

"But Heath! You were so sure! You got us all out here! What happened?"

"Aleja, I was amping, just like so many surfers who let surf reports and the promise of perfect waves turn their heads like Midwest tourists oogling b-grade whores in a Waikiki bar."

"Heath Larson, don't talk to me like that!"

"My apologies, Aleja, but I saw the wave models and thought we would get what we saw in the video. But I didn't think to check the prevailing wind direction, and so I blew it."

"Oh, come on, Heath, you saw the video from the plane! This place can get unreal!"

"Yeah, Ian, but from the original video you showed us you really couldn't tell exactly what the wind was doing to the waves. It looked offshore, but in waves this big there's a lot of spray coming off the top even if its glassy – or blown out. It wasn't sharp enough, so then you showed us two minutes of computer generated graphics that looked really amazing, but in fact was not real. You sold the whole thing like a tent-show barker selling snake oil, and you," he looked at Roberto, "bought the whole thing. And so did I."

He waved his hand around the compartment. Victor and Tina Sanchez had joined the group, and Mac Owens was standing in the bulkhead passageway.

"Sorry to interrupt your meeting," said Victor Sanchez, "but I've got to ask you to pull this whole show together right now. You either surf it or you don't. Either we stay, or we make ready for takeoff. What's it going to be?"

As usual, Tina Sanchez spoke up immediately after her husband's frank appraisal of things.

"Heath, why don't we deploy the waverunners and test all the equipment, especially the locators and the grid system. And Mac! Let's see the hoists in action and practice deploy and load-out. And who knows? Maybe the wind will change."

"Yes, maybe the wind will change," said Clark, looking for something, anything to get him off the hook.

"Yes, that's true, maybe the wind will change," said Larson was a hint of sarcasm and a look at Bruddah.

"Yeah, dey change," he agreed with a friendly smile, "Get stronga all day, jes' like island side. Dey steady and blow strong an' you can depen' on 'em. Dats why dey call 'em trades! Good for sailing! But not fo' surfing."

"Then you'd better git out there right now, Heath," said Mac Owens.

Larson gave his best friend another look. This time there would be no joking around as the minds of the two men met eye to eye to consider the situation. Nobody said a word, and when Bruddah spoke, he was talking to no one but Heath.

"We go geevum one short sesh. Keep in shape, yeah brah?"

"Ok, everyone, we'll work out all the systems, and we'll learn what we can in the next two hours," said Larson, surprising everyone with his about-face decision, "Captain Sanchez, does that work for you?"

"Roger that, Heath. You're in charge. What do you want us to do?"

The Chinese fire drill proceeded apace. Victor Sanchez monitored the weather radar and kept the engines idling while Tina Sanchez was on anchor watch to help him keep the *Skyhook* from swinging around during the sets. Mac Owens, with Mercante's help, deployed three Yamaha SUV Waverunners and fueled them. Bruddah fired up all the engines and Larson went through the electronics. Sonny-boy set up the boards and tow ropes and Gracellen got all the suits, safety vests and helmets organized. Laine and Rowe double checked all the emergency medical equipment and then got the cameras set up.

Ian Clark went to 'sunroom', opened the port-side dome, jumped up on the fuselage and climbed high onto the center of the broad wing. From there he had a clear view of the entire reef, an elliptical stadium of energy almost a mile long and three-quarters of a mile wide. He saw the trade wind chop, and he remembered his spur-of-the-moment story about offshore winds was based on nothing more than his needing a check with a lot of zeros on it. Now he was facing the possibility it might not be written at all. Then he thought of L.J. Merrill and realized he'd better stop thinking.

Larson and Bruddah had spent the entire flight from Papeete explaining his part in the whole thing, and it was time to get ready. He opened an aluminum case and powered up a high-speed laptop modified specifically for use with a personal locator beacon system. Every person on the water would wear a small transmitter and their positions would appear on the grid coming up on the screen in front of him and on digital displays on the waverunners. His computer also served as a radio unit to monitor and communicate with all the jetski drivers and with the *Skyhook*. It was the ultimate safety setup, and he felt the irony of being the guy in the middle of it all.

The three waverunners motored slowly away from the seaplane and out through the northern entrance of the lagoon. Heath and Bruddah were on unit one for tow surfing and rider retrieval and Laine and Rowe got unit two for safety and documentation. Gracellen and Noaloa had put aside their differences and were becoming fast friends in the face of the challenge of sharing driver duties on number three to gain experience with the big Yamaha in real conditions. The fourth unit was tethered to the cargo bay, ready to go in case of an emergency.

The wind had not increased, but the chop was undeniable. When they were well outside the impact zone, each driver went through a five minute double check of all on-board systems, including a comm check with the *Skyhook* and Clark. With all the locator beacons communicating with the laptop, everything was ready. Heath Larson was wearing emergency orange from head to toe: thick reef walker shoes, a lightweight wetsuit with padding around the knees, hips and elbows, and a thick lifevest. His helmet didn't have a radio, by choice. He didn't need the distractions, especially if he was inside a wave seeking perfect solitude, and so he had to raise his voice over the roar of the waves.

"We'll set out the grid, then two dry runs, and right back here for input. No deviations from plan, no fun and games. And that means you, Aleja!"

"Oh Heath, you're always such a crashing bore!" Her laugh eased a lot of the tension amongst the five men around her. "Anyway, Bruddah tells me after all this is over you're gonna retire and go longboarding at Malibu for the rest of your life! I'll get my revenge then!"

The big Hawaiian pulled his visor down and gave her a thumbs up. She turned to Laine who returned the signal. Noaloa and Rowe signaled their readiness, and Larson tapped Bruddah on the shoulder. They eased out into the open ocean as Bruddah slowly opened the throttle, mindful of the aviation fuel in the tank. Laine waited a few seconds, and then followed about twenty yards behind and ten yards to the left of the lead ski. Gracellen waited, then brought up the rear, maintaining the angled formation that precluded any collisions if a ski suddenly failed for any reason.

They came around the east side of the reef and rode up and over the large rolling swells well away from the surf zone. Clark monitored their positions on his screen, and at five second intervals he pushed a button on his control console to establish the outer perimeter of the personal locator grid system as the formation did a complete ring around the reef and arrived back at their starting point near the northern entrance to the lagoon. Clark's computer processed all the gridpoints to establish a coordinate system, and a grid of concentric rings was now displayed on not only Clark's computer, but also the displays on the consoles of each waverunner so that no matter where a surfer went, either riding on a wave or being swept underwater after a wipeout, the system could pinpoint the position of the personal beacon in an arena as large as twenty football fields.

When the formation arrived back at its starting point, the drivers moved in close so that Larson could clearly hear every word of the designated spotters, Bob Rowe and Sonny-boy Noaloa.

"Forget the lefts. Wrong angle. Too much west and too close to the reef," said Rowe, "The rights are much better, but the wind is dicey. Let's do the dry runs and take a closer look."

"Sonny-boy, what do you think?"

"Fo' reals, Heath. No go left, least not on dis swell. But da rights You can make, but stay doin' ollies coming down a face. No go inna tube."

Larson now had baseline perspectives from the two people who had never taken their eyes off the waves. He was ready to hear more.

"Aleja? Any input?"

"The right looks Rincon with a south wind. You can make it if you stay ahead of the double up wrap-ins, but if you get behind, you'll never catch up."

"Good analogy, Aleja, and good advice. Bruddah?"

"Barbie gots it right, brah. Maybe fun you get one. Not so fun it gets you," he said, and Larson knew that safety was on Bruddah's mind above anything else. He turned to the best jetski safety guy in the world.

"Randy?"

"Hold on a sec, Heath, I want to get some real data. *Skyhook,* what's the wind doing?"

"Holding steady at five knots, but I don't know what its going to do. I wouldn't count on it for much longer," said the voice of Victor Sanchez.

"Heath, Victor says the wind's ok, but we'd better play it safe and not count on it too much longer."

"Ok, two dry runs down the rights. Formation at wave-crest intervals. Here we go." Larson tapped Bruddah twice, and this time he opened up the throttle to seventy percent. Gracellen and Laine formed up at the same angle and followed him to the take-off zone. When they were all off the extreme southern tip of the locator grid, Bruddah led them in a wide circle to meet a new set. He set up on the second wave, staying out on the unbroken shoulder of the wave and concentrated on nothing but maintaining a course well away from the impact zone. Larson did nothing but watch as the swell felt the reef and the face steepened rapidly until its peak pitched forward into a breaking wave. Laine and Rowe did the same on wave number three, followed by Gracellen and Noaloa on number four. She had never seen anything like this in her life and she looked to Sonny-boy for some assurances.

"You think its thirty feet? Or twenty? Or how much?" she yelled over her shoulder, "It looks so much bigger when you see how much water is moving!"

"Yeah, Barbie, dats why twenty Hawaiian would be thirty at Malibu."

"Well, it looks a lot bigger than that! How big was the wave that won that XXL deal two years ago?"

"Who knows? Musta been eighty feet 'cause dey made out da check fo eighty grand."

"Well, this looks just as big. How come Heath never won it?"

"He hate dat stuffs. Said was stupid pay cash for courage. Dey try to git him in da ting 'cause he da best, but every year he tell 'em no way."

"Well, if Heath won't enter it, why do they even want to do it?"

"Dey don't anymore, Aleja. Da guy who won da eighty grand, he try' to surf one mo biggah last year so he get mo' money. But he drown and dey nevah find his body."

The drivers all stayed with their waves until they reformed back into rolling swells at the north end of the reef. Bruddah led them back up to the takeoff zone and the process was repeated on the next set of waves, only this time, they drove all the way to the *Skyhook* to take a break and talk things over. Victor Sanchez poked his head out of the cockpit window and gave Larson a thumbs up. He pulled back in and then Tina Sanchez did the same and pointed to the cargo bay where Mac Owens and Roberto Mercante tossed bottles of water to everyone. There was a lull in the waves, and everyone let their guard down a little to relax. Everyone except Heath Larson.

"Ian, any problems?"

"Some shadowing from the troughs, but overall it's working perfectly."

"How's the view from up there?"

Clark paused. He wanted to say "Overwhelming!" but thought better of it.

"Beautiful. Looks like the wind might be backing off a little."

"Randy, give me a data set from the *Skyhook*, will you?"

Ten seconds later, Laine had answers from Victor Sanchez.

"Good eye, Clark. Wind southeast decreasing to four knots."

"Bruddah? Think we can ride this place?"

"Gots plenny fuel, and we surf worse, brah. But not dis big not dis far from home. Maybe get a couple, tree maybe. Den outta heah."

"Aleja? Any more ideas?"

"If it was California, I'd be outta here right now and home under the covers waiting for the storm to hit. I hate surfing with wind chop coming at me."

"Bob, what's it look like through the viewfinder?"

"Give it a go, Heath. Just remember what Sonny-boy said."

"Yeah, Heath, ollie da chop and stay out ahead. Like Aleja say, you get caught behind, you fucked."

"I never said that, Sonny-boy! Goodness gracious, such language in the presence of a lady!"

She turned around and playfully slugged the former world champ in the arm. Once again, her spirit loosened things up for the men.

"Ok, two waves. Shoulder only. Aleja, station oh-two. You and Sonny-boy keep an eye on what I'm doing. Maybe you'll be next. Randy, oh-five, then form up when I come by and Bob, start shooting. Let's get on it."

The first wave of a new set exploded at the far end of the reef, and Heath Larson threw the handle of the tow rope out into the ocean. He checked to see that it was securely attached to the tow pillar on the back of the waverunner. Roberto Mercante slid a tow-board out of the cargo bay into the water. It was bright orange with yellow stripes around the rails for easy visibility. Larson dove off the ski, positioned his feet in the safety straps and grabbed the tow-rope handle. Bruddah looked over his shoulder and motored forward slowly. When the rope went taunt, he and Heath played a quick game of tug-of-war to insure the integrity of the handle, the rope and where it attached to the waverunner. Everything was a go, and Heath Larson was ready.

"Geevum brah!" he shouted, and Bruddah rolled on the power. The waverunner's big engine had horsepower to burn and Larson popped up out of the water like a water skier, a move he and Bruddah had perfected over the course of many years working together. Bruddah looked back, Larson nodded, and Bruddah headed for the takeoff zone. Laine and Rowe got going and followed Bruddah up the reef. Gracellen and Noaloa motored slowly to their station to wait for Heath's first ride.

Bruddah had his eyes on the horizon, turning in a wide circle to maintain speed while waiting for the next set of waves. They didn't wait long. When the first swell hit the reef, Bruddah was nowhere near it. He had studied the sets, and it wasn't until the last swell of the set approached the reef that he swung around and lined up an approach. He came in wide as the wall formed up into a centered peak over the reef. He glanced over his shoulder and Larson signaled for a launch.

Bruddah rolled on full power and carved a hard turn away from the wave. Heath Larson came around in a whipping arc going almost forty miles an hour. At the apex combination of speed and angle, he let go of the tow rope to match the speed of the wave with a margin of error before he began to slow down just as the wave stood up. He began gliding down the face of the rolling hill of water. No longer tethered to the machine, Heath Larson was now a surfer in every sense of the word.

The muscle memory from countless rides came to life instantaneously. He could see the white water from the previous wave. That told him where not to go. He made a long easy turn away from the impact zone. He angled sharply back towards the energy before turning away from it again to remain in the failsafe zone. Another cutback, another turn, another cutback. His sealegs were strong. He tightened the interval between turns and ran his board through a slalom course of moguls-in-motion across the face of the wave.

Bruddah was driving the waverunner parallel to Larson's track about twenty yards out on the shoulder. There was no way Larson would fall, yet there was no way Bruddah ever relaxed when Heath was up and riding. Ten seconds into the ride, Bruddah could see Rowe standing up on the back of the ski with Laine in full readiness at the controls. Rowe was seeing double watching Larson ride the wave. He could see from edge to edge across the horizon of normal vision, from the far left where the unbroken hump of the wave was formed to the extreme right where the wave was exploding across the reef. With a turn of a knob under his right hand, the steadicam mounted on his chest zoomed in to frame Larson alone in a transparent image projected on the inside of the visor. As the wave and surfer moved past them, Rowe hit stop and Laine fell into formation in the trough behind Larson's wave.

Larson kept turning and flowing until he neared station zero two where Gracellen and Noaloa waited. Gracellen had her hands on the controls of the waverunner, but Noaloa was standing up behind her, his arms in the air, cheering loudly as Larson swept into his last turn. Bruddah anticipated his move and got out ahead of him so the tow rope crossed Larson's path. With the grace of a ballet *pas de deux*, the two executed a perfect re-connect as Larson picked up the tow rope handle, leaned back, and Bruddah rolled on the power to get them back out to the takeoff zone.

Laine set up again at zero five and the entire process was repeated, with one exception. Heath Larson was starting to get stoked on surfing a wave unlike any he'd ever ridden.

He began to play with the trade wind cross-waves, at first jumping them as if he was on a skateboard, then banking off them to come around in extra tight turns back towards the maelstrom in the tube behind him. His rhythm was remarkable considering the size of the wave. Had it been at Waimea Bay or Mavericks, even the best surfers would have been racing for the safety of the shoulder. Not Heath Larson. He was, in fact, beginning to *toy* with the energy as playfully as if he was fooling around at Waikiki on some waist-high rollers.

Clark was watching it all from his perch on the wing and the sight of Larson having fun in waves almost four stories high was simply amazing.

"Hey, Mac! Tina! Victor! Check this out! Roberto! Get up here!"

Noaloa and Gracellen needed no such encouragement. They'd seen Larson surf before, but this was different. To watch a man riding a huge wave out in the open ocean was simply and truly 'awesome' in the most powerful sense of the word. And he looked like he was having a lot of fun.

Laine and Rowe, too, were transfixed by Larson's performance. They'd seen it all in more ways than one when it came to cutting edge surfing. But this was a master in his element, and the performance was only beginning.

Larson was tapping into power with skills acquired from riding thousands of waves and decades of dedication, his body always in motion while complementing the curves of the wave with pure balance and timing, all the way to a smooth conclusion right in front of Noaloa and Gracellen. He let go of the tow rope and slowly sank into the water. He leaned back and closed his eyes to fully absorb all the sensations of what he had just done. Bruddah waited at a distance, knowing exactly what his friend was doing and why, until he saw Larson's head come forward and an arm raised, the signal to come get him. Gracellen and Noaloa watched the ritual, as did Laine and Rowe. Then Heath got out of the straps on his board and climbed up behind Bruddah. He was obviously in a special space, but Sonny-boy Noaloa couldn't wait.

"Heath, maybe I go, yeah? Dat looked great!"

"If he gets to go, so do I!" said Gracellen.

Larson just smiled at the two surfers, but his first words were to the man who made it possible.

"Thanks for the setups, Bruddah."

"Same like home, brah. Dis place mo longer, maybe mo betta no wind."

"Yeah, and I think its glassing off a bit, Heath," said Bob Rowe. Laine confirmed Rowe's observation.

"*Skyhook* says the wind's down to three knots in the past twenty minutes."

Like a race car driver getting the feel for a track after a few laps, Heath Larson felt he could trust the wave to be free from surprises, at least for now.

"Ok, you two, go get ready and get back out here as fast as you can. If the wind stays down, we'll get you on a few. And check in with the captain and make sure he's in synch with the plan. Randy, Bob, let's go. Ok, Bruddah?"

"Yeah, but just a couple, brah. We no wanna push it da first time."

Heath Larson nodded, but with the cross chop dying down and the memory of his last wave still fresh, he was ready to redline.

From the cockpit of the *Skyhook*, Victor Sanchez saw one waverunner coming towards him and the other two heading back out to the other end of the reef. The wind had died down completely, and he quickly guessed what was going on. This was not the plan, and he didn't like it. His wife, however, was excited to see Heath heading out for more waves. As always she was thinking about the big picture that included not only the endowment fund, but the big payday under the contract with Wavelife.

When Aleja and Sonny-boy pulled up next to the seaplane, Mac Owens and Roberto Mercante were in the cargo bay door to greet them. After securing the waverunner to the seaplane, they helped the two surfers onboard so that they could get into their orange "flight suits" and double check their boards. Up on the wing, Ian Clark was happier than he'd been in a long, long time. Larson was shredding the place, Noaloa and Gracellen were going to join him, and suddenly everything was falling into place. And all thanks to a simple shift in the wind.

Larson took the whip from Bruddah and headed straight towards the reef. Unlike his initial approach on the previous waves, he didn't turn away from the building energy. This time he kept going.

He dropped down the face as the peak built up high above him. He could see the white water ahead marking the impact zone. He took a last look out towards the unbroken face where Bruddah was driving the waverunner. The chop from the trade winds was almost gone. Caution turned to commitment in the snap of a synapse. He was now in himself, and there was nothing else in the world except mind and energy.

Carve a turn hard off the bottom at full speed. Legs like truck springs absorbed the g-forces. Arms out, hands up, and leaned over, knees brushing the surface, slight arch to his back. Slingshot up the face, pause, then casual lean back, assess, then hard cutback to drive straight towards the wave's detonation point. Hit the base with two seconds to spare. Carve an arc at full speed, board at its design limits. Shoot out and up across the open face, relax . . . and look back at a liquid canopy arching into mid air behind him.

Heath Larson was beyond strategy, beyond calculation, responding with infinite articulation to a world of curving power and symmetry. Back to the bottom to gather speed. Another heavy g-force turn to the very top of the swell and the purest pinnacle of energy about to leap into midair. Launch off the lip and out into midair himself, weightless and detached. Free fall twenty feet, then re-connect down the face with a thousand tons of exploding power right behind him. Hard gouging turn and once again shoot out and up across the open face, this time towards a finale of mindless release.

Laine and Rowe came up outside of Bruddah to establish direct visual with Larson and witness the epitome of modern surfing's potential.

The wave was now halfway through its course. With a smile and a nod, Larson acknowledged the friend who made it all possible. Bruddah gave him a quick chaka with one hand and rolled on a bit more power with the other before pointing back to Laine and Rowe. Larson saw them and let his mind wander towards ego and performance. It was but a fleeting thought and he easily brought his focus back to himself to re-engage with the flow of his mind without any intrusions from the outside world.

He turned back into the heart of the wave for a final moment alone as the wave curved towards the entrance to the lagoon. Inside the tube for just an instant, Larson felt the energy dissipating and let his thoughts find equal rest. He emerged, and the wave was gone.

Heath Larson let his mind go where it always went after a great wave, conscious that all he knew only moments ago was gone forever and yet was waiting for him all over again, surfing in a realm all his own where the reality of time inside the wave became an absolute and centered experience. Then he snapped out of it, like he always did, when Bruddah was right there to meet him. Within seconds they were headed back out to the other end of the reef to do it all over again.

Victor and Tina Sanchez watched Larson from the cockpit of the *Skyhook* and were more than impressed by what they saw.

"You know, dad used to talk about grace under pressure," said Victor, "and I've got to hand it to Heath in that category. I bet he would have made a great pilot under battle conditions."

"Well, a wave isn't flak from anti-aircraft guns filling the sky, but I know what you mean, dear," said his wife, "One mistake and it could be all over, that's for sure."

Victor Sanchez watched Larson and Bruddah reach the southern end of the reef. He got out his binoculars to zero in on them, and immediately saw that the horizon behind them was no longer a sharp line. He glanced at the weather radar screen on the control panel in the PBY's cockpit. Across the southeast quadrant, a well defined form had appeared. It was a squall line, and from its shape he knew it was generating extremely fierce winds pushing ahead of the wall of rain.

The sea was glassy and smooth all around the *Skyhook*, but Victor Sanchez knew it was the calm before a storm. He flipped the intercom switch.

"Mac, Roberto, prepare for takeoff. Hey Ian!" he stuck his head out the cockpit window, "Get down off the wing. We gotta get out of here."

As the voice echoed throughout the fuselage over the intercom, Sonny-boy Noaloa and Aleja Gracellen looked at each other in disbelief. Mercante and Owens stopped helping the surfers with their vests.

"Roger that captain," said Mac Owens, "Ready in five minutes."

"But da waves is perfect out deah! And Heath say we go fo' surf! Fuck, I wan' go surfin'!"

He looked at Roberto Mercante, but the millionaire surfer was for once at a loss for words. Not so Aleja Gracellen, who always had her wits about her.

"C'mon, Sonny-boy, we'll be back soon enough," she said, turning to Mac Owens, "How can we help?"

"Sonny-boy, jump on tha ski, grab tha lift cables an' connect 'em. Aleja, help 'im get outta the water, stow all yer stuff an' strap in back in the 'sunroom'. Roberto, go help Clark, then cum back an' help me with the winches an' the side mounts when they get back in here. We gotta bunch a stuff to do, so let's all git!"

"Units one and two. Bruddah, Randy you guys hear me? Squall approaching. Black flag."

"Confirm black flag. Bob, we're outta here."

"Gotcha, Captain. black flag. Comin' in right now."

Bruddah turned away from the on-coming wave before Heath was in exactly the right place, figuring Heath would know exactly why the run was being aborted. He did, but his focus was on the wave, his last wave, and he didn't take his eyes off it. He kept the pressure on his board to increase the speed of the whip. He was living for nothing but his next ride, so far into his instincts that he was out of his mind, and yet in total command of his chosen reality. When he knew he had all the speed he needed, he let go of the tow-rope and sped towards the forming peak.

Bruddah felt the waverunner engine race and looked over his shoulder. He saw what Heath was doing and knew there was no stopping him. He let off the throttle and got on the radio.

"Randy, Heath taking one last one. We betta stay."

The ocean had turned to sheet glass. The waves were now a little bigger, with almost perfect shape. Bruddah and Laine turned to watch Larson maneuver perfectly into the peak. Then Bruddah noticed his waverunner roll awkwardly as a small swell came across the ocean's surface. He looked over and saw the same thing happen to Laine and Rowe. He glanced at Larson about to catch the wave when his waverunner bobbled again. He quickly realized the squall was sending out cross-swells on a different wavelength – and they were much stronger than the chop from the trades.

"Randy, we betta be ready. Mebbe this cross chop screw up da wave."

"Roger that, Bruddah. I don't like it."

His heart was pumping and the wave was building but his mind was far away inside a closed system of thought detached from the full spectrum of life around him.

Deep fading turn to the far side of the building peak. Sharp turn back and up into the very highest pinnacle of the wave. Pause, then aim straight down to the triangle of white water marking the detonation zone. Behind him vertical liquid rising ever higher to meet the reef. Ahead of him the base of power. Slight adjustment to his left into a perfect turn to the right and into the curved wave space arching over like a cathedral dome. Heath Larson entered his church and disappeared.

Out of the tunnel immediately in a blur of orange and yellow only to hairpin turn back into the huge tube. This time he remained inside.

All around him, a liquid sphere thirty feet in diameter spiraled and exploded. He adjusted his weight slightly and slowed his speed to match that of a universe his and his alone. He saw nothing ahead except the horizon running up into the wall that curved into the transparent roof far above his head. He was exactly in the moment with nothing to do but stand there and let his mind run free.

For almost ten seconds Heath Larson was motionless at thirty miles and hour. The wave began to feel a new part of the reef and responded with newfound momentum. Larson was ready for the change. His frame of reference, the open mouth of the tube framing the outside world, became ever more distant ahead of him even as he raced towards it. The inverse relativity of the moment enveloped his senses, and for Heath Larson, time stood still.

Bruddah was out on the rolling shoulder of the wave. He looked back for a second, but the angle prevented him from seeing his friend. Then a sudden wave about two feet high hit his waverunner coming out of the southeast. Seconds later it was followed by another almost twice as big. He almost lost control, but he recovered in time to gun the engine and leap over the next cross wave, almost five feet high. He realized what was happening, and for the first time ever he felt a deep anxiety about his old friend.

But Heath Larson felt nothing. His detachment was complete. All he knew was in and of himself. He was in control. He felt fully alive. He was exactly where he wanted to be: apart from the world and in his own reality.

The cross swells moved towards the heart of the wave, rippling across the face and changing the beautiful curves into broken chaos. Larson was so far back in the center of the tube he couldn't see what was happening. His ultimate freedom was about to become a disastrous trap as the symmetry of the world he trusted was instantly destroyed.

He barely felt the first cross-swell as it passed under his board. He paid it no heed and plowed through the second one with sheer mindless strength. Then the horizon disappeared from view as the next cross-swell completely transformed the wave, and the perfectly curved wall of the open tube ahead of him became a closing hemisphere of energy from which there was no escape.

The huge tunnel collapsed on itself and exploded in all directions. A cloud of spray was violently expelled fifty feet in the air. White water avalanched into a grotesque maelstrom. The wave seemed to pause in a moment of stasis before its forward momentum added more energy to the churning cauldron of seemingly limitless power.

The men on the waverunners waited for the world's best big wave rider to appear, but deep instincts of dread told their hearts he wasn't coming out. And there was nothing they could do about it.

Heath Larson was driven straight down through twenty feet of water in less than a second. His mind did not register a thing until the fins of his board were driven into the coral, followed by the board itself, and immense pressure forced him to his knees. Only then did he snap into awareness of his true reality when he realized he was thinking about what to do. He was strapped to the board. The board was impaled on the reef. In the snap of a synapse he knew there was nothing he could do, but it was too late to even admit that he was no longer in control. His mind broke free of its logic. An involuntary gasp and his mouth, throat, and esophagus filled with water. He couldn't expel it. His lungs convulsed. His heartrate tripled. The water around him calmed down, but he began to struggle, not able to breathe, not able to think clearly for the instant it would have taken to reset his mind with the logic of survival. Then he heard rumbling white water coming toward him. Then he heard nothing when the next wave came down hard and exploded his eardrums.

His body went into fight or flight panic. He could do neither as the final wave of the set sealed his fate. The float vest strained to bring him to the surface, but the foot straps held. There would be no release. He lost motor control of his body and his eyes rolled back in his head. His last conscious moment was strangely one of pure bliss.

Foam lay almost three feet thick on the slowly calming surface of the water. The waverunners could not go through that any more than a car can go through liquid mud. Even if Larson had come up, it would have been next to impossible to dart in and get him before the next wave bulldozed through the impact zone. Bruddah, Laine and Rowe watched the second wave of the set roll over where they'd last seen him, but they didn't panic. With Bruddah's experience, Rowe's EMT knowledge and Laine's mastery of big wave rescue, they were fully prepared personally, and the personal locator beacon system gave them all the advantage they needed.

But when Laine glanced at his display screen, he saw nothing. He pushed the reset, and got all the data about the waverunner, and then pressed the button to bring up the locator grid. Nothing happened.

"*Skyhook!* Rider down! Rider down! Where's the grid? I repeat, where's the grid? Bruddah, you got the locator grid?"

The Hawaiian looked at his screen, saw nothing, reset the display, and got the same results as Laine.

"Fuckin' bullshit! I got nothin'!"

"*Skyhook*, where's the grid? Where's the grid?"

Victor Sanchez heard the distress call, and his heart stopped.

"Randy, this is Victor. The grid is down. Repeat, the grid is down."

He'd ordered the crew to prepare for takeoff. He'd told Clark to get ready to leave immediately. Clark did, and turned off the system.

The worst case scenario for a big wave wipeout was unfolding to the horror of the three men on the waverunners. The last wave of the set followed through twenty seconds later. They would have to wait for the foam to dissipate before beginning search and rescue. Randy Laine began thinking fast. They had almost a mile of reef to deal with, and Larson could have been swept along by the wave that had eaten him, as well as the next two. And then there was the constant current from the motion of the giant waves. It was exactly why they had deployed the locator system, and now when it was needed most, it wasn't there. They only had a few minutes before the next set, the waves from the squall were getting bigger, and the wind was starting to come up. He ran through every scenario in his considerable experience within a few seconds and then took action as the last wave of the set rolled through.

"Bruddah! Go down to oh-two and wait for the last wave to go by. Give it twenty seconds, and then zigzag slowly into the wave field. Keep your revs up but your speed down. Don't let her choke. We've got to get a visual on him. Stay on the radio! Go!"

Bruddah took off. Then Laine remembered what had happened to Mark Foo at Mavericks. He had not come up because his board wedged itself into the undersea rocks and he had been unable to release his leash. Larson was not wearing a leash, but he was strapped to his board. Laine also remembered what had happened at Todos Santos when the rescuers had been unable to find the downed surfer because they overreacted in the tension of the moment and went searching without a plan.

So he and Bob Rowe waited the longest minute of their lives as the last wave of the set rolled through, waiting for the thick foam to dissipate sufficiently, so they could make headway without the waverunner stalling out. Rowe took the opportunity to detach the steadicam from his chest and remove his the helmet. He stowed the camera unit in a compartment, but the helmet wouldn't quite fit, so he strapped it loosely around a handhold. Then he positioned himself on the rescue sled and got ready to pull Larson aboard.

Laine turned towards the reef and went in slowly, looking down into the depths but unable to see much at first in the flat light of an overcast day. But the water was as clear as any on earth, and within seconds Laine's instincts paid off.

"I've got a visual on him, Randy," said Rowe,"I'll go get him."

Rowe peeled off his orange safety vest, threw it out of the way and dove overboard.

Randy Laine spoke into his headset.

"*Skyhook*, we've got him."

The wall of rain and wind was fast approaching the south end of the reef. A mile away, the *Skyhook* was taking off under maximum power headed north. Victor Sanchez was pulling her up fast while Mac Owens was controlling the throttles to redline the engines while making sure they didn't blow up. Tina Sanchez was on the radio trying to raise Tahiti air control.

"This is Victor Tango Three Niner Three. Mayday. I repeat Mayday. Request ambulance harbor entrance at fifteen hundred hours. Repeat. Mayday. This is the *Skyhook*. We've got a passenger with no heartbeat. Request immediate assistance our arrival. Over."

In the cargo bay, Randy Laine was administering CPR to an inert Heath Larson. Bob Rowe prepared the shock paddles of the defibrillator. Bruddah held the hand of his best friend. In the 'sunroom', Aleja Gracellen and Sonny-boy Noaloa were sitting across from Ian Clark and Roberto Mercante. They were not looking out the canopies as another set of huge waves roared out of the storm and exploded on the reef. They were not looking anywhere except inside their hearts with their heads bowed in prayer.

Part Two

Ancient Waves

June Gloom

The fog flowing in from the cold ocean was so thick Cheryl Corlund couldn't see the parking lot ten stories below. Whether looking out the window or at her immediate prospects, visibility was zero.

The only way things could be any worse would be if Heath had died. He survived, but when news of the trip hit the websites, within days Wavelife was in the crosshairs of the surf media. Everything about the reef and the LBO came out under a story line portraying her as the greedy CEO trying to steal a company by gutting it for her own benefit in a secret plan so ill-conceived a surfing legend almost got killed. And that was just the beginning.

The story went mainstream. Wavelife International became the Enron of the surf industry. In the clothing business where image is everything, the blowtorch onslaught by the media turned the brand into poison. Orders were cancelled, carloads of merchandise were returned and Wavelife's credit rating began to erode as confidence in her management abilities went into freefall. It was raining concrete, and then it got worse. The stock plummeted.

"What's the opening price?"

June Wilson looked up from her Blackberry. From the look on her face, Bill Massara knew the news would be bad. It was.

"All time low single digits. We'll be lucky if we're not junk at closing."

"Better withdraw the bid and notify the SEC," he said, "And then, well, there are other things you need to think about, Cheryl."

Massara's implication was clear. When it comes to the value of a corporation on Wall Street, perception can quickly become reality, and it wouldn't be the first time the market value of a corporation went south because of charges that were, in the end, entirely unrelated to the real value of the company.

Corlund spun around and drilled him with her frustration.

251

"Oh, you think I should get out ahead of the problem and resign?"

"Well, uh, it might be a better move than forcing the board to fire you," said Wilson, trying to give Massara some breathing room.

Corlund stared at her.

"You know, June, I'm not paying you to come up with that kind of advice."

Then she glared at the original target of her anger.

"And last time I looked, Bill, it still says CEO on my business card, so don't forget you still work for me."

That brought a quick, sharp glance from Dolly Artensa. Raised on the streets of South Central L.A. and a gospel singer on Sundays, she was a bedrock source of stability for Corlund in moments of crisis. Massara was well aware of the relationship between the two women. Her obvious disapproval of Corlund's attitude was a cue to Massara to go out on a limb.

"Correction, Cheryl. I used to work for you. I quit effective immediately."

Corlund turned away and looked out the window, but the June gloom was only getting thicker.

"So here's some parting advice, madam CEO. Be out of here lock, stock and barrel by end of business today. Submit your resignation to the board tomorrow. Roberto, too. Use your severance package to take a long vacation and let things sort themselves out. Remember, the board will have to replace the three of us, and that'll be awfully hard to do. I bet Black and Palua might try to run the company themselves for a while. But my guess is that they'll make mistakes, the stock will drop some more, investors will be screaming at them, and pretty soon they'll want out." He looked at June Wilson who knew exactly what he was doing.

"Then you tender a new bid," chimed in June Wilson, "You come in on a white horse and cash out the investors for dimes on the dollar. Then you re-org, re-brand, get people working again, and run the company as you see fit. In fact, if the price is low enough, you might be able to acquire all the assets without needing Lasserman or Vutara, assuming you can get some help from Ben Jeffries."

"That's a big assumption. I believe he dumped most of his Wavelife stock last week," said Corlund, so defeated and deflated she'd missed their points entirely, "I haven't talked to Ben since I saw him at the hospital on Maui, but from the look in his eye, I don't think he'd return my call."

"Oh come on, Cheryl, snap out of it. Just because your reputation as a CEO is now somewhere between Gordon Gecko and the wicked witch of the west does not mean this is end of the world," said Dolly Artensa, "I like the idea of your resignation. Honor is a best management practice, and there's a lot to be said for integrity as a CEO's most important core competency. So, I'm with Bill, and I quit, too, effective tomorrow."

That got Corlund's attention. There was nothing but a gray void in front of her, but if she listened to the people behind her and what they'd told her to do, she had a chance. And there was no other choice. She turned around to face her friends.

"Ok, Dolly, how do I get back on the block?" she said with a wry smile.

Artensa recognized the code in the question. "Back On The Block" was the title of the record Quincy Jones had released to announce his return to the music business. Whenever Corlund had needed unvarnished advice, that was phrase she used. Corlund needed a shot of Artensa's indomitable spirit, and sometimes that spirit worked in mysterious ways. The carpenter's nail routine had been Artensa's idea, as were a number of other highly effective routines that kept her boss sane over the years.

"Back," Artensa snapped her fingers twice, "back on the block."

She paused four beats, repeated the line, and began to snap her fingers in rhythm. Wilson and Massara didn't have clue as to what was going on, but Artensa was in rhythm and didn't think twice. Getting up out of her chair and walking across the room, she laid a rap on her boss.

Ok, CEO CC straight outta the OC,
here's the four one one – now you listen to me.
Convene the board ten aye em tomorrow
Tell 'em you've had enough of all this sorrow.
Your resignation is effective immediately.
And your team has quit too, and that includes me.
I ain't workin' for nobody else.
And without us here this place'll be hell.
And when that happens they'll begin to understand
that running Wavelife has nothing to do with surf or sand.
By then we'll have been back east and found enough money,
to come right back and buy this place, and I'll tell you, honey,
then we go into school clothes with Sonny and Aleja
as role models for kids who need to dream of being more than just a playah.
And we set it all up on a different synergy
Let's mix the salt of the earth with the salt of the sea
And Heath and Bruddah are part of this too,
and Wavelife becomes something honest and true.
Now if you think about it you'll be down with what I'm sayin'
You'll have to work harder from the heart day in – and day out
Getting real is what I'm talkin' about
The faster we leave the faster we're back
So, in brother Ray's words, Let's hit the road, Jack."

Wilson and Massara broke out into applause, but Artensa wasn't done yet. She stepped back and with a motion of her head to them the four joined hands in a small circle.

"Lord, help us now in this moment of change. We accept your will, and we beseech you for the strength to start again."

A sensation coursed through them that was palpable and extraordinary. But this was no tent-show revival, no healing of the lame in the aisles, no lost souls straining to find solace. No, with Dolly Artensa this was the real thing.

They dropped hands, and were silent for a moment as an entirely new energy filled the room that put a smile on Cheryl Corlund's face.

"Ok, now where were we? Yes, ladies and gentleman, for the moment I am still the CEO of surfing's largest corporation. Now, let's get down tonight, er," she smiled at Dolly, "I mean to business.

"June, you're contract with Wavelife is hereby terminated. Please vacate the premises immediately. When you get back to your office, there should be a call waiting for you about your next client," she pointed to herself then turned to Wavelife's former CFO. "Bill, your resignation is accepted. Please go to human resources and your exit processing. Good luck in your next position," she paused, "which just might include working with June if you'll be my personal business advisor. Why don't we all talk about it at lunch at my house, ok? And Dolly, please draft my letter of resignation and a goodbye message to the employees. And call Chad Roberts down in HR to have OUR," she paused to let the last word hang in the air, "exit processing completed as of ten a.m. tomorrow morning."

"Aren't you forgetting something?" said Artensa.

Corlund thought for a second, and then smiled in chagrin.

"June and Bill, my apologies. I forgot to say 'please'. I won't make that mistake again."

"That's my girl," said Artensa, "And while you're practicing your newly found and now permanent sincerity, you do have several calls to make."

She glanced at her watch to see what time it was in Hawai'i.

"Yes, I do, Dolly. Can you get Heath on the line?"

"Sure, after you talk to your husband and your children."

Since his return from the reef, Roberto Mercante had been unable to get much of anything accomplished. He'd gone through a lot in the past six months, including having to fire his entire surf team. But that was nothing compared to the shock of seeing Larson almost die at the reef. And after the withering attack on Wavelife in the surf media, he retreated to reconsider everything. Now he was slowly coming around by staying home and spending time with his teenage children. Then it was time for another shock from the wife and mother that had been so little of either for so long. The phone call lasted almost half an hour, and he felt some real hope for his family that hadn't existed for a very long time. So did Donny and Anna, though they were still a bit skeptical when the call ended.

Corlund went out and sat on Artensa's desk.

"Dolly, I think they don't quite believe we're really going to do this."

"They will after we get done with figuring this all out across your kitchen table, Cheryl. Remember, we're still on company time, so why don't you go home now and get things ready. Deep down I bet they've been waiting for years for you to come home and fix 'em sandwiches for lunch!"

* * *

254

The view from the front porch was spectacular in the early afternoon light, but there was nothing about it that made any difference to Heath Larson as he listened to Cheryl Corlund's question. He could have been in Topeka, Kansas for all he cared.

"No, I haven't been surfing, and in fact I might never surf again."

"Well, I can understand it might take time to recuperate, Heath, but - - - "

"But nothing, Cheryl. You can't recuperate from brain damage."

"What? The doctors in Tahiti checked you out. The doctors in Honolulu checked you out. Everything's ok. They couldn't find anything wrong, Heath."

"And they were right, up to a point. But a few nights ago I tried to get back into my reading routine and I couldn't understand what was on the page."

"Oh, come on Heath, you're still just a bit tired. You'll be ok."

"No Cheryl, this is serious. I can't understand Sartre anymore."

"Heath, nobody could understand him to begin with!"

"Cheryl, this is nothing to joke about. I was underwater for more than a minute before Rowe brought me to the surface. It took them another three minutes to get me to the *Skyhook*, and then another minute before Rowe got my heartbeat back to normal using the defibrillator. That adds up to almost five minutes of reduced oxygen flow to my brain. The generally acknowledged limit before brain damage sets in is three."

"Heath, you sound ok to me, and you passed all the psycho-motor skill and cognition tests to see if there was any damage. Maybe you need a little more time to just relax."

"Cheryl, relaxing is not going to help me ride big surf again because the foundation of my surfing goes much deeper than that, and you know it. So does Bruddah, and Sonny-boy and Aleja to a certain extent. But I've never fully explained it to you, or anyone, except for Ben that night in his library."

"Well, tell me about it, then. What is it, mind over matter or something like that?"

"It's not a cliché, Cheryl. Sartre wrote "Being and Nothingness" during the German Occupation of France during World War Two". He had just been released after nine months in a Nazi prison camp. He had spent the '30s becoming one of the most respected philosophers in France, but when the war broke out, he was challenged to put his tenets to the test. He came up with a philosophy of mental discipline to deal with the Nazi occupation, the rounding up of the Jews, and the executions of his compatriots in the Resistance. And I'm telling you Cheryl, "Being and Nothingness" gave me what I needed to surf big waves the way I do."

"Like Sartre was able to deal with overwhelming experience of the Nazi occupation. Ok, Heath, so you're telling me you pushed your surfing too far, you almost died, your brain is damaged, and you can't get back to the raison d'etre that allowed you to ride big waves to begin with. That really scares you, more than any big wave you've ever ridden, and now you don't think you can ride one ever again."

"Yes, and I'd just as soon keep it to myself, actually."

"Well, that might be ok for the part about Sartre, but I can tell you it will be big news pretty quick if you stop surfing, though probably no bigger than what's already been written about the whole thing."

Yeah, Bruddah told me it was in the papers, and Sonny-boy said it was all over the Internet, but I've stayed up here in the cabin and tried to forget the whole thing. No TV, no papers, no nothing."

"Lucky you, Heath. When word got out that you were hospitalized in Tahiti, the surfing press had a field day. It was nuts around here. They even staked out my house."

"Yeah, they tried to get to me, too. But Bruddah made some calls, and they left me alone."

"Like I said, Heath, lucky you, because here it only got worse. The press started digging into the company, and blew me up into headlines on page one of the business section. The reef, the cutbacks, the LBO, everything. Orders were cancelled, stuff got shipped back, and now Wavelife is in jeopardy of going under because the stock is practically worthless."

"But I thought - - -", he paused and realized the connection between Corlund's nightmare and his selfish desire to detach himself from the world. By being only in himself he had not made the wave, and that led to a catastrophe for a person who had never done him any harm.

"Cheryl, I'm so sorry. I, I can't tell you, I, just, it was just - - - "

"Heath, you don't have to apologize. In fact, it's all just as well. There might be a way out for the company, but only if I do something drastic. So I'll be resigning tomorrow."

"I got wiped out by a wave, and now you're going under too? Sounds like we're both paddling in, and its just as well, I guess."

"Heath, I don't surf, and I'm not paddling in. Dolly had an idea, and it just may help us find the one way out of our respective dead ends."

Cheryl Corlund knew she was out on a limb. There would be no way to get through to Larson unless his existentialism could be reinforced as part of the solution. But the solution to the entire problem had started with Dolly Artensa, and she had to find a bridge between the church-going Gospel singer and Jean-Paul Sartre. Then she remembered a name from a survey philosophy class from her freshman year at Harvard.

"Well, as I understand it, Sartre found himself ultimately boxed in by the airtight perfection of his version of existentialism. Isn't that what he finally discovered about his philosophy when he wrote 'No Exit'?"

"Not exactly, but keep going. I'm listening," said Larson.

"So what about Kierkegaard? He was an existentialist. Ever hear of him?"

Larson thought for a second. Why would she bring up the name of a Danish philosopher who, many years before Sartre published "Being and Nothingness", struggled with the dichotomy of individual identity versus Christian fellowship?

"Cheryl, don't tell me Dolly wants us all to be born again! And now that you've got religion, you're calling to convert me?"

"C'mon Heath, don't shortchange me or Dolly like that. But she thinks we can start all over again, and so do I, because there might be a way to put altruism and capitalism together the way Kierkegaard combined Christianity and existentialism. We can't detach ourselves from others, Heath, you with your Sartre, me with my corporate shield. We have to commit ourselves to a better world for everyone, not just ourselves. And I need your help."

Larson couldn't believe what he was hearing. Here was Corlund talking about riding a much bigger wave than he'd ever imagined. He knew her point was well taken about Kierkegaard's version of existentialism being a viable way out of his dilemma. And he was much easier to understand than Sartre.

"Ok, Cheryl, I get it," he said, "Whatever you want me to do, I'm there."

"First off, go surfing. Second, where are Bruddah and Sonny-boy?"

"On O'ahu. But I can get 'em back here by," he checked his watch, "I can have them here in about four hours."

"Ok, I'll call after I get home tonight. I want to make a business proposition to them, and you. We'll go over the details. Tomorrow is going to be a big day for all of us. Let me tell you what we've got in mind so far."

When she was finished talking to Larson, Cheryl Corlund went out to Artensa's desk to review her letter of resignation, the fax to the board members announcing an emergency meeting tomorrow, and the e-message to the Wavelife employees. Then she went back to the phone for another two hours. After hearing what Corlund had in mind, Aleja Gracellen had no problems resigning from Wavelife. She knew she wouldn't be missed in Orange County because there was no way the new leadership would be supporting the shelter. She had enough grant money in the pipeline to keep the doors open through the end of the year so the shelter was in no immediate danger. But the calls to Ian Clark and Tina Sanchez were nowhere near as easy. Though sympathetic to her situation, they weren't about to walk away from their contracts, even after Corlund talked in general terms about her plans. Thus having covered all her bases, it was now time to call Ben Jeffries.

"Cheryl, you know I can't do anything about all this anymore. Sometimes you just have to cut your losses and move on. It's always a pleasure to talk to you, and next time you're in New York, give me a ring, ok?"

"Ben, does Soren Kierkegaard ring a bell?"

"What?"

"You know, Kierkegaard. About a hundred years before Sartre's agnostic existentialism, he came up with something quite similar based on love of yourself, your fellow man, and the reality of God's love."

"What does that have to do with this phone call, Cheryl?"

"Well, Heath thought you'd be interested in what convinced him to hear me out about my plans. In fact, he wants to talk to you about them, too. Can you fly him to New York tomorrow?"

The mention of Heath Larson's name gave Jeffries pause. The memory of the night in the library on board the *Aeolusean* was indelible. He had flown to

257

Hawai'i to visit Larson in the hospital and make sure he was ok. Larson was a comrade-in-arms, and when he fell, Jeffries was there to lend support. Now, with the Wavelife stock in shambles and the LBO in the trashcan, Larson was the last thing on Jeffries' mind - which made it poetic justice that the mention of his friend suddenly got his undivided attention.

"Tell him my jet will be at the Maui airport tomorrow morning."

"Thanks, Ben. And on the way back, could you please make a quick stop in L.A.? There are some people who will be looking for work who would also like to talk to you, too."

"Cheryl, now what are you talking about?"

Jeffries listened intently as Corlund laid out a blue-sky scenario that quickly became quite logical after she explained everything that had happened in the office and on the phone.

"So that's the basic game plan, Ben, and it would be wonderful to have you on our team."

"I've got a lot of questions, Cheryl, but they can wait till we're on the *Aeolusean*. But since I know you'll have some good answers, we'd better get started right now. Have June and Bill call me at home tonight. I'll be up late. Which reminds me, tell Heath I've got a first-edition Kierkegaard for us to review when you all get here. See you then!"

Cheryl Corlund and Dolly Artensa were sitting on folding metal chairs by the window in the CEO's office. They were joined by Roberto Mercante who, for the first time in years, was holding hands with his wife. They'd come back after what had been the business lunch of their lives. It was well past quitting time and they were looking much worse for the wear and tear of the day's events. Armed with a bar code reader, Mercante had been locating everything they owned throughout the building and boxing it all up. Corlund and Artensa did the same thing on the tenth floor. They did not touch their computers, file cabinets, or any other source of corporate information. They were taking no chances. Their exit had to be quick, clean and above reproach. The boxes were date- stamped, sealed, and readied for shipment to their lawyer's office.

When Cheryl Corlund finally emptied her desk, she came across a book she'd kept since getting her MBA. She'd never opened it in all these years, but the view out the window into the swirling fog reminded her of one particular episode in the saga of Ernest Shackleton's heroic story of courage and determination almost a hundred years ago. Now that they were ready to walk out for the last time, she was finally going to use it in the CEO suite of surfing's largest corporation.

"Ok, team, this is pretty much it, except for one thing. Now, with all due respect to the good Lord," she nodded in Artensa's direction, "and the best management practices of Wall Street and the Harvard Business School, not to mention the savviest surfer I've ever met," she smiled at her husband, "I'd like to read a story about what happened to three people in much the same situation as that in which we currently find ourselves."

Mercante and Artensa sat down on some boxes as Corlund outlined the story of Ernest Shackleton's desperate attempt to rescue the men of his expedition after they had become stranded on an island off the Antarctic coast in 1914.

"They had no communication with the outside world at the time, so Shackleton decided to go for help. He hand-picked five men to go with him in one of their lifeboats, and their voyage across eight hundred miles of stormy seas to South Georgia Island is the stuff of sailing heroics. But that's not what I'm thinking about right now. They made it to the island, but there was a mountain range between them and the whaling stations. So they had to try and cross the mountains. With darkness coming on, they found themselves high on a windswept ridge with clouds coming up the slopes.

"Here, let me read you this one part," she said, opening the old book.

Within minutes Artensa and Mercante were transported far from the tenth floor of a high rise in the heart of Orange County as they listened to how the lives of three people came down to a moment where there was literally nothing but faith to see them through.

Corlund's voice had been steady and measured in reading the account. It softened as she came to the final passage,

". . .the possibility of the slope ending in a sheer fall occurred to us; but the fog that was creeping up behind allowed no time for hesitation. There could be no turning back now, so we linked arms and slid down in the fashion of our youthful days. When we stopped, on a snowbank at the foot of the slope, we found that we had descended at least 900 feet in two or three minutes. We looked back, and saw the grey fingers of the fog appearing on the ridge, as though reaching after the intruders into untrodden wilds. But we had escaped."

She closed the book.

"Of course, the story didn't end there. The three men had to battle across another mountain range, and then attempt two rescue voyages to get back to the island where they had left the entire crew of the expedition. But in the end, all were saved, with not one life lost, all thanks to a leap of faith."

Before anyone could say another word, the door was suddenly opened by the janitor pushing in his cleaning-cart.

"Oh, I am so sorry, so sorry. I come back later, sorry."

"No, please, that's ok," said Corlund, "We'll be out of here in a few minutes."

"Oh, thank you, thank you. This my last office and then I done."

"Well, compa," said Roberto Mercante, "You can be done for the night right now. We will clean up everything. Just leave the vacuum cleaner, ok?"

"Oh, I don't know. Big problems the boss maybe."

"You won't have any problems with your boss. I'll make sure of that."

"Thank you. Much thank you. You good people. Big surprise my wife I in the house early. I no see the children before they go bed a long time. Thank you. Buenos Noches."

"Amigo, un momentito, por favor." Mercante walked over to the man, opened his wallet, and gave him a hundred dollar bill. It was a far cry from the last time he tried to give a total stranger a c-note, but he realized that things were going to be a lot different from here on in.

"Para su familia."

"Gracias, jefe. Good night my friends."

The janitor closed the door and a warm light began to fill the room. The thick deck of clouds still hovered over the coast, but the rays of the lowering sun were starting to shine through a narrow gap of clear sky out to sea.

Almost a minute went by before Dolly Artensa broke the silence.

"How many men did Shackleton save?"

"All of them, Dolly. He didn't lose one. And we won't either. And we'll start with him. I'll call the janitorial service tomorrow and make sure he doesn't lose his job if Black and those guys start cutting back on everything."

"What about all the Wavelife people? What if the company implodes? What if the board screws up everything and this place goes under?"

"Then we just keep trying, like Shackleton, until we've done the right thing by all of them, Roberto, just like you did a minute ago."

The sunset's beautiful glow began to fade as the sun touched the horizon. Dolly Artensa turned away from the window, went over to the dimmer switches and turned them up full.

"Hey, you two, let's clean up this mess and get outta here!"

For Immediate Release

The conference table was littered with coffee cups and legal pads. A dozen large sheets of paper were taped on the walls, each covered with scrawling, handwritten text. Chairs were left at all angles by their former occupants. It was almost three in the afternoon, and the directors of surfing's largest corporation were still at lunch. They were in no hurry to resume what had become an increasingly contentious meeting triggered by Cheryl Corlund's resignation.

* * *

The entire issue of board governance of publicly traded companies had become front page news after the corporate melt-downs of a few years ago, but Wavelife had been so successful for so long that the company's outside directors had never really paid much attention to how the board was structured. The fact that the CEO was on the board and the chairman was her husband was not a big deal at the time. All that changed in a heartbeat when Heath Larson's heart stopped.

Fortunately, his heart began beating again, but now Wavelife was under a microscope. Writers used to doing surf star puff pieces began diving into documents they couldn't understand. It wasn't investigative journalism by a long shot, but the surf media was owned by the same conglomerate that published a string of tabloids across the country, and so a whiff of impropriety was transformed into a gale force wind of purported corporate malfeasance. Never mind that the leveraged buyout had been publicly announced. Never mind that the SEC was well on its way to approving the deal because it did indeed benefit the shareholders. Perception became reality, and when Corlund couldn't handle the heat and resigned, it took but minutes for the directors to realize they were now on the hook for investor losses stemming from their lack of supervision of the corporation. Then the word 'lawsuit' was mentioned and they all got on their cell phones to their lawyers. An hour later, they were back at the table and all agreeing on one thing: their only chance to stay out of courts was to take up-front responsibility for Wavelife's future by re-launching the company under their own management. The idea had merit, and with their respective backgrounds, they looked like the makings of a good team on paper. But by the time they'd adjourned for lunch, they'd accomplished next to nothing.

Steve Palua was the first to stake out a position since he had a lot to lose if the investors he represented lost everything. He argued for a makeover that would reflect a new commitment to the "core values of the surfing community", and that if they were ever to get their products back in the stores they first had to get the surf media off their backs. But Richard Black didn't like that idea at all. He wanted out of the surf industry altogether and pushed for getting more into street wear, even though Wavelife had no experience whatsoever in that market niche, because he figured they could turn a quick buck "selling all that X-treme hip-hop stuff" he saw on TV.

Bart Thomas wasn't a vision guy, but he knew the clothing industry inside out, and there was nothing about either idea that seemed viable long term. The more Palua and Black argued, the more he began to hold out for simply declaring bankruptcy. In language that turned the air blue, he tried to convince them that it happened all the time in the clothing business. But Palua was scared shitless over how his investors would react to Chapter Eleven, and Black's ego was unable to even consider such a defeat. Then Gunter Jacobsen weighed in and the meeting fell apart. First he came out against Palua and Black and proposed spinning off a division he could run that would concentrate on windsurfing and snowboarding. Then he remembered he wanted to get out of apparel altogether, so he picked up on Thomas' idea until he realized he didn't want a bankruptcy on his resume. The more he talked, the less he said, to the utter frustration of the others.

With Palua unwilling to consider any other points of view, Thomas becoming increasingly obscene, and Jacobsen unable to think straight at all, Richard Black finally had no choice but to suggest they all go their separate ways and get something to eat before returning to the board room for another try later that afternoon.

* * *

Black walked back into the empty conference room, well aware of the consequences if they didn't come up with something by close of business and equally aware of the slim chance of getting the other three men on the same page. He sat down at the head of the table and considered his options. Jacobsen was obviously thinking only of himself and was therefore useless. Bart Thomas, on the other hand, had made some forceful arguments against his idea of a hip-hop X-games transformation. His argument for bankruptcy, however, seemed premature, leaving them with nothing to work with, except Palua's proposal. And he had agreed with Palua on the most important point: they had to stabilize the stock and something was better than nothing.

Well, he thought, *I'm the chairman, and things are supposed to roll down from me, and not roll over me.*

He found a legal pad and tore off all the pages until he found a blank one. He wasn't going to wait for the others to return and muck things up.

His scrawl was barely legible, but the words were precisely what he wanted to say.

The board of directors of Wavelife International is pleased to announce the formation of a new management team. After a long and dedicated career in service to the corporation, we regret that Cheryl Corlund has tendered her resignation and will no longer be part of the Wavelife team. Roberto Mercante has also notified the board that he will be pursuing other interests effective immediately. Also leaving the board is Bill Massara, former Chief Financial Officer.

"What a bunch of bullshit," he smirked to himself, but he kept writing.

Please join me in thanking them for their exceptional contributions, and in congratulating the new members of the interim management team,

Now he had to do some thinking. Well, on second thought, not really.

Richard Black, former senior vice-president of Wavelife, and Bart Thomas, apparel industry veteran, will take over day to day operations of the corporation. Gunter Jacobsen, president of European operations, will oversee international markets. Steve Palua, legendary Hawaiian surfer, will be Director of Sales and Marketing. The formidable talents of this team will be committed to maximum return on the investments of our sharehoulders.

He sat back and read it out loud. The language was so generic he was almost embarrassed by its blatant plagiarism. Yet it would work, and that was all that mattered. He got out his cell phone and called down to the office he'd once occupied years ago.

"Public relations, this is Julie speaking."

"HI, Julie, this is Richard Black."

"Oh, Mr. Black, hello, how are you? Oh, right, probably not that good right now, I guess."

"No, actually, things are going to be better than ever. I'm in the boardroom and I need you to get up here right away. Or better yet, can you still take dictation?"

"Of course, Mr. Black."

"Take this down, put in on Wavelife letterhead, and get it out to the entire P.R. distribution list."

"Ready when you are, sir."

"I'm ready, Julie. Here you go. For immediate release - - -"

A Toe-Hold Position

"So tell me, Ben," said John Vutara, "Are we going down the tubes, or are we in the tube, or what is it those surfers say?"

"We've paddled in and we're back on the beach," laughed Jeffries, "They pulled the plug on the LBO yesterday. I don't anticipate the Feds wasting our time with any inquires."

"I tend to agree. Speaking of wasting time, anything else, Ben? It's getting a bit late."

"Two things: Corlund resigned from Wavelife and has some ideas about a start-up. She's coming to New York this weekend looking for capital."

"With all due respect, Ben, I can't imagine why you'd spend another minute thinking about working with her. I certainly won't."

"Just checking. What can I offer you for your time in all this?"

Vutara thought for a second.

"Three-fifty would do, plus another four-fifty for the - - -"

"How about a million and we call it even?"

"That will be just fine, Ben. I'll write off the company's time, otherwise I'd have to bill you for staff hours and all that. Much too much trouble."

"We'll get it over to you by courier tomorrow afternoon."

"No hurry Ben. Stay in touch," said Vutara, smiling at the thought of having just made about two hundred thousand dollars an hour for his involvement in the aborted leveraged buyout of Wavelife International.

"Will do, John, will do."

The call ended, and with it any attachment between John Vutara and Cheryl Corlund's new venture with Ben Jeffries. He picked up the other line.

"We're clear," he said on the conference call to Cheryl Corlund's home.

"And Peter?" she asked.

"Already done. He gave me a discount. Seven-fifty."

"What about Bruce Kaufman?" asked June Wilson.

"Well, I'd originally thought it might be good to bring him in on the deal. But I guess he didn't like the art on my walls or maybe there wasn't enough money in the deal or something. Haven't heard from him since. Have you?"

"No, not a word," said Corlund, "I guess he wants to build a mountain of money all on his own."

"Sure, let him try. And he'll probably do a good job at it for a long time. He still thinks he's immortal. Someday he'll learn he can't take it with him."

"Should we give him a courtesy call?" asked Bill Massara.

Jeffries furrowed his brow for a few seconds.

"I rather not waste our time, or his. He's pretty busy these days from what I understand."

* * *

"Mr. Kaufman, there's a Jack Richards on the phone."

"Thanks, Bonny. Oh, by the way, where are we having dinner tonight?"

"My place. I've got a new recipe I want to try on you."

"Well, if it is anything like the last time," Kaufman let the thought hang for a second to give his girlfriend a quick scare for the fun of it, "I'll be there with bells on. Things are always so delicious at your place."

Kaufman hated these in-house affairs, but he couldn't beat the convenience. It was better than the alternative of going to clubs – or worse. Still, sometimes he wished he could just find that special someone and settle down to domestic peace and tranquility. Well, it wasn't going to happen this time, but Bonny was a good cook – and lots of fun for now.

"Jack Richards! Sorry, old friend, but I guess I still owe you a call, don't I? I haven't talked to you since - - - "

"Since you needed some inside stuff about the surf industry for your meeting with Jeffries."

"Right! And a belated thank-you, Jack. You saved me a lot of money. What have you been up to?"

"Staying out of the market, Bruce, and staying out of trouble. But every once in a while, I get the old itch, and I was wondering where you ended up on that Wavelife deal."

"Out of it from the very beginning. They were going to pay way too much, and Ben Jeffries was so stuck on Cheryl Corlund he would have done anything she wanted. Not me, though. She's not my type."

"No I suppose not, Bruce, now that you mention it," laughed Richards, "But what did you expect, her to show up in an apron and offer you coffee? Anyway, I see where their price is down to single digits. I want you to buy me a toe-hold position."

"Oh, And why, may I ask?"

"Well, if you were a surfer, I could explain it to you."

"I always did like the way you think, Jack, but you must have salt water on the brain after all that surfing. Buying shares in Wavelife doesn't make any sense to me. Why don't you just burn the money instead?"

"Let's just say their new management will not be able to act with fiduciary responsibility to shareholders."

Kaufman knew exactly what Richards was talking about, and it wasn't about rescuing widows with their life savings tied up in Wavelife's stock.

"I see, Jack. Though a shareholder suit against a clothing company might be a bit dicey in court. That segment is always so volatile. They'll be telling the truth when they testify to complete ignorance of the realities of their sales projections."

"Bruce, thanks for trying to protect me, but as long as they're not trying to sell used burkhas in Afghanistan, they'll be worth something."

"Sounds like this is about more than just making money. How much do you want to spend, Jack?"

"I'll let you figure that out. Get one of your boys down at the trading desk to stay on top of the stock and get me in low. Send me the paper work as soon as you've made the transactions."

"And under what name?"

"Oh, I don't know. Why don't you go back and see how we did a few of those deals through, uh, Italy or the Bahamas or something. I can't remember that stuff anymore," said Richards, feigning ignorance of all the shell corporations they'd formed when he did this stuff for a living. Kaufman knew there was no way Richards' memory was failing him, but he double-checked.

"And we are to stay under the reporting levels?"

"Just like old times, Bruce," said Richards, "I don't want to scare the stock back up. We've got to keep it quiet."

"Will do. How's the family?"

"Donna and the kids are doing fine. Thanks for asking."

"Glad to hear it, Jack. Give them my best."

Jack Richards closed his cell phone and put it in the side door pocket of his SUV. He got out of the big car and walked across the parking lot to the entrance of OSOM's headquarters. He had come up a day early before another weekend of maintenance on the *Tom Swift* and training out in the Channel. He was about to open the lobby door when L.J. Merrill came out to meet him.

"Hey, Jack! Captain Bucher said we're skipping the run to San Miguel tomorrow. The *Mother Carie* is coming in this afternoon and he wants us to start working on launch procedures we'll use off South Africa. Plus he wants us to come up to speed on the Agulhas Current, so we've got to get some time in on the simulator! Jack, my man, we're really on our way!"

Jack Richards smiled for a second. He was going after Wavelife by land and by sea.

The *Aeolusean* Agreement

The people emerging from the long black limousines had been picked up by a Gulfstream V corporate at airports in Hawai'i and California, and now they were about to complete the last leg of their trip. Many had never seen the New York skyline etched against the twilight of a June night, and as they walked towards a private pier jutting out into the East River, they were captivated by the sight of the lights coming on in the City That Never Sleeps. A motor launch was waiting for them, as were two people in bright blue uniforms.

"Hello everyone! I'm John Frazer, captain of the *Aeolusean*. Hope you all had a good flight. Mr. Jeffries sends his regards and will be joining you early tomorrow afternoon. We'll be going on a short cruise down the river and then out to Long Island for your meetings tomorrow. May I introduce Robin Maguire, our chief steward."

"Yes, welcome! We've made special arrangements for the children and, of course, the teenagers. We'll sort things out aboard the *Aeolusean* so that everyone is comfortable. For those of you who were with us in Florida, we have taken the liberty of reserving for you the same suites."

"Why don't we just shuffle 'em up and everybody gets a different one this time?" said Heath Larson.

"Well, sir, with everybody's permission, we can certainly do that."

"Yes, please, I want the Polynesian one," said Aleja Gracellen, "You take the Greek one, Heath. After all if there ever was an Odysseus in all this, it sure has to be you!"

* * *

The day of her epiphany at Wavelife, Cheryl Corlund had brainstormed a new business plan on her kitchen table with her family, the spiritual guidance of Dolly Artensa, and the business expertise of Bill Massara and June Wilson. The first thing they completed was a mission statement "Riding With Grace Means Family First". It was clunky and still seemed to be about surfing, but it would do for now. Next, they answered two simple questions: Why are we doing this? What can we sell that people need?

First, they focused on the why: and it was all about true aloha, that is, generosity and sharing. Ideas flew back and forth about changing life for the kids of South Central, aiding the shattered and the homeless in Southern California, giving hope to at-risk kids growing up wrong in Florida and

Hawai'i, and changing the buying patterns of consumers who know the price of everything and the value of nothing.

Then came the hard part: how to use capitalism to accomplish those tasks. After a lot of what-if scenarios, they came up with a plan to sell clothes at affordable prices to working families using designs and marketing campaigns that inspired self-discipline and self-esteem.

Determining the corporate structure was next, and here they did something almost unheard of. The company would be owned by the Mother Ocean Foundation, originally set up for Aleja's shelter, but now to be expanded under a business plan and public stock offering coordinated by Ben Jeffries.

They began to pencil in numbers for a very tight, hardnosed, strictly business operation to compete in a market where the competition was already fierce. Bill and June tweaked the spreadsheets on their laptops and were eventually able to predict a decent return-on-investment for the backers and shareholders within a reasonable time frame.

With a business plan penciled in, they now had to turn their attention to exactly what they would be selling. The motto's words, "Family First," gave them the idea of involving their families and friends right from the start. They quickly thought of putting everyone together for three days of focus groups, research and business plan development. It didn't take long for them to decide exactly where they wanted to go after Mercante reminded his wife of their night on the Aeolusean. That decided, it was back to the office for them and Dolly Artensa to make calls, get their files in order, and pack up everything they owned in preparation for their last day at Wavelife International.

* * *

"So tell me what happened the day you all resigned," said Heath Larson, "It must have been pretty heavy."

"No, it wasn't that bad, not compared to what you went through, I suppose," said Dolly Artensa. They were sitting across from each other in the library an hour after everyone had come aboard and settled into their suites and guest cabins. But Artensa and Larson needed to talk about Cheryl Corlund, and there hadn't been a chance on the flight across the country.

"First off, I had to go to her house and get her because I didn't want her driving. I get there, honk the horn, no response. I go to the door, ring the bell. She opens it, and we've got problems. She hadn't slept and it showed. I threw her into a cold shower while I found an outfit that worked. Then I fixed her hair and got some makeup on her."

"But she sounded so together on the phone."

"Honey, its one thing to talk about changing your life. Its quite another to actually do it AND eat one big dose of crow AND like it. And Roberto! Good Lord, he was in worse shape than she was! I had the kids get him outta there – told 'em to get him down to the beach and force him to go out surfing and stay in the water until I called 'em!"

268

"Good idea, Dolly. He's not a bedrock kinda guy when he loses touch with surfing."

Artensa smiled with a knowing look.

"A surfer in the rag trade when things go belly up! What do you expect? Anyway, now we're gonna be late 'cause traffic's jammed on the freeway. We take a shortcut, and it is even worse. I'm driving but she's getting edgy about being late for the board meeting."

"Yeah, June told me about her walking through a blizzard in New York."

"Well, this time she can't walk, so she starts yelling at other cars and then at me. So I solved the problem right away. I slapped her."

"You didn't!"

"Oh yes I did, but not that hard and not without first warning her. But she was losing it and a meltdown was not an option."

"Then what happened?"

"She calmed down and - - -"

"No, when you walked into the lobby."

"A lot of people were standing around waiting for her to show up, and they weren't there to offer her any sympathy, let me tell ya."

"Thank God you went with her."

"Oh, He was there too, believe me, holding me up!"

"Why didn't she go in a back door and straight up to the board room?"

"When you write the tune, you face the music. And she'd been under so much pressure for so long that without some kind of clean release, she never would have found her spirit again."

The memory of his near death hit Larson right between the eyes, followed by another smack to the head at the thought of Cheryl Corlund giving him a chance to find his spirit again. That did it.

"I'm gonna need a drink for this. Care to join me?"

"Well, I'm not much for drinking, Heath."

Larson got out of his chair and walked towards the liquor cabinet.

"It's Ben's private stock - the best Scotch I've ever tasted," he said as he began to put some ice in a glass.

"Well, in that case, I'll take a short one, and hold the rocks!"

Larson laughed and walked back with glasses in one hand and the bottle in the other.

"May I propose the toast, Dolly? To courage and friends!" He poured from the bottle, they clinked glasses, and she took a sip.

"Whoa, this IS good stuff!"

"Dolly, say, "Geevum, brah, dis da kine stuffs!""

Artensa just laughed and they sat down.

"Heath, someday I'm gonna take you down to the 'hood for some real English as a second language!" she said, taking another sip, "Ok, Heath, now where was I?"

"Well, you walk into the lobby and - - -"

"There's maybe fifty people standing around. They see us come in and the place goes dead quiet. We keep walking towards the elevator, and for a second it felt like walking down an alley in the 'hood. You know something's gonna happen. And it did. Some guy, I think he was in accounting, steps in front of us and gets right in her face. Now, you'll pardon my French, but he said something along the lines of, 'You fucking witch – you fucked up everything! My stock is worthless!' Then somebody else steps in and starts in on her about jail and lawsuits. They're blocking our way to the elevator, and more people are starting to surround us."

"So what did you do?"

"I didn't move, but Cheryl stops and says in a very clear, loud voice, 'I am still the CEO of this company. You're both fired. Now, get out of here! Security!' she says, without taking her eyes off them.

"I look over at the front desk and wave to my friend Otis. Got him the job. Great guy. Used to play linebacker for USC. Teaches Sunday school at my church. So I yell out, 'Otis! There's two fired employees who are refusing to leave the premises.' You shoulda seen their faces!"

Larson looked at Artensa, downed the rest of his drink, and poured himself another.

"That's just like surfing big waves. Go for it and you've got a chance. Flinch and you're in big trouble."

"Oh she wasn't going to give an inch. She's tough as nails when she has to be. Anyway, here comes Otis and the crowd gets out of his way, fast. 'Ok, you two, let's go,' he says. They turn around looking like someone's just pulled a gat on 'em. He starts to herd them to the door. She follows them until she's in the middle of the lobby. She stops, turns around slowly and stares down the crowd. Then she says, 'I'll be meeting with the board in a few minutes and I assume they'll be running the company for the foreseeable future. If anyone has anything more to say right now, I'll be happy to forward your names. Otherwise, if you want to keep your jobs, I suggest you get back to work.'"

"Yeah, the board meeting! This is like hearing a good surf story! Here comes a big set!"

"So the crowd melts away and we get in the elevator. I hit the button, and the door closes. She looks me in the eye and she's gonna cry, I can just tell."

"Yeah, that would have been really bad! It would have smeared her makeup or something."

"You know Heath, you really need a woman in your life. Sometimes we just have to cry, and nothing is going to stop us. So I pushed another button to stop us on the floor below the board room. We get out and go straight to the ladies room. And we both cried for about five minutes."

"I wish I could do that sometimes," he said, finishing off his drink.

"Real men can, Heath, and do. Give it a try sometime, you big macho stud surfer you," she said with a smile that he couldn't help but share, "So we cry, and then we look at each other, and you're right, our makeup is completely ruined. So we start laughing, and then we cried some more and started smearing our faces and laughing and looking like two warrior women."

"Like Mel in *Braveheart*!"

"Heath, that was just a movie. This was real. And we didn't want the scene in the board room to be anything less than strictly business. So we cleaned up quick, but now she's looking like I haven't seen her for years. Serene, composed, and clear-eyed. She gets out the nail, kisses it for good luck, and off we go. We go up the stairs, open the door, and surprise the heck out of some more employees waiting by the elevator."

"What were they doing there?"

"Probably going to get in her face like the schmucks downstairs. But she ignores them and walks into the board room at exactly ten o'clock."

"Then what happened?"

"Five minutes later, she walks out, and that's that."

"Yeah, but what happened in the meeting?"

"Not a thing. It was strictly business, and she wasn't going to have it any other way. I'm sure they would have liked to work her over a bit, but she wasn't about to take any guff from them."

"And then?"

"We went down the elevator and straight to her car. She drove off the lot, turned a corner, and then pulled over a few blocks down the street. Then she called her kids at the beach, and we were back at her house by noon. When I left they were around the pool looking like a family for the first time in ages."

"So what's going to happen at Wavelife?"

"Heath, that's not our problem right now. They've got a board of directors with some heavy hitters on it and a building full of employees to work for them. We did our bit, we blew it, we fell on our swords, and now we move on. Which reminds me, I wonder what everybody's doing? I'd better go check on the kids, Heath."

"One for the road, Dolly?"

"No, thanks, I never finished this one! But when I see Bruddah," she said, "I'll send him down here. You can't be trusted with that bottle all to yourself!"

Roberto Mercante rubbed his eyes, sat up in the bed, and looked at his wife sleeping peacefully next to him. He thought of when they'd started out together selling surf trunks and bikinis to small surf shops up and down the California coast. They'd built up a huge company, lost it all, and now they were going to start all over again, only this time for the right reasons. He bent over and kissed her forehead. She opened her eyes and pulled him down to her for a long, luscious kiss. And for the rest of the afternoon, the husband and wife were nowhere to be seen on board the *Aeolusean*.

Nobody noticed their absence. They were all having the time of their lives on the megayacht. Dolly Artensa had brought along her two nieces, a nephew and his friend who had just been released from LA County Jail after doing six months for burglary. Aleja had brought two mothers and their children from the shelter, women who had come to the door with nothing and now had paid positions. June Wilson was with them talking about running the shelter while the children were in the pool with the kids from Hawai'i and the Massara children. Bill and his wife were talking with Bruddah's niece and two of his cousins on an upper deck enjoying the breeze coming in off the summer Atlantic with the New York skyline barely visible in the distance.

All the teenagers were in the games room where Sonny-boy Noaloa was showing a surprising talent playing ping-pong with Donny Mercante, who was no slouch himself. The boys from South Central couldn't get enough of the pinball machines, while the girls sat with Anna Mercante and Aleja Gracellen. There was a lot of talk about life in Malibu, Orange County, and South Central, and how surprisingly similar things were when spirit and motivation were eroded by too much money – or not enough.

Back in the library, Heath Larson was introducing Bruddah to the wonders of Jeffries' scotch while they perused rare volumes containing original accounts of Captain Cook's ill-fated voyages to the Sandwich Islands.

"Cross-cultural bullshit - and its still going on! I wonder if things would have changed if the haoles had left and never come back?"

"Yeah, well maybe not too late, brah. I call up some da big boys we go take ovah da airport. Native movement protest – one call we stop it all!"

"Not a bad idea. Mebbe even call in da Tui, get fo' reals!"

But Bruddah didn't laugh back.

"Fuck da Tui. Dey not Hawaiian. Dey say dey Hawaiian but where da aloha wid a bunch gangstahs? And look what dey do fo' da kids – show 'em be tough guys, guns, fightin' alla time, drugs. Fuck dat shit. Den dey gets money for dey clothing company and get bought off so build hotels onna sacred Ohana beaches? My family real Hawaiian. We hates dose guys. Mo' dan we hate Captain Cook!"

Larson wished he hadn't said anything as he watched Bruddah get out of his chair and walk across the library floor and look out the window. Then his old friend turned around.

"Say, brah, let's get offa dis boat go into New York, eh? We get Ben geev us one ride in da choppah."

"Sure, why not? I'll ask him when he gets here."

"Well, let's get on it, 'cause here he come!"

The chopper set down on its retractable landing pad in the aft section of the *Aeolusean*. The engine was turned off, the blades slowly stopped, and a door slid open. A group of children burst down the steps, followed by Ben Jeffries and his wife. She and Robin Maguire took charge of grandson Pierce and his friends. Jeffries went straight to the main lounge to touch base with the people who were integral to the success of the next three days.

Around dinner time a buffet was set out for everyone, including the staff and crew of the megayacht. When everyone had finished their food, Ben Jeffries stood up at one end of the deck and tapped a knife against a glass.

"I don't know when there has been a more lively group aboard the *Aeolusean*, and for that we have to thank Cheryl Corlund for quitting her job – and to Dolly Artensa for giving her a new one!"

272

Everyone laughed and clapped.

"Now tomorrow we have a lot of work to do, and there is no guaranteeing any of this will pan out. We are going to be taking off on a big wave, and as Heath and Cheryl can tell you, sometimes you don't make it."

The entire group went quiet, and that was exactly Jeffries' intent.

"I wish to propose a toast." Jeffries raised his glass. So did everyone else as they rose to their feet. Even the little kids picked up on what was happening and lifted their Shirley Temples. "To Heath Larson, my personal friend who almost rode his last wave! And to Cheryl Corlund, for giving him, and all of us, a new wave to ride!"

"To Heath and Cheryl!" said everyone in unison as they all took a draught from their glasses. Then Jeffries and the gathering sat down. Heath Larson and Cheryl Corlund stood up.

"Speech! Speech!"

Corlund was about to say something when her husband pulled her down into her seat and stood up in her place. "All she was going to say was, its all Dolly's fault!" he said, and everyone started clapping and looking to Dolly. Larson tried to sit down, too, but Bruddah pulled the chair back. "No, you go talk story, but make it short, brah, I wanna be Times Square by midnight!"

The big wave surfer gathered himself and walked to the front of the room.

"Thanks, everyone, and thanks Ben. I also want to thank Ben's wife, and Captain Frazer and the crew, and especially Robin Maguire for keeping all the young ones happy and for the suites that the rest of us – " he glanced at Cheryl and Roberto – "have enjoyed so thoroughly."

Roberto and Cheryl gave each other a kiss. Their two teenagers were cringing – and happier than they had been in a long, long time.

"You know, the last time I was floating on the ocean, I don't remember much. In fact I don't remember anything at all since I was just this far away from being dead," he said with a wave and nod to Bob Rowe and Randy Laine who had missed the Gulfstream but had flown in first-class during the day, "In the instant before I went under, I was so full of myself that I lost all contact with a simple fact – that I was human, just like everyone else on the planet, and just like every one of you. I thought I was master of my universe, until Mother Ocean took over, and suddenly I was nothing. And even that didn't matter to me then.

"But when you are trapped underwater and waves are slamming you towards death, you are completely alone. And sometimes it is only then you realize life is precious and should never be taken for granted," he said slowly, "Of course, by then it is too late as your mind goes black and no light comes on. But thanks to my friends, I'm here tonight, as we all are, to try and make the world a better place as best we can."

Everyone clapped . . . and there wasn't a dry eye in the house.

"We are here to create a new way of doing business as a corporation with values. I know that right now our competitors don't have a clue as to what we are doing, but when they get wind of us, you can be sure they won't make our jobs any easier. After all, that's what competition is all about. But we've got an edge on them that they'd never dream of – and that's why I am here – and that's why I convinced Ben to do everything in his power to support Cheryl's idea. Or was it Dolly's idea? So may I propose a toast? To Dolly Artensa – a true queen of soul!"

Glasses were raised and most were drained to the last drop.

"Now if you want to hear Dolly do "Respect", she will be down in the disco lounge later tonight. But for now, well, let me close with a couple of thoughts. There was a man on TV a long time ago called Mr. Rogers, and most of you kids probably never heard of him, but for some of us he, well, he was a pretty good guy. And he was once asked what he thought about looking back on his thirty years of trying to reach out to people, especially young ones. And he said, 'I don't know that, as human beings, we are made for the world we are making for ourselves'."

He paused to let the thought sink in all around the room.

"And then there was a guy named Ross Perot. He was very successful in his life, and one day someone asked him how he thought history should judge him since he was a self-made billionaire," he said, glancing at Ben Jeffries who had told him the story, "So he answered the question, but he didn't say anything about his accomplishments or his fortune. He simply said, 'Let's see how my kids turn out.'

"Well," he paused, "I think we're all here tonight to help make a world that IS made for human beings, using a corporation to get the job done. And if we do it right, then our kids, and our children's children, will be just fine."

The place was quiet for a second. Ben Jeffries stood up, as did everyone else. He shook hands with Larson, and the two titans gave each other a hug that would have crushed lesser men.

"Geevum brah, we goin' for it big time!" shouted Bruddah.

Everyone broke out in laughter and applause as the two men stood apart and looked out over the deck.

"Ok, Bruddah, now we go Big Apple!" said Larson.

The lights from New York were glowing on the horizon, but it was nothing compared to the glow of human beings ready for a challenge that they knew could possibly change the world – even if only a little.

Just about everyone was up early the next morning except one husband and wife who stayed in their suite and missed breakfast without a second thought. But when he heard an alarm clock built during World War Two coming in low to buzz the *Aeolusean*, Roberto Mercante made his sincere and profuse apologies to a not-quite sated Cheryl Corlund. He had a plane to meet, and she was beginning to understand his attraction to her first rival.

"Clem Charleton! Great to see ya! You haven't sold 'er yet, have you? You said you'd call first, remember?"

"I 'member Roberto, but after our little visit here, I gotta an airshow to do up on the finger lakes, an' I hear there's a lotta buyers up there," he winked, "so you'd better make a decision pretty damn quick, good buddy."

Another figure emerged tentatively from the seaplane. She looked around before stepping on to the tender that would take them to the *Aeolusean*.

"Hi, I'm Roberto Mercante. I wish we could have talked a long time ago."

"Well, let's get it right this time, Roberto. Wilson's surfing career almost did me in once, and I will not allow that to happen ever again!"

"That makes two of us, mom!"

Mercante stepped out of the way as the former world professional surfing champion gave his mother a long delayed hug and a kiss.

Then Clem's nephew emerged from the PBY along with his wife and three children. Mercante and Corlund had pulled out all the stops. They wanted every person that could possibly help them in planning their new business, including the owners of a mom-and-pop surf shop. And at Roberto Mercante's request, Tommy Pratte had brought along some samples of his innovative surf trunks.

Friday was a busy day mixing all the young people with their parents and guardians into focus groups on what was right, and wrong, with not only Wavelife but the entire retail end of the apparel industry.

Saturday morning was spent perusing dozens of clothing samples that Corlund had "acquired" through her Seventh Avenue contacts. After lunch everyone went off to New York for a matinee show on Broadway and a fun tour of the city well into Saturday night. Sunday was relaxed and slow aboard the *Aeolusea*n until the time came in the late afternoon for all the children and guests to go back to California and Hawai'i.

But for the principals of the new company, Monday and Tuesday were spent hard at the grindstone. Augmented by a small group of industry experts, Corlund and her team put together the steel frame of a new company. And if "Riding With Grace Means Family First" did not quite resonate yet, they had another card to play when it came to courage and resilience.

"It was a good idea then, and it's still a good idea, and we're going to do it," said Cheryl Corlund, "Let's go over everything that happened, starting with bringing Heath back to life, and going backwards all the way to the moment when Ian Clark first showed us the video."

The surfers, the executives, the backer, and Clem Charleton were all in the library of the *Aeolusean*. Sonny-boy's mom was there, too, sitting next to her son and re-claiming the role she once had as his best friend and surf coach. It took all morning to fully flesh out the after-action report of the events, from Larson's brush with death to Ian Clark's pitch meeting. When they were done, it was Aleja Gracellen who stopped them all in their tracks.

"You know, the footage we saw in the board room had a perfect left breaking. Being a goofyfoot, I couldn't take my eyes off it. Now Heath, you say the Navy wave action models were almost identical?"

"I checked back and figured out when Merrill must have shot the footage. There was only one Southern Hemi swell that came through just before Clark called Cheryl that could have produced the waves we saw. I got the computer graphics for it, and then when the May swell came up, I compared them. That's why I was so amped up. What are you getting at, Aleja?"

Sonny-boy Noaloa knew the answer.

"Aleja, you one smart haole chick! Da left shoulda been da kine - - -"

His mom pinched him hard under the table.

"Excuse me Miss Gracellen, but your suppositions are quite correct. If the prevailing swell size and direction were practically the same, and the sub-surface shoaling zone identical, then the quality of the lefts should have remained undiminished."

Everyone in the room did a double take.

"What?" said Noaloa, "What did you expect? Hey, it's the King's English with my mother sitting here. Isn't that right, Bruddah?"

"Dat's right, Wilson, and I tink you right, brah. Barbie, da left no good when we surf da place, but you tell you saw it perfect on da video, yeah?"

"Yes, Bruddah. Not only that, but on the photo trip, when the *Skyhook* banked away from the squall, I saw a reef in the distance and maybe another one even farther away – but the one closest to us had a left rolling along with an eye that didn't close."

"I wasn't watching that trip - - -" interrupted Noaloa.

"No, you were too busy watching yourself on Roberto's camcorder!"

"True, but when we were circling out there last time I thought I saw a circle of white water about ten miles away and one more way out on the horizon."

"I saw 'em as we were coming in," said Randy Laine, "but we were so stoked on what we had right in front of us that none of us gave those other reefs a second thought. Aleja, I think you may be right."

"Yeah, Heath, so we had to save your life because you were riding the wrong wave!" said Bob Rowe with an almost scolding tone to his voice. A few started to laugh but quickly swallowed their smiles when they saw the look of contrition on Larson's face.

"Well, Heath, maybe you should try again," said Cheryl Corlund, stepping in for him at just the right moment. He looked at her but didn't say a word. Her husband, though, did have something to say.

"I agree, Cheryl, except for three problems. Ian Clark and the exact location of the reef are still under contract to Wavelife. Same for Tina Sanchez and the *Skyhook*. And they have the permit."

"So what do you suggest?"

"Well, I remember the course from my time in the cockpit on the flights we made out there. The airspeeds, too. As for getting out there, well, Clem, how much would you charge for a charter to southeast of Tahiti and back?"

"Hell, that's a long flight. Cost ya 'bout," he paused, "Well, you know what they say, Roberto, if ya hafta ask how much - - -"

Mercante's excitement faded from his face as he realized just how expensive it would be to fly a PBY from Florida to Tahiti. Cheryl Corlund came to the rescue.

"However, Clem, if you donate your PBY to the Foundation and we hire you as her pilot, you get a tax write off AND a good salary. Is that right, Ben?"

"We'd have to account for all her uses and be ready for the scrutiny of the IRS. They would take a dim view of directors going on surf trips," said Jeffries sternly, "But since the *Skyhook* is already doing non-profit work, we can cite them as a precedent, especially if we assist them in their work down there."

"Well, that's a lot of flyin', so I'll need to train someone in the organization to fly 'er!" said Charleton.

"Good, Clem, and I know just the man for the job. Ok, Roberto, that problem's solved. Now, about the permit."

"Well, Clark got the permit for a hundred square miles all around the reef, so we'll just have to wait until it expires – in August."

A groan went up from around the room until Aleja Gracellen brought smiles back all around.

"That's ok! My dad told me once that the biggest day he ever saw at Malibu was towards the end of August. It came out of the Southern Hemisphere, so I think we still have a chance! Besides, I still want to surf those lefts, Cheryl, and you said that was part of the deal!"

Tuesday night was the wrap up – and a special ceremony took place in the library of the *Aeolusean*. First off, the board of directors of the Mother Ocean Foundation: Cheryl Corlund, Roberto Mercante, Ben Jeffries, Aleja Gracellen, Bill Massara and June Wilson, voted to expand the board to include Sonny-boy's mother, Clem's son-in-law, and Bruddah, who vowed to make sure real aloha was always at the table. Next, the official document to launch the new corporation was presented to the board for consideration. Not only did it include a section based on the Valdez Principles concerning the earth's ecology with respect to manufacturing, labor and materials, but it also established a commitment to the eco-*psych*ology of the communities where their products would be sold.

Cheryl Corlund and Ben Jeffries were convinced that corporate stewardship of basic human rights was good for business. For them, that meant establishing a presence in the marketplace by promoting values and behaviors that are less about buying power and ownership and more about a sustainable quality of life. They knew this was going to be no easy task. Using capitalism as a tool for altruism was akin to using a hammer to sculpt a flower, and they both made sure everyone understood the severity of the challenge.

Everyone did, and no one flinched. The document that came to be known as the *Aeolusean* Agreement became the opening section of the articles of incorporation for a new kind of company. And the vote was unanimous.

"A navigator is never trapped."

The afternoon tradewinds blew warmly from the southeast. Taveka trimmed his sail and sighted down a broad passage through two reefs. The southwest swells rolled under his voyaging craft with a steady motion. At this rate he would be home just after dark. Now that David had succeeded him as chief navigator of the Maruleans, he did not have to take part in the preparations for the rituals marking the beginning of winter. With nothing to do, he did as he pleased. He went sailing off in a random direction, and when he found what he was looking for, he went surfing.

He found fun waves to surf at a remote shoal near the far edge of the fishing grounds, leaving him to think about what life might have been like for him had he started surfing as a young man. He thought of what David had told him about Rabbit Kekai and Woody Harrison, men who had begun surfing before World War Two and continued to ride waves well into their nineties. Like them, he had discovered the peace of riding waves as a way to stop time. Now he was sailing away from those waves to face the passage of time once again. The only Marulean tradition marking the passage of time was the ceremony of the winter solstice, and this one would be his last.

A strange sensation of melancholy passed through him, like a cross swell slapping the side of a hull. The moment passed quickly. He was a navigator and his mind could pay little heed to such thoughts. His gaze was to the horizon, feeling the wind, current and swells, sensitive to any signs of change.

A dot of color caught his eye far ahead and slightly off his port bow. He maintained course until he was no more than thirty yards away. At first it reminded him of his youth during the war. More often than not a floating lifevest had contained the last remains of a corpse torn apart by sharks. It had always been a grisly task to get the dog tags or anything else that could be used for identification, but he did it by remembering that the anguish of families would be relieved by his retrieving something that could give them closure. And now, even after six decades had past, something inside him prepared for the worst. Then he saw that the lifevest was empty.

He altered course slightly and pulled the vest out of the water. It was not covered with algae or moss. It had not been floating at sea for any great length of time. He considered just how it ended up in these waters given the currents, winds and wave patterns of the Nebula Archipelago at this time of year. Then he remembered what David had seen in the sky over Ka'unua.

As Taveka's voyaging craft came through the passage, he was surprised to see almost the entire population of the Marulean sea people waiting for him. Normally they would all be at the southern end of the island preparing for the solstice ceremony that would begin in an hour, now that the sun was on the horizon.

He came closer to the shore and a dozen young people swam out to the voyager and scrambled aboard. They surrounded him with hugs and smiles as if he had just returned from a voyage of many years. The craft drifted ever more slowly until its forward hull finally kissed the sand.

Taveka looked at the crowd, all silent yet all smiling at him. Then Kalala stepped out into the water.

"Many thought that maybe you had embarked on your last voyage, Taveka."

"No, I have yet to see the albatross, Kalala, so I went surfing. How else is an old man supposed to find some peace and quiet around here?" he laughed.

The solemn homecoming quickly dissolved as happy children turned the voyaging craft into a place of play. Some began diving off the stern of the voyaging craft. Others began chasing each other around the decks. One discovered something he'd never seen before and with an innocent curiosity showed it to his friends as he tried to put it on.

"When the time comes, we will all be with you. Now can I ask that you be with us?"

"Of course, Kalala, but first you need to do something about these children!" They both laughed and Kalala clapped her hands. The boy dropped the orange lifevest where he'd found it and with all the others jumped into the warm water before joining his parents. Everyone began walking to where the solstice ceremony would take place at the southern end of the island. Only Taveka's own family remained behind as he stepped off his craft and came ashore. Luan hugged him and her children wrapped themselves around the legs of their grandfather. He picked up a child in each arm and looked at their father. But David Helmares was eyeing the object on the deck of the voyaging craft.

"David, your place is with the elders. We will talk later," said Taveka, "Come, Luan, I need to stop at my house before the ceremony."

They left David standing next to the voyaging craft. He saw the elders following the crowd in the distance. He could catch up to them quickly. He had a few minutes.

The lifevest was of an unusual design. It was similar to what he knew was used for water skiing, but the flotation partitions were narrower and smaller, as if the vest needed to be more flexible. It was surprisingly lightweight, and he felt some hard objects in its storage pockets. He pulled open a velcro flap. Inside was a small round plastic case labeled in white letters embossed on black plastic tape: 'Contrast Filter – Property of Bobrowesurfphoto.com'.

His mind began to race and his heart felt torn in two. He began to open a second pocket, but then stopped, realizing he'd already learned all he needed to know. He put the case back in the pocket and the vest inside the dome shelter. He knew he could not be distracted before the ceremony. He had chosen a new life with responsibilities to a people living far from the madness of modern civilization, though now much closer than they had once had been.

The next day David found his mentor mending some lashings on his voyaging craft. The fact that its owner's time was short was no reason for the craft to be allowed to decay. Taveka was as focused as if he had been planning a multi-island long distance voyage of a thousand miles just for the pride of doing so.

David sat down in the sand and watched the aged hands pull strong on the sennit cords. He automatically stepped in to help when an extra hand was needed, then sat back down until a second set of hands was required anew. No words passed between the two men. There was no sense of age, of youth, of teacher, or of student. They were simply two men of the sea with a task at hand needing no explanation. After an hour the work was done. Taveka went around to the prow of the craft. David thought he was getting ready to shove the tri-hulled outrigger out to sea and got up to help. Taveka held up his hand.

"No. For this you cannot help me. She will never touch land again. I must do this alone."

The job would have been immensely difficult for the two of them. To David it was clearly impossible that Taveka could do it alone. Then David caught himself, knowing it was time to learn yet another lesson from a proud man with a sharp mind.

Taveka sized up the distance to the water. He checked the tether between the canoe and its mooring tree. Then the old navigator went to the village's common work shed. After a number of trips he had assembled a large cache of small bags, a dozen roller logs, a long, stout pole, and another log about twice the diameter of the rollers. He positioned the rollers around the hulls, and then positioned the lever and fulcrum near the first roller under the forward prow of the main hull. He then a dug a hole in the sand, lined it with a bag, filled it with sand, and then gathered the top into a knot from which he extended a sennit rope. He looped the rope around the end of the lever, and then used his weight to push down on the lever, raising the hull a few inches. He tied off the lever to the rope and positioned the roller beneath the hull.

He repeated the process again and again until his voyaging craft was resting entirely on rollers. He positioned more rollers between the stern and the water's edge. Each action was, in and of itself, nothing strenuous. Slowly but surely the craft was now made ready to launch.

Taveka stopped and looked at the sun. Then he looked at the water's edge. The tide had come in almost a foot since he had begun the process. It was not yet at its peak.

"I have time before the tide. Let us talk."

"Where did you find the lifevest?"

"Where the winds and currents and swell had taken it."

"Where do you think it came - - -"

Taveka's look told Helmares the answer. He tried to soften the blow.

"There are two other reefs nearby. Maybe they were not at Ka'unua."

"And if they were?"

"That will not change what I will do there. And since I myself plan to surf Ka'unua - - -"

Taveka saw the look of surprise on David's face.

"Why not? I can ride waves. Why wreck a good voyager?"

"But the traditions - - -"

"David, traditions are not the past. The past is dead. Traditions need to be alive, and when we can add something of the present to them, we must. Otherwise we are trapped. And a navigator is never trapped."

David Helmares looked away to the horizon.

"David, you have decades ahead of you and you will always be challenged by currents of change. You came here seeking refuge from progress, yet even in the short time you've been here, it has become harder to fill the fish traps because the waters have risen. There are clouds to the south I have never seen before. The swells are not as constant yet sometimes they are more powerful than I can remember."

David turned to his mentor.

"I was listening to the BBC last night. There was a story about two speeches made recently by men running the biggest oil companies in the world. They both said the use of oil has reached a point where the momentum cannot be stopped."

"And what did they propose to do about it?"

"Pump the excess carbon back into the ground."

"Well, at least they are trying something new."

Taveka's tone brought a smile to David's face.

"Ok, Taveka, I get it. So, you'll go to Ka'unua when the surf is big?"

"Yes, David. I want to surf those waves, and I want to ride inside them. What better way to end my life?"

Taveka winked at David and they both had to laugh.

"Well, then we'd better pray for surf!"

"Yes, David, maybe it will be the biggest swell of my life. Or at least as big as the waves you saw when you were there."

"Well, you just might get it, Taveka. It was huge during that swell a moon ago. You know, you sound just like the surfer who once said if he had to die, he would die happily if it could happen in big waves. And he did."

"Oh, the Hawaiian who drowned in California?"

"How did you know about Mark Foo?"

"Same way you knew about the oil executives. The BBC always gleans these little nuggets that say a lot about the world."

"Yes, they'd understand the irony of him drowning with dozens of photographers and surfers around," said Helmares with a wry grin, "I'm sure he didn't plan it, but at least he died the way he wanted to."

"As I will, David, so when I don't come up after my last wave at Ka'unua, don't try to save me."

The smile disappeared from David's face.

"No David, remember I am doing this because it is our way. You and I are connected through my death and you cannot prevent it. There are no alternatives. That's the way it is David, and we must make our peace with it."

Taveka knew David understood him perfectly but that there was still something else troubling his former apprentice.

"And if there are other surfers there, try to make your peace with them."

"Taveka, shouldn't we be alone for a moment so important to both of us? And what if they - - -"

"What if they what, David? They'll let me die in peace, won't they?"

"Taveka, they take over surf spots and run everyone out of the water to film commercials. They hire guards to beat up people who don't get out of their way for their contests. They are capable of anything."

"So am I, David, when it comes to life and death, remember? However, since my riding waves at Ka'unua is about MY death, I'm not worried. You're the one who is going to have to solve the problems they bring with them, not me."

"And I will, Taveka, one step at a time. Just like you solved the problem of launching your craft."

Taveka looked at the water's edge and then looked David in the eye. Without breaking his gaze, he pushed the bow of the craft with a firm motion, launching it effortlessly down the slipway of roller logs into the quiet waters of the lagoon.

"Such is life, and such is death, David. People spend their lives solving problems, and if they are patient and think clearly, solutions present themselves more often than not. That is the proper path for a navigator. And when you get to the end of that path, death is but a simple and effortless motion from one world to another."

David watched his mentor walk down to the water's edge, push the craft further out into the lagoon, and leap aboard.

"However, I'm not gone yet, so let's make sure she doesn't drift away," he said, tossing a line to David, "And then I need to eat and rest a little."

"Yes, you did a lot of work, Taveka."

"The work wasn't hard. It's the talking that gets to me. Let's go."

Surf City

Richard Black gaveled the meeting to order. Gunter Jacobsen was on conference call from Munich, as was Bart Thomas from New York. Only Steve Palua and Black were actually in the conference room, along with the new CFO and the elephant he brought with him.

"Thank you for this opportunity to report to the board," he said. A former vice-president at Andersen before the Enron scandal, he was familiar with corporate meltdowns and well aware of how fast jobs could evaporate and subpoenas issued in situations like this. So he played a trump card just to get himself in the clear.

"And for the record, I have made copies of this report and forwarded them to each of you by registered mail.

"Now, without being too alarmist, the executive summary of my report is as follows: Wavelife International is headed for either Chapter Eleven or Chapter Seven. The company is highly leveraged at the present time. Inquires have been received by my office from six of Wavelife's seven lenders requesting meetings by end of business this week. Demands for factor loan payments have been received totaling thirty two million dollars. Cash on hand at close of business yesterday was eighteen million dollars. Attached please find detailed balance sheets and breakdowns across Wavelife's entire range of products and markets."

He continued to read in a monotone voice for another few minutes before Richard Black cut him off.

"Thank you very much for your report. If you will now excuse us, we need to consider our options."

"Fine with me. I'll be in my office if you need more information."

"No, I think you've provided quite enough to us for one day," said Black, who waited for him to leave before saying, "Who wants to go first?"

"That fooking bitch Corlund. She zet us up! She zaw zis whole zing coming, zent Larson out zere to get himzelf keelled, just zo she geet zee company cheap!" said a very upset Gunter Jacobsen, sounding like a European playboy just discovering his dominatrix wife had seduced his teenage girlfriend and now they were BOTH out to get his money.

"Gunter, keep it to yourself, ok?" said Black, "Even if you're right, Wavelife is a publicly traded company, and we're the board of directors, so we have to deal with it. What's your plan, Steve?"

"Since we're a publicly traded company," he said, carefully repeating Black's words, "we've got to protect the interests of the shareholders. We've got to come out fighting and make it look like we're headed for the top again.

We do that, we're executing our fiduciary responsibilities in the face of the previous management's malfeasance. You already sent out the press release, stating that we're going back to our core values, so that's what we do."

"How vill vee do zat? She fires ze zurf team, cut back awl markeeting, and she zays she did it for "protecting zee interests of zee shareholders," Jacobsen said, "Zen she comes at us wiz zee offer zu buy zee coompany, and ve all fall for dat. Now she's out zee door, scot free, und she can get zee company for nozing!"

"Keep yer shirt on, bub," said Bart Thomas, "Dis ain't over yet. What else ya got, Palua?"

"So, we come on strong, right now. It's just like surfing. We've been caught inside, but we're going to battle back. We blanket the surfing media with Wavelife p.r. We get with all the banks, stabilize the stock, and give our investors some breathing room. Then we set up Chapter Eleven as our fall-back position."

"The boys on Seventh Avenue don't like Chapter Eleven, pal."

"I know, Bart, but they'll really be unhappy if we end up in that Chapter Seven bankruptcy court downtown," said Black, "Keep going, Steve."

"Like I said last week, if we can get the surf media back in our pocket, and get our heroes back in front of the kids, we'll be cool, and then at least we can get to the fall shows."

"And then what?" asked Black.

"Yeah, and zen what?" chimed in Jacobsen.

"Then we sell a lot of paper and sell off all the excess brands like that chick stuff and the golf clothes and the skater shoes. The analysts will love the cash flow, the stock will go up and that will placate the banks and the factors. That cuts the losses of our investors," he looked at Bart Thomas, "We pay off certain debts right away, and we're off the hook. We can then either go Eleven or Seven or who knows what. But we need time. If we don't get it, we're screwed. Each of us will be fighting lawsuits for a long time."

"Ya know, I tink you have zumzing der," said Jacobsen.

Palua's plan rang a bell with Richard Black. As a consultant he could probably do quite well spinning off and selling parts of the company, so he stepped in.

"I have to agree with Mr. Palua. We simply have to defend the interests of the stockholders at this time. Do we need to take a vote, gentlemen?"

"Vote, schmote. I gotta make some calls to New York to keep the boys off our backs. Palua, you better know what you're doing here."

"I do. Gunter, get all the European surf press over to Huntington. Wavelife is coming back big. Get your sales people hopped up on "The Comeback Kid" angle. Sonny-boy Noaloa is gonna work with us. Richard, we're gonna take over at Huntington and he's gonna win the fucker."

"Gotcha covered, Steve. I can see the whole thing clear as day."

"And don't worry, Bart, I've got this all lined up like a perfect wave at Sunset Beach."

"What's Sunset Beach? Nah, never mind. Ok, Palua, you're the Duke now. Just don't wipe out. I got no pull if we end up in bankruptcy court."

"Not an option, Bart. We're not going to end up in Chapter Seven. That's just not an option."

* * *

"What you talkin' 'bout? Fo' real you askin' me go surf inna Huntington? You kiddin' o what?"

"No Sonny-boy, I'm not kidding you and I'm not asking you. I'm telling you. Your contract with Wavelife is binding."

Noaloa thought for a second. He'd seen footage of Steve Palua surfing big Sunset back in the day and had a lot of respect for him as a surfer. He'd met him at parties and knew he was a director of the company, but beyond that, Noaloa drew a blank.

"Sez, who, brah? What da deal here?"

"Well, you could ask Mercante or Corlund, and they'd tell you. Or how about Big K? I've got him right here."

"Why I want talk him? Brah, he gots nutin' to do wit my career. He one friend my dad, but dey not partta my life anymo'!"

"Oh but he is, Sonny-boy, because I'm in charge of your career now and he's working for me, as is Junior and some of the boys from the Tui. Here, talk to Big K."

Noaloa's heart jumped into his throat.

"Sonny-boy, brah, I tell you mo betta you lissen what Steve tell you. You no want problem. You no like problem. You do what Steve tell you, we no get problem. You no lissen, you get problem."

Sonny boy knew better than to say another word. It was one thing to argue with Steve Palua. There was no arguing with a guy like Big K.

"Anytin you say, brah, Let me talk one time Steve," he said evenly before taking a deep breath, "Yeah, Palua, what I gotta do?"

"That's better, Sonny-boy. We are going to get Wavelife back on top, with you leading the charge. There's a lot of people who have a real interest in your success so let's get down to business."

"So, you gonna make me one offer I no can refuse, yeah?"

"No, Sonny-boy, that's just movie talk. Just don't forget what Big K told you, ok? Now here's the deal. The board of directors is running the company, and I'm the guy running the surf team. We've got two jobs ahead of us: and the first one is win at Huntington to keep Wavelife's investors happy."

"What investahs? Brah, I get nothing for do wit investahs. Dats all stock market stuffs. Got nuttin for do wit me."

Sonny-boy's mom came into the room and was about to get on his case about the pidgin, but he put a finger to his mouth. He motioned her to come over to him and he shared the cell phone with her.

285

"Oh yes it does, Sonny-boy. You see, some people put a lot of money in Wavelife on my recommendation. Now if they lose their investment, they will not be happy at all. They sometimes get really upset when they are not happy. That's why Big K and the boys are working for me, to make sure the investors stay happy. Oh, and by the way, it wasn't easy to find you, but be sure and give your mom our regards. Am I making myself clear?"

"Sure Steve, anytin' you say brah," said Noaloa. His mom's eyes were like saucers.

"Good. You one smart boy. Now I'm booking you on United outta Orlando departing seven in the morning. We'll be waiting for you, so get there early because you don't want to miss your flight. You know Sonny-boy, you and I have a lot in common right now, so let's try to work together. It will be good for both of us if we do our jobs, you know."

"What, so we don' end up in da cane fields?" said Noaloa, with a laugh.

"I'm not laughing, Sonny-boy. See you tomorrow."

Palua put down the phone and turned off the speaker box.

"So far, so good," he said as he looked around the room at Big K, Junior, and the two men standing near the door. One had been translating the call in a slang of Mandarin and Japanese for the other. They looked straight out of a Asian gangster movie. Only this wasn't a movie.

*　*　*

Sonny-boy and his mom had flown back to Florida with Clem Charleton and the Pratte family after the meetings in New York. There was a lot of legwork to do to shore up MOF's plans, but now a single phone call had changed everything. The first thing Noaloa did was call Bruddah and Heath on his cell while his mom called Cheryl Corlund on hers. Both phone calls resulted in exactly the same conclusion.

"You go LA, Sonny-boy," said Bruddah, "An' we get everytin' ok later on, nobodys get hurt."

"Do what they tell you to do," said Heath Larson, "Dose guys play rough, as you well know."

"I'll call Clem," said Cheryl Corlund on the other line, "He'll come and get you. I know what's going on and I know all about Steve Palua. He's part of the reason Ben and I were going to buy all the stock. I'll tell you more later. Let me talk to Wilson, no – " she paused as a thought occurred to her, "No, I can't talk to him about Wavelife. Just tell him I said to do exactly what Palua wants and to honor his contract. And tell him its really important."

"I don't think we have any choice in the matter right now," said Sonny-boy's mom, "You know Cheryl, I should have stepped in when I found out about my ex being on your payroll. But I figured my son needed his dad in his life, so I kept my mouth shut. But now that Big K and the Tui are part of

286

things, we've got to do something. You know that those guys used drug money to start up their surf company, right?"

Corlund knew she was talking to one very savvy woman. "Well, this time the money was a lot smarter. They started buying real estate, and that's how Palua got involved. Da Tui was pretty much going nowhere in the clothing business, but Palua made some introductions, and next thing you know, they were all one big happy family."

"So that's how surfing got so big so fast over there!"

"Exactly. And when Palua's investors saw how well we were doing at Wavelife, they thought they could do it all over again. And stupid, greedy me, I fell for Palua's pitch about major investments in Wavelife in exchange for a seat on the board. He delivered as promised, and his people made a lot of money. Even when the stock sagged, Palua didn't say anything because he didn't want to attract too much attention. And truth be known, they would have done well if I could have used the leveraged buyout to cash in their shares. But now the LBO is off the table, the stock is down to single digits, and they stand to lose a lot of money."

"And that's the last thing Palua wants, that's for sure."

"So we just need some time. We'll come up with something."

"I'm sure we will, Cheryl. After what we did on the *Aeolusean*, I think we're capable of doing things Palua and his crowd could never imagine."

* * *

"So that's the plan, Sonny-boy. You're going to win. You are going to be the man, brah," said Steve Palua as he inched the on to the 405 leaving LAX. Sonny boy was in the front seat. Big K and Junior were in the back.

"What if I lose? What if I no even make it outta da first heat? What if da waves no good? What if the judges - - -"

"C'mon, kid, no matter what the waves are like, you know nobody can beat you if you're in top shape. And you will be. I guarantee it. We've got an Australian surf coach over here to get you ready. And don't worry about the judges, either, ok? And then after you win, we're going to that reef."

"You got Heath workin' fo' you too?"

"No, we don't need him. It's the new Wavelife, and its an all Hawaiian operation. And look at it this way. A bunch of American businessmen stole Hawai'i from us with shotguns in 1893, right? Now we are getting what's ours! It's our Polynesian heritage, Sonny-boy!"

"But what da deal wid da investahs?"

"You better leave them outta this, Sonny-boy. Now here's what we are going to do between now and Huntington, starting with having Big K and Junior as your twenty-four hour bodyguards."

* * *

Richard Black knew the truth of the ad business adage, "Half of all promotional money spent is a complete waste – but you never know which half." So he got going on their next step right away. Wavelife was going to go big at the Huntington contest, and nothing was going to get in their way. He made some calls and surprised the event organizers who, after Corlund had pulled all sponsorship dollars from the pro tour, now suddenly had to accommodate a heavy hitter demanding entrance to the party. They balked at first, but a call from the truckers and riggers union, thanks to Thomas and his East Coast friends, suddenly put Wavelife right where Black wanted to be. For the next three weeks, the four board members had their hands full. Thomas and Black prepared for the Wavelife blitz at the event. Jacobsen was rounding up press and buyers from around the world to be at the contest. And Steve Palua was in charge of the Comeback Kid.

Sonny-boy remembered the words of his mom and the message from Cheryl Corlund and did his best to cooperate during a steady stream of scripted interviews and staged photo ops. Palua had some P.R. experts giving him advice, and suspense began to build about Noaloa's comeback. Soon the surfing media got behind Wavelife bigtime and the brand was cool once again. Cancelled orders were reinstated, and thanks to Bart Thomas working the phones nonstop since their last meeting, the creditors stopped calling.

With a little more than two weeks to go before the contest started, Palua cut back on all media outreach and secluded the champ at a resort in Baja for an intense tune-up of his surfing skills, a highly controlled diet, and plenty of rest before the main event. The media campaign had been a success. Now it was time for the champ to climb in the ring and take back his crown.

The Aussie surf coach set up daily practice sessions that replicated actual contest conditions. Former Wavelife team members who hadn't jumped to other companies were re-hired and brought in to surf against Sonny-boy in heats in front of the hotel near Rosarito Beach. Having been fired by Cheryl Corlund while Noaloa stayed on, the former teammates were in no mood to go easy on him. Sonny-boy found himself on the losing end of several skirmishes for wave priority. Not that Noaloa had forgotten anything from his championship years, but there was no substitute for the dog-eat-dog heat conditions. The coach had the Wavelife surfers take it to the former world champ, and on several occasions he let Noaloa and his 'competitors' get into it on the beach with no holds barred for several minutes.

The idea was to stoke Noaloa's competitive spirit, but the strategy backfired. It was one thing to go through the motions of the media campaign. But when it came to real surfing, his heart just wasn't in it. He had spent too much time with Bruddah and Heath to suddenly shift gears and become a contest surfer bent on winning at all costs.

By the end of the first week of training, Steve Palua was worried. He decided his contender needed something to spark his performance. For the first time since picking him up at LAX, Palua gave Noaloa a cell phone and some privacy to call his mom and his friends to boost the champ's spirits.

Palua knew that Corlund, Larson, Bruddah, and his mom had told Sonny-boy to do his best because the jobs of hundreds of people were hanging in the balance. He'd explained that to Noaloa time and time again, but now Sonny-boy needed some more encouragement. He got it, and Palua's investors were happy when they heard the tapes from the calls.

"No, Sonny-boy, you no let 'em down no matta what! You show 'em how it's done, yeah? You geevum, brah!" said Bruddah.

"You're the best surfer in the world in contest waves. Do your best. You're the man now," said Larson.

"Everything's going to be ok. Remember how we used to surprise 'em at the contests in Florida? Do it for your mom, and take your mind off things in the evening, dear. Play some computer games or something."

"You can do it, I know you can. We all believe in you, and there are a lot of little kids who need a role model. And you can give them a lesson in courage," said Aleja Gracellen.

"Just shred the shit out it. Kick their asses on every wave. Don't give an inch," said Roberto Mercante, "Remember that video game we used to play and you just stomped me? That's the Sonny-boy you need to be."

"You need to get into the finals no matter what," said Cheryl Corlund, "Dolly sends her regards and says the Lord helps them that help themselves. So make the finals, and you'll make a statement of which you can be proud. Here, let me put Ben on the line."

"Sonny-boy! Good to hear from you! Best of luck at Huntington! And, say, my grandson Pierce sure liked playing video games with you on the web site we have on the *Aeolusean*. So log on as soon as you can. Ok, good to hear from you!"

Noaloa didn't quite know what to think of all the conversations, especially the stuff about the video games. His mom used to hate it when he played them, and he never played a video game with Mercante in his life. And then Ben Jeffries talking about his grandson Pierce? Sure, he and the twelve-year old had played some games, and the boy beat him several times. And after that first visit to the megayacht in Florida, they had played a few games against each other logged on to the web site, and kept in touch on the web site's message board.

A little light went on in Wilson Smith Noaloa's head. He had an internet connection in his hotel room. He'd tell Palua he needed to play some video games at night to relax. And he'd log on to the *Aeolusean* web site. He had no trouble remembering his password. "Geevum."

The next day, Noaloa was his old self, and his sparring partners felt the brunt of his new-found enthusiasm. Palua had a vanload of boards on hand, each with the Wavelife logo conspicuously positioned on the nose of the board, both top and bottom, so that no matter what the angle, any action photo of Noaloa on a wave was going to be a promotional shot for Wavelife. In contrast to the first week when Noaloa could have cared less what he was riding, he now went through them all, sometimes going around in a complete circle, trying to find the one that felt truly magical under his feet. It got so bad that at one point after a particularly disappointing ride, he rode to the beach, put the board between two rocks, and took a boulder and broke the brand-new custom surfboard clean in half.

By Friday, he had broken another four boards and discarded the rest before finally settling on a set of three. But Steve Palua didn't mind one bit. Everything was fitting together perfectly, and the Hawaiian who'd been a great surfer at Sunset Beach decades ago was looking forward to Huntington Beach as if his own surfing career was coming back big time.

Noaloa was paddling like a speed boat, beating his rivals to the priority buoy time and again, and stuffing them into losing with every tactic and maneuver in the book. He practiced one dirty trick over and over again, first used by a former world champ to outfox a rival into an interference call by taking off behind him at the last second, standing up for an instant, and then falling off as if his rival had caused him to fall. It was below-the-belt, but fair under the rules, and the win cinched his world title. He even had Palua take him to a boxing ring in Tijuana and work out with a speed bag and a real sparring partner. Noaloa was ferocious in the ring, landing punch after punch against the hand pads of a boxing coach. Then he put on some head gear and went a few rounds with a young Mexican contender, who was told to lay off the amateur surfer. But that only made Noaloa angry, and he started coming on so strong that he had to take a few shots to the head to calm down.

But Noaloa had made his point. He was ready to win, and win at all costs. Playing the video games on the *Aeolusean*'s web site had given him just what he needed to motivate himself. He made it obvious to everyone he wanted to win with all his heart and soul. And he made sure no one was more convinced of that than Steve Palua.

* * *

The beaches of Huntington run unbroken for miles, bordered by the small blue collar town of Sunset to the north and the glitzy wealth of Newport to the south. It is as grand a stretch of strand as can be found in Southern California, a ribbon of white running along the blue Pacific, punctuated only by the famous concrete pier that extends out from Main Street, Huntington's main drag. For fifty weeks a year, the pier stands like a sentinel out into the ocean, solitary and even a bit majestic. But for the last two weeks in July, the pier was consumed by a force that reduced it to little more than an exclamation mark for a marketing blitz that is beyond over-the-top.

The base of the pier disappeared under a city of scaffolding that accommodates media centers, sponsor hospitality lounges, skateboard and BMX ramps, judges towers, competitors ready areas, and bleachers for seventy thousand people. The setup takes almost a week, and bolting together all the scaffolding and walkways is only half the job. Once the skeleton was completed, the signage people take over, and all the scaffolding became a framework for an all out effort to cover every possible line of sight with a Wavelife logo, along with the signage sold to a pharmaceutical company, a European electronics conglomerate, and a hair care corporation. To top it off, huge advertising banners are hung like a corporate laundry line a hundred yards long from the beach to the end of the pier.

Wavelife's marketing team, after being decimated by Corlund's cutbacks, was reassembled into a sophisticated juggernaut unmatched in the surf industry. Thousands of goody bags were printed up with "The Comeback Kid" photo on one side and the Wavelife logo on the other. They were filled with a hefty dose of surf wax, pocket mirrors, cell phone shells, key-chains, cheap t-shirts, and a dozen more logo-stamped items from Wavelife. And thanks to Black's contacts on the City Council, Main Street was closed for the first time in history for a huge street party to celebrate the surf industry – and its resurgent corporate leader.

The overall effect of the Wavelife comeback campaign was immediately apparent. Stories were circulating about the afternoon of boxing in Tijuana and the take-no-prisoners attitude that left fellow Wavelife team members in awe. Palua encouraged them to share their experiences with other competitors over the weekend preceding the beginning of the contest. With Noaloa's picture plastered all over Huntington Beach, from the banners on the pier to the goody bags given out by the thousands, talk of the former world champ's return to competition was on everybody's lips.

* * *

The night before Noaloa's first heat, a caravan came north out of Mexico and arrived around ten p.m. at the hotel across the street from the contest. There were event parties all over town, but Palua needed his man ready for the next day. Noaloa was not going to object. He'd learned his lessons the year before, and he knew exactly what he needed to do to get to the finals.

Monday dawned gray and cold. A south wind came up early and the first heats of Junior Mens were surfed in marginal waves that were barely rideable. By mid-morning the sun began to break through, and the wind died down. It would come up again strong from the northwest in an hour or so, but for a brief period, the waves were about as good as they were going to get that day. Noaloa was in the first of the men's heats. When he paddled out, the general public had yet to arrive, but the stands were packed with seemingly everyone in the surf industry, ready to witness the comeback of the kid.

He did not disappoint. The horn sounded, and Noaloa immediately paddled into a wave that was barely breaking. Double carving s-turn, a quick air off a section, tail-slide three-sixty into a cover-up into a gouging cutback, all on a wave so slow and formless that ninety percent of the surfing public would have found it practically unrideable. Noaloa hopped the board across the flat section towards the shorebreak, setting up for a tube ride where there seemingly was no tube. He came out of the tiny pocket and busted a big air as the wave collapsed on the wet sand.

291

He was right back out into the lineup before any of the other three surfers had even caught their first wave. He glared at them as if they were interlopers in his private domain and then paddled away from the group towards the pier. No one on the beach understood his tactics until he came charging out from under the pier on a speeding knee-high shorebreak close-out. Once again, it was a wave in name only, but for Noaloa, it was enough to get a few seconds of blazing speed before launching an air with enough momentum to completely turn his board around at the apex of his flight and land perfectly balanced as the wave finally collapsed.

The crowd went wild. The other surfers seemed frozen in place. The kid was almost literally surfing circles around them – and they were highly paid professionals. Then he paddled right into the center of the group, smiling and quiet, but only for a second.

"Why you guys no paddle in? You no have a chance. I just got two waves an' I bet dey gimme eights, maybe nines. What you got?" They had no answers – because Noaloa was right. "Say, I tell you one ting. My two waves enough fo' me. You guys still no win you get tree. See you latah!"

Noaloa whipped his board around and proceeded to paddle directly to the beach. He took off his colored jersey and tossed it over his shoulder. He lifted his board high in the air and planted it in the wet sand. Then he turned around and faced the ocean, seemingly daring his competitors to beat him. Nobody in the stands quite knew what he was doing except for Steve Palua, who immediately sensed a P.R. bonanza in the making. He raced down the scaffolding stairs, ran to the water's edge, and raised Noaloa's right arm as if they were in a boxing ring after a knockout blow had stopped the fight.

A crowd of Wavelife flacks and models came out of the stands and crowded around Palua and Sonny-boy. Though there was still time on the clock, Palua had Junior and Big K lift Noaloa to their shoulders and carry him to the competitors waiting zone. The industry crowd didn't know whether to boo or cheer, but it didn't make any difference. Noaloa had made his point. The Comeback Kid was coming all the way back, and more. Wavelife International was alive and well, and the rest of the contest was going to be Noaloa's for the taking.

The next five days were unique in the history of contests at Huntington Beach thanks to Wavelife and Sonny-boy Noaloa. Without any world tour points, he had to start in the qualifiers, but that only whetted his appetite. He blazed through all his heats, and despite the bad surf, the event "was exceeding all expectations", according to event officials reading from scripts written by Wavelife's P.R. professionals. On Thursday he surfed his first heat against the touring pros, but that made little difference. When their turn came to surf against the Comeback Kid, not one could lay a glove on him. It was a performance for the ages, and the Wavelife P.R. machine was running like a locomotive on all cylinders. Noaloa and Wavelife were the toast of the town. Even the stock price began to climb. For the four men running Wavelife International, and especially for Steve Palua, that was the best news of all.

* * *

"How's the kid doing tonight?" asked Steve Palua, a flashy porn star on his arm and a cell phone in his hand. He was down in the bar of the Mandalay Beach Resort, the four star hotel across the street from the pier. The hotel bar was named the Golden Bear, after the bar where decades ago, when the area had been a hodgepodge of oil wells, surf shops, and tattoo parlors, Jimi Hendrix had played before he found the stardom that killed him. Palua was checking out one of his guitars on display, insured for two million dollars.

"Fine, brah, he playing video games wit Junior," said Big K, "Hey, Sonny-boy, Palua on da phone. You like talk to him o wat?"

Noaloa didn't even look up. He and Junior were locked into mortal combat on a big-screen TV.

"No, man, he's fine. He go bed early, be ready tomorrow. Win dis fuckah, get a big paycheck, everybody happy, no problem, yeah?"

"That's what I want to hear. I'll see you guys in the morning." Palua flipped off the phone and turned to his date. "Now, where did you say your friends were dancing?"

"Yeah!! Dat's one da kine Benjamin you owe me, Junior!" Sonny-boy had just kicked ass again.

"Sure champ, I pay you tomorrow, yeah?"

"Nah, fuck da money. Eh, what time it is?"

"Almost ten, champ. Bettah get some sleeps. Big day tomorrah."

"Yeah, Junior, you right. Eh brah, get me one magazine inna lobby? I like read. I need fo sleep."

"Sure brah, what you want?"

"Get me one Forbes or sometin' li-dat. I need fo learn bout money."

"I be back right away, champ."

Junior walked across the suite and opened the door where Big K was stationed outside. The two exchanged a few words, and the door closed as Junior headed for the elevator.

Noaloa waited a minute, and then opened the door.

"Big K, Junior go already?"

"Yeah, he down da elevatah."

"Say Big K, I need some cookies from da stoah. Room service send up da milks, but dey all outta cookies."

"Sorry champ, got my ordahs. Stay sit right here," said Big K.

"Yeah, I know. Buncha da chicks might come up and find me or sometin' right?"

"Sometin' like dat, champ."

The elevator door opened and two large security guards came out and walked briskly toward Big K. Their dark blue uniforms were stretched over muscles that said they had obviously played some big-time football in their day. Big K saw them and his heart started pounding, but not because he had a thing for uniforms.

"Hello, are you friends with a man named Junior?" said the guard with "Otis" on his name plate.

"Uh, no. Maybe. Wha da problem is?"

"He's down in the lobby. He didn't have enough money for his purchases, and asked us to come up and get you to bail him out."

Big K breathed a sigh of relief.

"Dat guy one kine stupid. I no can leave heah. He gotta fix his own problems."

"Sir, we need you to come with us, please. It will only take a minute, and we're sure everything will be just fine."

The two guards stood on either side of Big K, their legs spread wide, their hands on their hips, but smiles on their faces.

"Aw, hell, ok. Hey, Sonny-boy! Lock da door. Put on da latch. Don't let nobody in. I be right back."

"No problem. Hey, get me da cookies!"

Big K heard Noaloa lock the door. He tested the door handle. Then he walked with the two guards to the elevator door. Just as they got there it opened and out stepped a well-dressed man with an adorable woman in a coral silk dress on his arm. They'd obviously had a few too many, and they almost fell headlong into Big K.

"Oh sorry, sir, we're sorry. Aloha. We really are. Sorry. Aloha, we love Hawai'i. We spent our honeymoon there. Sorry. Aloha."

Big K glared at them as they stumbled past him and went weaving down the empty hall. He stepped into the elevator, the two guards right behind him. Otis pushed a button, and the elevator door closed. The woman straightened up and quickly knocked on Noaloa's door. The man went to the next door down, inserted the keycard, went inside and unlocked the door connecting the suite to Noaloa's. He came through it carrying his backpack. He turned off the lights in his room and closed the door behind him. They left the suite quickly, and put a "Do Not Disturb" hangsign on the handle of the adjoining suite. The trio ran down to the end of the hall toward an exit sign. Sonny-boy hit the crash bar of the door and held it open.

The man went to step through, but Noaloa held up his hand.

'Excuse me Heath, but ladies first, if you please."

Aleja Gracellen smiled, took off her high heels, and ran down the stairs.

"Let's see if you guys can catch me this time!"

"Wait, I can't hear you," said Steve Palua into the cell phone in his left hand, "Turn that down, will ya?"

"Why, I thought you wanted to party?"

"Not right now, I gotta take this call," said Palua, taking his hand off the steering wheel and punching the eject button while swerving across a lane on the 91 freeway and almost sideswiping an old sedan. The other driver leaned on his horn as he pulled up and gave them the finger. Palua's date gave it back. Palua was oblivious to the exchange as he yelled back into the phone.

"Now, what the hell did you say?"

"We came back up and - - -"

"What do you mean we? You were supposed to guard the door, Big K."

"Fuck you Palua, I no da babysittah. I stay leave him wit da door lock, and we came back he no answer da door. We pound it pretty good, too. Den we call da room and he no answer."

"Well, maybe he's asleep."

"Yeah, mebbe. Da lights is off."

"Ok, just sit tight. I'll be back in a while."

It was a few minutes past midnight before Steve Palua screeched to a halt in front of the hotel. He'd been chased by the angry guy in the old Buick for several miles down the 91, then off the freeway and around some surface streets in Garden Grove before finally losing him, only to realize he was lost himself. The bimbo was getting on his nerves big time so when they finally found the strip club, he just shoved her out the door, threw a c-note at her, and took surface streets all the way back to the coast. On the way he called the hotel manager, who informed him that in situations like this, the police would be called. Overdoses were not a common problem at the hotel, but the manager was taking no chances if the room turned out to be the scene of a crime or accidental suicide.

The manager was first out of the elevator, followed by hotel security in their coats and ties, the police and Steve Palua right behind them. Junior and Big K were looking like choir boys standing in front of the suite. The manager used a master keycard and opened the door, but the catch still engaged. Nobody responded to his demands for entry. He realized that the adjacent suite was connecting, but there was a DO NOT DISTURB hangsign on the door handle. Now he had a problem: kick down the door to Noaloa's suite, or disturb his other guests. Well, they told him in training that nothing was more important than customer service, not even the price of replacing a door. He nodded to the cops.

They put their shoulders to it and burst into Noaloa's suite. The lights were off. The video screen displayed the "Start Now" menu from a video game called "Fight to the Finish". The cops scanned the room, and then headed to the bathroom, expecting the worst.

"Nobody here, mack," said one, "What's all the big deal about?"

The hotel manager turned to Steve Palua.

"Yes, sir, what seems to be the problem?"

When the contest sound system cranked up with "Welcome to the Jungle" at eight a.m. the next morning, the word was out something was wrong in the Wavelife camp. Rumors spread fast at a surfing contest. Sonnyboy Noaloa's name came up just as quickly. It was not unheard of for a surf star to be missing in action the night before a big final. In fact, sometimes it was almost expected. Chicks, blow, whiskey, wine, and worse: the recipe may have varied from venue to venue around the world, but the combination of young surfers barely out of high school earning six-figure salaries while surrounded by mass media marketing hype created a potent brew for bad behavior. More than one up-and-coming talent had fallen victim to it all, and with Noaloa's reputation for partying till dawn, everybody figured he was up to his old habits.

But some of the veteran pros remembered the times Sonny-boy had shown up at the last minute and stumbled to the water with a hangover so wicked someone usually had to wax his board for him and help him put the jersey on. He would then paddle out and proceed to surf at a world class level and walk away with a big trophy and an oversized, cardboard check with a lot of zeros on it. No biggie, they laughed to each other. He'll be here. The final isn't until two, and there's a lot of money on the table.

They were right, up to a point. Thirty-five thousand dollars is a lot of money for winning a surf contest. But Steve Palua knew how much money was really on the table. He also knew his head was on a chopping block, and by noon he was panicking. Nobody knew where Noaloa had gone. Had he gone out for a night on the town and was sleeping it off in some sleazy hotel? Was he going to surprise everyone and show up at the last minute? The surfers were all trading "me and Sonny in Biarritz / Rio / Bali / Tokyo / Sydney / Durban" stories from last year's tour. The marketing people were cringing as thousands of people were walking around with "Comeback Kid" t-shirts on. The contest organizers were wondering just what they'd do if only one guy paddled out in "mano-a-mano" final. The worst-case scenarios kept getting worse, and they were looking for Steve Palua to tell them what to do. But his cell phone had long ago gone dead, so they couldn't find him. Which was the only strategy he had going for him at the moment.

He was in a hotel room with Richard Black and two Huntington Beach detectives. Upstairs waited Bart Thomas and several east coast associates. In another wing of the hotel the representative of Palua's investment group was cooling his heels with Junior and Big K. Jacobsen, the Europeans, and all the surf media were already across the street.

But Steve Palua was still in his all black Saturday night-on-the-town outfit, now sweat-stained and wrinkled, standing outside on the balcony looking at the contest on the other side of Pacific Coast Highway packed with Sunday traffic. Several camera trucks from local TV stations were parked down below. The P.R. flacks had called them with the offer of face time with the champ before the finals. But Sonny-boy Noaloa was 'not available at this time'. Palua remembered what he'd said, that he had it all lined up like a perfect wave at Sunset Beach. He cringed when he remembered that Sunset starts out looking like a perfect wave, but when it hits the inside reef, sudden and erratic sections usually nail a surfer whose overconfidence led him to think he could make it through all the way.

He heard a horn sound from across the street. He checked his watch. It was the end of the Longboard finals. There were only two more final events to go, the Women, and the Junior Men, before the Men's final. First call for Sonny-boy's main event was in half an hour, and time was running out. He had to think fast, and he did.

He led Black and the detectives from the room and down the back stairs and directly into the parking lot. Getting in an unmarked car they drove across the street to the contest. The driver had to flash his badge twice to get anywhere near the three-story high contest headquarters, and even then they had to walk another fifty yards to get to the nerve center of the giant event.

The four men went through a tent, not even pausing when asked for their badges. They climbed up a flight of stairs and stood looking out at almost seventy thousand people. They huddled with the contest director, a man who had seen it all at Huntington, including the riots of 1986. He knew the crowd was waiting for the main event, and after sitting all day in the hot sun with their cars parked miles away and the surf almost flat, the people in the bleachers were growing as restless as Romans waiting for the gladiators. He scribbled a paragraph on a white board. Palua and Black erased some words, changed others, and soon they had a script that worked for everyone. The contest director handed it to the announcer.

"Ladies and gentlemen, this is the first call for the men's final. First call for the competitors in the men's final."

No mention of names. No mention of the starting time.

When the Women's Final hit the water, the announcer stuck to the script. "Look at these ladies, battling it out in almost impossible conditions. Folks you gotta hand it to them, they are really trying hard out there." Throughout the heat he played up how bad the surf was, which was never done at a professional surf contest, and especially if the surf was getting better, which it was. The two detectives left the scaffolding, shaking their heads. One got on his cell and called downtown to put the force on alert in case the crowd got out of control. It had happened before, and it just might happen again.

The Junior Men's final was about to commence and the announcer was getting into the spirit of things with some ad libs of his own.

"And due to the surf conditions, officials are considering a delay of the event until the surf will allow these magnificent athletes to perform and entertain you in the best surf Huntington can offer."

The two contestants just looked at each other. There were some real sets starting to come in, easily the best waves of the entire week. They didn't know what was going on. Nor did Mick Lennox.

He had made it all the way through his bracket, and was slated to surf against Sonny-boy in the main event. Now he was in the competitor's ready zone, and when the Junior Men's finalists went into the water, there was no Noaloa getting ready at the other end of the tent. And then about halfway through the final he heard an announcement that made his blood boil.

"Ladies and gentlemen, we regret to inform you that due to deteriorating conditions, the finals of the Men's competition may have to be cancelled. We are speaking with the surfers themselves, Mick Lennox of Gnarlaroo and Sonny-boy Noaloa from Wavelife, and we'll advise you of their decision. But right now, the motocross guys are really turning it on and a great skateboard exhibition will start in a few minutes. And be sure to visit the concourse area where our sponsors will be giving away thousands of free prizes."

Lennox couldn't believe his ears. Nobody was talking to him, and Noaloa was nowhere to be seen. He knew something was screwy, but it was too late to figure it out now, and with five minutes before the final was to start, he grabbed his jersey from an official's hands and ran out of the competitor's area towards the pier. The two junior surfers were getting some outstanding rides as sets started to pour in out of the southwest. Lennox had one eye on the waves and one eye on his watch as he paddled out from the beach, staying underneath the pier and effectively out of sight.

The horn sounded, and the Junior Mens was over.

"Ladies and gentlemen, that concludes the Junior Mens event of the U.S. Pro Championships. We are still waiting for a decision as to whether the men's finals will be held due to the deteriorating surf conditions. We want the best waves for the best surfers, but it doesn't look like it will happen today. Please take care as you leave the event area, and drive safely."

A perfect set of five large waves began to form up outside. The crowd began to cheer as the powerful swells adrenalized the SRO bleachers and the thousands crowding the railings on the pier.

Mick Lennox paddled out from under the pier. A great cheer rose up from the crowd.

"Ladies and gentlemen. Due to the poor surf conditions, we regret to inform you that the Mens final has been postponed. The best skateboarders in the world are ready to start launching some fantastic maneuvers, and don't forget to visit the exhibitors mall and get your free prizes. Thank you for attending the Huntington Beach U.S. Pro - - - "

But no one heard a word over the roar of the crowd. The first wave of the set was close to the end of the pier and Mick Lennox was in position, ready to surf, contest or no. Suddenly the entire crowd was on its feet, but not in anticipation of Mick's ride.

A surfboard had been launched out into space from the middle of the pier. On the railing stood a man perfectly erect. The wave was getting closer. He stretched his arms out . . . and dove with perfect form into the sea. His entry was clean, and he came up right next to his board. The wave was now only a few yards away and looked like it was going to break right on top of him. He got on his board, took two strokes, and dropped down the face.

The crowd went nuts! The Comeback Kid was in the ring! But then the wild cheers of the crowd turned into one giant, "Huh?"

As the wave rolled down the length of the pier, banners unfurled, one after another, covering all the garish advertising draped on the pier. as Sonny-boy rode the wave in the classic Hawaiian style, erect, casual, in control.

When he was almost to the beach he kicked out and paddled back to where an astounded Mick Lennox was sitting on his board. But few of the seventy thousand people had their eyes on him. They were reading the text on the banners, as were all the competitors, judges, press and media people, Big K and Junior, the man from Palua's investment group, Gunter Jacobsen and the Europeans, Bart Thomas and the east coast boys and, of course, Richard Black and Steve Palua.

An Open Letter of Good-bye
To everyone in Surf City
From Wilson Noaloa

This will be my last contest, ever.
I was forced to compete because profits
took precedence over simple human decency.

To the people who forced me
To comply with their plans,
why don't you leave surfing alone.

To all my true friends at Wavelife,
and all the honest people at the company,
I hope you understand why I did this.

I hope to meet again with you all soon.
And we can start to work for a better future
for the surf industry and for modern surfing.

Contests can be a lot of fun,
most pro surfers are great guys,
as are many people in the surf industry.

But when the whole purpose of surfing
means less than SPIT to people making millions
And they don't even surf or love the ocean

Then I think its time to do something drastic.
So that's exactly what my friends and I have done.
After all, what do you expect from real surfers?

See you in the water.
Sincerely Yours,
Sonny-boy Noaloa

The crowd on the beach started to clap. And the applause got louder and louder until everyone was standing and cheering even though Mick Lennox and Sonny-boy just sat there as wave after wave rolled through unridden.

"Fucken a', mate, what the 'ell is this all about?"

"Jus' exactly what you see, brah."

"Well, are we going surfing then, or what?"

"Well, you heard 'em. Da heat cancelled! We no gotta do nuthin'!"

"Ya know, I never did like being a dancing bear in a gilded cage!"

The applause was sustained now, the crowd still on its feet.

"Ok, brah, we bot' go on dis las' one, we geevum one good show!"

"Yer on, mate!"

The two top professional surfers in the world took off simultaneously on the last wave of the set. The crowd leaped to its feet as they tore back and forth down the face, in perfect synch with each other, weaving figure-eight trails off the bottom, up into the lip, catching air almost simultaneously and spinning 360s as the wave rolled in towards the shore. A hollow section loomed ahead and they both disappeared into the tube. When they came out, they linked their forearms together and raised their free arms in victory. They disengaged and drove towards the shorebreak. Two powerful bottom turns, two massive launches up the face, and two surfers hung in mid air as the wave collapsed on the sand.

Sonny-boy turned and paddled back out to sea. From the other side of the pier a jet ski appeared and raced towards him. The driver did a hard turn as the safety man threw a tow rope to Noaloa. He grabbed it, and the ski began to gather speed. He looked back and saw Mick Lennox standing on the beach about to be mobbed. He waved to him, and Lennox jumped back into the ocean. Noaloa waved his arm in a circle at the waverunner spotter, the driver turned around and let off the throttle. Noaloa sank back into the water, Lennox paddled up next to him, they both grabbed the towbar, and the powerful Yamaha roared as it pulled the two surfers up and took off out to sea.

The crowd was astonished into silence until another roar was heard across the entire contest area. Heads turned, and coming down low over Main Street was a Catalina seaplane painted silver and blue. The PBY turned down into a perfect landing on the ocean just outside the pier. The jet ski and the two surfers powered up to it. The surfers got off their boards and were helped into the cargo bay. The ski roared off to the north at seventy miles an hour. The PBY's engines throttled up to full power.

The Catalina plowed straight out to sea towards the next oncoming set. As the first wave came rolling under the bow, she lifted into the air, gained altitude, and then did a slow turn back over the contest site.

Richard Black and Steve Palua were speechless. Then their jaws dropped as a figure leaned out the cockpit's starboard window and gave them the peace sign. The seaplane banked hard and headed west. As he left the pier behind, the pilot waggled the wings in salute.

"Say, Clem, can you show me how to do that some day?" asked Roberto Mercante from the co-pilot's seat.

"Sure, Roberto, but not with MOF property. You'll jes hafta get a PBY on yer own!"

Back in the 'sunroom', two dripping wet friends had joined three other surfers to watch Surf City recede in the distance.

"Hot damn," said Aleja Gracellen, "Did that get it or what?"

"Such language from a lady!" laughed Heath Larson, "But they've sure got problems now! I think we got our message across."

"Yeah, dey get da message," said Bruddah, "but maybe only make dose guys get worse."

A Signal from the South

The tall, silver-haired man ran down the canyon following the creek to the coast, to the beach, to the place where the land came to an end. He stopped at the very edge of the continent, a step from the sea. Turning to the mountains of Montecito behind him, he spread his arms to span the ridgeline, gazing at the heights where the hawks flew wild. He closed his eyes, and prepared to take his leave from the land.

Bowing his head in profound submission, Ray Seranen entered the ocean in the Chumash way, showing his respect by stepping slowly backwards until he disappeared beneath the waters of Fernald's Cove, a place of quiet never touched by the storms he knew were raging on the other side of the world.

He surfaced, moving through the still water seemingly without effort. He kept his body in graceful trim, gliding with the momentum from the rhythmic dolphin-kick of his legs. The V of his wake was broken only when he would raise his head now and again to breathe. Through the golden sheen of the cove at dawn he swam through waters protected as if this was the very birthplace of life itself, the place from whence we came.

Emerging from the sea, Seranen stood erect as the first rays of sunlight darkened his shadow across the wet sand. He lifted his shoulders up and back and pulled the morning air deep into his lungs. He began a sequence of liquid movements, weaving his arms, legs, spine and mind through a dance of one, turning and stretching, focusing inward, his closed eyes gazing at distant horizons. The world became a hemisphere of energy all around him, the step of his feet his contact with mother earth, the sea behind him a mirror of blue in the sharp, clear light of a new day.

He came to a final, still inner moment before opening his eyes, his daily morning ritual now complete. The Greek ideal was real to Ray Seranen. The health of his intellect depended on his being sound in body. He was now ready to face the daunting task of guiding men and women through the wilderness of the Southern Ocean.

He ran back along the edge of the sea and then turned up the creek without breaking stride. He passed through a tunnel under the highway and continued for almost a mile, stepping lightly around the rocks and boulders with the agility of a man a third his age, before leaving the creekbed and jumping up to the landing of a stairway hidden in the sage. High-stepping up the redwood treads, he emerged into the sunlight on a deck with a view from the Santa Ynez Mountains to the Channel Islands.

He stepped into the open shower and stripped in the warm wind that often blew from the land to sea on summer mornings. The cold water sprayed a rainbow in the bright light coming through the trees. He saw a red-tailed hawk circling high over a mountain peak, and he took the opportunity to imagine himself in the center of the continent, as far from the sea as one could get, with no knowledge of or connection to the oceans of planet Earth. It was a moment of consciously distancing himself from the world of work he was about to enter as chief meteorologist for the Order of Southern Ocean Mariners on this Monday morning.

Nine thousand miles to the southeast a fleet of six Alba_Swords was poised, on station and standing by, off the coast of Tierra Del Fuego. On Ray's signal, they would begin a non-stop voyage around the world. Under his guidance, they would play cat-and-mouse with the vast powers of the Roaring Forties, remembering all the while that the safe passages of the past were no cause for confidence. He and the commanders in the Roaring Forties Regatta would measure their risks accurately and listen to their instincts religiously, knowing the fate of the mouse that, in letting its guard down, does so for the last time.

Ray Seranen opened a thick oak door, brass fittings bright in the morning sun. He entered a room without windows, yet warmly lit by a system of louvres in the ceiling that moved with the sun to provide consistent lighting throughout the day. Soon he would lose all sense of local time while concentrating for hours on end to determine the fleet's precise launch zone off the coast of South Africa.

He closed the door, not to see the ocean again until dawn on the morrow.

* * *

For millions of people around the world, global warming was little more than hotter summers and increased electricity bills. Melting ice caps, the desertification of Central Africa, rising sea levels, and other anecdotal natural phenomena were all blamed on the "'greenhouse' effect", and there was a general perception of man affecting the weather for the worse.

Some meteorologists and oceanographers, however, saw these apparent symptoms as part of long-term cycles rather than man's comparatively short-term influence. They felt using hotter summers as conclusive evidence of global warming was little more than sound-bite science. They maintained the connection between man's excesses and climate change was much more complicated. Veteran meteorologist Ray Seranen was one of them.

He believed that as man's industrial development became a factor in global weather systems, there was one place where the effects would be extremely pronounced. Seranen held that Antarctica was the world's air conditioner, and that if forced to work harder to dissipate increased heat generated globally, the end result would be more activity in the storms tracks around Antarctica. Massive volumes of heated air circling towards the South Pole would create an imbalance that Nature would abhor with a vengeance. That fury would intensify the storms and winds across the ten million square miles of the Southern Ocean.

Seranen began to do research on Antarctic weather systems, the oceanic storms circling the frozen continent, and the resultant wave fields. He worked for two years mining massive data sets from hundreds of years of ships logs, Antarctic meteorological stations, and a variety of remote sensing satellites. He began to program computer models using formulas similar to those originally used to navigate spacecraft to the outer planets, and more recently to predict stock market fluctuations and trends. As his models began to correlate anomalies in Southern Ocean sea-states with temperature and gaseous emissions trends of industrialized countries, Seranen saw a bigger picture beginning to form connecting increased wave heights in the Southern Ocean with unstable weather around the globe.

However, there were gaps in his data. To guarantee the integrity of his models and projections, he needed real-time observations from Antarctica and the Roaring Forties, a vast network of data acquisition nodes throughout the most remote areas of the Southern Hemisphere to calibrate against the planet's most powerful winds and waves of the Southern Ocean.

Frank Bucher needed the same thing.

Bucher's theories about voyaging through the Southern Ocean could not be put to the test using weather data from commercial sources and space agencies. To venture through the Roaring Forties in winter, and ride safely ahead of the most powerful wave generating storms on the planet, he knew he needed something better by orders of magnitude. A conversation with Rick Vogel, the man whose research into swordfish led to the design of Bucher's voyaging craft, led the founder of the Order of Southern Ocean Mariners to Ray Seranen.

Ten minutes after they met in person, Bucher knew he had found the man for the job of OSOM's chief meteorologist.

"The only way this will work is if I have everything I need to do the job right," he said.

"What do you need, Ray?"

"A hell of a lot."

"Like what?"

"Like something that doesn't exist."

"Such as?"

Seranen scribbled a list on the back of an envelope. He read it over, made a few changes, and handed it to Frank Bucher.

"Let me know when you're ready to start on this."

Bucher began read the list aloud.

"Sixty four automated weather stations at sites arrayed strategically on the Antarctic continent. two hundred and fifty six data buoys all around the Southern Ocean. Data relay stations to feed information in real time to California. Computers with twice the capabilities of the National Weather Service. Anything else?"

"And all the people I need to do the job right," said Ray.

"Okay, you're on," said Bucher, and they shook hands.

But within a month they hit their first big snag. They submitted their project design to the National Science Foundation, the U.S. agency that controlled almost all the research in Antarctica. The response was something along the lines of "Great idea, guys – we'll process your app and with a little bit of luck you should be on the ice in about five years. First off, though, we'll need your entire project budget placed in escrow to get you a place in line."

Frank Bucher and Ray Seranen thought about it for all of a minute. Their response was predictable.

"To hell with that. We'll just do it on our own!"

The Antarctic protocol signed in 2002 by all the countries with scientific interests in Antarctica allowed private organizations unrestricted access to the frozen continent. Most of the time that provision was used by tourist companies. Now it was going to be used by the Order of Southern Ocean Mariners. To get their weather network up and running, Bucher and Seranen turned to men and women who had worked on The Ice for decades.

Seranen was familiar with the genealogy of the Ice Pirates, the nickname for the VXE-6 squadron of the U.S. Navy that, beginning in 1956, flew hundreds of missions ferrying scientists, equipment, and supplies to the South Pole and research stations all around Antarctica. He knew that in 1999 the squadron had been decommissioned for cost-cutting reasons, and although many of the Pirates were scattered to new assignments or retired, a good number were still living around the base that VXE-6 had called home, the Naval Air Station at Pt. Mugu, only a few miles south of OSOM's headquarters in Ventura.

Seranen and Bucher arranged a meeting with a group of retired Ice Pirates. To go back to Antarctica was no romantic dream for them by any means, but the mission was intriguing, the money was on the table, and there was no doubt that Bucher and Seranen were men of their word.

Within eighteen months, OSOM's Antarctic Meteorological Network was being tested, and a year later Seranen's research began in earnest with Bucher's first voyage around the Southern Ocean. And now, five years later, a lot of their success was due to the courage, judgment, brains, and determination of the resurrected Ice Pirates.

Eight years later, the envelope and the handshake had changed the world for both of them.

Ray got the information vital to his understanding of the world's climatic fluctuations, and he was able make all the weather-related decisions in support of Bucher's voyages around the world. Bucher pioneered a new frontier of adventure on planet Earth. Furthermore, Seranen's research on heat transfer and pressure gradients in the southern hemisphere drew immediate interest in the scientific community. He was able to quantify the connection between the waves of the Southern Ocean and changing weather patterns around the world. This was priceless information.

Seranen began to get calls from commodities brokers offering him six figure salaries to work them, but his research was not for sale to commercial interests. Instead, OSOM arranged for grants through the U.N. to underwrite a portion of the costs of OSOM's weather network in exchange for information that began to minimize crops losses while quantifying the effects of global warming.

Yet, for all its sophistication at gathering massive amounts of precise data from around the Southern Hemisphere, OSOM's data acquisition system was sometimes compromised by a force outside of Seranen's control that had its origins ninety-three million miles away.

* * *

Damon Waiya watched the satellite data display in OSOM's weather center on the ice in Antarctica. The Antarctic Meteorological Network system operator could feel his patience beginning to wear thin. Instead of real time weather telemetry from a satellite situated directly over the South Pole, he was getting nothing but garbage without the necessary data integrity necessary for the projection models waiting in Ray Seranen's computers. All OSOM had to show for a very expensive subscription to the INT-AT satellite data system was a scrolling message, "Due to meteorological conditions, all data links in your service area are currently inoperable. Our apologies for any inconvenience resulting from this temporary anomaly. See your user agreement for liability issues."

Damon took a deep breath, leaned back in his chair, and let his impatience drain away. He looked up through the skylight, watching the aurora australis shimmer in the darkness as the magnetosphere did a St. Vitas dance. Thanks to a massive storm on the surface of the sun, extremely dense solar winds were blowing through the atmosphere and nearspace over the southern polar region. Despite redundant systems designed to overkill specs, OSOM's data streams had become sputtering spews of ones and zeroes. From the Roaring Forties to the South Pole, it was as if there was a cloud of steel wool between the satellite and the ground.

This was a worst-case scenario come to life for the Order of Southern Ocean Mariners. Timing an encounter between the fleet of Alba_Swords and the waves of a powerful storm was not a decision easily made with a compromised data acquisition system. Unless the satellite datalink was re-established, it would be almost impossible for Ray Seranen to direct the fleet to an optimum take-off zone. A miss was as good as a thousand miles when it came to inserting the fleet into an orbit of the planet, and it was Damon Waiya's job to solve the problem.

So far, he had been able to come up with a jury rig. Waiya had re-configured OSOM's entire ANTMET network to funnel weather data to him at one hour intervals instead of instantaneously to the satellite. He then pushed the data packets up to Seranen using an undersea cable to the southernmost city of South America, Ushuaia, and then through the local telcom system to the old NASA telemetry station outside Santiago, Chile. From there they had a secure link directly to OSOM HQ in Ventura, and then to Ray's office up the coast in Montecito. This work-around might be good enough to get the fleet to a general take-off zone, but once there they would have to wait for the real-time data needed to execute a launch sequence. However, solar storms could last for weeks, and expecting the elements to cooperate was wishful thinking at best. In any event, the go/scrub decision would be Ray Seranen's call, not his, and that time had not yet arrived.

Waiya turned to a big flat panel displaying a 3-D map of the Southern Hemisphere. A pattern of green icons was arrayed over the Southern Ocean and Antarctica showing the location of each node of OSOM's automated weather station network. It was steady as she goes - for the moment – on the first day of the coldest and most violent month in the Great South. Though June 21 was technically the dead of winter, old hands knew August to be the time of "bad ju-ju" due to a lag in the weather extremes that did not coincide with the calendar. August was the month for the worst storms ever recorded on the Antarctic continent and, as a result, the best time for holding the Roaring Forties Regatta. Nevertheless, for the past three days it had been all quiet on the southern front.

This only heightened Waiya's anxiety. There would be no standing down for him, or Seranen, or the mariners aboard the Alba_Swords. They were at first stage alert, ready to react the moment an extreme storm event began its life somewhere near the center of Antarctica.

He walked to the display as all the icons continued to glow green. He looked closely at the AWS nodes on and around Dome Argus, a massive, bulging plateau of glacial ice fourteen thousand feet high near the center of the frozen continent. Dome Argus was the spawning grounds of the world's most powerful wind, the katabatic, a torrent of air that often reached speeds of over two hundred miles an hour blowing down and out to the Antarctic coast. Dome Argus was ground zero for the energy that, when injected into a low pressure cell over the Southern Ocean, would double or even triple the power of the passing storm, resulting in the huge swells sought after by the Alba_Sword fleet. For the moment, however, the data transmitted to Waiya's system center told him not a breath of wind was stirring on Dome Argus.

If you were standing on the Dome near the AWS this first day of August, you would no doubt marvel at the clarity of the view, the dramatic lighting of an Antarctic sunrise and the pristine perfection of the place. Except for the machine that looks like a NASA satellite sitting in the middle of nowhere, Nature untouched extends to all the horizons. In the atmosphere high above you, however, it is a different story.

Nature is reeling from man's excesses. Through the hole in the ozone layer, a massive swath of abnormal heat from the North is spinning down into the supercold Antarctic atmosphere. The two forces clash and spiral against each other into an accelerating cyclone drilling down out of the sky. It slams into the ice, and a monstrous wind is born.

But this is no ordinary katabatic.

307

The sound of a hundred freight trains shatters your silent reverie. Turning around, your eyes go wide with terror as a wall of wind comes out of nowhere at two hundred miles per hour. The katabatic smashes you to the ground, and you can't hear your own last words, "No! No! This isn't happening!" as the wind accelerates and literally blows you away.

Damon Waiya stood back from the display so he could see the entire automated weather station network, all its icons glowing bright green. Then one turned yellow - on Dome Argus. The AWS began to report meteorological activity sufficiently rigorous to trigger real-time data transfer. He stepped up to the display and touched the Dome Argus icon. A second panel on the wall lit up, showing the graphs of the instruments as they recorded what was going on in the middle of the nastiest place on earth. He stepped back so he could watch both panels at the same time while focusing primarily on the sensor indicators. Wind speed, direction, barometric pressure, and air density were all in flux, indicating a moment of accelerating phenomena. Then each gauge redlined. Barometric pressure fell to absolute minimum, wind speed went maximum. A red frame began to blink around each display, indicating the integrity of the sensors was being degraded. Then each gauge locked up, and the red border turned to an unblinking black.

Node failures sometimes happened for a variety of technical reasons, but Damon's instincts told him the AWS was dead not because of any transmission or network errors. He knew that the unit high on Dome Argus had been utterly destroyed.

Waiya spoke quickly into his headset mic.

"VXE-6 OPS, this is OSOM SYSOP. Reporting apparent catastrophic failure AWS-81.77. Repeat. Ice Pirates, this is Damon Waiya. Dome Argus node is dead. Stand-by."

Waiya went to the control console and sat down slowly. A few quick keystrokes, and the last thirty seconds of the data streams from Dome Argus were displayed on a third panel. He watched the sequence go from green to red to black. For a node to go down like that, something mighty must have happened. He ran the sequence again, but there was no denying that a truly awesome force had destroyed the AWS.

The sound of a Marconi wireless jarred him back to reality. Damon recognized the hand from the cadence of the dots and dashes. It was Ray Seranen, checking in over OSOM's secure frequency using Morse Code, the simplest communication system ever devised that forced OSOM members and support staff to think straight so that minimum signals contained maximum information.

Damon listened to the dot-and-dash sounds and continued to watch the array of green icons across the interior of Antarctica. With the exception of the small black spot that marked the death of the AWS on Dome Argus, all the other icons were still glowing green. His jury rig was holding, so far. He tapped a message on the brass apparatus next to the trackball on the console.

AWS 81.77 failure Anomaly unknown origin STOP
Event data transfer HQ initiated STOP Await instructions STOP

Eight thousand miles to the north Ray Seranen listened to the squawk box and jotted down the AWS locator code after the transmission ended. He read it a second time, then took a deep breath. His eyelids fluttered for a second, and then his pupils became like lasers.

Seranen turned away from the 'Sparks' station and went to the oversize globe in the center of the room. He walked around it, touching OSOM weather station icons in China, India, Brazil, and other global warming indicator sites. They comprised a distant early sensing system for massive atmospheric heat exchange events. Rows of data from the past forty-eight hours began to roll down a wall display, but he did not bother to read them too closely. He rotated the globe ninety degrees to put the South Pole at eye level. He stepped back to see the entire Southern Hemisphere while the data packet from Dome Argus arrived at the computer near his desk. Ray pushed the file icon across the screen to the input window of his global warming simulation scenario. Thirty minutes later, the printer rolled a sheet out into the tray, face up, with his worst fears staring back at him.

He sat down in front of his roll-top desk and read the printout a second time, the paper trembling slightly in his hands. His global warming models predicted a convulsive release of energy when the atmosphere, having been force-fed the poison of man's industrial excesses, would eventually have to disgorge the imbalance of energy into a river of supercharged winds. The onslaught of this monumental force would be heralded by a signal from the south in the form of an early warning from the coldest place on earth.

That harbinger of nature unleashed was, Seranen knew without a doubt, precisely what had just obliterated OSOM's weather station on Dome Argus.

The Ice Pirates

"Now that's cold!"

Pieter Kistenberg put the book down in his lap and looked out a porthole into Antarctica's winter darkness. With just a few pages from the war diaries of the vanquished German Sixth Army during the battle of Stalingrad, he was brought back to his usual self. He was three months into a winter-over on the Antarctic continent, and needed a mental tune-up now and again, even if it took reading about the horrors of the German defeat at the hands of the Russian avengers to put things in perspective.

Pieter Kistenberg was an Ice Pirate. Tasked with supporting and maintaining the integrity of OSOM's meteorological network in Antarctica and the Southern Ocean, the Ice Pirates knew that to get the job done required a rhythm of efficiency and camaraderie. The flight engineer always made sure he was personally prepared to meet the challenges of the coming day, and if it took reading about a World War Two battle that made wintering in Antarctica seem like a vacation in Hawai'i, so be it.

A knock on the door and Kistenberg kicked himself out of his bunk, landing cat-like on the floor of his homedome, one of many connected by a latticework of tunnels throughout OSOM's personnel facility at McMurdo Sound, near the Ross Sea south of New Zealand.

"Permission to enter?" It was his pilot, Rico Candelaria.

"Come on in, Suave."

Candelaria ducked through the portal with an easy grace. Like Kistenberg, he was in gym-rat shape, and his flight suit looked stretched around his arms and shoulders. He glanced at the title of Kistenberg's book.

"Ah mein freund, wie gehts mit der Wehrmacht?"

"Sold out by the Austrian corporal. First he prohibits Mannheim from going to the rescue, then he makes Von Paulus a field marshal so he won't surrender. Truly hell on earth. Makes this place look like Miami!"

Candelaria laughed and replied, "Well, sorry to report the skin diving trip has been cancelled, Pieter."

"Oh, so we'll just be lounging poolside again today?"

"Not quite. Damon needs to see us. Sounds like a node mission."

"Any idea where?"

"Not yet. I only got wind of it a few minutes ago."

Pieter felt a twinge of anxiety, but then he thought of what real pressure was: waves of tanks firing point blank at a trapped army, commanders in shock putting Lugers to their heads, stacks of corpses that were once comrades, the first steps of a death march to Siberia. He immediately straightened himself and smiled at Suave.

"Sounds like we're in for a bit of fresh air," said Kistenberg, grabbing two thick binders and his data pad.

Walking to the briefing room, the two men kept their minds free of any thoughts about what might lay ahead of them. Kistenberg and Candelaria were highly respected members of the Order who knew a thing or two about bravery and brains versus bravado and bullshit. They knew anxiety and stress were enemies best defeated by humor, and so it took them a minute to get through the door thanks to a hilarious "After you, Alphonse" routine.

"No, most excellent flight engineer, you have almost five thousand winter hours, and I a mere forty-two hundred. After you, oh grizzled veteran!"

"But oh pilot without peer, you've done touch-and-go medevacs at fifteen stations from Vostok to Cape Horn. After you, oh savior of the skies!"

On and on it went, until finally Candelaria played his trump card.

"But my dear friend, I must insist. Your boot heels are so polished that I've brought along my sunglasses so as to not be blinded in following you."

He smoothly whipped his shades out of his breast pocket and placed them smartly over his eyes.

"After YOU, my dear Alphonse!"

Rico swept open the door and Kistenberg stumbled through, laughing at his pilot's perfect "Gotcha!" It was pitch black outside, and Candelaria had obviously planned it all by having his shades at the ready, knowing that in the humor and absurdity of their little skit, they were reinforcing a bond that saved lives.

The room was smallish, with five armchairs arranged in a semi-circle in front of an oversize flat panel monitor displaying OSOM's meteorological network covering Antarctica and the Southern Ocean. Kistenberg and Candelaria joined the other three members of their flight crew, plane commander Mark Habeman, navigator Kathleen Drake, and loadmaster Mai Seqgen. Damon Waiya began his briefing.

"As you all know, we have been operating with a compromised data network thanks to Apollo doing the boogaloo in the magnetosphere. We now have experienced an anomaly that has Ray's utmost attention. Dome Argus went down about thirty minutes ago. The node experienced a catastrophic failure after transmitting highly unusual data indicating an ultra-powerful katabatic event. However, adjacent stations reported no anomalies and continue normal operations."

"That's a new one," said Habeman, "What's Ray got to say about this?"

"Nothing so far, other than a request for your consideration."

"Let me guess! With the Alba_Swords ready to launch, he wants all the data he can get, including Dome Argus," said Kathleen Drake.

"Can't he make do with what's still up and running?" said Habeman, glancing at all the green nodes on the display.

"No he can't," said Kistenberg, "and for good reason."

Everyone turned and looked at Pieter.

"I bet he thinks the AWS was destroyed by the first of a series of atmospheric convulsions as predicted by his global warming models. If his model is right, stronger ones are on the way, and they will power up katabatics beyond belief. And they'll all start up on Dome Argus."

"Damon, can Ray give us any predictions as to when we can expect the next one? We'll start working up a flight plan. Are the AWS guys running simulations on a replacement unit?"

"Not yet, but I'm going over there right now. As for when the next one is going to hit, I'm sure Ray is working on it as we speak. I'll have that information by the time the AWS unit is ready."

Waiya stood up and headed for the door. Candelaria rolled the trackball under his right hand and a cursor shot across the display. A menu bar presented icons, Candelaria made selections, and overlay graphics appeared one after another: color-coded surface wind arrows, the latest satellite infrared images of cloud densities, and isobaric contours of the interlocking high/low pressure systems spinning around the globe from the Roaring Forties to the South Pole. Another click, and it was all set in motion, running the past forty-eight hours in fast forward. Then the display froze at the precise moment that the node on Dome Argus went from green to yellow.

"Okay Rico, roll it back twelve hours," said Drake, "bring it up triple and center it on Dome Argus."

Candelaria was right on it. The screen wiped to black, then filled with the ice white of Antarctica's most inaccessible region. AWS-81.77 glowed green at dead center.

As the weather data was fed a second time into the program, the changes on Dome Argus were graphically displayed.

It was an eerie sight. A cyclonic isobar pattern appeared around the AWS. It started to rotate, and then spun faster and faster like a toilet flushing into a steep downward spiral. Then the gradients spread out and relaxed into calm. There was nothing on the screen but a black icon that had once been green. It had taken all of twenty seconds.

"Ouch!" said Mai Seqgen, "I've never seen anything like that before!"

"I have," said a very somber Pieter Kistenberg, "The models Ray generated from Eastern Pacific chubascos off Mexico combined with wind shear models from Tornado Alley in Kansas. You get downdrafts that hit the ground like steamhammers, then spray around in a spiral like a fire hose out-of-control until its direction stabilizes into a single path of power."

"Well whatever it was," Candelaria paused, "we're just guessing until we go on-site and find the AWS."

"Correction," said Pieter Kistenberg, "IF we go up there. Flying to Dome Argus means temperature, visibility, fuel, approach, landing, cargo off-load, take-off, and return issues. And if Jerry Phelps and the backup C-130 have to come get us, then we're all in trouble. Let's look at it this way."

312

He cursored the display into a three-dimensional horizontal view, and scaled it back to show their current location, their headquarters at McMurdo, at sea level on the Ross Sea coast.

"The target is at an altitude of fourteen thousand feet. It is almost a thousand miles away. The sun is above the horizon for only six hours. Available light on the ice will be quite limited unless it's clear, which it probably won't be. Landing and ice conditions are unknown. Surrounding weather systems are wildly unstable, and right now it is so cold up there who knows if we wouldn't just freeze dry on the spot."

The chief flight engineer looked around the group. There were some smiles at his attempt at humor. There was not a hint of disagreement in any of the faces listening to him intently.

"Approach path can't be determined until we're there and check the sasturgi ice patterns, which may be have been erased by the anomaly. We may not be able to land unless it is comparatively quiet and on-ice time must be minimized. Then we'll probably need to do a jet-assisted take-off to get out of there, with no guarantee that we'll still not have to burn way too much fuel to gain altitude in the face of," Kistenberg glanced around the group, "any unusual local breezes."

Everyone snickered at the Kistenberg's idea of "local breezes". It was like referring to a roaring freeway as being little more than a country lane.

"So, can we do it?" asked Mark Habeman, "Will half-an-hour be enough all around?"

The room was quickly filled by the sounds of laptop keystrokes clicking, pencils scratching and binders opening and closing. It looked like five students taking the final exam of their lives. Which in a way, it was. There was no margin for error. Creating an illusion of safety on such a mission would be a mistake that could kill them all.

Each Pirate was deeply involved in calculations, systems cross-checking, levels-of-criticality determinations, and some deep reflection as they leaned back in their chairs from time to time in contemplation. Then a flash of inspiration, and back at it they would go with a flurry of new specs and contingencies.

Nobody noticed when Damon Waiya re-entered the room and handed a slip of paper to Habeman. He glanced at it, and then passed it around the room. The margin of error for Seranen's projection was plus or minus sixty minutes. That put the mission deep into the safety red zone. Then again, they'd already come to that conclusion from their own calculations ten minutes ago.

Waiya showed no expression in the face of something that he'd never imagined could happen. The Pirates were calling it 'no-go'.

"Captain Bucher won't blink," said Candelaria, "He'll know that if we could do it, we would. But we can't. As the saying goes, 'No way in hell.'"

"Because that's exactly what we'd be facing if we tried to land at Dome Argus right now," added Mark Habeman.

"I'd give just about anything to see what happened to that unit," said Mai Seqgen, "except a life. And I'm sure everyone in OSOM will concur. If the Regatta hangs in the balance based on Ray's need for data from Dome Argus, then it's a scrub for the Regatta."

"To quote one old Pirate motto, 'I ain't pushing up a cross in this hellhole'," said Kistenberg, even as his thoughts ran to the frozen waste of human life at Stalingrad.

"Thanks for being frank, no pun intended," said Waiya, "I'll keep the AWS team on task with a replacement. If things change, they'll be ready."

"Say, why not do an airdrop? Or use an aerial unit? Deflate the balloon and float it down instead of up?"

"Might work. I'll get those guys to do some calculations on balloon pressures versus drop rates."

"What about parachuting them in?"

"Yeah, even better. We can come in low to help 'em survive impact. Can the AWS guys build a stripped down model that might make it?"

"I'll find out. Might have problems with transmitter antennas, but let's see what they can come up with."

Damon Waiya walked out of the room, followed by the Ice Pirates flight crew. They walked to Waiya's sparks station through the transit tunnels between the domes. They all crowded in and Waiya sat down to key a terse message to Ray Seranen, who would bounce it immediately to Frank Bucher and the captains of the Alba_Swords.

"81.77 Air drop only. Unit prep time unknown. Confirm."

Each Pirate tapped out their initials in dots and dashes, giving Ray Seranen the absolute concurrence warranted by the import of their decision. For the first time in OSOM's history, there was a distinct possibility that the Roaring Forties Regatta might be postponed indefinitely or cancelled outright.

However, nobody gave that a second thought when they considered the significance of the root cause of the situation. If Seranen's models were correct, a weather event of unimaginable proportions and power was on the horizon, the likes of which the earth had never, ever experienced.

On Station and Standing By

Frank Bucher stepped out of the sparks station into a raw winter's night at sea two thousand miles east of Cape Horn. The water was five degrees above freezing and the air ten degrees above zero. The wind was blowing Force Four and pushing high clouds towards the rising moon. The swell was out of the southwest at thirty feet every twenty seconds with a wicked cross chop moving across the open ocean. He was standing on a walkway forty five feet above the water line on the *Mother Carie*, a giant steel catamaran three hundred and fifty feet stem to stern with a hundred foot beam. The sea state conditions were hardly affecting the ship, but Seranen's message had serious implications for her cargo. Six Alba_Swords were berthed three to a hull, and their crews were getting ready to surfsail around the world. The *Mother Carie* was their launch platform, but now Bucher had to re-consider everything.

After coming out of the shadow of Cape Horn, they were now at a staging waypoint five hundred miles southwest of South Africa with sufficient time to set up their first surfsailing sessions ahead of the next front. A new storm would be coming through in about fourteen hours, and the crews of the Roaring Forties Regatta were on station and standing by. They were right where they wanted to be - until Seranen's message came through.

Bucher looked out over the moonlit seascape and read it a second time.

Antmet anomaly. Extreme katabatic event imminent.

Proceed cruise mode Agulhas only. Possible scrub R40R.

He considered his options. They could launch into the next front and run some sessions in the steep open ocean waves of the Agulhas Current off the South African coast. If Seranen's projections held up and all hell broke loose high up on Dome Argus, they could then retreat to the east coast of South Africa and pull into Port Elizabeth near the fabled points of Jeffrey's Bay. He smiled at the thought of surfing the biggest waves ever at J-bay, or even riding the perfection of Cape St. Francis at triple overhead. This was a fail-safe scenario that he could easily live with, so he spared a thought for a much more exciting alternative.

What if Ray's projections were accurate concerning a global warming weather event triggering surf of fantastic proportions? If their Antarctic weather network could get them accurate data in time, could they come up with a new launch plan? Could they surfsail the Agulhas, and then ride the biggest waves imaginable across the Southern Ocean? Waves that might be beyond anything ever recorded in the history of the seven seas?

"Come about, yer sailin' in dangerous waters," he muttered into the biting wind, knowing his imagination had run away with him. He tacked his attention away from speculation and back to reality by setting a temporary course to the galley for a cup of coffee on his way to the bridge.

The thought brought a smile to his face. The catamaran's regular crew was off watch on nights when the *Mother Carie* was in stand-by mode, a safe way to give the crews of the Alba_Swords an opportunity to share some of the larger responsibilities of OSOM's mission. Tonight it was the Russians' turn. He had a special place in his heart for them, and he knew their camaraderie was just what he needed right now.

They called themselves Team Zek because "zek" was the slang name for the inmates of the Gulag archipelago, a network of prison camps spread across almost a million square kilometers of Siberian wilderness during the reign of dictator Josef Stalin. Their ancestors were pioneers on the desolate coast where Siberia meets the North Pacific, fishermen who had to turn to subsistence living off the sea when the Soviet system collapsed. Despite such a seemingly bleak life, they were surprisingly cheerful and spirited, and when they saw what surfing was all about through some videos exchanged with Alaskan fishermen, they found a new arena to express the indomitable Russian zest for life. Throughout the Kuril and Aleutian Islands, they fished, surfed, and lived a wilderness existence not found anywhere else on earth. It was there they crossed paths with Frank Bucher and Charles Atkins.

The two men and a dozen founding members of OSOM were running short duration test sessions on Alba_Sword prototypes in the Gulf of Alaska. The Americans and the Russians hit it off immediately, and the fishermen-surfers from Siberia became the first international crew of the Order of Southern Ocean Mariners. They were quite simply the toughest sailors in the world thanks to their genes and Joseph Stalin, and they were exactly what Bucher and Atkins needed when it came to challenging the Southern Ocean in winter.

Bucher stepped through the watertight bulkhead just as a rogue swell hit the *Mother Carie*. He kept his balance easily, though a few drops of his coffee hit the deck. The Russians were all business and focusing on their tasks, except for the murmur of a running joke at the expense of the Australians off watch below. But when watch leader Rudolf Velelov saw him and his nearly fatal faux pas, loud laughter and biting sarcasm filled the air.

"Ah, Captain Frank Bucher! Vee vill have you scrubbing zee deck with a holystone after vee demote you zu cabin boy!"

"And since when does a man lose all rank for a minor infraction?"

The Russians all turned and stared at him. Then they all cracked up.

"Since always! Russian tradition!" boomed Velelov, and Bucher started laughing. The ribbing came with the territory, and he didn't mind it one bit.

"Ah yes, TRADITION!" He sang the word like Zero Mostel in 'Fiddler on the Roof', "The mother's milk of Mother Russia. I understand completely. It will not happen again. Can I humbly request a status report, comrades?"

Everyone got serious without hesitation.

"Steady as she goes," replied a smiling Misha Yevgenev, the navigator, turning the conversation around on a dime, "Easting at five knots, east north east seventy five degrees on course towards Agulhas staging zone."

"Helm equi-balanced," reported Yuri Konstantinov, the man at the helm, "Gyroballasts response time within spec. Minimum pitch and yaw through the sets."

"All support systems stable," added the first mate and chief engineer Ivan "The Terrible" Rostopovich.

"And plenty of surf! Even for a surfer like you, Captain!" The lookout, Ivan's wife Illyana, said without taking her eyes off the monitors in front of her showing the surf coming up behind the *Mother Carie*. There was a pause, and it gave Bucher his chance for a comeback.

"Thank you. These conditions remind me of stories about what the freighters went through on the Murmansk run. Lotta good American merchant sailors didn't come back from those mercy missions, you know," needled Bucher with a smile on his face, "just to save your Commie behinds after Hitler double crossed ol' Uncle Joe. But you got a good deal, and I bet you're still driving those old Dodge trucks around, aren't you? They run good over frozen tundra I hear!"

"Ah, Bucher, your American arrogance never fails to amaze me!" Velelov played an old role to the hilt, "Just because ve owed you our entire country in ze war debt does NOT mean you can, how do zey zay in your 'hood, you cannot DIS us and get away weeth it! Ve are ze new Russia! Or as new as ve Russians can get!"

They all laughed. All around them was raw winter power mixed with the wildest of oceans, but on the bridge of the *Mother Carie*, humanity thrived.

"Now, consider your friends from Down Zunder," continued Velelov, "Zey respect no one, and us least of all! Ve have had zeenough of zee cheeky Veekies! How about you zend zem to Kamchatka next winter? Special OSOM request!"

Velelov was referring to the Alba_Sword team from Australia, who despite their proven skills as fine mariners of the Southern Ocean, had to bear the brunt of being known as "Vickies", short for convicts, since Australia had originally been settled as a prison colony by the British. Of course, that was how the Russians settled Siberia. Stalin had shipped political prisoners and convicts to the end of the rail lines east of the Urals, leaving them with nothing but axes and the boxcars they came in, and so similar lineages fueled the rivalry between Team Zek and Team Oz.

"Zey zink zey are zo tough zose Aussies! Zend zem zoo our mother Siberia –Zen zey learn vat real convicts are. Vee Zeks vill teach zem!" harrumphed Rostopovich with a twinkle in his eyes.

"And if zey ask for explanations – vee vill give zem more Gulag justice!" chimed in Konstantinov, "Double their sentence! A tenner and another tenner! Twenty days in the Bering Straits on station! Vat vith prep and tear down and re-fit – Ha! ve vill use zem all winter!"

"Ok, boys, we need a reason for you invitation."

"Zimple," said Rudolf, "Vee vill invite zem zoo compete in zee Convicts Cup! Zee Zeks against zee Vickies – and as hosts vee vill show zem every courtesy!"

"That's good enough for me!" laughed Frank.

The Russians roared with laughter at the thought. It was all in good fun, but underneath was a thread of serious focus. The Russians were the lead team for executing Alba_Sword test runs from Russia to Alaska in the off season, and the Aussies would be under their command. Bucher smiled at the thought of the Russians and the Aussies having a go in the Bering Sea. As the tall ship mariners used to say when it got really raw, it would be 'Sailing with the bark on'.

"Zank you for your support, Frank", said Velelov. "Vee knew you vould zee zings our way. Vee are interested only in justice – another Russian tradition! Ha! HAH!!" He slapped his thigh, and off he went into a stream of Russian as they began to scheme their plans for the Aussies.

Frank smiled, finished his coffee, and stepped outside into the night as the half moon lit up the seascape, the same moon that he knew would just now be rising over the mountains behind his home in California.

Another rogue wave crashed into the *Mother Carie* from an odd angle and reminded Bucher of the decisions ahead of him. He knew the Russians would be up for a go no matter how big it got, and so the Aussies would have no choice but to ante in. And if Seranen's data was precise and the voyage plan exact, the Peruvians and the Germans would be receptive to the idea.

That left the two Alba_Swords from Ventura. He headed aft towards the starboard hull to visit with his crew on the *Tom Swift,* including the two able-bodied passengers who had brought along their surfboards. There was no need to tell them about Seranen's message right now since a scrub for the Regatta meant an end to the plans of Richards and Merrill. Then the thought of Richards' blank check crossed his mind. He stopped in his tracks. He realized canceling the Regatta was still an IF, and that he'd better talk to Charles Atkins about Seranen's message right away.

Jack Richards and L.J. Merrill were sitting in their bunks braced against the movement of the ship as seamen had done from time immemorial in rough seas. Unlike their seafaring forbearers, however, they had computers lightly strapped to their wrists.

The two able-bodied passengers were using small, thin laptops with narrow, rectangular screens to type entries into their personal logs. Handwriting was almost impossible in the Southern Ocean in winter, so OSOM's mariners used these digital logs to pass down time in heavy seas by keeping personal journals. For the past four days they had been kept busy with a wide variety of tasks, including taking their turn on the bridge of the *Mother Carie*. This was their first opportunity to get going on their journals, and they were making the most of it, and Jack Richards knew where he wanted to start his story.

```
I'll start with the passage round Cape Horn, though in
the end it was just a big rock at the tip of a
continent. Yet the ceremony was such that I thought we
were in the Sistine Chapel or something.
Bucher brought out the gold earrings, "to be worn not
with pride, but as a badge of humility" he said. They
don't want rounding the Horn to be some heroic feat or
some moment of victory. All the old hands seemed to
treat the moment as if it was their first, I guess in
honor of those who'd gone before only to have Cape Horn
make it their last. It was all a bit melodramatic, but I
guess that's the point. These guys are so prepared and
we are all so well trained I can't imagine anything
really fazing them, so I guess they have to go out of
their way to faze themselves.
We are now waiting for a storm and our first surfsail
session off South Africa. We're way more than halfway to
Merrill's reef if you go back to the shakedown cruise.
Four months of training with OSOM, all the secrecy to
keep Merrill happy, and thinking he's on top of
everything. Well he isn't, 'cause he still doesn't know
about the stock I bought or what is going to happen when
-"
```

Richards stopped typing, and erased the last two sentences. He closed his eyes for a minute. He knew the toe-hold position acquired for him by Bruce Kaufman was going to work exactly as planned. If Wavelife ended up in Chapter Seven, he'd have a seat in the bankruptcy court, though as a shareholder he would nominally be at the end of the line and would be lucky to get pennies on the dollar. But his loss would be peanuts compared to the suit he'd bring against the board of directors for bankrupting the company, a distinct possibility if Merrill could undercut Wavelife's plans to use the reef as the centerpiece of their P.R.

He ran the plan and the numbers through his head from several perspectives: perceptions on Wall Street and the surf industry, marketing cred in the surf media, Clark's treachery, shareholder lawsuits, and his costs to date. Nothing was out of spec. He started typing again.

```
It has all been worth it. Our first night on the
bridge of the Mother Carie was really interesting.
```

His keystrokes came in rapid bursts, but he was not interested in what was appearing on the small screen. He was just killing time, his mind on much larger issues.

L.J. Merrill was entering keystrokes very slowly though not because he cared about punctuation or capitalization. He didn't bother to correct any of his mistakes because he was much more concerned with making his log an account of his entire experience with OSOM, starting with the "sinking" during the shakedown cruise more than four months ago.

```
ian clark and frank bucher - i can think of no greater
contrast  specially the way bucher didnt rub it in out
off san miguel  I cant wait to see Clarks face when I
take down him and Wavelife in the waves that i found and
I will do it by sailing an albasword by way of cape horn
and not jumpjetting to tahiti in some corporate jet
```

when we sank on the shakedown I knew we were not going
to die panic sure seized up and helpless yes a junkie
coming down? done it a thousand times but going down in
a pitch black sea was like death itself until Frank came
up to the cockpit here we are seeing our lives flash in
front of us and frank bucher says I see captain satkins
didnt give you some important information before he came
below, so let me explain whats going on here
we noticed we were no longer sinking it was quiet and
still and we could hear waves above us and the moons
light was visible now and then in the troughs. I came
around first richards was still freeked I switched on
the cockpit lights so that bucher could see where he was
going but he was already standing next to me.
permision to take the helm, candidate? he said, and he
just flowed into the pilots station and I got out of his
way he reset the controls to what he later called sub-
surface cruse mode
richards shot off his mouth but big deal he had been
thrugh a lot
hey Im not paying for this shit. You guys better be able
to get me out of this And you can cancel the whole
fucking thing bucher
but bucher handled it well.
we thought youd enjoy some peace and quiet candadate so
just pipe down and stop your whinning
Well that shut him up for a second cause ive seen him go
off before when he didnt get his way
bucher said to me now candadate merrill you can take the
helm and please feel free to ask any and all questions.
well where do I start captain?
but richards just would not shut up
I will tell you where to start merrill Ask him why the
hell did he let you sink us And why didnt he tell us we
couldn't sink
because faith and team spirit make this whole thing go,
mr. jack richards and we like to determin your inital
baselines in those instincts early in the proces of your
evaluation. Oh dont worry jack, your outburst wont be
held against you in fact one of the things we look for
is if you can learn from your mistakes and of course you
need to make some for us to see how you respond
then his son came up through the hatch bucher turned
back to me and says looks like your watch is over You
are relieved
and that was that richards unbuckled his harness fast
the look on his face was something I had never seen
before something like rage embarrassment and cunning all
at the same time
the rest of the run was easy for us we stayed below and
hit the rack until our watch came up again I got some zs
richards didnt sleep at all and he didnt say a word
when we got back to ventura we had to record a verbal
acount of the entire shakdown cruse we then had to
handwrit a page on the best and a page on the worst
experience we had. they left us each in a separate room
told us where to put the tape and pages when we were
done then atkins said he'd call us in a few days and
that was that

When I got the call I told 'em to wait and that I wanted
Jack to hear it when I did I got ahold of him and we
met down at ALiso where it all started I called 'em
back and held the phone between us When I hung up jack
ws almost crying. hed thought hed blown it and so did I.
but now we are on the launch ship and things are going
well.

He looked out the porthole and thought of men a century ago looking at
the same waves, the same stars, and the character that had driven them
onward through these very seas, many towards certain death. He thought
about what had been going through the minds of Shackleton, Scott,
Amundsen, and their crews. He realized that conquest, ego and priority, the
things that framed the golden age of exploration, were the same forces
driving him and Ian Clark. He remembered Richards' quip about beating
Clark and Wavelife to the reef. He thought of himself as Roald Amundsen,
the noble warrior, with Clark in the role of Robert Scott, the foppish
dilettante, and their quest when the South Pole was the last great prize for
those two famous explorers at the end of the Golden Age of Exploration. He
knew it was a strech to compare Antarctic exploration to surfing, but still,
there was a parallel of sorts since the reef he'd seen was the last great prize in
surfing's era of exploration.

That gave him an idea. He knew Clark had been with Larson on the ill-
fated trip to the reef, but he was sure Clark was still determined to get out
there to cash in on his deal with Wavelife.

"Jack, I'm going to the sparks station. Got to send a message back to
California. Wanna go?"

"Thanks, but I'm gonna send some of this to my wife and kids and I'm
not quite done yet."

"I'll wait if you want?"

"Nah, I'll be a while. See you later."

L.J. Merrill made his way up to the communications station directly
below the bridge of the *Mother Carie*. He paused to take another look at the
Southern Ocean through a porthole before writing a message that would later
be sent in Morse Code by the ship's radio officer.

He used the exact words of Roald Amundsen when he put Robert Scott
on notice that a race was afoot. He made just one change regarding their final
destination.

"BEG LEAVE INFORM YOU PROCEEDING REEF. LJ."

He filled out the rest of the form. When he wrote the address he flashed
back to when he had last stood in front of Geosurf and Clark's office.

"And can you get it out so that it gets to Laguna Beach today?"

"Yeah, I'll send it to HQ and tell 'em to turn it around immediately.
Should be there in a few hours."

"And can you get his signature to make sure it ended up in his hands?"

"No problem. Must be pretty important, Mr. Merrill."

"It is, and thanks for helping."

L.J. Merrill went outside and ran into Frank Bucher coming down the stairs from the bridge.

"Cold enough for you, L.J.?" said the Captain.

"Just a bit brisk, I'd say. What's up with our voyage? Seems like everything is okay so far, no?"

"We're on standby until further notice," said Frank Bucher with a serious tone to his words, "and Mr. Richards?"

"Doing well, Captain. Been a changed man for months now," Merrill replied. Then he realized what Bucher had just said. A familiar stab of anxiety bolted through his brain. "Standby until further notice?"

"It means that we are on station and standing by. Nothing more, nothing less. Now if you'll excuse me, I've got to speak with Charlie Atkins."

Kamikazes

"Yes sir, he'll be with you shortly. Could I ask you gentlemen to please take a seat?"

"Well, tell him I'm here," said Steve Palua, "And tell 'em I need to see him right away."

"Uh, yes, just a moment," said the receptionist, pressing a blinking light on her phone console, "Good morning, Geosurf, please hold."

She put the incoming on hold and pressed the intercom button, but another blinking light came on. Distracted, she forgot what she'd just done and said the wrong thing to the wrong person.

"Good morning, Geosurf, please hold."

"Why should I hold? I own this place! What did you want?"

"Oh, I'm sorry sir. A Mr. Steve Palua is here with some gentlemen. He says he needs to see you right away."

"I bet he does," said Clark, annoyed at being interrupted during his morning e-trade session, but not surprised after what happened yesterday at Huntington Beach, "Tell 'em I'm busy and to wait and I'll be with them as soon as possible."

The line went dead and she punched the blinking light.

"Good morning, Geosurf, please hold," she said before looking up at the man looking down at her.

"Mr. Clark is quite busy right now. If you will please just be patient and take a seat, he'll be with you as soon as possible."

Steve Palua turned to the four men standing a few yards behind him and shrugged. As he did, the receptionist looked back at the phone console and handled the call on hold.

"Sorry to keep you waiting. Yes, how can I help you? . . . . . I'm sorry, I don't take reservations. . . . Let me put you through." "Good morning, Geosurf. How can I help you? . . . . Oh, I'm sorry," she said, forgetting to transfer the call. She punched two buttons and then another incoming. "Yes, how can I help you? . . . . Uh, he's in a meeting right now, can he return your call? . . . Your name, sir? . . . I'll give him the message."

Now somebody else was at her desk, but this time she knew the face.

"Hi Mike, how's it going?" she said wearily.

"Same old same old, Susan. But I've got something new for Ian. It's a priority telegram and he needs to sign for it personally."

"A priority telegram? What's that?"

"It's a new service we're offering. Part electronic, part in-person. When someone wants to send a letter immediately, but wants an actual signature like they'd get with a courier service, we can print 'em out in the truck and I handle it like a package."

"Ok, hold on a sec," she said, noticing the four men were now standing only a few feet from her desk, "Mr. Clark, you have a telegram that requires your signature and . . . Uh, . . .wait, let me check. Can't I sign for it, Mike?"

"Usually that's ok, but it's addressed to him and I need to see that he goes directly to him AND I gotta get his signature. So he has to sign for it."

"No sir, I can't sign for it – I'm not on the list . . . . Sir, that's not my fault I . . . Mr. Clark, I'm just trying to . . . "

Tears started to come to her eyes as Clark gave her an earful.

Steve Palua had heard enough. He turned and nodded his head at one very big and not very happy Hawaiian.

"Here, gimme dat ting," said a glowering Big K. He grabbed the clipboard from Mike's hand and walked towards Clark's office. As he reached for the handle, Clark came out, glaring at Mike and Susan.

"C'mon, you guys, I shouldn't have to be interrupted - - - "

He ran right into Big K and bounced off the brick solid Hawaiian.

"Here, sign fo' dis. And den we gonna talk bizness."

A shocked Ian Clark took the clipboard and scribbled his name. He gave the clipboard to Big K. Big K gave it to the Susan. She gave it to Mike. He gave her the envelope. She gave it to Clark.

"Uh, thanks, uh, Miss, Miss Gardner, would you please hold my calls?"

"That's Garcia, Mr. Clark. I've been here almost a month and you still don't know my name? Well, that does it. I'm going home."

"But its not five - - - "

"I know that but I'm tired of your crap. I quit."

Clark was stunned. Big K snapped him out of it.

"You heard da lady. She goin' home and you goin' back you office. We gots tings to talk about."

"Uh, yeah, sure come on in. Nice to meet you," said Clark, stepping back as Big K walked into his office, followed by Palua, Junior, Richard Black, and a man in a very expensive silk suit. Clark closed the door and walked to his desk. He still needed the other one-point-five to get in the clear so he did a quick mental run-through of the situation.

A day after the call from Cheryl Corlund announcing her resignation, Steve Palua contacted him and was gung-ho to get out to the reef. "We'll have to postpone the June 21 start date, but stay in touch and don't worry, we'll make it happen." But Palua and the Wavelife management team had their hands full dealing with the day-to-day operations of the corporation. He got through only a few times in July while they geared up for taking over the Huntington circus. Now it was late Monday morning and here they were, crapped out, because they hadn't known they'd been playing with loaded dice.

"Well, bad luck with Sonny-boy yesterday," he said, sitting down officiously behind his desk, "I never trusted him myself. I - - -"

"Ian, I'm not interested, so, let me do the talking, ok?" Steve Palua was in no mood for chit-chat about the disaster that could have only been worse had Noaloa's memo been addressed to him personally. But before he could say another word Richard Black cut him off.

"No, Steve, I'm the head of Wavelife, so I'll do the talking."

"No, respectfully, gentlemen, I'll do the talking."

The man looked small compared to Big K and Junior standing behind him, though his slicked back hair and red-tinted sunglasses added to the tone of authority in his perfect English. Clark couldn't pin down the accent, though he surmised Macao or Hong Kong would have been a good guess. One thing he knew for sure: both Steve Palua and Richard Black quickly stepped out of his way.

"Mr. Clark, my name is Parea Anasi. I represent investors with significant holdings in Wavelife International. We are now ready to work with you, but first I need you to describe the terms of the contract you have with Wavelife, all the events leading up to Mr. Heath Larson's accident, and your standing with Wavelife at this point in time. And be precise, please."

He pulled a micro-cassette unit out of his pocket and set it on Clark's desk. The red "record" light was already on.

"Well, I, I, - - -"

"Take your time, Mr. Clark. And speak freely, sir. You are amongst friends." Clark saw Black and Palua looking at the floor. "Junior, step outside and make sure we are not disturbed. Mr. Black, go with him and answer the phone. We certainly don't want to interrupt Geosurf's operations."

Ian Clark couldn't believe how fast Black and Junior got up and followed orders. As they left the room, he took advantage of the distraction to check the computer displays on his desk. His eye caught some movement in copper on the Malaysian market and the Euro was weak against the yen. He began to scribble some numbers.

"Big K, can you help Mr. Clark get started with our conversation? Mr. Palua, sit down, please. Over there."

The Hawaiian grabbed the pencil out of Clark's hand and punched off the power buttons on the computer displays. A minute later, Ian Clark was sitting like a chastened schoolboy in his leather chair in the middle of the floor. Anasi stood near the door leaning against the wall with his hands clasped in front of him.

"Mr. Clark, now, please start at the beginning. I need to make sure we all understand the facts of the matter, starting with L.J. Merrill's call to you from Santiago, Chile."

"How did you know about that?" said Ian Clark in the voice of a man suddenly feeling very ill.

"Mr. Clark, I'm asking the questions, not you."

An hour later, Ian Clark was feeling a lot better. The shock of having to deal with Parea Anasi had worn off once Clark realized there was only one way he was going to get the payoff he had envisioned the moment he'd seen Merrill's footage. For a while Anasi did nothing but listen until Clark tried to fudge some details. Then he was immediately hit with questions that made it clear Anasi already knew everything and was not going to put up with any bullshit. Clark played it straight from then on.

"Mr. Clark, I want to thank you for being candid and forthcoming," said Anasi, "After yesterday's events I can say the group I represent is now very interested in working closely with you to realize the full potential of your original proposal."

"Yes, I too hope to continue working with you, Mr. Anasi. I think we certainly have mutually beneficial interests and Geosurf can do a lot for Wavelife right now."

"Yes, Mr. Clark, I would now like to discuss the immediate future of your role in our business," he said, checking his watch," Mr. Palua, ask Mr. Black to step in and join us. It is almost noon and callers will expect your office to break for lunch."

Palua found Richard Black looking like he'd been trying to change the diapers on a dozen infants simultaneously. It had been a long time since Richard Black had fully understood the realities of front office work.

"Mr. Black, thank you for helping out in a pinch. I'm sure Mr. Clark appreciates your stepping in and solving his unfortunate personnel problem. Now, gentlemen, let me outline our immediate goals.

"One, Mr. Clark, please confirm the *Skyhook* and all equipment ready by the end of the week.

"Two, Mr. Palua, You have spoken highly of the Hawaiian surfers with whom you are associated. Get them ready to assist four of the surfers I added to the payroll. And get the surfers ready, too.

"Three, Mr. Black, you will prepare Wavelife International for bankruptcy proceedings. This evening I will be giving you specific instructions with regard to the position of the investors I represent. Gentlemen, any questions?"

Palua and Black were speechless. Not Ian Clark.

"Regarding my contract, Mr. Anasi."

"Yes, Mr. Clark. Well, as I'm sure your lawyer explained to you, the terms of the contract were quite specific. Only Heath Larson's name was on it, and no other names were added. Mr. Larson is no longer associated with Wavelife International, so it will be quite impossible for you to receive payment as specified by the contract."

Clark didn't know what to say so he tried to play hardball.

"So you're going to stiff me? Is that it?"

"Mr. Clark, though I realize Mr. Larson will not be able to ride a wave for us, I must hold you to the terms of the contract stipulating transfer of ownership of your company. You can talk to your lawyer if you want, but for now, let's try to work something out between us."

Now Clark was past playing hardball.

"Palua! You told me the Larson thing was no problem! You said there were other guys who were going to take his place!"

"Yeah, Clark, we thought a lot of things were going to happen, but as of yesterday, they won't. You can thank your old friends for - - -"

"Gentlemen," said Anasi with unchallenged authority, "Enough of that. Mr. Clark, the investors I represent appreciate the value of the reef to you. When our surfers have ridden their first waves at the reef, you will be compensated with one million dollars. That amount includes transfer of ownership of Geosurf Resorts to - - -"

"NO way! You're shorting me half a million and stealing my company? Do you know how much Geosurf is worth? No fucking way!"

Clark leaped up from his seat. He took a step towards Anasi, but Big K was right there to shove him back down in the chair.

"Mr. Clark, I know how much Geosurf is worth. And I also know why you sold the rights to the reef in the first place, including your problems with the IRS in this country and your problems around the world. Do you want more problems? Do I make myself clear?" he said, walking across the room, and raising his voice to almost a scream, until his face inches from Clark's.

Clark slumped back in his chair, knowing he was trapped. Anasi composed himself, straightened his suit, and looked over at the couch.

"Mr. Palua, you will be in charge of the expedition. Concerning the surfers representing our Asian markets, I understand they do not have experience in big waves, and I expect you to see to it they are given as much training as possible in the short time we have. You will also secure the services of cameramen with appropriate experience. We will use the reef for advertising campaigns in our Asian markets. I will speak to you more extensively on that point tomorrow."

"And the bankruptcy?" asked Richard Black.

"The liquidation of all Wavelife assets is my primary objective. However, the plan to exploit the reef and its inherent value to the company will be retained, as will ownership of Geosurf, by the investors I represent."

"You know, Mr. Anasi, I think I'm beginning to understand your line of thought," said Black, realizing exactly what Anasi was doing.

"Really? No, Mr. Black I didn't know. That is such a quaint habit you have in America. Always saying 'you know', as if by saying it the other person will be convinced of the truth of the statement. But then again, I also hear the word "really" a lot, which in my country is taken as an accusation that the speaker is lying."

Black was put back in his place just that fast.

"Now, Mr. Clark, be sure to contact the seaplane people and inform them of our intent to pursue the terms of the original contract. Mr. Palua, you have your instructions for now. Mr. Black, dinner at eight. My hotel. They do have the best blood rare steaks I've tasted in a long time. Big K, Junior, let's go."

Parea Anasi walked across the room, retrieved the micro recorder, turned and walked to the office door. He stopped just as Big K held it open for him.

"Gentlemen," he said, turning back to look at the three men remaining in the office, "I'll expect full and complete updates every six hours. This is now a hands-on operation, and I expect results."

He clicked stop on the recorder and walked out the door.

Steve Palua, Richard Black and Ian Clark didn't say anything to each other for a long time. Each had pushed his luck, and each had pushed it right over a cliff. There was an odd sense of camaraderie in the room.

"Palua, where the hell did you find that guy?" asked Clark.

"He found me. Six years ago I was selling real estate on the North Shore and he came along and bought a property or two. Next thing you know, he had some larger deals in mind, and things just started growing from there."

"So what's his angle in all this?"

Palua looked at Clark as if he'd just fallen off the turnip truck.

"Well, for starters, you have, or had, all these resorts all over the place. His guys have resorts, too. Now they have even more."

"But what about this marketing stuff?"

"Do I have to spell it out for you?" said Richard Black, "They have interests in large retail chains in Japan, Korea, Malaysia, and, of course, China. Their stores need merchandise and surfer stuff is big. And since it's all made in India, why should all the profits funnel through Newport Beach?"

"Huh?"

"With the market growth in their own backyard, Anasi's investors want to be in control of the entire operation and Cheryl Corlund played right into their hands. Her stunt with Noaloa will put Wavelife in Chapter Seven for sure. That's why we've got to spin off assets."

"Why?"

"So that there's as little as possible left over when the company ends up in bankruptcy court where creditors come first and investors are last in line. So your reef, and Geosurf itself, are the first items out the door."

"And they are going to use the reef for - - - "

"Same as Corlund. Make a big splash as part of a product launch."

"Yeah, but that depended on Larson and Noaloa riding the place!"

"Not anymore. All Anasi needs is photos and footage of his kamikazes riding forty foot waves as a backdrop!"

"But what if they get killed?" asked an incredulous Ian Clark.

"Then he'll build memorial shrines for point-of-purchase displays!"

It was just after five and Ian Clark had finally gotten through to Tina Sanchez. His entire afternoon had been spent being Geosurf's receptionist since the temp agency couldn't get him a new one until the next day. He silently reminded himself to be nice to the next one, though he knew his days in that office were now numbered.

"Tina, we're going to the reef, and right away. Are you ready?"

328

"Of course, Ian. I was waiting for your call. The waverunners are here and the *Skyhook* is perfectly operational, Ian, as per the contract. We're still in business and ready to go."

"Good. Two small revisions to the contract. A new signatory for Wavelife. And there will be four surfers instead of three and a different support team."

"Well, just as long as whoever signs it understands all the terms of the contract, and make sure he knows no more than twelve people."

"The contract's the same, only a Mr. Parea Anasi will be the signing it as your new client. And you'll be working with a Steve Palua."

"Ok, Ian, take care, and get me the contract ASAP," she said, a little worried about him, but still strictly business with a lot of money riding on the contract with Wavelife.

Ian Clark hung up with a sense of relief. All he had to do was get Palua out to the reef, watch a surfer ride a wave, and walk away with a million bucks. He thought about losing Geosurf and realized that wasn't such a bad thing after all. *Heck*, he thought with a wry smile, *maybe I can run a resort for Anasi and work on my golf game.* He began to straighten up his desk before going home. He noticed the Fedex envelope, but he'd had enough surprises for one day and put it on a stack of unopened mail. He put his jacket on and walked toward the door.

"*Oh, hell, wonder what it is.*" He turned around to get the red envelope. Inside it he found another envelope with a strange return address.

"What the fuck is the Order of Southern Ocean Mariners?" he thought.

He read the text of the message – and the initials of its sender.

His heart turned cold and his mind went blank until he connected the return address with why Merrill had used those exact words.

"Cute, L.J., pretty fucking cute," he said in a voice that filled the empty office. But his sarcasm rang hollow in the knowledge that even as Amundsen had waited until he was well on his way before cabling Robert Scott of his intent to be first to the South Pole, Merrill had kept his intentions a secret all these months and must now be already at sea en route to the reef.

Then Ian Clark remembered why Amundsen had won the race to the Pole, having been very prepared and absolutely methodical.

"So what does that make me?" he whispered, remembering the inept organization and hubris that lost Robert Scott the race – and then killed him.

The Long White Wings

The twins were pulling him in opposite directions and the grandfather in the middle could only laugh as he walked with them along the shore, one in the water and one on the sand. The little girl wanted to swim out across the lagoon, her brother pulled hard for exploring in the island's forest, and it was all Taveka could do to keep them in hand – and safe from their own adventurous spirit and curiosity.

"Now where are you taking your me? Shall we go out to the reef? Or in to the forest? Or up here! Now you can see everything!"

He scooped up a child in each arm and put them on his shoulders, still holding on to them carefully so there was no chance they would wiggle free and fall. They giggled in delight now that they were up in the air and could see much more of the world.

A second later he found himself regretting the consequences of his action, or more correctly his nose regretted it.

"Well I can see the two of you agree on something! When its time to go, you go!"

Off in the distance he saw the fleet of Marulean fishermen coming in across the lagoon, with the twins' father in the lead craft.

"Your father's home. We will go to him, and then I have to leave you until tomorrow."

"I was wondering why you were late. This certainly explains it!" said Luan as she saw David's center hull full of fish.

"We checked the commons reef and it was empty. Then I remembered that reef where we went on Easter Sunday - - -"

"Yes, I remember that reef quite well," said Luan, with a deep smile and a surprise for her husband – after his fish story.

"So I made a decision for us: to go there with the idea of shifting our village's fishing commons. And look what we brought back!"

David waved his arm down the beach, where other fishing craft were being off-loaded by the families of the men and women who had voyaged with David. Luan looked impressed - and bided her time.

"Did you go surfing? And how were the waves? As good as they were when we went there? Do you remember that trip, David?"

"I didn't go surfing. Do you see a surfboard? Do I ever go surfing anymore?" David let a little exasperation creep into his tone.

"Yes, David, I know, and I'm sorry you can't surf more," she said sympathetically, knowing there would soon be even less time for her husband to ride waves, "But here comes father with the twins. We better get the fish unloaded before he gets here."

"I know. He has to be going," he said with a tone of resignation.

"What a catch David!" said Luan, trying to cheer him up, "The old commons is empty, yet you find more fish than ever at a place we've never fished before. Did you think you'd be this lucky?"

"Well, I wasn't counting on luck. When we found few fish in the commons reef, some men thought it was because the sea level had gone up again and we hadn't changed the fences. But when we crossed the passage, I kept my hand in the water the entire way, and noticed several streaks of cold water. So I told everyone to sail back out into the channel and follow me."

"And you followed the streaks to our reef!"

"Exactly. Did I ever explain thermal fronts to you?"

"Yes David, I know, remember when you showed me all the electronic units on the *Morning Light* that you don't need anymore? You've come so far David, and I love you so much. And I have to tell you something, but finish your story first."

"Well, that's it, actually. The fish followed the thermal fronts into the lagoon and we got there before they figured out how to escape."

"We'll, that's two great trips you've made out there, and all because my father took a surf spot away from you!" she laughed.

"Don't remind me," he smiled at the memory.

"Well, you do remember that trip, don't you?"

"Yeah, the waves were really good!"

"Don't you remember anything else?"

"No, I went surfing, we came home. Oh, wait a second, I remember. "

"Yes, now you remember," she said, her face flush with a warm glow.

"Yes, you raised the sails all by yourself, and right on time, too!"

The strong Marulean woman pinched him with surprising force.

"Only because you didn't confuse me with your stupid 'helms a-lee' command! No, think, David, what else happened on that trip?"

"Uh, er, it was a nice sunset! We watched a nice sunset, didn't we?"

"Well if that's all we did, then I wonder how this happened."

She took his hand and put it on her stomach.

Their eyes met - and David realized he'd become a father. . . again.

"David! Good fishing I see!"

Taveka set the twins on the sand they wrapped their arms around the legs of a father still in shock over his wife's surprise.

"Thanks for letting me watch them. Is something wrong, David? Luan, is he sick? Luan, you better take care of him. Maybe he hasn't been surfing enough! I must go now," said Taveka smiling at his successor and his wife before turning to walk briskly up the beach.

"And looks like I'm going to be surfing even less!" whispered a man who couldn't have been happier as he kissed the mother of his children.

* * *

331

From the high perch on the ceremonial black rock, Taveka could see his home island in its entirety to the south, surrounded by its barrier reef, broken here and there by passes where the white water was interrupted by deep blue channels. Other reefs, atolls and islands extended to the horizon in all directions. It was his neighborhood, and he knew it well. He had seen it all his life, yet he was fully alert. The wind was blowing across the turquoise channel from the north. Long, low swells came out of the south. Flights of cormorants were circling in the distance. They were following a large school of fish being attacked from below. They were diving for scraps in the feeding frenzy, but they did not warrant Taveka's attention. He was waiting to see the kindred spirit of the navigators, and the great winged glider was a solitary hunter. I'karua always stayed above the fray, foraging on its own terms, its instincts unerring and ancient.

So Taveka continued to scan the horizon for the magnificent bird with the long white wings whose coming would be the signal to begin final preparations for his last voyage to Ka'unua where he would meet his end as gracefully as the wandering albatross soared across the sky.

His concentration was broken, though only for an instant, by the presence of a figure walking along the shore below him. And when he saw who it was, he felt a sense of comfort as Kalala came up to the base of the black platform.

"You're an old man, Taveka. Here, let me give you an extra set of eyes."

"Yes, Kalala, you may be right. Come on up here and we will watch together."

He had known her since childhood. She had been his wife's best friend. She became an elder when he became the navigator for their people. Few words passed between them until they started to joke about a game they played as children trying to be the first to see a particular fish in the lagoon or bird in the sky.

"I was the best in the village!" said the old navigator, laughing.

"Only because I always let you win," said Kalala, with a twinkle in her eye. Taveka responded to the challenge with a good-natured laugh.

"Well then, Kalala, what do you see ten voyager lengths to the south of the fishing grounds of your clan's ancestors?"

Kalala looked to the southeast. She could see the pass through the coral ring, and the change in color from the deep blue of the channel to the bright sandy green of the inner waters. She concentrated for a second, and then longer. For almost a minute she focused carefully on the spot almost two miles away.

"There's nothing there, Taveka. You're just trying to trick me like you always did!" she laughed.

"Ah Kalala, you missed your chance. Now you have no chance. "

'And why is that Taveka?"

"Because I'karua is no longer out there. She is here."

He gently lifted the elder's chin. Above them, circling in spirals on motionless wings, hovered the wandering albatross.

"I will convene the council for dawn tomorrow," said Kalala.

"I will be ready," said Taveka, without a trace of doubt in his voice.

Surfsailing the Agulhas

The open ocean swells were twenty-five feet high out of the southwest every twenty seconds. The *Mother Carie* was aligned bow-first into the wave trains and under half power to maintain her position. Launch conditions were optimal, and Frank Bucher had a green light from Ray Seranen to initiate the first phase of the Roaring Forties Regatta.

"Hey ho up and she rises -
"Hey ho up and she rises -
"Hey ho up and she rises -
"Surfing the Agulhas!"

The crews of the Alba_Swords were singing lustily while putting their backs into turning the capstans connected to a series of pulleys to move their crafts from the cradles in each hull of the *Mother Carie* to the launch zone amidships. The *Serena* was already in position aligned between the two hulls, hanging from overhead cables just above the water line, and pointed aft with her standing rigging locked down in the streamlined, "surfs up" position.

On the horizon, a wall of water appeared, followed by a dozen more.

"Initiate launch sequence," came Frank Bucher's voice over the loudspeakers.

The crew aboard the *Serena* double-checked their control systems and tightened the straps that held them firmly in their seats. They were ready for the takeoff. Now it was all in the timing.

The first swell rolled under the bow of the *Mother Carie* and through the two hulls. The launch support crew saw the *Serena* was still a little too high, so they backed off their capstan half a turn, using the mechanical advantage of the system to precisely lower the *Serena* another three feet to be in perfect position for the next wave. It came under the bow and Bucher sang out.

"Launch!"

The release clamps disengaged. The Alba_Sword dropped into the water ahead of the slope as the wave rolled through the twin hulls. The *Serena* was lifted to the top of the wave and Captain Charles Atkins gave the propulsion units a short burst. She slid down the face and rode the wave between the hulls, under the aft transom bridge, and out to sea. Frank Bucher smiled for just a second. His son was now at sea in the Roaring Forties Regatta.

"Permission to be relieved of duty, Captain?" Bucher said to the *Mother Carie*'s commander.

"Permission granted, Captain Bucher. And good surfing to ye!"

Frank Bucher left the bridge and proceeded to a capstan. There was work to do, and his Alba_Sword was last in line. Captain Adam Buchanan would now direct the launch sequences of the *Eden* from Australia, the *Ostrova* from Russia, the *Chicama* from Peru the *Seeadler* from Germany, and the *Tom Swift* from California.

The morning sun was low on the horizon. After becoming seaborne, each Alba_Sword had submerged to bivouac depth about sixty miles out from the very southern tip of the African continent. The Alba_Swords were maintaining formation and waiting to begin surfsailing the Agulhas Current where the twenty second swell period would shorten to fifteen, pushing twenty-five foot swells into tubing forty footers. The *Mother Carie* was well over the horizon. Once all the Alba_Swords had confirmed their system readiness, the mother hen had left her chicks to fend for themselves until, baring a scrub message from Ray Seranen, they would all rendezvous off the Kerguellen Islands a thousand miles and three days to the southeast.

"All vessels, surface."

The low frequency Morse code message went out from the fleet's flagship, the *Tom Swift*. The six Alba_Swords rose as one after a long set of swells had passed by overhead. The next wave train was fast approaching, but the crews still had time to double check everything.

Then the horizon to the southwest darkened. A large wall of deep blue water flecked with spray was moving towards the formation at about thirty miles an hour. The vessels were about fifty yards apart, their bows pointed to the east. The swell lifted them all simultaneously. About halfway up the slope of the forty foot swell, six captains hit their thrusters, and the Roaring Forties Regatta was officially under way.

"Can I get an engineering report, please?" asked Charles Atkins.

"Got it right now, Captain," said his wife, Margo, a fully-certified Alba_Sword systems engineer and aboard the *Serena* for the third time in a Roaring Forties Regatta.

"Go."

"From bow to stern all systems integrity confirmed within specs. Nose cone sensor data stream and fleet network operational. Bandwidth capacity usage twenty-two percent. Pectoral hydraulics at full pressure. Hydrofoil deployment within spec. Forward impellers generating forty two p.s.i. per sec. Propulsion system pressurization on automatic. Forward tanks at capacity. Pectoral lateral thruster velocities within spec. Forward trim and ballast transfer times within spec. Standing rigging pressure point sensors all reporting. We need to deploy in adverse conditions to complete report."

"Execute within the hour. Signal fleetcom our intent."

"Roger that. Continuing report. Main thruster system end-to-end report as follows. Main impellers at ninety five p.s.i."

"What about the - - -"

"Mr. Bucher, do not speak unless spoken too, thank you!"

"But - - -"

She elbowed him playfully, except she made sure it hurt a little.

"Never interrupt a lady, young man, it can be dangerous to your health! Now, where was I? Main Pectoral control response times, within spec."

Bucher and Charles Atkins smiled. She had skipped an item on the list, but it would come up later in the guidance and control section of her report. Some engineers designed their report sequentially bow to stern, others from the helm outward, and the Germans had come up with a concentric analysis process. The Alba_Sword was so completely integrated that it could be viewed in several different ways, all equally valid, almost like the application of differing medical philosophies to taking a physical.

Margo Atkins spent another five minutes going through her checklist. Everything was up to spec. There were no anomalies to report. The wave train was beginning to feel the opposing force of the current, and everyone was ready for "cruise mode" to end. The Serena was up to speed, and the Agulhas was dead ahead.

"Hey L.J.! It's blowing offshore!"

"No it isn't, Jack. The northeast wind is blowing straight against the southwest swell. Since we're entirely offshore and out in the ocean, the wind isn't blowing offshore. If the wind was behind us and following up on the swell, that would still be an offshore wind. The wind is blowing against the faces of the seas - - -"

"You mean the waves."

"Jack, we've gone through this time and again. We're mariners, and we call 'em seas, not waves. We're riding a sea right now, not a wave."

"Ok, but we're surfing! Nobody surf's a sea. And if the wind was at our backs, that is a following wind. If it's in our faces - - -"

"Jack, what's the big deal, man? You already know all this!"

"Yeah, but this is the real thing!"

"Jack, it was the real thing every weekend for the last two months!"

"C'mon, L.J., we're not running up and down the coast of California. We're not in the Channel. We're ten thousand miles from home and getting further away all the time! I'm just excited, is all, L.J. Humor me."

"Jack, we're on watch in a minute. Let's continue this on the bridge, ok?"

"Ok, it's not offshore because we're offshore. They are seas not waves, and I'm having the time of my life out here!"

"For what you paid for it, I hope so."

"Please L.J., let's not talk about money."

"Huh? Could you say that again? Did I hear you correctly? Isn't your name John Arthur Richards - - -"

"Watch change!" said Frank Bucher. Tak Kurosawa and Chip Bell came down through the hatch leading to the bridge.

"How's it going, guys! Hope you're not too stoked right now, cause if you are, you're gonna explode up there!" advised a very animated Chip Bell.

"Red watch, where the hell are you guys?"

The conversation ended abruptly. No one wanted to be on the bad side of the Captain, ever, on any ship, throughout the history of the seven seas. Aboard an Alba_Sword was no exception.

"Merrill, take the helm. Richards co-pilot. Execute."

The able-bodied passengers did exactly as they were told. L.J. Merrill slid into the helmsman's seat from the starboard side as Frank Bucher vacated to port. It had been practiced endlessly back in California, and Merrill had it wired. He had to, as did they all. There was no room for error in controlling an Alba_Sword on a wave the size of three story building.

"Ok, boys, I'm going below. She's all yours. Oh, and Merrill, try not to sink her this time, ok?"

The three men laughed at the reference to the shakedown cruise. After months of training and dozens of simulated emergencies, Frank Bucher knew his passengers were ready for the challenges ahead.

After an hour Jack Richards took the helm and for the first time in months, L.J. Merrill could finally let his guard down a little. It took almost twenty minutes to let go of the focus required at the helm, and he still had to remain alert as Richards' co-pilot. But the fleet was in formation, all system checks had been performed, all the maneuverability tests passed, and Richards had turned out to be a better pilot than anyone expected.

The wind was blowing straight against them. The Tom Swift was at one end of the formation. The wave was beginning to subside since the leading swell of a wave train was always decaying while the physics of wave motion dictated the slow appearance of a new wave at the end of the train. Before the watch was over, the entire formation would execute a loop to pick up a stronger wave two or three swells behind them. But for now, everything was steady state, and L.J. Merrill let his mind wander, like an albatross foraging across the trackless ocean, gliding on wave after wave, sometimes for a few seconds, sometimes for minutes. He floated above the events that had brought him to this point in his life and if he was mind-surfing his ocean.

The headland in Western Australia. The handshake with Clark. The library in Fiji. The porthole of the turbo-prop. His surfboards in the dumpster. His parents. The video camera under his bed. The Chapel. The crash of his high on a moonlit night in the Santa Barbara Channel. Standing next to Jack Richards hearing that they'd been accepted.

He slouched in his seat, and gazed to starboard. The other five Alba_Swords were all in cruise mode. He remembered what one of the Aussies had told him during training.

"Aye, Merrill, it's a great feelin' I tell ya, when all yer gotta do is let 'er glide forward, mate. Ya know she's ready for anything! Ya got the wind in yer face, massive energy at yer back, moving ya through space without any effort by you, yer shipmates, or the ship beneath yer feet. Yup, you'll be lovin' it the first toyim, mate! But then you'll forget all it took ya ta git there. Ya relax a bit too much. Ya start wishin' for something ta happen, mate. And when it does, yer always a bit surprised. Ain't that life all over, fair dinkum!"

"Mr. Merrill, what depth?"

Jack Richards had noticed a change in the handling of the *Tom Swift*. The wind was blowing more spray skyward. Forward speed had been reduced, yet the wave was now becoming noticeably more vertical.

"200 meter contour – continental shelf up ahead."

"Prepare to receive exact surfsailing instructions. We're coming into it."

"Aye-aye sir. Notifying watch below."

L.J. Merrill smiled at the exchange with Jack Richards, who smiled back, both feeling the energy of their friendship, born of need, fired by trial, scarred by contention, and now worthy of trust. Merrill shifted out of his seat and opened the deck hatch a fraction.

"Captain! Helm reporting sea-change!"

"Aye-aye, Merrill. Blue watch, follow me to the cockpit. Red watch, stay up there. You'll want to see this." Within minutes all five men were squeezed into the cockpit and it was time to get down to business.

"Where's the *Eden*?" asked Frank Bucher.

"Chasing the *Ostrova*, of course. They're about ten miles back. Picked up one of our albatross guides and decided to follow her while she forages."

"Tube rides?"

'Three. Even a doubleup for the *Ostrova*. Those guys are laying into it, that's for sure."

"Well Tak, good for them, but shall we show 'em how its done?"

"Aye-aye, Captain."

Chip Bell was riding shotgun to Tak's piloting, keeping an eye on the display showing the sea-surface topography for twenty miles all around them. In consort with the nosecone sensors in the other five Alba-Swords, the fleet shared a three dimensional, real time map of the sea state all around them as all the computers on the Alba_Sword exchanged information simultaneously. Bell was studying the sets ahead and astern to determine where the energy was focusing as the wave trains collided with the Agulhas Current. He knew what Bucher wanted to do, and he soon spotted just the place to do it.

"Tak, get us to port on my mark. Tight trim for about a minute. Then pull out and we'll jump wave to wave back out of this set. Frank, there's a big peak in the next set behind us. Just what you are looking for."

"Thanks, Chip. Gentlemen, everyone strapped in tight?"

Jack Richards and L.J. Merrill nodded as if they were about to leave the loading zone of the heaviest roller coaster anyone could ever imagine.

"Mark!"

Tak Kurosawa laid her over into a sharp turn. The Alba_Sword's starboard pectoral hydrofoil extended, the inside fin bit deep, and the *Tom Swift* came around on a dime. He went high for a bit of speed, and then down to the trough for another bottom turn. He touched the thrusters for two seconds, and off they went, charging down the line trimmed up high and tight against the wall of water forty feet high propelling them forward.

Richards and Merrill were about to get their first taste of the power and speed of an Alba_Sword in full flight. Bucher turned around and grinned from ear to ear.

"Ok, Jack, time to start giving you your money's worth. Take every tube you've surfed, roll 'em all into one, and I've got you covered in about two minutes. That's confirmed, Chip?"

"Affirmative, Frank. Here, take a look."

Bell hit a button and the infrared image on his display was duplicated on the inside of the cockpit dome for all to see. He used a pointer on his screen to show the crew of the *Tom Swift* where they were going.

"There she is. Could be the wave of the day. And looks like we'll be riding her three up."

Two small icons were moving across the display coming in from different directions and obviously headed towards the same wave. The *Chicama* and the *Seeadler* had been soloing on the same set as the *Swift*. Once they saw the *Swift* change course, they quickly saw the wave Bell had identified and read Bucher's mind perfectly.

"Oh man, are those guys gonna be on it, too?" asked L.J. Merrill.

'Sure, why not? These are not one-man tubes, or one-boat, I should say. C'mon, L.J., this is the fun part!"

L.J. Merrill smiled, a bit chagrined that, though the days as the lone surf scout were well behind him, he still had to get used to sharing the stoke of surfing freely without reservation.

"Kick out to port on my mark. Mark!"

Kurosawa hit the thrusters and brought the helm over. The *Tom Swift* went up the steep wall and came completely out of the water, all except her two rear stabilizers. She set down and immediately jetted towards the next wave in the set.

She went up the moving wall, banked off a graybeard cascade of white water, carved a bottom turn, and then another kickout. Kurosawa's rhythm was perfect. They covered hundreds of yards in seconds. He repeated the process for the last two waves of the set. They came down easy after the last one and saw the Peruvians and the Germans coming up behind them into the flat zone between sets. All three Alba_Swords were in the right place at the right time.

The next set was maybe a third again as big as the swells they had been riding. In the set, the fourth wave looked to be the one they wanted. The current rushing against it was pushing up peaks like a row of pyramids as far down the wall of the wave as the eye could see.

The Alba_Swords came into formation as the captains of the *Chicama* and the *Seeadler* let the *Tom Swift* take the lead. Though nobody in OSOM ever claimed priority when it came to riding waves in the Roaring Forties, everyone was happy to defer to Frank Bucher on a wave like this, knowing he was always good for a lesson or two when it came to surfsailing the Agulhas.

The *Tom Swift* jetted forward, her crew pushed back into their seats. Kurosawa now had the peak in his sights. A check turn to port, then a hard carve to starboard. The swell rose up behind them and the *Swift* stalled a little until she was within ten feet of the peak. Kurosawa paused for a moment of rest at the top, then a touch on the thrusters, and down she went like a big rig truck on the first hill of a roller coaster. Richards and Merrill were completely terrified. The *Swift* was going about sixty miles an hour at a fifty degree angle, the pectorals retracted for maximum speed. They didn't know what was going to happen next, but when they saw Bucher and Bell already leaning over, they quickly followed suit, using their legs to gimbal the seats at the most severe angle possible against the g-forces just as the *Swift* came to the trough. Kurosawa hit it on the button and the controls responded perfectly. The starboard pectoral fully extended and the *Swift* shot forward into a waiting cavern almost fifty feet high from top to bottom. He slowed her down a touch, and the sky disappeared above the *Tom Swift*.

Jack Richards and L.J. Merrill were awestruck tourists entering a cathedral. The roof folded over the Alba_Sword. The tunnel did not stay open for more than a few seconds, but it was long enough for the *Tom Swift* to squeeze through perfectly.

"Jack, L.J.! Take a look astern!" said Frank Bucher.

The wave re-formed, and another crest came over, collapsed, and spit out the *Chicama*. Ten seconds later it did it again, and out came the Germans. A triple tube, and everyone made it with room to spare, all on the same wave.

"Formation, Tak?"

"Yup, let the Germans lead. Frank, semaphore, if you please!"

Bucher tapped out the code for reverse field, tail boat becomes lead, execute at will. The bright semaphore light on the *Tom Swift* blinked on and off in a short series of dots and dashes. Confirming signals came immediately from the other Alba_Swords. The *Seeadler* turned hard back to starboard, followed almost simultaneously by the *Chicama* and the *Tom Swift*.

The wave was a monster almost four miles long, with peaks coming over and creating large caverns that enveloped the three boats time after time. For the next forty five minutes, the Alba_Swords went back and for the shredding the wave. Once or twice a boat was a little late on entry, resulting in a very wet exit. But forward momentum saved the day every time.

"Well, I wonder where they've been?" said Kurosawa.

The *Serena* suddenly pulled into the formation behind the Germans.

"Typical surfers! Always late!" laughed Chip Bell.

But Charles Atkins was having the last laugh as he signaled, "You shoulda been here an hour ago!"

Now there were four Alba_Swords carving turns and finding tunnels all up and down the line of a wave sixty feet high and three miles across. The Agulhas Current never stopped, and the wave continuously re-formed again and again until, after almost an hour, the swell began to lose some strength as subsequent waves in the train gained power and momentum.

"Gentlemen, anybody getting hungry?"

Frank Bucher felt it was time to grind and get in a nap before the afternoon session. Then it would be time for the able-bodied passengers to take a turn at the controls and see what kind of surfing they could do in a realm most surfers couldn't even dream of.

'Roger, that, Captain, unless someone wants to give it a go right now?" said Tak Kurosawa, directing his comments to L.J. Merrill and Jack Richards.

"Thanks, but we can wait till our watch this afternoon," said L.J.

"Yeah, I never thought I'd say it, but I've had enough tube rides for the moment," laughed Jack Richards.

"Signaling the formation," said Frank Bucher.

Five minutes later, all four vessels were submerged inside the body of a fifty-footer, riding the core energy like broadbill swordfish. Inside each Alba_Sword, there was just the barest sensation of motion and indeed it was somewhat quiet except for the booming of the wave breaking again and again, and the focused conversations of the crews methodically re-counting the high points of their morning session of surfsailing the Agulhas. Specific maneuvers and tube rides were the topics, and the banter of good-natured, yet constructive criticism left everyone ready for more that afternoon.

"You know what that reminded me of, Frank?"

"Kinda like Waikiki or something, Jack?"

"Yeah, or San Onofre, or that place up in Ventura, what's it called?"

"Yeah, Armandos."

"That place. One wave, tons of turns, sections, this way, that way, reforming, getting steep, backing off."

"But with twenty times the size, ten times the speed, and ride a wave for an hour, not a minute!" said L.J. Merrill.

The lowering sun was astern of the fleet, shining directly into the spray of the seas ahead. Richards and Merrill had surfed all afternoon, and now they could see dozens of rainbows in the spray ahead of them, lifting out of the back of the waves, dying and reforming to create a fantastic panorama with no equal anywhere else on earth. The six Alba_Swords had reformed into a delta formation on three waves, with the Aussies in the lead, followed by the two California boats, and the Peruvians, Germans, and Russians coming up behind. The formation was spread out across half a mile, and the rear boats could sometimes see the ones ahead sailing through the rainbow arcs. The symbolism was not lost on the mariners. It had been a rare day of perfect conditions in the Agulhas, and they were scheduled for more during the next forty eight hours.

Captain Cooper of the *Eden* signaled for fleet submersion. She peeled off her wave, did a large loop, and joined up with the second file. Cooper signaled her intent to repeat the maneuver. Both the California boats concurred. The three all looped out of their wave, timing their arcs to synch up with the following wave and insert themselves into perfect trim matching the speed of the *Chicama*, the *Seeadler*, and the *Ostrova*.

All six Alba_Swords were now on the same wave as the sun lowered behind them and the rainbows became fainter. There were two waves in the set behind them. On signal from the Aussies, all six looped back one wave, rode it for a hundred yards, and then looped back one more.

They were on the last wave of the set, and the next wave train was almost five miles behind them. A final signal from the Aussies, and the fleet of the Roaring Forties Regatta extended their forward pectoral units while beginning to fill their ballast tanks. The six Alba_Swords came to a rest and then, one by one, slowly submerged. By the time the next set of waves came through, the fleet was snug for the night after a day of surfsailing at its best.

Jack Richards and L.J. Merrill knew they'd just had a day of surfing unlike anything they'd ever known, but in contrast to the aftermath of countless surf sessions during years gone by, they were not chattering away about their experience. The silence of their shipmates was an reminder to the greenhorns that an unspoken tradition had to be upheld. To talk too much about their good luck and what they'd just experienced, or worse, to hope they'd be just as lucky tomorrow, was to incur a sailor's jinx that the seven seas never failed to inflict upon the greedy.

Throughout the fleet, the crews were all just as quiet, and no one dared speak of what the morrow might bring, one way or another. two men, however, though keeping the tradition like all the other mariners, were indeed pondering the future. The captains of the *Serena* and the *Tom Swift* were no less exhilarated by the day they'd just had, but both Charles Atkins and Frank Bucher were thinking about what might await them if Ray Seranen could determine the true extent of the power building over Antarctica.

Humility and Cunning

"Hey Bruddah, dis tool no work!"

"Speak English, Wilson! How many times I gotta tell you, dis is not da Westside, brah! You want me call you mom?"

Bruddah hated to invoke the mother's name, but somehow they had to cure the son of his self-imposed speech impediment. Sonny-boy rolled his eyes, but he got the message.

"According to your instructions, the specs call for a 13 mm and a torque capacity of 125 foot pounds. You gave me a 9/16 and a breaker bar."

"Sorry, 'bout dat. A 9/16 is da same a 13 mm, but you right on the breaker bar. Ok, we ask Clem. He know what to do."

Bruddah and Sonny-boy were working under one wing of the *Aeolus*, the silver and blue Catalina PBY once owned by Clem Charleton but now renamed after he had donated it to the Mother Ocean Foundation. The two Hawaiians were mounting the electric winches for the jetskis, as were Heath Larson and Roberto Mercante under the other wing. Clem Charleton had drawn up a set of rough plans and a sequence of steps that were easy to follow. Everyone was hard at work. They were on a mission, and there was no time to lose.

Charleton was working on the modifications to the landing gear for two more waverunners and not having an easy time of it. Mac Owens had already worked out the entire system, but since he had been working under the Wavelife contract at the time, Cheryl Corlund nixed any communication between Charleton and his old friend on exactly how to get the job done. She was not taking any chances. She was under no illusions as to who was in control of Wavelife and how rough they could play, both in and out of court. She knew the entire Mother Ocean initiative, born of altruism, was going to require a lot of humility – and cunning.

They had leased a hangar on the base at Pearl Harbor through Clem Charleton's old Navy contacts. To maintain secrecy, they never left the base even though the surf media knew something was up and was trying to get a story. But they never talked to anyone except when, from time to time, a few World War Two veterans stopped by to reminisce about flying the fabled Catalina all over the Pacific.

The tales they told were sobering, and Heath Larson in particular asked a lot of questions. The old flyers were living history, and the answers were sometimes accompanied by faraway looks.

"Hell, there is nothing you can do when you can die any second," said one, "So you find yourself thinking of your buddies. And when one of them gets it, sometimes you wish it had been you instead of him."

That kind of selflessness further revised Larson's understanding of existentialism, of "being in and for yourself", after having a long discussion with Ben Jeffries about Kierkegaard in the library of the *Aeolusean*. Heath had come to realize brotherhood is the only way a man can truly find honor in life, and though the old flyers may not have been philosophers, their wisdom was timeless. But there were limits to his sensitivities when it came to his fellow man, and he was not about to tell Bruddah and Sonny-boy that the tool they needed was already spoken for – until Clem Charleton forced his hand.

"Well, if ya need a torque wrench, ya need a torque wrench. An' I know we got one, and I don' have it. So if ya can't find one, well, ya'll capable young men. You'll figger it out."

"They have it!"

"That's right, Wilson! And you can have it when we're done with it," said Larson from the other side of the fuselage.

"Y'all heard the man, Bruddah. Say, while yer waitin' can ya gimme a hand with this side mount? Sumtin' ain't right."

"What's the problem Clem? You're a capable old man. You'll figure it out!" said Roberto Mercante.

Everyone laughed as Bruddah and Noaloa went over to help him. Larson and Mercante stopped what they were doing to join them and offer their two cents worth of advice.

"I know this is 'posed ta fit, but she just ain't cooperatin'."

"Maybe you had the bracket welded wrong," said Mercante.

"Well, if you ask me, your problem is the geometry of the struts."

Four surprised faces turned to Sonny-boy Noaloa."

"The design was calculated for the weight of the tires, not a waverunner. So retract the gear about 30%, and you'll have no problems."

Charleton stared at the mounting bracket and smiled.

"Hot damn, I bet you're right!"

"C'mon, Bruddah, let's get back to work and show da haoles how we get a job done island-style!"

Noaloa turned and walked away from the group. Bruddah exchanged looks with Larson and Mercante.

"Comin' Mr. Noaloa. Be right there, sir!" laughed Bruddah.

The men worked for the rest of the afternoon, sweating in the humidity of Hawai'i in August. The euphoria of Sonny-boy's "rescue" at Huntington Beach was long gone. They knew they had to get to the real reef as quickly as possible and m. ake good on their intentions to build a new breed of apparel company. They had to prove that the memo hanging from the pier was not just a one-time stab at the status quo. They had to come back quick and strong both in the water and the marketplace.

* * *

Six thousand miles away, it was just as humid and even more uncomfortable. Cheryl Corlund and Dolly Artensa were sourcing contractors from the ground up in the garment district in New York, and Seventh Avenue was a brutal as ever. For years Corlund had been out of touch with the bedrock grind of contracting for raw materials, cutting patterns, sewing garments and shipping them out the door. Those things never changed in the apparel business even if the business plan was radically different. Dolly Artensa had convinced her that schools are not the place for fashion statements. Clothes could be a lot of fun, but not at the expense of an academic and self-development environment, especially from Kindergarten through eighth grade. The Foundation's first goal was to go after that market niche with refreshing styles and colors, backed by positive advertising campaigns promoting the inner character, and not the external and fad driven reality, of children and young teenagers. To do that, they found their own character being tested again and again.

"I bet we could do a lot of this in L.A.," said Dolly Artensa, standing just outside a non-descript building that housed one of New York's largest clothing contractors.

"Of course we could, Dolly. Then again, we could always just go to China and get it over with, right?"

Corlund knew this was exactly the moment when capitalism confronted altruism, when it's a hundred and five and the humidity is a hundred percent and it all comes down to the flowering idealism of human values trying to mesh with the squeezing vise of price points. But she was determined to go back to the surf industry with a company like TierraDelFuego, which built up a very successful record in sales and social activism, donating one percent of its gross revenues to non-profit organizations. The only difference between TDF and Corlund's company was the former gave significant amounts of money to non-profit organizations whereas the Mother Ocean Foundation was a publicly-traded non-profit organization. It was a revolutionary business model, but given the success of investment funds that funneled money into socially responsible corporations, Corlund and Ben Jeffries felt the time had come to take it to a new and innovative level. As the founder of TDF had once said, "I never failed to make money being a good corporate citizen."

"But we're staying in country. We're not going to China. We can pay a decent wage to people right here if we do this right, and we will."

"Say no more, Cheryl. Ok, who's next?"

Corlund looked across the street and realized they were close to where her limousine had been stopped by the blizzard back in January.

"It's almost lunch, but let's try and get just one more out of the way. Who knows, maybe we'll get lucky."

345

There was no turning back now, although both certainly wished they could duck into the next subway station and get back to their hotel. Haggling with veteran garmentos in New York was exhausting, what with the shouting, histrionics, and negotiating for half-an-hour over something as simple as the number of loops per hole in each button. They always left on friendly terms, but so far only one of the four shops they'd visited would get their business. It was not an easy reintroduction to the realities of their industry.

Then providence stepped in for a second. Waiting to dodge traffic and jaywalk across the street, Dolly Artensa spotted a familiar figure getting out of a cab a half-block away. Cheryl Corlund was looking the other way and was about to cross the street when Artensa pulled her back abruptly.

"What are you doing?" said Corlund with some irritation in her voice.

Artensa pointed down the street.

"Shouldn't we go say hello?"

An instant later the two women were striding directly up to a graying man about to go into the building of one of the garment industry's most powerful money lenders.

"Bart Thomas! Good to see you! What are you doing down here?"

"Hello Cheryl, Dolly. I just might be asking you the same thing. That was quite a stunt with Sonny-boy and the seaplane, Cheryl. You know Wavelife is now headed for bankruptcy thanks to you."

"No way, Bart!" said Corlund, genuinely surprised, "You guys have got a lot going for you. Steve's a little green, but I'm sure you'll be able to get him on track. That was only one contest, and Sonny-boy is only one surfer. No biggie, Bart."

"It was, Cheryl. You know how much money it costs to put out the fall line. I gotta talk to the boys and they'll be asking twenty-eight points cause the banks won't touch us now 'cause the goddam surf media says we ain't cool anymore. Hell, we were cool last week! Surfers! You can have 'em!" said Thomas, suppressing a laugh.

"Well, Mr. Thomas, I guess we can agree on one thing. Trying to do business with the media on your back is a no-win proposition."

"Yeah, but you didn't have to jump ship that fast!"

"Oh yes she did," said Artensa, "You know there was no other way with her being barbequed in the press. Just because you guys blew it by letting Palua run the show doesn't mean Wavelife can't recover."

"Maybe you're right, but that ain't gonna happen. Palua's investment group is calling the shots, and I - - - "

Thomas realized he had just said something he wished he hadn't. Cheryl Corlund pretended she didn't notice, but of course she had.

"Now, Bart, we've worked together before. And had things been allowed to move forward, we would have still been working together. And who knows, maybe we'll get the chance to do so in the future. We are going to need some help with our new company, and we're looking to manufacture in country. Your specialty."

"Yeah, I heard you were up to something, but honestly Cheryl, I've got my hands full right now, and I couldn't get involved with anything attached to you."

"And you'd rather be working for Palua's people? That's not like you at all Bart. Since when does a New Yorker take orders from guys in aloha shirts sitting under palm trees?"

He had been looking Corlund straight in the eye. But her statement hit home, and he glanced away.

"See ya 'round, Cheryl. You too, Dolly."

Bart Thomas turned sideways and slid between the two women. On the streets of New York, sometimes being rude didn't really mean all that much, and the ladies didn't take it personally. There was compassion in their eyes as they watched the garment industry veteran walk through the doors of a lions' den on Seventh Avenue.

"Blaming you for his problems? That's not like him at all."

"He must be in a tight spot with Palua's people."

"And we were so close to buying them out."

"Maybe they'll take themselves out. And maybe Bart Thomas can be a part of it."

Corlund thought for a second.

"Remind me to call Ben during lunch, and Aleja, too."

"What about lunch? An army moves on its stomach, Cheryl!"

"We've still got that last call to make. Running into Bart Thomas was a one-in-a-million. We can't count on always being so lucky."

* * *

"Ok, hit the starboard switch, Roberto!" said Clem Charleton.

A head popped out of the cockpit window.

"Say, can you remind me which one is which. Port is right 'cause it has 'r' and 't' in the - - - "

Oily rags flew in his direction from four men all standing around a big jetski attached to cables descending from a wing. An electric motor engaged, slack was taken up, and the waverunner was lifted off the ground with surprising speed.

"Hold it!" The waverunner stopped.

"Give it three touches, Roberto!" said Heath Larson. The waverunner jerked upwards two inches at a time.

"Ok, strap the hold downs underneath her, guys!"

Sonny-boy Noaloa and Bruddah grabbed the web straps and crossed them under the waverunner to cinch them down on the wing supports.

"Ok, that's it. We're good all around," said Heath Larson, the acting loadmaster for the *Aeolus*.

"Yup, gonna do some flight trials tomorrah," said Clem Charleton.

347

"Yeah, and we go back Maui side get da locator set up. No want mo' problems finding anybody dis time!" said Bruddah.

"You know, somewhere between being humble and being smart, we just might make this whole thing work," said Larson.

"Well, you be da humble guy, brah, since dat one kine wave almost drown you big time. As for myself, I am going to demonstrate the advantages of strategy and research towards accomplishing the specific objectives of my new surfing career by executing - - -"

Three men stared at the speaker, and in a second a fast and nimble former world champion was being chased around the hangar by four men intent on teaching the kid a lesson to never mouth off to his elders. If they could ever catch him.

K2 - The Second Katabatic

Ray Seranen closed the thick oak door behind him. Normally he would have been looking forward to a good day's work. This morning, however, his daily ritual had done nothing for his peace of mind.

After the Agulhas sessions, there was a lot of excitement aboard the Alba_Swords and even more anticipation of continuing their surfsailing voyage around the Southern Ocean. Seranen's warning to Bucher about a possible scrub had come to naught, and Bucher saw no reason to deviate from their original plans. They were now on course southeast toward the Kerguellen Islands to a rendezvous with the *Mother Carie*. The mariners of the Roaring Forties Regatta were stoked.

Ray Seranen was not stoked.

The first katabatic had surprised him. The data from Seranen's early warning sensors around the world had reported a buildup of emissions, heat and particulate material in the atmosphere. Based on that input, his program should have triggered a warning of the event that had destroyed AWS-81.77 at Dome Argus. No such warning had been produced. Something was wrong somewhere, and Ray Seranen couldn't put his finger on it. Even after the solar storms had unexpectedly subsided, and all the communication channels were back to normal, things weren't adding up. Over the past forty-eight hours, his hot spot sensors were reporting skyrocketing levels of heated gaseous emissions, and still no forecast. There was only one conclusion to be drawn from the situation. There was a bug in OSOM's Antarctic Meteorological Network weather prediction model. He looked up at a picture on the wall of Grace Hopper, the patron saint of computer programmers who had de-bugged the ENIAC back in 1948 by walking inside the room-sized computer and finding a moth stuck between two metal contacts. Now Ray Seranen had to de-bug his system, and with the Alba_Sword fleet headed to rendezvous with the *Mother Carie*, he didn't have much time.

Six hours later, his bulletin board was covered with flow charts and the source code binder on the desk surrounded by print-outs. Copies of some sub-routines were tacked up in their place on the flow charts. He had mapped out the territory, found the areas he needed to focus on, and separated them out from the binder to examine them closely. He was like a spelunker going down into a cave, burrowing into the dense computer code layer by layer.

He took a lunch break around three, sitting out on the deck overlooking the canyon. It was a scorching day in the hills above Montecito, and feeling a bit drowsy after eating, he took a short nap in a hammock swinging in the shade under a California live oak. When he came to, his cleared mind caught a quick glimpse of the bug he was looking for. He was able to hold the thought just long enough to remember where it had come from: a story he'd once heard about a NASA moonshot in the early 60s.

Just after liftoff, the rocket targeted for the moon changed course and headed for Miami. It was immediately destroyed out over the Atlantic, and the error was eventually traced to Mission Control's guidance computer. It saw a (-), intended by programmers to be interpreted as a minus sign, but compiled by the computer as an ( ). Since that character was not allowed in that section of the code, the computer locked up, the rocket lost guidance, and the whole shebang went haywire.

He swung out of his hammock and within minutes was scrutinizing the series of sub-routines involved in katabatic event forecasts. He found one subroutine whose actions were entirely predicated on the (-) being interpreted properly. He ran a quick simulation of the subroutine. He did not get the expected results. He found the (-) in the code. He replaced the (-) sign with a ( ). Still didn't work. He put the minus back in. It worked.

He re-ran the subroutine twice more. No problems. He immediately initiated a full data run with sensor input from around the world during the previous forty-eight hours. Despite the massive processing power of his mini-mainframe, it was almost half an hour before a page of data came out of the printer. A quick scan of its contents sent Seranen to the sparks station without a moment's hesitation.

A second katabatic was going to be triggered on Dome Argus in less than two hours. The directional vector of the katabatic was unknown, but the wind would be blowing for at least twenty hours and possibly much longer at speeds up to two hundred and fifty miles per hour. It would definitely reach the Antarctic coast with enough destructive power to destroy anything man-made it its path.

"ANTMETNET ALERT LVL 10. K2 8177 <2hr. 175<WIND<250. VECTOR-?. 20H<DUR<-?."

Seranen was not given to hyperbole and rarely, if ever, sent anything of a personal nature when pure data was the only requirement. This time, however, he added a personal touch.

SHE IS COMING AND SHE IS COMING ON STRONG. SHE WILL KICK DOWN DOORS. ONLY GOD KNOWS WHATS NEXT. RS.

The dots and dashes took mere seconds to travel six thousand miles to Antarctica over OSOM's narrow band network. More seconds elapsed while Damon Waiya turned Morse Code into text. A minute later, all the winter-over stations around Antarctica received an unprecedented warning to batten down.

The column of wind spiraled in like a dive bomber out of control and slammed into the ice of Dome Argus. The wind mushroomed back up into itself, paused for a moment of stasis, and then avalanched outward across the ice like a river bursting through a dam. Half an hour later, Damon Waiya saw an icon on the display turn from green to yellow. It was the AWS closest to Dome Argus. He overlaid a transparent template on the display, tracing a

350

precisely calculated curved path, based on hundreds of katabatic events recorded by OSOM's network, from the point where the first AWS had been destroyed through the yellow icon. Waiya paused for a second, and looked at the predicted path. Then the yellow icon turned red. He began typing immediately.

"SOUTH POLE. KATABATIC VECTOR YOUR DIRECTION."

Then he went over to the VHF radio equipment to contact the Pole by voice. As he did so, he saw the AWS icon go from red to black and the next one in line for the Pole turn yellow.

Forty hours after the K2 hit the Pole, the mighty katabatic began to weaken. A damage assessment team shoveled its way out through the snow blocking most of the entrances to the old geodesic dome. They emerged to clear skies and mild breezes. It was a pleasant surprise. What they saw next was not. Steel towers were twisted like pretzels. Big snow cats were flipped over and upside down. And the South Pole's hundred million dollar research center, built to withstand twice the strongest winds ever recorded at the Pole, looked like the path of a hurricane through a trailer park.

By the time it reached the coast, the katabatic had spread out like a nautilus shell with a mouth three hundred miles wide. There it began to merge into a passing storm moving slowly across the Southern Ocean but in perfect position to receive the massive power predicted by Ray Seranen's models. Within six hours, an uninterrupted river of raw power, born of the excesses of an industrialized planet, began to strengthen the storm's winds. After twelve hours, what had been a typical Force One storm began to expand, and after another six hours, it had metastasized into a monstrous Force Five. Even as the battle between Man and Nature was still raging in a tornado-like column ten thousand feet high over Antarctica, the emboldened storm began to build up its first swells on an entirely new wavelength. The system was pushed eastward by the katabatic forcefeeding massive amounts of energy into the spinning low. Soon the center of the storm was trailing a wave-production zone longer and more powerful than any fetch ever recorded, like a comet trailing a spectacular tail. Only there was nothing beautiful about what the wind was doing to the sea – until the raw swells began to radiate out from their violent birthplace and emerge past the boundaries of the storm.

Throughout the entire event, Ray Seranen's computers had been fed a steady diet of data thanks to OSOM's network of weather stations and buoys. He compiled the entire data set into a swell generation model, and by the time the winds over Antarctica finally subsided, the storm was broadcasting well-organized bands of energy into the longest and most massive wave trains ever recorded in the history of the Southern Ocean, exactly as predicted.

The de-bugged program worked flawlessly, and Seranen knew the results would be good news for Frank Bucher.

* * *

LP 05E60S. >F5. GO KRGLN. LNCH PLAN<24HR. RS.

Frank Bucher read the terse communiqué and took a deep breath. The center of the low pressure system was well to the east, and as powerful as any ever recorded on earth. They were to go to the Kerguellen Islands, and Seranen would have a voyage plan for the fleet in less than twenty-four hours. He walked out of the sparks station and went up to the bridge of the *Mother Carie*. He shared the contents of the message with Charles Atkins and Captain Buchanan. They looked at the main data display console and a screen showing icons at the locations of the Aussies and the Russians in relation to the giant catamaran. Buchanan used the trackball mounted in the console to bring up a series of drop-down menus from which he selected "Rendezvous". Vectors were automatically drawn from each Alba_Sword to an intersection point representing the most efficient path for all three vessels.

"We better get the *Eden* and *Ostrova* on board right away," said Buchanan, "and then an all-hands meeting to lay out our options."

After dropping off the fleet for the surfsailing sessions in the Agulhas, the Mother Carie *had re-fueled in the Kerguellen Islands and shaped course back to the northwest to rendezvous slightly earlier than originally planned. This adjustment presented two alternatives to the six captains. They could haul out and await instructions from Seranen aboard the* Mother Carie, *or they could remain at sea and surfsail the remaining distance to the originally specified rendezvous point. The crews of the* Tom Swift, *the* Serena, *the* Chicama *and the Seeadler had decided to haul out. The* Ostrova *and the* Eden *opted to stay at sea, for a bit of sport, OSOM-style.*

Arrayed around the Southern Ocean were two hundred and fifty six floating automatic weather buoys reporting sea-state conditions by satellite signal to the computers at OSOM HQ in California. The network of floating weather stations also served as an array of racing buoys for the mariners of the Regatta. Every year, as the Alba_Swords of the Regatta coursed through the Southern Ocean, OSOM mariners refurbished the weather stations on the fly by replacing internal components and batteries, and updating software and communication systems and often used OSOM's albatross guides to find the most efficient paths between each buoy.

It was a badge of honor for a crew to R&R as many units as possible. Given the rivalry between the Aussies and the Russians, more than just bragging rights to the winner and increased data integrity for Ray Seranen were involved. They were battling it out over who would pick up the check for dinner, all expenses included, at the restaurant of the winner's choice in San Francisco at the end of the Regatta.

The message in Bucher's hands changed everything. When Rudolf Velelov and Helen Cooper received Bucher's news, the captains of the Ostrova and the Eden knew all bets were off and immediately altered course.

352

Twenty four hours later, all six Alba_Swords were aboard the Mother Carie going full speed ahead at forty-five knots towards a position calculated by Ray Seranen as being well within an optimum launch zone. In the messhall, the crews of the Alba_Swords were ready to listen to Frank Bucher, Charles Atkins and Adam Buchanan begin the most important all-hands meeting in the history of the Roaring Forties Regatta. Scuttlebutt had given everyone a pretty good idea of what was in the wind, literally: the opportunity to surfsail the biggest waves in the history of the Order of Southern Ocean Mariners.

The talk around the room was full of speculation. Jack Richards and L.J. Merrill were especially lit up by a level of energy that was putting their ideas about surfers as watermen in a whole new light. Modern surfing as they once knew it was looking more and more like a bubble gum sport compared to what OSOM was all about.

The meeting came to order when Bucher, Atkins and Buchanan walked to a white board at one end of the room. Charles Atkins began with an invocation.

"O Lord we thank you for the wonders we've seen as we make our way across your broad and powerful oceans and for being thrice blessed by the health and strength of our families, the skill and ingenuity of our fellow mariners, and the courage and humility that allows us to voyage safely in the Southern Ocean. Amen."

"Amen!" said everyone in the room, including Jack Richards.

"Now, to the matters at hand. Frank, you're up."

"Ray Seranen is tracking the biggest storm he's ever monitored. It is the second event predicted by his models of global warming, Antarctic weather, and the meteorology of the Southern Ocean. Code-named K2, it metastasized off the Weddell Sea after a massive katabatic wind was injected into what once was an ordinary Force One storm. Now it's Force Five, extremely well-defined, and moving our way. It is an extraordinary meteorological phenomenon, and we are in a position to experience something unprecedented in the history of oceanic voyaging, not to mention surfing." He winked at Richards and Merrill.

Bucher turned to the white board with a map of the Southern Ocean on it. He drew a diagram and wrote out some specs on the storm, prompting more than a few whistles and murmurs from the assembled mariners.

"We have a head start if we want to surfsail ahead of it, but just barely," he said without turning around, "Here are the issues we must address."

As he spoke, he wrote each topic heading on the board so that there was no confusion as to exactly what was on the table.

"One. Fuel problems. We need to run the *Mother Carie* at full speed to get to the launch zone. Depending on where we launch, if we launch, she might have to put back in to the Kerguellens, and catch up to us down course. Adam?"

"Worst case is that I'll have to wait for the system to pass and follow behind it. That will put this ship on the backside of K2, at least thirty six hours behind you, if not more. We won't be in range if you need us."

Bucher began writing again.

"Two. Storm Strength. K2's wind speeds are in excess of a hundred knots across a fetch almost four hundred miles long and two hundred miles wide. There is good reason to believe the area of the fetch will expand from eighty thousand square miles to four hundred thousand square miles before the winds begin to diminish some six to eight days from now."

A wave of astonishment rolled through the minds of even the most hardened OSOM veterans. Those numbers added up to thousands of open ocean swells each sixty to eighty feet high, if not bigger.

"Three. What's Next. There might be a K3, and it could be even stronger."

The buzz in the room was electric. It was like being told that the Rolling Stones were going to play at your local bar, and only you and friends were going to be there. And there might be some surprise guests, including U2 and Eric Clapton.

"We are on course to the Kerguellens. We have plenty of time to decide if we want to surfsail this event – or let her pass us by. We'll have more data from Ray in about three hours. From there he'll work up a provisional launch point for us along with trajectory options to New Zealand. Please caucus on your boats, and we'll reconvene here after dinner. Unless anybody's got something to add, that's it for the moment."

There was a moment of silence. Then everybody started talking at once in excited and awestruck voices until a single voice cut through the din with a deep, sonorous timbre.

"Frank, I've got something to add," said Charles Atkins.

He stood up and everyone ceased their chatter. Each person knew him to varying degrees, though the one thing they all held in common was well-known to him. This wasn't the Chapel, but he knew every person in the room would heed his words nonetheless.

"May I beseech each and every man and woman here to not say another word for the moment. Clear your minds and steady your hearts. Reflect deeply on the first time you and I shared a watch in the Chapel at OSOM HQ. Consider your thoughts as they were then before you give further consideration to what presents itself to us now."

The dinner dishes were cleared and the tables shifted around to form a dais at one end of the messhall. Chairs were rearranged in half circles with an aisle down the middle. A flat panel display had been mounted against one wall, displaying the OSOM logo and the pennant of the Roaring Forties Regatta. Everyone had two-page handouts covering the meeting's agenda and Ray Seranen's latest projections for the storm and the Regatta. A third page consisted of tear-off ballots. Adam Buchanan chaired the meeting.

"Since we last met, we've covered almost two hundred and forty nautical miles. The K2 storm has also been moving. Its fetch is now five hundred miles long. Ray Seranen will brief us in a minute. Before he does, let me make it clear to everyone there will be no chains-of-commands unless you agree to them. As of this moment your crew contracts are suspended. Once you have all the information you need, there will be a vote on the options, and even then, no matter the outcomes, you are still free to either remain aboard the *Mother Carie* or continue to crew aboard an Alba_Sword."

The screen behind Buchanan dissolved to a picture of the Shed at OSOM's HQ in Ventura where almost a hundred members of the Order had gathered. The two groups of people separated by ten thousand miles smiled and waved to each other. Then a third group appeared on the divided screen: Damon Waiya and the Ice Pirates in Antarctica. It was a video conferencing setup that OSOM used only on the rarest of occasions, and up to now never before during a Regatta.

The headquarters camera panned around and stopped when Ray Seranen filled the screen.

"Ok, you all know why we're all here. The fleet is in a position to intercept the largest wave trains in the recorded history of the Southern Ocean. The storm is currently generating seas of one hundred to one hundred and twenty feet in height at the epicenter of the fetch. Predicted parameters are as follows: the K2 storm will move straight east along the sixtieth parallel. Its fetch will eventually be expanded to a length of between seven hundred and eleven hundred miles long and two hundred to four hundred miles wide. It will be the biggest wave generating zone ever recorded. The winds will blow from ninety to one hundred and forty miles per hour across the fetch."

There was absolute quiet. Everyone knew the implications of Seranen's predictions were staggering.

"I have developed a scenario for the fleet that includes launch windows, wave propagation and height parameters, storm duration, and energy dissipation projections. You all have that information in front of you. However it is important for everyone to realize the limitations of the infoscape within which we are currently operating.

"What you have covers only what we know right now. My models indicate that at least one more weather event may be on the way. Without getting into rates of certainty vs. potential conditions, a K3 event centered in the Antarctic interior is highly probable within the next two hundred hours. Consequences for the fleet are currently unknown. So there you have it from my end. Please review your printouts carefully. Over to you Frank."

Frank Bucher was already in the speaker's chair, flanked by the captains of the Alba_Swords and Adam Buchanan. He looked to the right of him, then to the left, then straight into the camera.

"Thanks, Ray. Everyone needs to study the data carefully, but first let me play devil's advocate by saying it seems to me we will be like ants hanging on to the butt of an elephant on a rampage. Nature bats last and I don't want

355

to be swatted over the centerfield fence. So, my vote will be to cancel the Regatta effective immediately. Now, can anybody tell me why they are going to vote against me?"

For the next two hours, the debate went back and forth. The mariners of the fleet had caucused and their captains gave eloquent reasons for riding the surf from K2, along with data supporting assertions that the Alba_Swords were up to the task. They were countered by the Antarctic weather team. The Ice Pirates saw no reason to take any unknown risks when it came to Nature's fury. The OSOM members in Ventura were split evenly on both sides, but some strong points were made against the continuation of the Regatta. Nobody wanted to see bodies come home in boxes. . . or not at all.

Finally Adam Buchanan stood up and addressed the assemblage.

"As Winston Churchill once said, 'Democracy is a terrible system until you consider the alternatives'. Of course, there has never been such a thing as crews voting instead of captains ordering, but this situation is unlike any ever faced by mariners, as far as I know. So you all have your ballots. Your choices are these."

Buchanan wrote the options on the white board.

"One. We cancel the Regatta and I take you all home. After the sessions you had in the Agulhas, prudence might suggest there is no need to press your luck any further.

"Two. We pull in behind the Kerguellens and wait for the safer conditions.

"Three. We set up a launch and those who so choose go surfsailing as per Ray's voyage plan. If some Alba_Swords end up undermanned, we'll form up complete crews as necessary.

"Please number your ballots accordingly, and circle Y or N on each one. We'll adjourn this meeting for thirty minutes while the mariners mark their ballots. Ray, Pirates, thanks for the input and information. We'll signal a decision through normal channels in about an hour."

The Morse Code ticker began to issue its familiar short stream of auditory dots and dashes to waiting OSOM members in California and Antarctica. The message was short and concise. Ray Seranen and Damon Waiya were not at all surprised by its contents. Neither were any of the Ice Pirates or the people waiting at OSOM HQ.

R40R GO. UNANIMOUS.

As the *Mother Carie* sped to the launch area, voice lines and instant message boards were opened up from the catamaran to OSOM headquarters. The giant surf was soon to be news around the world, and the mariners of the fleet wanted their families to know where they were and what they were going to do.

Sophia Bucher grilled her husband for fifteen minutes concerning the *Mother Carie*'s fueling situation, submersion systems, possible course deviations, and a dozen more potential weaknesses in Seranen's plan, many of which Bucher had not fully considered. She had never doubted her husband in the past, but this time their son was involved and she hammered away until Frank began to doubt the whole thing himself. Only when she heard him waver did was she convinced her husband and son would be safe.

"Ok, you've got my blessing, Frank. Let me talk to Ken."

"Hi mom! I'll be all right and the *Serena* is in top shape."

"Ken, you didn't clean up your room before you left!" Sophia Bucher was smiling through her tears, "and your sisters are hopping mad about it! Now they won't clean up theirs!"

L.J. Merrill talked to his parents and reiterated his promise that this was his last surf trip. Jack Richards called his wife and kids, and slowly but surely families and loved ones in California, Germany, Peru, Russia, and Australia all had their fears sufficiently assuaged by the confidence of the mariners of the Alba_Sword fleet. It was not cockiness or fool's courage, but a function of the training and camaraderie, coupled with the technology and talent, of the Order of Southern Ocean Mariners.

Seranen's plan met with unanimous approval for two important reasons. One, everyone agreed they wanted to build slowly up to a maximum wave size that would be, given their experience with Alba_Swords to date, as big as anything they'd ever imagined they could surfsail safely. Two, the Alba_Sword mariners had the advantage of choosing the size of wave they wanted to ride. The course plan allowed the fleet to start off surfsailing seas with which all the skippers were familiar, about forty to fifty feet high on the sets. As the voyage continued, the captains had the option of pulling out and re-berthing with the *Mother Carie* or simply riding swells to the north and northeast towards ports of call in Australia. They could easily avoid what might be close behind them: thousands of graybearded walls stretching from horizon to horizon, each a hundred feet high – if not bigger. Everyone was stoked, because in the end nobody was stupid.

The sea was steely gray and glassy. The temperature was just above freezing. The wind was out of the east at ten knots. Ray Seranen had set up the launch window to take advantage of unusually calm conditions near the Kerguellen Islands while giving the *Mother Carie* a twelve hour window to put in and re-fuel at the OSOM station for the run to New Zealand.

"Hey Ho! And up she rises!
"Hey Ho! And up she rises!
"HEY! HO! AND UP SHE RISES!
Surfing to New Zealand!"

357

The crews were putting their backs into it and the winches were turning to launch the Alba_Swords on the most challenging voyage in OSOM's history. Everything was going smoothly just as it had during the first launch of the fleet off the coast of South Africa. A rendezvous waypoint was established at launch plus four hours to allow everyone to again shake out their Alba_Swords. An undersea bivouac would follow to give all the crews a chance to gather themselves and wait for the surf to come up. Ray Seranen had given them a twenty hour launch window when the surf would grow from twenty to forty feet. Each subsequent day the fleet could fall back to sets progressively larger so that by the time they were south of Australia, they would be surfsailing the biggest swells ever witnessed in the Southern Ocean.

Caverns in the Rising Sun

Part One: Gung-ho

"Try it again. I don't think they get it."

"Please I no you comprehend. Can repeat words again thank you!"

The translator hired for the surfers didn't know the vocabulary of surfing or the techniques of riding massive waves. The surfers were obviously bored, and Kai Woods wasn't getting his points across.

"Ok, tell them if they don't follow my instructions in certain situations, they will die."

The translator understood the sentence and did as he was told.

The four surfers shrugged.

Kai Woods was a transplanted Californian and one of the best lifeguards on the North Shore. He was a no-nonsense guy in the water and knew all the guys in the Tui, the tough-guy crew who had taken their name from the Fijian word meaning 'tribal elder'. Steve Palua was lucky to find him available when he needed a lifeguard whose word was above reproach and would be listened to by all. He anticipated no serious problems between Woods and the boys from da Tui who would be driving the jetskis. The problem was the four surfers added to the Wavelife roster by Parea Anasi.

Palua's investment group was convinced that *bushido*, a warrior code of honor in the Far East, could be the basis for a marketing campaign and corporate branding strategy. After they tried a version of it with the "Comeback Kid" boxing angle, only to have things end in disaster at Huntington Beach, the "surfer-as-fearless-warrior" angle was even more crucial to the marketing plans of the investment group. Combined with the tough guy Tui image and its lock on the Hawaiian surf scene, the *bushido* code of honor was exactly what Anasi wanted for marketing campaigns throughout the Far East. And Kai Woods was right in the middle of it all.

That morning he had started with some stories about Mount Everest and the climbers who, driven by 'summit fever', had perished due to their inability to distinguish between courage and stupidity. The translator couldn't understand what 'summit fever' meant, until Woods explained it simply: its when a climber forgets that getting to the top is optional, but getting back down is not. When the four surfers finally started nodding their heads, Woods thought he was getting somewhere.

Then he showed them the film, 'The Man Who Skied Down Everest', about the Japanese skier who tried to make a run down the long slope on the south side of the world's tallest mountain. The idea backfired. The surfers thought the movie was corny. The fact that the skier barely survived didn't register with them at all. Woods knew he had problems when some of the surfers even laughed at the part when the skier had to be rescued.

When they started up in the afternoon, the only thing that kept Woods going was the fact the men across the table from him were going to ride waves bigger than anything they'd ever seen. His job was to make sure they came back – even if they didn't seem to care whether they died or not.

"Ok, let's try this."

Kai Woods gave each surfer an egg and had them write their names on the eggs. Then he took them outside the house they had rented on the North Shore and turned on the garden hose. He opened the spigot, put an egg with his own name on it in his hand, and ran the stream of water just above the egg.

"Tube ride," he said.

The translator got the words across, The surfers said the two words in English over and over again.

Suddenly Woods directed the strong stream of water directly on to the egg. The egg cracked, then blew apart.

"Wipeout."

The translator didn't know the word, but the surfers were getting the point. But before Woods could repeat the demonstration about a wave's massive power versus a surfer's fragility with the surfers' eggs, two of them saw what was coming and smashed their eggs into each other. Then they laughed in his face.

It was obvious the gap between Woods and the Wavelife surfers could not be easily bridged in the short time they had. He felt they needed to be a lot less gung-ho and a lot more gun-shy about surfing the huge waves they were hired to ride. He told them to take another break, but then he called it quits for the day. He was getting nowhere, and so he took a long swim to think things through. When he got back, he called Steve Palua.

"Hold, on Tina, let me see who this is. I'll get rid of them and get right back to you. . . .Palua here. Oh, Kai, what's happening? Everything ok?"

Woods explained the situation. Palua glanced at Parea Anasi who fortunately was on a call to Hong Kong and not listening closely. Palua knew he had to get back on track, so he responded quickly in a muffled voice.

"Leave 'em alone, ok? We don't have time to train them thoroughly, and if they think you're trying to instill any fear in them, they'll take it as an insult. All we can do, Kai, is hope they'll know their limits. If they go past them, let's hope you can rescue them. If you can't, well, that's life. That's how Anasi sees it, and that's how they see it. You and I have got jobs to do, so let's not worry about stuff over which we have no control. Look, I gotta go."

"Ok, Tina, let's get back to business. Where were we? Are the waverunners and inflatables prepared?" said Steve Palua, speaking clearly for the benefit of Parea Anasi now once again listening to every word standing a few feet away in the hotel room overlooking Waikiki.

"Yes, the waverunners are mounted on the *Skyhook* and ready to go. All the equipment has been checked by Mac Owens. Have you had a chance to practice with the locator system?"

"No, we'll do that when we get there."

"Okay," said Tina Sanchez in a hesitating voice, "You might want to think about waiting a day or so to check the systems."

"Mrs. Sanchez, we are bringing a very experienced group of big wave surfers. They should have no problem riding the waves. All you have to do is get us to R.O.P. and we'll be just fine."

Sanchez quickly realized what had happened to Heath Larson was apparently of no concern to him.

"Yes, you're right, Mr. Palua. The contract is pretty specific when it comes to our responsibilities for your safety at the site. We'll be at the boarding buoy at six a.m. day after tomorrow. We'll have you at the reef, or R.O.P. as you call it, four hours later. We'll fuel the waverunners from our tanks, and off you go!"

"The jetskis run on aviation fuel? I didn't know that was possible. Can't they just be tanked up before we take off to save time when we get there?"

"No, Mr. Palua, they can't. That's a major safety issue. Oh, and while we're on the subject, don't forget that we can only refill your jetski tanks once, subject to Captain Sanchez' review of our fuel requirements."

"Oh, ok," said Palua. The look from Parea Anasi was not reassuring, so Palua came back at Sanchez to re-gain the upper hand.

"And the camera inflatables? What about gas for those? That's in the contract, Mrs. Sanchez."

"Yes, that's true. The gasoline for them will be transported in fire-proof bladder containers. Forty gallons, as specified." Tina Sanchez had a disconcerting feeling about Steve Palua and the new version of the Wavelife expedition. "And as per the contract, Captain Sanchez will make all decisions regarding weather and/or sea-state conditions. If he says we need to leave, you will be asked to board the *Skyhook* immediately. If you don't, we will simply leave you there and come back when it is safe and prudent to do so. That is clearly stated in the contract, as you know. Anything else Mr. Palua?"

"Just get us to R.O.P. and we'll worry about that stuff if and when it happens, ok?" Palua said impatiently. He didn't need someone warning him about potential problems at this point. The surfers were ready, the waves were going to be huge, and Parea Anasi was staring at him.

"See you in forty-eight hours, Mr. Palua, and good luck to you." She knew he would need it.

It was uncomfortably humid outside on the balcony overlooking Waikiki, but Ian Clark found it preferable to being in the air-conditioned suite listening to Steve Palua on the phone. Clark didn't care anymore that he was not involved in the business end of things with Skyrider. All he cared about was getting his money and getting out. If Palua wanted to do all the talking from here on in, more power to him. When the first Wavelife surfer finished riding his first wave, a million dollars would be transferred to one of Clark's 'business' accounts in the Bahamas. And that wave was just over the horizon.

As soon as the international surf reports began to make projections about the big storm stretched across the Southern Ocean southeast of Africa, Geosurf was inundated with calls from surfers wanting to fly to surf spots from Indonesia to New Zealand. WaveAlert analysts predicted the storm would remain strong as it moved east across the Southern Ocean and retain its strength in the window for sending huge waves across Polynesia. That was all Clark needed to hear. He called Palua, who had seen the projections himself, and within seconds the decision was made to meet the waves at the reef.

As for any other 'meetings' at the reef, he had said nothing to Palua. He got some info on OSOM and knew Merrill had figured out a way to get around the permit. But even if Merrill was there, it would make no difference to Palua. The boys from the Tui were always hired by Hollywood, ad agencies and pro contests to clear the water on the North Shore. With four waverunners, eight surfers, and two camera crews dominating the place, his old partner would have a tough time being the last soldier of the soul patrol trying to defend the place against the realities of life in the surf industry.

But that was not the problem he wrestled with on the balcony after hearing Palua talking to Tahiti, then taking a call from Kai Woods, and now once again talking contract terms with Sanchez. No, he was thinking of how Palua was using the initials 'R.O.P.', and he remembered thinking he was so clever coming up with the "Reef of Power" name going into that first meeting with Wavelife. It was pure moxie, and he didn't mind all that much when Heath Larson had immediately nixed that name when Mercante actually suggested using it. Then again he was not surprised when the investment group had liked the "Reef of Power" concept. They were betting their success in the surf industry on dominating the waves and using conquest and heroism as the key marketing concepts for their roll-out to consumers throughout the Far East. "Reef of Power" was perfect. Or as Parea Anasi said, "Why not give you the honor of naming it, which you did in the first place? We certainly won't call it Heath's reef, and since you are the man who brought it to everyone's attention in the first place, we will honor your work by using the name you gave it."

He heard "R.O.P." again and cringed. Anasi had shown him the bank account transfer receipt that would be activated by Anasi with just a few keystrokes on a laptop. Clark remembered his comment about seven figures sounding like chump change, and he was now little more than the chump they needed for the moment.

And I'm not the only one.

He hadn't heard what Palua had said to Woods, but it was easy for him to imagine why he'd called, and why Palua had lowered his voice. The four surfers had never done tow-in surfing – but that fact was going to make no difference whatsoever. He mentioned it to Palua, but was told that Anasi and his group had loved the Hollywood surf movie 'Big Wednesday', especially the ending where the hero almost dies in the biggest waves of his life. They were going to resurrect that theme, with or without the word 'almost'. Instead of training with jetskis, Palua told him, they had spent hours every day in martial arts sessions that, Clark surmised, did not emphasize character, sincerity and humility by any means, since those concepts were not part of the marketing plan.

Of course, none of those things were ever part of this to begin with, he laughed ruefully, remembering the snap decision he'd made between loyal humility and greedy betrayal.

He heard the impatience in Palua's voice at the end of his conversation with Tina Sanchez. Then Palua called the Tui guys and started talking story in pidgin. The cacophony escalated when Anasi got on another cellphone to update the "investors".

Clark put his hands on the railing, looked down twenty stories, and felt the exact same anxiety as when he had looked out the canopy of the *Skyhook* on the first flight out to the reef. Then he'd had a chance to level with the men close by and he didn't take it. He knew he wasn't going to get a second chance with the guys in the hotel suite. He looked down and stared at the beach far below. Then something caught his eye in the distance. The sun was lowering in the west, and the long shadows of the highrise hotels were touching the clear waters. To his right he could barely see a small park near the sands of Waikiki. In the center of the grass was the statue of surfing's most beloved ancestor, the man who stood for all that was right and noble in the sport and had been the ambassador of true aloha around the world.

Ian Clark just shook his head as the excited voices on the phones in the suite got louder and louder.

* * *

"Hold it right there, pal. Tina, can you come back here, please?"

"Coming, Mac, I'll be right there," she said while still in the galley. She had seen the waiting boat and the crowded afterdeck. It was just after sunup, the visibility was a bit hazy, but as soon as her husband feathered the props and the seaplane slowed down to glide toward the mooring buoy, she was out of her co-pilot's seat and heading to the cargo bay.

"Which one of you is Steve Palua? Oh, hi Ian, which one is Palua? You've got too many people."

"Hi Tina, uh, yeah, he knows that, but he's a bit sick right now."

The ride out to the buoy had been rough. There was big surf all over the South Pacific. The legendary reef at Teahupo'o, only a few miles away, was closed out. Going up and down in big swells with no forward motion was taking its toll, and the first to lose his breakfast had been the man in charge of the Wavelife expedition to the Reef of Power.

"Ian, you know the contract said twelve and - - -"

"Hold on, Tina, you're talking to the wrong guy. That's him there. Hey Steve! We need you right now!" A man on the other side of the boat stood up from leaning over the railing and came towards Tina Sanchez.

"Uh, hi, I'm Steve Palua. Uh, what's the problem? Why aren't we loading everyone aboard?" He turned and dry-heaved some phlegm over the taff rail. "Let's go! We're gonna make history today. Now what is the problem?"

"The contract said twelve passengers. You have more than that."

"So what? I'm sure you have plenty of room."

"Mr. Palua. I can take two extra people. We are not certified for more than fourteen passengers with the load we already have. At the per person rate in the contract, you will be charged an extra thousand dollars a person." She saw the camera cases for the extra photographers. "And your extra equipment will cost another thousand due to increased fuel consumption. We are not a 747. Every pound counts, Mr. Palua."

"Yeah, well, Clark said you were easy to work with and that everything would be ok."

Mac Owens had heard enough.

"Clark, why didn't you make sure these guys were within specs?"

"Mac, this isn't my deal anymore!" said Clark, holding up his hands to fend off Owens' anger.

"Mac, I'll handle this," said Tina Sanchez, noticing her husband's head poking out the cockpit window. If he got involved, the whole thing might explode. He didn't like surprises, and it wouldn't take much for him to just leave the Wavelife expedition in his wake.

"Now, Mr. Palua, let's be clear about this," she said, but Kai Woods had sensed the situation brewing, and stepped in front of Steve Palua.

"Kai Woods. I'm water safety. Steve, let me help out here, ok?"

Palua nodded weakly as he turned and walked to the other side of the boat where he retched another stream of stomach acid up his throat and over the side. Ian Clark stepped back quietly. He had a million bucks on the line and Kai Woods was looking like an ace in the hole.

"Ok, fourteen it is. Shigu, you stay," he said to the translator. He had been explaining the whole situation when he heard his name and translated it verbatim to the amusement of the Wavelife surfers, cool and smirking behind their wraparound sunglasses. They KNEW they were going, no matter what.

"But how you talk the surfers? They need me. You need me."

Woods looked at the cameramen standing near the Wavelife surfers. Anasi had made a deal with an Asian media conglomerate, and Woods knew they were as important as the Wavelife surfers. Maybe he'd be lucky.

"Either of you two guys speak English?"

"Yes, I can," said one of them.

"What's your name?" asked Kai Woods, relief palpable in his tone.

"Taz Nakamura. I was an exchange student at Pepperdine in Malibu a long time ago."

"Ok, we're down to fifteen. Who else doesn't have to go?"

Everyone looked at everyone else. Nobody said a word. Three big Tui guys would be driving the jetskis and had big wave experience. Palua had hired two veteran surfing cameramen from the North Shore who knew how to shoot big waves from jetskis. Then a fourth Hawaiian had been added for political and business reasons Palua couldn't ignore. The North Shore contingent looked impregnable. Kai Woods was not about to cross swords with them if he didn't have to.

"Ian, why don't you stay?"

"Cause I'm the only person who knows where we're going, Woods," he said defiantly before shooting a look at Tina Sanchez, who also knew the exact location of the reef but was bound by contract to never reveal its location, "AND I'm the only guy who knows how to use the locator system."

"Yeah, I know," said Woods, "Hey, Steve, you'd better get over here."

Steve Palua looked up, seasick and stressed. He'd heard it all but knew the Wavelife surfers were the key to the bushido marketing campaign. Their performance had to be documented at all costs. That left the boys from the Tui. He looked at the one he'd known the longest.

"Tony, brah, I'm sorry but - - -"

"No fuckin' way, Palua," said the muscular surfer, a veteran of many years on the North Shore and a founding member of the Tui, "I no come alla dis way an' no surf. An' I drive da ski mo bettah dan anyone."

Kai Woods knew Tony Aipua didn't drive a waverunner very well, but they were losing time and something had to be done. Of the other three Tui surfers, David Kahaio had the most jetski experience and had surfed big waves almost as long as Aipua. Ben Lalaoa was a great surfer, maybe the best of the three, though like Aipua he didn't have a lot of experience driving a jetski. But that didn't matter as much as the fact that he was hot-tempered and Woods knew that with Lalaoa, discretion was always the better part of valor. That left Keoni Padaca, son of a Tui heavyweight and added to the trip because Palua couldn't say no. But fortunately Kai Woods had an edge on him.

"Keoni, this not your day."

"Woods you no tell me I no go! My pops put me onna dis trip!"

"I know, and I'll answer to him. Just remember, you wouldn't even be here if it wasn't for me pulling you outta da rip at Sunset last year. Ok, Mrs., uh, I'm sorry, we haven't been introduced."

"Sanchez, Tina Sanchez," she said nervously, "and this is my husband, Victor Sanchez."

The commander of the *Skyhook* had just appeared in the cargo bay door.

"Tina, we got some problems here?"

"No, I think everything's ok."

"Then Mac, why aren't we loading up?"

365

"Jes' workin' out sum last minnit details, capt'n," said Owens, covering for Tina Sanchez. They both knew when he was on the verge of losing his cool and she took her cue perfectly.

"Yes, Mac's just working out some last minute details, dear. C'mon, we've got to talk about a new fuel profile for the flight, so let's go back to the cockpit, Victor. Ready in a few minutes, right, Mac?"

He nodded as Tina Sanchez pulled her husband away from the cargo bay door. Ian Clark breathed a sigh of relief. But when Owens hesitated since he didn't quite know where to start while looking down at the boat full of people, a big pile of surfboards and a lot of equipment, Clark saw a chance to get back in the game.

"Ok, everyone, this is Mac Owens, the flight engineer on the *Skyhook*. He knows everything about this plane, and he's the guy figured out the mountings for the jetskis. What he says, goes, ok?"

Owens didn't know what to say, and Clark kept going.

"Now, we have to distribute the load properly, right Mac? I remember how you wanted it last time, but first let's take care of Steve. Kai, why don't you and Mac take him forward, and get him some of that great seasick stuff. In fact, better get some for all of us, ok Mac?"

Kai Woods smiled. Mac Owens looked at Clark and nodded his head.

"Clark, you got this covered?"

"Yes, Mac, I do. We'll get the boards in the back, the big boys up front in the galley, the camera guys and their stuff in the 'sunroom', and the surfers in the cargo bay. And we'll be ready in five minutes."

The lumbering Catalina needed an extra five miles of ocean to get aloft, but an open ocean is an endless runway for a PBY. Due to the weak southeast trades and the extra weight, Victor Sanchez did not have it easy getting the *Skyhook* airborne. His problems were compounded by the fact he had to conserve fuel at all costs, and one way to do that was a long, slow gradual takeoff. The fuel budget had been calculated for a twelve man payload. Now, with the extra weight, he had to worry about every gallon. Once they were finally in the air, Tina Sanchez left her co-pilot's seat and went to the galley with more to say about the fuel problem.

"With the unexpected payload increase," she said, careful not to look at the burly surfers, "I had to work out a new fuel budget. We'll be able to get you to the reef, and we'll fill up the waverunners, but only once. We won't be able to refill your tanks because with all this weight, we'll use more fuel to take off and return to Tahiti."

"What if we want stay? What if da surf really good?" asked David Kahaio.

"If we refill your tanks, we'd have to leave the waverunners, or - - -" she paused, knowing the original contract allowed for multiple trips and the costs were covered by the terms of the contract, "Or we can re-fill your tanks, and leave you guys out there with food, water, and a big liferaft for shelter. We'd fly back to Tahiti, refuel, and with no cargo coming back, we'd have plenty of fuel and food for you to keep surfing all the next day and then takeoff with everything loaded up the way it is now."

"So we got no problem! We use alla da fuel, you fill us up, we keep surfing, you go get mo gas, come back, and we surf some mo! Dis gonna be one da kine surf trip!" said Tony Aipua.

"Sounds ok," said Kai Woods.

"Sounds great!" exclaimed Ian Clark, "Now let's just hope the cameramen brought plenty of film. Take a look down there!"

The ocean was "corduroy to the horizon." Incredibly long, evenly spaced hills of water were lined up one after another, coming out of the southwest for as far as the eye could see. They didn't look like they were moving at more than thirty miles an hour, and in fact the only indication they were not motionless was the wide borders of white water all around the reefs to the north. Last May those reefs had been fringed with waves breaking around them. Now some of them were almost completely buried in whitewater.

"Sheezus, Clark, it looks pretty big down there," said Kai Woods.

"Yeah, dis gonna be one da kine session," said a very stoked Ben Lalaoa.

"But no biggah dan outside Log Cabins!" added Tony Aipua.

"We gonna geevum good!" cheered David Kahaio.

Two hours later, Lalaoa's excitement was long gone, as was that of Aipua and Kahaio. They were just now beginning to understand how far out in the ocean they were going. But their machismo code was inviolable, and none of them said much except an occasional, "Dis one long way out to dis buggah." And they had to be stoic for another reason as well. They'd always had to respect Heath Larson for the what he'd done in big waves, but they resented him nonetheless. The Tui boys saw themselves as the true defenders of big wave traditions, born on the North Shore, that Larson had never been a part of. They needed to prove they could surf waves that had almost killed him.

In the cargo bay, Taz Nakamura was getting to know the four surfers he would be filming. He had shot some surfing events in Japan and had spent a season on the North Shore. He knew getting good surfing footage took years of experience, but a freelance photographer always answers his phone and always says yes. Like the North Shore surfers, he didn't let it show, but Taz Nakamura was becoming increasingly concerned about the job as the flight wore on. He sensed no fear behind the attitude and the sunglasses. Only one of them seemed to have any concept of what they were going to do, but more than once he seemed the odd man out of the four surfers.

The other cameraman was completely involved with the manual of the new digital video camera he'd brought with him. Nakamura quickly realized the guy had never used it before, but when he said something about it, the TV guy told him in sharp tones not to worry because the guy had years of experience filming sporting events for network TV and was a professional who knew how to do his job no matter what.

The cameramen from Hawai'i, Brad Halley and Craig Bishop, were much more relaxed. A big time assignment during the North Shore off-season was a godsend for them. They didn't mind the long flight. It gave them more time to check all their equipment. They were making good money and they knew Aipua, Kahaio, and Lalaoa. They had shot footage of them for the Tui ads and promo videos. The chance to come along on a trip like this could only increase their chances for even more work in the future with da Tui and Wavelife.

Kai Woods was with them in the 'sunroom'. He was looking out the Plexiglas dome at swells moving across the sea surface a thousand feet below. The more he looked, the more he felt like a fireman approaching a forest fire in the distance as winds whipped the flames into an inferno. When he first got the call from Steve Palua, he'd felt he was up to the job. But the training sessions with the Japanese surfers had gone nowhere and there had been almost no time to talk to the guys from da Tui. He knew he needed help, and so he called Randy Laine. He wanted to talk to a guy who'd been out to the reef, and just as importantly he needed some good advice from the man who knew more about tow-in surfing safety than anyone else on the planet.

But for two days there was no answer. Then Palua called and said they were flying to Tahiti in forty eight hours. Woods had tried to get in a safety session with the Tui guys, but they were so amped getting new boards made for the trip that only two showed up, and their "too-cool-for-school" attitude was as disconcerting as the arrogance of the Wavelife surfers. With time running out, Woods knew he was headed for trouble. He finally connected with Laine visiting family back in Virginia, and as soon as he had fully explained the situation, Laine's simple advice confirmed Woods' fears.

"Don't do it. Don't go. It's suicide."

"Randy, there's big money behind this. Palua is making it sound like the most important surf trip in history. The Wavelife guys are gung-ho and the Tui guys are just as psyched. We're going no matter what. So give me some advice, Randy."

"Use the locator system. Make sure it works. Don't ride a wave until it's all set up. The place is huge. It's three times the size of Jaws. Imagine Cortes Bank with waves twice as long as Hanalei Bay. We got lucky with Larson. It wasn't even that big, maybe twenty, twenty-five. His wave did a spooky clamshell, so maybe you can't trust the wave to stay perfect. Play it safe. Keep 'em on the shoulder, get the P.R. shots, and get out of there in one piece. It's a big place. You can get lost like little kids at a carnival. You have no reference points except the seaplane. You have to use the locator system to know where you are. And don't surf the lefts no matter what. They may look rideable when you get there, but that side of the reef must be really sensitive to swell direction. And if an odd set came through from a slightly different angle, you'd have big problems. Make sure you set out the locator grid before anyone rides even one wave. Ride in formation, one wave at a time. two skis on safety every time there's a rider up. Don't let anyone vary from the game plan. Larson and Bruddah are the best. Rowe and I know our shit. We thought we had it wired, yet Heath almost died out there. What does that tell you?"

Laine's words echoed in the thoughts of Kai Woods over and over again. As he looked out the Plexiglas dome at the endless lines coming up from the Southern Ocean, he wished he could just call a halt to the whole thing right then and there. Then he decided he'd better try.

"Fuck this bullshit. This ain't gonna work, you guys."

"What? What's the problem?" said Brad Halley, who was looking at his watch and was startled by Woods' words.

He looked them both in the eye and laid out everything on his mind. He reiterated Randy Laine's advice hoping the cameramen could be enlisted as allies in his cause. When he was done, he knew they understood the situation, but their replies told him he was not going to get any help from them.

"Well, let's wait till we get there. You've handled the North Shore outer reefs, and big Sunset, Waimea, Laniakea. This shouldn't be all that bad," said Craig Bishop.

"And the Tui guys have surfed Alligators, Avanlanche, big Makaha," said Halley, "Aipua has been over to Mavericks a couple of times, and all three of them went on a run to Cortez way back when. They know their limits. They'll be ok. The Wavelife guys? They're pro surfers. They'll do what they're paid to do. So what's the problem?"

"Look at it this way, Woods," added Bishop, "You're doing all you can. If you put too much fear in our hearts, we'll all get nervous and make mistakes. Just relax, and maybe it'll turn out to be a dream session for all of us."

"Maybe, and maybe it'll be our worst nightmare. It's going to be much bigger than the swell when Larson was out here. If we can't do this right, we shouldn't be doing it at all. I gotta talk to Palua."

Kai Woods got up and left the 'sunroom' to go forward. The cameramen were suddenly concerned not for their safety, but for their paychecks.

Woods made his way forward to the cargo bay. He saw Nakamura and thought to say something. But the guy was working for Palua, and so Kai Woods kept going forward. He stopped momentarily to talk to Mac Owens and was glad he did.

"Say, I'm sorry this whole thing is so messed up, and the more I think about it, the more it worries me," said Woods.

"Yup, seems like ya might be bitin' off more than ya kin chew. And jes' remember when y'all leave this plane, we don' hafta risk our lives to save y'all. This ain't Mount Everest. We getcha to the mountain, but we ain't gonna climb it. If y'all git in trouble out there, t'aint none of our business. Sez so right in the contract," said Owens, looking Woods straight in the eye.

"Yeah, that's what I figured. Actually, that's just what I wanted to hear."

He proceeded through the galley without saying a word to Clark or the North Shore guys. He knew Clark was just in it for the payday at this point, and he'd already pissed off the Tui guys by keeping Padaca off the plane, even though there was no alternative. He entered the cockpit. Victor Sanchez was all business.

"Next time you come up here, ask permission. We've got our hands full and can't be distracted."

"Sorry, I just need to talk to Palua."

"Go ahead, but hurry up."

Kai Woods wedged himself into the forward compartment.

"Steve, wake up, we've gotta talk. It's real important."

"Wha, wha, what's important? Are we there yet? How's the surf?" Palua was groggy and it took a few seconds for the words to register.

"No, we're not their yet, but the surf is going to be huge."

"So? That's what we want. What's there to talk about?"

"Steve, this is insanity. We're not acting like a team, nobody is listening to me, and the surf is going to be bigger than when Larson almost died."

"Oh, fuck, Woods, don't start that whining shit again."

"Palua, I'm telling you, we're not ready. Somebody's gonna get hurt, or worse. People can die when it's this big."

"Woods, we already had this conversation. If guys die, that's their business. Just like mountain climbers, you know? They don't need playground monitors. Just do your best and you'll get paid."

Woods had a flashback to the movie he'd shown the Nisei surfers. He remembered the words of Owens, and he also remembered the disaster on Mt. Everest back in 1996 when eight people died in two days.

"Palua, if you don't pull the plug on this right now, I want out."

"Then stay on the plane and stay out of the way. The North Shore guys can take care of themselves, and the other guys know what they're doing. Maybe you don't agree, but that's the facts."

Woods stood up to see the ocean through the small lookout bubble dome. There were thick lines of raw energy in the ocean for as far as the eye could see. He had to make a decision right then and there. He was a surfer who had a healthy fear of the ocean. He was also a lifeguard who saved those who didn't.

"Ok, Palua, you've got me. Even when we black flagged the North Shore two winters ago, I still had to go out and save some idiot at Waimea. We threw him in jail when I got him to the beach. He got his thrills, and I almost got killed. That's my job, I guess."

"Yes, Woods, that's your job. And you're making more money in one day here than you make all summer sitting in a tower watching tourists getting their toes wet. So make the best of it, ok?"

The sun was no longer coming through the portholes. Ian Clark checked his GPS. They were on course, but something felt wrong, and he knew what it was. They were losing daylight. Sanchez was going slow to conserve fuel, and even with the fall-back scenario of a return flight, he was taking no chances. Clark took a look out a porthole. The swells in the ocean were a little harder to see given the vertical angle of the sun, but he knew they were much bigger than last time. He felt a twinge of real fear, remembering how close Heath Larson had come to being killed. Then he remembered the money.

Maybe it wouldn't be that big. Maybe it will be safe and easy to ride the place. And all I need is for one guy to catch one wave.

Then Clark remembered one important difference. Heath Larson and Randy Laine had run the show last May. They'd formed a team and demanded discipline of everyone else. Larson owed his life to real professionalism, the kind that was in short supply on this trip.

An hour later, Clark checked his G.P.S. He closed his eyes for a second, and then looked out the porthole. He saw the reef easily, though it was still many miles away. He went to the intercom.

"Ok, guys, we're almost there. It's just coming up on the horizon."

Victor Sanchez felt the plane wobble a bit as all the surfers scrambled to the nearest window to get a view of what was ahead of them. When they did, no one said a word.

The waves were stretched across the ocean from one horizon to the other, curving here and there as they refracted off submerged shoals until they approached the reef and their energy focused on it like a line of soldiers re-forming to attack an enemy fort. The flanks moved onward, but at the center, two forces were going to engage in a confrontation of immense power as the timeless motion of the sea was challenged by the immovable planet. Neither side ever won, but in the battle zone between them, the passengers of the *Skyhook* were looking to find the surfer's dream.

The only passengers who had any idea of the size of the waves were Kai Woods and Ian Clark. They noticed how far apart the waves were, the long interval a sure sign that the surf was huge, as big as anything Woods had seen in Hawai'i. Clark saw how much wider the white water zone was around the reef than it had been in May. The waves were breaking in deeper water, but the shape was still perfect.

Victor Sanchez banked the *Skyhook* to the north. This was his second landing at the reef with the waverunners, and his approach pattern was identical. He came spiraling down in a series of slow, wide circles. His first pass allowed the surfers a complete view of the entire arena below them. Only then did they begin to realize just how big the place really was. Kai Woods thought of the world's most famous big wave arenas - Jaws, Mavericks, Cortes Bank – and he realized all of them put together would still not compare to what he was seeing.

They could see the beautiful colors of the interior lagoon, but the reef itself was invisible. Broad borders of white water ran down both sides of the reef for almost a mile. The outer edges were clean and even. There were no irregularities, jumps or jags.

"It's perfect," said Ian Clark over the intercom.

His pronouncement broke the spell in the cargo bay and the 'sunroom' where everyone began to point and talk to each other. They could see inside the tubes of the waves - when the barrels weren't spitting out clouds of spray. One wave, going down the east side of the reef, spit four times, and yet the curl line peeled perfectly.

The Reef of Power was everything they could have imagined, and more. The long flight was forgotten. All the anxiety built up over the past days and weeks disappeared into thin air. Steve Palua was mesmerized. The Hawaiians were as stoked as the Japanese were animated. The cameramen were scrambling to get vantage shots using every camera and lens they had. But Kai Woods clearly understood Randy Laine's words to the bottom of his soul.

"This place is amazing, Ian. Let's make sure we don't screw it up."

"Uh, yeah, Kai, it's amazing. We'll be ok," said Clark, but his attention was on the GPS unit in his left hand and a scrap of paper in his right.

He'd spent another five thousand dollars with the computer guys, assisted by an oceanographic topographer, to try and nail down the exact location of the reef Merrill had shot. He looked again at the GPS unit. Slowly he crumpled the paper into a tiny wad. The numbers still didn't quite match. The place below them wasn't the reef discovered by L.J. Merrill. It must be, Clark knew, one of the zones of white off to the east. Then he smiled when he realized he had discovered this reef and, in fact, had not stolen anything at all from L.J. Merrill. He laughed at the irony of everything that had transpired over the past three hundred days. He was suddenly a happy man, and he shared his sense of victory right away.

"Kai, this is going to be insane! We're gonna make history today! Okay guys," he said over the intercom," Let's get ready to set down. Oh, and by the way, last time I was here, the conditions were a bit sketchy. But today is bigger, better shaped, and there's no wind. This is the best big wave ever in the history of surfing, period. And it's all ours."

A series of cheers and hoots echoed throughout the fuselage until the no-nonsense voice of the plane commander cut it off.

"Mac, confirm passengers and cargo ready for set down."

"Ok, boys, strap in! Ian, Kai! Get 'em ready! Flight. All cargo secure. We'll be go for setdown in a minute. "

"Roger that. Starting final approach in one minute."

Victor Sanchez repeated his landing pattern by lining up with the opening at the north end of the reef. He lowered the pontoons from the tips of the wings. He set the *Skyhook* down gently until he heard the keel slicing through the glassy surface. He touched the throttles back a hair but kept her nose up.

"Pontoon contact," said Tina Sanchez.

He let the nose come down, and the flying boat was no longer flying. Sanchez used the throttles to steer her into the protection of the reef at the northern entrance to the lagoon. He throttled all the way back, and the heavily laden *Skyhook* came to a rest.

Ian Clark went into strictly-business mode as soon as he un-snapped his seat belt. He clearly remembered how Larson had led the charge in May. He knew the drill, and he was ready. This was now his reef, and he was going to take command.

"Ok, guys, let's all get up on the wing. You can see the place and I can tell you exactly what we are going to do. Follow me."

Palua and Woods exchanged puzzled glances with each other and the Hawaiians, who themselves weren't quite ready to be taking orders. But Clark had been there, they hadn't, so they would listen to him, for now. When they got to the cargo bay, the Wavelife surfers were changing into their new lightweight wetsuits in a variety of bright colors keyed to produce vibrant resolution on TV screens. The camera guys were each doing four things at once in the 'sunroom'.

"Wait a sec! Taz, tell 'em to wait, we've got to plan this out a bit, ok?"

Nakamura translated, but the Wavelife guys only slowed down a little. The TV guy was already shooting with his new camera in one hand while looking at the manual with the other.

"Hey you guys, can I get you to stop for a second! We have a lot to go over, and it's important!" Clark said with authority, "Follow me up on the wing. Don't step on the flaps, and don't sit on the engines. They're still hot."

Clark opened one of the Plexiglas canopies, stepped up to the fuselage and guided the men up to the broad wing of the PBY. A minute later he wanted to get started, but everyone was looking right past him at the huge waves breaking perfectly down both sides of the reef.

"Hey! Listen up! All of you!" Clark shouted above the roar of the waves, "Now sit down and pay attention!" That got their attention, but just barely. "Ok, guys, I got you all here, and now I'm going to get you the best waves of your lives. Here's what we have to do."

Clark's moment of glory was short-lived.

"Hey, we know what to do, brah. Get da gas in da skis we go surfin'," said Tony Aipua.

"Who gonna drive me?" asked David Kahaio.

"What about the inflatables? I gotta have my hands free to shoot," said Brad Halley.

"I'm going on a ski," said Craig Bishop.

"Hey, we got to get these guys out there first and get some establishing shots for TV," said Taz Nakamura, translating furiously for the TV guy.

"I'll do the talking here," said Steve Palua, "I was surfing big waves before most of you guys were even born. Now, let's start with - - - "

"Let's start with the safety procedures," said Kai Woods, "I need everyone to - - -"

"Who made you the guy to give orders, Woods?" said Ben Lalaoa, "Palua put this whole thing together, and I think - - -"

"No, I put this thing together," said Clark, raising his voice almost to a scream, "and I'm the only guy who knows how to get this show on the road."

"Fuck dat! Last time you here, Larson almost die! Why we listen to you?"

Lalaoa stood up and crossed his arms. The Wavelife surfers began to chatter away while looking at Clark.

"Ian, you got us here, but I can take over now," said Steve Palua, who stood up next to Lalaoa.

"Steve, listen, I know what I'm talking about. Now here's what you guys have to do."

Clark felt a hand gently move him slightly aside.

"Starting with paying attention, and that means each and every one of your boys, Palua. And if you got any problems with that, I'll dump you and alla them in the water and leave you here for a few days. You got that?"

Nobody said a word, least of all Steve Palua.

"Now, sit down and shut up. My wife's got something to tell you," said Victor Sanchez. The surf was roaring in the background, but the power in his voice came through loud and clear. Clark couldn't have been more surprised if L.J. Merrill himself had suddenly come to his aid. Sanchez stepped aside for his wife to stand between him and Clark, with Mac Owens right behind her.

"I have a signed contract with Mr. Palua," she said, holding up the four page document, "We have delivered you to your destination. However, you are still onboard, and therefore you are still under the command of Captain Sanchez. What he says, goes. Victor?"

"Now listen good 'cause I'm only going to say it once. And you better be translating this right, pal," he said, glancing at Taz Nakamura, "Heath Larson almost died out here, and he knew what he was doing. You guys don't know shit from shinola. Hey, translator, tell your friends there to pay attention. My dad fought in World War Two and - - -"

"Yes, Captain, yes, give me a second."

Nakamura let loose with torrent of words that immediately got the attention of the Wavelife surfers. Their smirks quickly disappeared.

"Ok, now, here's what you are going to do to disembark from my aircraft. Clark, who's the main guy for the jetskis?"

"Tony Aipua," he said, nodding at the big Hawaiian.

"Ok Mac, that guy's your assistant. Get the skis fueled and tethered. Who are the camera guys?"

Halley and Bishop stood up.

"You get the zodiacs in the water and fuel 'em. Ian, what about the locator system? Did you test it?"

Sanchez looked at Clark with a clear message in his eyes.

I won't screw up this time and neither will you.

Clark shook his head and then looked at Steve Palua.

"Ok, you must be the guy who signed the contracts. Who's the lifeguard?"

"Uh, he is," said Palua, pointing to Kai Woods.

"Go and get the safety vests," said Sanchez, "Check 'em all out, and then get the locator system squared away. Is that what you want, Ian? 'cause from now on Clark's in charge, and what he says, goes. Make sure you all listen to him," said Sanchez, pointing to Clark, "As commander of this aircraft I'm giving him full authority here. Now get going."

He turned around and went back down through the canopy, with his wife right behind him. Mac Owens gestured to Tony Aipua who stood up and followed Owens, leaving Clark to address the rest of the men.

"Taz, get all your guys in the galley and get 'em focused, if you can. Kai, we're gonna make sure these vest locators work before we hand 'em out. David, go all the way aft and get all the boards in the water. Open the hatch back there and tether 'em together. And double check all the fins and footstraps on each board. Steve, help Craig and Brad with the zodiacs and the camera stuff. Palua, you help 'em cause you'll be driving one of them. Oh yeah, Taz, make sure the TV guy is ready to go. Craig, let's get you in a zodiac and start shooting around the plane. Then we'll go to stage two. Kai? You get the last word here because this whole thing has to be about safety first."

The lifeguard appreciated Clark's words more than he knew.

"We are all responsible for each other. Don't forget it." He looked made eye contact with the Hawaiians. He wanted them to know he was issuing a personal challenge to them. "If we do this right, we'll make history. If we screw up," he turned to watch a set of thirty foot waves roll in, "we'll, we're not going to screw up, ok?"

The sun was pushing across the sky into afternoon. Almost two hours had passed since Victor Sanchez had given Clark the backup he needed. The safety runs had been done, the grid set out, the helmet radios checked, the displays on the waverunners were accurate, and the surfers were behaving themselves. Everyone had followed Clark's orders exactly, and both he and Woods were beginning to feel things just might turn out ok.

Then it was time for Ben Lalaoa to get the first real wave of the trip. It was in the thirty foot range, and he stayed well out on the shoulder. His ride was greeted with hoots and cheers by the entire crew following in formation down the wave on the four waverunners and two zodiacs. Ian Clark, sitting on the wing of the *Skyhook*, tracked the cluster of personal locator beacons across the grid on the laptop. When they all reached the inside station, Tony Aipua pulled in and picked up Lalaoa effortlessly. The first wave had been ridden. They'd done it.

As ordered, the entire crew came back to the *Skyhook*. Palua pulled up his zodiac under the cockpit window.

"Say, Mrs. Sanchez, you can make that call now, please," he said before seeing Clark on the wing and giving him a thumbs-up. Clark took a deep breath and sighed. He was now a free man with a million bucks waiting for him to start a new life. He came down off the wing and into the cargo bay with all the watercraft floating nearby.

"Ok, guys, listen up, and Taz, if you need me to slow down, let me know, ok? Oh, wait a sec, hey Victor, what's on the weather radar?"

"All clear all directions," came one voice from the cockpit, and then another.

"Ian, Mr. Anasi sends his regards. Your arrangement has been concluded. I have a confirmation number for you."

"Thanks, Tina," he said. Clark felt another rush of exultation. Then he turned his attention back to the men under his command.

"Ok, now we're ready for stage three."

Clark proceeded to call out names and assignments that would give them a chance to double check all the cameras and equipment with the Hawaiians riding a few waves and the Wavelife surfers watching. Then they would get an hour of waves to themselves with Kai Woods driving the fourth waverunner. The camera guys were either in the zodiacs or on the backs of the jetskis.

"And if I tell you guys to do something over the radio," Clark said, "don't think twice. Just do it. I can see everything from up here and on the locator display. We make no mistakes and you get the best big wave surf session ever. That's the deal. You ready?"

A resounding "Yeah!!!" came back before it was drowned out by the roar of engines as the waverunners and zodiacs headed back out to sea.

For the next two hours, the waves never changed. It was a Hawaiian thirty foot, and flawless. Everybody was perfectly willing to stay clear of the impact zone. Nobody wanted any part of the heavy energy that chased them down the line on each wave. It all went like clockwork. The euphoria on the faces of the surfers was visible on wave after wave. Different boards were tried. Riders sometimes did weaves on the same wave. Kai Woods was always alert but relieved that it was all going so well.

Then the first waverunner ran out of gas. It was Kahaio's, running along an easy shoulder in front of one of the Wavelife guys. He hit the reserve switch and called out over his helmet mike to Clark. He'd told them to be checking their gauges, but in all the fun and excitement, he knew it was inevitable that at least one guy would forget to stay vigilant. As agreed, everyone cut short their runs and headed back to the *Skyhook*. It was time to make a decision. They would have to leave now, or they could fill their tanks, stay overnight, and have the *Skyhook* come back in the morning with more fuel, food, and film. Ian Clark had no doubt what the vote would be.

A half hour later, the waverunner fuel tanks were all topped off, as were the portable tanks of the two zodiacs. Mac Owens deployed one of the twelve man liferafts and maneuvered it toward the inner edge of the reef lagoon where the water was only knee deep. He and Clark rigged the shade tarp over the raft and off-loaded all the food and water they'd brought on the trip.

"Heck, ya got yer own island paradise here, Ian! Now all you need is a dame or two and you'd be set!" he laughed.

The cameramen changed all their batteries, boxed up all the film and digital image cartridges, and made a few agonizing decisions about what to take since they couldn't keep their big cases with them. They knew whatever they didn't have would for sure be needed, but the *Skyhook* would be back early the next morning, and Palua's instructions made it a little easier.

"Tomorrow we'll start by shooting the Wavelife guys. I want all the raw footage we can get. We want to put together a TV show right away when we get back."

Taz Nakamura translated for the TV guy and the surfers. Their eyes lit up like neon lights.

"Say brah, you got plenty a me an' da boys?" asked David Kahaio.

"We shot you guys from every possible angle, David," said Palua.

"That's right," said Brad Halley, "We've got four hours in the can. Gonna have some heavy home movies when we get back Island side."

"Ok, we're all clear on the weather?" asked Kai Woods.

"If we weren't we wouldn't be doing this," said Victor Sanchez, "We'll be back by nine tomorrow. If something happens, you got a portable radio in the life raft. It puts out an emergency signal to us."

"What, in case you need rescue us?" laughed Tony Aipua.

"Well, this is pretty unusual, and you never know what might happen," said Tina Sanchez, "but your contract allows for this contingency and you guys voted to stay. Just don't forget what happened to Heath Larson."

"Dat guy tink he so smart alla time. We no dat stupid in waves dis big," said Aipua.

* * *

The surf camp was floating in knee deep water near the northern entrance to the lagoon. Jetskis and surfboards were arrayed all around the liferaft. The accommodations were cramped, but nobody complained. They passed food around and talked about the waves they'd seen and ridden. The surf was perfect, the weather ideal, the water warm, and there would be more tomorrow. Hours of film and digital images were in the can and headed back to the people who wrote the paychecks. Thanks to the money of a corporation and the engines of the jetskis, they were living the surfer's dream.

"Dis place da best wave in da world!" said Tony Aipua, "Mo' perfect dan anytin I evah see dis big."

"Tomorrow I gonna get one da kine tube ride," said David Kahaio, "Mebbe get ten o' dem!"

The talk only got bolder as the sun began to go down. After gassing up the skis, they had done a few more runs with the Wavelife surfers followed by the Hawaiians towing each other into some macking sets. But Steve Palua called a halt late in the afternoon. He wanted the waverunners to have plenty of fuel the next day. Now he was going to explain why.

"Ok, guys, listen up. Here's the plan for tomorrow. We're going to get an early start, and I mean really early."

"Say brah, mebbe dat not so good idea," said Ben Lalaoa, "Island side we wait an hour, mebbe two, see what da swell doing, watch da conditions. Dat dawn patrol stuff ain't safe inna big waves."

"Yeah, Steve," said Kai Woods, "I gotta agree with Ben. If the conditions are going to be good all day, what's the hurry?"

Taz Nakamura was translating as fast as he could. The Wavelife surfers were paying close attention. To them it seemed as though the Hawaiians were objecting to Palua's plan about making a film because they wanted to get the best waves. But Palua wasn't going to back down to the Hawaiians. His motives were pure – purely commercial, that is.

"Because we need to get all the footage we can right as the sun is coming up. We need to be shooting at dawn, and we need to keep shooting for at least an hour. Every wave, every tow-in run, every angle."

"That means we gotta be out there at first light," said Brad Halley. He knew the logistics from a cameraman's perspective and the timing involved to insure they got the stuff the director wanted.

"Whatever it takes, you guys are here to do it. Now, here's the deal. Tony, David, Ben, Kai. You guys will each drive a ski. No, wait. Everybody get out of the raft."

"Say brah, what dis about?" Ben Lalaoa was never one to cooperate if he didn't have to.

"Its called blocking a scene," said Craig Bishop, "we're going to set up the actors with the props, assign the cameras, and make sure everyone knows their place when the director yells 'Action'!"

"Thanks, Craig," said Palua.

"Fuck, I ain't no actor! I ain't gonna do dis bullshit!" said Lalaoa.

"Then you don't get paid, brah," said Palua, "The guys writing the checks didn't send you out here for a vacation. So what's it gonna be?"

"But, Steve, dis is surfin', brah!"

"After we get what I want, you can surf all day long. I need enough footage to make a TV show - - -"

"And the working title is 'The Surf of the Rising Sun'," said Ian Clark, knowing full well exactly what the whole thing was really about.

"Yeah, thanks Ian. That's the idea, Ben. You in or out?"

Ten minutes later, each driver was sitting on a waverunner. The two Hawaiian cameramen were assigned to ride with the two best drivers, Aipua and Kahaio. They had their equipment in their hands. Then Palua put a Wavelife surfer on the back of each of the big waverunners with a surfboard under his arm. The other two cameramen got in one zodiac. Clark, with the locator system, got in the other. Palua stood back and looked at the cast and crew. He got out a camera and took a few pictures.

"Hey, Steve, let me get one of you," said Clark. He got out of the inflatable and walked across the coral. Palua gave him the camera and then stood in front of the assembled group while Clark snapped several images.

"Hey, Steve, where you gonna be?" asked Aipua.

He went over to the zodiac with the two cameramen in it.

"I'll be with these guys."

"Ok, guys, say geevum!" said Ian Clark. The surfers started to raise their boards in the air, the Hawaiians flashed the "chaka" sign with one hand and their helmets held high with the other. The cameramen held their equipment in the air. Clark snapped a half-dozen images.

The sun was getting close to the horizon. The huge surf had created a soft mist in the air, and the light was fading fast. Clark thought he better get some more with a flash. He wasn't familiar with the camera, and in trying to figure it out, he fumbled it and dropped it into the water. A groan went up from all the men, and Clark looked mortified as he bent over and reached down to retrieve the camera.

"No problem, Ian! It's waterproof! Take some more shots!" said Palua.

Clark got the flash working, and with everyone suddenly stoked all over again, he got another dozen images of the men and their equipment as the sun disappeared into the mist. He put the thin camera in his safety vest. It still had a few frames left in its memory and he figured he'd get more shots tomorrow as the sun was coming up.

"Ok, now let's double check everything. Safety vests, tow ropes, helmets, locators, everything. Get it all ready to go, and leave everything right where you'll be tomorrow. Taz, get the cameras loaded and ready in the zodiac. Brad, Craig, yours go on the skis. Tony, make sure the boards are strapped on the back, and Kai let's do a comm check and test the locator beacons and the entire system one more time, ok?"

Everyone followed Clark's orders without complaint. Thanks to him, they were surfing the most perfect big waves they'd ever seen.

Darkness came on quickly. Kai Woods had rigged up a light at the top of the pole holding up the tarp covering the life raft. Small fish from around the lagoon were attracted by the soft orange glow of the canopy that created a cozy bivouac for night. The crew inside was still excited, and for almost an hour the talk was nonstop as they finished off the food, fortifying themselves for the big day tomorrow. But after a while they quieted down, and soon nothing could be heard except the constant roar of the waves all around them, like jet engines that, after a while, are no longer heard by the passengers. They were exhausted and all fell asleep quickly.

The nightlite was left on as the monsters roamed around the perimeter of the Reef of Power. Safe in the lagoon, the men dreamed of surfing the huge waves surrounding them, riding inside giant liquid tunnels at an unknown reef deep in the most remote reaches of the South Pacific.

* * *

Part Two: Caverns in the Rising Sun

Ian Clark's eyes opened slowly. In the dim glow of the nightlite he could see men all around him still sleeping soundly. He gathered his thoughts and checked his watch. First light would be about an hour. He awkwardly rolled over, raised his head and peered out under the tent flap. A thin crescent moon was barely visible through the haze and he could hardly see the stars, unusual for a night sky in the South Pacific. He noticed the sound of the surf had stopped almost entirely. For a second he thought maybe it had gone down.

An explosion shattered the silence. It was the first wave of a set, and though he was a mile from the impact zone, it seemed louder than any wave he'd ever heard. The volume of sound increased as the wave rolled towards him down both sides of the reef.

Clark pushed the stopwatch button on his watch at the next explosion to time the intervals between the waves. He pushed it again at the next. And the next. And the next. The interval told him the surf was huge, and the explosions didn't stop for another three minutes. The last of the waves rolled past the northern end of the reef, and it was quiet again. Another head peered out from under the tarp.

"It gonna be real big, yeah brah?" said Tony Aipua, wide-awake.

"Yeah, I think so. We better get this show on the road."

"I help you today, brah," said Aipua with a wink before he pulled his head back under the tarp and bellowed a wake up call, "Ok, guys, time to geevum! David! Ben! Let's go! We gotta get da jetskis ready. Palua! Dis whole ting yo idea! No mo' sleeping, brah!"

"Uh, yeah! I'm up! How's the surf?"

"Pretty big, brah. Pretty big."

A dull, gray glow was growing in the east. The men were getting their bearings and slowly gathering around the equipment waiting for them. Ian Clark tried to marshal his troops.

"Ok, everybody get to your ski. Camera guys, into the zodiac. Let's stay on plan, everyone, just like yesterday, ok?"

"Wait a sec, I think the drivers should get the skis going first, and then we'll load 'em," said Steve Palua, now wide awake and ready to be the director on the set.

"So which is it, Palua? Load up or start the engines?" Tony Aipua was only adding to the confusion.

"Tony, you guys get your engines running. Taz, start the outboards. No, wait, I'll do it. Taz, get your cameras ready and make sure the TV guy is ready to go, too. And tell the surfers to get on the skis."

"And tell 'em to put on their vests!" added Kai Woods.

An engine started, then stopped. Someone fell over in the water and started cursing. One of the Wavelife surfers couldn't find his safety vest. Another decided he wanted to ride a different board. But soon all the engines came to life and a thick cloud of noise and exhaust surrounded the men. The jet fuel burned rich and the carburetors were coughing and sputtering fumes as throttles were rolled on to rev up the engines again and again. Then a new set came down the reef and the powerful roar of the surf added to the confusion.

"Taz! Get those guys on the skis! Brad, you ready?"

"Fuck yes, Craig! Let's get going! The light's coming on!"

"I can't get the engine started!" said Palua Ian Clark went over to help. The TV guy was reading the manual for the camera strapped around his shoulder. Clark had to get his attention to get him to move only to hear a stream of curses directed at both him and the camera.

The light was coming on, and the men could clearly see each other through the smoke and mist. Yet with no wind to clear the air, the colors of the boards, skis and wetsuits were muted as if they were in a shadow on an overcast day.

"Hey, Brad, I think the light's gonna be shitty! This mist sucks!"

"Yeah, I know, but Cecille B. DeMille wants what he wants!"

"Okay, guys, I'm going up the lagoon. Stay in radio contact, ok?"

Ian Clark revved the outboard and turned away from the campsite. He motored a little ways out into the lagoon, stopped, and turned on the computer and the locator system. Then he spoke into the microphone.

"Ok, raise an arm if you can hear me."

He saw all the drivers, cameramen and Palua raise their arms.

"Ok, play it safe. Don't do anything stupid. Kai! Stay on top of it. Palua! Make sure everyone follows the plan!!"

"What plan?" yelled Kahaio, "We goin' surfin, brah!"

The Hawaiian gunned his engine and led the group out of the lagoon entrance. For a second Clark was a bit proud of what they were doing until he saw Steve Palua gesturing to the TV guy to show him where to point the camera – and a cloud of exhaust trailing behind the ragged formation.

Ian Clark gunned his outboard, turned in a tight circle and rolled on the throttle. Straight ahead of him, at the far end of the reef, he could see a wave almost forty feet high coming over in a pyramid peak. The huge wall began to break in both directions. Clark watched the right, and it was breaking perfectly. He turned his head and looked at the left. He saw a massive section break unexpectedly and close out the wave completely.

"All drivers! Don't surf the lefts! It's closing out on that side," he said into his helmet radio.

"Yeah, Clark, we're only going to surf the rights anyway. We need the rising sun to shine on the waves," said Palua nonchalantly.

The rest of the set powered through. Clark was awestruck at the view from this angle. Yesterday he had been sitting on top of the *Skyhook* at the northern entrance to the lagoon. Now he was almost to the southern limits of the inner waters. It was the difference between watching a pretty good hitter from center field and standing on the pitcher's mound with Barry Bonds at the plate.

He put the motor in neutral and checked the locator system. The locator beacon dots were showing in the lower left of the grid as the group went around the reef. Then they blinked out. Then they reappeared in a slightly different place. Then they blinked out. He checked the battery indicator, but he had enough power. Then he realized he was now floating directly on the sea surface instead of sitting on the wing of the *Skyhook* fifteen feet above sea level. The surf was so big it was interfering with the signal.

"Palua, this is Clark. We've got a problem."

The comm system was open mic all the way around. Palua was talking to the cameramen in his zodiac and the ski drivers all at the same time. They were talking back to him, and to each other. Clark realized an even bigger problem was shaping up. Steve Palua was giving orders off the top of his head as the formation motored south around the reef.

"Yeah, Clark, what do you want? No, Taz, don't shoot them yet. We're going to get a shot of them coming out of the entrance. Hey, Ben, circle around me for a second. We've got to get some specific shots. Tony! Come back around, ok? Yea, what's the problem, Clark?"

"I'm coming out there. The waves are too big for the locator system if I'm in here." But Clark's message got lost in the crosstalk.

"The surf is a lot bigger, Palua!" said Kai Woods, "We gotta talk!"

"Everyone! Come over here! We've got to get some shots right away!"

"Hey Brad, what's your f-stop?"

"Everybody get a warm up wave! Then stay down by the entrance! Wait till you are all together! We've got to get a shot of you coming out!"

"Why didn't we do that already?"

"Can't we get it later? Craig, I'm at f/4. There's not enough light!"

"Nobody take off until I'm in position. I gotta reset the locator system from a new reference point."

"Hey, am I imagining this, or is this still the same set?"

"Palua, maybe we better go back and wait for the seaplane."

"Ok, we've got about five minutes before sunup. Everybody get a wave. Red, Yellow, Green, Blue. In that order."

"No! Yellow goes last!" said Taz Nakamura, "This guy's got to color balance his camera!"

"Ok, red, green, blue THEN yellow!"

"Tony, get your guy in the water and whip him into the next one! Look at that wave! My God!"

"Nah, get in line behind me – let's circle back up to the peak. And stay on the shoulder!"

"Palua this better be worth it. This is insane."

"Just follow my directions. Taz! Why aren't you shooting?"

"You've got me driving."

"Oh, ok, start shooting. I'll drive!"

"Palua, what's Japanese for get in the water?"

"Hell if I know. How about Banzai?"

"Banzai! Go for it!"

"Hey not there, David! I'm gonna slice your tow line."

"Not if you wait a minute."

"Fuck, is this set ever gonna end?"

"Drivers, switch your console to the locator display."

"Which button was that? Oh, I just turned it off! Wait, okay, got it!"

"Ok, I'm going on this one. Brad, is he ready?"

"Yeah, but I'm not."

"Red team, go! Green, rider up and ready."

"He can't get his foot in the straps."

"Blue team ready. Rider up. Let's go!"

"Blue team wait! Stop! No! Go! I said GO! Green, catch up to him! Ride down to the entrance! Taz, what they hell is going on with this guy?"

"Nothing! He's got image!"

"Everybody go!"

"Fuck! What happened to my gas? That can't be right. I had plenty."

"Don't worry about gas. Yellow team go!"

"Rider down! He missed the pull-up!"

"Fuck, this set is still going! I've never seen anything like this!"

"Go! Yellow! Go! Everybody get a wave! Get down to the entrance and wait for my signal!"

The chatter never stopped as each driver positioned his surfer, accelerated, and within seconds there was a rider up on each wave.

Ian Clark positioned himself in deep water at the edge of the grid set up the day before to encompass the entire reef. As soon as the *Skyhook* returned, he knew he'd have to set up a new grid for just the rights to gain back a margin of safety.

"Sunrise in one minute! One minute!"

"Palua, you've got at least another five minutes! The haze is gonna block the light."

"Hey Palua! These guys are talking to each other! HEY!!! HEY!!! Palua, what's the word for shut up? They aren't ready!"

"Get the sun as it comes up! Start shooting!"

"Whew! That set finally ended. Man, this place is unbelievable!"

"Sunrise! Everybody start filming! Roll cameras!"

"Palua! Wait! Aw, fuck, who cares! Brad, this is nuts!"

"For what he's paying you, just do what he tell you to do!"

"He doesn't know what he's doing!"

"Shut up, Bishop, and turn on your camera. Here it comes!"

The set had lasted for almost five minutes. Now the ocean was calm, except for swirls of foam and little whirlpools here and there. All eyes turned to the east and strained to see through the gray haze laying thick on the water. The horizon line was indistinguishable. There were no rays from the sun spreading skyward. There were no overhanging clouds reflecting light down on the surfers. There was no wind. Except for the swirling currents running over the coral down both sides of the reef, there wasn't a sound except that of engines idling.

A small red dot appeared, seemingly suspended above the ocean. It grew in size but did not rise upwards. It glowed through the heavy mist, brighter and brighter, while it base began to broaden.

"All cameras rolling! Get it! Get it! Ok, drivers, pull-up your riders and come slowly towards me. Taz! Pan across from the sun to the riders."

"Hey, wait! My guy got his tow line tangled!"

"Rider up! Here we come!"

"No! No! All together! All together!"

"Tony! Circle around!"

"Kai get out of the way! David get the fucker up on his board!"

"Ben, shut up!"

"C'mon! C'mon! Taz! Is he getting this? Taz!"

"How do I know what he's seeing?"

Steve Palua grabbed the TV guy and turned him towards the surfers. They had formed up and were coming straight at the zodiac.

"Slow down! Move over! Spread out! I can't see the surfers! Taz! No! Don't shoot the surfers! Keep shooting the sun, and then pan around!"

The red eye of the sun cast a baleful glare on the confusion of the surfers. As the waverunners went past, Ian Clark tracked them on his laptop. The ocean was flat, the locator beacons were close, and everything was working perfectly. The formation went to the southern end of the reef. The rising sun was now above the mist and casting a surreal light across the surf zone. Then the entire southern horizon seemed to rise up as a wave train approached the arena where the surfers and cameras were waiting.

"Say brah, dis gonna be one big set!"

"Fuck! Look da first one!"

"Oh my god! Punch it!!"

The waverunners avoided the first wave by speeding to the safety of deep water. They let the next wave go by, too. It was ten feet bigger than the first one.

"Sheezus! Hey Clark, what's the shape like down there?" The waves were unlike anything they'd seen so far, and Kai Woods wanted a scout's eyeview down the lineup. But the only thing Steve Palua wanted was the opening sequence of a TV show with the rising sun shining on heroic surfers riding incredible waves.

"Ok, each surfer on a wave! This is what we came for! Brad, Craig, its money time! Taz! This is it! Geevum!"

Ian Clark had yet to respond to Woods' question. He was mesmerized watching a wave so big, so powerful and yet so perfect it defied description, even by a man who had sold surfing perfection for years. He'd never seen anything like it in his life, and neither had anyone else in the history of surfing. Then he remembered Woods' question.

"Kai! It's perfect! The first one peeled, and the second one – is – just – just – – Palua! Palua!! Tell 'em DO NOT GO IN THE TUBE! STAY ON THE SHOULDER! That's the most amazing thing I've - - - Look at that fucking WAVE!"

He remembered the camera in his safety vest, and as the wave went by he took a picture through the huge open mouth of the spinning tunnel leading back down into a liquid cavern lit up by the rising sun.

The set lasted almost five minutes. Each wave was at least forty feet high, measured vertically. The slope of the faces was three times as long. The Hawaiians had never seen surf this perfect on a scale this big, but they were driving fast jetskis running aviation fuel and weren't too scared of the situation. The Wavelife surfers, on the other hand, were in a world they could never have imagined. They were going to ride waves whose raw power was beyond anything they'd ever dreamed of. They had no idea what a wipeout was like in surf like this. They had never paid the price for a mistake in such waves and it was too late for explanations from either Woods or the Hawaiians. And then Steve Palua made things worse.

"Ok, we got a problem. The orange safety vests! We can't see the Wavelife surfsuits. We need to do some runs without the vests. Yeah, we can do it. Drivers! Come over here. Taz, explain to them what we're doing."

Kai Woods' instincts went to red alert.

"Steve, make sure they stay on the shoulder! Make 'em promise! We'll never be able to get 'em! Palua, the foam is three feet thick inside! Palua, are you listening to me?"

He wasn't. He was talking to Taz Nakamura who was talking to the surfers who were talking to each other while the TV guy filmed everything and the Hawaiians waited.

The surfers took off their vests – with the locator beacons in the pockets.

"Palua! What about the locator beacons?" asked an incredulous Ian Clark.

"Uh, don't worry. Just leave 'em in the vests. Just a couple of runs for the cameras. We'll put them back on right away."

"Hey, Steve, Clark's right. Have 'em stuff the beacons down the front of their wetsuits," said Woods.

"Nah, that's gonna take too much time. Let's just get some easy shoulder runs, ok? Just a couple, and then we'll just put the vests back on. Ok guys?"

"Palua, you fuckin' nuts! But if dese guys wanna surf wid no vest, I tow 'em in," said Tony Aipua.

"You da boss, Palua. Whatever you say, brah," said David Kahaio, shaking his head.

"My guy smiling! What da fuck he tinking?" asked Ben Laloa, knowing he'd never get an answer.

"Palua, just one run, ok? This shit is crazy!" said Kai Woods.

"Brad, you getting all this?"

"I'm almost out of memory, Craig. You?"

"Got about twenty minutes left. Hey Palua, why don't we take a break and wait for the plane?"

"Yeah, c'mon, Steve, we've got all day."

"Just a couple more. Ok guys, here comes a set. Oh, and try and get two guys on the same wave this time. Yeah! Get two guys on one wave, and two guys on the next wave. We'll follow you down the reef! Taz, tell the TV guy what we're doing! Ok, let's go! two on a wave! Now!"

The waverunner drivers looked at each other.

"Kai, we go me and you," said Tony Aipua, "David, go wid Ben. We geevum one time and dats it! Fuck dis bullshit!"

The formation of four waverunners moved down the reef, followed by the zodiac. The surfers were slaloming on the shoulder, as instructed. As they went by Clark, he snapped two more pictures of Palua steering the zodiac with the waverunners and surfers barely visible as they sped by. He checked the camera and it had two more frames left in the memory. He put it back in pocket of his safety vest.

When they got to the end of the run, Palua wasn't happy.

"No, that ain't good! The skis are too much in the picture! One more time and drivers! Peel off and get outta the way! This is the last one, ok guys! Wait a sec, come on over. I want Taz to talk to 'em."

"Palua!" screamed Kai Woods, his instincts on overload, "They aren't wearing vests and if they fall we won't be able to find them!"

"Yeah, Palua, what the fuck are you doing?" yelled David Kahaio.

"Earning my paycheck! Now shut up you guys!! We'll just get one more and then wait for the plane!"

The drivers pulled the Wavelife surfers over within earshot of Steve Palua. He began to explain what had happened on the first run with Nakamura translating. He also told them this was going to be their last wave. The four surfers immediately started snapping back at Nakamura. The TV guy's ears perked up and he stopped his camera.

"Steve, they're pissed! They wanna surf! This is a matter of honor for them. They think you're trying to protect them like children. They say they can surf as good as the Hawaiians. They - - -"

The surfers began screaming at Nakamura who translated word for word.

"We are not cowards! We do not need your protection! We will be heroes for our country! We will be famous on TV!"

"Tell them this is only the last wave for now. We need to wait and get more gas and film from the seaplane."

Taz Nakamura did as he was told. two of the surfers started pointing at Palua and shouting.

"Steve, they don't believe you. They think you will let the Hawaiians surf and not them."

"Tell them one more easy run, we wait for gas, and they will come back out here right away," explained Palua, but when Nakamura finished his translation, the Wavelife surfers made no attempt to hide their disdain. And they weren't the only ones.

"Palua, what you talkin'? I no gonna drive dis ting all day! I brought two da kine boards fo' go surf!" said a growling Ben Lalaoa.

"When the plane gets here, we'll figure out the day, ok? Right now, let's just get one more wave!" said the increasingly frantic expedition leader.

The waverunners accelerated back out to the takeoff zone. As they went by, Ian Clark heard the surfers screaming over the roar of the engines. The Tui guys looked determined. The North Shore cameramen looked nervous. On the zodiac, the TV guy was fumbling to change a setting, and Taz Nakamura was barely holding on because Steve Palua was running wide open trying to keep up with the waverunners. For a moment Clark thought of a Hollywood film set gone haywire. The director was harried. The crew was pissed off. The actors were insulted. The cameramen were running out of time. And the safety guy was freaking because they were violating all the rules.

Then Ian Clark saw the set coming and remembered what had happened the last time he had heard the words, "One more wave."

The formation entered the takeoff zone. Aipua and Woods lined up exactly as before, and within seconds two riders were up and gliding down the slope of the first wave.

"Ok, peel off! Peel off!" yelled Palua, his voice maxing out the microphone and barely intelligible, "Get way out on the shoulder! That's it!"

The two surfers saw the waverunners turn away from them. The same thing happened on the second wave. Now four surfers were all up simultaneously on successive waves. The first wave hit the reef and began to explode in peeling perfection towards the surfers riding safely in the deeper water. For a moment they looked at each other before they all looked directly into the power coming at them and screamed the oath of the bushido warrior.

The surfers on the first wave sliced hard turns towards the reef. They dropped down to the bottom of the wave and turned as hard as they could. The other two surfers did the exact same thing. They all wanted to demonstrate they were world class surfers who didn't need to be protected from big waves. Taking off their safety vests had only served to embolden them.

But one of the surfers on the second wave lost his nerve almost immediately. When he had a clear view of the maelstrom in the cavern of the wave, he quickly turned back and headed for safety. Kai Woods saw what the guy did and cut over to get him. The surfer grabbed the tow handle and allowed himself to be towed into deep water. He looked back over his shoulder in shame. He had failed the code of bushido. His friends would be riding to glory, and he would be forever branded a coward as long as he lived.

The three remaining surfers had what they wanted, what they had trained for. They were brave and not afraid of death. They were young and did not know the value of life. They were good surfers, but they were no match for a power beyond their comprehension.

The lone surfer drove deeper towards the tube. He felt his own soul stained by his friend's disgrace. He was mad with determination to defend his honor. His bottom turn came around perfectly at high speed. He went to the top of the wave, so far above him that by the time he had elevated forty feet, the roof of the wave was beginning to come over.

The pair of surfers were just as saturated with bushido, but their turns were too tight and didn't give them the speed they needed. They crouched low and tried to eke out more speed from their boards.

The lone surfer tried to turn back down the wave. His outside rail caught an edge. The board lost all speed. He tried to force the board forward. It came loose, and pointed back down the wave. Straight down.

The paired surfers were racing for their lives. The roof of the wave was above their heads, then ahead of them. One looked up and panicked. The two boards collided and the surfers fell sideways. And then, with their feet strapped to their boards, they went up and over with the cascading lip.

The lone surfer fell through mid air to the bottom of the wave, landing head-first just ahead of the guillotine lip. The pair were flung out into mid air in an arc almost sixty feet in diameter. When the lip hit the trough, they hit with it.

"No! NO! NO!!!" Steve Palua was watching it all in the slow motion of disbelief. Then adrenaline flooded his mind.

"RIDERS DOWN!! TONY! DAVID! BEN! GET 'EM! NOW!"

But the men on the waverunners didn't respond to Palua screaming at the top of his lungs. For a moment they were overwhelmed by the reality around them as the disaster began in earnest. The bodies of the surfers were driven straight down into the coral. Necks snapped, backs broke, rib cages were crushed. The waves then lifted the corpses up and brought them around inside the cylinder of the tube and slammed them back down a second time.

With Palua screaming for them to do something, Ben Lalaoa jammed on his throttle. He forgot the ski was running on aviation fuel and it fishtailed wildly. It took him seconds to regain control but not before his waverunner bogged down because the impeller unit was sucking foam. He gunned his engine beyond redline. It blew up. The next wave was right on top of him. He bailed out. He and his waverunner suffered the same fate as the three surfers.

Aipua and Brad Halley saw Lalaoa go down. They realized his mistake. David Kahaio didn't see it. He made the same mistake, though he was lucky and somehow got some traction in the foam. He saw where he was and tried to do a hard turn to get out of the impact zone. On the back of the waverunner, Craig Bishop wasn't ready for the turn. He flew off into the water. Kahaio realized what happened and stopped. But then he saw the next wave coming right at him. He gunned the engine to get over the lip. Bishop tried to dive under the wave. Kahaio bailed out, but both men, and the jetski, were sucked up the face and then over the falls and down into the guts of the wave. Clark saw their beacon units disappear as the two were driven deep underwater. The next wave rolled over them before Clark saw the beacon dots begin to rise to the surface. The next wave rolled through and the beacon dots were gone. When they didn't show on the screen after a few seconds, Clark knew there was no chance he'd ever see those men alive again.

Now three surfers were gone, lost without locator beacons and nowhere to be seen. two drivers were down, their skis bouncing wildly in the mass of exploding white water. One photographer was underwater, his skull a mass of pulp and bone protruding from the helmet.

Kai Woods stayed calm. He had raced fifty yards out to sea and disconnected the tow rope of his surfer. The guy was screaming, but Woods knew he had work to do.

Aipua was speeding along the edge of the impact zone, trying to get a visual on something, anything. David Kahaio floated to the surface. Aipua went to get him. Halley reached down to pull the Hawaiian on to the rescue sled. He turned him over, saw his face, recoiled in horror and let go of the corpse.

"Get him in! Get him in!" screamed Aipua.

Halley was catatonic. Aipua elbowed the photographer out of the way, knocking him overboard in his adrenalin panic to save his friend. He leaned over to pull Kahaio up on the sled. He saw his friend's skull. He didn't see the next wave towering over him.

388

Palua was driving the zodiac down the reef looking for the fallen surfers. He thought he saw one. He turned and raced towards the yellow splotch of color. It was the headless torso of one of the Wavelife surfers.

Palua screamed. His hand came off the throttle of the outboard. The TV guy was still filming, pro that he was. Taz Nakamura saw another wave approaching and had the sense to grab the outboard throttle. He rolled on the throttle. Too fast. The engine flooded, and stopped. The wave lifted them to its very crest. The TV guy was still filming. Palua fell out of the zodiac. Nakamura threw his camera away and jumped off. The zodiac went up, up to the crest. Then it went down, straight down in the powerful waterfall of the crushing wave. The TV guy was looking through his camera to the bitter end.

Palua and Nakamura somehow floated up and over the lip. The next wave was headed straight for them.

Kai Woods raced down the point, looking for floating vests. He saw them, but could not get too close to the impact zone because the foam was so thick. He turned around and went back up to the takeoff zone. He knew he had to wait until the last wave of the set went through. He checked his locator display. He saw dots here and there but they were fading on and off and he thought it was an electronic problem. He pushed a button to reset the system but instead the ski control console came up. The gas gauge still read empty. He brought up the locator display again and saw nothing. Woods looked up and saw why.

Ian Clark wasn't waiting for the foam to dissipate. He was tearing into the impact zone to try and save the cameraman and Steve Palua.

He got to Palua first.

"Get in! Get in!" he yelled.

"Fuck! Help me! Help me! Get me outta here! Help me!"

"Grab the rope! Grab the rope!"

Palua grabbed the rope on the float of the zodiac with both hands.

'Get in the boat! Taz! Taz! Swim! SWIM!!" yelled Clark.

Nakamura began to stroke for his life. The wave was forty feet high, identical to all the others. Breaking in the same place. With the same power.

Nakamura saw the crest above him. He dove at an angle to get under it.

Ian Clark tried to pull a panicking Palua into the zodiac. The former surfing legend clawed at Clark's arms. Clark shook himself out of Palua's death grip. Palua kept struggling and had one leg almost in the zodiac. Neither man saw or felt the wave lifting them skyward.

Palua fell backwards out of the zodiac and down the face of the wave. He hit the bottom and all the air was slammed out of his lungs. But he was still conscious as the wave began lifted him skywards.

Ian Clark also felt the wave lifting him upwards. He had watched Palua fall out of the zodiac into the vast void below, and for a second he thought he would just float over the back of the wave. He relaxed for an instant. He was safe, sitting in the zodiac, the lip of the wave having passed beneath him.

Then he sensed something terribly wrong. The wave was still cascading forward, and he felt the zodiac being sucked with it straight down. Below him he saw nothing but exploding power as he descended into the detonation zone.

The last wave of the set was breaking down the reef. Kai Woods gunned his engine and followed it. The foam in the impact zone was dissipating. He began to strain to see the bright orange of the floatation vests worn by all the drivers and the cameramen. Suddenly he saw what he was looking for. He went in slowly. He got to the orange vest. There was nothing in it.

Now the foam was almost completely gone. He saw the backs of several vests. He went to the first one. The man was face down. It was Tony Aipua. Woods stopped to get him. He tried to get the big Hawaiian onto the rescue sled. He tried to roll him over on to the sled. He saw Aipua's face. His eyes were bulged out of their sockets, blood was streaming from under his helmet. His mouth was locked open.

Woods left him and kept going, hoping to save a life before starting the grim task of dealing with death. Another vest. Another body. It was Brad Halley. The camera was still strapped around his neck. Its body was wedged up into the helmet. Only his eyes could be seen over the camera housing that had been jammed straight up through his jaw.

Woods saw another vest. He was losing his grip. Randy Laine's words pounded in his brain.

"Don't go. Don't do it. It's suicide."

He rolled on more power towards the next body. He pulled up next to it and slowed down. He leaned over the ski to see if he could somehow reach the body. He didn't notice his engine quietly stutter to a stop. It was the other photographer. He was dead, as was the engine of the waverunner. Woods stood up and rolled on the throttle. Nothing happened. He tried to start the engine. It turned over and caught with a roar. He opened up the throttle. The engine died. He tried to start it again. It turned over. It never caught. The gas gauge was finally telling the truth. Another set was coming in a few minutes. There was only one thing left to do. He dove off the dead jetski and swam towards the last place he saw Nakamura. He got a visual on him. He waved. Nakamura did not wave back. Woods swam hard. He shouted. Nothing. He reached the photographer. He was not breathing. Woods quickly put a finger on his carotid vein. There was a pulse. He began CPR. He never stopped. He floated up and over another set of ten waves. He got lucky. A rescue sled, torn from a waverunner, was floating nearby. He pulled Nakamura towards it. He never stopped the CPR. Another set, but now he had Nakamura half on the sled. He never stopped the CPR. Another set. He was near the lagoon entrance. He kicked and breathed into the mouth of Taz Nakamura. He never stopped.

* * *

Part Three: Clark's Reef

The passengers were all eyes out the portholes. The translator was jabbering away into a high powered cell phone doing a direct, live interview with a TV station in the home of one of the Wavelife surfers. Parea Anasi was actually smiling. Everything was going according to plan, and his phone calls to Hong Kong, Newport Beach, New York and Tokyo had been pleasant experiences. Keoni Padaca was particularly excited as the stories of endless perfect waves had him almost jumping out of his skin. Big K and Junior didn't surf except on huge longboards in Waikiki, but they were looking forward to seeing their Tui brothers shredding the huge waves.

Victor Sanchez began to circle the reef while Tina Sanchez timed the intervals between the sets. The *Skyhook* banked around in a clockwise circle giving her a perfect view of the entire lagoon and surf zone below. Looking down from her co-pilot's window, she immediately sensed something wrong.

It was obvious there had been a massive increase in energy over what she'd seen the day before. The waves looked a LOT bigger. She was overwhelmed for a second before she came to her senses and was able to comprehend the new scale of things below. It was then she realized what was wrong, and a powerful alarm sounded deep in her heart.

She could see no waverunners cutting ahead of the riders. The lagoon was empty, except for a splotch of international orange near the entrance and some tiny splotches of color here and there. Some were bright orange, some yellow, some florescent green. They were the colors of the lifevests – and the Wavelife wetsuits.

"Victor, come in low and slow and drop her in right behind the reef. We can't wait for a lull. You've got enough seaway in the wave shadow. Go straight into the lagoon entrance."

Victor Sanchez was immediately alerted by the tone in his wife's voice. He glanced at his wife. She was staring down at the reef.

"Sea surface conditions? Apparent wind direction?" he asked, thinking to jog her into a normal landing cadence of information exchange.

"Uh, Victor, just get us in there as fast as you can."

"Tina! What's wrong?"

"Victor, get her down as fast as you can."

"Mac, confirm passengers ready for set down. Starting final approach."

"All passengers secure, Flight. All cargo secure. Go for setdown."

"Roger that. Ok, we're going in."

The seaplane taxied slowly into the mouth of the lagoon at the northern entrance to the reef. The roar of the engines subsided, replaced by the thunder of the waves cascading in rolling explosions as wide, open caverns collapsed into avalanches.

Tina Sanchez reached over and grabbed her husband's hand.

"Victor, I think we'd better talk to the passengers right now and keep them on board. Mac! Deploy the Avon and fire up the engine. And get all the medical gear in her including the DF unit."

"Where is everyone? Did you see them when we circled?"

"Victor, I think we've got a disaster on our hands."

The small rubber inflatable sped to the big orange survival raft. The flaps were closed. There was no movement, no hands raised to greet them. Eight surfboards were still tethered to the raft, floating gently in the morning sun. It all looked so peaceful, and for a second both Tina Sanchez and Mac Owens thought everything was going to be ok.

They pulled up along side the raft. They lifted the flap. Sitting up against one side of the raft was one of the Japanese surfers. He was staring straight ahead, talking in low tones, obviously in shock. Laying flat on his back was Taz Nakamura. Over him was the kneeling figure of Kai Woods.

"I've still got a pulse on him. Gotta keep him going. Did you bring the defib unit?"

Owens scrambled into the raft. Tina Sanchez handed him the DF unit.

"Where are all the others?" she asked.

"Out there someplace," said Kai Woods without even looking at her, busy doing everything he could to save at least one life.

"I'd better go with you Tina," said Mac Owens.

"No, stay here and help him," she said, with an odd tone to her voice. She didn't want to stay and watch them bring a dead man back to life as had happened three months ago. It was a memory all too vivid for her. Yet somehow she also knew what she was going to see next would be with her for the rest of her life.

She backed the little runabout away from the raft and began a slow circle of the lagoon. She was alone, surrounded by an amphitheater of fathomless sound from the waves breaking all around her. The water inside the lagoon was a smooth aquarium of beautiful, natural colors, a backdrop against which manmade, artificial colors quickly caught her eye.

She saw large, shattered shards of the plastic shells that had once covered the waverunner engines. She saw the fins of a surfboard and the board's tail section broken off with the thick wood stringer protruding a foot out from the shattered foam and fiberglass. A completely deflated zodiac was pinned to the reef by its outboard engine. Twenty yards further, a twisted and mangled waverunner was on its side, its keel broken in two as if a giant hatchet had been used to try and cut the waverunner in half.

A few yards from the wreck of the ski she saw what looked like a floating lifevest. She slowed the engine, and then stopped entirely. She jumped out of the runabout and walked waist deep across the rough coral until she was about fifteen feet away. The first thing she noticed was several schools of tiny colored fish swimming all around the vest. Then she saw why.

Her mind flashed to the stories her father-in-law had told Victor, stories about retrieving the remains of downed pilots during the war. She remembered how his eyes would begin to glance from side to side and he would change the subject and start talking about the beautiful fish swimming around the shredded corpse of a young man. "Funny thing, that, you know. There would always be little schools of tiny fish around the body. All the colors you can imagine. Like in a tank at a pet store."

She splashed back to the Avon, fired up the engine, and drove the runabout up and down the east side of the lagoon. There was wreckage everywhere, several helmets floating oddly in the lagoon, and lifevests floating in shallow water with bodies in them. From a distance she saw part of a bright yellow wetsuit – and part of a body still in it.

She came back to the survival raft and bounced off it with a jarring motion. Mac Owens lifted up the flap. He started talking rapidly.

"We got a clean heartbeat. The surfer is pretty broke up. Kai is runnin' on autopilot. What about - - -"

Owens looked into the eyes of Tina Sanchez and saw the nightmare.

"Kai, I'll be right back. You'll be ok?"

"Yeah, we saved him with the DF. Good thing we brought it. We'll need it if - - - " Woods looked at Tina Sanchez and knew there was no reason to say another word.

Owens got in the runabout and pushed off away from the raft. He started up the motor and headed back to the *Skyhook*. When they arrived, Victor was waiting in the cargo bay door. He saw the look on his wife's face. Then he heard her words.

"Three in the raft. They'll make it. One confirmed dead on the reef. I think it was one of the Hawaiians. Broken waverunner shells, busted boards, and lifevests that - - -"

She stopped talking and started crying.

"Tina! Throw me the line. Tina!"

His wife looked up at him. She held up both arms and he lifted her into the cargo bay.

"Sorry, Victor. I, I just, we've got to do something. Victor!"

"Victor, you take care of her," said Mac Owens, "I'm goin' back to git Woods and the other two. Then we've gotta lotta work ahead of us, Capt'n. Nobody else made it."

Tina Sanchez collapsed in shock. She began to sob uncontrollably. Victor wrapped his arms around his wife and lifted her to her feet to stop her convulsions.

"Is something wrong, Captain? Where are the surfers?"

Sanchez looked at the man standing in the hatchway to the 'sunroom'. He heard the engine of the runabout rev up.

"Mr. Anasi, fourteen men decided to stay here. At this time, three of those men are alive in the life raft. Mr. Owens just went to get them and bring them aboard. We have one confirmed fatality. Remain in the aft area and return to your seat. I will update you as necessary."

"What do you mean, you will update me? Who do you think you are talking to?" Panic began to well up in Parea Anasi.

"Mr. Anasi, return to your seat in the aft section. Now!"

Anasi didn't make a move, or couldn't, but Victor Sanchez had no time for any more explanations.

"Listen, Anasi!" he said in a rising voice as adrenaline started to rush through his veins, "When I return, if you or any of your party is not buckled in their seats, I will lock you in back there for the rest of this flight. If you don't do what I tell you to do, I'll take any actions I deem necessary to guarantee the safety of my crew and this aircraft."

"What the hell does that mean?" said Anasi sarcastically.

Sanchez kept supported his wife with one arm. With the other he reached up to a box bolted high up on the bulkhead. He flipped open the latch and slipped his hand inside. He turned back to face Anasi.

"I've got to find eleven bodies and get 'em to Tahiti. Now move!"

Sanchez kept the forty-five pointed downward. Then he flipped off the safety lever and looked Parea Anasi straight in the eye. He nodded towards the hatchway. Big K, Junior and Keoni Padaca moved back into the compartment as Anasi came towards them.

Sanchez held his wife gently as he kicked the hatch closed. He put the gun in his flight suit and with both arms around his wife, made his way forward to the galley. He sat her down and comforted her. In a few minutes she calmed down and spoke to him in a halting voice.

"I'll be, I'll be ok. It was like what, like what your father used to talk about, Victor. The whole place is so beautiful, and there's all these colorful fish swimming around. And then you see a body, or parts of a body," she said slowly, shaking her head.

"Just stay here, Tina. When you can, try and raise Papeete. Tell 'em we'll be overdue and will update them in a few hours."

"Ok, Victor. Ok."

The Captain of the *Skyhook* stood up and walked back down the fuselage, thinking about his father and the things he'd seen that he never talked about.

Mac Owens brought Kai Woods, Taz Nakamura, and the Wavelife surfer back to the *Skyhook*. Victor Sanchez got in the runabout with Owens. It took them almost two hours to find and retrieve the intact corpses of Tony Aipua, David Kahaio, and Ben Lalaoa. The passengers back in the 'sunroom' stayed there the entire time, except when Owens and Sanchez needed Big K or Junior to help them lift the corpses into the plane.

Kai Woods got something to eat and drink and then went up on the wing with a walkie-talkie and binoculars to help Sanchez and Owens. He thought about Randy Laine's words and he realized the whole thing was doomed from the moment he had tried to get through to Steve Palua about the real dangers looming ahead of them. But there was no getting through to him, and Palua's words echoed in Woods' mind.

"If guys die, that's their business."

Sanchez and Owens eventually found the remains of the other Wavelife surfers and the crushed helmet of Craig Bishop, with shattered fragments of his skull protruding from it, floating in the lagoon. Near the remains of the second zodiac they found an arm with a wristwatch Woods recognized as belonging to Brad Halley.

And the surf never stopped. The warm tropical sun burned off the mist. Walls of water fifty feet high were breaking perfectly for almost a mile down the east side of the reef with the flawless perfection of every surfer's dream.

Towards noon Kai Woods saw what looked like a feeding frenzy near the mouth of the lagoon. Ten minutes and two dead sharks later, Owens and Sanchez pulled the half-eaten corpse of the TV guy out of the water. Sanchez had to shoot several more sharks threatening to eat their way right through the rubber floats of the runabout. The sharks followed them right up to the *Skyhook* and Mac Owens shot a few more. They had to wait a while before going back out to search for more remains.

They found several body parts half-eaten near the mouth of the lagoon. By process of elimination, it became clear to everyone on the *Skyhook* that the sharks had been feasting on Steve Palua.

And the surf never stopped. The lefts were now completely closed out, though the rights were still breaking perfectly with some sets now topping sixty feet. They made several runs around the reef, staying well clear of the impact zone, and once they thought they saw a flash of orange before it disappeared inside a huge tube.

Victor Sanchez was barely able to take off in the gathering darkness as the huge waves turned his runway into an obstacle course. The *Skyhook* flew on a course to the north to pick up the trade winds and get back to Tahiti as fast as possible. They had the corpses and various body parts of ten men aboard. They never found Ian Clark – or his remains.

Sea-change

The smell of the sea was different. The low shroud of mist on the southern horizon was unlike anything he'd ever seen, and if he could have asked Taveka about it, he would have been told same thing. But as the chief navigator of the Marulean sea people, David Helmares was now on his own. From the moment Taveka saw the long white wings of the wandering albatross, no words could now pass between them.

Their voyage to Ka'unua was imminent, and that alone might have been cause for David's sleepless night. However, he was wide awake and fully alert due to the unusual power flowing through the entire Nebula Archipelago. His ears were tuned to the frequencies of the waves breaking on reefs up to a mile away. By candlelight he was making entries in a small notebook in the navigator's code of symbols as taught to him by Taveka for use on extraordinary occasions to quantify a record of wave and weather phenomena. He remembered questioning his mentor about the system since so much of the knowledge of the navigators was passed down through oral traditions or sheer experience. Taveka's answer had surprised the apprentice.

"Someday you'll be able to keep it all up here, but for now, write down what you need to remember. New facts have a way of floating and dissolving over time. When the ocean shows you what you have never seen before, better to fill your brain with memories that can't be represented by codes or symbols."

In the silence between sets, David reviewed the last three days of his log. In addition to the wave height and interval notations, he had sketched numerous cross-hatched wave patterns as the large swells had refracted through myriad shoals near the home island of the Maruleans. He remembered when Taveka had shown him several logs made over his lifetime, including one from August of 1968 that David recognized as a record of the swell from the same storm that had produced the biggest waves ever at Malibu. David's current notations were similar, including the way the progression of entries clearly portrayed an inexorable increase in wave size. But Taveka's log had finally indicated a peak, and then a decline, in the storm energy. David's log had yet to indicate any reduction in the power emanating from what undoubtedly was a storm of far greater proportions.

He checked the position of his time-keeping reference stars. He started a new entry when the silence was broken by a sound like a cannon shot as the first wave of a new set broke on a shoal almost a mile away. As the set of waves came closer, he tuned his ear to discern the individual explosions on the reefs leading to his island.

Then he heard an entirely different sound, coming not from the ocean, but from the sky. He knew exactly what it was but let the moment of recognition pass without a second thought. He would not be distracted from the polyphonic rhythms of the swells and the movement of his reference star. When the set of waves ended, he completed his entry in the silence of a lull. Then and only then did he look in the direction of the receding sound. He saw a ghostly silhouette moving across the dome of stars. It was easy to spot. Colored running lights were blinking on the wingtips. David thought of the lifevest Taveka had found, but before he could ponder the situation any further, another set announced its arrival and he returned to his work.

Taveka was laying on the ceremonial platform where he had slept every night since seeing the albatross. In his dream-trance the beat of his heart matched the rhythms of waves breaking all around him. Then the waves stopped, and he had the distinct sensation of his heart slowing down until a last heartbeat echoed like the distant roar of a wave far out on a barrier reef somewhere in the South Pacific.

He was happy in the stillness. Then the silence was broken by a new and different sound, familiar yet out of place. He allowed it to bring him back to wakefulness. The low drone from high in the sky made him think of David and the changes ahead for the sea people of Marulea. The very nature of the thought was all he now needed to realize he was no longer a part of their future. He smiled, and he knew it was time.

He opened his eyes and hopped down from the platform to the sand. He began to walk with dispatch and resolution along the shore towards the village in the distance. Within minutes he was in front of the house of his daughter and his grandchildren. His successor was sitting on the porch, barely visible in the candlelight. He walked towards him until he was only a few feet away. David looked up, then stood up. Their eyes met. Then Taveka blew out the candle. Seconds passed in the darkness. Each man turned away knowing the tasks now to be performed.

David Helmares went back into the house. Taveka resumed his strong strides towards the lagoon. The final process of succession had begun.

By the time David returned to the porch with Luan and a torch used for night fishing, Taveka was launching his surfboard from the edge of the water. They lit the torch and carefully positioned it open to the sea but protected from the wind. When Taveka was halfway out to his voyaging craft, he looked over his shoulder at the village, knowing he would see nothing but darkness and a single flame, burning brightly.

A minute later he was aboard his voyaging craft and lashing his surfboard securely alongside the shelter dome so that it did not affect the balance of the hulls. Then he was still for several minutes to absorb the movement of the craft and the strength of the wind before readying his sails for the voyage. He hauled on his anchor line. When the coral weight was securely aboard, he looked up and saw the torchlight flicker before becoming bright and steady again. But the light itself had not wavered. A mast with shortened sails had passed across his line of sight. The light flickered again, then was blocked out entirely as the wind filled the sails of David's voyaging craft.

Taveka smiled. This was going to be fun. He put his tiller hard over and his sails caught the wind. He'd made a bet, and now the race was on. If he won, his successor would have to do the laundry of his grandchildren for a year. If he lost, well, Taveka knew he was not going to lose, not to a surfer from California, and certainly not to a voyaging craft carrying an extra passenger, even if she was his daughter.

The two craft shot out of the reef pass and soon the single torchlight was below the horizon, Taveka slightly ahead with David and Luan shadowing his course. All around them surf was breaking white over unseen coral shoals while glowing phosphorescence coalesced across the sea like galaxies across the night sky. The navigators felt the currents begin to strengthen and adjusted their course against the stars that would guide them through the night across the Nebula Archipelago. There were still many hours to go before dawn, and five days to go before Ka'unua appeared on the horizon.

K3

"Takeoff checklists?" asked plane commander Mark Habeman.

"Done, all systems within spec," said flight engineer Pieter Kistenberg.

"Do we have latest from Seranen on the K3?"

"Roger that. No change. Within twelve hours and counting," said navigator Kathleen Drake.

"MET NET system integrity confirm?"

"Confirmed. All AWS icons green. Replacement units aboard and ready for deploy," said loadmaster Mai Seqgen, "One at 8177, three on the way to the Pole. One open item. Pole managing office asked Damon if we could set down and evac some folks. Some of 'em want out, and they want out now."

"Well, can't blame 'em. Lucky they hadn't dismantled the old dome yet," said Kistenberg, "'cause it will still have to be home for a while until we can get them out of there safely."

"Mai, comm them to sit tight until afer K3 blows through," said Habeman.

"Hopefully not while we're out there."

"And hopefully not when we come back here. Come to think of it, Pieter, can you work up a fuel profile to a New Zealand pub just in case?"

"MacTown to Dome Argus to the Pole to Christchurch? No can do without a partial re-fuel at the Pole, but we can't set down there. So we're coming back here no matter what. Will get you exact numbers ASAP."

"Thanks. Ops weather report?"

"Perfect. Summer conditions. Highly unusual," said pilot Rico Candelaria.

"Backup ready?"

"Confirm OSOM C-130-2 on standby."

"Roger that. Comm the tower we're go for takeoff. Rico, if you please."

Candelaria touched the throttles ahead. The ski Herc taxied slowly out to a sheet of blue ice near the main Antarctic polar supply center at McMurdo Sound. He used the four big engines to turn around at the end of the runway before pushing the throttles all the way forward. A minute later the Hercules was aloft and accelerating up to maximum airspeed, her crew knowing they had to stretch her performance envelope if they were to have any chance of completing their mission ahead of the next katabatic event. They also knew it would be more powerful, by orders of magnitude, than the forces which had laid waste to the South Pole facilities. And they knew patching up OSOM's network was the only way they could buy enough time to broadcast warnings to all the outposts around Antarctica, and especially those that would be in the path of the K3.

The flight up to Antarctica's highest ice plateau was startling in its ease. It almost seemed as though the entire continent was resting after the K2 event. Visibility was unlimited in the low winter light, and at twenty thousand feet the crew of the *Osomair* had a rare view of the Transantarctic Mountains from horizon to horizon. It was summer weather in August, but the Ice Pirates never let their guard down. When they arrived at Dome Argus, the reason for their vigilance was confirmed. What looked like a bomb crater ten miles in diameter was centered around a blasted and jagged ice surface. Leading from the crater, straight towards the South Pole, was a gouge in the ice two miles wide.

They shot a roll of aerial photos with a camera that stamped each frame with date, time and GPS information before a final flyby to drop the new AWS unit to the ice. The parachute deploy went smoothly, and the unit was sending back data without a hitch. Rico Candelaria was in constant contact with Damon Waiya at OSOM's ANTMETNET ops, and at first Waiya thought there had to be a problem with the AWS.

"You sure, Rico? I'm getting variable winds at twenty knots, temp ten below zero, barometric at nine fifty six. You could have a beach party out there!" he said to over the HF voice channel.

"Yeah, but there's no beach! It looks like someone took a massive pickax and tore the place up before gouging a riverbed straight to the Pole!"

As the *Osomair* flew to the Pole following the path of the K2 katabatic, the Ice Pirates dropped three more AWS units to replace the ones destroyed in order to give the Pole a margin of warning in case the K3 came the same way with more destructive power in its winds. But when the C-130 began to circle the Amundsen-Scott South Pole Research Facility, it looked like there wouldn't be much left to destroy. The outlying science and data sector towers, arrays, and facilities were completely obliterated. The main research facility looked like it had been ripped apart by a giant knife opening up a sardine can.

"Good God, what a mess!" said Pieter Kistenberg, operating the aerial camera to once again document the destructive power of the K2 event.

"And every last piece of wreckage has to be taken off the continent!" remarked Ken Habeman, "But at least we're not looking at planeloads full of coffins going home."

"Yeah, and they were going to dismantle the dome two years ago and ship it out under that same 'take out the trash' agreement. Thank God for the bureaucracy of international paper pushers!" said Roger Drake.

"You know, we better get out of here fast. This is just too spooky. Rico, contact Damon. Any news from Argus?"

"OSOM ANTMETNET ops, this is *Osomair*. We're over the Pole. Damon, anything coming in from Argus?"

The voice of the sysop filled the cockpit.

"Not a thing. Quiet as a nursery during nap time."

"Anything from Ray?"

"Yes. K3 is imminent. Atmospheric loading is at K2 levels plus sixty percent and rising. Upper level winds are accelerating towards Dome Argus. Same scenario, and no telling where she'll go after she hits."

The sun was moving along the horizon without touching it. The lighting hadn't changed since they'd chuted the first AWS down to Dome Argus four hours ago, and now they were halfway home after their recon over the Pole.

"*Osomair*, this is METNET ops. *Osomair*, do you read me?"

"Go ahead, Damon. What's cooking?" said Mark Habeman.

"AWS 8177 just blew up. Repeat, 8177 down just like K1, only faster."

"Copy that. Do we have a vector yet?"

Damon Waiya looked at the glowing network of icons spread around the Antarctic continent. Even as he spoke, another AWS icon began to glow yellow and its data gauges began to flux.

"*Osomair* confirm potential vector through network node point 77.93. Repeat AWS at 77.93 reporting accelerating conditions."

Waiya flipped a switch and opened a broadcast channel to all the outposts around Antarctica.

"All hands Antarctica, this is OSOM ANT MET NET broadcasting an urgent bulletin. Stand by for details."

On the Hercules, Kathleen Drake grabbed a dryeraser marker and a navigator's map of Antarctica. She laid a clear sheet of acetate on it that was already marked with the graceful curve of K2's path, almost as perfect as a nautilus shell, from 81.77 to the South Pole and then out into the Weddell Sea towards South Africa. She then shifted the acetate around, lining up the curve from 81.77 to 77.93. The curve overlaid the Russian research station at Vostok, for many years the site of the coldest temperatures ever recorded. She continued to trace the projected path inside of Dome C, the site of the Concordia research station supported by the French and the Italians. From there it continued unimpeded until it intersected with the coast at the Ross Sea – and the McMurdo station.

"OSOM MET NET, *Osomair* here. Damon, K.D. here. Project K3 path through your location."

"Roger that, *Osomair*. Was just about to tell you the same thing." Waiya flipped a switch that opened a voice channel from his tiny headset mic to MacTown operations.

"Attention all hands. OSOM ANT MET NET reporting Force Five katabatic. Path outbound from Dome Argus through Vostok. Projected path through McMurdo. All personnel move immediately to reinforced structures. Repeat. Katabatic imminent. Assume duration and wind speed double of previous event. Assume potential loss of life."

Everyone who heard the warning was well aware of what had just happened to the South Pole Station during the K2 event. Now an even more powerful katabatic was going to wreak havoc at Antarctica's largest inhabited facility at McMurdo Sound.

"*Osomair*, this is MET NET ops."

"MET NET, this is *Osomair*. Affirmative. What's up?"

"Just got a call from senior NSF manager. He was ready for the bad news. He wants to evacuate the hospital and get everyone else out of here that we can squeeze into your bird. Eighty pax on the manifest."

"Are you loading up Jerry and the *Hawk*?"

"Negative, *Osomair*. Until you get here, C-130-2 still your backup, but we've already counted those seats in the evac plans. You'll have about an hour on the ground before the K3 gets here. Maybe less. What's your fuel profile?"

The implication was clear. Refueling the Herc and on-loading a full cargo of passengers at the same time was going to require ground personnel, who would not have much time to get to safety before the katabatic arrived.

"Got it right here, but not with eighty passengers. Will get back to you on that. Over and out," said Habeman, "Mai, better get the cargo area ready for some guests. Pieter, got that fuel profile for Christchurch?"

'Right here. We'll be down to thirty minutes air time when we land. We'll need a re-fuel of eighteen hundred pounds, assuming a tailwind of eighty knots across the Ross Sea to Christchurch."

"Ok, now add eighty pax to that profile."

Kistenberg stiffened just a touch. With the extra load, they were back to the edge of safety. Maybe over it.

"Mark, recommend immediate shift to maximum endurance profile. And guessing we'll need an extra thousand pounds of fuel."

"Of course, Pieter, if we slow down now to conserve fuel - - -" Kathleen Drake paused to let the implications sink in. Rico Candelaria confirmed them.

"We push back our ETA and have even less time to gas up even though we'll need more fuel. But maybe we can use the frontal edge of the K3 to help us get off the deck."

"That's cutting it close, said Habeman, who then took Candelaria's idea a step further, "Pieter, include Rico's suggestion in your calcs, and also a tailwind of two hundred knots to roughly sixty degrees south latitude. Get the final numbers to me for trans to Waiya. We'll get out of there one way or another. Jerry, too. Our hangars aren't bomb-proof."

Everyone realized what that meant. They'd seen the destruction at the South Pole from the K2 wind. The same thing was going to happen to their home town in less than two hours.

"Pieter, got that fuel profile?"

"Affirmative. Using the K3 to help get us off the ice and then fly with it into the K2 system, we'll need twenty four hundred pounds. And that's flying max endurance profile all the way to Christchurch."

"Rico, anything come to mind about this whole thing?"

"Negative, Ken. It will be low and slow across the ocean, but if we time our takeoff and get some help once we're aloft, we'll be OK."

"Kathy, go get Mai, then contact Damon and confirm the pax manifest. Then give him Pieter's fuel requirements. And get an ETA on the K3, please."

The trail of AWS icons from Dome Argus to McMurdo Sound told Damon Waiya all he needed to know. Except for the two closest to the OSOM facility at MacTown, they were all black. And of those two, one had just gone from yellow to red. It would soon be dead, leaving the last icon, just on the other side of the Prince Albert Mountains, still glowing green.

Osomair, this is ops. Mark, you've got about an hour. I'm down to the last AWS at 76.158."

"We'll be on the deck in about fifteen minutes, Damon. Re-fueling ready?"

"Yeah. Pax too. It's gonna be tight, Mark."

"Actually, the tighter the better. Less fuel wasted waiting around. In fact, we're gonna wait till she hits. We need the tailwind to get us off the deck."

The approach into Willy Field at McMurdo station was a familiar routine for the Ice Pirates. The landmark mountains were like old friends, and the lights at the base in the growing darkness were friendly as ever. It was home, only this time they wouldn't be staying, and in fact they had to leave as soon as possible.

The *Osomair*'s landing was textbook. As soon as the C-130 came to a halt, re-fueling began. The rear cargo bay ramp was lowered so that rows of web seats could be rolled in and locked down. Then the evacuees loaded aboard, including two stretcher cases placed in the bunks behind the flight deck. Everything was going smoothly. Grace under pressure was a tradition of the Ice Pirates. And the pressure was on.

"*Osomair*, this is ops. AWS 71.158 just went black. Last indicated wind speed was one fifty before total failure. She'll be coming over the mountains in about fifteen minutes."

"Roger that, Damon. Gonna be a lotta work to fix the tear in the net this time, that's for sure," said Mark Habeman.

"Yeah, after a couple dozen round-trips from Christchurch just to get us barely operational again," said Waiya, knowing what had happened at the Pole.

"We'll make sure first on the list is several pallets of New Zealand beer."

'Thanks, Mark, we'll need it. Gotta go. We're gonna hunker down in cargo containers the facilities guys bolted together and cabled into the rocks. You're cleared for takeoff, Mark."

"Thanks, Damon. Out."

The voice radio went dead.

"Pieter, how we doing on the fuel load?"

"At safety threshold, Mark. Another five minutes should do it."

"We've got fifteen. Tell the ground crew to hit it directly to the container depot when you're done. I'll keep an eye on the Prince Alberts. As soon as the stars disappear, we're cleared for takeoff. Rico, assume a tail wind of zero nine zero knots. Mai, everyone strapped in?"

"Affirmative. Eighty pax plus two stretcher cases. The life rafts will be a bit cramped."

The Ice Pirates all knew when it was time for a few jokes.

"Oh, you mean those bulky things I threw away last year?"

"What life rafts? We don't need no stinking life rafts!"

"Let's see, if we contact Ray and he contacts Bucher, we can ditch near the fleet and get a ride without getting too wet!"

"Yeah, I always wanted to try that surfing stuff!"

Across the McMurdo Sound from MacTown, the Prince Albert Mountains stood sharp against the deep blue Antarctic sky. The air was so clear that stars were easily visible just above the line of peaks. Rico Candelaria and Kathleen Drake were in the pilot seats of the Hercules. Pieter Kistenberg was going through the takeoff checklist with them. Mark Habeman had a pair of binoculars trained on the range of white peaks about twenty miles away. It was a crystal vision of Antarctic beauty at night, and the Ice Pirate allowed himself a rare moment of emotion.

"I'll never know how a place so beautiful can be such a killer," he said.

"Well, its just Nature's revenge on us," said his wife, "We want to know so much, we want to prove ourselves to ourselves over and over again, and we're lucky if we even stop to think what we are doing. And when we don't stop to think, we either kill the planet or ourselves."

The four Pirates on the flight deck were all silent for a second, the only sound the idling engines waiting to pull a big machine into the sky and take them and eighty-two women, parents, and patients to safety.

"I feel like I'm waiting for an army from Mordor," said Habeman, "and here it comes."

He was watching the lowest point in the mountains, the Taylor Valley. Stars began to disappear as a wall of gray rose up and filled the space between Lister Mountain to the east and McNeish Peak to the west. The flood of wind and ice particles grew, lapping up the sides of the valley towards the peaks. Now other low spots in the range began to fill in, and within a minute the entire Prince Albert Range was under assault. It would not be able to hold back the invasion about to pillage the largest man-made facility on the frozen continent.

Habeman touched on the switch activating the C-130's intercom without taking his eyes off the incoming wall of power.

"Hello everyone, this is the captain, Mark Habeman. We will be taking off shortly, so please make sure your seat harnesses are secure. And then double check the person to right of you and the person to the left of you. As soon as we're aloft, I'll be back and get things squared away for our flight to Christchurch, New Zealand."

He clicked off the mic. The mountains were now completely covered with a towering blanket of ice and snow blowing down their slopes like an avalanche. K3 would arrive in less than a minute.

"Rico, we'll be at nil and nil on the takeoff."

"Aye-aye, skipper. I won't be able to see where I'm going either ahead or above. That much less to think about, the way I look at it!"

The outlying buildings disappeared from sight. Then the anemometer on the C-130 stirred. Within thirty seconds, it was blowing forty knots from the port side of the plane.

They were on the Williams Ice Shelf, the frozen sheet of ice used only in emergencies during winter-over operations. It was one big runway in all directions. Since taking off in a ninety knot cross wind was not the kind of foolhardy stunt that kept pilots and passengers alive, Rico Candelaria applied power to the two port engines, and the Hercules came around to put the K3 on her tail.

A hellhound gust roared past the cockpit. The plane moved forward slightly. The wind speed indicator pushed past sixty. It was time to go.

"Rico, if you please."

Co-pilot Kathleen Drake pushed all four throttles forward, but only to fifty percent. Using half throttle was a highly unusual plan, but they wanted to save as much fuel on the takeoff as possible and with an unlimited runway, they could get away with it.

The plane instantly accelerated.

"Full flaps." Long ailerons built into wings swung up into position.

"45 knots."

"Fifty-five knots. Sixty. Sixty-five. Seventy." Drake was calling out the speeds. They hit a rough stretch of ice and the skis chattered and bounced.

"Throttles up fifteen percent," said Ken Habeman. She pushed the four levels forward two inches.

Candelaria felt the front of the plane go light under his controls.

"Eighty knots. Pieter, any scrub issues?"

"None."

"Ninety knots."

"She's all yours, Rico."

Candelaria pulled the yoke control towards his chest. One hundred and fifty thousand pounds of men, women and machinery lifted off the ice.

"Forty feet. Sixty. Eighty. One hundred. One thirty. One fifty."

"Circle to port at a thousand feet," said Habeman, "Let's get a last look."

The entire Prince Albert Range had been reduced to a mere speed bump by a force now just beginning to find the weak points in over a hundred buildings, smothering the huge facility as if it didn't exist. One building, however, was still visible, standing on a rise overlooking the oncoming devastation. It was the square, wooden home to the Scott expedition and had stood intact since the beginning of the twentieth century. As they leveled off and set a course to safety, the Ice Pirates wondered if this was the last time they would ever see it again. They would be flying right back as soon as the K3 abated. Just what would greet them upon their return was something they weren't going to think about until they had to.

"Pieter, fuel profile?"

"Fifteen percent above safety, Ken, assuming maximum endurance profile to Christchurch. Nice takeoff, Suave!"

"Hey, I did the throttles!" said a smiling Kathleen Drake.

"Well, it was my idea in the first place!" grinned Candelaria.

"Yeah, but it only worked because I got the passengers all praying in the right direction!" said Mai Seqgen, and laughter filled the cockpit.

"Speaking of which," said their leader, touching the button on the intercom, "Folks, this is Commander Habeman again. I hope you've said your prayers for the folks we left behind. If you have, you can now unbuckle your harnesses, but do not remove your survival suits. We aren't planning to do any surfing down there, though as it turns out there are OSOM mariners who are. But of course, they are surfers, so what do you expect? Probably too many wipeouts has filled their brains with salt water. But we'll wish them luck as we take our hot showers and stretch out on clean sheets in," Habeman looked at Kistenberg, who held up six fingers, "six hours plus the time it takes for the shuttle buses to get us to our hotels. That's all for now."

It was a night flight of quiet reflection and steadfast vigilance of all systems. Three hours out they passed the Point of Safe Return without a second thought. Of course, on this flight, there was no PSR since there was nothing safe to return to. That never entered their minds. They were Ice Pirates. They were the best, they would always complete their mission, and 'pushing up a cross' was never an option.

When they passed over the Antipodes Islands, they contacted terminal operations at Christchurch. They were now safely in New Zealand airspace, and the alien wilderness of Antarctica seemed a world away.

The Ride of the Alba_Swords

Ten thousand feet below the *Osomair*, five of the six Alba_Swords were now hauled out aboard the *Mother Carie* in the lee of the Antipodes. Only the *Serena* was still out to sea, though closing fast on the final waypoint of the Regatta's voyage from South Africa.

Margo Atkins and Patty McRane were in the cockpit having a great time running her across the last of the K2's big swells. Below decks, Ken Bucher, Charles Atkins, and Nelson Roberts were shooting the breeze in the foc'sle in the time honored custom of mariners off watch. Dinner was coming up, and by the time a watch change would be scheduled, they'd be aboard the *Mother Carie*. With only food and their port of call to anticipate, it was that rarest of times for a sailor at sea, a respite of true peace filled with easy conversation and camaraderie.

"Hey Kenny, whaddaya got there?" Charles Atkins saw the young mariner paging through a book.

"Oh, it's this old publication I got from Mr. Vogel when he found out I was going on this trip. It has the whole story about how he came up with the swordfish idea for surfboards. Plus it has articles on stuff I never knew about surfing. Mickey Dora, artificial reefs, these guys in New Jersey that got arrested for surfing. Here, take a look."

Ken Bucher closed the book and tossed it across the passageway. A surprised Charles Atkins caught the spiral-bound volume.

"Thanks, Kenny, but I didn't have to see it."

"Go ahead, I've read it twice."

Atkins had never seen the publication before. After a few seconds he realized it was formatted sideways, like a calendar, except it was almost three hundred pages long. He flipped it around and began to pay close attention to the table of contents.

"Hey!" said Roberts, checking his watch, "Dinner at six bells, mates. And since I'm the duty cook of the day, I'd better get on it."

"Great," said Bucher, "I'm hungry! What's for grind?"

Roberts laughed.

"You're always hungry! Its pasta casserole with steamed broccoli and a salad."

"Well, can I just have an extra helping of the casserole and uh, - - - "

Atkins had found something to pique his curiosity in the publication, but he still had a word for the young sailor.

"You gonna eat yer greens, boy! Yo mama didn't raise you to pick and choose what's good for you!"

Bucher laughed and thought of his mother in her garden ten thousand miles away. He'd eaten his greens all his life, and now, even when he had taken giant strides towards being his own man, he was still living with her common sense.

"Okay, okay. Nelson, need any help?"

"Sure, Kenny. Mr. Atkins, what's our ETA on the *Mother Carie?*"

He looked across the aisle, but Charles Atkins was suddenly oblivious to his two shipmates. Roberts saw the captain's furrowed brow and knew it would be best not to bother him.

Charles Atkins had seen and surfsailed his share of big waves. He was familiar with the European Space Agency's study, called MaxWave, designed to quantify the existence of rogue waves and determine the safety and economic implications when ships sink because of them. He was fully cognizant of Ray Seranen's use of that data in his global warming sea-state models and how OSOM had made contributions to the body of knowledge with its research in the Southern Ocean. He felt he was up to speed on all the current theories and information. But now he had unexpectedly found an article that drew his undivided attention, an article that he had never seen before, first presented at the 9th Annual Offshore Technology Conference in 1977 by Dr. Joseph Goldman. It had been reprinted in the October 1993 issue of the Mariners' Weather Log, and now included in the meteorology section of the Groundswell Society's Second Annual Publication. With the possibility of a K3 event still looming, Charles Atkins had a very direct interest in the answers to the question posed by the title of the article, "How High Can Giant Waves Get?"

Dinner came and went without Charles Atkins joining his shipmates. In the cockpit, the ladies were doing a "Thelma and Louise" imitation that had Bucher and Roberts in stitches. Every once in a while they'd throw the helm hard over just to bounce the men around, though the style and grace of the *Serena*'s response was nothing less than awesome. Margo Atkins and Patty McRane were in the top rank of Alba_Sword surfsailers, and they weren't above showing off a bit just for the fun of it at the end of a long and memorable voyage.

The *Serena*'s captain was not part of the fun. Alone in the softly lit interior of the Alba_Sword, Charles Atkins was in deep concentration, taking notes, scrolling through the data recorder of the *Serena* and reviewed imaging of some particularly big sets from the past two days. The more Charles Atkins read, the more acute his level of alertness became.

He reviewed the last of the communiqués from Ray Seranen. The K2 storm was stationary at the intersection of the Date Line and the sixtieth parallel, midway between New Zealand and Antarctica. Swells were still radiating out across the entire Pacific, but the storm's days were numbered.

Or not, thought Atkins. *What if another katabatic came roaring down off the ice?*

He knew Seranen's predictions about a K3 event, but as yet there had been no news of it, nor would there be until the *Serena* was hauled about the *Mother Carie* and Atkins could get an update from Frank Bucher. But that would not be for another few hours, and instinct told him he might not have a moment to lose. He began to sketch diagrams of storm scenarios for the next ten days on clear sheets of acetate laid over charts of the Southern Ocean and Antarctica. He quickly saw some significant differences between what had happened with the K2 storm and what could happen next.

If Antarctica kicked down another big wind to mix with the remnants of the K2 storm, the resulting low pressure system would have an elongated north-south fetch to it, not east-west. It would remain practically in place and would not trend eastwards. And though the new storm would not last as long as the K2 storm, it would be far more intense.

Atkins compared his diagrams to the illustrations in the article. The similarities were impossible to ignore. He took careful note of Goldman's methodology and was familiar with the math underlying the computer model's parameters. He could find no gaps in the study's logic, nor could he poke any holes in Goldman's conclusions.

Now he was certain of the potential for a real storm to develop that would match the hypothetical maximums predicted by Dr. Goldman. He began to read some passages aloud, almost as if he was delivering a sermon in the Chapel, to *hear and feel* Goldman's exact words.

"A maximum combined sea state of 219 feet is possible . . . a maximum combined sea state of over 200 feet may not be the ultimate in expected storm conditions . . . If storm motion is taken into consideration, an addition of up to 20% of maximum conditions is possible . . . As a passing note, during the construction of this model, comparable pressure gradients were found in the Gulf of Alaska. We hope this is a passing coincidence.

"We cannot yet accurately predict the storm wave forces at the breaker height. Since the maximum storm wave at the breaker height has been measured so infrequently and modeled for only small waves in tanks, the velocities and accelerations, (especially the vertical components) that make up force data must remain theoretical estimates."

Atkins paused for a long minute. He took a sip of water before finishing with the study's final paragraph.

"Climatic variations presently apparent in the form of worldwide areas of drought and deluge . . . There is great concern that we are either in a long-term cyclic variation or a short term irreversible trend . . . The use of dynamic models to arrive at extremes becomes increasingly important when we question where all the extremes have yet to be experienced.

Atkins closed his eyes. Goldman stressed the use of increasingly dynamic computer models. Bucher and Seranen had gone after real-world data sets. And now there was a chance, a good chance, that Goldman's hypothetical extreme sea states, with waves two hundred feet high and bigger, could intersect with the real world of the Order of Southern Ocean Mariners.

"What are you reading, dear? We're coming up on the *Mother Carie*," said his wife, fresh and vibrant after a great surfsailing session.

One look at her husband, and smile on her face disappeared.

"What's wrong, Charles?"

The *Mother Carie* was riding at anchor in the lee of the Antipodes with all the Alba_Swords safely aboard. As chance would have it, the OSOM mariners were keeping the time-honored tradition of the tall ships, except when life and limb are threatened, by not sailing on God's day of rest. It was Sunday, and a man of the cloth was about to address the ship's company. However, it would not be a sermon. Charles Atkins had information that every OSOM mariner needed, and the sooner they got it the better.

"By now I'm sure you all know our Antarctic facility was heavily damaged by the third katabatic event predicted by Ray Seranen. Designated K3, it is still blowing and, like its predecessor, is presenting us with decisions to make. Thanks to Frank Bucher, we took advantage of what K2 offered us: the opportunity to complete six days of surfsailing on waves as big as any ever seen in the Southern Ocean. Now comes a similar situation and I bring you news about K3, though instead of stepping into Frank's seven league boots, I'm going to need my dancing shoes," quipped Atkins, drawing a laugh from the room. Atkins dancing skills were no secret to anyone who had spent any significant amounts of time at OSOM HQ, which meant just about every person in the room. "In fact, what I've got in mind involves a bit of choreography for us all. Someone hit the lights."

The first slide on the screen showed a map of the Southern Hemisphere. Atkins went through a short explanation of Seranen's theories on global warming and his predictions of a series of catalytic events centering on the highest, coldest place on earth. He laid out the chronologies of the K1 event on Dome Argus, the K2 event and the destruction at the South Pole, and finally the K3.

"Chutting in a new AWS unit over Dome Argus was critical in warning the Russians at the Vostok research station about the K3, and getting enough warning to those folks at MacTown to batten down everything."

"Ah, ve Russians again taking the brunt of the invasion! Ve can live through anything!" Rudolf Velelov's interjection prompted more laughter and a looseness that made everyone all the more ready.

The next slide was a map bordered by Antarctica, New Zealand, Polynesia and South America. The latest satellite photo of the K2 storm, along with the current location of the Roaring Forties Regatta fleet were superimposed on the map.

"When the K3 hit the coast here," said Atkins, using a laser pointer, "Its winds were stronger than any ever recorded in Antarctica. That power is even now revitalizing the K2 low pressure system."

A wave of excitement went through the room, and Atkins made note of it immediately.

"And I'm sure right now everyone here is ready to continue surfsailing around the world. But will you want to do that on waves that will be twice as big, or bigger, than any of the K2 storm waves? Do you want to see waves like this?"

The slide changed, and suddenly there was dead silence.

Atkins had prepared the slide to provide the mariners with a scale image of what a two hundred foot wave would look like – with a forty-five foot Alba_Sword riding down its face.

"Now let me continue, but first a quick thanks to Ken Bucher for loaning me a publication containing an article that allowed me to get a handle on the whole thing."

"Well, no thanks necessary Captain," said Bucher from the back of the room, "I was lucky to run into Mr. Vogel, and he was lucky to have a copy of the Groundswell Society publication on him at the time."

"Yes, Ken, I guess Pasteur was right after all. 'Chance favors the prepared man'. And thanks to the article, we may be lucky AND prepared to surf waves of almost unimaginable size. What is ironic in all this is we'll be using information developed by the oil industry for purposes of insuring offshore drilling platforms around the world."

For the next fifteen minutes Atkins went through the graphics and highlights of the Goldman study. He had extracted key phrases from the article as bullet points, ending with Goldman's observations about the need for increasingly dynamic models to fully understand the physics of ocean waves.

"And that is my point of departure, ladies and gentlemen, for proposing that we turn the Roaring Forties Regatta into a full-fledged scientific expedition to investigate the waves of the K3 storm."

Atkins paused for a moment.

"I'm talking about ending the Regatta right here and now, and shifting into an entirely different operational mode requiring precise choreography and perfect coordination. It will be innovative, balanced in its fundamental simplicity, and yet majestic. So in putting this whole thing together, I thought about a meeting between the improvisation of Miles Davis, the smooth soul of Smokey Robinson and, from Richard Wagner," he paused with a smile at the German crew of the *Seeadler*, "the dynamic of 'The Ride of the Valkyries', since it will take a lot of energy, style, and power to pull this off."

He waited for the murmur across the room to die down.

"I've devised a set of course plans under the title 'The Ride of the Alba_Swords.' I still have to work out some details and then send 'em all to Ray for review. Right now I want to share my thinking with you before taking another step," Atkins did a quick James Brown 'up on the good foot' routine, "But I feeeeeel good about it, so let's see what you think."

The crowd hooted and clapped at Atkins' antics, knowing he was trying to set them up with a sense of ease and relaxed assuredness. If he had to fight fear and anxiety, his plan would never get off the ground.

"Now, with all due respect to your excitement about all this, if we had not surfsailed the past six days with flying colors, I would have had serious second thoughts about this proposal. But as my better half said, 'We can always sit this one out', so let's see if we can get a consensus."

Another slide came up on the display showing a re-org of the Regatta into three distinct data teams.

"Our objective is to acquire an invaluable body of real time, real world information that up to now could only be approximated using high-speed computers and simulation programs. We will gather data at the edge of our planet's limitations concerning wave generation, energy, height, speed, mass, interval, duration, and decay. We will explore the K3 wavescape in three simultaneous phases.

"Track A will be for the *Serena* and *Tom Swift* on the primary energy vector up into Polynesia. The *Chicama* and *Seeadler* will be on Track B, following a the great circle route across the Southern Hemisphere, and Track C, for the *Eden* and *Ostrova*, will run dead east on a course to Cape Horn and through the Drake Passage.

"Each track will offer unique opportunities to study the wave energy of the K3 event. Track A follows the narrow bandwidth of K3's biggest waves. Track B courses from just outside the storm's perimeter on a curved path to the South American coast. Track C covers follows wave trains that could theoretically circumnavigate the entire Southern Ocean several times without before dissipating."

The slide shrank into a small box in the upper left. The rest of the screen now displayed the proposed voyage courses.

L.J. Merrill was sitting off to one side with Jack Richards, Chip Bell and Tak Kurosawa. When he saw the proposed course for the *Tom Swift*, his heart almost leaped right out of his chest.

"Jack, we're going right to it!" he whispered to Richards sitting next to him. Richards looked closely, tracing Track A upwards with his finger into the most remote zone of atolls in all of Polynesia. "It's almost as if the storm wants us to get to the reef," said Merrill, who then smiled when Atkins seemed to confirm that belief.

"The storm is dictating the terms here. These paths are my best guesses as to where the energy vectors of interest will be given the timing and direction of the power injected by the K3 katabatic into the still potent remains of our old friend, K2. So that's the nuts and bolts of it. If we adopt my plan, today is the end of the Regatta. From here on in, we dedicate our Alba_Sword voyaging skills to a purely scientific study."

"A good plan, Mr. Atkins," said Cecilia Huarcaya, the engineer for the *Chicama*, "we'll show our German friends some points in Peru where the waves will look like pages in a book."

"Yes, Cecilia, we'd love to see the real Chicama with you. One question, Charles. What about the *Mother Carie*? Who does she follow? And does she still meet us at Cape Horn to ferry us back to Ventura?" said Otto Von Luckner, captain on the *Seeadler*.

"She's already spoken for, Otto. The NSF needs our help, and they've got it. We have offered this ship as a cargo platform to assist in the rebuilding of MacTown and the South Pole and we are sending OSOM's C-130 cargo planes back south full of relief supplies."

"So, vee go around the world, the Zeks and the Vickies, and zen vee race to California! Ha! What say you Helen?"

"No worries, mate!" said the Captain of the *Eden*, "and the loser pays for the winner's tickets home!"

A question came up that brought everyone back to the business at hand.

"Why the pairs? Wouldn't we get more data by spreading out?" asked Nelson Roberts.

"Good question. I had thought of spreading all six of us out in a radial array. But in pairs there is data acquisition back up. Plus sailing alone would not be, uh, prudent, for want of a better word. Tell you what, I've made a copy of the Goldman study for each crew. Please consider it required reading before we reconvene on after dinner. And hold your questions till then. Ray is already working on my idea, that is, of course if you are all interested. Can I get a show of hands? Good! See you at dinner."

The meeting broke up into excited groups. L.J. Merrill and Jack Richards were all smiles as they walked towards Frank Bucher.

"Well, Frank, do I owe something to Atkins for getting us to the reef?" said Richards, trying to be funny while turning the topic deftly towards his real objective.

"If anything, you owe the storm, Jack. But surfers can never even begin to pay for the waves they ride, and since we're going to be surfing thanks to a storm strengthened by the ecological nightmare of global warming, well, who knows exactly what you owe, or to whom you'd write your check!"

"Yeah, Jack," added L.J. Merrill, "maybe you'd better start paying your debt by getting rid of your urban assault vehicle and buy a hybrid."

Bucher smiled, as did Richards.

"Speaking of checks, Frank, can we conduct some business? You said it would be wait-see at best, and we've waited, and now it looks pretty good."

"You got it with you, Richards?"

"Right here, Captain, right where it has been this entire voyage just waiting for you to say the word." Richards opened the breast pocket of his OSOM uniform. He pulled out the check, and handed it to Bucher. L.J. Merrill handed him a pen.

"Thanks L.J. Now, Jack, you know this is non-refundable, right?"

"A deal's a deal, Frank. Go ahead and fill it out."

He bent over the table, wrote the date and a number on the check. Then he wrote two words on the amount line. He straightened up and extended an arm straight at Richards with the check plainly visible.

413

"Any problems with that, Jack?"

Richards barely glanced at the number before looking Bucher straight in the eye.

"I gave you a blank check to fill out. You did. Deal, Frank."

Bucher folded the check and put it in his pocket.

"Here's your pen back, L.J. See you guys after dinner. Oh, wait, there might be a problem that you guys haven't thought of."

Richards never made mistakes, especially with his own money.

"Oh, and what might that be?"

"We're going to your reef, and you just paid for your ticket. But what are you going to do when you get there?"

"Uh, we're going surfing, of course! What else would we do there?"

"Maybe just stay on the boat and watch."

A suddenly perplexed Jack Richards turned to his surf guide who was momentarily caught off guard. But then, just like the old days when he found himself in a tough spot, he thought about surfing and a strategy came to him.

"No, Frank, we'll be out there. We've got the big wave boards we need thanks to your turning us on to Vogel's swordfish designs, and we've done a lot of sprint work during our paddling sessions. We won't be getting in early, but we'll be able to make the drops, and those big fins will hold the bottom turns. We think we're good up to thirty-five, maybe forty feet. So what are you talking about, Frank?"

"Jeez, Merrill, didn't you hear Atkins? Do you have any idea how big it's going to be when we get there?"

L.J. Merrill's gut instincts of only moments ago were now subsumed by the problem of surfing REALLY big waves. He had to think fast, and he did.

"Actually Frank, I figured you could tow us in if need be. The *Tom Swift* has the acceleration on full thrust, and I think she's got at least ten runs in the auxiliary tanks without affecting her capacity. Shouldn't be a problem."

"Good thinking, Merrill," said the Captain, "You are an excellent guide. Jack, be sure and give him a generous tip when you get home. Guys, I got stuff to do. See you back here for dinner."

Bucher turned and walked over to the white board where Atkins, Adam Buchanan and the other captains were gathered and discussing the launch window and sequencing.

"He's up to something, Jack," said Merrill, "He knew we'd talked about towing-in. He got your check, and then he comes on with some 'minor detail' shit? Reminds me of all that chit chat at Razors, remember?"

"Oh, I don't know about that, L.J.," responded Richards, just to have something to say as a retort, "What could he possibly have up his sleeve now except my check for five million dollars?"

For the second time in ten days, a conveyor belt of energy connected the atmosphere over Antarctica with the waves of the Southern Ocean. Once again everything man-made in its path was damaged or destroyed. But there were some significant differences between K2 and K3.

414

The former was a storm of huge proportions, but still a storm that behaved in a predictable pattern given the history of meteorology in the Southern Ocean. K3, on the other hand, was a phenomenon that up till now could only have been imagined by a computer. It was a combination hurricane and tornado with an elongated eye almost two hundred miles long. It was an oval racetrack instead of a merry-go-round, with a heavy whip section on its northwest turn. That fetch zone acted like a catapult releasing massive pulses of energy along the narrow bandwidth of Track A, even as the storm's rotation, still powered by its supercharged concentration of wind, continued to spawn smaller swells for Tracks B and C, if heights approaching one hundred feet could be called "small".

Ray Seranen worked a twenty four hour shift, not including his morning run/swim and several naps in his hammock, to produce voyage plans for Atkins. He re-designed OSOM's storm simulation software to replicate Goldman's model. Then he factored in the K3 event's wind speeds and duration. Finally he simulated what the storm would do after absorbing all the wind. His report to Atkins was eagerly awaited, and Atkins was able to share its contents with the OSOM mariners after dinner.

"As you can see," said Atkins, pointing to the display on the wall behind him, "K3 is a lot different than K2. Please notice the oval eye of the storm. This is something rarely seen in the Southern Ocean. And also notice the change in the storm from twelve hours ago, to this minute, and then on out for the next forty eight hours."

Atkins filled the screen with one graphic at a time to give everyone a sense of the storm's motion.

"Ray's running a full projection through the OSOM computers at HQ to produce a time-lapse of what the storm will do. But for now, we think this is all we'll need to get going. Let's look at image number four, and I'll show you how we are going to choreograph the flights of the Alba_Swords."

The final graphic filled the screen. Along the outer edge of the system were three Alba_Sword symbols lettered A, B and C.

"As you can see, the locations of the launch zones are about one hundred and fifty miles apart from each other. At the top of the storm, straight up the Date Line, is the launch for Track A. Track B starts here, and Track C all the way over here. Now the rub is, we have to launch Track C first, then B, then A - for science purposes. Tracks B and C are for long distance studies, and so those boats will use the same reverse leapfrogging technique to ride bigger and bigger waves as they are generated from the storm over time. Track A is about gathering data from the biggest waves imaginable."

L.J. Merrill glanced at Jack Richards, who didn't take his eyes off Atkins but elbowed Merrill in return.

"Captain Huarcaya and Captain Luckner have been gracious enough to go along with the plan. And I'm happy to report the hot-blooded sporting rivalry between the Russians and the Aussies will continue twice around the world while racing to AWS units across the Roaring Forties."

The round of applause was not unexpected, though welcomed nonetheless. It wouldn't have taken much to upset the plan, and Charles Atkins breathed a small sigh of relief before turning to Adam Buchanan.

"Captain, will you say a few words about our next steps?"

Atkins sat down and Buchanan took the helm of the meeting.

"First off, all ashore that's going ashore in one hour. We can get chopper to come get you, so after the meeting, please let me know if that will be necessary. Next, to arrive at the Track C launch point, we'll have to weigh anchor within the next two hours. We are still working on the timing at that launch zone versus elapsed time to B launch and then A launch. The word 'choreography' is quite apt in this situation, and Charlie Atkins had done a masterful job laying out our steps. Frank, you got anything?"

"Only that I think turning the Regatta into a full-blown science mission is a step up for the Order. Riding waves isn't everything," he glanced at Merrill and Richards, "and this is an once-in-a-lifetime opportunity, thanks to Charlie. Ok, do we need ballots, or will a voice vote suffice? All interested in joining "The Ride of the Alba_Swords" science expedition?"

Thirty hours later, the *Mother Carie* was on station at the launch area for the Russians and the Aussies. When they arrived at the starting point for Track C, the swells from K3 were just beginning to roll through the launch zone. They were no more than thirty feet high, but using the loop maneuver and timely undersea bivouacs, the *Eden* and the *Ostrova* would be riding waves two to three times that size in the next four days shaping course straight across the Southern Ocean to Cape Horn. The waves would be as big as any ever recorded in the Southern Ocean, but the course was a familiar one, and the crews of the two Alba_Swords were over the horizon within minutes of launch.

The ride to launch zone B was as rough as predicted. The Peruvians and the Germans launched without a hitch. Track B was a long haul across waters not normally travelled by Alba_Swords, but the Peruvians were going home, and the Germans were very interested in the Great Circle Route research angle. They were looking forward to clear sailing across deep seas with only a few islands anywhere near their course. Their opening day waves were in the fifty foot range. They too would be looping back to ride the biggest swells and then measure their decay to the coast of Northern Peru where, all things being equal, the *Chicama* and the *Seeadler* would be riding twenty-footers near the site of ancient temples with friezes on their walls depicting curling waves and the ocean full of groundswells.

With two-thirds of the Regatta mariners gone, there was a somewhat eerie echo down the long hulls of the *Mother Carie* as she sped towards the final launch zone. The *Serena* and the *Tom Swift* were the breeding pair of the whole OSOM concept of transoceanic voyaging, and the captains were their designers. Still, there was a sense of uneasiness on board the giant catamaran that affected everyone.

Neither tracks B or A presented any extraordinary challenges, but Track A was something else again. Atkins and Bucher decided a video conference with Seranen was a good idea as they raced to their launch zone. And indeed, Seranen had some things to say to the mariners, and in particular Charles Atkins and Frank Bucher.

"Nobody's ever seen two hundred foot waves. You'll be headed straight towards shoaling zones where those waves will be breaking even if the water is four hundred feet deep. You'll be in areas where surface wave refraction from underwater canyons and ridges will build up peaks that may approach three hundred feet. There are seamounts all over the place down there that may be like trap doors and cause whole sections of the waves to hollow out and collapse with enough power to crush an Alba_Sword."

Nobody said a word aboard the *Mother Carie*. Frank Bucher looked at Charles Atkins, who took his cue and delivered a response to Seranen's well-considered criticisms.

"Frank and I thought about those issues, Ray. That's why I assigned Track A to our boats. We'll respect our limits and stay well within them."

"Are you sure? What if you have to bivouac? The Alba_Swords can't handle the pressure, as you well know. Or are you going to ride inside the swells like swordfish, going thirty knots or more, but for how long? What kind of P.S.I. can the bow tolerate, especially since all your data acquisition instruments are only inches from your pressure points? You'll have to surf night and day, with no mistakes because you won't be able to handle the waves that may be only a few hours behind you. My models tell me the energy is going to peak fast on Track A. So where's your safety margin? What are you going to do about the waves behind you?"

Seranen had found the one flaw in Atkins' plan. The capability to submerge and cruise like swordfish INSIDE the body of the wave, or simply run silent and run deep beneath them, was what made the Alba_Sword voyages possible in the first place. Now that strategy was out of the question.

Margo Atkins and Patty McRane looked at each other, realizing they hadn't thought of that. Neither had Chip Bell or Tak Kurosawa. The four OSOM veterans were suddenly reduced to rookies. And the rookies? They were now alarmed. All eyes turned to Frank Bucher and Charles Atkins, who didn't even blink.

"We have a specific reef as our primary target. Once we get there, we are going to stay there and use the Alba_Swords like floating research platforms to study the waves. If need be, we will have a safe anchorage in the wave shadow behind the reef or, if necessary, within its interior lagoon."

L.J. Merrill and Jack Richards looked at each other. Were they talking about Merrill's reef? There was one way to find out.

"Hey, can I say something?" L.J. Merrill stood up.

"Correct me if I'm wrong Frank, but if the reef you're talking about is the one I discovered, how do you know it has an interior lagoon? I never showed you the video, and we've never discussed it. It does have a lagoon, but I don't know how deep it is. And as for the surf, I saw the place at about twenty-five, maybe thirty feet. That was what Jack and I were planning on surfing. And even if it gets a lot bigger, we can tow in as per our conversation. But I don't know what's going to happen if the surf gets as big as you say it will. So are you talking about the reef I discovered, and if so, how do you know what's going to happen when we get there?"

"Yes, L.J., it's the reef you discovered, and it will be a safe harbor for us," said Bucher, looking Merrill straight in the eye. Then he turned back to the video camera.

"We'll be ok, Ray."

Merrill's jaw dropped. Bucher turned and spoke directly to the legendary surf scout and his employer.

"You gave it away with your excitement over Charlie's original course plan, because within that path, there is only one place that would have the perfect waves that you, and your so-called competitors, seem to want so much."

L.J. Merrill was almost visibly apoplectic. First Ian Clark had burned him. And now Frank Bucher?

"Yes, L.J., I know EXACTLY where it is. And make no mistake, if it wasn't on the route Charlie drew up, we wouldn't be going there. This surf is just too big to mess around, and the science too invaluable to ignore, for us to alter our course for you guys. You just lucked out, here, L.J."

"But how did you figure it out, Frank? I worked on it for years!"

Everyone from the two Alba_Swords was now transfixed by the two men. Ray Seranen could only watch the confrontation, his part in the conference now temporarily moot.

"L.J., there are data resources that you can't get to. We can. This ship is a former U.S. Navy vessel. We have access to underwater topo maps that are highly classified because Navy submarines need to go anywhere."

He turned away from Merrill to face the camera and Ray Seranen.

"We needed to know if we could follow the energy vector safely. We knew we couldn't bivouac, so we knew we'd have to find a safe harbor," he turned back to Merrill, "If your reef hadn't filled the bill, we would have modified our plan and we never would have gone to your reef."

Merrill was dumbfounded. The K3 storm had allowed Bucher to figure out the location of his reef and know what he'd find when he got there. However, he was nowhere near as upset as Jack Richards, who suddenly realized he'd been snookered. He'd given Bucher a check for five million dollars to go to Merrill's reef - when they were going there anyway.

"When Charlie first showed me his plan and the energy vectors," continued Bucher, "We got 3-D underwater topos of the shoaling zones within his voyage plan. That's why I can talk about your reef with some authority, L.J., because I know where it is and I know what it looks like."

The two able-bodied passengers were dumbfounded. Bucher didn't miss a beat getting back to Ray Seranen.

"Ray, what are we looking at?"

Seranen was slow to pick up his cue. He'd never dreamed that Frank Bucher would pull a fast one.

"You will be launching in sixty footers. I believe, and Captain Buchanan correct me if I'm wrong, but that is pretty much the upper limit of the *Mother Carie*, correct?"

Buchanan, too, was perplexed by the sudden turn of the meeting involving Merrill's reef. But he snapped out of it when he heard the words "launch" and "sixty feet" in the same sentence.

"Actually, we couldn't launch in waves that big with a full load. We'd be too low in the water and the boats would not clear the transverse platform across our stern. With only two boats, and all the weight forward, I think we'll be ok. But anything bigger, and we'll have to scrub the launch."

"Then that certainly makes timing an issue, because the seas are going to double in size within twenty four hours. And they will only grow exponentially. Frank, you sure about where you are going?"

Seranen had never questioned Frank Bucher's judgment before, and the words felt strange coming out of his mouth.

"We'll be able to ride out the entire swell, and get all the data we could ask for. We may even surf a few sets while we're there. There's no chance the entire ocean around the reefs will close out. If there was, we wouldn't take the risk. Charlie and I went over this twice. We'll be ok."

He turned to the crews in front of him.

"Anybody got anything else?"

Bucher knew what the answer would be, but he also knew there was something else in the silence. What was once seen as a scientific expedition was now something quite different. Everyone had known bits and pieces about L.J. Merrill and Jack Richards. Now the story had come out, and the reaction of the two able-bodied passengers was hard to ignore.

The women were quiet. Margo Atkins thought she knew her husband, but something in this whole thing wasn't quite right. Patty McRane didn't know what to think, and her fiancé was eyeing her with a "What have you gotten me into here?" expression. Ken Bucher was still trying to digest what his father had done. He had never known him, and his uncle, to be anything less than honorable. Now they had come off as something less than that. They had not been dishonest, but somewhat crafty, and he found himself feeling something of the moment when heroes turn out to have feet of clay.

Jack Richards still couldn't believe that Frank Bucher would use them the way he had. But five million bucks brought his old cynicism out of retirement. Questions flooded his mind. Had Atkins and Bucher known where the reef was all along? Did Merrill give them the data just to get his money as payment for being allowed to join the Order? Did they all set him up to get his money?

L.J. Merrill felt exactly the same as he had that day in front of the Geosurf office, as if he had been played like a fiddle. Now, after all he'd gone through, he felt like a chump all over again.

Within hours the *Mother Carie* was rolling up and down in an awkward motion. The sea-state was so powerful even the huge catamaran was having problems. And Adam Buchanan was not about to keep his thoughts to himself as they prepared to launch the last two Alba_Swords on board.

"Frank, I gotta tell ya, we're both pushing it here. You've got a place you say will provide you safe harbor no matter how big it gets. Well, my safe harbor is eight hundred miles from here, and I'll be running with this cross swell the whole way. I don't like it, Frank."

"Adam, once you get us in the water, you can get the hell out of here and be drinking New Zealand beer in a pub day after tomorrow. I'll be two thousand miles to the northeast in three days and sitting in a lagoon waiting for the surf to go down. We're not doing this for the fun of it, Adam. There's a lot of science to be done - - - "

"And a five million dollar check to cash."

"Yeah, well, so what? Merrill's reef just happens to be the ONLY place we could find a harbor without getting into all kinds of trouble in the archipelagos to the west, north and east of the reef. With these conditions, I'd never go anywhere near French Polynesia. But we've got a chance to follow the main energy vector out of the storm, and get a lot of science on the way. And when it gets too big, we have a safe harbor."

"Well, Frank, all I can say is, just this once – and never again."

"That's right, Adam, never again. We were faced with the same decision NASA had to make years ago when an extraordinary solar system alignment would permit the Voyager tours of the outer planets. This is our chance to voyage in a situation almost as rare, if not more so, since it might NEVER happen again, period. Charlie and I know what we are doing, Merrill's reef is our failsafe position, and our crews are with us."

"Oh I don't know about that, Frank," said Buchanan, "I think you'd better have a chat with your man Richards."

"This is nuts. He can keep his five million bucks. You can have your reef. I want out of the whole fucking deal. I'm not gonna let that asshole snicker at me when we get there."

"Jack, this is no time to go soft. We're going, and that's that."

"Maybe soft has nothing to do with it, L.J.," said Chip Bell.

"Maybe he's in over his head," said Kurosawa, as if Richards wasn't even there, "It happens all the time, though normally we determine a person's profile when it's early in the game as opposed to when it's too late."

"What do you mean, too late? If I want out now, then end of story. And I want out."

"Gentlemen! Let's put our backs into it!" said Frank Bucher bouncing down the stairs with a jaunty look in his eye. He saw Kurosawa, Bell, and Merrill straining at the capstan – with Richards off to one side, hands on hips and feet apart, waiting to confront him.

"Merrill! What the hell's wrong with your client? And why aren't you holding his hand? He looks a bit bent, I'd say!"

"I'm going surfing at MY reef. Fuck you and your Navy maps. Maybe you set me up and maybe you didn't, but I'm going no matter what. You got a problem with Jack, you deal with it, CAPTAIN!"

The capstan jerked forward as L.J. Merrill heaved ahead forcefully. Bucher turned and took a step towards the millionaire. Richards stood his ground defiantly, obviously measuring the distance between the two men against how hard he could connect with the Captain's jaw.

"Yeah, Jack, I know! You're pissed off! You paid us to take you to a place we're going to anyway. So take a swing! If that will make you feel any better, be my guest!"

Bucher took a step forward. The millionaire cocked his clenched right fist and fired. Bucher met it in midair with the palm of his hand.

"Go ahead, Richards, try again! I won't block it this time!"

Richards tried a left jab. Bucher waited until the last millisecond, then tilted his head to let the punch go past his ear.

"Tell you what, Jackie Wallet, when we get home, what say you and I go down to the Seventh Street Gym in Oxnard. Head gear, gloves, referee, the works. Ten rounds. You knock me down, you get your money back. I knock you down, you pay another five million."

Jack Richards didn't move a muscle, and there were no words behind his clenched teeth.

"You think about it, Jackie."

Bucher took his place behind a spoke on the capstan. "Let's go guys, we don't have a moment to lose," he said, without even a glance at Jack Richards, before singing out the first words of the old sea chantey.

"Hey! Ho! and," he shoved against the spoke, "Up she rises! Hey ho and," he shoved and shouted, "UP she rises!" The capstan began to revolve.

Then the last empty spoke was given a shove so hard the other four men almost lost their footing.

"HEY HO AND UP SHE RISES!" Jack Richards' voice echoed loudly off the steel walls as he kept on pushing with the strength of two men.

Within minutes the *Tom Swift* was in position. An hour later both she and the *Serena* were in formation. A set of sixty footers came through, and two Alba_Swords were on their way with Charles Atkins and Frank Bucher at the helms. They had faced new challenges time and again since founding the Order of Southern Ocean Mariners. Now they were on a course that would take them close to wave energy of unimaginable proportions.

Two days later, the two Alba_Swords were halfway to their target. They were riding a set of waves about seventy feet high from trough to crest. The surfsailing was awesome in the truest sense of the word. Earlier that morning their forward scan sensors had found a series of seamounts, and all the skills honed in the Agulhas were brought to bear carving through giant half-pipes of water about a hundred feet high.

Frank Bucher and Charles Atkins never left the cockpits of the *Tom Swift* and the *Serena*. They would catnap at times, and had their food brought to them. Like the captains of the tall ships in the Roaring Forties a hundred years ago, they knew that one mistake without an instant and correct response from the man responsible for all the lives on board could spell disaster from which there would be no escape.

On board the *Tom Swift*, Chip Bell was standing the last minutes of his watch. There had been little chance for small talk, but during a long trim run, Bell broached a topic still sensitive since the launch two days ago.

"Frank, you really gonna take on Jack Richards?"

"Chip, someday I'll have you over to the house and you can read some of the captains' logs from the Cape Horner days. Richards got off easy. And yes, if he's up for it, so am I. Besides, we could always use another five mill, and he wouldn't miss it any more than he did the money he gave us!"

"Ok, Frank, if you say so. But maybe you should share some thoughts with Merrill. He's still pretty bent about the whole thing. And take it easy on the bottom turns. The hydraulic pressures are redlining."

"Yeah, I expect they are. Oh, and Chip, please try to raise the *Serena* will you? We need to cross-calibrate our sensors again this watch."

Chip Bell went below, and a minute later, L.J. Merrill had joined Frank Bucher in the cockpit. The waves were turquoise and aquamarine fading to royal blue from their crests to their troughs, The *Tom Swift* was going almost forty miles per hour across the clean face. The sun in the mid afternoon was warm and the Alba_Sword was in full 'surf's up' trim.

"Steady on four-five degrees, helmsman."

"Aye-aye, Captain, four-five degrees northeast, sir, dead on. A word with the captain?"

"Go ahead sailor."

"Richards was a club boxer, you know."

"Yeah, I know. We checked his references. But I was counting on him being a bit slow after being out of the ring for such a long time."

"Well, he doesn't like people to mess with him over money. You can expect him to take you up on that boxing match."

"Maybe, maybe not. We checked his tax returns. He's gonna need the writeoffs this year." Bucher turned to watch the trail of the Alba_Sword spin out endlessly across the wave they were riding. "Say L.J., did you believe me when I told you this was the only course we could take to get the maximum data from the storm?"

"No, and I still don't," said Merrill, never taking his eyes off the bow of the Alba_Sword or the compass, "Somehow you figured out something, and I don't know what it is. It took me years to figure out where I could find the last, most perfect wave on earth, and all of a sudden you know more about it than it do. Do you know what that feels like? You chase something for years, you find it, and then someone comes along and breezes right through a door it took you years to open?" Merrill paused, "But then again, I'll admit there is a world of difference between the last guy who ripped me off and you, Frank."

"You must still be holding a grudge about Ian Clark if you think I ripped you off. Maybe we took Richards for a little ride, but not you, L.J. The storm told us where to go, and we really had nothing to do with picking the course we're on. And that's the truth, L.J. So what is it about Clark?"

"He owes me big time. And when I see him, he better be ready to pay up. And it has nothing to do with money. I just want to see the look on his face when he finds out I beat him to the reef."

"What for? To shame him to his face? He knows what he did, and so do a lot of other people. And don't forget, Amundsen beat Scott to the Pole, but Amundsen regretted his victory for the rest of his life."

"Well, Scott had it coming to him, didn't he?"

"Nobody deserves to die the way he did, L.J. And in the end, Scott became a hero, and Amundsen never did quite regain his honor."

"Well, I've got my honor, Bucher, and as for Clark, there's nothing heroic about selling out to the surf industry."

"Well, I wouldn't be so quick to judge the man, L.J. People do things for the damnedest reasons, and as I recall, your life wasn't all that altruistic either, now was it, Mr. Surf Junkie?"

"What's that supposed to mean?"

"Come off it, L.J. We both know what you were doing for years was nothing more than an addict getting high over and over again, right?"

"Yeah, but - - -"

"No yeah-buts, Merrill. You've changed a lot since I first met you, but your fixation with Clark is bullshit. So get over it. If you've learned anything at all from OSOM, you know that honor has a lot to do it."

"That's a laugh, coming from you, after what you pulled on Richards."

"I haven't cashed that check yet, now have I?"

"Well, no, but - - -"

"But what? And if it's such a big deal to him, then he and I will settle it man to man in the ring. Simple as that."

"Well that's what I've got to do with Clark."

"Its not the same thing, Merrill, and you know it. Maybe Richards is a bit edgy about his five million, but the way you are messed up about Clark is much more serious. If you don't get control of it, you'll lose something deep inside you that you might never get back. So give him a chance, L.J. and you just might be the better man for it."

"Thanks for the advice, Frank. I hope I remember it when I see him."

Crosscurrents at Ka'unua

The glow of the lowering sun was weak in the west. The wind was from the wrong direction, blowing cold and damp against the struggling sails. There was no pattern to the swells. The fast and true sailing at the beginning of the passage was no more. David Helmares had begun this voyage with confidence, the sad reason for it notwithstanding. He knew the guiding stars to follow, no matter the currents or storms, from when he had first sailed to Ka'unua. He'd completed the tasks he had accepted as his destiny, knowing that someday he would have to return to witness his mentor's passing. Now the task ahead of him was ebbing his will. The sullen weather and difficult voyaging added to the ache in his heart. He found himself fighting to maintain his wayfinding skills against the both the elements of Nature arrayed against him from without and the unrelenting sorrow of his soul from within. And he was losing.

No words had passed between him and Taveka, as tradition prescribed, once I'karua had signaled the beginning of the succession process. In that moment of change, Helmares lost his friend's counseling, his laughter, his admonitions, and his encouragements. After years of apprenticeship, the student was now to become the master without a word of parting, a conversation of goodbye or even a little joke about it all. His mentor was no longer needed by the Maruleans, his duty to his people complete, their identity forever enhanced by the decades of his presence. Now a new leader was supposed to be ready to play his part in the life of the sea people, but that man was beginning to doubt himself, and only the last words of Taveka kept David's mind on an even keel.

"Never give away the last of yourself to things you cannot control. No matter how much the sea takes out of your heart, you must not let it touch the still moment inside you that IS you. Find your star, hold it close, and use it like a blazing sun to defend yourself. If you use it well, nothing will defeat you. If you doubt it, anything can."

The cold wind would soon fulfill its promise of clouds to obscure even the brightest of stars throughout the dark night ahead. The ultimate test of a wayfinder's skills was about to begin. There was nothing that could be trusted in any direction except Taveka sailing ahead of him, but soon David Helmares would have to find his own guide through the growing darkness.

Luan said nothing to him. She was fully aware of the fight going on inside the man she loved, but she dared not break his concentration.

The sky and sea were gray going black. The wind began a low whistle in the rigging. The voyager seemed fixed in place, assaulted from all sides by slapping chop and short steep waves that seemed to be laughing in derision at

David Helmares. A sudden squall filled the air. Swirling spray stung his eyes. He could barely see beyond the prows of his craft, yet he searched and strained to maintain visual contact with Taveka's voyaging craft ahead of him. He became increasingly afraid to lose his last and only guide. Then a final glimpse came and went, and he was alone.

A rogue wave crashed onto the deck, knocking him off balance and breaking his grip on the tiller. The long piece of wood, left free for just an instant, swung wildly away from him before slamming into his stomach as the voyager lurched off course under the pressure of the wave. Helmares stumbled, slipped and fell. A foot slid off the side of the hull and he was down to one knee reaching in vain for the tiller and control. The tiller swung again and he barely warded off the blow aimed at his head. His eyes shut tight in fear. He was exhausted, beaten, full of sorrow and now shame at the defeat but moments away, a defeat from which some men never, ever recover.

The prows of his voyager went high in the air. A swell rolled under the hulls and lifted the stern before dropping down again. David Helmares saw the tiller swinging wildly. The voyaging craft was now at the mercy of the sea, helpless and dangerously adrift as was he, cowered into a fetal position, completely inside himself as a last solitary retreat.

But there he was suddenly not alone.

What about your children? And their mother? What about the child inside her? What about her love for you? What about the man voyaging ahead of you, who trusted you and is able to die in peace because that trust was well-placed? Here they are, because here is their love for you, and yours for them.

The thought was the last and only thing he had, but it was not going to be drowned by a sea, or blown away by a wind, or confused by storms or frightened by the night.

There was love inside him, and though it may have been the last thing of consequence that defined who he was, it was all he needed. He focused on it and fanned its glow as if trying to bring life back to a cold and dying fire. And a spark appeared.

He did not stop his thoughts. They began to extend outwards, to his parents whom he had loved, and who had loved him. The spark caught and a flame appeared. Stronger and stronger he poured on the memories of all the years of his life when kindness and generosity had been exchanged between him and other human beings. The flame danced, and old friendships appeared in its light, feeding it and making it brighter to illuminate the way for even deeper memories to come out of his past, memories of all the students who would never forget the best teacher they ever had.

David Helmares felt the fire's warmth. It lit up his eyes behind their closed lids. Then it would be contained no longer and the bright light of the love inside him forced his eyes open wide.

He saw the tiller and put both hands on it. He gathered himself and got to his feet. He spread his legs and stood firm, warming all his muscles in the fire now burning strong inside him.

The wild and open ocean was dark all around him, but nothing could dim the light from his eyes. A wave lifted the prows, and the voyager was very much off balance. David reacted by shifting his weight against the tiller. When the wave left the sterns of the hulls, they came down together. His response had come just in time to give him a moment in balance. Twenty five seconds later, another swell lifted the voyager, and again David Helmares took the swell at an angle coming towards him, but left it evenly and balanced as it flowed behind him.

The wind increased in strength. Lightning flashed far to the east. The chop was all over the hulls. He remained steadfast, waiting for the next swell. He counted the seconds, and at the last instant, he pushed against the tiller. The prows went high in the air, but evenly this time.

Now he had it. Now he had his wayfinder's guide after first finding his soul's guide within. The squall came down hard, but David Helmares was smiling, almost laughing now. His full sails drained fresh water and he cupped his hands for a drink. Another swell came at him head on, but with his hand firm on the tiller, he was making headway by plowing squarely into the constant energy coming straight at him. He knew he was on course for good.

"Luan! Luan!" he called to his wife. The rain was coming down hard, and the noise that muffled his words, "I need help with the sails!"

Her bright smile came out from under the shelter dome on the voyaging craft. She knew her husband had withstood his challenges, and she dispelled the last of his intensity with a touch of humor.

"Oh, I'm sorry honey, but my nails might get damaged! Do I have to?"

Helmares responded perfectly to his wife's well-timed quip.

"Yes, and not only that, but I need a kiss, right now!"

"Aye-aye, captain!"

The rain began to back off, and the wind shifted as the squall moved on. David stayed at the tiller as Luan swung the sails around. Then a star appeared, and David took immediate note of its position off his mast relative to the next swell. The wind really began to kick up, and Luan struggled with the sails to give their voyaging craft even more speed. Soon they were flying forward, and more stars appeared. David saw a part of the constellation he needed. It was lower in the sky, and would disappear before dawn, but it pointed to a path of stars he traced up to the apex of the dome above him. As the great track of stars wheeled overhead, he would watch each set on the horizon. When the last star touched the sea, they would be at Ka'unua.

* * *

"I thought we all better talk after what just happened out at the reef and what we're going to do next," said Heath Larson. His mind was very much on the new low pressure system between New Zealand and Antarctica and he had everyone on a conference call, including Mac Owens, who was now in Hawai'i. It took him a second to remember that there was something more important to understand before he began to talk about going on a surf trip.

426

"Mac, can you tell us what happened?" he said, but the words came out stiff and leaden, as if he was suddenly a bit ashamed of his original reason for the call. And Mac Owens didn't make it any easier for him.

"Well, I, I don' quite know where to start, Heath. An' fact is, I'd rather not say much t'all. Why do ya wanna talk about it, Heath?"

But Mac Owens knew why. Rumors were beginning to circulate in Hawai'i and the surf industry that something bad had happened to the Wavelife expedition, but no one outside of Tahiti knew any details. With a morgue full of corpses and body parts, everyone involved was placed incommunicado while Tahitian officials imposed a complete media blackout, knowing the deaths of eleven men would quickly be big news throughout the South Pacific, and then throughout the world. They wanted to know exactly what happened before the world media descended upon them and had initiated a formal investigation into the entire episode. It was immediately determined that Victor Sanchez had acted in accordance with all aviation laws, and the Tahitian air ministry, with whom he'd worked closely over the years, honored his request to be allowed to take his wife home. Sanchez knew both he and his wife needed time to recover from what they'd seen: in some ways even Victor's father never fully recovered from what he'd had to do more than sixty years ago. Officials also gave Mac Owens permission to get on a jet to Hawai'i after taking a full statement from him. Not so Kai Woods, Anasi or the men who had flown out to the reef. They were still in Tahiti under a polite form of house arrest.

Aleja Gracellen sensed the tension and stepped in.

"How are Victor and Tina?"

"Back home, Aleja. but 'fore y'all start askin' a buncha questions, I just can't tell y'all a helluva lot, 'cause that's the deal I made with the Tahitians. What I can tell ya is that guy Palua was givin' orders, he made sum mistakes an' things got outta hand."

"Randy Laine called me after he talked to Kai Woods. Said the whole thing sounded like a disaster in the making." Larson's clumsy attempt to get Owens to open up was cut off by a trenchant question.

"Mac, can you tell us how many went out there?" asked Ben Jeffries, sitting in his office with June Wilson and Bill Massara.

"Fourteen."

"Who came back?" asked Sonny-boy Noaloa.

"I cain't speak ta that 'cept ta say 'twas a cameraman an' a surfer an' the man who saved 'em."

"What about Ian?" asked Cheryl Corlund, sitting with Dolly Artensa in a tiny office in Newport Beach.

"Cheryl, I think ya kin figger the rest fer yerselves."

"Lord have mercy on their souls," said Dolly Artensa.

For quite a while it seemed like the silence would last forever in Hawai'i, New York, and California as everyone was lost in their own thoughts about what role they had played in the death of Ian Clark and ten other men.

"I'm sorry Mac. You're right. So what do we need to talk about Heath?" said Cheryl Corlund, putting Larson on a spot from which there was no exit except by honestly going forward.

"Those guys were surfing the wrong reef. We looked at the DVD again and Aleja was absolutely right. The place we surfed is not the place in the video. It has to be one of the two reefs to the northeast. There is a new storm right now that will give us a second chance. I think we should get out there."

"Not so fast, Larson," said Roberto Mercante, standing up to Larson after he'd put Mac Owens on the spot about what had happened, "You said that once before and you almost died. Now other people said it and they're dead."

Mercante's sudden sobriety startled everyone.

"Roberto, I'm sure Ian learned from what happened with Heath," said Aleja, "But maybe those guys cornered him. Or maybe he took them to the wrong reef on purpose."

"All I know is, Palua and those guys were playing for keeps, and maybe they got what they deserved," said Sonny-boy.

"Sonny-boy, nobody deserves to die just so some crooks can make a goddamn buck," said Ben Jeffries.

He looked at Massara and Wilson, whose knowledge of Palua's investment group had helped him fully understand just why Cheryl Corlund had tried to pull off the LBO in the first place.

"So why do we even need to go back out there? We aren't looking to make celebrities for public consumption anymore, are we?" said Dolly Artensa. The gospel singer from South Central was, once again, playing devil's advocate. The business team knew it was a good question. The surfers knew it was a good question. But one person had a quick answer, because she was exactly between the two camps.

"No, Dolly, that's not in the business plan as I understand it. But I am, and if you want me to be a role model, this is as good a time as any. If we do it right, we'll take the media spotlight that'll shine on us and reflect it on to the issues we believe in."

The phones went silent again. Larson knew contemplating another trip out to the reef so soon was pushing it. But it was a risk he had to take.

"Thanks, Aleja. Everyone, please, let me explain a few things. Over a week ago, I got a call from a friend in Western Australia, and when he told me how big the surf was, and how fast it came up, well, uh, I was uh, - - -"

Ben Jeffries smiled at Larson's reticence because he understood Larson's inner turmoil quite well. Bruddah, too, understood why his friend was suddenly at a loss for words, so he broke right in, knowing that it would be easier on Larson if he didn't have to talk about himself.

"Yeah, brah, you start pacing 'round da house. You call Randy. He not home. You get onna computa. Check Navy website. Now I tink you gonna explode. You get out da maps. Check da swell angle like you did da last trip. Den you really go nuts."

"Yeah, I guess I did. Surfing is such a cruel mistress, sometimes."

"Oh, and what do you know about mistresses?" asked Aleja Gracellen with a purposefully innocent tone to her voice that accomplished her goal when she hear some muffled laughter on the speaker phones.

"Uh, nothing, only a figure of speech."

"Yes, Heath, we're sure that's how you meant it," said Artensa, picking up where Aleja left off, "being the fine church-going man that you are."

Bruddah and Sonny-boy looked at him. Now Larson was in trouble and Bruddah couldn't bail him out this time. After explaining to Artensa all about Kierkegaard, existentialism and Christianity, he'd promised her he'd start going to the little church down in the valley.

"Uh, yes, exactly, Dolly. Thank you. Now, as I was saying, - - - "

"Yeah, he fine man go church alla time. Put ten dollah in da plate. Gonna sing in da choir next week," said Bruddah.

"Oh Bruddah, you're going with him? Oh praise be!" said Artensa, "and Sonny-boy too, no doubt."

"Uh, yes ma'am, absolutely. Good for the soul. Excellent sermons!"

Now the surfers were really in trouble. But before she came to their rescue, Cheryl Corlund glanced at Artensa who smiled knowingly at the surfers' flimsy story.

"Well Heath, I guess that storm was something special."

"Yeah, Cheryl, it was, and I started amping. But then I realized we weren't ready. The waverunners were still in boxes, and we hadn't tested them with the mountings on the *Aeolus*. Then I got a call from Randy Laine after he talked to Kai Woods. He filled me in on the whole thing, and I started to have flashbacks about how my impatience and ego had almost killed me. Talking to Randy settled me down pretty fast, I'll tell ya."

"Thanks for the confessional, Heath, but let's get to the point, ok? There's a new storm and more waves coming, right? So, have you called Randy yet? How about Bob? "What about the plane? Are you ready?" said Gracellen, "'Cause I'm ready!"

"Sonny-boy?" asked Cheryl Corlund.

"I concur with Aleja," said Sonny-boy.

"He mean he go surf one kine big wave geevum fo' da cause," said Bruddah.

'Thanks for the translation, Bruddah!" said Cheryl Corlund, "Clem? Is the plane ready?"

"Yup, sho' is," he said, "Plus we got Mac ta' help us, so I'm ready ta file a flight plan. Jes say the word."

"I think Aleja spoke for all of us," said Cheryl Corlund, "Anybody got anything more to say?"

"Yes," said Dolly Artensa, "When we get off the phone, I'd like for everyone to stop for a second and say a prayer for Ian Clark and the guys who died out there. And then ask the Good Lord to give us His blessings."

"And offshore winds!" added Aleja Gracellen.

A loud "Amen!" filled the speakerphones.

Dawn came clear, bright and warm. The blue sea was now calm and smooth as the long low 'guiding' swell continued to roll out of the southwest. The two voyaging craft were much farther apart than at any time during the passage to Ka'unua, but neither was in any way off course. Their destination was close at hand, though still four or five hours away on this windless morning of an day long anticipated.

But Taveka knew he wasn't going to die today, and probably not tomorrow, and maybe not for while.

Ever since he had become the chief navigator of the Marulean people, he had known what was going to happen when he lowered the sails of his craft for the last time. And over the last two years of his life, he had worked to be in control of the exact manner of his death. He had, almost mischievously, modified the tradition so that instead of sailing his voyager into waves to meet his death, he was going to ride a surfboard into the heart of the ocean through the tunnel of a big wave.

That wave would not break at Ka'unua on this day. The waves rolling beautifully down both sides of the reef were barely waist-high.

A mile north of the reef David and Luan had lowered their sails and set several sea anchors. They would only approach Ka'unua on the day of Taveka's passing, and that was obviously not going to happen on this calm morning.

Soon the sun was straight overhead and hot on Luan's bare skin and David began diving to spear some fresh fish. She was keeping an eye on his bubbles coming up from the deep even as she watched the surface of the sea for sharks. She raised her head and shielded her eyes from the sun. No sharks, no wind, nothing in any direction except the masts of her father's voyaging craft off in the distance in the center of the lagoon. Intermittent waves of a quietly surging sea washed around the edges of Ka'unua.

Luan sat back down as David came up with yet another fish on his spear.

"Well, I never thought I'd be happy that the surf was flat, but then again, I guess that doesn't make this any easier, does it?" he said.

"No it doesn't. Dad is probably laughing about it, I suppose."

"I wonder if anyone ever dies when they want to."

"Will you want to when you are the man waiting in the center of Ka'unua, and our son is sitting out here?"

David Helmares was not surprised by his wife's question. He thought of his son, and another child on the way. He thought of what had saved him last night when he was beaten down to the last remnants of his character.

"When that day comes, I will have only one wish. I'll want to make sure my love for you and our children and our people was left as strong as I could make it. And that love will never die. So I'll face my death as your father has shown me. And I'll show our son. That's the chain, and I won't be the one to break it."

"You, David, are becoming more a Marulean man than ever. Now, how about one more fish for dinner?"

"Coming right up!"

Helmares adjusted his diving goggles and dove back down to hunt for another fish. Luan sat smiling at the thought of her husband's past and their future together. She stretched her arms over her shoulders, then felt the baby inside her kick a little. She looked back over the side of the voyager to check on her husband's bubbles. She could see him deep, and he appeared to have another fish on his spear. She sat up, and glanced toward the reef where her father waited for waves.

As she did, she saw something floating past the tips of the tri-hulls. She looked a little closer, and saw what it was.

David Helmares could hear his wife's screams while still fifteen feet below the surface. He kicked harder and the screams became louder.

"Luan! What is it?"

He lifted himself out of the water and grabbed his wife with both arms. She turned to him and buried her head on his shoulder. He held her tight, said her name, and kissed her on the forehead. She acknowledged the kiss and held him tighter. Only then did he look over her shoulder.

He saw the dome of a helmet about two inches above the surface of the blue glass sea. Something was pushed up into the helmet. Extending down into the clear water was a neck severed cleanly just above the shoulders.

Taveka watched the sails being raised and by their set he knew the voyaging craft was coming his way. Minutes it entered the lagoon, David at the tiller and Luan standing well forward.

"Father! We need your help."

He saw his daughter was very distraught, but he could not speak to her.

"Father. We need to break the tradition of silence. David can't, but I must. And I am not going away until you talk to me, father!"

Taveka thought carefully about why the tradition of silence existed. It gave others a true sense of the finality of his dying while he was still with them. It avoided lots of idle talk that might dissuade the navigator from completing his responsibilities. But his daughter needed him.

"Wait till I tell your mother what kind of child you turned out to be! Breaking rules, ruining traditions, never giving a man any peace."

"Yes, I'm exactly the woman you get when a man like you is her father."

"Hmm, I never thought of it that way. Our ancestors won't be happy."

"Tell them it won't happen again," said Luan, looking her father straight in the eye until she realized the utter truth to the words she had just spoken.

"No, I suppose it won't," he replied, looking at David.

He let the craft drift forward until the two men faced each other.

"What do you need, David?"

He told his mentor what Luan had seen. He said nothing more. The understanding between the two men went without saying.

"Luan, stay here – you've seen enough. David, come aboard and bring your sharpest knife. Sometimes all we need to do is cut away a piece of their uniform with their name on it or their dogtags - - - "

He stopped the memories in their tracks. He looked at his daughter, and then looked out to sea where their search and retrieval would begin.

"It must have been a big group if they needed a PBY. We may have much to do, but we have a lot of light left and there's not much wind right now."

They found the floating helmet, and David broke off a vertebra from the neck. It was all that would be needed to identify the victim, and at least next of kin would have some kind of closure. Using the surfboard to retrieve some items while the voyager went after others, they collected floating shards of four different surfboards, one with a foot still inserted in the straps. Once again, David broke off a bone and kept it. They found a nearly intact foam sled, the kind used behind waverunners for rescuing surfers, and another helmet, empty. They saw the remains of several sharks, including one whose mouth was stuffed with something. The back half of the shark was completely gone, and Taveka took it upon himself to cut away more of the shark, revealing a hand extending out its throat. The hand had a ring on it. He cut off the finger with the ring still on it.

The wind began to come up as the afternoon wore on. Still they searched back and forth across the zone near Ka'unua where swell, wind and current had left a trail of debris and remains. Here and there they found plastic shards or part of a windshield or a fragment of a wetsuit.

Just before dark David saw a lifevest floating upright in the water. Taveka saw it, too. The vest contained a torso. The head had been torn off. Both arm openings were slashed with the deep slicing cuts of sharks' teeth. The spine protruded from the bottom.

David put the surfboard in the water. There would be no need to pull the floating hulk aboard the voyaging craft to do what was necessary. He was about to step down on the board, when Taveka stopped him.

"Sometimes I thought it was better to find them like this. When they were crushed in their planes, they often appeared asleep. Sometimes I didn't want to touch them because I thought they were going to wake up. I was fifteen the first time, and it took me almost four years to eventually learn that they weren't ever going to wake up. Let me do it."

The old man stepped onto the wide surfboard, sat down, and paddled slowly towards the floating remains. He leaned over and rolled the torso towards him so that he could open the vest. As he did, he felt something in one of the pockets. He held the vest with one hand and opened the pocket flap with the other. He pulled out a small camera and held it up for David to see. Then he tossed it over, but he missed and the camera went into the water. It floated, and David bent over the edge of the voyager's hull to retrieve it. Taveka continued to open the vest. There was no necklace or chain or anything else that could be used for identification until a shirt was revealed. It was soaked in blood, but there was a logo on the chest that could just barely be seen. He cut the shirt away and held it in one hand. He began to backpeddle away, when David called to him.

"Taveka, better get a vertebra, too."

"Yes, you are right. We didn't do that back then. I'll get the vest, too."

David carefully organized everything as Taveka raised sail. He placed the vertebra in the shirt, and wrapped everything else they'd found in a small piece of sail cloth. He wrapped the vest around the bundle and used a length of sennit rope to secure it into one package whose contents were now safe. He placed the camera in the vest pocket and closed the flap.

Taveka went into the shelter dome and opened the compartment where, long ago, he had placed the box of offerings to his ancestors. From it he removed his time-worn carving tools, the first coil of sennit rope he had ever made as a boy, and a large bundle wrapped in an old piece of duck canvas, waterproofed with candle wax and tied tightly with sennit line.

"You were going to get all this stuff anyway, but I needed it all with me on my last voyage."

David placed the bundle of remains and fragments deep in the compartment in the center hull. He put the wood panel covering securely in place, and covered it with a mat.

"Leave it in there. You and I must never touch it again. When you get back to our island, leave this craft outside the lagoon. Then tell Kalala everything. Let her take over from there. You will have done your part. She knows what to do until arrangements can be made to get it directly to someone with the proper authority to receive it."

The sun touched the western horizon and disappeared quickly. Within half an hour, stars began to populate the canopy overhead. The two voyagers were lashed together, floating within the protecting coral ring of Ka'unua. The waves were getting a little bigger as a full moon was rising in the east. The two navigators and the woman who connected them were sitting on the platform of Taveka's voyaging craft. They were eating the fish David had caught while Taveka talk about the reef to the southwest.

"It has always been a place of taboo, even as Ka'unua has always been a place of peace. Here, there has never been a shark that we didn't know. With all our ancestors still here, this place is safe. But that reef," he gestured to the southwest, "is where we never go."

"There must have been a lot of them, and a lot of equipment," said David. He recounted the items he'd seen, and Taveka added a few things to the list.

"Yes, you can get a lot of people and equipment into a PBY."

"You never told me anything about seaplanes, father."

"No, I've never talked to you about the war and what I did when I was young. And I'm not going to now. David knows a thing or two, and someday you can ask him. But as for the seaplanes, did you ever hear of the people who fly around helping families and kids between Tahiti and Fiji? They have a PBY. Maybe you'll see it someday."

"Looks like I'm going to be seeing a lot of things someday that I've never seen before," she said.

David frowned at the thought, but then something occurred to him.

"Maybe not. The waves must have been huge, and with the sharks feeding on the corpses, the news might keep people away."

"You think so? I don't. I think this is the beginning of a new era for our people, and I hope your being a Californian will help."

Silence settled on the voyaging craft like wind dying in the sails. David and Taveka gazed into the future, but Luan looked out across the lagoon at the waves breaking perfectly along the reef. The moon was shining directly into them, and their white water trails were luminescent. She thought of how her husband had often moved in his sleep as if he was paddling a surfboard, or rising up to see waves, or talking about riding the liquid curves with an almost blissful look on his face, the same look she had seen so many times after they had made love. She looked at the two men and decided to change the subject to something far less serious than the future of the sea people.

"David, have you ever, uh, *surfed* in the moonlight without me knowing about it?" Luan asked with a slight tone of accusation. She winked at her dad without David seeing her do it.

"Of course, but, - - -" stammered David, taken aback by a question that had nothing to do with what they'd been talking about, "I mean, no, uh, you've always known where I was at night after I, uh, I mean you and I, I mean why would I want to go surfing instead of - - - "

Taveka had happily given up his little girl to the man who made her a woman and a mother, but they were still so close they could read each other's minds. He played his part perfectly.

"That's ok, David, I won't say anything to her. We'll just call it navigator stuff," said Taveka, with a grin matched by his daughter's, that told David the two of them were in cahoots.

"Uh, yeah, Luan," he said with a 'Two-can-play-that-game' tone, "That's navigator stuff. Can't tell you. Sorry!"

They all laughed, and in the joy of the moment, Taveka suddenly realized where the idea had come from that had sparked Luan's question. He stood up behind her and looked out at the waves. He watched two or three roll all the way down the reef.

"David, please un-lash your craft from mine."

"May I ask why?"

"You may ask, but I don't have to tell you."

Taveka looked at the waves and then looked at his long, wooden surfboard lashed under the cross members. Then he looked at David, who realized what Taveka was going to do.

"Are you ever going to stop surprising me?" David asked incredulously.

"Yes, and quite soon, actually. But not tonight. Let's get going. I want you to show me some things."

David Helmares paddled the last few yards to the voyaging craft where Taveka and Luan had watched him ride several waves in the moonlight. He had displayed the exact same technique on each one, showing Taveka how to adjust speed with precise changes in the body's center of gravity, shifting his weight to accelerate then slowing just a touch to perfectly match the pace of the wave brushing past Ka'unua, even to the point of putting his arms up over his head to elongate the curve of his body while gliding in perfect harmony with the wave.

He stepped up from the board to the voyager in one spry motion.

"Show off!" said his wife, laughing at her husband's last little touch of agility and style.

"That's how you do it, Taveka," said David Helmares, "You keep your feet together and use your arms high above you, with your back in an arch so that you can shift your center of gravity just so and keep the nose from pearling while staying exactly in the sweet spot of the wave."

"That's what he's doing in the other picture you have on the *Morning Light*, isn't it?"

"Yes, the one of Mickey Dora. Between him at Malibu and Joey Cabell at Tamarin Bay, its all you need to know about perfect poise and style on a small wave. Ok, your turn."

Taveka was all business as he lowered himself to the deck of the board floating next to his voyaging craft. With time remaining before his final surf session, he wanted to reach a new level of skill.

"Now don't try to do it with your feet together," advised Helmares, "Just work on the arch. Get the feel of the speed against the shifting of your weight. And slowly! Too much arch and she'll race right out from under your feet! Just stay with the wave the whole way. The spray coming off the nose of the board is your guide. Just the barest stream is what you're after."

"And please watch me and tell me if I make any mistakes. I don't want to be a, uh, what did you call 'em?"

"A kook!"

"Yeah, I don't want to be a kook on my last wave! The ancestors would be insulted!"

"How would they know? They've never surfed!"

"David, they would know. When it comes to balance and harmony with the ocean, believe me, they would know."

Taveka paddled his board away from the voyager towards empty waves shining white and deep blue. He rode two of them to practice the techniques of trimming his board for maximum speed. David hooted in approval across the open water. The old man then got ride after ride, sliding across the small, clean, waves as they broke flawlessly down the reef. Soon the moon was almost overhead and illuminating the entire reef. Taveka ended a ride and did not paddle back out. He was as excited as a man could be, but though the spirit was willing, the flesh was now weak. He knew his limits and lived within them even in the last days of his life.

"You never cease to amaze me, Taveka," said the student-now-teacher as he lifted the board out of the water, placed it across the hulls, and then offered his strong arm to pull his mentor on deck.

"I think I've got it. I can't do it with my feet together like you did, but the speed and the arch and spray off the nose, yes, I've got it."

Luan had watched her husband and father ride every wave.

"David, maybe someday you can teach me how to do that."

"Well," he touched her full stomach and smiled broadly, "The arch might be a little hard for you right now."

"Yes, and my grandchild might throw your balance off!" laughed Taveka, "You know how kids can do that without even thinking about it!"

Above their bright and full laughter came a fresh, new sound far different than the steady, washing noise of the small waves breaking along the reef. It did not register with Luan, but David and Taveka heard it quite clearly.

"Let's go back inside the lagoon. I think the surf is getting bigger."

"Yes, David, that's what you said earlier. Maybe two or three feet bigger since we got here."

"Yes, my dearest daughter, but now there's something else coming to Ka'unua. Something new is starting up, and daylight will tell us more." Taveka smiled at David as a wave came down the reef easily six feet high. It lifted the voyaging craft and setting it back down almost abruptly. There were two more waves just like it, one halfway to the southern tip of the reef, and then a third even further up the reef, just starting to break in the moonlight.

The sun was still well below the horizon to the east. David and Luan were asleep in each other's arms on their craft, floating about fifty yards from the voyager of Taveka. Despite the strenuous hours of surfing under the full moon, Taveka was alert and awake. The swells were far, far apart. He felt the emptiness between them innately. He had been tuned to the rhythms of the ocean for decades, and yet this rhythm was substantially different from any he had ever felt. Though they were now twice the height of a man, Taveka's instincts told him these waves were but infants. They would continue to grow steadily, from youth to maturity to full adulthood. And somewhere behind his instincts, a distinct feeling existed that their size and power would expand to a fantastic height and strength. And when those ancient waves came, he would welcome them warmly on the last day of his life.

"David, David! Wake up!"

He heard the whispered voice through the last moments of his sleep. He immediately knew who it was, and where he was, and why he was there. A wave of dark emotion flooded through his mind, and his heart went heavy. He unwrapped Luan's arms from his chest, and sat up in the shelter dome. He knew he would have to wake her soon, but he thought letting her sleep for now was all he could do for her on this day so long expected.

"Yes, Taveka, I'm coming. I am here. I am here for you."

"Good. Quickly, now, David."

Helmares came out of the shelter. He looked to the south and saw a set of waves, each over ten feet high. He was suddenly confused and looked at the side of the voyaging craft where his mentor kneeled on his surfboard.

"Taveka, uh, I'm ready, but - - - "

"Good, let's get going," he said excitedly, but when he saw the sad look on David's face, he backpedaled for a moment, "Oh, yes, well, it is not big enough today, so I want you to show me more techniques."

Helmares' expression changed entirely.

"You what? I thought - - - "

"Don't think so much, David. Let's just going surfing. Tomorrow, or the next day, or the next, I will think about my last wave. Right now the waves are still babies and I want to go and play with them. Do you want to go?"

* * *

Fifteen hundred miles to the southwest, the waves were not babies. They were seventy feet high for the second day in a row and perfect for high performance surfsailing. Some brilliant maneuvers had been executed, yet the Alba_Swords stayed on course, knowing a safe haven awaited them in a little more than seventy hours. They were not going to be late. Eight hours behind them, the waves were easily a hundred foot high. Another Eight hours back, the open ocean seas were half again as big. And the mariners aboard the Alba_Swords *Tom Swift* and *Serena* knew the probabilities existed of much bigger waves even now being spawned off Antarctica.

* * *

"We have to go back in, and right now," said David, barely pulling out of a ten-footer near where Taveka sat on his voyaging craft.

"Why? You rode that wave well. I can do that, I'm sure of it."

"No, Taveka, you would fall for sure."

The old man was a bit offended.

"And why is that may I ask?"

"You may ask, but I don't have to tell you. Now help me with the board, and let's go back in the lagoon."

"Now we can go back out there," said David, setting the board down across the cross members of Taveka's voyaging craft.

The old navigator came around to the rear of the surfboard and put his eyes close to the tail. Then he slowly moved his head backwards, with one eye closed. Then he repeated the process with the other eye.

"You missed a spot," he said.

The long board was a masterpiece of craftsmanship. David had spent many hours with Taveka building its interior framework using bamboo strips, and then surrounding the wing-like assemblage with solid wood, seasoned and strong. He had purposefully designed it so that it would be wide and easy for Taveka to use for learning the basics of surfing. Yet in the back of his mind he knew that the waves of the Nebula Archipelago were world class, so being able to re-shape the nose and tail, and even change the rocker, were possible thanks to the wood's extremely tight grain making it almost waterproof.

David frowned, but after grabbing the rails of the board with both hands, closing his eyes and feeling the two curves slowly to a final center point at the tail, he realized Taveka was right. He looked at the few inches in question.

"Yes, you're right, but we don't have a fine grain wood rasp."

"We will in just a minute."

Taveka grabbed his goggles, and dove off the side of his voyaging canoe. Fifteen minutes later, David had successfully used his new tool to make the rails of the surfboard perfect. When he had said something to Taveka about breaking off the coral, the old man just shrugged his shoulders.

"My ancestors know what it's for."

The wide tail of Taveka's board was now a narrower 'diamond tail'. They continued to work, thinning out the last two feet of the board to reduce its buoyancy and give the board more bite. Then David addressed the shape of the nose by narrowing its outline to reduce its bulk and gain more control. Finally he streamlined the profile of the fin and reduced its thick foil slightly to give the board more forward thrust. The two men were excited and admiring their handiwork when a voice of reason snapped them out of it.

"Are you two ready to eat?" said Luan, "or are you going to starve yourselves like children who are too busy playing?"

"Now, that's what we want," said David, cross-stepping with flair after completing a great ride down the reef in the early afternoon, "She's responsive without being wobbly. Tail slices with authority. The fin works perfect. She's ready when you are Taveka. She'll give you the control you'll need."

"All the way back in the tube? Let's see if you can disappear and make it out. I want to be sure your new design works all the way."

"Back in a minute, Taveka," said David with a joyful feeling of anticipation that he'd never quite known before. He was about to get a perfect wave all to himself, and try to ride back in the tube as deep as he could get, and doing it all for someone else besides himself.

The board had its own momentum. Two strokes and to his feet. He leaned back to slow the board, then extended his arm forward, lowered his shoulder and accelerated down the face that was becoming more vertical second. A hard, sharp first turn off the bottom, the diamond tail cutting into the base of the wave, the fin flowing perfectly while providing stability and direction. Up the face, the wall extending ahead, speed now a critical factor.

Another carve off the bottom, and then under the roof of the cylinder, board fitting the inner curves of the wave perfectly. The wave seemed to pause, and he stepped hard on the tail, raising the nose in the air, then into a crouch deep inside the spinning tube, looking out of the tunnel as his mentor watched his every move. He emerged from the wave as it backed off in the deep water down by the lagoon's entrance. He paddled back out to where Taveka was waiting.

"Thank you, David. I'll have all the control I need. Now give me the board and go back and get your wife. And take your time, I won't need you to come back out here for two hours or so. I've got to practice."

"Any suggestions?"

"Yes, help me out of the water."

"No, about the board, Taveka!"

"No, I don't think so, but I am awfully tired. What a thing to do with your life! The more you ride waves, the more waves you want to ride, and the more waves you ride, the more tired you get, except your mind refuses to listen to your body because it gets more and more excited!"

"Yeah, yeah, yeah. What else is new?" David smirked playfully, "Here, let me go ride one or two. I think its getting bigger again."

"Yes it is, but it is still not big enough to kill me. Maybe tomorrow, or the next day, or who knows? Maybe I'll just surf out here forever!"

"Now what?"

'The nose is still too fat. It needs to be pulled in to more of a point so it will catch less wind and will not affect your balance in fast turns. And the rail needs a little less curve to fit the wave better."

"Well what does that mean? If that's what you need to ride bigger and bigger waves, then we'll end up with a long narrow, pointed platform that goes like a rocket ship!"

"You learn pretty fast for an old man!"

"How are we going to eat if all you do is surf? We have only enough food for maybe four days, and how will we get more?"

"Don't worry, dear, something will happen."

"Yes, and remember soon you will only have to feed yourselves. Now let me have some more of the fish stew. I think the waves will be even bigger tomorrow, but - - -"

"But still not big enough for you," laughed David.

"No, I think that will be another three days at this rate."

Luan was just about to give the two men a piece of her mind when she realized that in three days, her father would be gone forever.

"Well then, tomorrow you are not leaving me in here to float around in the lagoon. I'm going out there to watch you, and with all this talk, you guys better show me some good surfing."

439

"Don't worry, dear. It might be fifteen, twenty feet on the sets. But it is so perfect I - - -, hey, I know! Let's go surf the other side of the reef tomorrow! We haven't done that yet!"

"Always something new, right, David?" laughed his wife.

"Yes, I taught him that, but that's navigator stuff, so don't blame him!" said Taveka.

* * *

"So we can't get a permit until the other one expires?"

"That's correct, Mr. Larson. We are sorry for the delay," said the official in the Tahitian Maritime Ministry's office of special permits.

"Well, can we do the paper work today so that it will be ready?"

"No, that would be premature. We must wait until the permit in the name of Wavelife International has expired before we can proceed with your application."

"But Wavelife - - - "

"Yessir, I know what you are going to say. However, we have our laws regarding the issuance of permits for special activities inside the territorial waters of our nation, and I'm sure you want to cooperate with our laws," said the official.

"Excuse us, sir, while I have a word with Mr. Larson," said Mac Owens as he pulled the surfer aside and spoke in a quiet but very firm voice, "Heath, don' say 'nuther word. They're under a lotta pressure over what happened ta Clark an' Palua. If he thinks fer even an instant ya woodn't wanna cooperate with 'em, we ain' never gonna git a permit."

Owens turned back to the maritime official sitting behind his small wooden desk in the windowless concrete room with a fan barely circulating the air above them.

"Thank you very much fer yer time," said Mac Owens, "and we'll be happy to return to see ya day afta tomorrah."

"Yes, Mr. Owens, and thank you. We are all very sorry for what happened to your friends. And Mr. Larson, we are happy to have you back to visit us after your accident last May. It is not good for tourists to die in my country, and I know you will be very careful this time. Oh, and Mr. Owens, don' forget to make the necessary your arrangements regarding the usual fees and charges that accompany an application of this type. Here, here is my card. Come back in two days and ask for me. Goodbye!"

The two men stepped outside into the sweltering sun of August in Tahiti. Once again, Heath Larson was learning the lessons of patience, though not as easily as he thought he would.

"Now what? This is just so much crap!"

"This is jes a miner detail, Heath, an' you got sum 'vantages ya don' even know 'bout. He knows yer name, an' he knows me, an' brother, that's like gold down here. 'Sides, we got lots to do. Hell, I bet the permit gonna be ready fo' we are!"

Larson wasn't going to be mollified quite so easily.

"What was that he said about fees and charges? How much is this gonna cost us? And what necessary arrangements?"

"It ain't gonna cost you a cent, Heath. We gotta go an' open a bank account right now an' Cheryl needs to put fifty grand in it, an' that's gonna take twenny four hours. Plus we gotta git all tha paper work from tha *Aeolus* an' everybody's passport numbers ta operate a charter inside their airspace."

"How did all this happen last time? I can't believe all the stuff we gotta do."

"Ian Clark did it all. Geosurf had an account fer their surf resort, an' the *Skyhook*'s bin flying 'round here fer years. An' even with all that squared away, when we flew y'all in there las' May, it cost twenny grand to pull that off on the spur of the moment. An' Clark had to eat that since nobody wanted to tell ya 'bout it after what happened to ya."

"Mac, at this rate we'll never make it for that swell."

"Didn't that 'tude getcha in trouble last time? Now jes' take it easy, an' we do first things first. How bout sum lunch?"

"I dunno know, I'm not that hungry."

"Heath Larson, ya know what yer problem is?"

"No, Mac, what's my problem other than getting a piece of paper so we can go surfing?"

"Yer problem is that yer too big fer anyone ta slap some sense into ya. Now y'all listen to me! We ARE gonna eat lunch. An' then we're goin' to the bank, an' we're gonna start the money process. An' then to the hotel an' git everybody organized fer tomorrah. An' yer gonna do what I tell ya ta do 'else I'll have Bruddah tow yer ass out ta sea tied to one of yer surfboards an' you can jes paddle back ten miles or so. Now fly right, buster! Yer gittin' a second chance, an' you aint gonna blow it if I have anytin' ta say 'bout it."

* * *

David Helmares was up an hour before dawn on the third day of their sojourn at Ka'unua. Luan was wide awake the moment her husband moved away from her.

"I am going to scout around the entire reef. If your father wants this to be the day, I'd better first understand what he'll be facing."

"Have the waves changed?"

"Yes, Luan, I feel today is very different."

Helmares kissed his wife deeply. She was bearing their third child, and he did not take leave of her lightly. But today he was the chief navigator of the Maruleans from the moment he opened his eyes, and he had a responsibility she understood well.

Without even looking at the waves he dove off the bow of his voyaging craft and swam across the lagoon, the warm water comfortable and his muscles strong and supple. He could hear the surf, but did not look to see the

441

waves. He only looked down into the water between each breath. He was starting his day by immersing himself in a different world, away from the waves, and closer to Taveka's ancestors. He reached his mentor's voyaging craft. He was not surprised that Taveka was still sleeping after seven days of challenges and exertion that would have taxed any strong man. The surfboard was resting on the crossbeams. David pulled it down into the water and rolled himself onto its deck.

"Take your time."

David did not reply to Taveka's voice coming from inside the shelter dome on the voyaging craft. There was no need for words to pass between them until he had something to say. He shifted to a kneeling position and began to paddle with the strength of his entire body. He used the sun to stay on course and never looked up as crossed the quiet lagoon surrounded by a sea-change in the size and consistency of the new day's waves. The weight of the board provided extra momentum across the water, and before long David arrived at the lagoon entrance. He kept paddling and soon felt a slight change in the water temperature and noticed the board responding to a different texture on the surface of the sea. He stopped paddling and let the board glide on its own until it came to a floating rest. For a minute or more, David closed his eyes and sensitized himself to the open ocean. He felt the currents and the roll of the swells. He listened for the changes in the slap of wavelets against the board. He inhaled deeply to determine how much sea spray was in the air. Never once did he look around to get his bearings. He was a navigator, and as such he made sure all his senses were tuned to the ever changing sea.

There was no doubt the surf was very different today. Now he would find out just how different.

The ocean was quiet around him in the lull between sets. He laid down on the surfboard and paddled with just one arm until the sun told him the board was pointed on a new course around the east side of the lagoon. He began to paddle with both arms at the same time. Between each long hard stroke he paused to let his senses gather information. Then he heard the sound of a wave breaking at the other end of the reef. He continued paddling, listening to the wave breaking as it came towards him. He adjusted his course slightly away from the reef. He heard another wave break off in the distance, and then he felt gravity pull against him as he went up the unbroken slope of the first wave. He counted the seconds it took before he reached the crest, where the early rays of light caught the corner of his eye, before he slid down the back of the wave as it continued its journey to the north.

Then he counted the seconds before he went up and over the next wave, and the next, until the entire set had passed beneath him. Without ever seeing the waves, he knew they were twice as big as the day before, and the interval between them had increased. Several sets came and went, but he never looked at them. He just kept paddling across the ocean's surface to absorb its character without thinking.

Finally he knew he was closing in on the impact zone by the initial sounds of the waves breaking over the southern apex of Ka'unua. For the first time, he stopped and sat upright on the board. He slowly raised his head and used his shadow across the board to point it straight south. He took note of the slight difference in the sun's position from when he had last been to this very place, a skill he had learned early on in his apprenticeship. He sat and looked out to sea with his gaze exactly on the horizon. He felt the rise and fall of the first swell of a new set and heard it break maybe fifty yards behind him. He stayed tuned to feel the interval of the waves. Now that his sensitivity to the ocean was fully developed, his first thought was of the seas between Ka'unua and the birthing place of the swells far to the southwest. His second thought was one of love for his wife and children. His third was for Taveka and the decision he'd made about the end of his life. He considered the sum total of all he'd come to understand since he'd left the lagoon, and he smiled.

The ocean was balanced and the power of the waves benign. There was a hint of imminent change, but Ka'unua was not going to be a place of death today. He lay down on the board and set a course toward the entrance to the lagoon down the western side of the reef. He never looked up. He never changed his cadence and was never surprised by either a set or its waves. When he was back where he started, he stopped just short of his voyaging craft and spent several minutes coming out of his navigator's trance. He left the surfboard floating between the hulls, lifted himself up to the deck, and kissed his wife as she put her arms around him.

"Well, I don't know if he's ever going to want to die now. Today he's going to ride waves unlike any he's ever seen."

"Is it big enough to - - - "

"No, Luan, it's not big enough to kill him, but it IS big enough to give him a day full of surfing's purest promise."

* * *

A fresh morning breeze was springing up across the harbor at Papeete as the surfers and the flyers went over the day's tasks ahead of them, the first of which was to meet with Kai Woods. The Tahitian officials had finished questioning him, and though they were still maintaining a news blackout over what happened to the Wavelife expedition, they allowed Woods to brief the Mother Ocean team before his flight back to Hawai'i later that morning. The permit fees were a big part of why they were going to allow another expedition to take place, along with the absolute assurances of a persuasive Mac Owens and a humble Heath Larson that this time there would be no close calls, nor any chance for a repeat of the Wavelife disaster. To that end, Kai Woods was eager to tell them everything he could.

"We had everything going for us except common sense," said the lifeguard, the horror of the experience still visible in his eyes, "and if we had just taken our time and not been in such a hurry, all those guys would still be alive today."

"Or if Steve Palua wouldn't have been under the gun," said Sonny-boy, "You were right, Bruddah, what we did at Huntington only made things worse."

"Now that you mention it," said Mac Owens, "Victor told me he had to pull a .45 on that guy Anasi to get him to cooperate."

"Kai, did you ever tell those guys what I told you?" asked Randy Laine.

"Several times. Palua just brushed me off. Said I was insulting their code of honor by trying to tell them to be careful. He said Anasi and the investors knew exactly what they are doing, and that if the surfers didn't care about dying, that was their business."

"Well," said Roberto Mercante, "What we went through last May is nothing compared to what's in store for them."

"Yeah, well, we almost did the same stupid shit. If Wavelife hadn't been in so much trouble, you and Cheryl wouldn't have bit so hard on Clark's idea. We wouldn't have had the money for the skis, the seaplane, and all that, and I wouldn't have almost died," said Larson.

"Naw, be honest Heath. Nobody had anything to do with what happened to you except you. That was your own fault," said Randy Laine, "and same for those guys who died."

"He right, Heath," said Bruddah, "Da Tui guys too macho, da Wavelife guys too bushido."

"Kai, what happened to Ian?" asked Aleja.

"Last I saw of him, he was going after Palua and one of the cameramen with him. The other TV guy must have bought it when their zodiac was caught inside, and Ian was going to get Palua and the guy I saved."

"Where were you?" asked Randy Laine.

"I was coming down the reef, and I could see guys in the white water, but the foam was so thick I couldn't get 'em until the set was over. They went into the impact zone, one after another, and they never came out."

"Dose guys nevah lissen nobody," said Bruddah of his fellow Hawaiians, "dey lose dey cool just like that."

"I guess Lalaoa went in to get his surfer, and then Kahaio went in to get Lalaoa, and then Aipua went to get Kahaio, or something like that. I couldn't see exactly what happened. Randy, you were 100% right about everything, but one thing I never would have dreamed of was when Palua wanted footage of the surfers riding without their vests."

"He what?" Heath Larson was incredulous.

"He told them to take their vests off so their surfsuits were easier to see for the cameras."

No one said a word for a few seconds. Kai Woods had another thought.

"Well, it might have worked, actually, if Palua hadn't been so intent on shooting footage at sunrise. But then again, the Hawaiians wanted to go surfing and it was almost impossible to deal with the Wavelife guys. Now that I think about it, we only got as far as we did because Captain Sanchez backed Clark when we first got there."

"Yeah," said Mac Owens, "that was a shocker. But I guess Victor still felt 'sponsible fer almost losin' Heath an' he knew someone had ta tell those guys what ta do. Ian got 'em so far, but then Palua blew it."

"Clark did everything he could," said Woods, "And I tried, but when those guys felt they'd been insulted by us trying to keep 'em safe, and then Palua tells 'em to take off their vests, well, the whole thing just turned into a house of cards."

"What about the guy you saved? Why didn't he kamikaze like the others?"

"I didn't ask him because I don't speak Japanese. But Taz told me the guy said he saw the face of some goddess or something inside the wave. He was pretty freaked out."

"I bet he saw Quan Yin," said Aleja.

"Who?" asked Sonny-boy.

"She's the goddess of compassion and mercy in the Orient, or something like that."

"Oh yeah," said Clem Charleton, "I bet that was it. There was a pilot in World War Two who missed hittin' one of our battleships 'cause he said he saw 'er face in the clouds. I don' know 'bout that stuff, but I guess that surfer is alive today 'cause of somethin', just like that kamikaze pilot who ditched into the sea rather than kill himself."

"I tell you one thing, though, it was so perfect out there," said Kai Woods with a distant look in his eyes, "When we got there it was just unreal, both sides of the reef. The next day, the rights were forty foot like they were coming out of a machine."

"Yeah, but da lefts dey no good," said Bruddah.

"Yeah," said Woods, surprised, "How did you know?"

"Because the same thing happened in May," said Larson.

"So, you're going to try and surf the rights again?"

"No, we're not going back to that reef. It's the wrong place."

"You're kidding me! All those guys died at the wrong reef?"

"That's right. The waves were perfect on both sides of the reef in the video that started this whole thing," said Aleja Gracellen, "I wonder if Clark ever knew he'd ended up at the wrong place."

"You mean he didn't know where the video was shot?"

"Apparently not, since it was shot by L.J. Merrill," said Mercante.

"So that's what the deal was. I saw him looking at his GPS unit and a scrap of paper just as we got there and for a second he wasn't smiling at all. But then he started laughing, and next thing I knew he was totally stoked."

"Well, this time, Kai, we're going to the right place. It's still a business deal I'm afraid, but we've learned our lessons both in and out of the water. Maybe we'll get unreal waves and maybe we won't," said Larson, looking out across the harbor and seeing a lot of white water on the barrier reefs, "But the swell's coming up fast, and our permit should be ready in a few hours."

"You think I can ride those waves?" Taveka had seen big waves in his lifetime, but he had never looked at them through the eyes of a surfer.

"If you want to. The waves are perfect. They will not surprise you. We changed the shape of the board. It will not fail you. If you want to die today, you can, but a good surfer would not be at risk out there today."

"I am a good surfer, and I will not die as a, uh, what was that word?"

"Kook!"

"I will not die a kook. I will ride these waves, and I will continue to ride them until Ka'unua decides its time for me to join my ancestors."

"Taveka, that does not sound like the tradition of the wayfinders as you taught it to me."

"It is not. I taught you the traditions as they were for all my ancestors, and the tradition of facing death with courage has not changed. Changing how or when that is done will not require any less character of me, or you, or of your successors. And remember, David, as soon as I die, I will be re-united with my wife, and what more could I ask for? But that will not happen today, because I have chosen a different path to her side. So now that I am a surfer and have a craft that will not fail in the waves, I will not die today."

"Then go surfing, father."

"I will, but you will have to stay here because there is no wind to fill your sails. I will ride these waves by myself. Can I have my board now, please?"

For an instant, David was caught offguard by his mentor's direct and decisive statement. But only for an instant. Then he realized there was only one board, and that the surf was REALLY good.

"Maybe you can loan it to me when you are done."

Taveka thought for a moment.

"I have changed my mind. Go and ride two of them. One on each side of the reef. I will watch you from here, and then I will swim down to the entrance and you can give me the board."

"Thank you Taveka, that is very generous of you."

"Generosity has nothing to do with it. I want to see where you sit and wait for the waves, and I want to see how you ride them. And if you make any mistakes, I will see exactly what not to do."

David Helmares remembered so many lessons taught to him in exactly the same way. And sometimes Taveka would purposefully make a mistake and then ask David to identify it.

"Okay, Taveka, and I will make one or two mistakes just to see if you are watching carefully!"

The navigator smiled at his apprentice.

"How dare you play tricks on an old man on him in the last days of his life?"

"Well, now that you are a surfer, there is no reason for me to make it any easier on you!"

David backed away from the voyaging craft, and paddled over to where his wife was sitting. She put her finger up to her mouth.

"I don't want to hear any of that navigator stuff, David! Just do what you are going to do. And I love you very much!"

The sun was almost straight overhead, and the surface of the sea was so glassy it was difficult to see the waves coming in. The interval between the waves was longer than it had been the day before, and that meant the surf was still going to get bigger. Taveka's prediction about the swell was accurate. The waves were easily twenty feet high and peeling off in long, perfect arcs. Once they began to break there was no way to catch them before their faces became concave. However, in the last seconds before the rolling ocean swell peaked up over the reef, there was a tiny moment of opportunity in a very small take-off zone. It was there that David Helmares was sitting, in exactly the right place, at the southern apex of Ka'unua.

In California's big waves, he had used combinations of landmarks to triangulate his position. As the surf would get bigger, he would use new markers and angles to tell him where to catch the waves and avoid getting caught inside. At Ka'unua, there were no landmarks. Yet even with nothing but ocean all around him, his skills as a navigator enabled him to know his exact position.

A set loomed on the southern horizon. David paddled slowly toward the reef. He stopped and thought about Taveka. Could he paddle as fast as David? What if he paddled for a wave and didn't catch it? Or too far in and the wave caught him?

David stopped and a sly grin spread across his face.

"He wants to be a surfer. He'll figure it out."

He paddled two more strokes, and turned around to face the first wave of six, each twenty feet high, moving silently in the last moments of their life before exploding over the coral of Ka'unua.

He decided on the fourth wave. He floated up and over the first two waves of the set. He turned his board around as he went over the third.

He started paddling slowly towards the reef. He felt the slope of the wave lift him. He paddled harder. About half way up the face of the wave he used all his strength to dig deep just as the wave was becoming steep. The momentum of the surfboard took over and it began to slide down the steep face on its own. David immediately got to his feet with a few moments to spare before he had to decide which way to go on the wave. He remembered the first time he saw videos of Peahi in Hawai'i and how perfect the rights were. Then on an historic day early one winter, Laird Hamilton had gone left, which until then no one had ever done.

Sure, why not?

He leaned back a little and turned his shoulders to the left. He dropped his rear knee to within a foot of the board, executed his turn and set a course all the way down the face to the flats. There he carved a long turn back up to the top. About ten feet from its crest he leaned forward and went back down to the base of the wave, repeating the combination ten times during a long and very fast ride. Taveka's board was all it needed to be, not only to catch the wave, but to stay with it all the way down the reef. Almost a minute after he had started his ride the wave transformed itself back into an open ocean swell at the end of the reef. David did a slow and gradual exit turn and seconds later, the wave was gone from him forever.

He paddled back out to the take-off zone ready to catch a wave to ride down the other side of the reef. The waves were perfect and there would be no surprises. He took off facing down the line of a blue wall. He was ready to take some chances. He waited until the wave was very steep. He only paddled twice. He had much more speed dropping down the face. His initial turn was fast and sharp, the subsequent off-the-lip maneuver quicker and more precise. The drop was breathtaking as he drove to the bottom again. He laid into a casual arching turn. Halfway up the face he turned back down to the very base of the wave where he carved a hard turn at maximum speed. He leaned back a touch, and then did a cross-over step up into trim position. He let the roof of the wave pitch out over his head. This was his last wave, and he wanted to show Taveka what a really deep tube ride was all about.

"If I surf the east side of the reef, I can get inside the wave. If I surf the left side of the reef, I can enjoy many turns and relax."

"For an old guy you're pretty sharp. You're practically a surfer! Now Taveka, what mistakes did I make?"

"Coming in so soon."

They both broke out in laughter.

"Correct. I should never have listened to your request to ride only two waves."

"David, you are the chief navigator of the Maruleans. You don't have to listen to me anymore."

"That's right Taveka. But more importantly, I am also the chief surfer of the Maruleans. And you just made your first surfer's mistake, thinking you could understand this place by watching me on only two waves. You should have let me ride the place for two hours! But no, I will indulge your impatience, my student. So get out there, oh wise and all-knowing sage of the South Seas, and be ready to swim a few times!"

Taveka only rode the rights. He waited for the last wave of a set and that was very smooth and easy to ride. And then, like every surfer, he was a little too ready for another. His excitement affected his judgment, and seconds after he'd caught his next wave he found himself inside the tube almost immediately. He was surprised at how fast it happened and lost his bearings. He hesitated and lost speed. He sensed his mistake immediately. He knew there was no chance to recover. He bailed out off the tail of the board and swam for the bottom to avoid the heavy turbulence just behind him. He came up easily in the still water behind the wave but then began paying a price for his impatience by swimming under the last wave of the set. And that was the easy part. The wave pushed his board all the way down the reef. It took him almost forty five minutes to retrieve it.

Another wipeout occurred just after he caught his next wave and made it to the bottom, too late to carve a turn. He realized his mistake and dove deep to emerge out the back of the wave as he'd done the wave before. When he came up, he got lucky. Somehow his board had popped up and was only twenty yards away. And since he'd hadn't made the same mistake twice of not waiting for the last wave of the set, there were no more waves coming, and he had the luxury of swimming lazily to retrieve his board.

On the next two waves he had ample opportunity to practice the graceful "hood ornament" arch, as David called it. The way the wave filled his mind while so poised was the real wonder of the stance. The moments of perfection lasted for what seemed liked minutes instead of seconds as he absorbed the full value of perfect balance in a still, poised position with the power of a big wave exploding so close behind him.

After four hours, three good waves, two wipeouts and a long swim, Taveka came back through the entrance to the lagoon. The late afternoon sun was still bright in the western sky. Taveka was glowing almost as brightly.

"Father, you don't look like a man only a few days from his departure to the next world," said Luan, "and you don't surf like one, either!"

"Luan, if I keep surfing these waves, you may never get rid of me!"

Their hug was as warm and joyous as any they had shared in all her life, and Luan could not have been happier for her father.

"Well, you are now a real surfer, Taveka. You took your lumps and paddled back out for more. And you certainly have many more waves in you, that's for sure. But there will be no surfing for you tomorrow."

"Oh? And why is that, David?"

"Because surfing has narrowed your mind to the exclusion of reality. What my mother worried about happening to me has now happened to you."

"And that is?"

"All you are thinking about is surfing. Look to the east, Taveka."

The wise old man turned away from the sun. Far out to sea a line of black clouds had appeared.

"And now look at the waves, Taveka."

A ruffling chop was beginning to cross the faces of the waves. They were a little bigger, but their crests were crumbling instead of breaking cleanly. While Taveka had been paddling from the entrance to the lagoon to the voyaging craft, the conditions had changed completely.

Taveka turned and looked at his surfing mentor with a frown on his face.

"But I was having so much fun!" he complained, with a touch of humor to his tone.

"Ah yes, the curse of perfection! Tomorrow the waves will be ruined, and you will have to find something else to do with your life!" said a veteran surfer who had been riding waves since he was fifteen years old and knew what he was talking about.

The tanks of the *Aeolus* were almost full. The jet skis were ready and tested. Everyone had completed their tasks prepping the boards, the locator vests, and the safety gear. The paperwork for the *Aeolus* was completed in record time thanks to Owens' long-standing friendships with Tahitian air authorities. Only the permit stood between the surfers and the last, best big wave arena on earth – until Clem Charleton delivered the weather report. He passed around the weather fax fresh from the cockpit of the *Aeolus* showing the edge of a storm moving westwards about five hundred miles east of Tahiti.

"If it blows through fast, we might get lucky," said Mercante.

"Or we might get out there and find it too junky to ride," said Larson, with a pessimistic edge to his voice.

"Well, ya know that permit might take all day. Figger two hours per signature, an' we need three of 'em, so mebbe by the time we're ready, she'll blow on thru," said Mac Owens.

"Yup," said Clem Charleton, "I wouldn't bet on goin' surfin' tamorrah."

Heath Larson bit his lip for the tenth time in the last hour. He glanced out the porthole at the barrier reefs outside the harbor. The surf was easily twice as big as the day before, and getting bigger.

* * *

In the last light of the day, David, Luan and Taveka had removed all the lines holding their masts upright and collapsed them flush with the decks. They lashed the two voyaging craft together in the shallows of the eastern side of the lagoon. They set out extra lines in an array of purchase points on the reef. Ka'unua would protect them from the waves, but not the winds. They made sure there was no chance they would be swept over the extremely shallow coral that formed the protective ring around the lagoon. They knew if that happened, they would then be pushed sideways into the impact zone of a rising swell where their chances of survival would be slim. Just after dark, strong gusts of horizontal rain heralded the coming storm. They retreated to their shelters, safe within a lagoon surrounded by an ocean about to go mad.

There was no dawn the next day. The storm's intensity had only increased throughout the night. David and Taveka huddled under a tarp watching the huge surf through the rain and spray.

"What do you think? Almost twice as big as yesterday? Or is it just the storm adding its own energy?" thought David aloud.

"The swell is bigger, but not doubled – not yet. David, you were right yesterday. Surfing does things to your mind, doesn't it? I should have sensed this change coming yesterday an hour before you did."

"Yes, Taveka, surfing blinds you to the obvious all too often."

* * *

'See what I mean, Heath? If we hadda gone out there right away, we'd a been right in the middle of this," said Mac Owens, looking out a porthole of the *Aeolus*, snug in Papeete harbor tied up to a permanent buoy to weather the storm, "An' 'stead of us all bein' scared shitless, we spent the whole day sittin' nice an' dry in an office watchin' good people type up papers while apologizin' fer the delay."

Heath Larson had nothing to say in reply. He had been so focused on surfing he hadn't paid attention to the possibility of a sudden change in the weather. He had tunnel vision in a very real way, wanting life entirely on his own terms deep inside the tube of a huge wave. That willful ignorance had almost killed him once thanks to the comparatively small waves of a passing squall. Now a real storm was coming from the exact same direction, almost as if to remind him the ocean will always accommodate anyone who has to learn their lessons the hard way. He became well aware of how his antsy impatience about the permit meant he still hadn't learned his lesson completely. Thanks to Randy Laine and Bob Rowe, he had survived his own arrogance, and yet he still had to wonder if he was going to need them again.

"So what it gonna do tamorrah?" asked Bruddah.

"Well the bad news is it will still be raining and windy," said Clem Charleton, "The good news is, that's what it's gonna be like here in Papeete. Out where we're goin', it should be sunny, clear, and - - - "

Aleja Gracellen was the first to clearly realize what he was saying.

"And offshore winds!"

* * *

"This cross chop is starting to get pretty wicked, Tak," said Jack Richards, helming the *Tom Swift* on his watch with Tak Kurosawa strapped into the cockpit seat.

"Yeah, must be a big storm blowing east to west up ahead," he said.

"Well, if we just had a weather fax or satellite hookup, we'd know what was up ahead, wouldn't we?" asked Jack Richards with just a hint of exasperation.

"Jack, my man, we don't want to know, remember? This is how they did it for hundreds of years, and with just one little radio in your hand, you can throw all those years away. This boat can handle anything, and as long as we stay in front of what's behind us, we don't need to know what's up ahead."

"Well, you guys knew where to go when Frank got that Navy data!"

"Jack, we like to think we aren't stupid!"

Below decks, Chip Bell was playing ping pong with Margo Atkins on the *Serena*, bouncing limericks and tongue twisters back and forth in Morse code. She was making a concerted effort to improve her touch, and she needed to practice with someone. Ken Bucher was on deck of the *Serena* with Nelson Roberts and Patty McRane, taking his turn at the helm. The waves were pushing eighty feet, and after almost two weeks at sea, they didn't seem all that unusual to the young surfer or his shipmates.

451

The skipper of the *Serena* was sitting in the extra seat in the cockpit. Charles Atkins was going over his calculations and the last update from Ray Seranen. The K3 storm was roaring still. Wave trains chasing the two Alba_Swords had increased substantially in keeping with Seranen's model. Sets to one hundred and sixty feet were emerging from the zone of generation in a narrow bandwidth almost exactly as predicted. The data acquisition plan for the biggest waves in recorded history was working and their ETA at the safe harbor of Merrill's reef was now less than thirty hours away.

* * *

The storm began breaking up just before dark. David Helmares stood on the deck of his voyaging craft watching the surf until he could no longer see the waves. The deep swells from the south were now pushing forty feet with some bigger sets – and the storm surf was subsiding. He knew tomorrow would be clear, the winds would die down, and then breeze up from the perfect direction: straight into the faces of the breaking waves exactly as they did the day he had first come to Ka'unua. Tomorrow the surf would be perfect. It would be the day for Taveka to reach his limits, and then go past them.

* * *

The harbor lights of Papeete were bright in the night. The wind had grown stronger, though the rain had abated. Aleja Gracellen looked at her portable alarm clock. It said 4:44 a.m. and was playing the strong, classical music she had programmed into its MP3 player. She got out of bed, dressed quickly, and knocked on the door of Randy Laine and Bob Rowe. They were ready and waiting, and soon the three of them were downstairs walking purposefully through the hotel lobby. They had parked the rent-a-car right outside, and fifteen minutes later, they were in the *Aeolus'* zodiac motoring across the harbor to the waiting seaplane, her interior lights glowing brightly.

A half hour later, the engines of the PBY roared to life. The sky was still dark, but on the horizon ahead, just above the water's surface, a touch of gray softened the black. Clem Charleton taxied the *Aeolus* out of the harbor, the propellers biting deeply into the wind coming straight out of the east. The headwind was a blessing and a curse. It gave the wings more lift, but threw more chop against the hull. The extra drag of the waverunners was also significant. It took almost five minutes to get up to speed, and another two minutes before Clem Charleton was finally able to lift the heavily laden seaplane free of the ocean. The sky was clearing ahead for a small group of surfers on the dawn patrol of their lives.

* * *

452

"Luan! David! Wake up!"

The chief navigator and his wife came out of the shelter dome to a sky full of stars. The winds had died in the night. The razor sharp eastern horizon was glowing with a dark orange hue. The moon hung just above where the sun would soon appear. David looked up, and saw the waves. Then he tilted his head back to see the tops of them.

"Taveka, do you know how big it is out there?" said David with a worried tone. He looked down at a man smiling like a little boy. Taveka had surfed twenty foot waves two days ago, but his joy was that of a child knowing something wonderful was going to happen.

"Of course I do, David. What more could I ask for? I'll see my wife today. My ancestors are already preparing my welcome. Look!"

David and Luan looked over at the center of the lagoon and saw a circular pattern of tiny waves forming again and again in expanding concentric rings.

"I have a task to perform while the sun rises. When I come back, we will talk. Then it will be time."

David knew tradition prescribed that the navigator should begin the last day of his life by sailing once around Ka'unua. He realized Taveka planned to keep the tradition by paddling around the reef. He took a long look at the wavescape around them and knew there probably wasn't another surf spot on earth where the waves had exactly the same shape at five feet as they did at twenty-five feet. And now he was looking at waves almost three times that size and the shape was STILL perfect. It was daunting to comprehend the sheer scale of Ka'unua, but he understood what he was seeing. The fields of white water surrounding both sides of Ka'unua were almost a hundred yards wide. He looked down at his old mentor below him kneeling on his surfboard. But now their relationship had changed, and so he didn't think twice about schooling his surfing apprentice.

"Taveka, I understand your excitement. The ancestors are indeed excited at your coming. We don't want to disappoint them, or your wife. You will not paddle your surfboard around the reef."

Taveka's face lost its smile. Luan had never heard her husband speak to her father with such authority.

"Completing a circle of Ka'unua will leave you exhausted by the time you get back. You will save your strength for your last wave. You will make one passage around Ka'unua, as tradition prescribes. Taveka, come aboard. Sit on the bow with your daughter and enjoy the rise of the sun. You will see the greatest beauty any surfer has ever witnessed on this planet. I'll navigate for you for one day, your last day, so that you may have your final wish."

The smile returned to Taveka's face.

"Yes, David, you are right. I am just too happy to think straight this morning. I was here over sixty years ago with my father, and the memories are strong. I am changing the tradition he taught me, because I am a surfer, and he was not. I am a surfer, you are my mentor, and I will listen to you."

Sunlight was streaming through the portholes of the *Aeolus* and shining on the faces of passengers and crew. The last clouds of the storm were behind them. Ahead the world was open and clear in all directions. But the roar of engines pulling the PBY to her destination was the only sound heard aboard her. The passengers had all made this flight before, yet their silence was not one of boredom or complacency. They were three hundred miles from their destination. Their thoughts were all over the map.

From his co-pilot's seat, Roberto Mercante had a spectacular view, but the former chairman of Wavelife International was seeing very little. With the *Aeolus* on auto-pilot, he was now little more than a passenger falling through a trap door of memories and self-doubt. This was his fourth trip to the place that once was going to save his company. It had killed the man who had made a deal with Wavelife International. He remembered the first meeting, Clark's arrogance and his own. He remembered the first flight to the reef and his call to his wife telling her it was everything they needed and more. He grimaced at the thought of those words. He wanted to stop remembering right then and there. But his conscience would not let him off the hook so easily. What about the trade shows? What about the second trip to the reef, a photo op arranged for the sole purpose of locking down a billion dollars in financing? And then the trip in May when Larson had almost died, and for what?

He looked down at the ocean and knew the surf was going to be as big as anything ever witnessed in the history of surfing. He should have been stoked and ready to go. He knew MOF was a fresh start giving him a second chance, but self-doubt had him trapped inside a very small, very tight, and yet very powerful sphere of anxiety.

"Pilot to co-pilot," he heard over his headset. The words did not register with him for a second.

"Hey, co-pilot, keep an eye on her, Ok? I gotta go take a leak," said Clem Charleton from his pilot's seat. He didn't, but he'd recognized the change that had come over Mercante. Mercante was wearing an old Geosurf t-shirt, and Charleton figured things out right away.

"Uh, yeah, sure, Clem, no problem," said Mercante distractedly.

"Bullshit, Mercante. Now lissen, an' lissen good. Mac Owens has been ridin' herd on Heath Larson, an' looks like I'm gonna do the same fer you. Ya don't have time ta git sentimental flyin' a PBY. Yer friend Ian Clark ain't coming back, y' understand?"

"No, no, I'm ok, Clem."

"No sirree bob, yer NOT ok, but ya will be in jes' a few seconds. I'm putting you in command of the *Aeolus*. She's fulla folks trustin' their lives to you, an' that 'ncludes me. She stays on auto-pilot, but if sumtin' happens, the first decisions are gonna be yours. So throw all them memories right out the window, y'hear?"

"Yessir, captain."

"This plane was built fer military purposes, not sentimental sightseeing. She's on a mission right now, as are you. You got that, Mr. Mercante?"

"You can depend on me."

"Good, because if I thought you were lyin' to me right now, you'd be going out that window with alla the crap that was on yer mind a minute ago!"

"Without a parachute?" said Mercante with a sheepish grin.

"Wipe that smile off yer face, co-pilot. What's yer heading? What's yer altitude? Airspeed? Engine temperature? Oil pressure? Manifold pressure? Fuel consumption?"

"Uh, er - - -"

"Or should I ask ya when was the last time ya saw Ian Clark? Now do you understand? Have all that info to me in a minute, from memory, Mr. Mercante."

The captain of the *Aeolus* took off his headset and swung down out of his seat and through the hatch in the bulkhead leading to the galley.

"Oh no, not this again!" he said just loud enough to get the attention of Heath Larson, Sonny-boy Noaloa, Bruddah and Aleja Gracellen. The four surfers looked at Clem Charleton with the same empty stare he had just seen on his co-pilot's face.

"Y'all got a lotta memories, doncha? Well, lemme tell ya sumtin'. This plane weren't built for memory lane excursions. She wuz built to fight an' win a war. Tha people who flew 'er back then had a lot more ta think 'bout than jes a surf trip, or makin' clothing, or runnin' a shelter. They were fightin' fer their lives defendin' our country. That's why this plane was built inna first place. Now she's here to help y'all fight fer what you believe in. An' that's mighty hard to do if y'all start second-guessing yerself. Jes like Roberto up there ruminatin' 'bout ol' Ian Clark. The man was what he was, an' I'm sorry he's gone, but he ain't comin' back. I've lost a cupla' buddies over the years. I know how Roberto feels. This ain't the time fer it. I told 'im ta snap out of it, an' he's gonna do what he's told on this aircraft. Get my drift?"

The four surfers were now looking up at him. Charleton knew he'd made his point, so he chose his next few words carefully.

"Heath, make us all some breakfast, woudja please? This man's army moves on its stomach. Bruddah, you and Sonny-boy find Mac and tell 'im to keep you busy fer the next coupla hours."

"And what should I do?" asked Aleja Gracellen.

"Go up front an' sit in the pilot's seat 'till I get back. I hear tell you do a good job runnin' the shelter, so yur already a capt'n in sum ways. I wancha to ask Roberto each an' every question ya kin think of 'bout the *Aeolus*, hear?"

Clem Charleton never took his eyes off them.

"Bruddah, Wilson! What are you waitin for? Now git!"

Everybody jumped to it as Charleton went to the intercom.

"Co-pilot! Gimme them numbers! What's yer engine rpm? Does that jive with yer manifold pressure? What if it doesn't? What's the problem? Ok, ya got a VIP up front with ya, now. I'm leavin' the intercom on, so gimme them numbers, now! And then explain 'em all to yer new student."

Charleton went aft and found Bruddah and Sonny-boy with Mac Owens.

"Keep 'em busy Mac! Can't have any dead weight on this trip!"

Mac Owens knew exactly what his old friend was doing.

"I was jes' 'bout ready to cum git 'em, Clem! Lookit this mess," he said with a sweeping gesture at what actually looked to be a very orderly cargo bay full of tow-in surfing equipment, "Never seen such disorganization. Looks like a buncha surfers were in charge of all this! We gots sum cleanin' up ta do!"

Charleton squeezed through the cargo bay and entered the 'sunroom'. Randy Laine and Bob Rowe were in a lively and animated conversation going through their equipment with a studied but professional nonchalance.

"Whew, finally! Now you boys look like y'all know what's what 'round here. Hell, them folks up front made this flight feel like we're goin' to a funeral or sumtin'."

"Well, the surf is gonna be really big, and Clark's dead," said Randy Laine, "I guess you can't blame them for being a little preoccupied."

"I shore as hell can! It's only surfing! What's the big deal?"

* * *

"Course, helmsman?"

"Northwest, sir, forty-five degrees dead on," said Ken Bucher.

"What's our speed?"

"Thirty-nine knots."

"Good. We'll be pulling in behind the reefs around three this afternoon. Message from Ray says the storm imploded ten hours ago, a little sooner than the Goldman model predicted. Max wave size was about one ninety."

"So no two hundred foot waves?"

"No, not unless they start refracting on us."

"Then what'll we do?"

"Hope the Navy data is correct."

* * *

The wind was stronger now that the sun was beginning to warm the air. David Helmares tacked back and forth in the lagoon to gain speed. He timed his exit perfectly. The voyaging craft shot out through the lagoon entrance on an angle, immediately gaining enough seaway to come about and sail towards the southern end of the reef.

Now that he had a clear view of them, he knew the waves were easily as big as anything he'd ever seen on videos from Cortez Banks, Mavericks or the outside reefs of Hawai'i. He also knew he had no way of telling how big they REALLY were. Seventy feet? Eighty feet? One set came through that step-laddered from forty to fifty to sixty feet in the first three waves. Then eight more waves came through at around sixty feet before a lull that lasted about ten minutes. The next set had fifteen waves in it, and each was way bigger than sixty feet. But no matter how big they were, each wave rolled around both sides of Ka'unua with perfect shape.

"So where am I going to take off, David?"

"That's what we are going to find out, Taveka."

Taveka noticed the tone in David's voice was very sober.

"Well, just make sure you get me killed without me becoming a kook."

David couldn't help but laugh at Taveka's attempt to lighten things up a little. "No way can we let that happen! What would your ancestors think? So first we'll go see what the takeoff zone looks like. You'll have to catch your wave out there, and in exactly the right spot while it still has slope to it, but before it breaks. Once the lip starts coming over and the tube is formed, it will be impossible to get in without getting pitched."

"Getting pitched?"

"Yeah, when the wave catches you and throws you out into mid-air. That happens to kooks when they can't paddle fast enough. Problem is, the swell is still moving with a lot of speed and momentum. Plus there's the wind coming up the face."

"What if I can't paddle fast enough? Then what?"

"Then you'll die a kook unless I can think of something. But as I recall, someone once told me a navigator is never trapped. So don't bother me right now! The talking is getting to me!"

The two men exchanged broad smiles.

"Yes, father, don't bother the chief navigator. Just be a surfer, do what you are told, and watch the waves!"

Taveka looked at his daughter and loved her all the more for her words, reminding him that he was a mariner who was simply going on a new voyage. He was with his loved ones, and they were not grief-stricken as people often are when thinking only of themselves. David and Luan were not worried about their tomorrow on this day. They were fully in the moment with Taveka, and he was ready to die a happy man.

Luan went forward to adjust and trim the foresail. Taveka thought of the few times he and Luan's mother had sailed together. He would soon be sailing with her again, thanks to a man for whom he had nothing but respect. He looked back at David Helmares standing at the tiller. There never had been a man like him in the history of the sea people. His faith in the surfer from California was complete, even when it came to the time and manner of his own death.

For two hours they sailed in wide circles around Ka'unua while David kept a constant eye on the sets breaking down both sides of the reef. He remembered seeing a picture of what was once the biggest wave ever ridden on the North Shore of Oahu. It was a beautiful day, the surfer was wearing a yellow wetsuit on an orange surfboard, and there was an almost surreal quality to the photo. Now David was seeing wave after wave of the same size breaking on both sides of Ka'unua in mirror-image perfection. It was a surfer's ultimate dream, though for him it was a big problem with no apparent solution. Taveka wanted to die with dignity, under control, and fully aware of his body and senses right through to the last second of his life. And there was no doubt the waves had more than enough power to accommodate him.

The sun was almost to its noon zenith. They were well to the south of Ka'unua. The wind was holding steady, and David was certain it would last the rest of the day. Several sets had come in over the past hour, six to eight at a time, with lulls lasting up to ten minutes between them. But then came a longer lull, and after an almost fifteen minute wait, a set came through with twenty waves in it. The only constant was the size, shape and interval between the waves themselves, and David concluded he'd learned all he could about the waves and their powerful encounter with the sacred reef of the Maruleans. He put the voyaging craft into the wind, lowered the sails, and ate some food and drank milk from several coconuts they had with them. It was in that moment of stillness a solution came to the chief navigator.

"I've got it! Luan, please raise the sail. Taveka, sit all the way back on the end of the center hull so you will have a clear view behind us."

The voyaging craft gathered speed quickly. David went far out to sea to meet a set almost half a mile from Ka'unua.

"Here we go!"

Helmares pulled the tiller towards him and Luan dropped the sails. The voyaging craft came around perfectly and began to slide at an angle down the wave. David pushed the tiller away from him, turned back towards the reef, waited a few seconds, then pulled the tiller to re-set his course down the east side of the reef, where the sun was illuminating rainbows in the spray of the waves. The craft began to race across the wall stretching ahead of them. David knew exactly where he was, and as the peak began to stand up close behind the voyaging craft, David kept his hand steady on the tiller.

Taveka gazed in awe as the very highest peak of the wave, some eighty feet high, leaped out into mid air, forming a tunnel unlike anything he had ever seen. He began to smile, and then laugh, transfixed to his very soul.. He pointed at the liquid world turning over and over, always changing and always the same, a vision inside a perfect wave of fantastic proportions seemingly close enough to touch. He was beyond ecstasy, beyond all physical sensation, his mind, body and soul captivated by the sight of so much energy so very close. The wave broke perfectly for almost a mile until the final section of the wave collapsed with a resounding slap as the liquid roof caved in, expelling all the air from its powerful core and drenching Taveka with spray.

David guided the craft up and over the now quietly rolling hill. He was about to ask Luan to raise sail when he saw she was already at the task. David pulled the tiller towards him, and the voyaging craft exited the wave.

Taveka was simply and wonderfully awestruck.

"Can I go inside that wave? David, am I going to catch a wave like that?"

David looked at Luan as if they were dealing with a child whose innocence was heart-stopping.

"Yes, Taveka, that's where you are going because now I know how you are going to catch your wave."

"Oh, good! Let's get my surfboard and you can tell me what I have to do."

* * *

"There it is," said Roberto Mercante. From his vantage point in the cockpit of the *Aeolus*, he was the first to see white water on the horizon. A minute later, he saw a second, and then a third area of white against the ocean's deep blue.

"You sure, Roberto?"

"Affirmative, captain."

"Good! Go forward, keep yer eyes on yer targets an' be a spotter fer us. Mac! Come on up an' gimme a hand, ok?" said Clem Charleton.

"Read your mind, Clem!" Owens was standing right between the two seats in the cockpit.

Roberto Mercante took off his headset and turned with a smile to Mac Owens. It was a moment of true emotion for both of them, but they didn't say a word. Owens settled into the co-pilot's seat and put his headset on. A quick glance across the console told him the *Aeolus* was doing just fine. Roberto Mercante went to the compartment forward of the cockpit. Charleton had installed a Plexiglas dome that blended into the hull of the Catalina. From this forward vantage point, he could see perfectly in all directions. He hit the intercom button.

"We're here," he said. Heath and Bruddah went to the windows in the galley area. Aleja and Sonny-boy were in the 'sunroom' with Randy Laine and Bob Rowe. The intercoms were open throughout the plane and they could all hear and speak to each other.

"Confirm three reefs, Clem?"

"Got 'em, Roberto."

"Come around to starboard and spiral down lazy to a thousand feet around that first one."

The *Aeolus* circled in. Everyone in the aft section now had a clear view of seascape below.

"There it is."

"But, but, its gone! Where's the reef?"

"Hey, it much mo biggah!"

"Oh good Lord, look at that wave!"

"There's no lagoon! It's completely gone!"

"Da surf so big da place no can handle it!"

"That can't be the reef we surfed!"

"It is," said Heath Larson grimly as saw where he almost died.

"But, it was so perfect!"

"Yeah, was. That swell was nowhere near this big," said Randy Laine.

"Unbelievable!"

"Believe it. The place we surfed doesn't exist, at least not today."

Mac Owens was staring down out of the co-pilot's window. Though he was not a sentimental guy, he couldn't take his eyes off the place that was so attractive at first, had become even more wonderful and enticing, only to turn out to be very dangerous, and in the end a place of tragic death.

"Clem, hold your altitude for another go-round."

"Roger, that, Roberto. Say, y'all goin' surfin' down there?"

Nobody on the *Aeolus* quite knew what to say. Finally, Heath Larson spoke for all of them.

"Not today. And never again."

The reef once sold to surfing's biggest corporation as the last and best big wave arena on earth was now completely obliterated by rolling avalanches of white water. A quarter mile beyond what once was the take-off zone, waves were collapsing in huge sections like buildings in an earthquake. The reef where eleven men died a week ago was now buried like roadkill beneath an eighteen-wheeler. It was being erased clean, over and over again, by waves three times as big as the one that almost killed Heath Larson. Only an intermittent circle of turbulence in the center of the huge zone of white water revealed the location of the reef, a place of many memories for the surfers on the *Aeolus*, now a place that no longer existed.

"Clem, take her back up to two thousand and head due east. We'll be where we're supposed to be in about two minutes."

"Roger that, Roberto."

* * *

The last wave of a set came down the sunny side of Ka'unua, huge and perfect all the way to the end of the reef where the tube finally imploded like an exclamation mark at the end of a sentence. There was a pause, and then the energy reformed back into a rolling liquid hill moving silently through the sea on its transoceanic voyage. David used the swell's motion to gain some speed before coming around and heading towards the mouth of the lagoon. It was going to be an easy entrance into the lagoon with the wind at his back. He glanced up at the pennant on top of his mast, fluttering in the breeze and telling him the wind was holding from the same direction. Beyond his telltale he saw motionless wings high in the sky.

"Taveka! Look, here comes an - - - "

He did not finish the sentence. The wandering albatross would not look that big at that altitude.

"David, what is it?"

Luan knew something serious had stopped David's mind in mid-thought. She saw him looking high in the sky to the west. She turned and looked in the same direction. Taveka saw them and was confused for a moment. He thought they were going through the entrance to the lagoon to get his surfboard. Then his mind found itself, its old self. He raised his head and saw, and then heard, a memory flying right towards them.

* * *

460

"That's it! THAT'S the place!" Roberto Mercante could clearly see the elliptical reef dead ahead. The waves were like spokes on a wheel, radiating around a beautiful lagoon with clean precision. He had seen this vision once before in a conference room on a gloomy day so many months ago. Except these waves were twice as big, if not bigger.

"Clem, let's do a slow circle to starboard. Keep her at two thousand."

"Holding pattern at two thousand, roger that, Roberto."

David finally blinked and saw they were sailing towards the coral.

"Luan! Drop the sail!"

His wife quickly responded to the command and the voyaging craft glided slowly to a stop in front of the lagoon entrance.

"She's a PBY, all right," said Taveka.

"We gotta wait for a set. It's a lull down there right now. Clem, can we maintain holding pattern?"

"Sure, we kin, since yer payin' fer the fuel. Continue holding pattern."

"What are they doing?" asked Luan.

"They're in a holding pattern waiting for a set. They already checked the sharks' reef. It must be closing out. Now they are taking a look at Ka'unua."

"Let's go get my surfboard. There's plenty of waves for everyone, and I only need one."

"Pretty long lull," said Sonny-boy Noaloa.

"Then it will be a pretty long set. Be patient," said Randy Laine.

"You too, Heath," said Aleja when she saw Larson biting his lower lip.

"Maybe they'll go away," said Luan.

"Not when they see a set. They know what they are looking for."

"I'll talk to them. I can take care of this, David. Ka'unua is the home of my ancestors. They'll understand, won't they?"

"Here comes a set! Look at those waves!" said Bob Rowe in disbelief.

"One – two – three – four – five – six – seven! " counted Randy Laine.

"Look how she jackin' like one kine pyramid!" exclaimed Bruddah

"Oh, yeah! Look at the left, Sonny-boy!" screamed Aleja.

"There's your open eye! That's the one you saw!!" yelled Sonny-boy.

"But this is twice as big!!" shouted Roberto.

"And still perfect," said Heath Larson in a very soft voice.

461

David saw the first swell of a set peak up, pitch out, and split into two perfect waves. His wife sensed his tension like heat from a building fire.

"David, maybe they're just taking a look."

"Of course they are. And they just found what they wanted."

"Maybe they forgot their surfboards!" There was no response from David Helmares. Taveka dropped all pretense of humor. "Now, David, isn't this exactly what we talked about? What you felt that last time you were here? Are you feeling it again?"

"Those are the best big waves on the planet. It must be sixty, eighty feet down there, and it's perfect," said Heath Larson with a voice of authority no other surfer in the world could match.

"Dis place mo bettah dan anythin' in da Islands! Da rights AN' da lefts dey perfect! Dis da place, brah!" said Bruddah.

"Yeah, Heath, looks like you're finally going to get what you wanted," said Randy Laine, "And we're not gonna make any mistakes this time."

"Hey! What's that inside the lagoon?" exclaimed Roberto, "There's something floating in the lagoon! Some kinda Polynesian trimaran!"

"Fergit about that one inside the lagoon," said Clem Charleton as he circled the PBY into a final approach, "What are y'all gonna do 'bout the one down there in front of the entrance? It's floating right where we gotta go!"

"I bet they've seen us by now," said Luan, standing on the prow of the center hull and shading her eyes from the noonday sun.

"I'm sure they have. And no, Taveka, they didn't forget their surfboards. Those are jetskis hanging under the wings."

"Well, David, that's better than the bombs those seaplanes sometimes carried during the war."

"You think so? I don't. Ka'unua is our sacred reef, but that will mean nothing to them."

The *Aeolus* came around and did a wide figure eight to set up an approach to Ka'unua from the north. The timing was critical. They needed a lull to set down on the flat water and taxi into the protective wave shadow of the reef in line with the entrance to the lagoon.

"Here they come. What are you going to do, David?"

"I don't know. I just don't know. I know what I want to do, but I hope I don't do it."

"I guess we both test ourselves today, David."

"Clem, drop 'er down quick. I'll shut down the engines. We're gonna stay out here fer a while."

"Gonna be pretty rough when them waves start up agin."

"That's ok. We're gonna stay out here till our passengers figger out what they wanna do.

"Hey, passengers! Strap in for a landing! Roberto! Get the hell outta there! You'll see all ya want soon enough!"

Everyone quickly strapped themselves in place.

"What are we gonna do? What if it's their reef? What if we can't surf here?" asked Sonny-boy Noaloa.

"Take it easy, brah! Dey probly my cousins mebbe. I go talk story wit 'em. Mebbe no problem."

"Well, at least they didn't come right up on top of us."

"They know they've got problems. They know."

"Why? How do they know that? We haven't said anything to them."

"Because, Taveka, they come from a world where nobody trusts anyone else. And for good reason. That's why I came to live with you."

"Ah, and now you have brought that to Ka'unua."

"Brought what?"

"Suspicion."

"What am I going to say to them, Heath? Why don't you go?"

"Aleja, this could be a really delicate situation. You've got the best reasons for being out here. And well, you're, uh, you're uh - - -"

"What, I'm a woman?"

"No, I was going to say you're not a professional surfer. After what happened at the other reef, that might make a big difference."

"Yeah, they must know about what happened to Clark and those guys."

"You guys can't be serious! Heath, you're the guy who made this whole thing work in the first place."

"Well if that was the reason, then Roberto should go."

"No way. If they heard the whole story, and that I'm here asking for a second chance? No way."

"Hey! Y'all back there better hold on ta sumtin. Here come's a set!"

They were in very deep water, and the wave was not going to break. But as the swell approached the *Aeolus*, Charleton gunned the engines so that she would not slide backwards down the rolling hill. The fuselage tilted skyward, and everybody inside was thrown to the rear of the galley compartment. She tipped up and over the top and then floated down the back of the swell.

"Yeee hahh! Ride 'em cowboy!" The rebel yells from the cockpit did nothing for the passengers' peace of mind. "Here we go agin!"

Thirty seconds later, the next wave came. And for the next six minutes, the set rolled under the *Aeolus*. Clem Charleton and Mac Owens were having a good 'ol time using the engines to survive the oceanic roller coaster. Finally the set subsided and Owens went back to the galley.

"Hey, y'all better figger out whatcha wanna do. Me an' Clem kin do this all day, an'd its kinda fun. But that ain't gonna get the cows milked, ya unnerstand?"

"Aleja, please, you go."

"Typical men. When it comes to a real man's job, the only man for the job is a woman, is that it?"

"Tell ya what, Barbie. I go wit you. You do da talkin'."

"Ok, Bruddah, let's go."

"Well, they seem to know what they are doing. And if they were going to confront us, they would have come in here instead of riding out those swells."

"Yes, Luan. Thank you. I will wait to see what they are going to do next."

Taveka immediately noticed the tone in David's voice and challenged the emotion behind it with a pointed question.

"And what if they need the shelter of Ka'unua to protect themselves?"

David didn't quite understand why Taveka would ask such a question. But whatever the reason, he already had his mind made up.

"They didn't have to come here. Let them live with their decision."

"Did you like being tough with other surfers in California, David?"

"No, Taveka, I didn't. And I won't now even if I have to."

"What does that mean?" asked Luan, surprised at her husband's attitude.

"Ask your father. He learned about being tough a long time ago. Ask him about the war, Luan."

"Is this a war, David?"

"I don't know yet, Taveka."

'Why don't we take a jetski?"

Mac Owens and Bruddah were starting to clear a space in the cargo bay to inflate the zodiac.

"Because they don't have any fuel in them."

"Well, you've got fuel right there!"

"Dat fo' de outboard, Barbie, no can do."

Aleja Gracellen was in no mood to take no for an answer.

"So I have to wait for you to inflate the zodiac, mount the motor, and all that? Listen, I know how to drive a jetski and I want to get this over with. Heath! Can you run a jetski on the outboard gas?"

"Uh, yeah, you can, but - - -"

"Thanks! Mac! Bruddah! You heard him! Mac, open the cargo bay and get the hydraulic thingy ready. Bruddah, where's the gas?"

"But, Aleja, - - -"

464

"Do I have to start using foul language? Let's go!"

Mac Owens opened the cargo bay door just as Aleja Gracellen ducked under it. She gingerly stepped out on to the edge and then took a step up onto the wing support, and then over to the waverunner mounted next to the wheel wells of the PBY. She sat down and took a look at the controls.

"God bless it! Where's the keys?"

'Right here, Aleja!" said Owens.

Gracellen turned around and grabbed the keys from Owens' outstretched hands. All she needed now was the can of gas.

"How much time before the next set?"

"Who knows? Mebbe five minutes?"

"Ok, this thing better work. Bruddah, gimme the tank."

Bruddah handed her the five gallon can of gas. Gracellen stretched back down to the waverunner and poured the five gallons into the tank.

Heath Larson's head now poked through the cargo bay door.

"Aleja! Crank it once. Then crank it twice. Then stop."

"Ok, once, twice. Now what?"

"Mac! Lower away!"

Aleja Gracellen found herself slowly lowered into the water. She released the clamps, and the waverunner started floating away from the *Aeolus*.

"Ok, crank her up!"

Gracellen hit the starter, and the waverunner's engine caught and turned over right away. Then she gave it some throttle and it backfired.

"No! Go slow! I set the injectors for aviation fuel, so don't open it up too much. It will get you there, but go slow!"

"Hey, here comes a set!"

Bruddah saw the first wave was standing up at the far end of Ka'unua.

"Bruddah, c'mon, lets go!"

"No Barbie! She no run dat good! I mebbe too big! You go!"

"Bruddah, I will never forget that you stood me up on our first date! Bye!"

"David, I think they are trying to respect us."

"That's nice, Taveka. Maybe they will go away."

"David, maybe you guys should talk some navigator stuff about this."

"No Luan, there's nothing to say."

Taveka knew he was right, but Luan gave it one more try.

"David, let my father help you."

"No Luan, he's helped me enough. I'm his successor. This is my responsibility. I'll know what to do when the time comes."

"Here it comes, David," said Taveka. He pointed to the seaplane. Above the sound of the distant engines they could now hear a different, higher pitched sound. One of the jetskis was detached from the plane. A plume of black smoke trailed behind it as it turned and started to come directly towards them.

From the other direction, the first wave of the set rolled past the entrance to the lagoon, followed by a dozen more.

465

Aleja Gracellen could see nothing but a rolling hill of water sixty feet high all across the north end of the reef after the first wave of the set had broken down both sides and had re-formed into a swell. She opened the throttle as far as she dared and went up the slope ahead of her to the swell's crest.

"Oh my God!"

She had a clear view of Ka'unua. It was like being at one end of a giant Coliseum. Massive waves, bigger than anything she had ever seen, were coming down both sides of the reef. And there were more behind them. Down the back of the wave she went. Behind her she heard the engines of the *Aeolus* roar for an instant before the sound was muffled by the massive swell between them. The next wave was a little bigger, and Aleja Gracellen started laughing.

"Sure, why not? I can do this! Stupid engines! Stupid gasoline!"

The engine coughed a backfire.

"Oh, I'm sorry, I'm sorry waverunner! You're a good jetski and you've got a good motor. We'll make it!"

She patted the waverunner and faced the next swell as the *Aeolus* came down the back of the previous wave. For a second she thought the roar of the seaplane's twin Pratt&Whitney engines was like parents cheering for their child, the little engine that could.

For the next ten waves, the *Aeolus* and the waverunner rode out the set with Clem Charleton and Mac Owens having fun and Aleja Gracellen suppressing panic by turning into a little girl having fun. Finally the set ended, the ocean went flat, and the woman who danced with the sea approached a beautiful lagoon and the Polynesian voyaging craft guarding its entrance.

"Well, they made it. And here comes someone to say hello."

"Fucking smog! Goddamn it! Look at that black smoke!"

"David, don't look with your eyes. Look with your heart."

"She made it! She made it! That chick's unreal!!"

"Hey, guys, more sets like that one and we're gonna have big problems leavin'. We only got so much fuel, y'know."

"Well, that's not such a bad idea, actually. We can leave the waverunners, go back to Tahiti, get more gas, and come right back tomorrow. Surf should still be pretty big."

"Roberto, mebbe no gonna be a tomorrah for us out here," said Bruddah, "Mebbe we shouldn't here at all."

"Thank you very much, sir. I'd better go. I'm running low on gas. I'm sorry we came here, and we will respect your wishes."

"Remember, do not enter the lagoon. Anchor your plane in the entrance. Everyone stays aboard until you leave, and you must never come back."

"Goodbye, and thank you."

"Got it!" said Kenny Bucher, carefully holding the sextant with which he had just taken a noon sight to determine their position.

"Nice going, Kenny. You have a greenhorn's luck to get a horizon in waves like this! Care to do the calculations, too?"

"Yessir, Uncle, I mean Captain Atkins, I'd like to try."

"Ok, and we'll check your numbers against your dad's. Margo, could you please signal a request to the *Tom Swift* for their calculations of our position?"

Half an hour went by before Kenny Bucher handed a slip of paper to Charles Atkins. Five minutes later, Margo Atkins handed a slip of paper to her husband. He compared them and smiled at the young sailor.

"Margo, please signal back his numbers are accurate, though he was about five minutes slow in getting them to us," said Charles Atkins.

On the *Tom Swift*, Frank Bucher smiled at the message from Atkins. He went up to the cockpit where L.J. Merrill and Jack Richards were intent on maintaining trim across a wall of water eighty feet high.

"Gentlemen, ETA in less than three hours. You guys bring wax with you?"

Ancient Waves

"What did you say when he asked why we were here?" Heath Larson hammered Aleja Gracellen with yet another question.

"I told you, Heath, remember? About MOF and that we have a permit from officials in Papeete? And I told we will fully respect his decision."

"What kind of guy was he?" asked Roberto Mercante, "Did he ask anything about Wavelife?"

"He looked me straight in the eye the entire time," she said, noticing that Larson's eyes were darting around nervously, "And no Roberto, he didn't ask about Wavelife. He listened to what I had to say and then he told me what I've told you. And that was it."

"Did he say we can't surf here?" asked Sonny-boy Noaloa, "I mean, it is perfect out there, and I know we could surf it safely."

"No, he did not say we couldn't surf here, Sonny-boy. He said we have to stay on the plane."

"Then why didn't you ask him if we could go surfing?" Heath was getting insistent.

"Heath, why would I ask him that if he said we have to stay on the plane!"

"But why do we have to stay on the plane?"

"I told you! This is a sacred place!"

"But he said we can't go in the lagoon! Why can't we go surfing?"

Aleja Gracellen was not going to be grilled any longer.

"Heath, you go and ask him! Maybe you'll make a better impression that I did!" she said, standing up and taking a step towards Larson, "After all, you're the guy who - - -" She stopped short of saying something she knew she'd regret just as Mac Owens stepped between them with the smooth touch of a Southern gentleman.

"Who is gonna back off and leave the lady alone, right Heath? Aleja, you did jes fine. Anybody else got any more questions?"

"Yeah, one," said Larson, his frustration overpowering his self-control, "If he doesn't want us here, then why didn't he tell us to leave now?"

Mac Owens was out of patience.

"Heath, why doncha jes shut yer trap, ok? He don't want us to die tryin' ta git outta here. He saw us set down an' he knows how much weight we're carryin' an' he knows how big the surf is!"

"Mac's right. The elder said something to him about that, because I was sure he was about to tell me we had to leave right away."

"So now what can we do, Aleja?" asked Roberto Mercante.

Aleja Gracellen stood up and drilled him with a silent stare while the thunder of massive waves filled the galley.

"No, Roberto, it's not WE can do, it's what YOU can do. I've done my part, and so if you'll excuse me, I'll be back in the 'sunroom' taking a nap. And I'll thank you for my privacy in advance."

She got up and left a group of men not knowing what to say or do next.

"David, I am ready. We can go now."

David Helmares was looking at the seaplane floating in the entrance to the lagoon at Ka'unua. He was eating the last of his fish, slowly and methodically chewing each mouthful without taking his eyes off the PBY.

"You can go now, Taveka. I cannot."

"David! What's wrong with you! Why not?"

Helmares ignored his wife. He was not going to be distracted. He stood up, lowered himself into the water, and began swimming to the other voyaging craft using a sidestroke to keep the seaplane in sight.

Luan looked at her father and saw that he was taking absolutely no notice of David as he swam away. He was looking straight at her.

"Luan, if he is in conflict, you must not interfere or think anything less of him for his words. He is my successor. He is the navigator of our people. He finds his way on his own terms, and that is who he needs to be."

"Father, I - - -"

"Luan, what concerns him is more important than how I die. The future is confronting him and our people," he said, taking her hands in his, "And that future includes the life of his children and the woman he loves. I am no longer a part of his world, Luan."

Taveka rose to his feet. She began to stand up but he gently put a hand to her shoulder and a finger to his lips before he kissed her on the forehead. They both knew there were no words for what passed between them in their final seconds together.

Then he stepped lightly on to his surfboard, dropped to a kneeling position, and pushed himself away from the voyaging craft without looking back. He paddled to the southern apex of the coral formation in the center of the lagoon. He slid into the water and dove for the bottom. When he touched the living coral of the ring that had grown during his lifetime, he carefully placed the necklace of the navigators where it would someday be found by his grandson. He blew a stream of bubbles into the clear water, and he was instantly aware of his ancestors surrounding him. His face broke into a broad smile, and he floated to the surface.

He started to paddle across the placid beauty of the lagoon towards the entrance. His strokes were firm and continuous, and his surfboard was gliding smoothly. Yet he was not fooled by the ease of the moment. He knew everything would change as soon as he left the protection of the Ka'unua. As he paddled he smiled at a thought that this PBY did not have machine guns protruding from the twin domes behind the wing or from beneath the tail. It was painted silver and blue, not black or camouflage. It had come to Ka'unua not as a warbird, but merely as transportation for people who were not out to harm anyone. Its broad wing came close to spanning half the width of the channel, so he paddled at an angle towards the eastern side of the entrance. Then he saw two men in the cockpit, reminding him of those who flew the Catalinas during the war. They were good, brave men. Maybe these pilots were, too.

Taveka stopped paddling. The waves were not going anywhere. His death was a foregone conclusion. He had all the time in the world. Even on the last day of his life, his curiosity remained undiminished.

"Hey, he's coming over here!" said Mac Owens, watching Taveka respond to his wave from the cockpit of the *Aeolus*.

"Well, 'course he is! He certainly wasn't going surfin' out there, that's for damn sure!" replied Clem Charleton from the pilot's seat.

"Ahoy, PBY, permission to approach?"

"Ahoy, surfer, you have permission."

"Thank you. It has been many years since I was this close to a Catalina. You have taken good care of her."

Clem stuck his head out of the pilot's window.

"How do you know her?"

"From the times we'd rendezvous with a PBY after we'd hidden sailors and pilots from the Japanese. And the times when we'd help recover the remains of the men who didn't make it."

Neither Mac Owens nor Clem Charleton knew what to say in response. Sometimes veterans don't like to talk about their combat experiences, and so they took no chances.

"Well, aren't you a little old to be going surfing?" It was all Charleton could think of.

"No, not at all. I have been surfing for more than two years now. Keeps me young. Do you surf?"

"Uh, no, I don't. But all the passengers we got aboard shore do. Funny sport. People will do jes about anythin' to ride a wave."

Taveka laughed heartily. "I know what you mean. I hope you all have good luck and that your friends find what they are looking for. Goodbye!"

"Uh, where are ya goin'? You aren't going out there, are ya?"

"Yes I am. I have a wave to catch."

"Well, I hope ya know whatcha doin'. You kin get killed in them waves!"

Taveka smiled broadly.

"Yes, I know. Goodbye!"

Taveka maneuvered his surfboard away from the seaplane. Mac Owens and Clem Charleton didn't say a word watching him leave the protection of Ka'unua. A minute later a set rolled through and he disappeared from view.

"Clem! Let's git up on the wing! I bet we'll still be able ta see 'im from up there!"

"Yeah, an' maybe our passengers might be interested, doncha think?"

Charleton left the cockpit and went back to the galley area. Six men were sitting around the table about as frustrated as they could be. They had not seen Taveka paddle by since watching the waves had only made them feel worse.

"Say, you boys don' look too busy. Why doncha come on an' we'll set a spell up on tha wing. Never know jes' whatcha might see. C'mon, we'll go up through the cockpit canopy. Can't disturb a lady, you know."

Nobody moved, but Charleton was ready for their sullen response.

"Seems like you boys forgot what we talked about flyin' out here. This plane ain't built fer crybabies. So let's go guys, 'an that's an order."

Minutes later, the men on the *Aeolus* were sitting on the broad wing of the seaplane. They had a spectacular view of the elliptical reef, the wide fields of white water surrounding it, and eighty foot waves breaking with almost mechanical precision.

"Mighty big waves, ain't they, Clem?" said Mac Owens.

"Yup, you'd hafta be plumb crazy ta go out there," said Clem Charleton.

"Naw, with jet skis, we surf waves dis big, no problem," said Bruddah.

"Yeah, and it's perfect! And with offshore winds! Why don't we just go out and see if that guy does anything? I mean, what can he do with nothing but a sailboat?" said Sonny-boy.

"Sonny-boy, this isn't our place," said Heath Larson, now sobered up after he blew it with his questions to Gracellen, "We're not going surfing and that's that."

"Yeah, I s'pose nobody should be out there," said Mac Owens, "an' specially without a lifeguard an' jetski an' all."

"Unless they were a-tryin' to kill 'emselves."

"Oh, yeah, Clem, that's right. Now I git it."

"Get what? What are you guys talking about?" asked Roberto Mercante, but the two flyers played deaf.

"Yup, Mac, but he didn't seem that crazy to me!" said Charleton, glancing towards the breaking waves, "Matter a fact, he looked ta me like he knew 'xactly what he was doin'."

"Who knew what he was doing?" asked a confused Heath Larson.

"That guy we jes' talked to. Said he was gonna ride a wave."

"What guy? There's nobody out there!" said Mercante, his voice dripping with disbelief.

"That's where yer wrong, Roberto. Y'all better take a good look."

Mercante was about to say something until he saw Charleton's eyes and realized he wasn't kidding. He stood up just as Taveka disappeared from sight in the trough between two waves.

"Where, Clem? I don't see anyone!"

Taveka re-appeared paddling hard up the face of the last wave of the set.

"Better look agin, Roberto, cause there he is!"

Taveka slide down the back of the wave. With no more waves coming in for the moment, he was clearly visible as he paddled without hesitation towards the southern end of the reef.

Six dumbfounded men saw what they just couldn't believe. Not a word passed between them until Bruddah's Polynesian instincts gave him a clue as to what was going on.

"Aleja said dis sum kin sacred place."

"Yeah, but what's he doing out there, trying to kill himself?" said Sonny-boy Noaloa.

"Yeah, he'll never catch a wave," said Heath Larson with a hint of disdain in his voice, "The guy must be nuts."

"Well, Heath, I wouldn't be so quick ta judge the man," drawled Mac Owens, "there's a tradition in sum dese island societies when tha elders start gittin' on, 'stead of stickin' 'round an' bein' a burden on their families, they jes' git inna old outrigger an' sail off an' never come back."

"Well, if that's what he's doing, he's got more courage than any man I've ever met," said Randy Laine. He wasn't speaking to anyone in particular, but Heath Larson heard every word.

"Hey, Bob, why don't you get your camera and shoot some footage?" said Roberto Mercante.

"Well, if Mac's right about why he's out there," answered Rowe, "and this is his sacred reef, then I'm not going to steal anything from him and put it in a camera for us to stare at someday."

"David!" Luan cried across the water to the other voyaging craft, "He's out there! David! He's paddling out to the waves. Aren't you supposed to be watching him?"

There was no answer from the man laying flat on his back under the shelter dome, but David Helmares was not asleep. He was quite awake, thinking through a problem much more intense, and with much greater implications for the Marulean people, than whether or not he saw Taveka die.

The next set approached and it took Taveka a long time to paddle up and over each wave. He was glad he'd listened to David and rested while reconnoitering the surf zone around Ka'unua this morning. There was no fear in heart, though he did know his limits as a surfer. And he knew that when he went past them, he would be reunited with his wife.

As he went up and over each wave, Taveka looked into the liquid tunnels rolling down the reef. Even after a lifetime at sea, he'd never seen anything like it. The sun lit up prisms of rich colors in the spray all around him. He smiled at the beauty of the experience, yet he was very aware of the challenge he faced. He kept well away from the impact zone even though the waves, though massive, never varied from their path. He was taking no chances that a rogue wave might surprise him and crush him to death. He was not going to be a victim of circumstance. He was a man with full knowledge of exactly what he was doing, and he would carry that knowledge to his last instant.

The next set formed up well to the south of Ka'unua. He closed in on the area where the swells first felt the reef. With a lifetime of instincts and hard-won knowledge surging through his mind, he watched the first swell stand up into a peak before breaking evenly in both directions. He didn't move. He let all the waves of the set go by, including the last one. Then the sea was quiet, and he remained motionless in the trance of a navigator for several minutes until a smile finally crept across his face. He was ready.

He looked to the south and waited until he saw a change in the horizon. Then, and only then, did he close his eyes and let his mind begin to gather a lifetime's memories, starting with his last words to Luan less than half an hour ago. Nothing was forgotten, not a day, not a year, not a person, nothing. The power of his intellect made each image sharp and clear, and he did not stop until he came to the moment when he had been here, so very long ago, to witness the death of his father. He saw the wave that killed him, and then he opened his eyes.

The next group of swells was approaching Ka'unua. The horizon was no longer visible. He summoned all his emotions attendant to courage and fortitude. He snapped back into the sharp and agile mind of a navigator about to face his ultimate challenge. The bloodlines of his ancestors began pumping tirelessly through his muscles. He paddled to the impact zone before turning to face the set. The first wave towered above him, and he began paddle with all his strength to maintain his position. He never stopped - as wave after wave came through - until he knew the next would be the last.

With his father at his side, he turned to catch the wave. He felt himself lifting up and he dug ever harder with each stroke. The long slope formed and gravity began to give his board more momentum. He could see the white water marking the point of impact ahead of him, and for an instant he could see all of Ka'unua, the home where his soul would soon come to rest. Spray began to blind him, but he kept paddling and paddling. He could see nothing, but he felt everything. It was his wave, and he would now ride it to his wife's open arms.

The ocean and the reef were his allies. The wind was not.

It came up under the nose of the board. Taveka felt the opposing pressure and paddled harder. He felt his forward motion increase. He felt the board begin to slide down the wave. He pushed himself up to his feet. He stood erect. He had the wave he wanted.

The wind blew Taveka back off the tail of his board before it blew the board up in the air and over his head. Seconds later he heard the explosion as the peak impacted and the wave started to follow its path around Ka'unua, without him riding deep inside it on his way to everlasting peace.

The shower of spray raining down seemed to mock him. Disappointment filled his heart. He had been perfectly balanced between the immense power of the ocean and the sacred reef of the navigators. For an instant he had been in the time and space he so desired. Now the wave was gone, and he was not where he wanted to be. Then a small grin began to grow on his face.

"Ah," he laughed to himself, "This is what I get for changing the tradition! The wind is not the enemy of a voyaging craft, but surfboards do not like wind. So now what?"

He looked out across Ka'unua. He felt his father still with him as he gazed at the circle of coral in the lagoon where his ancestors awaited him. He felt the pull of his heart. He wife now knew he was coming. He watched the wave leaving Ka'unua, re-forming into an ocean swell on the far side of the PBY. A memory crossed his mind, but then he realized she was no longer a warbird. Those were not bombs under her wings.

"Yes! That's it!"

He envisioned his last moment anew, and felt both his father's approval and his wife's happiness. He was a wayfinder even to the last, and he had just found a new way to get to where he wanted to go. He was still a navigator, and a navigator is never trapped.

* * *

"Can you believe this wind? It is going to be so good!" said Jack Richards at the wheel of the *Tom Swift*.

"Just keep her on course, helmsman! You're going almost forty knots and here comes a shoal," said L.J. Merrill, concentrating on the sensor display as they raced across the face of the open ocean swell.

"You think you guys might let me get one or two rides when we get there? Or is this place exclusively for paying guests?" said Frank Bucher.

The men laughed at the thought, and the memories of the session at Razorblades during the shakedown cruise came to their minds.

"Sure, Frank, just don't have Charlie raising the black ball flag until we're done, ok? For five mill, you owe me a lot of tow-ins, no?"

"As long as your check's good, Jackie, and I'm sure it is. Say, L.J., you ready to go surfing?"

"Fucking-a, I'm ready!" he replied with bravado. Suddenly his excitement turned to anxiety when he thought of Clark's treachery. Then all the days, weeks and months of his quest for revenge cascaded through his mind.

"Uh, how much longer?" he said, almost to himself.

"You'll be there in a little less than an hour, L.J."

* * *

"Can you believe that! He really wanted it!" said Roberto Mercante.

"Dat guy got mo' balls than alla us put togetha!"

"Yeah, Bruddah, but what he doesn't have is a chance in hell with the wind like this," said Heath Larson.

"Unless we tow him in," said Aleja Gracellen, joining the men up on the wing after watching Taveka's failed takeoff with binoculars through the 'sunroom' observation domes.

474

"No way! A Polynesian elder at his sacred reef? The last thing in the world he would want to have anything to do with is jetskis."

"Well, here he comes, Heath, and this time, YOU do the talking!"

Taveka paddled under the wing and came to a rest alongside the cargo bay. Nobody knew quite what to say until the obvious came to the mind of Roberto Mercante.

"You, uh, you really wanted that wave, didn't you?"

"But you never would have made it!" chimed in Heath Larson, "Uh, I can, I mean, uh, we thought, uh - - -"

Taveka paid no attention to stammered comments about the obvious. The solution to his problem was right in front of him, and his determination had hardened his concentration to a razor's edge.

"Ahoy Captain! Permission to approach?"

"Granted, sir," said Charleton.

"I understand you use this," Taveka touched the waverunner mounted on the landing gear, "to help the surfers ride these big waves?"

Everyone was stunned by the question posed in all seriousness with a voice full of authority.

"Uh, yes, that is what we use them for," said Heath Larson.

"Thank you young man, but I wasn't talking to you," said Taveka, "Captain, I would like to request your assistance. I need to catch a wave, and the wind will not let me. Can you arrange for one of your crew to pull me into the wave I want, using one of those?"

"I'm not in a position ta help ya out with somethin' like that," said Clem Charleton with a voice full of respect for Taveka's personage. He looked around for a second and had an idea and he knew who should be the guy to make it work.

"But I believe it can be done. Whaddaya think, Bruddah?"

"Captain Clem, you tell 'im I give 'im one tow in, but we gotta get some straps for da feet."

"I brought an extra set," said Sonny-boy Noaloa, well aware that he too shared the blood lineage of Polynesia.

Sir, I have two men willin' to help ya. If you would like ta come aboard, we'll git ya started. My name is Clem Charleton, and may I introduce Bruddah and Sonny-boy."

"Thank you, Captain. My name is Taveka."

Taveka's voyaging craft was still secure against the eastern rim of the lagoon. David was still beneath its shelter. His own voyaging craft had drifted a little in the wind while Luan watched her father paddle across the lagoon and out to the waves. But when Taveka missed his wave, Luan raised sail and soon the two voyaging craft were side by side.

"David! He didn't get the wave he wanted! He's coming back in."

David Helmares barely heard the words. He was in the trance of a navigator facing the challenge of determining a course into a wildly unknown future. He needed to be sure of himself and his instincts. He let a very small part of his mind respond to his wife's words.

"He'll think of something. He won't ask me because I won't help him. He knows why."

Luan knew better than to say anything more. She realized this process was nowhere near a conclusion, and it was all she could do to keep her mind from slipping into a vise between her father and her husband. She needed a thought to hang on to, and when she found it, she raised a sail to put some distance between the two voyaging craft. But before she headed towards the center of the lagoon, she left her husband with the sounds of a spirited laugh and exactly the words she needed to say.

"Oh, right, navigator stuff! I should have known!"

The wooden board was a marvel of construction. The surfers had never seen anything like it, especially how the nose and tail had been recently reshaped for better performance in big waves. Now it would be modified a final time with the footstraps Sonny-boy Noaloa held in his hand.

"Where do you stand when you ride it?" he asked.

"I prefer to stand here, like this," he said. He stepped on to the board and positioned his feet close together about two feet back from the nose. Then slowly he arched his back, and with his hands held just so over his head, he became the epitome of surfing's grace and balance.

"But I suppose we will have to make other arrangements," he said, stepping down off the board, "Sonny-boy, let me have those, please."

Noaloa, like everyone else, was a bit stunned not only by Taveka's hood-ornament pose, but also by his take-charge attitude. Taveka examined the footstraps briefly and put them near the nose of the board. Then he laid down prone on his board, positioned himself where he normally paddled, and popped up to his feet.

"Here is where I stand at the top of the wave."

Sonny-boy put the straps over Taveka's feet. When he carefully marked the holes where bolts were normally used to secure the straps to the board, he quickly realized he had a problem. Just as quickly he had a solution. He removed the straps, and Taveka stepped off the board. Then Noaloa dug deeper into the canvas bag and came up holding a small surfboard repair kit.

"Normally we drill holes into the board, but your board is hollow, so I'll have to attach them with some fiberglass and resin. It cures in the sun so we should be ready in a little while."

"I thank you for your help, Sonny-boy."

"Uh, you're welcome, sir, but may I ask you to call me Wilson, please? My full name is Wilson Smith Noaloa."

"Thank you Wilson. And may I ask you to introduce me to the rest of your friends?"

Bruddah was standing behind Noaloa and knew Taveka was purposefully giving the respect of an elder to a young man. That fact was confirmed when Taveka winked at him when Sonny-boy began his introductions to Heath Larson and Randy Laine standing in the cargo bay, along with Aleja Gracellen who had now joined them.

"Yes, Aleja, I am sorry we were not able to exchange formal greetings the last time we saw each other, but I hope you understood the circumstances at that time."

"Perfectly, Taveka, although I had a bit of trouble getting these men to understand!" she laughed.

"Yes, I can imagine. Excuse me Wilson, please continue."

"And up on the fuselage, we have Bob Rowe," who waved his hand at Taveka, "and Roberto Mercante."

Taveka nodded to Rowe, but when he saw the shirt that Mercante was wearing. The expression on his face changed from greeting to concern. He had seen that shirt before.

"Captain, with your permission, may I have a word with Roberto Mercante? And may I speak with him alone?"

"Why, uh, of course, sir," said Clem Charleton with the same look of surprise that was also on everyone else's face.

Half an hour later, the galley was still buzzing with conversation between the flyers, photographers, and surfers. The cargo bay had become a workshop where two men of Polynesian lineage were working carefully thanks to a new appreciation of their heritage. But back in the 'sunroom', two men from opposite ends of the world were close to tears.

"I do not know how the life of your friend came to an end, but I hope he passed away peacefully before his body was attacked. That is why we have always avoided that place. I am sorry for his family."

"I don't think he had any family. He never mentioned anyone in all the time we worked on our plans or during our trips out here."

"Yes, I remember your visits. I saw the PBY in the moonlight last October and then we found a lifevest in May. We thought you had come here since the vest was not shredded by the sharks. You were very lucky both times. And now here you are again, and that is why my successor made his first decision about you. Even now he is still trying to understand it all. He is over there on my old voyaging craft and concentrating with all his strength because the future of these waters, and of my people, will depend on the decisions he knows he will have to make if and when this all happens again."

"Well, he won't let us surf here and we're not supposed to come back. May I ask why?"

"Roberto, the fact that you are asking that question is why David told you to not come back. And it is why he has to be prepared when you do, or others do. You see, we have many traditions and customs that guide our people. It is not for you to understand them all. And yet those traditions can change, and David has to be prepared for that to happen."

"Yes, but why won't he - - -"

Taveka raised a hand.

"Please, no more. Time will provide you with some answers. For now, there is something more important for you and I to do, and do immediately. It will relieve David of a burden, and it is important to me." He pointed to the waverunner that Aleja had used. "Do you know how to drive this?"

"Why, yes, but it needs fuel."

"Good. I ask that you please get it ready so that you can come with me to my voyaging craft and then bring me back here."

Mercante could not have been more surprised, but Taveka did not give a second thought to what he was doing. He knew the ancestors were watching with approval. Death had no power over their curiosity or sense of honor, and since honor was the reason for the waverunner's mission, Taveka knew they would see nothing wrong about a modern machine crossing the sacred lagoon of Ka'unua.

"Roberto, I need you, and only you, to come with me to my voyaging craft. There is a tradition that must be observed, if you are willing. I ask you to become a guardian of your friend's remains, and those of others that died with him, along with items that may be of importance. And no one but you may touch what you will bear to the families of the dead."

The roar of the waves prevented Luan from hearing the waverunner motor quietly past her. She was sitting beneath the shelter dome on the voyaging craft in the center of the lagoon, using her father's ancient tools to carve a piece of soft coral to focus her mind in the quiet space between her father and her husband.

Near the southern edge of the lagoon, the explosions were almost overwhelming. Yet the sound of the jetski's engine was unmistakable to David Helmares even though his trance was complete. He was living his first visit to Ka'unua while concentrating on the bundle of remains and objects in the hull only a few feet away.

Mercante held the waverunner steady against bow of the center hull. Taveka stepped lightly to the deck of his voyaging craft without even a hint of emotion. He never thought he would stand on her again, but his mind was far too active to be reduced to sentimentality. The voyaging craft was nothing but wood and sail to him now, albeit with a very precious cargo aboard.

David Helmares was completely aware of what was happening though he remained motionless in his trance. Taveka went under the shelter dome, stood still for a moment, and then pulled back the mat and removed the plank to reveal the orange life vest wrapped around a bundle of items. He motioned to Roberto to join him and pointed to the compartment.

Mercante saw Helmares but Taveka grabbed him by the shoulder and pointed to the bundle with a forceful gesture. Mercante lifted it carefully and Taveka pointed to the waverunner. Then he looked at David and just for a moment the hint of a smile flowed between the two navigators.

* * *

"Margo, please signal the *Tom Swift*. Tell Frank to check his sensor imaging."

Charles Atkins had been wholly focused on the display looking for channels to safety and the danger zones to be avoided. As they closed in on their destination, he began to notice discrepancies between the real-time displays and what he'd committed to memory from the Navy data. Finally he did a screen-for-screen comparison between the sensor images and the topo maps. Not only did they not match, but instead of there being only one reef ahead, his latest imaging showed him three.

Frank Bucher had not been monitoring his display, but when he got the message from Charlie and saw what was really ahead of them, he realized the implications and immediately went to the cockpit where Richards and Merrill were helming the *Tom Swift*. They knew something was wrong when Bucher brusquely ook the helm and turned the Alba_Sword out of the wave.

"Gents, the Navy data is wrong. Only one reef was indicated, but there are three. Now I don't know which one is yours, L.J., but sensor imaging of the first one shows nothing but a nightmare. It's completely closed out."

"So what are we going to do?"

"We'll be in range for a detailed imaging of the second reef pretty soon. We're too far away to tell right now, but it looks like its handling the swell."

"And if it isn't?"

"Then we've got problems. Imaging of the third reef looks almost identical to the first one. So we're headed to the one in the middle, boys."

"What if it can't handle what's behind us?"

"That's a good question, Jack. I'll have an answer for you soon enough."

* * *

"We're ready, Taveka," said Sonny-boy Noaloa. He'd attached the straps firmly to the navigator's board and topped off the waverunner's tank with aviation fuel.

"Thank you, Wilson." He turned to Roberto Mercante standing behind him in the cargo bay. "Remember, no one but you can touch what you have in your hands. This is how we venerate those who have died without peace in their hearts. We must give their souls rest as best we can until their remains are safe with their families."

Roberto Mercante only nodded. A man who had been glib all his life was completely at a loss for words.

Taveka stepped off the seaplane to the deck of his board. He put his feet in the straps while still holding on to the *Aeolus*.

"You guys got plenty of waves out there, that's for sure!" said Bob Rowe, in the unusual position of watching amazing waves without a camera in hand.

Taveka said nothing though he looked up and smiled at the people on the wing. When he saw Aleja Gracellen he bowed his head slightly.

"I think he only needs one, Bob," she said quietly as she raised a hand in a silent goodbye.

"Boy, this is weird," said Randy Laine, "I've spent years keeping surfers alive, and now I have to sit and watch a great man ride a wave to his death."

"You think this is weird for you?" whispered Heath Larson, "How do you think I feel? He's truly courageous and you aren't going to save him. I was truly stupid, and you saved me!"

Mac Owens and Clem Charleton were standing on the fuselage just in front of the engines apart from the others. Taveka gave them a thumb's up and they both snapped off military salutes to a man they knew was a real hero. Then he turned to the business at hand with instructions for Bruddah and Sonny-boy.

"I only want one wave, the last wave of the group. As soon as I am riding it, please turn off your engine."

Sonny-boy played out the tow line as Bruddah slowly maneuvered the waverunner away from the seaplane. Taveka was standing with his feet in the straps. He bent over and picked up the handle with one hand, holding on to the *Aeolus* with the other. Bruddah pulled the line taut. Noaloa was expecting Taveka to fall, but with his knees bent he was ready, and just as the line went straight, Taveka let go of the *Aeolus*.

"Ok, Bruddah, he's got it," said Noaloa as Bruddah rolled on the power slowly. Taveka instincts took hold, and he leaned back to keep the tow rope taut. Then he gave a thumb's up to Noaloa.

A set was pounding down both sides of the reef. For the men on the waverunner the sight was not at all unfamiliar, yet the fact remained they were taking a brave man to his death. And though they felt strengthened by their Polynesian bonds to Taveka and his timeless dignity, the experience was deeply humbling. With serious and somber expressions on their faces, Bruddah and Noaloa towed the navigator across the deep water north of the lagoon entrance to give Taveka a chance to get his sealegs as a tow-in surfer. Then they came around in a wide circle. Noaloa was watching Taveka handle the curve, and suddenly he couldn't believe his eyes. Taveka's smile was so broad and bright he seemed to be almost laughing.

"Bruddah! He's having a good time back there!"

The last waves of the set rolled down the reef as Bruddah, Sonny-boy and Taveka cruised to the south. All three of them could not take their eyes off the sight of huge tubes breaking perfectly, one after another, until the last wave rolled past them.

Bruddah reduced speed and circled out to sea to await the next set.

"Chip! What's she looking like? Are we a go on this set?"

"The bottom looks great, Frank. Every wave in that last set was perfect!"

"Tak, is this the wave we want?"

"In this set it certainly is. We've got seven waves ahead of us, nothing behind. All systems are up to spec, and so no there's no reason to pull out that I can think of."

480

"Uh, maybe we should circle around and wait for the next set and, uh, check the shape from a better angle," said an increasingly nervous L.J. Merrill, standing with Jack Richards below decks watching Chip Bell's display reveal the perfection of the reef. Though he was concentrating at the helm, Bucher couldn't help but overhear the comment.

"Why bother, L.J.? Didn't you already see this place from the air?"

"Yeah, Frank, but maybe we should give it another look just in case!" yelled Richards up through the hatch, giving Merrill a bit of support.

"C'mon, Jackie, You want your money's worth! Doncha want to get every wave you can?"

"Yeah, but - - -"

"But what? Are we not surfers?" roared Bucher as he accelerated the *Tom Swift* down the eighty foot face for even more speed.

The first swell of the set approached Ka'unua, its building face appearing as if the entire ocean was rising towards the sky. Bruddah did a wide circle well clear of the impact zone to set up a practice run down the reef. Taveka maintained the strain on the tow rope and gave a thumbs-up to Sonny-boy.

"Frank! First wave over the shoal! Something's on the screen, but can't tell what it is. You want the display up there?"

"Negative! I've got all the visual I need! Tak!"

"On course, Captain!"

Taveka sensed what Bruddah was doing and gave Noaloa another thumb's up. Then the roar of the jetski's engine was drowned out as swell exploded into two perfect waves.

"First wave clean and perfect! Both sides of the reef! Shoaling zone absolutely even," said Bell, his voicing ringing out loud and clear, "Anomaly still displayed. Don't know what it is."

"Bruddah, he's ready."

They pulled out of the wave down near the entrance to the lagoon. Everyone was waving their arms from the top of the *Aeolus*.

Taveka was a little kid having the time of his life. This was almost too easy. He would have to apologize to the ancestors, but in the end he knew they would all want him to tell the story again and again.

"Number two perfect!!! Here comes number three! Same size, same speed, same shape!"

"You know L.J., you truly did find the best big wave in the world. This place doesn't look real it's so perfect!" marveled Jack Richards.

"It better be real," muttered L.J. Merrill, feeling a familiar twinge of fear that he was going to be let down again. But seeing was believing, and he was able to shake it off by staring at the screen and the perfect waves on display.

"Bruddah, we better get him set up."

Bruddah looked over his shoulder and hesitated. He was about to send a man to his death, but Taveka only smiled and pointed out to sea.

The big Hawaiian turned back and rolled on the power.

"Frank! I think we're too far back for the rights. Charlie's definitely going left, so we'd better open a bit of room between us and then follow him down the west side of the reef."

"Got it, Tak! A big right-go-left bottom turn coming up! Hold on!"

Bruddah swung wide around wave number six as he gave his gauges a final check. He saw wave number seven just starting to feel the reef, and behind it, the last wave of the set. He began his launch arc to set up a wide curve that would position Taveka exactly where he needed to be. Sonny-boy saw that the navigator was in perfect form, leaning back to keep the rope taunt and his board under control. He pointed out to sea, and Taveka nodded his head enthusiastically.

"Ok, Bruddah, he wants it!"

Wave number seven stood up vertically and pitched out into a perfect pyramid of liquid power. Two angled crests separated into giant tunnels that began to roll down opposite sides of Ka'unua.

"All hands! Secure for takeoff!"

Frank Bucher saw the back of the wave that had broken ahead of them. Then both Alba_Swords were lifted up the face and began to drop in. He glanced to his left and saw that Charles Atkins had readied the forward fins of the *Serena* exactly as he had done on the *Tom Swift*. When he looked back, he saw a jetski towing a surfer.

Bruddah looked up and saw two streamlined ships, looking like huge swordfish, coming down the face of the wave. One carved a turn to the left. The other was coming straight at him.

Sonny-boy Noaloa didn't see the Alba_Sword, but he knew something was going on when saw the expression on Taveka's face change from joy to awe, and then to determined readiness for the speed of the whip.

482

"Hard to port!" screamed Bucher, jamming the *Tom Swift* into a turn that almost flipped her over. The spray from the Alba_Sword drenched the jetski as Bruddah banked the waverunner into a full 180 turn.

Bucher hit his thrusters full blast to get out of the way of the surfer. He looked back and for a second his eyes met Taveka's. Then the *Tom Swift* joined the *Serena* in flight formation. Noaloa now saw the Alba_Swords but quickly looked back at Taveka who was watching them as he came around the arc and accelerated into the wave. He looked at Sonny-boy, and with a final smile to the young man, he let go of the towbar. He turned his head to face the wave and his past ceased to exist.

This is the wave. I have the speed. I can feel it. I have this wave. I HAVE IT! Now, turn, TURN!

His mind went blank at the sight of the wave ahead of him, but the feeling in his heart could not have been more beautiful. His ancestors touched his soul and instinct became his guide. He envisioned his course across the building wall of water and his wife waiting for him at the end of his final voyage.

"David! DAVID! HE'S ON THE WAVE!! DAVID!!!"

The navigator snapped out of his trance. He came out from under the shelter dome. His entire range of vision was filled by a wall of water – and more. To his right he saw two ultra modern vessels speeding down the face of the massive wave like flying torpedoes. To his left he saw a waverunner racing in the opposite direction.

David Helmares was sledgehammered simultaneously from two opposite directions. A sensation of being surrounded tried to force its way into his mind. It didn't have a chance. His self-control was complete. He saw his path clearly ahead. The two forces faded to nothing at the edges of his gaze as his keen eyes focused on the surfer perfectly positioned at the apex of the giant wave. He smiled as he whispered, "A navigator is never trapped."

The wave towered to the sky as his old friend and mentor began a long, beautiful turn. The board held its edge and gave Taveka the control he needed to set the board on a path that fit perfectly into the concave face of the wave.

"Nice turn! You did a good job changing the tail, David!"

Luan stepped up and put her arms around her husband to watch her father's last wave. Her mind was fresh and there was joy in her heart, knowing the happiness of her father.

The curve of the translucent roof created a constant cylinder of space revolving perfectly into a giant tunnel. It was almost impossible to see him, but the track of the board told the story of Taveka's ride. He was now at the very bottom of the liquid wall standing eighty feet high. Then the white wake turned away from the impact zone as the navigator set a course straight and true. Gradually he began to disappear inside the cathedral. The track never wavered. For one last instant they could see Taveka poised with his body arched and his hands held high in the air. Then he disappeared forever into the heart of the wave.

The wake left by the surfboard could barely be seen in the curving roof of the tunnel. As the wave peeled down the reef, Taveka's trail was still visible, getting closer and closer to where perfection exploded into chaos.

The wave reached the final section of the reef. The course of the navigator never varied. The mouth of the tunnel expanded from a spinning circle into a wide-open ellipse. Taveka was exactly where he wanted to be, inside the deepest part of the giant wave. Then the mouth of the tunnel snapped shut as the roof of the wave collapsed into a massive avalanche of whitewater exploding in all directions. A huge cloud of spray hung in the air for several seconds. And then the wave gathered itself, and rolled on.

The white water backed off and the energy reformed into an ocean swell that was new, yet ancient. It was once a perfect wave eighty feet high, and yet it was never more than grain of sand in the universe, nor its life anything other than a moment of mystery, an infinitesimal slice of time just long enough for a man to begin his journey towards eternity.

David and Luan held each other close, still looking down the reef as the last of the wave dissipated completely. The seaplane was visible to the left, and for an instant they could see the waverunner heading in across the fields of white water now scattering in the currents.

Then the baby moved in Luan's womb, and David felt new life soon to be born. He was about to say something, but Luan put a finger to his lips.

"I'll take care of our child. You go take care of our people."

* * *

The Alba_Swords surfed the wave all the way down the reef while staying well out ahead of the perfect tube rolling behind them. They pulled out when the strength of the wave finally began to subside. The propulsion systems were powered down for the first time since they'd launched from the *Mother Carie*. The vessels were finally coming to a rest, but Frank Bucher had no illusions about the conflict about to take place.

"Tak, signal Charlie. We need to talk as soon as possible."

"Frank, you gotta talk right now," said Kurosawa, nodding to the hatchway leading below. Bucher knew exactly what he meant.

"We're here! We made it!" Jack Richards was feeling flush with the rush of a victory hard fought and nobly won, a feeling he had never quite known before. He had done something the hard way, the right way, and now he could let himself feel a sense of honest satisfaction. He couldn't contain himself as he came up to the cockpit. "Hey Frank! Thanks a million! Or should I say five million! That was a great wave! Next time can we watch from the cockpit? What a turn!"

Richards's excitement turned to confusion when he saw no satisfaction or joy on the faces of Bucher or Kurosawa.

"Hey! C'mon! This is what we've waited for!" There was no reply, but when Bucher nodded at something in the distance behind him, Jack Richards turned around while L.J. Merrill made his way up to the cockpit.

"How was that wave! This place is perfect! Its eighty feet and perfect!" Merrill was as excited as a man could be. The long journey was over, all the planning and effort rewarded, the reef as perfect as he had imagined, and now he was there. "Was that unreal or what! We're going to ride the best big waves on earth!" he exclaimed as he stepped up on deck.

His euphoria was met with stone quiet. He stopped in his tracks. The eyes of the three men were looking right past him. For a second he didn't know what was going on. Then a feeling he'd known far too many times began to drown his heart.

"Hey, you guys, what's the deal? Jack! What's going on?"

"Well, uh, L.J., you better - - -" Jack Richards could not say another word. He nodded his head and darted his eyes, silently telling the legendary surf scout to turn around.

A second later, L.J. Merrill felt a sharp pain stab from his heart to his soul.

* * *

"Can somebody say something? I don't know whether to laugh or cry!"

Aleja Gracellen's words were the first to break the silence of the stunned people up on the wing of the seaplane. The death of Taveka would have been enough of a life changing experience on its own. To have two ultra-high-tech sailboats, shaped like swordfish, in formation riding across an eighty foot wave down the west side of the reef was just too much. Now not only were they trying to make sense of Taveka's death, but a whole new reality had just been forced upon them like a tag-team slap down that had them reeling.

"You know, I thought I'd seen just about everything when it comes to surfing, and no disrespect, Heath, but what he just did puts it all in a little box that I'll never think about ever again," said Bob Rowe.

Larson tried to reply, but no words came to him. Nothing from his career as a surfer or his deep knowledge of existentialism seemed at all significant compared to the courage and commitment of a man on the last wave of his life.

"Yup, that's one helluva way to go out, at the time 'an place of yer own chosin'. That's how I heard those old navigators used to do it, and I guess some of 'em still do," said Mac Owens.

Bruddah and Sonny-boy climbed aboard the *Aeolus*. They were ashen faced. They had just helped kill the noblest man they had ever met.

"You guys ok?" asked Roberto Mercante, still holding the bundle Taveka had given him and not ready to try to put into words what he had just seen.

"This whole thing is just gettin' too much," said Sonny-boy Noaloa, still remembering the final smile on Taveka's face, "I'm kinda losing it here."

"I think we all are," said Randy Laine.

"Who dose guys?" said Bruddah in a low, dark voice.

"I betcha they're asking the same thing 'bout us," said Clem Charleton.

"What difference does it make who they are after what Taveka just taught us?" said Heath Larson.

The waves continued to break in loud, roaring continuums of sound, but Larson's words hit home for everyone on board the *Aeolus*. They all realized it was more important to come to grips with Taveka and his death rather than have their emotions tangled up in the reality of their new neighbors.

The pilots went forward and sat in the cockpit, busying themselves with stuff that didn't mean a thing, all the while talking here and there about what they knew of PBY's flying in the South Seas and what true courage was while fighting a war. Randy Laine and Bob Rowe went to the galley and made themselves something to eat. To watch a man with no lifevest, no backup ski, no experience, and yet no fear was something that had yet to sink all the way in for the lifeguard and safety expert. The two Hawaiians went swimming for a long time around the seaplane, immersing themselves in the only true reality they had in common heritage with Taveka. The former chairman of Wavelife International sat up on the wing with the bundle in his care, lost in a wide open world of thought, glancing now and again at the white water on the horizon where Ian Clark had died, and then over at the last section of Taveka's wave.

The best big wave surfer in the world and the woman who danced with the sea found themselves in the observation compartment, sitting on the bench seats opposite each other. Every once in a while, Aleja would try to find some connection or understanding that they could hold on to, and Heath Larson knew much of what she said rang true. Yet he said very little in reply, his thoughts swirling around Roberto Mercante and the bundle of remains, then about surfing and what it had done to his life – and to Ian Clark. Gracellen's words cut through his confusion somewhat, but he wondered if he would ever understand something completely outside the philosophy he had used so successfully inside huge waves.

Eventually Aleja realized Heath had drifted off to a place she could not follow, and inwardly was glad she could now just think for herself. She turned away from him and looked out across the lagoon as another set of massive waves peeled down the reef with flawless shape. Her first thought was of the tiny waves of Santa Monica and the little girl running waving to the dolphins.

As for Larson, he was riding with Taveka on the navigator's last wave. His existential underpinnings had been completely whipsawed by the courage he'd witnessed and the simple reality of riding a wave as a last expression of life. A smile came at the thought of the discussion he would have with Ben Jeffries about what they needed to learn from Taveka's last wave.

* * *

"Hey, you! Who the fuck are you?" L.J. Merrill didn't care that his big wave surfboard had almost speared a hole into the aluminum fuselage of the PBY. He didn't even see it happen because he was looking up at Roberto Mercante sitting on the wing. "What are you doing, here? Why don't you just get the fuck outta here, now!"

"Hey, wait a minute! Hi, I'm Roberto Mercante," he said, trying to gather himself, "You know, uh, we - - - "

"Oh, the big shot himself! Well, funny to meet you here! Bring the whole team, did you? Where's Heath? Where's Sonny-boy? What, no photographers?"

Then it all dawned on Mercante.

"You're L.J. Merrill, aren't you? Uh, I think you and I should talk, ok?"

"What for? Fuck you! You can't buy me, off like you did Clark! And where is that son-of-a-bitch? Hey Ian!" he yelled at the top of his voice, "You on this fucking airplane?"

Within seconds Heath Larson and Aleja Gracellen were in the cargo bay. Merrill looked up at them with a sneer on his face and was about to say something when Randy Laine and Bob Rowe appeared, followed by Mac Owens and Clem Charleton who shouldered their way past the photographers.

"Say, pal, I don't let anyone insult this plane," said Clem Charleton.

"Oh, you must be the chauffeur for these rich assholes!"

"And just who the hell are you?" said Mac Owens.

'I'm the guy who found this place! Now why don't you just fly your fucking plane outta here! And where's Clark? Where the fuck is he, Mercante?"

"You must be L.J. Merrill," said Aleja Gracellen.

"That's right, and who the hell are you? Some whore along for the ride?"

Bruddah and Sonny-boy had seen someone paddling across the channel from one of the boats. When they heard the yelling, they started to swim back to the *Aeolus*, and fast.

"Her name is Aleja Gracellen, and I'm Heath Larson."

"Oh, Mr. Big Wave Hero. What are you doing out here? Didn't you learn your lesson last May? Stealing can get you in a lot of trouble!"

Merrill turned around. The two Hawaiians were only yards away and swimming right at him.

"Oh, here's the big time surf star! And his thug body guard!"

"Bruddah! Leave him alone!" Mercante yelled, "Bruddah! Don't!"

The Hawaiians stopped short.

"He's right, Bruddah," said Heath Larson, "Leave him alone. We've got more important things to deal with right now. Roberto! Why don't you handle this, ok? Seems you need to straighten this guy out on a couple of things."

Larson's words gave everyone pause and they gladly followed his lead. Bruddah pushed Merrill's board out of the way to clamber up into the cargo bay with Noaloa right behind him.

"You watch you mouth, brah," said Bruddah, but Larson pulled him around and pushed him through the hatch leading forward. Everyone slowly followed them without even looking back.

"Okay, Mr. Big Shot Millionaire, just me and you, since I take it that lying piece of shit Clark isn't here, is he?"

"Hold on, L.J., I'm coming down there. And no, he's not here, not exactly."

The first wave of a set rolled past the end of the reef as Roberto Mercante came down off the wing with some difficulty since his hands were full. The roar of the waves was no match for the rage of L.J. Merrill.

"What do you mean, not exactly? Where is he? He fucking double-crossed me and when I see him he's gonna wish - - -"

Merrill's heart stopped him in mid-sentence when he remembered what Frank Bucher had said to him. The moment of silence was all Mercante needed to begin speaking slowly and carefully.

"Well L.J., maybe he regretted what he did, but we'll never know."

"What do you mean by that? Where is he?"

"He's dead."

"Yeah, right, he's not dead," said Merrill, unable to say the words with a sarcastic sneer fueled by another outburst of rage, "Fuck you, Mercante! Get the fuck outta here, now!"

"L.J., Ian Clark is dead. I know he's dead. I have the proof right here."

"What's that?"

"It's his lifevest. And inside - - - "

"Inside are some vertebrae we took from the pieces of bodies left over after the sharks got 'em." Both men turned to see the voice coming towards them.

"And there's a camera in the vest pocket, and there's some vertabrae that can be used for DNA identification wrapped up in a Geosurf t-shirt just like the one he's wearing." David Helmares said directly to L.J. Merrill.

"Who are you?" The rage was gone from Merrill's voice as his mind began to collapse like a wave hitting the sand.

"I am the chief navigator of the sea people of Marulea. This is Ka'unua, the sacred reef for fifteen, no, sixteen generations of navigators."

"But, but, why, what - - -" The words were barely above a whisper.

"I could ask you the same questions, but I already know the answers. You're the guy who flew over this place last October. Just before sunset, remember?"

The last wave of the set re-formed into a swell, the wind began to die down, and the men were surrounded by silence.

"Now, there has been enough talk for the moment," said Helmares, "And there is still much to say. But we must not have any conflict here. Please."

"Yeah, L.J., let's all just back off," said Mercante.

But L.J. Merrill did not hear a word. He could barely see the men speaking to him. His breathing was short and shallow. His mind was so beyond overload that he could do nothing but act on instinct. He lay down on his surfboard, barely able to get his legs out of the water. He gripped the rails for a moment. The water touched his hands and he let them fall into the sea. Muscle memory took over, and slowly he began to paddle away.

Mercante and Helmares watched him until the silence was shattered by the first wave of a new set. They turned to the south and watched the biggest waves of the day begin to march down both sides of the reef.

"First I give you permission to stay until the surf goes down," said David, shaking his head, "and now not only have others arrived, but the surf is only getting bigger."

"Uh, yeah. Sorry. Uh, my name is Roberto Mercante. And we're all sorry, and, but I mean we're all sorry about what happened to Taveka, too."

Helmares smiled.

"He's lucky I built that board so we could pull in the nose and tail. Otherwise he would have spun out and died a kook!"

Mercante couldn't believe his ears. But before he could say another word, David Helmares was moving on.

"I'm going to go get my wife, and we'll bring our voyaging craft down here. We must understand as much about each other as we can, including them," he said, pointing to the two boats on the other side of the channel, "and him." L.J. Merrill was still paddling across the channel.

"I don't know, David. He's really upset about us being here."

"Yes, I can understand why he's raging. I was pretty pissed off when I saw his plane. I'm going to swim over to those boats and get this whole thing out in the open for everyone at the same time."

"Have 'em come over here. There's plenty of room up on the wing."

"Good idea. See you in a little while."

"I wonder what happened. He's barely moving his arms," said Jack Richards softly as he passed the binoculars back to Frank Bucher.

"I've never seen revenge take over a man like that," said Tak Kurosawa.

"Well, maybe he got it all out of his system," said Margo Atkins.

"Let's hope so," said Chip Bell.

"Maybe that guy who swam up outta nowhere had something to do with it," offered Ken Bucher, "I wonder where he came from?"

"From across the lagoon," said Charles Atkins, pointing to the two voyaging craft.

L.J. Merrill paddled his board up to the side of the *Tom Swift,* floating a short distance from the *Serena*. The two boats were loosely tethered and sea anchors had been set out instead of dropping regular anchors into the coral. Every once in a while Patti McRane gave the Serena's thrusters a touch to keep the two boats apart and yet in position. Merrill's shipmates had joined the crew of the *Serena* after Frank Bucher suggested it might be a good idea to give him some space. He knew they were watching him but he never looked up as he climbed the rope ladder and went below.

"Maybe I'd better go talk to him," said Jack Richards, but Frank Bucher touched his arm and shook his head.

"He's got a lot to think about. And so do we. Charlie, we'd better signal HQ that we're here. See if Ray has anything for us."

"Aye-aye, Captain," said Atkins, smiling at his wife, "We've got a new Morse code expert on board. She'll get right on it."

The thought of contacting their home port gave everyone a chance to take a deep breath and get their minds back to the reality of their voyage, and for an instant there was a feeling of release in the cockpit of the *Serena*. Then L.J. Merrill surprised them all by coming back up to the cockpit of the *Tom Swift*, toweling himself dry and calling across the water in a loud voice.

"Uh, there's this guy swimming over here. He wants to talk to us."

The words were barely out of his mouth when the mariners in the cockpit of the *Serena* heard a voice behind them.

"Ahoy visitors! I am David Helmares, chief navigator of the sea people of Marulea. Permission aboard?"

The Nebula Archipelago

The north wind from the passing storm had stopped blowing just after Taveka's last wave. A cloud of mist now hung over Ka'unua. The shape of the waves was still perfect and the water still clear, but the colors had changed from turquoise and white to dark blue and gray. Each of the quiet people sitting up on the wing of the *Aeolus* was seeing something different as they watched the huge waves. To the surfers, it was the most perfect big wave surfing arena on earth. The sailors hoped it would be a refuge from the power of waves two hundred feet high. To some it was a place where a courageous man had willingly met his death. To others it was nothing more than a death trap. One feeling, however, was shared by all: everyone felt out of place.

L.J. Merrill sat alone out near the wingtip. Jack Richards was a few steps away next to Tak Kurosawa, Chip Bell, their captain and his son. The couples of the *Serena* were close to the port engine. Seated near the other engine were Clem Charleton, Mac Owens and Roberto Mercante, with Randy Laine and Bob Rowe right next to them. Sitting as far as possible from L.J. Merrill were Heath Larson, Bruddah, Sonny-Boy Noaloa and Aleja Gracellen. The crews of the *Tom Swift* and the *Serena* had not been welcomed aboard the *Aeolus* with any real enthusiasm. The death of Taveka and L.J. Merrill's tirade still hung in the air. Varying degrees of anger, sadness, fear, and frustration were not going to make this meeting any easier for the visitors to Ka'unua.

David Helmares was helping Luan step up to the fuselage when the first of wave of a set began to break almost a mile away. It took several seconds for the sound of the detonation to cross the lagoon, but he did not turn to look until Luan was standing safely next to him. Then, with their backs to the people on the wing, the husband and wife watched the waves surround Ka'unua with a crescendo of power and sound until, minutes later, all was silent again. They turned around and introduced themselves.

"I am David Helmares. This is my wife, Luan."

"My father was Taveka, the chief navigator of Marulea. My people live across the Nebula Archipelago," she said, "David was born in California. He has now succeeded my father."

Luan sat down as David began to speak.

"For centuries the Maruleans have inhabited ten thousand square miles of Polynesia's most remote atolls and islands. We are on paper with the Tahitian authorities, but essentially we are off the map by our own choice. I don't know how you got your permit, but I suspect it is because the officials in Papeete didn't know exactly where you were going. And even if they had, I'm sure money still talks.

"And so here you are. This is Ka'unua, the sacred reef of the navigators. It is our Valhalla, if you can understand that," he said, seeing some confusion in the eyes looking at him, "Think of this place like Mt. Everest once was to the Sherpas, before it became Mt. Everest. They called it Chomolungma. It was a sacred place for them, but now people go there to conquer it or die trying. Over time, change came to Chomolungma. Now, thanks to one man, change has come to Ka'unua."

He didn't look at L.J. Merrill. He didn't have to.

"For the moment I have nothing to say to him. I will tell you what I said when I saw his plane fly over Ka'unua last October."

Everyone stirred and leaned forward.

"I was here to complete tasks set before me as part of my becoming the chief navigator of the Maruleans. I came here alone, with no compass to guide me. I came as a wayfinder, to the reef where the souls of navigators preceding me now rest. It was a holy moment for me. And then I saw the flash of metal in the setting sun. It took me a few seconds to figure out why a plane would be all the way out here. When I did, this is what I said."

His eyes swept across the people on the wing. The last person he saw was L.J. Merrill before he looked up at the sky.

"Out! Out!! GET THE FUCK OUT OF HERE!"

David Helmares screamed, and for several minutes, he filled the air with rage and obscenities just as he had once before. He never looked at the overwhelmed people on the wing until he finally stopped and slowly made eye contact with each and every person - except one.

"What I said that day to a man I couldn't see, and who didn't hear me, is still alive in my heart," he continued, his voice now subdued, "And so you now have an idea why I did not welcome the people of this seaplane. Obviously I did not want them here, and today least of all. Today I was to witness the death of my mentor, the man who preceded me as chief navigator. The father of my wife. Had you not arrived, I was going to launch him into his final wave using a voyaging craft to give him the speed he needed. But your coming was something I had to deal with, and he knew that was more important than his death. Still, he wanted to die on his own terms, so he got you to help him. And he did, and I saw it. So that is done.

"Now what? Do I let the boats anchor? Do I let the seaplane stay? If so, why not let you all go surfing? If the guy who got you all here wants to go out, do I stand in his way? And then what happens? Where would it end? Or do I really have any power at all to stop you from doing anything you want?

"You see, I know you have legal standing here, with your permits such as they are. But no one has ever been here except the navigators of the sea people. This is a sacred place. And I don't know if there was anything sacred about why you all came here," he paused, "or what you are going to do with your knowledge of Ka'unua once you leave."

"When I first found the sea people, they questioned me for almost three days about every aspect of my life. They did this because they needed to know who I was. That process will not take place today because those people are not

492

here. However, it is still the responsibility of the chief navigator to understand all he can before deciding what course to take in their name. And so I will ask you two questions. Why are you here? And what will you do with your knowledge of Ka'unua when you leave?"

He held up the coral carving Luan had made with her father's tools.

"I will give this carving to the first person who wants to speak. All others must listen. When that person is finished, give it to the next person, and so on, until all have had their say. You may talk as long as you like, or you do not have to say anything at all. When you are done, I will have the information I need to make a decision."

David heard the first wave of the next set approaching. To the sharp eyes of many on the wing, it looked bigger than anything they had seen so far.

"You will have to speak loudly, please. Who will go first?"

Jack Richards raised his hand. David tossed the carving to him with a perfectly accurate throw that surprised everyone, including Richards.

"I'm here because I wanted to surf huge, perfect waves and because I did not want a big corporation to use this place for its own benefit. I wanted to get here first and steal their thunder. But when Heath almost died and you and Cheryl resigned, Roberto, I upped the ante. I bought stock in Wavelife knowing Black and those guys would be unable to run the corporation properly. I planned to initiate a shareholders lawsuit to drive them into the ground. But as it turns out, they did it themselves. So now I am here only to go surfing, and when I get back home, I will be permanently retired from the stock market so I can try to be a better husband and father."

An astounded Roberto Mercante raised his hand. Richards stood up and walked over to him and handed him the carving. No words passed between them, only an extra moment of pause.

"I was the founder of the company he's talking about, Wavelife International, I first came here for exactly the reasons he described. And because of those reasons, I lost my company, and men lost their lives over there," he said, pointing to the reef in the distance, "The greed and ambition that caused their deaths are very familiar to me. But now I am here to help communicate the spirit of surfing to people who need inspiration."

"An' we're the good ol' boys that been flyin' him out here," said Mac Owens. No one had any problems hearing the strong voices of Mac Owens and Clem Charleton talking about their experiences bringing people to Ka'unua. Their honesty and character came through loud and clear, giving the next person the courage to ask for the stone carving.

"I once wanted to surf the reef where Ian Clark and ten other men died," said Heath Larson, "And I wanted it so much that I died, too, except that I was brought back to life thanks to my friends. But it was not a wave that almost killed me. It was my own excessive sense of self. And now I want to do the same thing as Roberto. I am still learning the lessons of that day and hope that I can also share with others the inspirations, and not the hubris, of surfing. And thanks to these two men, I have my life ahead of me to accomplish that goal."

He walked over to where Randy Laine and Bob Rowe were sitting and offered them the carving.

"Well, I'll be brief," said Randy Laine, "I came here to make sure nobody dies. But then I had to watch Taveka do just that on his last wave, and if I work with people in the future who get some big ideas about who they are and what they want to do, the first thing I'm going to tell them will be about the time I learned about real courage."

"Yeah, Randy and I were pretty blown away watching Taveka's last ride," said Bob Rowe, "and though I have taken a lot of pictures of some of the most amazing surfing ever, I refused to do so when Taveka paddled out. What he did puts everything I've ever seen in modern surfing in a new perspective, and from now on I'll always have the most amazing ride I'll ever see right here to remind what true character is all about."

The words of Laine and Rowe rang true across the wing, prompting Margo Atkins to speak about OSOM's mission and introduce its members one by one, all of whom were happy to let her speak for them, including Frank Bucher. Then she handed the carving to her husband.

"Let me start by saying that if it wasn't for me and the storm that made these waves, we wouldn't be here." He briefly explained the background of the Alba_Swords, the presence of L.J. Merrill and Jack Richards, and how they came to arrive at Ka'unua. He explained the K3 storm, as the last wave of the set rolled by, leaving him to complete his words in silence. "We know there are bigger waves still to come. It will be half again as big by dawn, and there may be waves twice as big as what we are seeing by tomorrow afternoon."

David never took his eyes off any of the speakers. Behind them he could see the swells re-forming past the northern end of the reef. He spoke for the first time since the carving left his hands.

"Yes, that last set was about ten feet bigger than the waves this morning. It is getting bigger, just as you say."

With everyone now sharing thoughts of the ocean's energy, the carving went to Sonny-boy and Bruddah. They spoke about their Hawaiian roots and what had happened when they had assisted Taveka. Sonny-boy also had some things to say about Wavelife and pro surfing and Bruddah talked about Maui and his partnership with Heath Larson. In the end, they both said the same thing concerning what they would do with their knowledge of Ka'unua: the waves meant little to them compared to what they had learned from Taveka about the courage and character they wanted to share with young people in both Hawai'i and Florida.

The set subsided and once again, the quiet was deeply felt. Then Bruddah handed the carving to Aleja Gracellen. She chose her words carefully in recounting everything from the first meeting at Wavelife to what she was doing only a few days ago working at the shelter when she got the call to drop everything because it was time to ride the biggest waves of her life.

When she saw the next set coming she brought her words to a conclusion.

"If I can do anything to help people in need, then it seems like riding perfect waves is the least I can do. There is a way to turn surfing into something that benefits people besides us. We can take the media spotlight shining on us and turn it around to illuminate problems we feel deeply about. And if my surfing gives people inspiration as they try to surf their oceans, even if they are a thousand miles from a beach, then I thought maybe I would be doing some good. I just don't know if I want to surf that!" she said, hearing an explosion a mile away of the first swell splitting evenly into two perfect waves each over eighty feet high.

Then she looked back across the group, but there were no raised hands. She returned the carving to David Helmares. He looked at the waves, and then the carving. Then he caught the eye of the man sitting alone at the far end of the wing. He stood up and walked over to L.J. Merrill.

"Your turn," he said, and handed him the carving.

Merrill began to speak in a soft voice. The roar of the waves drowned out his words. Only Jack Richards could barely hear him, though his eyes never broke contact with David's. He never stopped talking, except to brush tears from his eyes, something only David could see.

The last wave of the set rolled through. All was quiet once again, except for the voice of a man speaking from his heart.

"I have a promise to keep to people who love me. I have ridden enough waves on this trip to last the rest of my life. If I surf the waves of Ka'unua while we are here, it will be in memory of a man who was once my friend. It is not for me to accuse or forgive him. Ian Clark is dead, and may his soul rest in peace. When I leave Ka'unua, I will always remember what surfing, as wonderful as it is, can do to people who forget its blessings. Believe me, I know, and there are eleven dead men who came out here because of me who are lost to their families and friends forever.

"Riding this place, and using its waves the way I have used waves around the world, was an obsession for me. Not any more," he said before looking at Jack Richards, "I hope. I hope I've learned that the only way for anyone to truly deserve surfing's blessings is to share them with others. Maybe Ian and I were doing that in the beginning when we started Geosurf, but in the end we were both consumed by our own selfishness. And so we both lost ourselves. I became addicted to surfing's perfection, and he found himself trapped selling that perfection to the highest bidder. Ian is now dead, and this is my last surf trip. That's all I got to say."

The silence was now complete. L.J. stood up and walked across the wing until he was close enough to toss the carving gently back to David. He looked with empty eyes at the people on the wing, from Aleja Gracellen to Jack Richards. Then he hung his head and went back to where he was once again alone with his thoughts.

It was several minutes before an explosion broke the silence, sounding the arrival of a new set at the southern tip of the reef. Only then did David Helmares begin to speak.

"I thank you all for your words. You have given me all I needed to make my decision. Now we must think about the surf. The lulls this morning were almost ten minutes long. This one was less than six. The waves have doubled in size every day for the past three days. Taveka called them babies when this swell started. He said they would one day become ancient. I thought that day had come, but now it won't be until tomorrow?" He looked at Charles Atkins.

"Yes, and it is our hope that this reef will provide us a safe harbor from which we can observe the biggest waves ever seen by man."

"And what if Ka'unua fails to protect you?"

"Then we will find protection elsewhere."

"We hope!" added Frank Bucher.

"And what of the *Aeolus,* Clem?"

"Well, David, if we gotta get outta here, hell we'll just wait fer one of those two hunnerd footers an' use 'er like a launch ramp!"

For the first time in hours, if not months, a bit of humor washed relief through many hearts on the wing of the *Aeolus.* Then Mac Owens made everyone laugh.

"Yup, gonna do a late take-off an' fly 'er right thru one of those tubes. Hell, if Taveka can git out there, so can a coupla rebel pilots! 'Cept we're gonna kick out 'for we buy the reef 'cause we ain't trained anybody ta take our place yet!"

He tipped his hat to David, who returned the gesture. In that moment, David sensed a bond begin to form between himself and the flyers. He looked over at L.J. Merrill and the bond grew to include him. Then David felt the beginnings of an equilateral balance between the Maruleans, the Mother Ocean Foundation and the Order of Southern Ocean Mariners. He looked at the sun. They still had two hours before sunset, the dark gray of the wave faces was turning to a deep blue in the rich afternoon light, and the innermost limits of the tubes were starting to glow from the rays shining down the tunnels.

"You may all stay as long as you like. Ka'unua is not going to suffer from your presence. And if you want to go and ride these waves there is no reason for you not to." He stood up and turned to his wife to help her to her feet.

"In fact, I'm sure the ancestors are curious to see you ride waves now that my father has made surfing a new part of their traditions!" laughed Luan.

* * *

Roberto Mercante was on the wing of the *Aeolus.* The locator system was at its very limits, but the grid established around the reef displayed clearly on his screen, as did the beacons in the lifevests of all the people on surfboards and jetskis around Ka'unua, including L.J. Merrill and Jack Richards. The *Serena* was floating about a mile south of the take-off zone. She was acting as observation buoy, recording information about the shoaling, refraction, and dynamic power of the waves, and sending signals to the *Tom Swift* with wave heights and counts for each set.

With Randy Laine and Bob Rowe riding safety and Bruddah towing him, Sonny-boy got the first ride. He played it safe for the first part of the wave towering ninety feet over his head. Through the middle section of the wave, he cut back slightly so he could see the lip starting to peel far above him. Then he stood perfectly still before arching with his hands over his head, a salute to Taveka and the soul of a man he would never forget.

On the other side of the reef, Frank Bucher surfed the *Tom Swift* across two waves to give L.J. Merrill and Jack Richards a first hand look at the wall of a ninety foot wave as seen from the cockpit of an Alba_Sword. After the second wave, the *Tom Swift* paused for a few minutes behind the reef. The two surfers got out their boards, threw them over the side, and then began to paddle the distance up the reef, going up and over huge waves with nothing but their arms to power them. There was no doubt they would need a tow to catch the giant waves, but they wanted to pay at least some homage to the idea of surfing without machines.

Bruddah brought Sonny-boy around to the takeoff zone where Heath Larson waited with Aleja Gracellen.

"Wilson, is this anything that a lady should be doing?" she asked.

"By all means, mademoiselle, by all means. The thrill of the encounter will saturate all your senses."

"Ok, Heath, but I want to go left!"

Out and around the takeoff zone went the three jet skis. Heath Larson towed Aleja Gracellen into wave number six of the set. He kept an eye on her, as did Bruddah, Noaloa and Randy Laine. Bob Rowe had his eye on her, too, filming the wave as the woman who danced with the sea flew across a huge liquid stage of curving turquoise, poised like a ballerina at the top of the wave before dropping toward the bottom to lean into a curving track accentuated by the graceful line of her extended arms. Halfway down the reef the formation went past L.J. Merrill and Jack Richards paddling out. Moments later Aleja finished her wave, and without a second's hesitation, Randy Laine raced back and offered the two men a tow to get them up to the takeoff zone.

"I appreciate the effort you guys are making," he said, "But the sun's going down, the surf is coming up, so grab a line and let's get you out there!"

"Thanks, Randy," acknowledged L.J. Merrill, "But if we get just one wave, that's all we really need."

"And I paid five million bucks to OSOM, so let Frank Bucher tow us!" laughed Jack Richards.

Out from behind the entrance to the lagoon came the *Tom Swift* with two new passengers, David and Luan. Chip Bell had just received a message from the *Serena* about the biggest set of the day headed for Ka'unua. Bucher gunned the thrusters and powered up the reef to the takeoff zone. When he came up next to Richards and Merrill, Tak Kurosawa threw them each a tow line connected to the transom of the *Tom Swift*. David and Luan were fascinated by the Alba_Sword, especially since using a sailing vessel to tow a surfer was something David had in mind that very morning, although it seemed ages ago.

Wave number four was pushing a hundred feet according to the *Serena*. It looked a lot bigger when L.J. Merrill and Jack Richards rode it together, safely out on the shoulder, along the perfect reef of Ka'unua.

Sonny-boy rode another right and went through a tube so big it almost looked like the jet skis could fit inside it with him. They re-grouped near the *Aeolus* where Owens and Charleton had joined Mercante after re-setting anchors all around the seaplane.

Now it was Heath Larson's turn, with Aleja driving. It was a singular moment for both of them. He had not ridden a wave since the one that almost killed him. She was now entrusted with the life of a man looking to regain his faith in himself and did not take that trust lightly. But although it was a serious moment for Larson, she knew he'd appreciate getting a healthy dose of her inner spirit. And since she was in control, he didn't have any choice.

She redlined the engine and gouged a trail of white water in the ocean like a dragster burning rubber off the line. Larson was barely able to hold on to the tow bar. She knew how fast she could go on the big Yamaha, and within seconds she was zooming around at almost sixty miles per hour. But Larson was game for Aleja's test of his mettle, and the run back up the reef was more performance slalom water skiing than it was a surfer getting a tow. When they got back to the takeoff zone, Aleja saw the *Serena* on the top of what she knew was going to be another hundred footer when it hit the reef.

She jammed a long curving power turn, as Laine and Bruddah came up the reef, to whip Heath Larson across the face of the forming pyramid. He let go of the towbar and carved a hard turn against as he dropped down the face. He saw the white water of the impact zone two hundred yards ahead of him. He set up a continuously curving turn, the apex of its arc almost fifty yards from the impact zone, that would take him back up to the top. He paused and felt his entire being lit up and ready to ride as he always had.

He repeated the exact same maneuver, this time coming within twenty yards of the impact zone. One more turn and this time he grazed the edge of the white water with so much speed that in the blink of an eye he was back up to the top of the wave. For a second he paused again, and everyone looked to see what the legendary surfer would do next, hoping he was no longer interested in simply standing alone inside a giant wave. Larson felt all eyes on him, and he knew why. It was a moment of truth. He responded, and a new authenticity rose within him. What once was a longing for solitude had been replaced by the limitless boundaries of distance and speed in graceful arcs. His track began to complement the beautiful curve of the breaking tube, and everyone breathed a sigh of relief. The last section began to loom ahead, but he did not drop back down the face of the wave. He simply turned off the top and exited cleanly and safely as the wave imploded over the inside section. Heath Larson had learned his limits, because Taveka had shown him what happens when you go past them. Yet Taveka's act was one of courage. His time had come. Heath Larson felt he had a lot more to do with his life before he faced that final challenge.

The jetskis circled around him and came to a stop as the last wave of the set rolled under them. Larson smiled at Bruddah and Sonny-boy, but he saved his words for Aleja Gracellen.

"Ok, Aleja, you made your point," he laughed, "I hereby pronounce myself a changed man, ok?"

"Finally!" she smiled, "Now don't forget, when you come to Malibu, you'll need some training! Probably about three weeks worth!"

Then another set came through, and the shadows of the huge waves began to extend across the lagoon. An hour had gone by with waves seen and ridden unlike any in the history of surfing. But unlike most amazing surf sessions, everyone knew when to stop. There was no longing for "one more wave" after they'd truly felt the phenomenal wonder of waves ten stories high, shaped as if by a machine, powered by a storm two thousand miles away that had more in store for them on the morrow.

When the sun touched the western horizon, everyone was back on the wing of the *Aeolus* watching it go down. Another huge set came through. The sun was visible through each successive trough between the waves, until the largest waves began to block it out. The last wave was so big and its base so broad that by the time it had passed in front of them, the sun was gone.

For a few hours after dark, the lights from the Alba_Swords and the Catalina PBY mirrored brightly across the lagoon of Ka'unua. The men and women spending their first night at the sacred reef of the Marulean sea people were conscious of not only where they were, far out to sea in the remote reaches of the South Pacific, but also the extraordinary circumstances in which they found themselves. Yet despite the landmark surf session in the late afternoon, there was no adrenalized excitement amongst the surfers and sailors once the last light of day was gone into the night. Everyone ate quietly, and within a few short hours, the lights dimmed and all slept deeply in their berths.

On the platform of the voyaging craft in the center of the lagoon, Luan slept soundly as did the child within her womb.

Not so her husband. His inner calm kept him awake. He was sensing change in the ocean, and between brief snatches of sleep, he was fully alert, once again in the trance of the navigator. It was the same powerful state of mind he'd summoned to hold himself together in the face of the seaplane's arrival and Taveka's imminent departure. He knew he'd been lucky Aleja Gracellen had been his first contact with the surfers. Otherwise he might have made mistakes from which there would have been no return to grace. But once Taveka had ridden his last wave, he readily assumed the role of leadership for which he had trained. The *Aeolus* and the Alba_Swords, having come to the reef for waves and revenge, had been absorbed into his thinking almost effortlessly. All it took was the tortured soul of L.J. Merrill speaking words of regret about Ian Clark, the man ultimately responsible for all the visitors to Ka'unua, who had paid the ultimate price for his folly. David Helmares knew there was no cause to extract anything more from the soul of L.J. Merrill or anything else from those who were here because Merrill had seen Ka'unua from the air so long ago. He felt the approval of his course of action by Taveka and the navigators, and through his half-closed eyes he saw the lights reflecting across the lagoon as those of campfires going back to the dawn of history, giving warmth to the faith and hopes of human beings.

Throughout the night David never slept for more than a few minutes at a time. He remained tuned to the rhythms of the waves around the reef and the movements of his voyaging craft in the wind inside the circle of Ka'unua. Then, just as a crescent moon began to rise an hour or so before first light, he sensed a change. He felt a tiny swell roll under him.

It would not have been noticed by anyone other than one trained and practiced in using the slightest wave motion to gauge the ocean's changes. Many seconds passed. Another swell came through the hulls. The message was clear. Ka'unua was losing its ability to resist the energy of waves.

He felt a cold breeze begin to spring up from the southwest as the black of night began to soften. The roar of explosions was all around him, reverberating through the trillions of water molecules floating in the air from the relentless onslaughts of oceanic power exploding in precision paths around Ka'unua. He looked out to the south where the stars on the horizon were being obscured by each successive wall of water. He looked over at the *Aeolus*, the dim glow of her cockpit lights shimmering across the lagoon. Then his eye caught the silhouette of the Alba_Swords, and he thought he saw some movement.

Two sets came and went before he saw a white wake coming straight towards him across the lagoon. At first he thought it was a jetski, and even so he watched it with a welcoming emotion that he realized felt wonderfully refreshing. Then in the growing light he soon saw not the profile of a waverunner, but the flat outline of a surfboard. He could not imagine how anyone could paddle a surfboard that fast, but he didn't ask questions when Frank Bucher came up alongside the voyaging craft. Helmares reached down, their hands held strong, and in one motion, Bucher was on the platform. The eyes of the two men met and did not let go. Nor did their grasps.

"You didn't get to ride any waves, yesterday," said Bucher.

"I rode a lot of waves yesterday without ever getting wet."

"Well put. We have tried to build our Order on the honor you showed us."

"I had a good teacher."

"Yes, maybe someday you'll have time to tell me about him."

"Yes, maybe someday."

"I have a gift for you in appreciation of your kindness to us."

"Frank, it was easy once I felt the pain in the heart of L.J. Merrill. And then, of course, there's a lot of beautiful waves all around us to smooth out the rough edges. It's the most amazing swell I've ever seen."

"Maybe the most amazing swell ever. And that's why I'm here. You have yet to ride a wave, and I would like to give you that opportunity."

"How can you do that? Tow-in surfing is just not my style. I learned a lot by example from Taveka, but I think how he caught his last wave was one lesson I'm going to ignore."

"I understand. Let me explain. When you were aboard the *Tom Swift*, I noted your curiosity about its systems, especially the propulsion units. I have modified that technology for a surfboard. I have never used it in surf over fifteen feet or so, but the speed it can give you would be enough to get into these waves. I would like to give it to you."

He pointed to the board floating next to the voyaging craft.

"It is not for bombing around like a waverunner, but used properly, it can open up new realms of surfing for you."

The surfer in David Helmares leapt at chance, like an excited teenager with a new board, to go and try it out on a surf trip with good waves guaranteed.

"You're on, Frank! And now that I think about it, I'll get to show Taveka something new! Meet you back at your boat in about twenty minutes. I'll get the other voyaging craft and we'll go around the reef and give it a good look."

David ducked back into the shelter dome and whispered to his wife.

"I've got to go check the surf. I'll be right back."

She pulled him down to her and kissed him deeply. Then she let him go. She knew it was navigator stuff.

David swam across the lagoon to Taveka's voyager. He had done nothing to exercise his muscles for several days, his sailing notwithstanding. Now the stretch of his arms and the rhythmic breathing of his lungs refreshed and energized him. He came up to the old craft of his mentor. He knew every inch of it. With its cargo now removed and given to Roberto Mercante, the craft exuded a warm, familiar welcome. He quickly raised the coral anchor and released the lines securing her to the reef. The foresail went up easily, the tiller went hard over, and David went slicing across the lagoon towards the Alba_Swords silhouetted against the stars until he dropped sail and drifted up to the *Tom Swift*. Bucher handed him the board. It felt no heavier than the board he had made for Taveka. It was not a featherweight by any means, but that was often an advantage in big waves. He admired its fluid lines and was about to thank Bucher when the gift turned into an exchange for a favor.

"Say, I've got some friends and do you think they can come, too?"

David Helmares laughed as memories of countless surf trips in his first car came to him. He had the only wheels in his group of friends for a while, and as soon as the word got out that he was going surfing, his buddies were always ready to jump in.

"Sure, Frank! As long as they pay for gas!"

"Ok, I'll be right back. Oh, and don't worry! They aren't bringing their boards!" He could barely get the words out while trying to keep his voice down and laugh at the same time. He tiptoed across the deck of the *Tom Swift*. He tapped three times on the porthole of the *Serena*. two figures emerged, jumped across to the *Tom Swift*, and followed Bucher. David heard whispers in the darkness.

"Charles Atkins, captain of the *Serena*. Permission aboard?"

"Ken Bucher, able-bodied passenger, the *Serena*. Permission aboard?"

Helmares had to stifle his laugh.

"Only if you guys brought some wax! Sure, let's get going!"

The two stepped down lightly to the outer hull and tightroped across the beams. Bucher stepped down to the voyaging craft and pushed away from the *Tom Swift* in one smooth motion. The voyager drifted towards the entrance and a set came through so they no longer had to whisper.

"Thanks David. Next time we'll go in my car, I mean boat!"

David Helmares was quick with a rejoinder.

"What next time, Frank? Maybe you guys are kooks and I won't want to be seen with you. Let's find out! Charlie, the foresail. Young man, the main! And you, Frank, got that board lashed down?"

"Aye-aye, sir!"

"Good! Then you're the ballast. All hands! Raise sails and hold on!"

The voyaging craft accelerated towards the mouth of the lagoon. Her passengers were amazed at the speed. The crescent moon was well above the eastern horizon. It would not be long before first light. The roar of the waves was deafening, but it was no competition for the laughter of the men.

"How many times did we do that as kids? Sneaking out of the house, rolling the car down the street so it wouldn't wake anyone!"

"Frank! We had to roll it because it wouldn't start!" laughed Atkins, "That's why we always had a carload – we needed the muscle to get 'er going!"

"Oh man, how many dawn patrols to Oxnard from Santa Monica," David reminisced, "and then up to Rincon for the afternoon."

"Or camping out up at Jalama!" grinned Bucher, shaking his head, "and trying to sneak past Floyd into the Ranch! And now look at us! I sure hope this endless adolescence is good for something!"

Young Ken Bucher was, as always, absorbing all he could. He listened to the camaraderie of the men in the stories they told. He studied the design of the voyaging craft and the way her sails caught so much wind she almost seemed like she could fly. And, of course, he was seeing waves bigger than anything he had ever imagined, though while looking at their crests, he took note of several constellations that he'd never seen before.

Helmares set a course to the deep water where even the biggest waves of the previous days had been reduced to rolling hills with gradual slopes. He wanted to get a first impression of the true change in the ocean. After going up the steep face of but one swell, his instincts were confirmed.

"It's a lot bigger, guys."

"That's ok! You're the guy going surfing! We're just gonna watch, bro!" said Frank Bucher with a wicked grin.

"Yeah, gee, thanks! Hey, wait a minute! How do I know that board even works?" Helmares could barely suppress a smile.

"Charlie, the man doesn't believe the board works as advertised. A demonstration, if you will!"

Atkins stepped lightly along the center hull and unlashed the board. He pressed his hands onto the deck and wrapped his fingers around two shallow handholds. He squeezed them, and a small string of LED indicators glowed green across the nose of the bright yellow board.

"Ok, Mr. chief navigator of the Marulean sea people," said Frank Bucher, in a car salesman's voice, "Allow Captain Charles Atkins of the Order of Southern Ocean Mariners to personally demonstrate the advantages of being the proud owner of an Alba_Sword surfboard!"

502

The voyaging craft was trimming at an angle across a big swell standing up in very deep water. Suddenly Charles Atkins leaped off the outer hull with the board pointing down the slope of the wave.

David Helmares couldn't believe his eyes. Atkins and the board accelerated with an amazing jolt of speed. Atkins stood up, did a hard turn, and there he was riding the wave right next them!

"Now, what else can I show you, David? How about some turns! And some soul to go with 'em!" yelled Atkins as he slalomed down the face with his inimitable style and flow.

""Hey! That's my board! Give it back! The sun's coming up and I gotta go surfing before I go to work!" said David Helmares, laughing louder than he had in a long, long time.

The eastern sky was getting brighter, clearly illuminating waves so big the men had to look up at the crests. They were still in deep water and nowhere near the massive energy of the breaking waves. Or so they thought.

"Hey! David! Punch it!"

Helmares saw the wall standing up sixty feet above his mast. He helmed hard over and filled his sails with wind.

"It's really big out here! Maybe we should go in!" teased Frank Bucher.

"Naw, I got it all under control!" laughed David Helmares, smiling even as the next wave stood up a hundred feet high. The sun touched the horizon, and from almost a mile out to sea, the men could observe the rights of Ka'unua. The waves were still holding great shape, though yesterday's perfection was gone. The offshore wind out of the north had switched to a southwester just breezing up and beginning to texture the wave faces with fields of tiny bumps. From high on one crest David looked all around him and saw that the entire ocean was beginning to show signs of upheaval.

"Hey, I better get one or two waves, and then we should get back. It's going to get pretty heavy today."

"Yup! That's what we figured! Here, let me take the tiller! Charlie, show him how to use the handles. Kenny! You're on the sails. Let's get out there!"

For an instant David Helmares couldn't quite accept what was going on. But there was something about Frank Bucher's utter self-confidence, Atkins' sharp and precise manner, and the steadiness of Ken Bucher that immediately put him at ease. They were a team par excellence, and if he was to be the beneficiary of their spirit and generosity, it was something not to be missed.

"Ok, David, when you grab the handles, the lights glow green. When you turn them like this, off she goes! She'll give you a five second burst. Then she shuts down automatically. That's all you need. Once you're on your feet, stay low until you're halfway down the slope. Then the trick will be to time your first turn, like a soloist coming in on an orchestra."

Atkins had never seen David Helmares surf before, so he added a cautionary note.

"When we've ridden waves this size on the Alba_Swords, one thing I learned is to adjust my rhythm to the size of the waves. Set up your bottom turn in the biggest arc you can imagine and flow all the way to the top. When you drop back in, don't go rigid. Stay loose and keep turning in rhythm."

"Thanks for the tip, Charlie. I get it. There are a lot of notes to each measure, so don't come up short."

"Yeah! Something like that. Its music on a whole different scale, so you've got to adjust your chops, as it were."

"Will do. Frank! Get us a hundred yards dead south of the impact zone!"

With an expert's advice well heeded, David Helmares felt fully prepared. From that moment on, he never gave a second thought to what he was about to do. With Bucher at the helm, the voyaging craft coursed out to sea. The wind felt much stronger, and since Atkins and Bucher guaranteed the surf was going to get bigger, he knew he didn't have much time.

"I want to get a test run. Wave number three of the next set. Follow me down a ways and then come get me when I kick out! See ya, guys!"

Helmares grabbed the board and launched off the outer hull. The horizon lifted above sea level. The next set was on its way.

Helmares grabbed the handles and turned them. He was ready for the acceleration and the board shot forward. Just as Atkins said would happen, the thrust shut down after five seconds. The board had incredible glide. David knew this whole thing was going to work.

The first wave of the set was as big as Taveka's wave, but David ignored it. The second wave showed the true character of the set. It was easily a hundred feet high if not bigger. David now knew what to expect of the remainder of the set.

Wave number three was still about two hundred yards away. He turned the board around and began to paddle hard towards the reef. He felt himself being slowly lifted skyward. With the wind coming from slightly behind him, he was not blinded by spray. He saw the entire ring of Ka'unua, with the Alba_Swords and the seaplane at the far end of the lagoon. Then he noticed he was looking DOWN at the lagoon almost half a mile away.

He waited until he was near the threatening crest of the swell. He turned the handles, and the board shot down the face of the wave. He looked up and saw he was about halfway to the impact zone. When the propulsion system shut down, he was going so fast he just held on for a second, like a beginning surfer taking off on his first big one. Then he jumped up into a low crouch and entered into a new dimension of surfing, feeling a sensation as primal as that which he'd felt on his very first wave ridden so long ago.

He saw the edge of the impact zone to his left. He turned to his right. The wave had some bump to it, but nothing he couldn't absorb with his knees flexed. He was under no illusions about trying to ride close to the giant tube behind him, at least not on this wave, as he raced for the shoulder. With its shape derived from the broadbill swordfish, the board had unbelievable momentum. He had never experienced anything like it, but he was not slow to use the special qualities of the board right away to carve a few turns before cruising out and over the top of the wave. Looking out to sea he saw the rest of the set. With luck he knew he could get the last one.

Bucher came up fast and Ken dropped the sails right on time before the voyaging craft did a sharp turn and slowed almost to a stop. David handed the board to Atkins standing on the bow and pulled himself aboard near the stern.

"Raise sail! Let's get the last one of this set and then we're outta here!"

The wind was getting stronger. Frank Bucher had quickly mastered the voyager and instinctively had her running at top speed back out to the take off zone. There were only two more waves in the set when they got there, each a monster, but still with ridable shape.

"See you guys all the way inside! Let's ride it together, but stay way out there so I don't hit your wake!"

David Helmares launched himself with a powerful leap off the transom of the center hull and immediately began paddling furiously. Bucher put the helm over as Atkins and his son trimmed the sails to stay out ahead of David Helmares on their last wave.

The navigator set his course towards the impact zone. He felt himself lifted skyward. He twisted the handles. The board accelerated. He matched the speed of the swell. The thrusters shut down. He stood up. He was surfing.

David Helmares let his imagination run free. He went to the bottom of the wave and did a hard turn, careful to draw it out all the way up to the top of the wave. Down he went a second time, his stance rock solid and the board responding perfectly. He carved the hardest turn of his life, but quickly wished he had a little more bite in the tail as he felt it go a bit squiggly on him. He backed off the throttle and thought of Taveka's board and how they'd modified it until it was exactly what his mentor needed. Far down the wave in front of him he saw Taveka's old voyager. Then he knew all the navigators were watching his every move, so he decided to show them something special.

The tube was coming over behind him. He saw the edge of the impact zone and turned towards it for just an instant before slicing the board into a soul-arch turn that left him completely inside the barrel. For an instant he was blinded by the morning sun until he saw the huge wall turn translucent blue. With unmatched grace and poise, he carved a series of beautiful turns inside the wave with the power of the ocean at his disposal and an audience of his peers cheering him on.

The wave was now going into its final section. David smiled at the thought of his mentor entering the final tube of his life. He turned around, and for an instant he caught a glimpse of the liquid cathedral that Taveka had chosen to enter. Then his surfing instincts took over, driving him forward with a series of check turns to gain all the speed he could. The giant wave collapsed behind him, expelling a huge cloud of spray from its mouth that almost knocked him off his board. He crouched for balance and held on until the wave began to re-form into a rolling hill of water, now free of Ka'unua to continue its journey across the open sea.

David cut back towards his left. Frank Bucher did the same, both trimming across the flats until they were in front of the lagoon passage. They matched their slowing speeds, and with a final flourish, David stepped aboard the outer hull exactly when Charles Atkins picked the board up out of the water. Bucher came about and the voyaging craft was suddenly gliding calmly into the lagoon with four passengers grinning from ear to ear.

"Ok you guys, see ya for breakfast. Gotta go check on the wife! Later!"

The passengers dove into the water and the voyaging craft accelerated across the lagoon under full sail. At the last instant David dropped the sails and steered the voyager right into place next to his own. He tied the two craft together and hopped across the hulls. He slid under the shelter dome and laid down next to his wife, all in one motion.

"So, how was your sesh?"

David Helmares was so stoked he didn't think before opening his mouth.

"Unreal, honey. My new board works great!"

"New board? What new board? You never told me you were getting a new board! And you told me you were just going to check the surf, not ride it! We'll have to talk about this later," said his wife as if he was in big trouble, and it took him a second to come around.

"Hey, wait a minute! How did you know I was going surfing?"

"What, you think I'm going to let you go out there without knowing exactly what was going to happen? Frank Bucher had an idea, I liked it, and that's all you need to know for now."

The sun was now well above the eastern horizon. Heath Larson, the first person up on the wing of the *Aeolus*, took a look out to sea immediately knew nobody would be surfing today. Not only was the southwest wind kicking up white caps out to sea, but the surf was now so big that it didn't look like surf at all. He thought of what surf was around the world, lapping under a deck of a beach house in Malibu, or rolling gently across the reefs of Waikiki, or splashing the tourists on the beaches of France in August. This was not surf. This was an ocean transformed.

A set was just starting to come in. The first wave almost blocked out the entire horizon from east to west. The wave began breaking directly in front of Ka'unua with good shape in both directions. But no pyramid peak had formed up in the takeoff zone. It was just one giant wall all the way across.

"Well, Heath, whatcha got goin' out there t'day?" asked Mac Owens as he climbed up on the wing.

"Well, you could surf it if you had to. But when it looks like this in the islands, its better to be on the beach wishing you were surfing than be paddling for your life wishing you were on the beach!"

Owens laughed at Larson's re-wording of the old pilot's maxim. Bruddah and Sonny-boy joined them, and the big Hawaiian could only shake his head when he saw the size of the surf.

"Dees waves too big. Gimme one kine fun wave Waikiki we get home. No jetski, no rescue guys, just sum fun cruisin', brah."

"Yeah, but it's still got good shape! You could make those waves!"

"Not with this wind, Sonny-boy," said Larson, "It's only getting stronger, and there's already a cross chop out there."

"Yeah, but guys surf Mavericks with the wind from the same direction."

"True, but right now these waves are twice the size of any Mavericks wave I've ever seen."

"And it IS going to get even bigger!"

The men on the wing were surprised to hear Charles Atkins' voice with Frank Bucher and his son right behind him. They came up on the wing and were dripping wet.

"Don't tell me you guys were out there?" exclaimed Larson incredulously.

"Yeah, you really missed it! It was perfect at dawn!" said Frank Bucher. "Hey, why don't you all come over for breakfast? It's going to be one helluva day!"

The cockpits of the Alba_Swords were designed to accommodate three people. There was little room to spare, but that didn't bother any of the crew members and guests eating and talking and gesturing at the waves coming out of the south. After a good night's sleep, everyone was in high spirits.

Nelson Roberts was duty cook on the *Serena*, with Tak Kurosawa doing the same on the *Tom Swift*. Clem Charleton, Mac Owens and Randy Laine were below decks getting a tour from Ken Bucher and Chip Bell. L.J. Merrill was sitting with Roberto Mercante out on the foredeck of the *Tom Swift*, talking about Merrill's ideas for co-op surf camps under the flag of the Mother Ocean Foundation. Aleja Gracellen couldn't have been happier getting away from a planeload of men and visiting with Margo Atkins and Patty McRane.

Heath, Sonny-boy and Bruddah were being tortured by Atkins and Bucher about how they'd REEEALLLY missed it.

"Man, that David Helmares! No jetski! In the tube! How long was he in there Frank?"

"Oh, at least twenty seconds! I had to stop counting!"

"And boy, those bottom turns! Best big wave surfing I've ever seen!"

Bob Rowe was shooting stills and video at the same time. He was out on the bow of the *Serena*, getting a shot looking across the crowded cockpits toward the south. What he saw stopped all the conversations in mid sentence.

"Hey!!! Everybody! Look south! You guys below! Get up here!"

A long lull had allowed the surfers and sailors to almost forget about the surf. But the surfer's maxim, "The longer the lull, the bigger and longer the set" was never more true than at that moment.

The first swell was clearly visible almost a mile outside the takeoff zone, a solid wall of deep blue water with a ruler-edged crest extending across the horizon from east to west. The very top of the wave began to feather, almost as if it wanted to show off for the spectators by breaking in unbelievably deep water. Then it calmed back down momentarily before entering the shoaling zone of Ka'unua. There it began to reveal its true power by crashing down all at once across the takeoff zone. It was the first close-out wave at Ka'unua.

The white water rolled forward and didn't stop until it was rebuffed by the reef, though once again the wave seemed to have a mind of its own, as if it wanted to ignore Ka'unua entirely. It had to back off, though not without sending a message in the form of a small swell that rolled clear across what had been the untouched inner waters of the lagoon. On either side of the reef the wave went unchecked and broke erratically in huge formless sections.

The second wave of the set completely erased any semblance of Ka'unua as a surfing zone, and another rolling swell disturbed the inner lagoon. Then far outside in the deep water, where the *Serena* had anchored the day before, the third wave actually capped over. A beard of white water fell down its face and rolled forward until the monster smothered the entire surf zone with exploding white water.

Nobody said a word. The swell from the first wave had now come all the way across the lagoon. It rolled under the Alba_Swords and lifted them up in the air. They came back down with a sudden thump. The message was unmistakable, and there were ten more waves coming on strong in case anyone wasn't entirely convinced. The day of reckoning had come to Ka'unua.

David Helmares saw the swell coming across the lagoon. Although the voyaging craft went up and over it with ease, he was not distracted from the real issue he now faced. There would soon be no shelter in the quiet inner waters of Ka'unua. He ducked back under the shelter dome. Luan knew exactly what was going on.

"I'll get everything ready. How much time do you think we have?"

"I'm not sure. There's never been surf like this. I'm going to put your father's craft over the coral circles. Then we'll go talk with our guests and figure out how to keep us all safe."

Charles Atkins was trying to figure out the same thing. He knew how big the surf was going to get. What he didn't know was exactly how the bottom of the ocean southwest of Ka'unua would affect waves now arriving from the K3 storm. He had used the *Serena*'s sensors to map the bottom while on station as a surf report buoy for the sunset surf session of the previous day. Later he compared his imaging with the Navy data, and once again, the Navy map was inaccurate to a significant degree. That left him no alternative but to conclude that the refraction potential at Ka'unua was completely unknown. Of one thing he was certain, however. While his seabed imaging may have been serviceable when determining the shoaling and refraction processes in waves up to a hundred feet, it was almost certainly a whole different story this morning. This wave confirmed his fears, and he didn't wait for the last wave to go by before commanding everyone's attention.

"I was hoping it wouldn't happen, but this set is telling me it will. The seamounts and canyons south of here are beginning to affect the size of the waves. We knew we could expect waves this afternoon that will be twice as big as yesterday based on what we knew about the storm that made them. What we didn't know was how those swells would be shaped as they came towards Ka'unua. Now I'm sure we can't count on shelter at Ka'unua when the peak energy pulses show up later today. I'm pretty certain that where we are anchored right now will be under fifty feet of white water by dark."

"But, but, how can it do that?" asked Aleja Gracellen, "If it's flat here when its eighty feet, why would that happen if the surf is only twice as big?"

"Good question. Yes, it is only doubling in size, but the amount of water below the surface can increase by a factor of eight. The entire ocean starts to move in really big swells, and the sea bottom starts to exert exponential forces on the waves."

"Oh, yeah, that's right. My dad used to tell me about how that works in Oxnard," said Gracellen, "It can be flat at Zuma and six feet up there."

"Exactly. Silverstrand's a great example," said L.J. Merrill, "thanks to the underwater canyon at the entrance to Port Hueneme. Black's does the same thing. And there are a lot places around the world where the deep sea bottom changes the surf completely. In fact, that's why we're here."

Merrill had everyone's attention as he explained how he found Ka'unua.

"I looked all over the world for a place like this, at the confluence of a subsurface system of seamounts and canyons, exposed directly to open ocean wave trains. From the data I had, which of course was NOT as good as the Navy data," he glanced at Bucher and Atkins who smiled with sheepish grins and downcast glances, "I knew this area could be holding big waves. Then I found ships' logs and, uh, other stuff that of course I can't reveal - - -"

"Yeah, stuff he hasn't even told ME about that cost me a bundle!" said Jack Richards with a hearty laugh that cracked a lot of smiles all around.

"Hey, I was a pro when it came to being an addict, what can I say? But those days are over, I hope. Anyway, it took me a long time to figure it all out, and then get a chance to fly close enough to get a look. I tried to get Ian to let me reconnoiter this place with the *Skyhook*, but he was too far gone down the road to riches. So I had to wait, and I lucked out, though I guess in the end he sure didn't, God rest his soul."

Merrill suddenly stopped talking and looked out to sea. Then he looked at Charles Atkins.

"So, Captain Atkins, as you were saying?"

"Uh, yeah, L.J., you really did an amazing job finding it the way you did. I'm pretty sure there's not another wave in the world that can hold the exact same shape from ten feet to a hundred feet. But now we've got the biggest swell in recorded history. If we were a hundred miles to the east or west, it would not be nearly as big given the narrow broadcast band of the storm's most powerful winds. That's why we came here – to acquire some maximum numbers. We thought we could do it safely. Now I don't think we can."

"So what are the options?" asked Heath Larson.

"As scientists, sailors or surfers?" said Sonny-boy Noaloa perceptively.

"As scientists, we stick it out to the bitter end, send data till we drop, and get our PhD's posthumously. As sailors, we get the hell out of here right now. Head for the deepest ocean we can find around here and hope there are no surprises. But with this wind coming up that's a pretty rough option, if at all."

"I'm gonna git us sum info 'bout that right now," said Clem Charleton. He dove off the railing of the *Tom Swift* and swam back to the *Aeolus*.

"Yeah, we like to keep it simple on an Alba_Sword, so we don't really know what the wind is going to do. But worst case? As sailors we'd make it, but it wouldn't be any fun."

"Well, then, sounds like we're stuck being surfers!" said Margo Atkins.

"Sorry dear, but you're right," said Atkins, gazing again to the south, "Here comes another set."

The voyaging craft floated above him against the blue sky as David dove deep to the center of the coral circles. There was no tradition for him to follow in doing this, but he felt happy with the idea of touching the sand with his hands where his offerings to the ancestors rested. When he reached the bottom, he saw the carvings, right where he had left them, now buried a little deeper but still visible. They would sink over time until the next navigator, David's son, would bring sixteen offerings of his own. He thought of his mentor, and happiness filled his heart. Taveka was now with his wife and his ancestors, leaving him to face the changes at Ka'unua and make the necessary decisions about what course to take as chief navigator of the Maruleans. Had he made mistakes, he would have felt admonition, or remorse. But no, the navigators were satisfied with how he had faced the challenges and he had their blessing. He exhaled some air, and the bubbles danced and played up to the surface. It was time to follow them, but as he surfaced his happiness changed to a feeling of farewell. Then his mind was filled by a single clear thought.

"Come back soon and visit us. And bring your friends."

David paddled his new board slowly away from Taveka's old voyaging craft now secured by a single sea anchor above the coral circles. He stopped and looked back for an instant. Then he laughed when he knew there was one navigator's tradition that would remain intact.

After all, Taveka," he said, aloud, "You told me Ka'unua means 'the reef that eats the old outrigger', and we can't let the reef go hungry, now can we?"

He turned and began to paddle in earnest. Glancing over his shoulder, he saw another wave closing out across what had been the takeoff zone. Within seconds the wave pushed over the coral and turned into another swell rolling across the lagoon. Then he realized what his new board could do.

The next swell in the lagoon was almost three feet high. He looked back through its transparent face and for a second he saw, in the beautiful colors reflecting through the crystal clear water, a circle of sixteen images. Fifteen were almost identical to the carvings he'd offered to the navigators. One was the smiling face of a man he'd never forget.

He twisted the handles. The board shot forward. Seconds later he was standing erect, riding the rolling swell across the lagoon. He put his feet together, arched his back, and raised his arms above his head in the same hood ornament pose that Taveka had learned so well.

"Hey! Look at that!" exclaimed Margo Atkins.

Everyone turned and saw David Helmares riding an unbroken, rolling swell across the lagoon angling towards his voyaging craft, set against a backdrop of unfathomable power, a vision never to be forgotten by the visitors to Ka'unua. They had gathered on board the Alba_Swords to determine their next course of action.

"Let's wait till he gets here," said Frank Bucher, and then we'll talk."

"Well, one thing I kin tell y'all right now," said Clem Charleton, treading water next to the *Tom Swift*, "The s'wester gonna come up to fifty, sixty knots. Seems your waves are somehow pushin' up their own weather!"

"What if we use the *Aeolus* as a scout?" said Roberto Mercante.

"That's exactly what I was going to suggest," said David Helmares, now with Luan in the cockpit of the *Tom Swift* after bringing their voyaging craft across the lagoon.

"Even though I know all the reefs, atolls, and seamounts between here and our home island, I don't know what will happen when waves this big come sweeping through the Archipelago."

"Yes, and it's unfortunate these waves are so big. We planned to take my father's voyager back with us," said Luan.

"You mean you were going to sail it alone?" said a wide-eyed Aleja.

"Of course! I am the daughter of a navigator. And I am the wife of a navigator!" she said with a laugh.

"Ok, let's get this straight," said Frank Bucher, "We are going to surfsail north through the Nebula Archipelago with David as our guide and the *Aeolus* scouting ahead to avoid any surprises."

"Yes, we don't want surprises, such as trap-door suck out sections across two or three miles of undersea ridges six hundred feet deep!" said Tak Kurosawa.

"Exactly. And the further north we go, the more we can count on wave shadowing to reduce the size of the waves," said Helmares.

"Unless," said L.J. Merrill, "the sea bottom starts funneling the wave energy and we find ourselves riding a building wave, not a diminishing one."

"And if it does," said Frank Bucher with a pause, "Then - - -"

"We count on the *Aeolus* to see far enough ahead and get us out of trouble," said Helmares, finishing Bucher's sentence without hesitation. The two men looked at each other and realized their minds were right in synch.

"How are we going to communicate?" asked Chip Bell, "We've only got Morse code on board, and you guys only have VF radios."

"No problem, brah!" said Bruddah, "We got da kine helmets! Got da radio inside!"

"And with the direct line of sight, the signal will be loud and clear," said Randy Laine.

"But what about your voyaging craft, David?" asked Bob Rowe.

"We are sailing her home, one way or another. We've got a following wind. We'll be able to keep up just fine!"

The word 'we' stuck in his mind for a second. He thought about his wife, and the child inside her. Then he thought of the man who had done a very good job of sailing his voyaging craft that morning. That gave him an idea to discuss with Luan and Frank Bucher.

"That settles it, then," said Mac Owens, "I got a seaplane ta prep fer takeoff. How long we gonna stay here?"

"I think we have at least two, maybe three hours," said David Helmares, "We're safe now, but we want as big a wave as we can get going north."

"That's good thinkin'," said Charleton, "We kin see ahead, an' if yer on the biggest waves, the ones in front of y'all will tell us a lot more than if they ain't so big."

"So we wait for the first set of the peak of the swell? Maybe around three this afternoon?" said Jack Richards.

"Taveka's voyager is our indicator. When the wave comes that devours her, we go," said the navigator.

* * *

The sun was high overhead. Taveka's voyager was riding up and over the swells in the lagoon. The sets were 'stair-stepping', each wave bigger than the last, but as long as Taveka's craft held its ground, everyone stayed focused on their jobs.

Clem Charleton was using his radar to measure the first wave of a set while the line of sight across the lagoon was unimpeded. Number one had just measured one hundred and fifty feet high with the crests of the next three waves easily visible behind it. During a lull he checked in with Mac Owens.

"You sure this is gonna work, Mac? Never seen anythin' like it!"

"Aw, c'mon, Clem! Used ta do it alla time during the war! Strap a coupla them JATO bottles back behind tha wings, set 'em off, an' yer' airborne jes like that!"

"Yeah, but why'd they stop usin' 'em? Tell me that mister PBY expert!"

"Well, they were kinda unstable, but I never heard of a jetski blowin' up!"

"Okay, jes' make sure ya got 'em under control!"

"Clem, I been plannin' this out fer a long time! She's gonna work jes fine, don' you worry."

Owens was addressing the weakest link in their plans. Without a lifting wind, the takeoff run of the *Aeolus* was a problem, but Mac's idea of using the waverunners to execute a jet-assisted take-off was the perfect solution. The big Yamahas had horsepower to burn, and Mac had reinforced the landing gear mounts against just such an occasion as this. Now all he had to do was re-set the hydraulics and rig up a throttle control system, though like the JATO rocket bottles used in the war, they had to work the first time because he wouldn't get a second chance.

David discussed HIS idea with Frank Bucher and his wife. Luan was going to fly in the *Aeolus*. Frank Bucher was going to sail on the voyaging craft. With a baby in her womb and a fifteen hour trip ahead of them, she and

512

David had given careful thought to the challenge they faced. If there had been no alternative, they would have made the best of it, come what may. But David had seen the skill with which Frank Bucher had handled the voyager, and when he broached the subject, Bucher accepted willingly. Then they shared their plan with everyone else.

That left only four men aboard the *Tom Swift*. Tak Kurosawa became the commander. With a berth open, Chip Bell nominated Sonny-boy Noaloa as his watchmate. "He's smart as a whip and has great reflexes. And I understand he's a pretty good surfer, and this is all about riding waves, isn't it?"

Noaloa was now aboard the *Tom Swift*, and Bell was running him through a crash course on crewing aboard an Alba_Sword, with Merrill and Richards contributing tips as necessary.

"You'll love it, Sonny-boy! L.J. picked it up right away, though he did sink us the first time!" said Jack Richards.

That gave Roberto Mercante an idea. "Why don't we use the waves to push more of us home instead of aviation fuel? Can you squeeze another man on each Alba_Sword?"

"Well, do tell, Roberto, now that's a pilot's kinda thinking!" exclaimed Clem Charleton.

"And I can take someone," said Helmares, "Say Heath, you want to ride the biggest wave of your life?"

So Bruddah joined the crew of the *Tom Swift*, Randy Laine was brought aboard the *Serena*, and Heath Larson joined Helmares and Bucher on his voyaging craft. Bob Rowe was going to be filming the whole thing from the observation compartment of the *Aeolus*, with Aleja and Luan serving as lookouts up front.

"I've got no problems with my wife telling me where to go," said David.

"And I'm SURE Heath won't mind putting his life in the hands of capable and confident women," said Aleja.

"Charlie and I do it all the time at home!" Frank Bucher's smile was not shared by an almost blushing Heath Larson, who just shrugged his shoulders while remembering what Dolly Artensa had said to him long ago about needing a woman in his life.

"Comm check, *Aeolus*, comm check, please," said the navigator.

"*Aeolus* here," said Roberto Mercante, "Hear you loud and clear."

"Try an open channel," said Clem Charleton, sitting next to him.

"How do you adjust the volume, Roberto?"

"Hold on a second, David, let me get through to Tak and Charlie."

A minute later, Roberto Mercante was in his element carrying on three conversations at once.

"Take off the helmet and you'll see a dial inside. Plus put it on standby once we get going. Saves the batteries."

"How long they good for?"

"Good question, Tak. Hey Randy! Batteries for the helmets on the boats?"

"Good for eight hours continuous use. But we've got spares."

"Got 'em right here," said Bob Rowe, "I'll bring over right away."

"And how waterproof are these things?"

"Good to fifty feet, David."

"Say, David," said Charles Atkins, "You better let Frank try the helmet. He's got a big head and it might not fit!"

"Thanks for the advice, Charlie. Hey Frank, you sure your head's gonna fit inside this thing? Charlie said I'd better check!"

"Sounds good all around, Clem," said Mercante, "*Tom Swift*, out, *Serena*, out, hey, what's your handle, David?"

"Call me Ishmael! Nah, uh, let me think. How about *Dreamboat*? Yeah, that works," said the navigator.

"Ok, everybody power down. Pop in the new batteries when you get 'em. We'll do another check in an hour."

The sun started its westering path. The *Aeolus* radar was now measuring first wave heights at one hundred and eighty feet. Taveka's voyaging craft was barely making it up and over the swells threatening to break in the lagoon. But somehow she kept her prow facing into the energy, almost as if Taveka and his ancestors were aboard her, fearlessly facing wave after wave. They knew the reef was hungry, but it was not dinner time, not yet.

About two thirty in the afternoon, everyone suddenly found themselves with nothing essential to do. The radios for the helmets of the helmsmen were ready to go, and the communication channels were linked to the cockpit of the *Aeolus*. Clem Charleton had his takeoff flight plan clearly in mind. Mac Owens knew the jetskis were going to work thanks to Randy Laine re-wiring their ignitions and connecting them to toggle switches that Mac would control from the cargo bay. Roberto Mercante had given their plan some more thought, and now each man on the *Dreamboat* was going to wear a lifevest with a locator beacon in it. An obvious thing to do, but nobody had thought of it until almost the last minute. Then Aleja brought up another point.

"Won't we be traveling all night? Isn't that even more dangerous?"

"Actually it isn't," said Luan, "David will have his stars, and we'll be able to see the reefs much more easily from the white water breaking over them."

"Yes, but now that I think about it, let's have the Alba_Swords keep their running lights on," said Bob Rowe, "So I'll always have a visual on them."

"And I've got a torch I use for night-fishing," said David Helmares.

Then the quiet of a long lull spread across the twenty one people aboard the Catalina seaplane, the Alba_Sword vessels, and the Polynesian voyager.

It was David Helmares who broke the silence.

"We're gonna need some sailing room to get up to speed, so I think its time we weigh anchor. Between the sharp eyes guiding us from above and the steady and responsive hands on the tillers below, we're as ready as we can be. Just everybody take a minute, and say a few words to someone somewhere.

514

Let them know we each may need a little help on the way. Ask them to come along, at least in our hearts and minds, until we get home sometime early tomorrow morning."

A few minutes passed, and many a quiet "Amen" was heard as each person floated a prayer up to the skies above or the waters below.

"Raise foresail!"

"Raise main!"

The voyaging craft of David Helmares leaped forward, its sails full of the strong, cold wind coming out of the southwest.

"Hard to starboard!"

Larson and Bucher quickly adjusted the sails, and the *Dreamboat* headed out to the eastern side of Ka'unua.

"Control systems up! Thruster systems up! Hydraulics! Rig for surfsail confirmed! Raise the sea anchors! Cast off bowlines! Cast off sterns!"

The Alba_Swords came to life, the decks were cleared, and the *Serena* and the *Tom Swift* headed to their launch positions.

"Ok, Roberto, start 'em up!"

The Pratte & Whitney engines began to turn over, belching a bit of black smoke until they caught and came up to speed.

"Mac! Y'all set back there?"

"Aye-aye, Clem! Lowering away."

The two waverunners settled down gently on either side of the *Aeolus*. Thirty seconds later, both waverunners were idling rapidly and under control.

"Ok, let's cum 'round an' go back up in tha lagoon jes a bit. This wind'll be blowin' us forward, an' I wanna catch that wave an' git airborne right away. Think yer dad's ancestors gonna be ok with that, Luan?"

"Of course! Navigators, and they are always ready for something new."

"Looks like they're all set, David," said Heath Larson.

Helmares had his radio helmet on. He heard Heath, and he heard something else at the same time.

"Roger that, Heath. Bruddah says, "Geevum brah!!""

David Helmares brought the voyager around and off the wind, ready to get all the speed he could. The horizon to the south began to grow dark, as he'd seen it do so many times in the past three days, starting with the day Taveka rode his twenty footers right up to today's dawn patrol surf trip. Throughout it all, the waves were a constant presence against which all things were measured. Now it was time to leave Ka'unua and once again the waves were the focus of his attention. His voyaging craft was almost a mile and a half to the south of reef, near the area where Charles Atkins had positioned the *Serena*. Yet the waves were beginning to stand up even further out to sea.

The first one broke top to bottom in almost four hundred feet of water. The white water was a hundred feet high and a three hundred yards across when it hit the furthest tip of what once was the takeoff zone. But the reef would not budge, and the energy seemed to part to either side. A mighty swell re-formed just inside the reef. Taveka's voyaging craft went up and over it, but its tethering line snapped at the peak.

"Taveka's voyager is floating free, David!" said Frank Bucher.
"Got it, Frank! Here comes another one! Everyone! Hold your positions!"

"Good Lord!" exclaimed Aleja.
"Steady everyone!" said Roberto Mercante, "We're right where we need to be. She'll be eighty feet when she gets here."
"Clem! 'member that patch we laid down in the parkin' lot in Orlando?"
"Sure do, Mac!"

The next wave was beyond belief. Born near the limits of Dr. Joseph Goldman's projections of a two hundred and twenty foot wave, it had decayed a little during its journey across the Southern Ocean to the Nebula Archipelago. However, thanks to the seamounts focusing on Ka'unua, the wave was breaking in over five hundred feet of water. And again, Taveka's craft somehow floated up and over the re-form that almost broke as it rolled towards the seaplanes and the Alba_Swords through the lagoon.

"David! We're goin' on the next one!"
"Roger that, Clem. Alba_Swords?"
"*Serena* ready," said Margo Atkins.
"*Tom Swift* ready," said Tak Kurosawa.
"Ok, we're all on it. See ya in a while! Heath! Hold on to the cross member! Frank! Right next to him!"

The third wave of the set was seemingly limitless in its power. It crushed through the impact zone of the previous two waves and bore down on Ka'unua. This time the wave did not hesitate or reform when it felt the apex of the reef, and Taveka's voyaging craft disappeared like a small toy beneath a landslide.
Halfway down the mile-long lagoon, the wave seemed to pause for just a few seconds before backing off into a giant rolling swell eighty feet high, smooth as glass, and exactly what the *Aeolus* needed.
"Roberto! Count us down! Mac! Together on his signal!"
Bob Rowe was filming from the back of the plane. He didn't know if anyone was ever going to see what was coming through his viewfinder, but if he had to die a happy cameraman, this would do nicely.
"Not yet! Not yet!"
The swell was only twenty yards from the tail of the *Aeolus*.

516

"Steady! Not yet!"

The slope of the wave came under the tail. The seaplane was lifted skyward. Roberto called it on the button.

"Three, two, one – Go!"

Clem Charleton threw the throttles forward, and three thousand horses came to life. Mac Owens hit two toggle switches, and the powerful jetskis added their thrust to the roaring engines. The keel of the *Aeolus* dug into the wave. She rose to the top of the swell, and then down the slope she went. Within seconds Clem Charleton had all the power and speed he needed. He pulled back on the controls, and the *Aeolus* lifted free of the wave, airborne at eighty miles an hour and ready to fly for the next two thousand miles.

Back in the 'sunroom', Bob Rowe heard the rebel yells over the roar of the engines. Then the wave collapsed over the last curves of the elliptical reef and exploded all across the coral before freeing itself of Ka'unua forever. But unlike all previous swells, it did not reform cleanly, and fifty feet of white water continued to roll down its face as it moved into the deep water where the *Serena* and the *Tom Swift* were waiting.

"All thrusters, now!"

The Alba_Swords dropped down the face just ahead of the white water, quickly coming up to speed to ride the majestic power of the massive wave.

L.J. Merrill, the third man in the cockpit of the *Tom Swift*, was on the heaviest wave of his life. It wasn't a perfect tube, and he was sharing it with others, but it knew it was a great way to end his entire surfing career. He looked up and saw the *Aeolus* circling like a giant albatross, its long white wings stretched and relaxed, gliding above to give guidance to those below. Far down the line he saw the *Serena* with two women at the helm. Now all he needed was for the *Dreamboat* to join them, and L.J. Merrill's sense of family and belonging would be complete. This was his final step in leaving his addiction, and the memories of what had happened between him and Ian Clark, in a past he would never re-visit again.

"Did those guys go? Hey, Tak, what about the *Dreamboat*?" L.J. Merrill felt a familiar sensation of anxiety hit him where it always had, right in the heart. "Scout! What about the *Dreamboat*! David! Where are you? Roberto, where are they?"

"Hey, *Tom Swift*, next time don't drop in on us, ok?!"

"What the heck?" exclaimed Tak Kurosawa, his hands on the helm.

"Yeah, we were on it first! Who are you kooks? And what are you doing on my wave!"

Kurosawa looked to his left, and a big grin broke across his face.

'They're right behind us L.J.!"

Merrill turned and there was the voyaging craft of David Helmares, slicing along the very crest of the same wave that propelled the Alba_Swords. His anxiety disappeared as fast as it had enveloped him. His heart felt a profound joy, and he knew there was no longer a monkey on his back.

The *Aeolus* flew lazy circles around the three vessels surfsailing their way north. Mac Owens had an idea, and half an hour later the intercom box in the forward compartment was patched into the comm network so that Luan and Aleja could talk directly to the people at the helms of the sailing craft. It wasn't long before they saw four patches of white water arrayed across their path. The formation cut to the east around them, and for the rest of the afternoon executed a series of course changes at the direction of the women on the PBY to avoid one shoaling zone of reefs and atolls after another.

Nobody paid much attention to the sunset, marred as it was by a heavy layer of spray across the surface of the sea. But David Helmares was the first to pay attention when his stars begin to appear. Had he known the GPS coordinates of their destination, he could have easily given them to Clem Charleton and they all could have followed the *Aeolus* with ease. But David didn't know them. He was the chief navigator of the Marulean sea people, and his knowledge of the stars did not need to be supplanted in any way. The stars were always there, and they were never wrong. For the time being, nothing made by the hands of man could make the same claim.

Night gave Luan and Aleja a remarkable view of the galaxies above and the nebulae of reefs and atolls below. Long streaks of phosphorescence appeared behind some reefs as the huge waves stirred up microscopic organisms from the sea floor. When a ridge of white appeared on the horizon, the women quickly realized it was a reef of real danger to the surfers on the wave below. David checked his stars and then led the Alba_Swords over a submarine canyon that provided a pass of safety through the hazard. When they'd made it through, Frank Bucher took the helm and Heath Larson trimmed the sails, giving the navigator a chance to close his eyes, though his senses never slept. Once or twice he sat up, seemingly still asleep, to tell Bucher or Larson to pull in a sail or lay off the tiller a degree or two.

At midnight the watches changed. Luan went to the galley to catch a few hours sleep. Mac Owens came forward and spelled Roberto Mercante. Clem joined Aleja up front, and the Southern gentlemen kept the young lady from Malibu entertained with stories about his days courtin' Southern belles that left her laughing for hours. Bob Rowe was long gone in the back, but his watch alarm would have him up with hours to spare before the morning arrival at David's home island.

On the *Tom Swift*, L.J. Merrill and Jack Richards were at the helm, with Sonny-boy and Bruddah squeezed in behind them. The four men, once dead set against each other, now had a lot to talk about, and their conversations ranged from their love of the sea to high performance tube-riding to sharing the stoke of surfing with new generations of surfers.

Ken Bucher and Nelson Roberts guided the *Serena*, with Randy Laine on deck alongside Charles Atkins. At one point, Atkins took the helm and motioned for the three men to strap in and hold on. He then called to his wife below, and the *Serena* was filled with the sound of the Funk Brothers, the Motown house band. He began to choreograph the surfing of the *Serena* to

"Come See About Me" and "The Way You Do The Things You Do". Soon the women below were singing along, though they knew better than to be anywhere but strapped in their bunks as the Alba_Sword carved and swooped across the dark blue wave that rolled on and on.

Course changes, watch changes, stars setting one by one: the passage home ran all through the night as the swell began to slowly lose its some of its power. The *Aeolus* provided unerring guidance as the Alba_Swords did a loop to the following wave. David Helmares was awakened for the maneuver and with plenty of wind and speed, the *Dreamboat* followed the *Tom Swift* and the *Serena*. Then he'd resume the sleep of a navigator, restful and yet always alert.

The crescent moon rose in the east, adding its beauty to the heavens. Dawn was not far off, and everyone knew that their voyage would be over when the sun touched the sky of a new day.

As they came closer to the home waters of the Maruleans, the wave lost more and more of its power to the reefs of the Nebula Archipelago. The change brought David out of the shelter dome. He looked for his stars and called for a course change around a small group of reefs just over the horizon. The wave seemed to respond to David's new course and built up again. From the *Aeolus*, Luan was able to see the channel leading to the place of her birth. She saw how the swells were bouncing from one side of the channel to the other. David then gave instructions for one last course change, and the work of the *Aeolus* was done.

Light, in the east, began to brighten the horizon. David Helmares took the helm and had the Alba_Swords set up behind him. He edged along one side of the channel where the wave was still forty feet high and breaking along the shoals connecting several atolls to each other.

Suddenly, the surfers were looking into the open tunnel of their wave as it peeled along the reef to their left. For almost ten minutes they rode in formation before David executed another course change. The Alba_Swords followed him across the channel so they could watch tubes form and reform along another set of shoals. A final slicing run across the face of the wave, still twenty feet high, and the home island of the Maruleans came into view as morning light filled the sky.

The children were up early, as usual. The teenagers taking care of them were still sleepy, but they had no choice except to follow the little ones out the door. Then their eyes opened wide as the twins ran down to the lagoon.

Through the reef pass came two strange sailing craft. Then they heard, as did all in the village, a sound that most did not recognize except the elders who never forgot that sound from their youth. Within minutes the entire village was watching a Catalina PBY come in for a landing behind the Alba_Swords.

The modern vessels and the seaplane were such an awesome sight that no one noticed the voyaging craft in their midst. No one saw two men step off and a woman step on. But as the craft came in through the reef pass, two little children began to look at it with a special sense of wonder. Then their caretakers saw what the little ones sensed.

The voyaging craft slowed and glided to a stop near the water's edge. The toddlers saw their mother and father and splashed heedlessly towards them. Within seconds each was in the arms of a parent, their faces covered in kisses. But like all small children, they could be held still only momentarily, and an instant later, they were straining in their parents arms, their attention now totally captivated by the sight of the *Aeolus*, the *Tom Swift*, and the *Serena*.

David and Luan turned around, and the twins strained further to get to the objects floating on the clear blue water. Then a set came through, and perfect eight foot waves framed either side of the deep water channel where the Alba_Swords now rested near the PBY.

"Well, we better figure out if we are going to let them stay."

"What's this we? You're the chief navigator. That's your job. I'll take the children home. See you when you're done."

David pushed his voyaging craft out from the beach and raised a foresail. He slowly gathered speed, gliding through inner waters where a dozen Marulean fishing and voyaging craft were moored along with the boat he had built with his own hands. He thought of the first time he had come into this very lagoon in her, an unexpected visitor to the sea people. It was a far cry from a single-handed sloop to a PBY seaplane and two Alba_Swords, but the problem was the same for him now as it had been for Taveka. He had to reconcile maintaining the integrity of the Marulean culture with the arrival of visitors with whom the Maruleans, at face value, shared nothing.

A set of waves came in from the horizon. He watched them break perfectly on both sides of the reef passage, with the visitors floating in the deep central channel. He turned and looked back at the beach where more and more Maruleans were now coming down to the water's edge. David was almost literally between two worlds. Then he saw one wave peel with such perfect shape across the reef that for a moment he was not a Californian, or a Marulean, or the chief navigator, or a husband or a father. He was simply a surfer, and he watched the wave with a special eye of appreciation.

"That wave was perfect!" he exclaimed, and in the instant of recognition that comes when a man's soul is truly touched by the ineffable wonder of nature, he knew what he was going to say and do next.

"Wow, look at those waves!"

"I wonder if we can go surfing?"

"I bet he's going to show us where we can anchor."

"Look at all those people on the beach."

"No wonder he left California and never went back."

"I could stay here the rest of my life."

Everyone had questions to ask and things to say to David Helmares. None, however, had any idea of what he was about to say to them.

"Ahoy, visitors! You do not have permission to land here. You do not have permission to anchor in these waters."

The tone of David's voice was a shock to them all. David looked at the Alba_Swords and the PBY and made sure everyone could see and hear him.

"We are not at Ka'unua. There we were far out to sea, alone with the ocean and her endless power. Now we are here, in the center of the Nebula Archipelago, where the Marulean sea people reside. As you can see, they are on the beach. And I am their chief navigator. I brought you here to safety, and only for that purpose. Now I must act in their interests."

"Of course, David," said Aleja, quick to understand exactly what he was doing, "Remember when I first approached you at Ka'unua?"

"Yes, I remember that, Aleja, and your respect for us then is what I must ask of all of you now. When I first came here, Taveka did not let me land. I could not drop anchor. There are no visitors to the Maruleans, given the reefs and atolls for hundreds of miles all around this island. Nobody sails through this part of the South Pacific. Yet there I was, just as you are here today.

"So Taveka asked me who I was, and I tried to explain my voyage, show him my papers, and all that. But he was not interested. He wanted to know who I was as a person, as did the elders and all the inhabitants of this island."

"Immigration can be one tough buggah." Bruddah elbowed Sonny-boy.

"Yeah, Bruddah, and the thing was, until they understood me almost better than I know myself, they would not let me anchor."

"So what do you want us to do?" asked L.J. Merrill.

"At Ka'unua I was able to welcome you only after making sure of my instincts and my responsibilities to the Maruleans. Now I must do the same. Clem, the swell's going down fast, and you should have a clear seaway for a takeoff by noon. Frank, Charles, I can prepare you a chart to get out of here, and believe me, you will need to follow it closely."

David looked across the decks of the Alba_Swords and into the cargo bay of the seaplane. Faces that had just been so full of life and vitality were now confused, somber and dejected.

"If you want to go ashore, you will have to explain yourselves, one at a time, as I did many years ago. Once all the questions have been asked of you, the elders and I, along with our people, would have to decide if you can stay."

"I don't know how that would work for us, David," said Margo Atkins, "There's a lot of us, and we've still got a long way to go."

"Yes, Margo, that's true. And even if you'd been invited, visitors need to send heralds ahead of them, with gifts and ceremonial offerings. If I was to be that herald for you, well, I couldn't do it right now because I don't know each and every one of you well enough to perform the task properly."

"So we're back where we started, aren't we?" asked Jack Richards.

"No, Jack, we've all come a long way, I think. We've all done something wonderful together, but that only goes for us. But the people on the beach would have one way to try and understand who you are, Jack, and that is to ask every question they can think of and have you to tell them everything about yourself."

Richards looked away at the thought of what the Maruleans might think of him after three days of questions. Roberto Mercante was equally ill-at-ease at the thought.

"We understand, David. I think every one of us truly knows exactly what you are talking about," said Heath Larson, also uneasy about how he would explain himself.

"Thanks, Heath. We have sailed together, and we have surfed together. And maybe the day will come when we all, the Maruleans, OSOM, and the Mother Ocean Foundation will inhabit moments of life with our hearts as one. But I am only the chief navigator for the society of my wife and my children. I advise the council of elders, and though my life is with them, they have nothing in common with you at the present time. Maybe there will someday be a way for our cultures to find understandings and friendship that will withstand the obstacles of human failings. Maybe there is much to share someday between us, and maybe the time will come when we will try."

"But now is not the time, is it, David?" said L.J. Merrill.

"No, my friend, it isn't."

The navigator's craft drifted towards the Alba_Sword. Everyone was quiet as the two men shook hands. They didn't let go for a long time while looking straight into each other's souls. Then they nodded to each other as the voyager began to drift away. Soon David could see everyone again.

"Frank, Charles! Thanks to you and your crews for being such gracious guests at Ka'unua. Clem, Mac! Thanks for the hospitality you extended to Luan and the guidance through the night. Randy, thanks for keeping everyone safe out there, and don't let that footage get out of hand, Bob."

David Helmares then turned to Roberto Mercante.

"You have a special charge from Taveka, and maybe after you take care of what he gave you, you'll find that the Mother Ocean Foundation is only the beginning. I'm sure he knew what he was doing when he trusted you."

Roberto Mercante had no words in reply. With the legacy of Ian Clark in his hands, and they both knew it was a solemn charge.

"And Jack, you once helped a man in need, and in the end I think that helped you more than anything. Thanks for bringing him here so that we could meet each other, and if you want to come back, bring your family."

"I don't think that will happen for a long time, David. I've got a lot of things to do with them, and surfing is not high on the list."

"Yes, I can understand that. Heath, you ever want to surf out there again, you come get me first, ok?"

"Will do, David, and thanks for the one wave I really needed."

"There's more waves out there, Heath. There will always be more waves. And don't forget, we've never checked the third reef out there."

Helmares saw the twinkle in Larson's eye and both men smiled.

"Aleja, if there was one person who I think would be able to find a welcome amongst our peoples, it would surely be you."

"Thanks, David, but I gotta get back to the shelter. Tell Luan I'll never forget her."

"I will, Aleja. Bruddah, keep an eye on our reformed surf star, ok?"

"Will do, David. We Polynesians gonna stick togeddah!"

"We gonna geevum good for Taveka when we get back!" said Sonny-boy.

"Anything you do in his memory will work. I'm sure of it. In fact, I've only been able to think clearly about the situation right now because I remembered what Taveka did the first time I came here. He didn't get ahead of himself, or give in to my impatience. He did what had to be done, though that only made things harder for me. I was his apprentice for a long time and tried to gain as much of his wisdom as I could. And I'm trying to use that wisdom now. I wish there was an easy way to bring you all into the world of the sea people. I wish there was a way to make that happen right away. But as L.J. said, now is not the time."

David saw another set was coming in to the reefs.

"We all have challenges ahead of us. Life will always be coming at us like sets of waves that never end. Yet our problems will always be a little easier to deal with if we stay in touch with the timeless ocean."

Three perfect waves were peeling down the reef. David knew there was nothing more to be said when he found himself looking at the surf instead of the people in front of him.

"So, since we've said our goodbyes, why don't we go and surf some of these waves? I've got a new board I'm dying to ride, and there are a couple of classic pintails and a fish stowed away on my boat. Who knows what our cultures may find in common, but surfing together is a good way to get started. I think we heard the warning of the waves at Ka'unua. Now let's go and play with them to learn their songs."

Epilogue

The Mother Ocean Foundation was able to acquire all the assets of Wavelife International in bankruptcy court. The first thing Cheryl Corlund did was keep everyone working at the headquarters in Newport Beach and Dolly Artensa became head of human resources. Richard Black and Gunter Jacobsen were last seen in Europe doing telecom deals, and Parea Anasi was last seen selling suits in Hong Kong. Bart Thomas and Ben Jeffries kept an eye on the bottom line, and publicly traded non-profits became a new trend on Wall Street.

Aleja Gracellen's shelter continued to expand thanks to Bill Massara and June Wilson becoming active managers of the Foundation's non-profit division. This allowed Aleja to resume dancing in the waves at Malibu, and when not working at the shelter, she pursued a university degree in Fine Arts.

Sonny-boy Noaloa met a girl he'd had a crush on in junior high, and with his mom's blessing, was soon happily married. Mick Lennox was his best man. He never surfed competitively again, being too busy in both Florida and Hawai'i working with Bruddah on stay-in-school programs for at-risk youth and they both helped Kai Woods with waterman's training for pro surfers.

Heath Larson became a frequent visitor to the sea people of Marulea. He became a beloved uncle to the children of David and Luan, and they eventually started to surf the third reef on occasion. But when the surf got really good, they always paid a visit to Taveka and the navigators who could always be found surfing inside the biggest waves at Ka'unua.

Roberto Mercante became chief pilot of the *Aeolus* after Clem Charleton retired and flew her as a sister ship to the *Skyhook* doing missions all around the South Seas, including ferrying young Maruleans to the Skyrider Foundation where they continued their education thanks to Victor and Tina Sanchez. And Mac Owens kept both planes in the air.

Charles and Margo Atkins began to seriously collect straight six soul patrol vehicles from the sixties that were always on loan to visiting OSOM members from around the world. Tak Kurosawa and Chip Bell went back to work at OSOM and Nelson Roberts and Patty McRane became inseparable after deciding to postpone their marriage indefinitely.

The *Serena* and the *Tom Swift* were once again nestled in their slips at Ventura Harbor when Ken Bucher returned to university in September. Ray Seranen and the Ice Pirates received awards from all the countries doing research in Antarctica. And Frank Bucher now had to deal with his daughters demanding to go on next year's Roaring Forties Regatta.